# HORROR USA: CALIFORNIA

## AN ANTHOLOGY OF HORROR FROM THE GOLDEN STATE

JEAN ANKER    PETER E. APERLO    GABRIELLA BALCOM
RICHARD BEAUCHAMP    CHLOE BECKETT
LAWRENCE BERRY    JON BLACK    LAURA BLACKWELL
DUANE BRADLEY    N. M. BROWN    R. BROWN
KOURINTHIA BURTON    DOMINICK CANCILLA
SARAH CANNAVO    PATRICK CANNING    STUART CONOVER
DAVID DANIEL    CHARLIE DAVENPORT    CRAIG DEUTSCHE
SIDNEY DRITZ    MADISON ESTES    J. P. FLORES
MATHEUS GAMARRA    KEN GOLDMAN    ELANA GOMEL
SCOTT HARPER    CINDAR HARRELL    JASON MARC HARRIS
JUSTIN HUNTER    KEVIN JONES    EDWARD KARPP
JOHN KUJAWSKI    MIKE LERA    JP MAC    P. F. MCGRAIL
SYDNEY MEEKER    MERCURY    TREVOR NEWTON
JANE NIGHTSHADE    CHARLOTTE O'FARRELL
EVAN PURCELL    C. C. RAVEN    MARIANNE REESE

ALANNA ROBERTSON-WEBB    TROY SEATE    JEFF SEEMAN
WILL SWANSON    TAMIKA THOMPSON    GREG TURLOCK
DJ TYRER    GABRIEL VALJAN    CLAY WATERS
KATHERINE WIDICK    FRED WIEHE    LORNA WOOD
YVONNE

Edited by
GABRIEL GROBLER & R. C. BOWMAN

SOTEIRA
PRESS

SOTEIRA
PRESS

# CONTENTS

Cult Classic                                                    1
The Horror in the Plaza                                         5
The Golden Gods of Hollywood                                   13
The Warriors of the Sand                                       25
Cat                                                            40
Mark of the Bruja                                              52
Smoked                                                         67
Let Me Introduce the Demon Inside You                          73
Gemini Dreams                                                  78
Santa's Village                                                92
Crossroads                                                    103
The Black Band                                                115
One Last E-Ticket Ride                                        119
Melicious Maladies                                            125
The Pale Tenant                                               131
Do You Wanna Play, Mommy?                                     139
A Cold & Lonely Evil                                          141
Theda and Me                                                  147
A Murder of Crows                                             159
How Canals are Taught to Eat                                  161
The Last Royal                                                165
Conflagration                                                 176
Beach Boy                                                     184
Rosa Castilla                                                 191
Industrial Breeding Process                                   197
It Comes to Drink                                             201
Shadow Man                                                    206
The Lost Cabin                                                214
Soul Toll on the Bay                                          218
Rock 'n' Roll Eats its Children                               220
Fry Machete's Monsters, Munchies, and Mayhem                  236
The Cactus                                                    245
Roads                                                         253
She by the Sea                                                257
The Cutting Room                                              266
Stray                                                         276

The Huldur                                   283
South Command                                290
The One Thing I Can Never Tell Julie         297
L.A. When It Bleeds                          306
California Doubling                           322
The Dead Road                                327
Angel Republic                               331
Night In Willow Wash                         344
Downtown San Diego                           348
Don't Pick the Oranges                       358
Somewhere Short of Paradise                  360
The Unheard Sound on Deardroff Road          371
The Nowhere Place                            375
My Grandpa's Best Friend                     388
Every Day is a Parade                        392
Movie Magic                                  402
The Wrath of Okeanos                         409
Retribution                                  415
Kissing Off Amber                            423
Gertrude On Olympiad Drive*                  432

*MORE FROM SOTEIRA PRESS*                     433

# HORROR
# U S A
# CALIFORNIA

# CULT CLASSIC

## CHARLOTTE O'FARRELL

The movie I starred in back in 1988 was never screened, but it's more famous on the internet than anything else I've worked on. Or maybe that should be "infamous."

After what happened on set, the studio would never get away with sending the movie to theaters, even if they'd been able to finish it with the footage they had.

Instead, the once-great, now-defunct American Classic Pictures quietly shelved it. They had us sign agreements never to tell our stories to anyone, under threat of never working in Hollywood again. They hoped the whole thing would disappear. Mostly, they managed to keep the story out of the press—with one or two exceptions. They couldn't have predicted the internet sleuths decades later, who would obsess over the existence (or not) of the movie, and dig up whatever they could find.

Sometimes I thought about commenting anonymously on these forums, but when ACP was still in business, I worried about getting sued. Besides, I think I've kind of repressed it over the years. Wouldn't you?

It was supposed to be my big break. The fourth in the midlist slasher franchise "The Springtime Ripper," the movie was made towards the end of the slasher boom but was still a major draw. ACP knew it was a surefire money-spinner, even if the returns were getting lower—and the reviews harsher—with every outing of the black-caped, cleaver-wielding bad guy. The original had been about a killer who struck around Easter, dressed in a costume similar to the common portrayals of Jack the Ripper. Since the real Ripper murders didn't take place at Easter and the movie only had basic references to the time of year in which it was set, I assumed they picked it because it was the only major holiday that didn't yet have a slasher franchise attached; Christmas, Valentine's Day, and Halloween were all taken.

I never expected to hear back after my audition for the role of Claire, the main female character's nerdy best friend who died in the final half hour of the movie.

Tommy, the director, had barely looked at me as I ran through my lines. So, getting the part felt like a dream. Finally, my ticket out of waitressing and cleaning job hell! This was what I'd moved halfway across the country to L.A. for. I could see my name on posters outside every theater in the world: Alice Susan Primrose, actress at last. I walked down those famous streets on a high for weeks, finally feeling like a somebody.

When I arrived for my first day on set, it was like stepping into a dream. ACP was one of the most prestigious places in Hollywood back then. The Springtime Ripper movies helped establish this reputation, but it was no longer their main focus—our film had been downgraded to one of the smaller lots. It didn't matter to me. I had stars in my eyes.

I sat in makeup with Ella Heage. One of the original horror heroines who'd made her name in the slasher boom of the early 1980s, she'd moved on to other projects, but still faithfully returned every sequel for another fight with her caped enemy. By now, her character, Jessie, had survived three knife battles, an attempted drowning, a burning house (set on fire, of course, by the Ripper) and the loss of countless friend groups. And all before setting off for college, poor girl.

The latest screenplay saw the unlucky Jessie move to California under a new name to live with her aunt and uncle—being unknowingly followed by the Ripper. There was some exposition at the beginning to explain how the Springtime Ripper was still alive and killing after being locked in the burning house in the last sequel, but that's expected in slashers. Fans accept it. It's the price to pay for another fun onscreen massacre.

Ella herself was wonderful. After all her success I'd expected someone a little more, well, stuck-up. But she was so supportive, even telling me stories of her own first day on set: "The budget was trash on the first one, sweetie, you wouldn't believe it." She wasn't much older than me, maybe five years my senior, but she'd landed the Jessie role so young that her acting experience made her seem like she was from a different age. I was in awe.

"Just don't sweat it. You'll be fine. You're here, you made it," she said with a wink when her makeup was done and her beautiful blonde locks styled to perfection. As she walked out the room, I felt dizzy with excitement.

The first scenes were establishing shots of Jessie and Claire sitting on a bed having a sleepover. Tommy, the director, was demanding, shouting increasingly aggressive instructions at us to say one line more clearly or tilt our heads a certain way. Ella kept rolling her eyes at me in a "just ignore him" sort of way. After four movies, she probably tuned a lot of the crap out.

It was mostly fluff that wasn't going to be used, but I enjoyed the acting chemistry between us; it gave me a good feeling for the rest of the movie, despite Tommy.

That didn't last.

Since everything's shot out of sequence, the next scenes were completely unrelated. If I hadn't had the script, I would've had no idea of the story by the time we came to the famous scenes about two weeks into filming. It was Jessie's fight scene with the Springtime Ripper. It wasn't quite the final climax; that part was only a few pages from the end of the screenplay, but this sequence was still full of tension. My character was killed shortly before but was still in shot, so I had to play the most undemanding role an actor can have: corpse.

Well, it seems undemanding. It was actually kind of hard to stay still for that long, only breathing in shallow bursts that the camera wouldn't pick up. My neck ached after one take. We took a break after three, and there I was again—lying on my back on the floor, show runners positioning my body so it didn't look different to the first three takes. I was just glad I didn't have to keep my eyes open.

"Where is he?" I heard Ella demand, her usually calm voice cranky. I sneaked one eye open to take a look.

Zack, the stuntman-turned-actor who had played the Springtime Ripper since that famous original, wasn't known for his punctuality. But going missing mid-scene was a stretch even for him.

I saw Ella with her arms folded, standing straight as the makeup staff put the final touches to her face and the crew adjusted the lighting and sound equipment.

"Ah! About damn time!"

She threw her hands up in the air as the Ripper appeared in full costume. Face covered by the black mask. Costume top hat covering his hair. Cleaver in hand. He said nothing; he just casually walked to the set and was directed to his position by a runner.

Tommy called action. I closed my eyes again.

At first, it all seemed okay. The grunts as the Ripper lunged at "Jessie." Her stage screams. The bumping as they wrestled across the bedroom set.

The first of Ella's genuine screams will stay with me forever. It made me jump so hard I nearly opened my eyes. Gee, her acting was getting better than ever, I thought—that one sounded real! Then another scream, louder than before, that ripped through us all. No way was this stage shouting.

I opened my eyes. A blood splatter shot across my face, soaking me in red. A different red than the gooey mess the studio produced to look like blood.

It took a second for my eyes to adjust to the horrifying sight silhouetted against the harsh set lights. The Springtime Ripper, chopping into a cowering Ella with a real cleaver, cutting off her arm in chunks. The growing panic from the crew as they raced forward, finally realizing this was really happening—but not before the Ripper buried his cleaver in Ella's forehead.

Three cameramen wrestled the Springtime Ripper to the ground. I sat up slowly, drenched in blood, watching crew scream for help as they cradled Ella and made futile attempts to save her.

There are many versions of this story circling internet forums, of the spectacular, gory story of Ella Heage being hacked to death by a crazed stalker in a Ripper costume on the set of her latest movie. But they all include one detail which I remember so clearly: in the middle of the carnage, I looked straight at the one remaining stunned camera guy behind the equipment, and shouted: "Turn the fucking camera off!"

The aftermath is a blur. The mask was dragged off the cackling madman, revealing a face I vaguely remembered hanging out near the studios before filming began. Police arrived. Ambulances. We found Zack knocked out in his dressing room, where the stalker—disguised as a workman—had stolen his costume. We were taken to a secure property miles from anywhere and told never to reveal what had really killed Ella. The story of a "tragic on-set accident" was brought out first. There was no trial; rumor has it the ACP put considerable pressure on to make sure the killer was quietly locked away in a secure psych unit and never spoken of again.

I got small parts in Hollywood after that. I'm lucky, and rare, to have been able to make a modest living through my acting for most of my life. In leaner years, I've turned to teaching acting classes to other young wannabes. Sometimes I'll see one who reminds me of a younger me—or worse, a younger Ella. And at those times, I'll fear the exposure that'll come to them if they succeed in this business, in this fake but beautiful town. You just never know who's watching.

As for the internet experts on "The Springtime Ripper 4?" Let them speculate. They're right that this happened, and the footage existed once. What became of it, I don't know. Some of it must have survived for the legend to build. If there are any copies out there, I would want them burnt.

I won't be doing any interviews after this. I've said all I want to. Generally, I think I recovered okay from the horror of that day. Maybe I've just pushed it down and tried to forget, and maybe it's come out of me in other ways. But I didn't leave L.A., and it didn't stop my love of acting.

There's one thing I've steered clear of, though, and I don't think you can blame me.

I never, ever audition for horror movies.

# THE HORROR IN THE PLAZA

## PETER E. APERLO

Is that too tight, Miss? I'm sorry. I don't wanna hurt ya... at least—you know what I mean. You gotta stop squirming around, now. It ain't gonna help. I know you're one of Marco's girls, but that don't matter. It don't matter one bit. In fact, that's why I—I gotta do it, and that's all there is to it. Don't look at me like I'm some sorta monster. I ain't no monster! Yeah, I'm holed up in this crummy, two-bit room on the tracks, with a face like you never seen, but I ain't no monster. You oughta thank me. You would if you knew what's coming. 'Cause I do.

I wasn't always like this, you know, all balled up and fidgety. I had a good thing going when I joined up with Tony C. back in '23. Now, I don't blame Tony for what happened. He was as surprised as we was. Before that I was legit, working crab boats up in Frisco. But you got good years and bad years in crabbing, and Tony was offering good cash money, running boats from the ships off of Malibu and whatnot, bringing in the good stuff. Mexican, Canadian, whatever. And there ain't no bad years in that racket. Got me a new Packard, a coupla new suits, and enough spending money so I wasn't sitting at home alone with the Grand Ol' Opry on Saturday nights. Hobnobbed with movie stars and all that. This town don't care how you get your money, as long as you got some. Tony used to say we was keeping a hundred and twenty million people from poisoning themselves with bathtub gin, and he was right. We wasn't hurting nobody. Nobody was putting a gun to their head to buy. Blind pigs, country clubs—we supplied 'em all.

Then things turned sour with Farmer. You heard about all that, right? No? Prob'ly too young. Cripes. Don't look at me with them eyes. Look out the winda or something. Watch the trains.

Farmer Page's running all these games around L.A., see? And we's supplying him, got it? Now, he's got a beef with Tony over price or something, I never found out what,

5

and pretty soon the fireworks start up. Machine gun war is what the papers was calling it, only I ain't never seen no choppers get taken out to play. Not on our end, anyways. There was fellas playing like they was from Treasury and pulling all kinds of hooey, but we just wanted to make deliveries without bothering nobody. Then Tony C. gets sent up, and I'm working for his brothers, but it ain't the same. It wasn't so fun no more. It got to be like you couldn't trust nobody.

All's I know is me and Louie is making a delivery clear out past Glendale, someplace I never been before, supposed to be some movie star's ranch or something. Anyways, we pull up and these goons come busting out of a barn with bean shooters pointed right in our faces, telling us to reach, and calling us dago bastards and whatnot. It was a setup from the start, and it didn't take a college boy to figure out real quick these weren't no percentage bulls from the LAPD. These fellas was County, and we ain't got no pull with County. And they didn't bat an eye before doing the foxtrot on me's and Louie's faces, and enjoying it more than they should.

That's how I ended up in that shiny new jail they got up in the top of that Hall of Justice downtown. They give you a pretty view, but you can't go nowhere. Nice, huh? So, I'm supposed to be sent before this real bluenose of a judge, and my mouthpiece is working on a change of venue and whatnot, and in the meantime, I'm stuck under glass twiddling my thumbs. I musta been there three months before they foist a cellmate on me, this skinny greaser from across the river in Lincoln Heights, a guy named Flaco. Strictly small potatoes. Got hauled in for some two-bit job at a five-and-dime. He don't talk much, mostly sad about disappointing his mamma, but he can play a mean game of euchre. Could, anyway.

But they ain't gonna just leave us be to sit back and enjoy ourselves on the taxpayer's nickel. Oh, no. There's this Mrs. Sterling, see, and she gets it in her head that Sonoratown oughta be cleaned up, on accounta it being where the city started and all. The first church is there in the Plaza, you know? But it's all a filthy pigsty, with crummy old buildings and mud for streets, and people throwing crap in the gutter like they're living in the Old Country or something. They even had to do a Pied Piper act back in '25 'cause the place was lousy with rats. Anyways, instead of torching the whole stinkin' place, she wants to fix it up all pretty and invite the tourists in so they can pretend like they're south of the border down in Mexico or something. So, Mrs. Sterling talks the city into it, but they don't wanna spend no money on fixing up a bunch of crap, so Sheriff Traeger is oh so generous and volunteers all the saps he's got in the County lockup to help out. That's how me and Flaco got chained to a bunch of other sorry fellas dark and early one cold November morning, and marched down to that place where if God knows about it, He's pretending like He don't.

The Plaza gots this big fountain in it, only it don't work. There's a buncha Mexes lounging around like they got nothing better going, but they all screwed once they seen us and the bulls coming. There's a coupla Chinamen, too, over on the eastside, near Alameda, pushing vegetable carts and whatnot. This big Kraut bull named Stammherr peeled Flaco and me off, gives us a coupla shovels, and sent us into this old brick job called Franconi House. That's what it said over the door. Used to be a low-rent

6

boarding house—and I mean real low-rent—but they kicked the bums out before we got there. He told us to clear out the cellar, calling us "ladies" like it's a big joke he just thought up, but I'm wondering what's the shovels for. I found out quick.

These half-rotted old steps go down to the cellar, which is maybe twenty by twenty. It gots this round brick ceiling, like you might see in church—a little, crummy, old church. You could smell that cellar long before you got down there. It's the smell of a place you don't go into unless you gotta. They used to keep wine in it, back when you could, but all's there is now is busted barrels, busted furniture, and filthy, black muck up to your knees. Coupla wet winters and the place is swimming. Even after the summer we had there was still mud, and the furniture and bric-a-brac had gone all mushy with stuff growing on it. There's just this one little grate up at street level that lets in a few slivers of light if the sun's right. We get this weak little lantern from the bulls, but it throws more shadows than light. They gotta measure the kerosene out every day like it's gold or something, prob'ly 'cause they think we's gonna drink it.

We start by prying out the big stuff and stacking it in the street. They gots this truck that comes around at the end of the day to haul it off to the dump or somewheres. Then we gets to put our shovels to use and try to find the floor, filling up buckets and dumping them in the street. There's animal parts like bones and fur in that muck like somebody's been chucking their garbage in there, or maybe things just got stuck and died, like that Brea place over on Wilshire. A group of Society folks come around once to gawk at us. I don't know if that Mrs. Sterling was with them, or else I'da thanked her for the opportunity. We's all pretty ripe by the time bath day rolls around. But I ain't complaining too bad, since it was better'n crabbing, and at least we got outta the cooler for a bit. Back and forth, back and forth, cell to cellar, cellar to cell. That's how it went for four days, until Flaco found that well.

He's scraping out the muck in a corner to get down to the floor, which is brick like everything else, when he hits some wood planks that somebody'd spiked down right into the mortar between the bricks. He gets all excited like I never seen, and calls me over. When I get there, he taps the point of his shovel down on the wood and it makes this dull, hollow thud, like there ain't nothing underneath.

"Do you know what this is, Nicky?" he asks me.

"I dunno. A hole somebody wanted covered up?" I says.

"Not jus' a hole—a *well*. I bet it goes all the way down to the Zanja Madre!" he says, and starts chopping away at the planks, which is pretty easy 'cause they're mostly rotted through.

Now, I didn't know what this Zanja Madre was at the time. It sounded like some mountains or something, and I thought he'd gone screwy looking for mountains under-ground. But Flaco tells me it's the old water system from back in the Pueblo days when Mexico was running things, and Spain before that, but they stopped using it a bunch of years ago. His people was around here a long time, and his grandfather used to tell him stuff about them days, along with stuff *his* grandfather used to tell *him*. Flaco says this Madre thing used go all around the city, bringing in water from the river, and if we could get down into it, maybe we could lam it outta here. Not having a lot of faith in

7

the machinery of the criminal justice system from what I seen so far, that sounds like a plan to me, so I help him clear away the wood.

What we got when we was done is a round hole about two and a half feet across, with bricks around the sides going down into the dark. It was too dark to see very far, even with our crummy lantern. I drop a rock in there, and pretty quick we hear a little plop, so it don't sound like it's too far down to the bottom. Flaco goes first on accounta it's his plan and he's the skinniest. He uses his legs and arms to press his back against side, making his way like he's Santy Claus going down a chimney or something. Pretty soon I don't see him no more, and I'm getting nervous 'cause the bulls is due to come by soon, but then he yells up that he's on the ground and for me to come down. I tie the lantern to a sleeve of my work jacket and lower it down, and with him jumping up he can just grab it. Seems the well is only about a dozen feet deep, so I get into position and start the Santy Claus routine. About halfway down, my foot slips on the slimy bricks and I catch the express train down, scraping my forehead on the way.

Flaco was smart enough to step out of the way, and when I put my skull back together, I could see he's crouched over in this little tunnel maybe four feet high. It's arched over with brick, like a pizza oven, which is funny 'cause it's a little hot in there. You'd expect a well or sewer or whatever to be chilly, but that place was warm and stuffy, with the air pressing in all around you like a wool blanket.

"We are in it now, amigo. I don't think we can go back up if we wanted to," says Flaco, and I gotta agree. The tunnel we're in goes both directions further than our light can show. There's only about an inch of water in the bottom of it, and as much mud below that, so moving around's not a problem, except it gives you the heebie-jeebies if you touch the sides with the slime and mold and whatnot. The smell's not much better'n the cellar, either. After getting our bearings, we can tell the tunnel runs kinda north-south, and we decide to run south for no particular reason. We had a fifty-fifty chance and still crapped out.

We don't go very far before we come across a dog carcass, musta been laying there a coupla months, and a lotta the bones in the middle was missing. Flaco gets all excited again, on accounta he figures that if a dog can get in, we can get out. When he's right, he's right, I had to give him that. We walk I gotta figure maybe another block and then we seen this hole that's been punched through the bricks up around where the ceiling starts to curve, about two feet up. It's a pretty small opening, but you could get in if you tried. Flaco thinks we should go in, but I'm thinking about that dog and what coulda made that hole. I says we should look for a bigger way, something somebody built, not some animal burrow that you don't know where it's gonna go. Besides, we should get as far away from that well in the Franconi House cellar, just in case the bulls decide we're worth following down here. Flaco agrees, and we keep feeling our way forward, all hunched over like Lon Chaney.

All of a sudden, Flaco blows the lantern out, and it's blacker than black. I can't say boo before he puts a hand over my mouth and I hear him whisper, "Chinos." I try to push his hand away, but he's stronger than he looks, and anyway I find out what he's talking about pretty quick. It sounds like people arguing or something up ahead, and from around a bend we can see a dim light. It's getting brighter and bobbing around, like somebody's coming with a lantern. That's when I noticed the rotten smell weren't so bad here, that there was this sicky-sweet smell grabbing at your nose and mouth. You've tried a little poppy smoke in your day, aintcha? Aintcha? Yeah, so you know what I'm talking about. It turns out there's these three Chinamen dragging something in a bag—I ain't sayin' it's a body, and I ain't sayin' it ain't—and they're chattering away all excited like three monkeys in the zoo, like they don't expect nobody else to be down here.

I get it real fast that the tongs are using the Madre for whatever they need to use it for. Prob'ly comes in pretty handy for moving stuff around, I bet. Anyhow, I don't wanna stick around and get a tour, especially since these fellas don't look too social and they're toting around some nice-size cleavers. Flaco gets the same idea, and we start backing up, real nice and slow. I don't remember if it was me or him who stumbled, but there's this splash, and the Chinamen go quiet and we both act like statues. When they start shining their light down the tunnel at us, we hoofed it lickety-split back the way we come. The Chinamen send up this war cry that woulda made Genghis Khan proud and come splashing after us.

We was crawling as much as we was running, bumping into walls and rocks and whatnot. Flaco was in front, and I'm getting water and muck kicked up in my face, but I'm not complaining 'cause I hear them fellas getting closer and their light once in a while bouncing around near me, and I just keep going. All of a sudden, something grabs me by the left arm and I end up on my ass. It's Flaco, and he's inside that little hole we seen earlier, and he's pulling me in. What can I say? I went.

It wasn't all moist like I figured. The ground was dry and hard like it'd been dug out a while ago, but it's still like being in a sausage casing. I crawled forwards and he crawled backwards, faster than I woulda figured in a tight spot like that, but then we had motivation, didn't we? This little tunnel or burrow or whatever turned back and forth and up and down. There was some even littler holes that branched off, but we stayed to the main route. Once or twice the light flashed in at us, but the Chinamen didn't try to follow. I could hear 'em whispering back there at the entrance, and I don't know what they was saying, but you could tell just from their voices they was scared of something. We didn't stop, though.

The tunnel slopes down for a long time, and I'm starting feel like I can't breathe down there. Pretty soon, though, I hear a little yelp, and don't feel Flaco in front of me no more. I'm whispering his name and cursing him to God and anyone else who'd listen for leaving me in the dark, when I see this little light up ahead. Yeah, it's Flaco, and he's got that crummy lantern of ours going again. He's grinning at me, standing outside the little tunnel. When I get closer I can see he's in this big old cave or something, a helluva lot bigger than where I'm at. He helps me out and we take a look around. Now I ain't no park ranger or nothing, but it looked like a real cave, like nobody dug it out, only it gots these wavey-like stone steps leading up and down. You couldn't see where nobody chiseled 'em out or nothing, and they was all smooth like

9

polished marble, only they wasn't. Naturally, we decided to go up, but we don't get too far.

Maybe a dozen or so feet up and around a bend we find this big rock and a lot of little rocks and whatnot blocking the stairs. Now this rock had chisel marks on it, along with a big crucifix carved right into it, only it was kinda sideways. All around the crucifix was these carvings of stars and tree branches and whatnot, and it all just gave you a weird feeling like you didn't want to touch it, even though all it was was just a big rock. There's some writing on it, too, in these crazy-looking letters like you see on a church, but it's in Latin, and the nuns back home can tell you that wasn't my strong subject. But Flaco says it says something about a devil named Yang-Na. That don't sound like no devil I ever heard of, but Flaco says it was the name the Indians used to call L.A. before it was L.A. -another thing his granddad told him. And then he remembers something about them old Spanish priests sealing up some Indian demon or something inside the ground, something them Indians used to pray to, and they built the Plaza Church right on top to make sure it don't come out no more.

We were quiet then for a little bit. Then I says, "It's all a bunch of hooey, that's what it is—a boogeyman story to scare little kids into eating their vegetables and whatnot. In fact, if anything, I bet those priests was hiding something down here they didn't want the Indians to find, maybe gold or jewels or something like that." Now Flaco's a superstitious type, and he don't take to my line of thinking right off. He was all for crawling right back in that tunnel and taking our chances with the Chinamen. But I told him, "Look, it ain't gonna hurt nothing to go and have a quick look-see what's down there. Maybe we might even find another way out. Sometimes you gotta go down to go up." In the end, the stupid bastard listened to me and we went down the stairs.

With our little light you couldn't see much, but I seen some marks on the walls that was beginning to convince me that maybe somebody did carve this place out. They wasn't chisel marks, more like gouges, like you'd get if you dragged a rake across half-dried cement. They wasn't everywhere, but they was all headed in the same direction we was. The other thing I noticed after a coupla minutes was the smell, and a crab fisherman never forgets the smell of the ocean. Flaco smelled it, too, and even though we was miles and miles from the harbor, for some reason it made us happy and excited like there might be a way out down there. And if anything, the tunnel we was walking down was getting bigger. We also spotted a coupla rats skittering around at the edge of our light, so we figured they gotta have a way in. Funny looking rats, though—faces smooshed in kinda like pug dogs, and they was all mangy looking. It kept getting warmer in that damn hole, too.

Then we round this corner and the walls go away and it's all blackness, but the stairs keep going down. It's this big cavern, see, the size of one of them fancy theaters like they got down on Broadway. Only it's dark like before the picture starts, and our little lantern ain't helping much. We hear this noise that sounds kinda like water slapping against a dock, only slower and quieter and not with a regular beat—and every once in a while there's this "thunk" like if you dropped a tuna into a mud puddle.

We was curious about what was making those sounds, and of course we wanted to get the hell out of there, so we went down the steps a bit to see what we could see. We stopped when we seen stuff moving at the edge of the light. Not just those mangy rats that was running around, but there was these gray shapes squirming around in a big pool of watery mud. They looked like seals or something, only more clumsy. This muck was all around, and from where we was standing, it looked like it covered the whole floor of this cave. That is, except for this big rock in the middle. We could just make it out at the edge of our light. It was the size of one of them freight cars outside, only rounder with spiky pieces sticking up all around. The seal things was bunched up thicker around it, and quite a few was clambering and sliding over it or just laying on it. They was rooting around with their snouts, looking for stuff to eat, and every once in a while they'd find something and bury their faces in the mud caked all over that rock. Pretty soon there's this humming, real soft like, but getting louder.

And I coulda sworn that big rock moved, just a little.

I turn to Flaco to see if he seen it, but he ain't there, and I ain't in that cave no more either. All of a sudden, it's all sunny and I'm on this beach. It don't feel happy like some picture postcard, though. Far to my right and left, the land curves out to sea to these headlands, like I'm at the end of a big bay. It coulda been Venice Beach, only there ain't no piers or sunbathing tourists around. There's only these brown, long-haired people, all of them naked and not caring about it, walking past me, headed for the ocean. They're all singing in some language that I don't understand, but somehow I do. The song's beautiful and it's ugly, but mostly it's frightening, but I still gotta hear more. They stop about waist deep in the water, singing their hearts out like a bunch of Methodists. Even though it's hot out, I'm shivering, but I don't know why. Pretty soon I find myself walking toward the ocean, too. The people turn to look at me as I come, and they all got these big eyes that don't blink, and big, blubbery lips that keep singing that damned song.

By the time I get down to the water, the sun is almost down, turning the sky and sea all pink and purple like the insides of some gutted fish. I get the feeling we're all just waiting for something, all happy like it's Christmas morning or something. I don't even notice, but the singing's all died down and now they're just saying this word, over and over again, only real low like a whisper you're afraid somebody might hear.

"Yang-Na, Yang-Na," is what they're saying.

I felt the thing before I even seen it. The surge of water, the black bulk of it approaching, like a whale about to broach. I stiffen up, my heart thumping in my chest, but I can't look away. I'm screaming at myself in my mind to turn around, to run like hell, but it's like my legs don't work no more, or at least they don't work for me no more. Things are swimming around my legs now, gray, slippery bodies sliding up against my ankles and between my thighs. That big rock is rising up outta the water, and something's telling me to come on in, that I'm hot and thirsty and my skin is so dry and cracked. I know deep inside it ain't true, but it sounds so good, that it'd be such a relief. I'd be outta the County lockup, outta the life, just floating, floating without a care, you know? Before I know it, I'm up to my lips in the salt water, but I don't care. I'm ready to take a drink.

Right about then I heard Flaco scream.

Bam! I'm back in that cave, and I can just make out his face before them gray seal things pull him under. I'm only a few feet away, but I'm in the muck up to my neck and them things is holding me back. They're holding me all gentle, but there's too many and I ain't moving. He's screaming, screaming with mud pouring in his mouth, and he don't stop until he's covered and there ain't no more bubbles. I got that picture in my head still, and it ain't going nowhere.

That's when I start struggling, fighting like I don't know what, trying to shake them things off and get back to shore. They ain't being so gentle no more, showing me teeth all jagged and brown. To be honest with you, I don't know what I done or how I found the strength to lam it outta there. The only thing I remember before I got out was taking one last look at that big rock, and I seen this one eye like a dinner plate looking back at me.

I don't know how I got outta the Madre. I came to, down around near the Seventh Street Bridge, and found myself rolling around on the mud bank. Luckily it was night-time and pissing down rain, or I woulda been picked up for sure. That's when I noticed my leg was bleeding, and you could see teeth marks from them things. It didn't look too bad, though.

I been holed up here ever since then. First I got the sores, then the peeling started, but then in the last week or so, my fingers and toes started going, one by one. The hair, too. Don't hurt, though. Kinda feels good, like after a sunburn, you know? You pull off the old skin and there's a whole new you under there. Still, I know it ain't pretty. The only time I've been out is to get you.

This ain't personal or nothing. It's just... It's just that I'm yellow, okay? I couldn't off myself if I tried. So, this is the way it's gotta be. It's real sharp, and I hear it don't hurt none. And don't worry about your folks being worried sick and not knowing what happened you. I'm gonna shout about what I done from here to Santa Monica! And I don't care if Marco's goons put a slug in the back of my head for it, or if I gotta do the hemp dance up at Folsom, but somebody's gotta do it for me. Do it right, and do it quick.

You hear where they're talking about clearing out Chinatown, digging it up to put in a shiny, new train station? Miserable saps don't know what they'll find under there. But that ain't it. The whole town can rot and fall off into the ocean for all I care. I gotta do it now 'cause there's still a little bit of *me* left in here, see? That thing down there wants me by its side, forever and ever, grooming it, feeding it, making it happy. And every day, a little more and a little more, Christ help me, I'm starting to think that's what I want, too.

Now, hold still.

# THE GOLDEN GODS OF HOLLYWOOD

## KATHERINE WIDICK

My heels clicked on the pavement in a rhythmic pattern that belied my haste. It was dark, darker than it should have been considering the moon was full. That was the way of things in the glooming. The streetlights were useless. The few poles that were left in this part of Hollywood had long since sputtered and died. Garbage tumbled down the alley. The papery ticking sound it made raced me home.

The chilly pellets dripping from the clouds didn't bother me. The tin canisters, hidden in my coat, were safe and dry. That was all that mattered. Sneaking my loves out of the theater had been risky, but what choice did I have? They belonged to me as much as I belonged to them. The thought of someone talking to them the way I did, loving them the way only I could, made me crazy. When some interloper tried to destroy them, I slipped over the edge. But I was back now.

When I reached the scratched-up, off-center door that led to the rooms I rented, I paused to fish the key out of my pocket. As soon as I grabbed hold of the small, metal object I felt it slip through my fingers. I caught it before it finished its descent. Once the key was in my hand and I reached to unlock the door, my weight shifted, and I lost my balance on the crumbling step. The grip I had on my tins loosened. One of the canisters tumbled to the pavement, landing in a puddle of piss and grime. A strangled cry escaped me. I rushed inside, set my treasures down on a chair held together by duct-tape, then sprinted back outside.

"God, don't let me be too late," I sobbed as I scooped the canister from the odorous muck. Holding it to my chest, I ran back to my rooms. I had to get inside before *they* saw what I was doing. I had no idea who it was that watched me. I'd never seen anyone hiding in the shadows. Still, I knew *they* were there. Always.

Once inside, I grabbed my last clean towel, or maybe it was my only towel, I couldn't remember, and bundled the canister in its faded warmth.

"It will be okay," I muttered. "I'm so sorry. You know I love you; you have to know that. You're my favorite." As soon as the tin was dry, I placed it on the table next to my projectors. James deserved a place of honor; after all, he was my true love, my real true love. How could he not be? He was the one I had given my virginity to.

I was eager to get started. My men needed to be set free, but first I had to take off my tattered coat and blood-soaked clothes. I needed to look my best for when James and the others came to me. I only had one good dress left. It was from another time, another, more decadent place. I'm so glad I'd saved it for such a special occasion. When I slipped into its cream-colored satin folds, it would be as if I were putting on my wedding dress.

As I finished my ablution, my mind wandered back to when I first saw James. He was embedded like a god high on the black and white screen. I was one of only a handful of folks who still sought out the old ones. Most people wanted color and action. They wanted sex and mindless entertainment. Nowadays, no one wanted to invest their senses in the soul of a movie.

I used to think that people like me, the ones who were enraptured in the golden age of Hollywood, would understand how I felt about the movies. They didn't. Oh, they talked a good talk. They thought they knew the old ones. They didn't. Only I did. I was the only one willing to give my heart, body, and soul to the ones I adored. So far, only one of my golden screen gods had shared my body. That was about to change.

"Soon, my darlings," I crooned as I ran my fingers over the aluminum tins that held the celluloid bodies of my loves. I could feel their combined heartbeats thumb against the pulse of my fingers. I could hear their voices in my head. The pride in their words told me I had done good.

"Yes, I saved you. Just as the five of you saved me so long ago."

Ever since the owner of the Olden Throw Back Theatre had passed, his family had let the once golden palace run to ruin. The facade had faded to a rainbow of colors not found in any artist's paint box. The floors were unstable. Whenever I snuck inside, I had to watch my step lest I fall through the decaying planks and impale myself on some moldy stage prop hiding in the basement. The faded black curtains surrounding the splintered stage hung in rotten tatters. The seats were nothing but springs poking through red velvet fabric. The building was condemned, but I didn't care. There was risk involved. I knew *they* watched my every move but what else could I do? My soul survived for the solitary purpose of granting my paramours their freedom. Each morning, at 3:00 am, I left my dank rooms and headed to the theater. I left during the witching hour because the veil was at its thinnest then. I knew in my bones that the supernatural forces haunting me would have other things to attend to during that time. Until five, when the witching hour ended, I would be free from *their* never blinking eyes.

This time, when I went to visit my darlings, a thought niggled at the back of my mind telling me that tonight would be different. It was as if I could smell something sinister in the air. Normally, when I was out at this hour, *they* left me alone; it was the only time I felt at peace. I knew *they* wanted to drive a wedge between my loves and me. *They* wanted us apart. I could taste the jealousy dripping from *their* life force. Before I left, I lit a candle, prayed to whatever god might be on duty that night, then slide a knife into the only pocket in my coat that moths hadn't eaten completely away. The alley leading away from my rooms was hidden in blackness. I had to feel my way through its depths. Hesitantly, I placed my hand on the brick wall that guarded the abyss. A thick, slimy substance oozed through my fingers. Each night it was the same. One day, when the sun's rays were strong enough to pierce the smog and darkness, I went outside to investigate the nefarious goo. There was nothing there but cold, hard brick.

My progress was tedious. I could feel *them* tracing my footsteps. Evidently, that night, I was *their* thing to attend to. Trying to fool *them*, I ducked in and out of doorways and hidden alleys. I doubled forward then dropped back. Once, I even headed home. When I got to my rooms, I spun around and sprinted to the theater.

I knew right away that something was off. The rusted hinges of the main door lay separated from the wooden frame, causing it to stand frozen in an incomplete fall. As I ducked through the unsafe entrance, I heard voices. Making my way further into the theater, I followed the sound until I could hear what was being said.

"Do you think there's a market for these old black and whites?" A male with a deep, coarse smoker's voice asked.

I inched closer. I was scared, not for myself but for my loves. At first, I wasn't sure where to go. Then I noticed a thin trail of light coming from my left. I held my breath and tiptoed that way, not stopping until I saw an obese man standing near the stage. He was holding a canister between his fingers. The hair on the back of my neck bristled as fear claimed me. "No," I whispered. "Leave them alone, they're mine." No one heard me.

"Nah, it's just a pile of shit. I can't believe people paid to watch this crap."

"I know, right? It had to be old people. They probably have no idea modern, colored picture shows exist." The fat man's companion laughed. I used the sound to cover the squeak of the floorboards as I moved closer. I didn't stop until I was near enough to touch the smaller man, the one holding a flashlight. I hid in the shadows and fumed as the larger man began tossing around the canisters.

"Not sure why the hell we had to wait until the middle of the night to come here… oh, that's right, my sister wouldn't let you out of the house."

"Your sister's a bitch. Now tell me what the fuck we're supposed to do with all this junk," flashlight man snapped at his companion.

"How dare you call my loves junk," I muttered under my breath.

"Did you hear something?" Flashlight man asked.

"Just the ghosts of people who died of boredom while watching Uncle Frank's crappy old movies."

"Old age and boredom will get you every time. I bet no one under seventy ever set foot in this place."

"Idiots." I wasn't old. I'd just turned twenty-one. Though to be fair, the dunderhead was partially right. My soul was old. No, that's night quite accurate. My soul wasn't

15

old; it was gone. I'd used it as fodder to feed my loves. My mind was wandering. It had been doing that a lot lately. It was as if the movie reel in my head had pieces of celluloid burned away. I pulled myself together so that I could listen to what the men were saying.

"I think we should just leave them here. This place will be flattened by noon. What's a little more rubbish?" flashlight man said.

"Not sure why Aunt Kay wanted us to come here and give this shit hole a final sweep. Ain't crap worth saving in this godforsaken tomb. Why don't you head home to Darla while I finish up? Heard her bitching to my wife that you ain't never around. Besides, if she wakes and finds you snuck out…"

"It's three in the morning. That, and the bottle of wine she guzzled before, bed means she ain't waking till at least noon. I *will* take you up on your offer, though. It's past last call but Mickey will open up for me, in more ways than one."

"Hope Darla doesn't find out about your side piece."

"From your mouth to God's ear."

"Yeah, well, I hope God's ear is closed to the sounds you'll be making, and your priest's ear is open to your confession."

"Screw you."

Both men moved toward the entrance. I followed them. While they stood talking by the busted door, I hid behind a grease-covered popcorn machine that had stopped working years before I discovered the theater. From there, I watched the skinny adulterer leave. When the fat man headed back into the viewing room, I crept out from behind the oily beast and inched toward an alcove situated mere inches away from the man.

"What to do with you?" he asked as he picked up a canister. "Guess I could take you with me. Maybe some antique dealer will give me a few dollars. If not, my kids can use you to start a bonfire."

"They don't belong to you! They're mine! You're not taking my darlings!" I screamed as I pitched forward and drove my knife into the man's back.

"What the f—" he began as he reached around and tried to pull the knife out from between his shoulder blades. I was too quick for him. Before he could finish his sentence, I pulled the knife out then jammed it up and under the left side of his rib cage. I laughed as he fell to the floor.

Sitting next to the dying man, I said, "Let me tell you a story. You might be a pig, but even an animal deserves to know why it died."


You see, one night, when I had fallen asleep cuddled in a seat in the loge, your uncle locked up without making sure the theater was empty. That's the night James first came to me. I'm talking about James Cagney. With your unholy distain of the old ones, I'm sure you've never heard of him. Anyway, I had fallen asleep during the second showing of my favorite movie. When I woke, I made my way to the projection booth. I had to see the movie again. I wasn't sure why, but the desire to see James burned through my brain. I knew how to work the projector; I ran it a few times when your uncle's hired boy didn't show up. He gave me free passes whenever I helped out. That night, as I threaded the fragile celluloid through the teeth of the machine, I thrilled at the thought that for once it would be just me and Jimmie.

"*Angels with Dirty Faces*, one of the best," I whispered. "If I'd been in the flick with you, Jimmy, I never would have let you turn bad. I would have found a way to save you. You wouldn't have needed that stupid priest, even if he was an old friend of yours. You would have had me."

"Is that right, doll?"

"What… who…" I spun around. The light of the projector blinded me, and I couldn't see well enough to put a face to the silken voice.

"Over here, doll. Close your eyes for a minute. When you open them, you'll be able to see me."

I turned toward the front of the theater just in time to see James Cagney step off the screen and onto the stage. At first, he was huge, his body matching the size of his celluloid image. I left the projection booth and ran down the stairs to the theater floor. Still half blind, I ran right into Jimmy. Thank God he was human sized, though at 5'5" he towered over my 4'10" frame. He grabbed me in his arms. My vision cleared. I gasped at the sight of his beautiful red hair. I hadn't expected that. Sure, after all the time I'd spent studying him, memorizing every detail of his life, I knew what color his hair was. Still, nothing had prepared me for the actuality of seeing the real thing. The eyes that stared into mine were deep and soulful, so dark that I wasn't sure if he even had an iris. Despite his height, he was built athletic and strong. Before I knew what was happening, he scooped me up and carried me to the stage. He laid me in the middle of the rough, uneven floor.

"I've been watching you," James said. "Yeah, doll, I've been watching you for a long time." The words fell off his tongue in honey dipped heat.

"I love you," I blurted out.

"That makes me want you even more."

"Oh…" Warmth spread across my face at the thought of being loved by this man, this god. I was a virgin. Soon that antiquated term would no longer apply. I settled back on the unsanded wood as Jimmy ripped open the front of my dress. After pulling a knife from his back pocket, he cut the front of my bra and watched my breasts tumble free. With a mischievous grin plastered on his face, he pulled off my panties. Next, he stood and began removing his clothes. Like the refined gentleman I knew him to be, he folded each piece before placing it on the floor. He was hard and ready for me. No foreplay. No preamble. Just wetness and need as he entered me.

I woke to the flap, flap, flap of unthreaded celluloid beating itself to death against a steel gray movie reel.


At some point, while lost in my reverie, I'd pulled the dead man's head unto my lap. I was absent mindedly running my fingers back and forth over his eyelids in order to keep them shut. The souls of the dead can seep through open eyes if you aren't careful. When that happens, the dead haunt you forever. With a sigh, I continued my story.

"God, what happened to me?" I asked the empty theater as I lay there on the stage. I waited for an answer, but none came. My body ached. The pain woke me from my dark haze, and it all came back to me. He'd come to me. I'd played with his beautiful red hair and stared into his dreamy eyes as he hovered over my body.

"Nah, it couldn't have happened. It was just a dream, a fantastic dream," I whispered as I stood. That's when I noticed my dress was shredded. I was naked underneath the ragged fabric. When I tried to take a step, I felt a tight pull between my legs. Looking down, I saw a trail of dried blood gracing my inner thigh. I needed to pull myself together. I walked off the stage, then sat on one of the theater's threadbare seats. As soon as my bottom hit the chair, I felt the slivers.

"It was real," I exclaimed as I ran my fingers over my lips. James Cagney, the James Cagney of *Angel's with Dirty Faces* and *The Strawberry Blonde* and many other wonderful films, had come for me. He'd kissed my never-before-touched lips. He'd taken the virginity I'd once offered up to him while watching one of his films.

Finished with my story, I sneered at the dead man as I pushed his head off my lap. Leaving him there I stood, walked over to the discarded reels, and began sorting through them. Most were just movies with long-forgotten actors lying dead among their dreams. It didn't take long to find the ones hiding the ghosts of my loves. As I held the canisters close to my heart, it dawned on me that I was standing in a no-trespassing, condemned building with the body of a man I had killed.

"Come on, Edna, you have *got* to stay focused," I admonished myself. "What would Jimmy do?" I mumbled till I laughed. My mantra had a much more sinister tone then the one chanted by Christians. Once I settled, an idea came to me.

"Fire. I can use the celluloid to set the theater on fire."

"What about the body, doll face?"

"What? How are you here? There's no movie playing."

Jimmy smiled at me as he maneuvered me over to the nearest wall. He pushed up my skirt, ripped off my panties, then thrust into me. As he moved inside me, a voice in my head told me to gather up the dead man's blood and take it with me. I would need it to resurrect my loves. As soon as Jimmy climaxed, he disappeared. Alone now, except for the corpse, I could sense that the sun had begun chasing the moon. I was out of time. Racing over to the dead man, I grabbed one of the canisters. Dumping out the soulless reel, I used the lid to scoop up as much blood as it would hold. Securing the top to the bottom, I placed the blood-filled vessel on top of the canisters I planned on taking home. Hoping that the dead celluloid would burn hot enough to disintegrate bones, I opened up the canisters and dumped the reels on top of the corpse. I dropped a lit match on top of the movie mountain, grabbed my loves and the blood canister, and headed for the door. With trembling hands, I held my beloveds and prayed that the bones would be gone by the time the firemen arrived.

"We'll take care of everything, little lamb, don't you worry your pretty damned soul," an incorporeal voice sang in the night.


After creeping out of the building, I ran over to the broken-down park that took up residence next to the theater's parking lot. I sat on a rusted carousel that had long ago spun excitable children around until they puked.

"You'd think city hall would have removed this broken piece of crap," I whispered as I used my feet to slowly turn in a circle. Since no sane parent ever brought their little ones to this neighborhood to play, I guessed it wasn't a priority. Besides, the powers that be had long since forsaken this part of Los Angeles.

It had just started to drizzle when I heard the ear-piercing whirl of a fire truck's siren. Afraid I'd be seen, I leapt off the carousel and moved deeper into the park so I could hide in what could loosely be called trees. It wasn't long before I grew bored with waiting. Afraid to leave the safety of the gnarled foliage, at least until after the rescue units had gone, I allowed myself to drift back to the early days spent with Jimmy and my other loves.


After James made love to me that first time, I snuck into the theater every night at exactly 3:15 am. I still patronized the theater every evening so as not to arouse suspicion, and I always made a point of saying goodbye to Frank, the owner, before making the dangerous and dismal trip back to my rooms. Since my return trip was always deep into the evening, I could feel *their* eyes boring into my brain. Once home, I tried to get a few hours' sleep before the witching hour struck three. My mind always raced from thought to thought and chased away sleep. At three, when the ones who watched me were occupied with other tasks, I ran to the theater. Using a key I'd stolen off the back wall of the closed-down concession stand, I slipped inside.

The theater had three projectors. One of them only worked some of the time. That meant I could only let three of my loves out. James was always with me, always. The others didn't seem to care that he was my favorite. After all, he was my first love. They understood the bond we shared.

I would alternate the others. Sometimes I played Rudolph. I knew he wasn't strong enough to come down from the screen. Still, he could talk to me and his rich Italian accent floored me. I couldn't wait to touch the silken strands of his dark brown hair. His eyes were supposed to be brown. Legend had it that they matched the color of his hair. Even though I had yet to see him in color, I knew what to expect. The library was a wonderful thing, a place full of useless knowledge that fueled my existence. He was younger than the others, but that didn't matter, at least not to me. I longed to feel his 5'11" frame wrapped around my waiflike body.

"Piccola ragazza, you are one of the world's great beauties. Bellissimo," he said from the screen. Rudolph Valentino looked stunning in his sheik's robes.

"I love you in *Four Horsemen of the Apocalypse*," I gushed the first time I talked to him. "It's my favorite."

"Why are you playing *The Sheik*, then?" he asked.

"I couldn't find *Horsemen*," I said with a laugh.

Being a creature of habit, whenever I let Rudy out of his canister, I let Charlie out too. Despite his underlying melancholy, he was good for a laugh. When I wanted to talk to Charlie Chaplin, I played, *The Great Dictator.* I was anxious for him to be able to materialize. Having a thing for hair, I wanted to run my fingers through his tousled, black mane as his baby blues took in my nakedness. I usually didn't like men with moustaches, but his made me all tingly inside, which made me like it very much.

Some nights I liked to pair up Douglas Fairbanks with Fred Astaire. I loved a man in tights and what better image than Doug up on the screen leading Robin Hood and his merry men? As for Fred, I thrilled to the thought of him sweeping off the screen, grabbing hold of me, and twirling me around the room. I knew I would be all clumsy feet, but as gifted of a dancer as he was it wouldn't be long before I'd become his new Ginger. When I wanted to see Fred, I played *The Broadway Melody of 1940*. It transported me back to the golden age of Hollywood, an era I should have been born in. Maybe I had been. I couldn't remember. That would explain a lot of things. No, that wouldn't have been possible. I was only twenty-one and the year was… it was… I couldn't remember.

Sometimes, Jimmy wanted me all to himself. When that happened, I didn't even take the others out of their tins. They understood. Jimmy was their leader. With my help he would give them the strength to step down from the screen.


When I came back to myself, I saw that the firemen and police officers were gone. No one had come looking for me, or if they had, they never found me.

For a second, I set down my canisters so I could stretch my limbs and release the cramps in my hands. Within seconds I heard rustling in the bushes behind me and knew *they* were near.

I picked up my loves and ran to my rooms.


I was finally home. As soon as I changed clothes, I could be with my loves. I'd barely finished buttoning up the front of my elegant satin dress when I heard a banging, explosive sound coming from the first of my two rooms. With no time to step into my peep-toed, sling back shoes, I rushed out of my bedroom only to find all but one of my projectors smashed and laying on the floor.

"What happened?"

"I don't know, doll," James said as he turned toward me. He had been peering out my small, soot-smeared window. It was to the right of my wood burning stove, and caught the pollution my only heat source spewed out.

"Did you do it?"

"I may play a criminal on the big screen, but I would never destroy someone else's property. You hurt me with such thoughts."

"I'm sorry, Jimmy. Truly I am." Before either one of else could say anything, another voice joined us. It came from a dark spot behind the table.

"Finally, I get to look into your eyes and caress your beautiful face. Come to me, *bella bambolina*, my pretty bird."

Rudolph stepped out of the shadows and sauntered over to where Jimmy and I stood. Fingers still entwined with Jimmy's, I reached my free hand out to Rudy. He took it, turned it over, and kissed my palm. Jimmy let go of the hand he held and gently pushed me into Rudy's arms. When his mouth met mine, he nipped at my lower lip, forcing me to open up to him. Before I could process what was happening, I was sitting on my faded yellow loveseat and my dress had been hiked up to my waist. I knew the precious satin was crushed. I didn't care.

I felt Rudy enter me. Nearly lost in his rhythmic movement, I was startled when a hand began stroking my leg. I looked down and saw Fred lean into me. He began running his tongue up and down my leg. The gesture should have been unseemly. It wasn't. There was something backwardly erotic about it.

"Come join us, Doug," Jimmy said as he sat down next to me. I heard the front door close. Heavy footsteps trudged on the floor. I turned in the direction of the sound and saw Doug lumbering toward me. There was something a little off about the way he moved.

Before I could give it much thought, Jimmy tilted my head back so that he could reach my lips without bumping into Rudy. I wanted to concentrate on the man making love to me, but my senses were overloaded. Jimmy kissed me long and deep. When he let me come up for air, I glanced down at Fred then over at the window. I could barely see it from where I sat, but the quick glance I stole sent shiver chills down my spine. There was a figure standing behind the smudged glass. It was large and misshapen. *They* had finally decided to make an appearance. My mind was spinning. I felt drunk and confused.

"What's happening?"

"This is what you wanted, isn't it? Or have you changed your mind?"

"What are you talking about, Jimmy?"

"You wanted the others to come to you. You wanted all five of us to make love to you. Did you not realize there would be a price to pay for such hedonism?"

"I thought my love brought you through the veil."

"It did, in a way," Doug said. I noticed he was holding the only canister that wasn't lying open on the table. As he opened it, blood leaked from the sides. He carefully lifted it above his head then poured the contents over the six of us.

Blood spattered into my eyes. I felt the thick, cold liquid seep between my legs.

Sliding my hand down my body, I accidently locked my fingers in someone's hair. The hair felt thick and curly. That's when I knew Charlie had replaced Rudy inside of me.

"Stop. This is all wrong. This isn't how it's supposed to be!" I shouted.

"Oh, but I'm afraid this is *exactly* how things are supposed to happen."

"Who said that?" I asked as the words echoed though the room. Laughter bounced off the walls. That's when I knew *they* had orchestrated the whole thing. *They* had taken over my life. It was never James Cagney making love to me. None of the men playing with my numb body were who I thought they were. My celluloid loves weren't touching me; the real gods of old were.

I heard the clanking sound of a movie reel turning. The men or whatever *they* were heard it too. Momentarily distracted, the golden gods released me. I stood and walked over to where the only surviving projector rested on the table. The film spinning on its reel started playing on the uneven building blocks of my wall. A figure I didn't recognize appeared on the screen. Soon he—I think it was a he—was joined by several other misshapen forms.

"We've been watching you," the thing on the screen said. "Since you were a toddler, we've followed and controlled your life."

"Why?"

"You're special. Part of today's world, yet from another time. We knew you were what was needed to bring us home."

"This isn't your home!" I yelled.

"It was, once. It will be again, once we are strong enough to seize control from the lesser beings that inhabit this plane. You, Edna, are the catalyst that will make us strong again."

I screamed as the ones I thought I loved disappeared. One by one, *they* began stepping out of my wall. Sanity drifted away as darkness fell.


EPILOGUE

"Police! Open up! Ms. Worthington, if you're home and able to come to the door please let us in."

"I don't think anyone's home."

"The private dick her father hired said she hasn't left the place in over a week."

Heavy footsteps echoed down the alley from where the two police officers stood.

"Have you found her?" a man frantically called from the darkness.

"Shit, it's her father. What now?"

"This can't be the place. My daughter would never stay here," a disheveled man said as he joined the officers. "Edna had enough money to buy whatever she wanted. I refuse to believe this hellhole is where she chose to stay."

"Sir, I'm Officer George Kinsey and this is my partner, Officer Sean Gale. I know this must be hard for you, but this is the address your private investigator gave us."

"Then someone must have kidnapped her. My daughter would only stay in a place like this if some criminal was holding her prisoner."

22

"Nothing in our investigation suggests that, sir."

"Officer Kinsey is right. As I see it, we have two choices. We can call for backup in case there's something illegal going on, or we can force the door open and take a look inside."

"Don't you need a warrant?"

"No, sir. No one has seen your daughter in days. You yourself suspect foul play. Edna isn't answering the door. That's probable cause."

"Do it."

Officer Gale ran to the squad car and grabbed a small battering ram out of the trunk. Both officers mounted the decaying steps that led to the door.

"Sir, you need to step away from the building and let us handle this."

"That's my little girl in there!"

Despite its precarious position in the frame, it took four tries before the ruined door gave way.

Officer George was the first one to enter the room. "Oh, my God!"

The second his foot touched the blood-soaked carpet at the base of the door, the odor of unwashed flesh and human piss filled his nose. Green, mucous coated vomit sprayed the brick wall across from the door. Small yellow chunks landed on Mr. Worthington's shoes. George didn't care.

"What the hell?" the distraught man said as he gagged up his lunch. The pungent, acidic smell of his vomit did nothing to lessen the stink of the alley.

"I'm sorry, sir, but I can't let you inside until after the coroner gets here." Officer Gale said in a shaky voice.

"Are you trying to tell me she's dead, my Edna's dead?" the father screamed. "What happened to her? What happened to my little girl?" He wiped a hand across his vomit laced mouth.

"I think we need to wait until the coroner and his team arrive. They're better suited to answer your questions," Officer Kinsey said in what he thought was a firm and comforting voice. It was neither.

"I need to see her."

"This area is a crime scene now, sir. It's imperative that we leave everything as it is."

"No!" Edna's father pushed past the officer and ran inside.

There on a threadbare rug lay his once beautiful princess. Before she ran away from his dark palace, the world had been hers. After her mother had died, he'd sacrificed everything for Edna. He called upon the old ones to watch over her, and begged them to bring his wife back. *They* said that could be easily done if he was willing to pay the price. He promised them anything.

Afraid to get closer, he backed up to the doorway and stared at Edna's lifeless corpse. Cream-colored maggots crawled across her pale skin. The flies that sired them poured from Edna's mouth. Her legs were splayed apart in a way that highlighted the bloody white substance oozing from her core.

Something moved inside the gapping chasm that once held her heart. Entwined in the fingers of one hand was a torn strip of celluloid.

Unable to take his eyes off her rotting body, Edna's father felt his mind slipping away. Nothing that he saw made sense to him and he needed it to. His life was about numbers and data and dark secrets that only he knew.

Collapsing to his knees, he crawled over to Edna. Then he leaned down and placed his blood drained lips against her screaming mouth.

An inhuman sound escaped from him as he stood, mind slipping away. "Why?" he screamed.

"You said you'd pay any price," a soundless voice echoed in his head. Reminding him of the promise he'd once made.

"Not this," he sobbed as he collapsed back to his knees. The world went silent.

Time passed in achingly slow increments. The coroner had long since taken the desecrated body of his daughter. When the investigative team arrived, he'd been escorted out of the building. Now his hollow shell stood in the alley. Someone had thrown a blanket over his shoulders. He hadn't noticed. Even after everyone else had cleared out, he remained standing in front of Edna's door. In the hills above him, the fading words of the Hollywood sign glowed in the distance. He glanced at the letters, but their meaning was lost on him. A small, still-functioning part of his brain told him that he couldn't leave. *They* would be coming for him.

His soul was already gone, so he didn't so much as flinch when a hand touched his shoulder and snaked down to his chest.

"Hello, Peter," someone who sounded very much like his dead wife whispered in his ear.

# THE WARRIORS OF THE SAND

## JANE NIGHTSHADE

"If there was ever a *true* ghost town, it's Shelby," Marina read out from her smartphone, "up in Mono County near the Nevada border."

Kyle kept his eyes resolutely on the road, both hands on the steering wheel. "Hmmm," he grunted in reply.

Undaunted, she continued reading from a website article about historical Shelby: "A hundred and fifty years in the past, Shelby had a thriving goldmine and a population of about ten thousand souls. However, after the mine played out, Shelby's fortunes ebbed, and then the last few diehard residents abruptly left during the Great Depression in the early Thirties."

The couple drove east from San Francisco toward Mono County: he, a prosperous corporate attorney and she, a freelance commercial photographer. It was a long and unfamiliar drive for both of them, toward a landscape they didn't even know existed until a week ago, when Marina had heard about it from a friend in her advanced landscape photography course.

"If I sell any of the Shelby photos, the whole trip is tax-deductible," she reminded him, as they headed toward the semi-isolated badlands of the sparsely populated county.

"Damn." Marina's data connection abruptly died as they started to hit remote countryside. "That's the end for now of my travelogue on Shelby."

"I guess it's nice to know I gave up my weekend for a tax deduction. Why are we going to *this* place again?"

"Because Shelby is *different* from the other old mining ghost towns in California. Mainly, because of how it was *left* by the people who lived there. With canned foods still sitting on the kitchen shelves, the tractors in the fields, the cars parked in the street.

"There were even neatly made beds in the hotel's bedrooms, and full whiskey bottles stacked in the saloons. Nobody knows *why* the people of Shelby left so much behind. But it was completely vacant by 1931."

"This is interesting *why*?"

Marina sighed. "You're so hopeless. Don't you have any curiosity? Why am I with such an unromantic boyfriend?"

"Because of my inescapable charm, clean hygiene, and impeccable dental work," he said, turning briefly to favor her with a toothy grin.

"That must be it." Marina rolled her eyes in mock-contempt. "My friend says the State Parks Service took over, and decided to preserve Shelby just as it was left, a piece of living history. The only people who ever really go there are movie location scouts and artists or photographers, like me. Maybe the occasional history buff."

They arrived at their motel in Mono City, some twenty miles downwind from Shelby, on Friday night; it was mid-spring and the weather was chill and blustery. In the morning, after a full night's sleep, Marina collected a Shelby guide pamphlet from a small stack at the front desk. She also borrowed an old book about the town from a desk in the lobby. She scanned the book over breakfast at their motel's adjoining Silver Dollar Pancake House, reading out little tidbits of information to Kyle over poached eggs, as he pretended to listen.

"Listen to this—it wasn't on the website!" she cried. "There were several notorious lynchings in the history of Shelby, and the judge who presided over the 'frontier justice' was actually named Lynch. Philip Lynch. Isn't that a weird coincidence?"

"Yes, I suppose so," replied Kyle in a detached voice; he was busy reading the *New York Times* on his smartphone. "Good thing they've got free Wi-Fi here, to my ever-lasting shock and awe."

"You're just not into this, are you? I always attend your tacky legal events without *kvetching*—now it's *your* turn to support *my* career."

"Yes, dear." Kyle didn't look up from his digital version of the *Times*. Normally, he only logged onto the Internet to read the *Times*, the *Bleacher Report*, and the *Wall Street Journal*.

"You'll like it better when we actually get there. I'm sure it'll be really interesting and cool, almost like being in an old spaghetti Western." She hummed the theme from *The Good, the Bad and the Ugly*, which Kyle pointedly ignored.

She returned the old history book to the motel's desk clerk after breakfast. The young man looked up briefly from a portable TV, where he'd been watching a gameshow. "You can't take nothin' out of Shelby," he admonished her, placing the book aside. He spoke with an odd inflection over the words *you can't take nothin'*, and Marina took note of it defensively.

She protested, "Of *course*. I would *never* disturb anything at a State Park! It's against the law to take things from the parks."

"Well, in that case, have a good trip with your lawyer boyfriend," came the laconic reply, over the sound of a female contestant screeching hysterically about the price of Tide.

They pulled away from the motel parking lot a few minutes later, and Kyle reminded Marina that Shelby really was a ghost town in the middle of nowhere. "It won't have Wi-Fi or even voice service," he pointed out. "No checking the Internet every five minutes on your phone."

"You don't have to remind me of it, I know," she retorted, as their car continued to creep up the serpent-shaped, two-lane road to Shelby. "I *do* spend too much time on the Internet, and I *am* trying to break the habit."

She looked out of the passenger's side window and watched the road turn lonelier, and the landscape on either side become more forbidding, more wild.

"I've only been on a few minutes today so far, to see what the rating was for my 'Kitler' photo of Mr. Smuggles."

"What the hell is a *Kitler?* I'm almost afraid to ask."

"A Kitler is a cat who looks like Hitler," Marina explained. "There's a whole website devoted to them. You post a picture of your Kitler and then other people vote on its resemblance to Hitler. There are thousands of cats posted there."

"For fuck's sake, that is just ridiculous. What a way to waste time."

"The last time I looked, just one person had voted on Mr. Smuggles, and he only got a 4.5 out of 10. I guess he doesn't really look all that much like Hitler."

"For fuck's sake," repeated Kyle.

"You already said that."

"I meant, for fuck's sake, we're here. Unless I miss my guess, there lies Shelby over yonder in them thar hills."

He gestured toward a hulking arrangement of weathered wooden buildings, painted a faded rusty brown, looming out of the monotonous scrub landscape. "They almost look like Norman turrets brooding over a desert battlefield from the Crusades. *Ahoy Saladin—*"

"It's the stamp mill, silly!" Marina exclaimed. "That's where the mine workers brought in the rocks and boulders for crushing. Then they would extract the gold and silver ore from the crushed rock."

Kyle followed the map in Marina's guide pamphlet to a small kiosk and parking lot marked with the Parks Service's logo. "No rangers are around," he said. "That seems odd."

Marina left a five-dollar bill in a donation box at the kiosk.

"What a lonely job for a ranger," said Kyle. "Imagine being stuck out here by yourself, day in and day out, in a broke-ass ghost town that looks like this."

"Some people might see a rare beauty in the bleakness and solitude," retorted Marina. "Let's go walk around a bit and look for a place to set up the tripod and other equipment for a shoot."

They headed in the general direction of the looming stamp mill, crossing an overgrown field in which sat a weather-beaten cabin. A vintage truck was rotting away in the field, with gray-green prairie grass bursting out of its cab and engine.

"Who would leave behind a truck like that?" wondered Marina aloud. "It would have been valuable in the Depression years. Especially with money so hard to come by in those days."

"Couldn't say," replied Kyle. "Maybe it broke down, and the owners didn't have any money to have it fixed."

They followed the map, cutting through waist-high fields of grass, encountering yet more abandoned old cars, plus rusted-over farm- and mining equipment, until they found the main street.

"This is creepy. We're the only ones here," said Marina. The main street was not paved; it was a long stretch of windswept sand, with dilapidated buildings on either side. Some of the buildings were listing to one side badly; all were weather-beaten, with paint and varnish peeling off like flayed animal skin, and decaying in inglorious silence.

"Looks like Gary Cooper might be coming down the street soon at high noon..." said Kyle.

"It really does look like that, doesn't it? Like a Wild West movie set. And yet people actually lived here for almost eighty years. There was a church, a school, a hotel, even an Odd Fellows hall."

"Let's check out some of the buildings."

They walked into the Shelby General Store, taking in shelves that were still lined with canned goods and dusty old glass bottles. They saw a wooden planked counter with a cash register in rusty metal scrollwork sitting on top, several upright flour and barley barrels, and an old-fashioned coffee grinder ready for customers who didn't exist.

"I don't get it," said Marina. "Why would they leave the food behind? The guide pamphlet said the heavier stuff was left because it was too hard to move down the hill, but what about the food? Who would leave cans of food and coffee behind? Or bottles of medicine? People would have been destitute during the Depression—surely *someone* would have taken the food and medicine."

Kyle shrugged. "I dunno, really. Hey, there's a saloon! Let's go."

"Look at the sign; its name is The Golden Fleece. Must have been very grand in its heyday!"

Inside, a hulking and elaborate pool table dominated the main room; it had a felt top of a still-vibrant light blue shade, and mahogany legs carved with sculptures of rearing lions. Nearby was a wall-rack of pool cues. A long time ago, someone had left two of the cues on the felt covering, as if the players had just set them down to order something from the room's long bar, which was made of dark, dust-covered wood.

The two visitors exclaimed at the mirrored shelves behind the bar—ones that contained an impressive array of spirits, in addition to bottles of syrups and tonics, beer, and champagne. At the bar's far end, a phantom barman had placed a glass decanter and a grouping of shot glasses, each stacked bottom-side up. The barman had turned a solitary shot glass upward, as if waiting to be filled.

"These are very cool," said Kyle, picking up the upturned shot glass. "Wouldn't they look great above the bar at home?"

"*Kyle*! Don't touch anything!"

"Can't I take just one home with me, as a souvenir?"

28

"No! Of course not!"

"Why not?"

"It's *stealing!*"

"It isn't—no one owns this stuff. They left it all here."

"It belongs to the Parks Service now," reminded Marina, firmly. "What would happen if everybody took a souvenir? Soon nothing would be left."

"I didn't see anything in the guide brochure about not taking things. Nor at the parking station," protested Kyle.

"*Hmmmm… you're right.* Usually they put up a sign warning you not to take anything away, even if it's a pinecone or a wildflower. But, anyway, it's wrong, so put that shot glass back. Let's go over to the old hotel—it looks interesting."

Kyle grumbled and made an exaggerated show of putting the shot glass back on the bar. He followed Marina reluctantly outside and down the street to the Shelby Grand Hotel, a three-story brick structure that stood next to the Oddfellows Hall. Unlike the Oddfellows Hall, Kyle pointed out, the hotel wasn't listing crazily to one side. From the street, the building appeared sober and true—even still somewhat habitable, after a little cleaning up.

"What was that?" cried Kyle, all of a sudden.

"What was *what?*"

"I dunno," he said. "I thought I saw something hanging from a window at the jail across the street. Like a body. With bony bare feet, jutting out of a saggy pair of pant legs."

"There's nothing there," said Marina, firmly. "You probably saw a whirlwind spiral of sand. I've seen several since we've been here. Maybe you've got a guilty conscience."

"Guilty about what?"

"Everybody has *something* to be guilty about. Let's go into the hotel."

"Hey, look," said Kyle, after pushing open the front double doors of the Shelby Grand. "The front desk still has room keys in its cubbyholes. And there's a bell and an antique typewriter on the counter."

Marina looked around with a look of awe on her face. She pointed to a little corner off the desk, which housed an ancient telephone switchboard. Some of the lines were still plugged into their moldering, respective slots.

"I wonder what it was like a hundred years ago. People milling about in the lobby, the switchboard operator connecting calls, the bellhops in shiny buttons rushing to get the guests' luggage," she said dreamily. "So romantic! It must have been something to see."

"Yeah, so *romantic,*" said Kyle. "There would be no air conditioning and no deodorant. Everyone would smell like B.O. The street would be full of horseshit. *You'd* be wearing a long dress with ten petticoats underneath, even in a hundred-and-five-degree heat."

"Well, I'd be *used* to it because that's all I would have known. Look over there!"

She gestured toward a long console table in a prominent corner of the lobby, with a glass case on top running the length of it.

"That must be where they keep *The Warriors of the Sand!*" exclaimed Marina. "I read about it in the book at the motel."

They went to look at the case. Marina wiped the dust off the glass top with a corner of her jean jacket. Inside, the case contained a plaster cast—so long it was made of three separate plaster sections—of a stunningly beautiful sand drawing.

"It's a *masterpiece!*" she exclaimed. The plaster had captured a scene of Indian warriors riding out for battle in full regalia, with their painted mustangs, feathered lances, Henry repeating rifles, and quivers of arrows.

"It's remarkably lifelike," she said. "All done with just a sharpened stick and wet sand. There's something almost *religious* about it. If you look at it long enough—it's almost as if—I swear—you could see them moving. With the ponies all nervous and tossing their manes, and the war regalia flapping in the wind."

"So what was the story on this thing?" asked Kyle.

"Apparently there was a young man named Scribbler Jack, a half-white, half-Indian who would make extra money by drawing scenes in wet sand in the street for pedestrians and bar patrons," Marina answered. "The hotel manager's wife was entranced by this particular scene, and she ordered that plaster be poured to preserve it before the wind blew it away."

"I wonder what happened to Scribbler Jack? Seems a shame if this is all that's left of his remarkable talent."

Kyle absentmindedly stuck his hands in the pockets of his anorak. "Hey, what the —it's gone!"

"Gone? What's gone?"

Kyle looked abashed. "I took one of the shot glasses after all, from the saloon. I grabbed it when you weren't looking and stuffed it in the pocket of my anorak. But now it's not there!"

"You *stole* it? How *could* you?"

"I'm sorry. I didn't mean any harm. I just really wanted a souvenir. But now it's gone, and I don't know how that happened."

"It must have dropped out on the ground while you were walking around. We can find it if we retrace our steps. Then, when we find it, *we are going to put it back exactly where it was before.*"

"Okay, okay, Miss Prissy-Face."

They retraced their steps, all the way back to the Golden Fleece. There was no sign of the shot glass on the ground they covered.

Inside the saloon, they looked all over the floor, near the pool table, under the barstools and then—on the old bar itself.

At the far end of the bar, the grouping of overturned glasses and the whiskey decanter was still there. Including the solitary, upturned shot glass, waiting an eternity for a ghostly refill, just as it had looked when they first entered the saloon.

"Can't be," said Kyle. "I *took* the one that was right-side-up."

"There must have been *two* upturned shot glasses," answered Marina. "We just didn't notice it at the time."

"No, there was only *one*."

"You must have dropped the other one," she said stubbornly, sweeping the floor again with her eyes.

"I'm taking it again," said Kyle.

"*Kyle!*"

"It's just an experiment. I'll put it back afterward, I swear." He grabbed the upturned shot glass and stuffed it back into his anorak pocket. "Shouldn't you be setting up your equipment and getting some shots? You're going to miss the best light."

"All right, let's go get the stuff out of the car," she said. Kyle noticed she didn't seem particularly interested in photographing Shelby anymore.

"What I really want to do is just go back to the Shelby Hotel and look closer at *The Warriors of the Sand*. I'm sure I hadn't yet *begun* to see all of the exquisite details."

"You looked a long time already."

"I guess I'll have to take at least a few quick shots out here," she grumbled. "But the real story's in the hotel with the sand cast. I wonder if I've got the right equipment to shoot it properly."

She and Kyle cut through the fields again, past the rusting cars and farm equipment, back to their lonely car. It was still the only vehicle parked in the lot. Kyle opened the trunk and took all the photography equipment out. He shouldered the tripod while Marina grabbed her favorite camera, and they set off once again to the town, wading through the abandoned pastureland.

"Maybe we should start at the church," she said. "I could see if a greeting card company would want to buy a shot of it for Christmas cards."

The church formed a simple wooden structure with a peaked roof and a steeple; it was weather-beaten, with most of the white paint peeled off, and slightly listing to the right. It supported a plain iron cross on top of the steeple. Against the backdrop of the bleak, yellow-green-gray hills and surrounded by abandoned fields, the church would translate well to photography, Marina told Kyle.

"Here," she added, indicating a spot in front of the church. Kyle set everything up as instructed. Then he straightened and stretched, putting his hands absently again into his anorak pockets, while Marina adjusted her camera on the tripod.

"It's *gone!*" he cried. "Marina, the shot glass is gone again!"

"Are you sure?" she said, plainly irritated. "You must have dropped it in the field while you were lugging the tripod around."

"Maybe so," said Kyle. "Call me crazy, but first I'm gonna go back to the saloon and see if it's back in place at the end of the bar."

Marina shouted, "*Oh for fuck's sake!*" but Kyle had already started loping back down the sandy main street toward the Golden Fleece saloon and couldn't hear her words. Reluctantly, she ran after him into the saloon, leaving her tripod, camera, and other equipment behind.

"There it is!" said Kyle. "It's back in its place at the end of the bar!"

This time Marina didn't dispute the number of shot glasses at the bar. "You're right. There were five downturned ones and one upturned one. And that's how many of them are there *now!*"

"What's going on? What *is* this place?"

"You know something... I've been thinking—that clerk at the motel told me '*You can't take anything out of Shelby.*' I thought he was warning me about taking souvenirs... But what if he meant it *literally?* That you can't, *physically*, take anything away from here?"

"But that's crazy, Rina—just crazy." Kyle shook his head. "Maybe I should try to take something else, one of those old bottles... for instance..."

He slid behind the bar and grabbed a tonic bottle off one of the shelves.

"Mornin', folks," came a steely, hard man's voice from behind them.

Kyle and Marina turned to see a figure silhouetted in the doorway of the saloon. When the figure moved closer, they saw a man in an old-fashioned uniform: a dark-blue, brass-buttoned jacket, light blue pants and muddied tall boots with spurs. His wide-brimmed hat bore the crossed-rifle, brass insignia of the U. S. Cavalry on the hatband. He lifted it toward Marina politely, and she could see he had blue eyes and a bright red beard, mustache and eyebrows.

"Um, good morning," replied Kyle, somewhat spooked. "My girlfriend here is a professional photographer. And I suppose you're the ranger from the Parks Service who looks after this place?"

"I'm the *caretaker* here, yes," said the man in uniform.

"Oh, I see. Do they make you wear that as part of the living history exhibit?" asked Marina.

"It's required for my position, yes," answered Red-Beard, with a nod. "I see you've got a bottle there in your hand, sir. You weren't planning to run off with it, were you?"

Kyle's face flushed red, almost as red as the ranger's beard. "Umm, no—not really. I was just looking at it." Hastily, he placed it back on the bar.

The ranger nodded. "You can't really take anything out of here anyway," he said. "Most people around these parts know that."

"What do you mean?"

"Everything here's stuck here, just like them warriors in the glass case at the hotel."

Kyle and Marina looked at each other in disbelief, and Kyle snorted a strangled little laugh of nervousness.

"I don't follow you," said Marina. "What's the connection with that?"

The ranger crooked his stern mouth into the trace of a faint half-smile.

"Let's set down a piece, I don't have anything else to do today, unless some other folks come by, and it don't look like that'll happen."

Red-Beard nodded toward a dusty saloon table with some rickety chairs around it. "Them chairs are okay to set on. In case you were wonderin'."

"This I gotta hear," said Kyle, taking a seat at the indicated table, and Marina followed suit.

"It started with Scribbler Jack, the half-breed drawin'-boy. As was the usual case in

32

those days, neither the white side nor the Indian side wanted much to do with him. His mother's people, the Paiute, decided he was bad medicine because he could draw figgers that looked real, like the white man's art." .

The ranger sighed and sounded almost sad.

"The Paiute didn't like them figgers at all. There was a rumor goin' around the Indian camps that the white man's pitcher box could steal a man's spirit, and I guess some of 'em thought Scribbler Jack's figgers were more of the same. They weren't alone neither—when the pitcher boxes first came to town, even some white Christian folks were scared of them. 'Unholy graven images' said some. As for Scribbler Jack, he kinda made a bargain with his tribe; he promised he'd only draw his figgers in the wet sand. When the sand dried and the wind came up, the figgers would be gone. They weren't permanent-like, so any spirits they stole would be released with the wind."

"He made a pretty good livin' round here, drawing his figgers in the sand with a sharp stick, settin' out a tin cup for folks to show their appreciation. He liked to set up in front of the hotel because a lot of fancy folk ate there."

"But he wouldn't draw on anything but sand?" asked Marina, fascinated.

"Aye—Scribbler Jack would never draw his figgers on paper, or anything else permanent, even though some of the fancy folk offered him money for it. He only worked in the wet sand."

"But—but—he let the warriors be preserved..." she protested.

"There was no *lettin'* about it, Missy," said the ranger, shaking his head. "Jack worked till sundown on a hot Sunday afternoon to draw them warriors, pouring the water on the sand a little bit at a time. Folks crowded around him to watch, eggin' him on. They were all excited, pointin' and shoutin'—'*Oh, those warriors, look how real they are, those horses, those hooves!*' It was a real sight to see.

"Unfortunately for Scribbler Jack, it was *too* good a sight to see. The hotel manager's wife said it would be a crime to let them warriors go back to the wind, when the sand dried out. 'It's a masterpiece!' she cried. 'We can't let it go.'"

The ranger paused for a moment, and an expression of discomfort flitted over his face. He rubbed his upper right arm, somewhat absently, with his left hand. "Excuse me for a piece, I get *pains* sometime in my arm," he apologized. "I dunno why, but I get them now and then... I must be pretty old by now—I've been here a long, long time."

Kyle cleared his throat. He made a face to Marina that said *not right in the head* and she nodded back, with a faint, knowing smirk.

The ranger continued his story after a few moments, the pains apparently gone.

"She screamed for someone to get the plasterer and he came a-runnin', even if it was a Sunday. Scribbler Jack kept objectin', mind you, but nobody wanted to listen to a half-breed. When it was all done, he snuck into the hotel several times, tryin' to destroy them plaster casts, but he was always caught. Then they got that glass case and locked it, and that made him even madder. He tried one last time, goin' there with a big rock at night to smash the case, but the manager caught him and shot him. Shot him right there in the lobby of the Shelby Hotel. Claimed it was self-defense, and Judge Lynch was happy to oblige and let him go. Ol' Jack was taken to a bunk at the old jail and that's where he died. Poor fella had to look at ol' Barefoot Burke hanging' from a window upstairs while he passed."

Kyle pulled back from the table in fear. "Barefoot Burke? Hanging from the window?"

Red-Beard nodded. "One of Judge Lynch's specials. Got his neck stretched that morning. He never wore shoes. Looking' at that thing probably hurried poor Jack to his final reward. Why'd you ask?"

"I *saw* a man hanging from the top window, while we were walking to the hotel. He had long, bare feet."

The ranger rubbed his sore arm again. "It coulda been a dust spiral," he finally allowed. "Plays tricks on the mind. Barefoot Burke has been gone a very long time, I reckon."

"That's what *I* said. But what about Jack?" Marina interrupted. "And the warriors and the plaster casts—?"

"Well, that's what I've been *tryin'* to tell you. Before he died, ol' Jack told the Doc, *'This town'll be locked in as long as them warriors are locked in that glass case.'*"

"*Locked in*? What did he mean by that?" asked Marina.

"It happened kinda slow-like, after that. But people started noticin', as the years wore on. A load of ore would disappear on its way to Mono City. When the ranchers tried to drive their beef out, the cattle would spook and stampede. It kept gettin' worse, and people started leaving, first just a trickle, then a flood. Some of their things would disappear when they tried to leave, and eventually, it got so bad, people were just leaving' everything behind, except the clothes on their back. But nobody wanted to talk about what was happening', because they didn't want to admit there were things that couldn't be explained by their Bibles.

"And that's why you *can't* take anything out of Shelby. You can try to take that there tonic bottle—" he nodded at the bar where Kyle had left it— "but that ain't gonna do no good."

Kyle and Marina sat in silence, trying to make sense of the ranger's tale.

"Thank you for the story," said Marina, finally. "That was worth the trip up here, just for that."

"'Tain't nothin', ma'am." He rummaged inside his jacket and consulted an antique pocket watch. "It's past noontime. Time to get back to my rounds. Afternoon, ma'am," he said, standing and tipping his hat again to Marina.

The ranger nodded at Kyle and then walked out of the saloon.

"Well," said Kyle finally. "That was quite a story. I guess it's time for us to be going, also. Your tripod is waiting for you back at the church, m'lady."

"Yes, I guess we'd better go."

They walked out onto Main Street and saw that the sun was high in the sky; the ranger's timepiece had been accurate, for its age.

"That's funny," said Kyle. "I don't see old Red-Beard anywhere on the street. He only left about two minutes ago."

34

"Maybe he knows a shortcut." Marina spoke in a distracted tone. "He probably knows this place like the back of his hand. You know what, Kyle?"

"What?"

"It isn't *right*, what happened to Scribbler Jack."

"Yeah, I know. A terrible injustice—letting the manager off for killing him."

"That's not what I meant. Yes, that part was terrible, but it's the fact that they wouldn't respect his wishes about *The Warriors of the Sand*. It wasn't right to lock them up like that."

"*Lock them up?* You can't tell me you believe that nonsense? It was clearly made up just to discourage people from taking things. That ranger has probably told it to hundreds of visitors."

"Well, if you don't believe it, you can always go back inside the saloon and try to take that tonic bottle out to the car. And what about Barefoot Burke?"

A dark, fidgety look passed over Kyle's face. "Uh, no thanks, I've had enough of that saloon and its contents. Enough of this whole place, as a matter of fact. And I probably read about Barefoot Burke somewhere and just didn't remember it. You don't seem too enthusiastic about taking photos anymore, anyway. How about we just go back to the motel in Mono City, have a bite to eat, and get some rest? We can come back tomorrow."

Marina sighed. "Okay. I just can't get my mind off poor Scribbler Jack, though. It's like they *violated* him. The whole town just looks different now. Maybe tomorrow it'll be different."

They retrieved the tripod and other equipment from outside the church and then trudged back to the little Parks Service kiosk where the rental car was parked.

"We're the only car here," said Kyle. "How'd that ranger get here?"

"He probably lives somewhere close by, just off the highway. He probably walks to work when the weather's good."

"Yeah, probably," said Kyle.


All the rest of the day, Marina gave off an air of being distracted and ill at ease. Kyle attempted to cheer her up, but she could only manage a few weak smiles—even when he called up the Kitler website, and reported that the rating for Mr. Smuggles had improved to 5.3.

"Well, that's nice for the cat," she said in a bland voice.

Kyle was mystified. "Since when is Mr. Smuggles 'the cat?' You dote on that creature!"

"Piffles," she harrumphed back.

She went to bed early, pleading exhaustion, and he went up a bit later, after a drink at the motel's little bar. They watched an old episode of *Star Trek: The Next Generation* on the motel's all-too-basic cable service, and then turned out the lights at nine-thirty.

Marina was troubled all through the night. Kyle had never known her to talk in her

35

sleep, ever, and they had been living together for more than two years. But that night she did talk in her sleep, muttering words that clearly concerned Shelby and Scribbler Jack, although he couldn't quite make out their meaning.

*Paiute War* and *bluecoats* and *horse soldiers*. And even some garbled words of an unidentifiable foreign language. Marina didn't fall into a real sleep until a good deal after midnight, but when she did, she slept deeply until morning. She woke to find Kyle hovering over her with donuts and hot coffee on a tray from the motel lobby.

"Good morning, sweetie," he said. "Want some hot coffee?"

She sat up in bed. "Smells really good, even for motel coffee. Thanks!"

"You had a terrible night last night," said Kyle, sitting down on the side of the bed.

"Really? I don't remember anything at all."

"You kept saying nonsense about the Indians, and then there was one part when you apparently started talking in Klingon."

"Did I?" Marina laughed. "Well, I'll tell you, I *was* a little *spooked* by that ghost story the ranger told us yesterday."

"Oh, I knew you were. Look, sweetie, I've been to a few of these old Gold Rush towns, and the locals do whatever they can to bring in the tourists. They tell ghost stories; they dress up like Annie Oakley and Buffalo Bill; they claim that Joaquin Murrieta or some other desperado used their town as a hideout. That ranger just did his job *too well,* and besides, he probably didn't realize he was dealing with a delicate artistic temperament like yours."

"But what about the shot glass you tried to take out of the saloon? You have to admit, that was *very* strange."

"I've been thinking about that. I think it fell out of my anorak pocket both times, just like you said it did. It fell on the ground, and the ranger was walking around on his rounds, and he found it twice and put it back. That's the only rational explanation."

"I guess that could be," admitted Marina. "He sure showed up at the right time, didn't he? Like he'd been watching us for a while and knew what we were up to."

"That's my girl." Kyle leaned over and gave her a quick kiss. "Do you still want to go out there and get your photographs?"

"Oh, yes!" said Marina, suddenly alert, back to her old, enthusiastic self. "It looks like it's going to be a wonderful day, too, much nicer than yesterday. The light will be gorgeous."

They drove back to Shelby, and this time, Marina packed both of her cameras in the trunk, plus the tripod: the big camera for taking landscapes on the tripod, and a smaller one for shooting interiors.

They parked in the Park Service's lot, in the same spot as they'd done the day before. Once again, theirs was the only car in the lot.

"I hope we don't see Ranger Rick today," said Marina. "There was something about that cavalry uniform, and the way he wore it, that creeped me out. It didn't look like it came from an online re-enactment catalog. Like it was homemade, or something."

"I hope we don't see him either. He clearly thinks we're troublemakers."

They unloaded the car and strode through the abandoned fields toward Shelby. "Look at all the wildflowers! Aren't they beautiful? I didn't even notice them yesterday. And the sun's so bright, even the stamp mill looks kind of cheerful."

Once again, they found the church, and Kyle set up the tripod and Marina adjusted her big camera on it. She took several pictures of the church. "These are gonna be good," she said happily. "I got some of the wildflowers in the foreground.

"Okay, that's about it for the church. Kyle, why don't you take the tripod and the big camera over to the school? I want to get that too. And while you're setting up, I'm going over to the hotel with the other camera to get some pics of the interior. I love that old typewriter on the front desk counter—how much do you think that thing weighs? It looks like a rock."

Kyle looked a little uneasy at talk of the hotel. But Marina seemed so cheerful and enthusiastic, that he relaxed. "Sure, I'll meet you over at the school once you are finished at the hotel."

They gave each other a short kiss, and then parted after reaching Main Street. Marina headed one way toward the hotel, and Kyle went the other way to the school.

The school building was a handsome structure, Kyle told himself, as he unfolded the tripod and set it up in a likely spot, and affixed the large camera to it. It was one of the better-preserved buildings, a two-story wooden clapboard structure with a copula on the roof that contained what looked like the original cast-iron school bell. He walked all the way around it and then peeked inside. He saw a few rows of wooden desks in the main classroom—the old-fashioned kind with inkwells in the corners—and an antique map pulled down over the chalkboard, showing the borders of the nation circa 1880. The walls were lined with shelves filled with crumbling books, and there was a prim rolltop desk in one corner.

Kyle heard something moving behind him, and turned quickly. It was only a small cloud of dust and sand kicked up by the wind. "Dust spiral," he recalled Marina lecturing, before. "They do get around."

Then he noticed that at his feet was a drawing in the sand. He bent and looked closer. It depicted a pair of eagle feathers, crossed at the quills, exquisitely drawn. "Someone's been here!" he told himself. "Hell of an artist. Maybe they were here yesterday after we left. But how'd this drawing survive the wind?"

Later, he sat on the steps of the school building to wait for Marina to come back, thinking troubled thoughts about the curious feather drawing. He waited a long time, and then eventually consulted his watch, amazed to see that he'd been waiting for an hour and a half.

"I should go over to the hotel and see what Rina's up to," he said aloud. "She doesn't have that much time to shoot before we have to drive back to the motel, pack up, and then hit the road for the city."

He jogged over to the old hotel, feeling a kind of dread with every stride. He stopped shortly in front of the Golden Fleece, thinking he'd heard someone moving about inside, and wondered if the red-bearded park ranger was lurking about, watching them. But then he moved on; the first priority was to see if Marina was all right, or if she needed help. When he reached his destination, there was a strange field of pewter sky and charcoal clouds around the hotel, and the building itself looked dark and forbidding.

"Where did all that sun go?" he wondered. "How did we ever think that hotel was charming and quaint?"

He jerked open the grand old double doors, and slipped inside the lobby. In the gloom, his eyes located Marina after a moment or two; she was standing in the corner, near the glass case that held *The Warriors of the Sand*, and there was something about her stance that wasn't quite right. He approached quickly and saw that she was standing on the carpet in a ring of white powder, surrounded by broken pieces of some white thing. Her small camera was on the floor next to her, still in its case.

Then he noticed that there was a good deal of broken glass on the floor around Marina too, mixed in with the white dusty powder.

"I had to let them *out*," she said, in the same dreamy, preoccupied manner she had shown the previous evening. "It wasn't right."

Then he saw what had happened. She'd taken the heavy old antique typewriter from the front desk, and used it to smash open the glass case. With the case destroyed, she'd removed the three adjoining plaster casts of *The Warriors of the Sand*, and smashed them also, leaving broken plaster pieces and dust all over the threadbare carpet. The typewriter, now mangled and twisted, lay nearby.

"*Rina, for God's sake, what have you done?*" Kyle cried. "You've *vandalized* it!"

"It belonged to Scribbler Jack," she said. "It didn't belong to the hotel, don't you see? I *had* to do it."

"We need to leave, now!" Kyle cried, grabbing Marina's arm. "I think I saw the ranger over at the saloon. He could come in here any minute, and then you'd really be in trouble. This could mean a huge fine or even jail time! You've destroyed valuable state property."

Marina smiled an odd, crooked half-smile, as if unaware of what she'd really done.

"You act like you've lost your mind!" he cried. "Yesterday, you almost took my head off for wanting to nick a lousy little shot glass!"

He picked up the small camera and pulled her along by the arm with his free hand, out onto the verandah of the old hotel, keeping his eye cocked for any sign of the red-bearded park ranger. He squinted down the sandy length of Main Street—

"What the—?"

A huge cloud of dust rolled straight toward them: thick, advancing yellow-gray dust and swirling sand. And the sun was bright again, incredibly bright, almost blinding.

As the cloud came closer, Kyle could hear a kind of dull pounding, which made a faint collective roar, and then he heard high-pitched whooping of shouts in some peculiar tongue, and he saw, for the first time, the flashes of the sharp hooves and the fiery snorting nostrils, the buckskin-clad legs kicking painted mustang flanks, the sun glinting off the fittings of scores of raised Henry rifles, and the polished stone heads of arrows fitted to a hundred raised bows...

"*I had to let them out, don't you see?*" said Marina in a strange, mechanical, pleading voice, from beside him. "*It's what he wanted.*"

"But they're coming right toward us!" screamed Kyle, and then his voice was strangled in the dust and sand.

Across the street, the solitary red-bearded man in cavalry blue moved out onto the creaking boardwalk in front of the saloon, and silently watched the mustang ponies gallop past in an enormous cloud of dust and sand. An ancient memory stirred in his consciousness.

"There's nothing I can do now—it's a full-on Indian warrior raid and you poor folks ain't gonna get out of it," he said to the cloud of dust, sand, whooping figures, and horses. "Such a pretty girl and nice young fella." He shook his head with a regretful motion, and started to rub his painful right upper arm. "I remember now—it's from that arrow I took back in the Paiute War of Eighteen Sixty-Ought."

# CAT

## MIKE LERA

Carrying the little plastic cage by its handle, Rebecca sprinted up the non-operating escalator, panting, face fraught with dread, a pang of fear hitting her chest like electricity the more she contemplated *Charles* wandering from the subway terminal.

Wandering into the world.

Rebecca was thirteen, petite, wrapped in rugged street clothes. Jean jacket, faded pants and dirty tennis shoes. Head harnessed with a linty beanie, her long black hair hanging past her shoulders, dangling along her heavy backpack that bobbed up and down as she ran.

Her brown eyes were teary, stinging with sweat, and she could see portions of North Hollywood as she approached the top of the stairs. Piles of buildings jutting the dark sky beyond Lankershim Boulevard, scattered streetlights glowing with a yellow hue above them, diffused by a thin two a.m. fog.

She halted at the top of the steps, her moist palms resting on the rubbery hand rails, feeling the cool air from the desolate parking lot outside, listening to the high-pitched choruses of distant subway trains below.

*Need to check all floors,* she thought.

Rebecca scurried back down the escalator, back inside the subway station. Reaching the top floor terminal, she maneuvered over turnstiles and proceeded quickly down a flight of stairs, to the mid floor. Train tracks lay on both sides of the platform. Thick yellow pillars and cement benches lined the middle. The beige checkered floor was spangled with black stains like a mechanic's garage.

Rebecca rechecked the bench area where she had fallen asleep earlier, dozing into a much-needed two-hour nap. Where she awoke to find Charles's open, empty cage beside her. Where her initial instinct told her he was stolen. Where she quickly discarded that idea.

He would have screeched; she would have heard him.

No, Charles was clever. He had a knack for tinkering his way out of things. He'd done it many times before, ever since he was young. Always fidgeting, tinkering with the latch on the cage's little metal door. She always found it so adorable when he batted at it with his little harmless paw, like a puppy puttering a small toy.

Aside from all this, Rebecca would have heard someone approaching; the sound would have roused her from her nap.

*Her father had trained her well for that sort of thing.*

All that mattered now was that Charles was gone, and this was not good.

She reached into her pocket and dug out a white plastic bottle containing Charles's special pills. She checked her watch. It was well past his med time.

There was a hollow place in the pit of her stomach, warm like the air. "Please, God... pleeeease..." Rebecca whimpered. Then she said in Russian, "I need to find him *now*!"

She had been in the U.S. now for three years and lived in Northern California with her family. This had been her first official trip to Los Angeles, and as a thirteen-year-old, she wished that her current excursion could have been a nice, fun visit to Venice Beach, Universal Studios, or Dodger Stadium. Not running away from home, fleeing The Place.

Fleeing from her uncle and brother.

Dashing down another flight of stairs, Rebecca entered the station's bottom level terminal, which had only a single train track. More pillars aligned the middle of the platform, and Rebecca could hear voices behind one of the last pillars. Youngsters laughing, goofing around. Rebecca would normally avoid strangers at this hour, especially in a place like this, in a city like this. But Rebecca was desperate.

She took a deep, centered breath. Walked past a few pillars, her nostrils ensnared by the raw pungent smell of marijuana. At the last pillar, she found two teenagers, male and female.

The boy was a tall, heavyset Latino, about nineteen, bulky as an ape. He wore sunglasses, a black Rams cap and a dark winter jacket. The girl was slightly younger, a Latina with long reddish hair and red lips. She wore a tight "Punisher" shirt with a faded white skull and carried a canvas knapsack.

The teens silenced when they saw Rebecca approaching.

Her heartbeat was in her throat, yet she stayed poised, resting the plastic pet cage on a bench beside her. In her foreign accent, she said, "I was wondering if you have seen my cat."

The boy replied, "Uh... naw."

"Where you from?" the girl asked, dropping her sack. Rebecca took a slight interest in the girl's tattooed fingers as she put a marijuana joint to her mouth. "You like, Persian or Armenian?"

"Homegirl sounds like Dracula," the boy remarked, coughing up cannabis smoke.

The boy and girl chuckled, gave each other fist bumps.

41

"I'm Chechen," Rebecca replied, firmly, her stare now stoic. "And I'm from Dagestan."

"W'zat? 'Taco stand?'" the boy blurted out.

"Tha's cold, Grizzly," laughed Maga, playfully swatting the boy on his big arm. Closing a hand on her joint, the girl said to Rebecca, "Watch this, chica," and with the other hand, made a "gun" and "shot" the closed fist. "Pew!" she sputtered. She opened her hand; the joint was gone.

"I'm Maga—means magician." She eyed Rebecca's backpack. "Let's try your bag." A moment later, the suggestion became an order. "Give it up."

Grizzly's smiling face had evolved into a hard stare.

Rebecca remained mannequin-stiff as Maga stepped closer, overwhelmed by the older girl's aroma of marijuana and onion breath.

Maga lifted a tattooed hand toward Rebecca's shoulder where a strap of the backpack had been harnessed. Rebecca gazed into the girl's cool, dark eyes. But the second Maga put her hand on Rebecca's shoulder, the second she touched her, something inside struck Rebecca like an electric jolt, awakening a *demon* deep within her that had long lain dormant, tucked away in a locked cage... now unleashed.

Rebecca grasped her attacker's index finger, gave it a quick clockwise twist, until... *Snap!* Maga wailed.

Rebecca followed with a punch to the nose. Maga fell to the floor, blood gushing.

Grizzly launched himself at Rebecca. She sidestepped with careful coordination and connected with a side kick to Grizzly's knee cap, sending him down on one knee with a yelp. Before he could rise, she gave him a martial arts-style open-handed thrust to his Adam's apple, knocking the air from his windpipe.

Grizzly grasped his neck, gasping as though choking on a bone. Rebecca grabbed the back of his shirt and withdrew an Ontario Apache folding blade from her back pocket, flinging it open like someone straight out of *Soldier of Fortune* magazine.

A flash of memory flickered in her mind. A glimpse of her father, one of her last "sessions" with him. *Victor or victim,* he'd said.

Raised in Dagestan, a Russian republic warzone rife with separatism, organized crime and ethnic tension, Rebecca and her brother were schooled in military combat the way other children are taught how to ride a bike, hit a ball or swim.

Taught. Trained. Prepared. Radicalized. Immersed in marksmanship, blades, hand-to-hand combat, and explosives, their father filled with an inexpressible hope that his children might also spread their *cause*. Protect their *cause*. Die for it against anyone or anything outside of it.

Rebecca held the knife to the gagging Grizzly's throat, seconds from slicing him. Because it wasn't a nineteen-year-old boy she was seeing—*it was that Russian soldier who had gunned down her father while walking home from the market, mistaking him for a Chechen extremist who had bombed a Russian army jeep just days before.*

Continuing to hold Grizzly by his shirt, Rebecca's mind flashed with more memories.

Recollections of her gentle mother, whom Rebecca loved, and the "old house" in Fresno, California where they lived, shortly after their arrival in the U.S.

The sight of her sweet, gentle mother on hospice care, lying weak in bed. Her mother presenting her with a gift on her 10th birthday.

A kitten.

"Please, care for him," her mother told her, handing her the gray and black-striped little cat. Her first gift that wasn't a weapon. "Love him. Be kind. Please, Becky, be... kind. *Dah-rah-gah-ya.*"

Her mother's last words to her.

Still holding the knife to Grizzly's throat, Rebecca glanced at the empty cat cage on the platform bench, as though roused from a trance.

She peered down at the fat boy, then looked at the knife, her grimacing face untightening; the demon within her tucked back into its crate. "I don't have time for this," she muttered coldly, shoving Grizzly to the floor.

She needed to get Charles.

Grabbing the cage, she sprinted across the terminal, to the staircase.

In her periphery, Rebecca spotted Maga taking something out of her knapsack. Seconds later, she was pointing a .9 millimeter at Rebecca. *BAM!*

Pieces of plaster flew off a wall behind Rebecca. She blitzed up the staircase, back to the mid floor, her heart trip hammering. She ran across the platform, to a nonoperating escalator ascending to the top floor terminal.

Rebecca climbed the long flight of metal stairs. She repeated in her head, *Should have killed them. Should have killed them both.* Her father's words echoed in her mind: *Victor or victim.*

As she neared the top of the staircase, she heard sounds. Inhuman sounds, identical to a meat-depraved wild beast chowing on well-anticipated carnage, and she slowed her pace. Peered just over the landing.

A large foyer was before her, white-walled and brightly lit. And there, in the middle of the room, a tall, skinny boy lay on his back staring at the ceiling, the top of his bald tattooed head facing Rebecca. Strips of gash marks lay across the top of the boy's head, deep and nasty.

At the boy's side was a small animal—*a cat.* A skinny, gray and black-striped house cat, its front paws mounted upon the boy's stomach, its little head looming above him. Rebecca wasn't close enough to see exactly what the animal was doing or what was going on. But one thing was certain—this animal was Charles.

Cage in hand, she stepped off the escalator and onto the floor, a look of confused glee smeared across her sweaty face. She listened to the cat's low grumble-gripe noises. Its head jerked as it hovered over the boy. Rebecca crept closer, and saw blood. Lots of it, pooled on the youngster's stomach, and she realized—or rather confirmed— that her lost cat Charles was tearing his teeth into a boy's belly.

Just looking at the gruesome scene made Rebecca's teeth hurt. Her blurry eyes fought to adjust as the cat's jaws closed and crunched through the teenager's tattooed skin, pulling tendons like wires, blood spilling onto the floor. She fell back a step, all her muscles tensing into tight guitar strings. She felt as if she had suddenly stepped into a dark, horrifying fairy tale.

"Oh God, Charles," she whispered. Tears choked her voice, squeezing it, blurring it. And staring at the cat, her cat, her Charles, her first panicky impulse was to call him.

She reached into her pocket. For the pills. The pills, however, weren't worth squat right now.

The creature stopped its feasting and turned its pointy-eared little head toward her.

A thick, continuous guttural groan rumbled in its chest, a sound unlike that of any normal cat. Charles gazed into Rebecca's grimacing face, his large green eyes settling magnetically on her. His bloodstained, whiskered mouth tightened into a humorless grin as he hissed. His teeth were like a row of yellowed fence spikes, caked with human carnage. His face was twisted and wild, a crazed caricature of a nice, gentle domestic cat. Combined with his gray and black-striped coat, the snarling creature made Rebecca think of a miniature Maltese tiger.

*Uncle!* Rebecca's mind fluxed. *Uncle, you sick twisted man!*

Shortly after her mother's death three years ago, Rebecca and her older brother went to live with their uncle in Sacramento, California. A former genetic researcher, her uncle owned a ranch-style home surrounded by acres and acres of land, a sort of compound Rebecca always referred to as The Place.

Memories of The Place flickered in her mind like lightening. Particularly the Workshop, as Rebecca had called it, a laboratory of assorted animals ranging from monkeys to sea creatures to hawks and other birds.

Memories of...

—*Test subject #0110, "the mouse," placed with a large Indian cobra, the little rodent viciously and efficiently biting off the snake's head...*

—*Test subject #0142, "the octopus," tossed into the shark's tank, pulping a Great White's bones to bits with its tentacles...*

—*Test subject #0198, "the tarantula," put into a cage with a road runner, the bird bitten so many times, blood dripped from its lifeless beak...*

Charles approached her. Rebecca took a tentative step back and set her backpack on the floor. Her nerves were like tripwires that triggered land mines. Her breath came to a painless, complete stop. No movement in her legs, her tripwire nerves setting off explosions down the core of her spine, shutting off all signals. Her hands became stupid blocks of dangling flesh.

The cat was now twenty feet from Rebecca, its back arched—a furry little Quasimodo on all fours. Its gray and black hair stood on end. Its pulsating, watery eyes never left Rebecca's bulging brown ones. Deep, hissing groans emanated from its body. Saliva and blood dribbled from its chin as it slinked forward, almost languidly, readying its attack.

In a slow sort of whimper, Rebecca whispered, "Ch-Charles...?"

A voice from behind her jumpstarted her nerves, causing her to drop the cage.

"What the hell?"

Rebecca turned around.

44

Maga stood before her, face and shirt matted with her own blood, .9 millimeter in hand. Grizzly limped at her side, clutching his throat. Their eyes bulged, mouths gaping with terror and disbelief at the bald boy lying lifeless across the room in a pool of blood.

They didn't, however, notice the bloodied cat approaching.

"Tha's Sleeper!" Grizzly shouted, his eyes darting rapidly between Rebecca and his dead friend across the foyer.

Maga pointed the gun at Rebecca's face, her own face twisted with discombobulation and anger. "What did you do to Sleeper?"

Rebecca held a blank stare. Her combative instincts urged her to snatch the weapon. Point it back at her assailant. Blast her. But Rebecca was spellbound. Dazed from seeing what her pet Charles had become.

Maga shouted, "Answer me, you little—"

A horrid, high-pitch screech seized everyone's attention. An instant later, a ball of gray and black fur bolted at Maga like an arrow shot from a crossbow.

Maga fired an aimless shot from her pistol, but it was more of a spazzed reaction to the cat landing on her breast. Charles's long claws dug deep into her flesh, blood oozing. Then he gave the screaming girl a fantastic swat to the face with a powerful paw, and a good portion of Maga's skin ripped off. Like removing the top layer of a pizza, revealing the sauce and lumpy crust beneath. The gun fell from Maga's swaying hand and slid across the foyer floor.

Maga collapsed, Charles remaining on her chest. The cat went to work on her neck, sank its teeth in easily, blood spraying. Rebecca and Grizzly, meanwhile, watched with dropped mouths and wide eyes. Watched as Charles ripped out her throat and sort of . waved the flesh and limp veins around in his mouth in playful triumph.

Emitting shrill gasps from both horror and nausea, Rebecca and Grizzly ran across the foyer, bolted down the escalator. They paused at the mid-floor terminal, panting as they faced the escalator in fearful anticipation. Grizzly withdrew a large hunting knife from a hidden pouch.

But they heard nothing. Saw nothing.

Until…

A gruesome howl hailed from above.

The small cat descended upon them from the top floor balcony like a muskrat paratrooper jumping from a plane, Charles's blood-outlined mouth making him resemble a demonic cat-clown.

He pounced on Grizzly, who flinched away absurdly, like a kid getting his first shot. Then there was a *shhllick* sound, and the cat instantly bounced off Grizzly's chest and fell to the floor. It screeched and scrambled about the platform, Grizzly's knife lodged deep in its shoulder, blood trailing and flailing about.

Then the knife came out of the animal, landed on the floor, and Grizzly and Rebecca gawked stupidly as Charles slid over the platform edge into one of the train track gullies, completely out of sight.

Silence.

No movement of any sort. Rebecca and Grizzly waited for the cat to leap out again. But it didn't.

Rebecca fixed her gaze on the gully wall. *He's hurt... bad.*

She wanted to save him. Get him off that track. Get back on the road she was on and continue their journey together.

But good ol' Mr. Logic-Reason slapped her upside the head.

Charles was sick. Dangerous. And if she loved him, truly loved him, she would let that stab wound finish him. Let the next train end him. She wondered if she should have even taken him with her when she escaped from The Place.

Her thoughts were cut short by a slow, hideous sound drifting from the gully. A low, powerful growl, like a combined lion, bear and gorilla. A bellow echoing throughout the entire terminal.

Grizzly took an involuntary step back. He picked up his bloodied knife off the floor, trembling.

Another growl, and it was apparent by now that these were not noises produced by a small house cat. Rebecca understood what was happening. *The further the excitement, the further the process,* her uncle had said, after his work on Charles had been completed six weeks ago. An expert in the field of molecular genetics who had once used animal models to "save human lives," Rebecca's uncle had created his greatest masterpiece, now in full bloom. Which was why he constructed a neurological drug to sustain Charles—special pills—before it would be time to officially unleash him on certain... targets.

Of course, a subway terminal at 2 a.m. wasn't what her uncle had planned.

Rebecca spotted a floor-to-ceiling elevator in the middle of the platform, a large square structure with silver metal walls and two adjoining metal doors, resembling a giant safe. She forced her legs to take her there.

She slapped the UP button, arm trembling like a track under a train. *Bing!* The elevator's double doors opened. She dashed inside, pressed the HOLD button, glanced at Grizzly across the platform.

But Grizzly just stood at the center of the platform, gaping at the track gully.

"Come on!" Rebecca screamed.

Grizzly didn't budge, eyes fixed on *something* emerging from the gully, something Rebecca was unable to see from the elevator cab.

Again, she heard the horrific growls and groans echoing from the train tracks. Watched the knife drop from Grizzly's hand. Then, as the elevator doors began to shut, she saw it. Huge, grayish, the size of an ox, blitzing across the platform, hitting Grizzly like a freight train.

The doors closed. *Bing!*

Rebecca stood there, unmoving. Listening to Grizzly's screams. Listening to the beast, its roars like an angered dragon, puma and T-Rex all shouting in harmonious concert.

And suddenly... silence.

Finally, she raised her hand to press the UP button, and then...

*BA-DOOM!*

The entire elevator shook. Rebecca stumbled, wobbling like a three-legged chair. She steadied herself, again attempted the UP button.

*BA-DOOM!*

Another jolt, both metal doors denting inward, the elevator lights flickering. Then another jolt, the doors protruding further. Then another, this time knocking Rebecca to the cold, dirty floor. She reached up and finally managed to press the UP button. The lift, however, remained stationary, so damaged it could go nowhere. There was another jolt, this time from the side, forcing Rebecca to the opposite wall. Then another hit, from behind her, the protruding wall nudging her to the center of the cab.

Her mind clamored, awash with fear, heart thudding heavily in her chest. Yet she stayed still, remembering one of the key elements her father taught her for basic survival: calmness. Listening to the outside roars, Rebecca remained at the cab's center, breathing in harsh gasps while the elevator shuddered and screeched.

And all at once, the battering stopped.

Rebecca waited. Sat in the quiet for a while, stared at the dented walls. Her mind drifted. Images of The Workshop entered her head.

Fragmented memories of...

—*finding Charles's empty cage in the lab...*

—*entering the Restricted Area, walking down that long bright corridor that resembled the sanitarium wards she'd seen in movies, squared holding cells with thick glass on either side of her...*

—*cougars in these cells, pacing back and forth...*

—*jaguars in others, staring straight at her...*

—*tigers, cheetahs, and other wildcats being wheeled down the corridor on gurneys, heavily sedated, stitched up at their stomachs...*

Fragmented memories of...

—*one particular cell, where she placed a trembling palm on the cold thick glass, her eyes welling up...*

Rebecca opened her eyes.

She rose from the elevator floor, bathed in sweat, her scrambling thoughts beginning to find traction. She attempted the button once more. The dented doors opened, but only partially.

Rebecca peered through the narrow opening, carefully gazing at the entire second floor platform.

Blood and flesh and mesh everywhere. Body parts galore, a piece of a tattooed hand sliding down one of the pillars.

She heard a deep wail somewhere, like a wounded whale.

She stepped out of the thrashed elevator cab. Machinery smoke assailed her nostrils, and her feet sloshed through puddles of blood. She saw a pillar that was halfway dismantled and riddled with giant claw marks. Chunks of tile and concrete lay everywhere, together with glass. Cement benches were cracked and out of place, and a large square directory lay flat along the floor.

47

And there, before her on the platform floor, the animal lay on its side. It was calm and still, facing away from her.

It was the size of a rhino, its thick tawny fur colored grayish-black, sporadic dark stripes throughout, matted with gore. Enormous pointy ears sprouted from its large head like devil's horns. Its long, snake-like tail flapped about.

Rebecca walked slowly toward the creature, and had a soundless gawk when she saw half of Grizzly's head lying on the floor, his half-opened eyes staring straight at her. The coppery smell of flesh and carnage engulfed her, and her world tipped, like she'd just stepped off a spin-out ride. She let out a short, queasy cough as she walked around the large beast, getting a full-frontal look.

Its body was extremely lean, legs incredibly thin. Its paws were the size of car tires, with nails that simulated shark's teeth. The animal's head was amazingly large, and seemed disproportionate to the rest of its body, almost as if mounted from a different animal. It reminded Rebecca of a sphinx.

Her brows sank low when she noticed multiple thin, red-tipped *tranquilizer darts* sticking out of the creature's body. She glanced around, searching for the darts' shooter, but saw no one.

She jerked suddenly as the animal lifted its groggy head toward her, desperate to pounce on the ripe piece of human meat standing before it. But the drugs were too strong, so it just lay there facing Rebecca, giving her a full view of his face.

Its eyes, which took up a good portion of the face, were bright yellow like twin suns, split vertically by thin black pupils. Mad eyes, senseless, fixed unhesitatingly on hers. Its enormous jaw hung wide, as though for a slow gusty yawn, displaying teeth the size and shape of icicles. Foul breath rushed out, hot like an oven. The nose was sloped, smooth and wide, and long fur hung around the sides of the head. There was a green swampy stench about the beast.

Rebecca looked up as if awakened from a deep sleep, and saw someone down the platform step out from behind a staircase. A muscular male figure wearing black boots, tactical pants, a black military-style jacket, a black cotton mask. He held an assault rifle. Said into an earpiece in Russian, "Got 'em."

She gave the dark figure a blank stare. A combination of fatigue and a desperate need for a moment with her animal thwarted her panic.

She stepped closer to the drugged beast and knelt, her cold heart hammering in her ears. She gazed into the creature's somber face as it fought to keep its eyes open.

And then, something happened.

The beast's legs retracted, bones popping like snapping wet wood, together with the squishy sounds of tissue and other organs, the creature emitting long groans of pain. Its long heavy fur receded into its skin, along with its lengthy whiskers. Rebecca's eyes bulged as the creature's entire body shriveled and shrank like a burning piece of paper, and laying its head on the floor, it stared straight at Rebecca, its bright yellow eyes transitioning to light green. Finally, its eyes closed, and the animal slipped into sedation.

It continued to shrivel and shrink until… her little cat Charles lay before her.

Her heart staggered. She instinctively grabbed him and held him in her lap. Gently rocked him, resting her chin on his soft, bloodied, sleeping head, pulling the darts from his body.

"Now you have eight more," she muttered, smirking through tears.

She looked up at the muscular figure in black, now joined by another figure. A young man, it seemed, in the same type of uniform, wearing a mask, carrying a rifle.

The young man walked to the girl and cat, knelt before them.

Rebecca stared at the man's shrouded face with the somber look of someone who had just come from traveling in blistering heat, struggling to maintain at least a semblance of control.

The young man slowly raised a gloved hand, carefully pulled a sweaty hair strand away from Rebecca's face. His lips peeked out of a mouth hole. The corner of his mouth moved upward into a slight grin, and Rebecca's chest surged with warmth. They shared the same mouth. The same smile.

But Rebecca refused to smile. Gazing at the young, twenty-year-old man, she remembered that day at the Fresno hospital three years ago, before her move to The Place. Before the Workshop. Before Charles's treatment.

She remembered...

*Standing at her mother's hospice bed, the young man beside her.*

*The man walking away without a word, face filled with contempt and rage, giving one last glance at his dying mother before joining the roughly shaved, baggy-eyed fifty-something man at the doorway, walking out with him...*

She remembered...

*Charles bathing himself thoroughly on her mother's bed.*

*Her mother's final words to her, "Kindness, child," in Russian, voice low and weak, tiredly handing Charles to her. "Show him... kindness."*

Rebecca could have taken off the young man's mask. Stared into his face.

But she left his mask alone.

Rebecca took her stare off the young man and placed it back on Charles, still in her arms, and stroked the sleeping cat's blood-matted fur.

She observed the large lumpy surgical scars across Charles's stomach that he received six weeks ago. Examined the little black serial number—0129—tattooed on the inside of his ear.

The girl and the young man remained in the quiet.


Rebecca stood at the kitchen counter of her new home, poured Purina nuggets into a tray, then stirred in tuna. She took out a small container from her pocket, emptied out two white pills, mixed them in with the rest of the cat food. She set the container on the counter.

Entering her bedroom, she found Charles perched in his usual place—the window sill.

He liked looking out at the world.

Rebecca set the tray down, beside the litter box. Charles hopped down and galloped to his food.

At first, Rebecca's temporary "parents" had not been too keen on having a cat. But they were quite taken by Rebecca, and though they knew little about her past or her family, they wanted desperately to help this traumatized orphaned girl have a better life. And so Charles stayed in her room while she was at school, coming out only when she was home.

It was Trish, her fifteen-year-old "sister," whom Rebecca kept Charles away from.

Rebecca knelt beside her cat, pet him while he ate. Gently rubbed his stomach.

She felt the large, lumpy surgical scars he had gotten at The Place, and they opened doors in Rebecca's mind once again.

Fragmented memories of The Corridor…

—*Standing with tears before that glass cell, staring at the slender gray and black-striped "borrowed" subject sedated and stitched up at the stomach—Charles—almost lifeless on the cell floor.*

Memories of…

—*The roughly shaved, baggy eyed fifty-something man standing behind her, his reflection in the glass, wearing his wrinkled, stained lab coat over a ruffled dress shirt and tie, cigarette dangling from his mouth, his arm around the young man, both excited as two children on Christmas Eve.*

—*That baggy eyed, uncouth man in his wrinkled lab coat saying, "The first of a kind; a step above assault rifles and bombs."*

*Her uncle.*

Rebecca fixated on Charles as he ate his breakfast. Appraised the remarkable creature before her. She was appalled at her uncle's abominable creation, yes. But she couldn't help but feel a strange sense of morbid admiration for the man's work. A morphological hybrid. The most magnificent display of gene manipulation and DNA conglomeration in history.

She touched Charles's shoulder, stroked the stab wound Grizzly gave him, now stitched up. Her thoughts reverted back to the events at the subway terminal one month ago. Back to the young man with the cotton mask and assault rifle.

She was still perplexed at how he allowed her to leave the subway terminal… *with* Charles. Perhaps it was her affection for the animal. Perhaps it tapped into that last bit of human still left in him, touching what remained of his former self deep within, wanting desperately for his *sestra* to have no part of her uncle or The Place or even him.

Perhaps the young man understood the "gift" Rebecca was given by her mother on her 10th birthday.

Charles looked up at her. Gave her a brief stare, munched loudly on food. Then went back to his meal.

Rebecca peered at the floor, at the front page of a crumpled newspaper:

**NEW TERROR ALERT:** Attacks Against U.S. Military Members, FBI Issues Strong Warning

*In a joint intelligence bulletin issued overnight by the FBI with the U.S. Department of Homeland Security, officials strongly urged those who serve or served in uniform to monitor anything that may reveal their identity and home address to violent extremists and domestic terrorists...*

She folded the newspaper, placed it inside Charles's litter box.

She frowned.

*Kindness* her mother chanted in her head.

She gave Charles her usual goodbye kiss on his head. Then she stood up, slung her backpack over her shoulder.

"Crap in my shoes today," Rebecca said. "and you'll have seven lives left." And with a smirk, she left her room.

She exited the house, crossed the lawn, on her way to catch the school bus.

Rebecca didn't notice Trish—her fifteen-year-old American "sister"—watching her through the kitchen window. Watching her with a razor-edged stare, one eye black and blue underneath the lining, a cut on her lower lip. Remnants from the girls' last encounter.

Had it not been for Rebecca's mother's ever-echoing words, *kindness*, things could have gotten ugly.

Trish grabbed the container of Charles's pills, which Rebecca had carelessly left on the counter. Then she took out a container of Reager's Jelly Beans from her pocket, all black and white, identical to the cat's pills. She poured the rest of Charles's pills into the garbage disposal, along with the black jelly beans from the container. Finally, Trish filled Charles's pill container with the white jelly beans. She sealed the lid, placed it back on the counter.

With a beastly grin across her fair-skinned face, Trish watched Rebecca trudge down the sidewalk. Examined Charles's container of "pills," a glowing aura of curiosity within her to see what would happen to Rebecca's beloved kitty, now without his meds.

# MARK OF THE BRUJA

## JP MAC

An ambulance howled down Fundament Way, siren wailing into the cool spring night. Coasting along in the bike lane, Craig watched the emergency lights flash into the distance toward St. Benedict's Hospital. Leaning down to unclip his cycling shoes from the pedals, Craig felt uneasy. He recalled last night's bad dream where, riding in a peloton, he'd crashed and snapped both ankles like chop sticks.

Hopping off his bike, he removed the cleated shoes before walking the Diamond One Clarity up the curb and leaning it against a telephone pole. Craig forgot the dream, still aglow from the praise of his peers. Stuffing cycling shoes into his backpack, he walked his bike up onto the sidewalk, angling toward home.

The Chula Vista Apartments stood like a three-story stucco prison for the elderly, low-income workers, or those just starting out, like Craig. Every window featured burglar bars. On the inside of the barred window was a quick release lever. Should fire erupt—always a possibility with the ancient wiring—the building residents could open the bars from inside and flee onto one of the many exterior fire escapes, and down a ladder to safety. Craig had never bothered testing the levers on any of his own windows. He figured eighty years of being painted over probably rendered them useless. But with Los Angeles engulfed in another real estate frenzy, you couldn't find cheaper rent.

From the shadows, a hulking figure emerged into the front entrance light. Wearing a football jersey and baggy running shorts, the youth's thick hands held a skateboard and an opaque plastic trash bag. The big kid gripped the bag and smacked it against a stucco wall.

Once. Thrashing and pained yelps.

Twice. A yelp.

A third time. Thrashing.

A fourth. Quiet in the bag.

Craig yelled, "Hey, Abdi, you better not be hurting some dog. I'll call the cops."

"Back off, bitch."

Laying his bike on the grass, Craig darted forward in his socks. He grabbed at the trash bag, but recoiled. Abdi's legs, arms and neck were covered in suction marks. *What was this kid doing to himself?* Abdi's eyes were red THC-marinated slits as he shoved Craig, knocking the fledging writer-director backward onto the lawn. As Craig wriggled out of his backpack, Abdi was able to unlock the front door and enter. The front door locked automatically behind him.

Cursing, Craig Heebner fumbled in his belly pouch for his lobby key and was soon inside the Chula Vista Apartments. Past the lobby and elevator, in the first-floor hallway beyond, he saw Abdi. Flipping Craig off, Abdi stepped into Apartment 102 with his skateboard and silent plastic bag.

"Hey, asshole."

Darting forward past the mailboxes, Craig failed to notice paint-spattered work boots. Tripping, he flung out both hands like Superman as he fell onto the lobby tiles.

A giggle. The smell of stale beer. "'Eebner, whaz'sup?"

Sitting, Craig scowled back at a grinning Porfiro Zavala, legs splayed, back against the mailbox. The old man's white hair was in disarray as if electrified, his dark brown face creased with wrinkles like a desert arroyo. Craig scowled in disgust and examined the friction-burn on his palms.

Call the cops on Abdi? Craig hated to see living things hurt. Notify the landlord that Abdi was killing animals outside the building? But that might result in trouble for Festanya. *What in the freaking world was a hottie like her doing with an overgrown high school dropout?* Rising, Craig hurried back outside to snag bike and backpack before they were stolen. Meanwhile, still on the floor, Porfiro Zavala muttered in Spanish, struggling to rise like a legless man on a toilet.

Back in the lobby, Craig sighed and stashed bike and backpack against a wall near the elevator. He approached Porfiro. "Interesting Friday?"

"Koreans fire me, hire some *cholo* for less."

Craig extended an arm. "Grab and I'll pull."

Together they maneuvered Porfiro to his feet. Setting the wobbly housepainter against the mailbox, Craig dipped down and retrieved the man's black lunchbox.

"You okay, 'Eebner."

Arm around Zavala's waist, Craig steered him out of the lobby and onto the stained blood-red carpet of the first-floor hallway. Drawing parallel to Apartment 102, Porfiro said, "Better to die from poison than serve a bruja."

"What's that?"

"*La joven gordo* has the signs. He serves the bruja."

"Abdi? He's a stoner. A loser. He used to deliver pizzas around here. They were always cold, and he'd bitch about the tip."

"Little children will vanish soon like in Sonora. I remember."

The two men stopped in front of Apartment 103. Like a jeweler examining a ruby through a loupe, Porfiro examined a key ring, finally plucking out the key to deadbolt and door. In a breath rich with the fragrance of Pabst Blue Ribbon, he said, "They hate salt. Holy Water. What is pure is not for them."

"Too much sodium is bad for blood vessels."

Moments later, Craig decanted the fluid old man inside.

"You okay, 'Eebner."

"Sorry about the job. Tough break. Don't forget your lunch box."

Porfiro cradled the lunchbox like a football. "It starts soon."

"Go straight to bed. Hey, what's a bruja?"

Porfiro lowered his voice, glancing over Craig's shoulder at the door to 102. "Witch."

"Festanya? Come on, she's hotter than Fukushima."

"Form of a woman, but also monster, demon. A night traveler. Careful, 'Eebner."

As the old man's door slammed, Craig chuckled. Witches were middle-aged white women dancing naked in in the backyards of 4,000 square-foot houses north of Sunset. He'd heard Porfiro's family was either dead or estranged, leaving the poor guy alone with beer, and now, unemployment. It must suck to be old.

A short elevator ride later, Craig wheeled his bike into unit 202. Muffled chanting rose once more from Festanya's apartment below. Just like last night.

Twenty-four hours earlier, Craig had been tapping away in his living room, fleshing out characters. *Lethal Blow* would be more than another cheap nonequity play produced on a badly lit stage in a dumpy theater with uncomfortable seats. Craig's contemporary drama about political and sexual unfaithfulness in a San Francisco mayor's race—a cross between Harold Pinter's *Betrayal* and *Othello*—would be his big break. Craig believed a demonstrated skill at suspense and emotional braiding would open industry doors. He imagined himself writing on shows for Netflix and Amazon. In time, he'd produce and write his own original works. But for now, the pressure was on to finish a draft for tomorrow night.

And that's when the new idiots downstairs had begun to chant. The noise enraged him with its eerie, disturbing syncopation. Still in biking spandex and Swiftwear Aspire cycling socks, Craig had stormed downstairs. Rapping sharply on the door to Apartment 102, he waited.

Wearing a tattered bathrobe, Abdi answered. The kid's stump-like neck featured a suction mark the size of a bathtub stopper. Dashes of blood encircled the wound, now starting to trickle into the collar of the terrycloth robe. Craig winced. "What happened to you?"

"What do you care?"

"You live here now? I thought you delivered pizzas?"

"I quit. What's it to you?"

The kid's face reflected smugness, contempt, and sexual satiety. Craig gritted his teeth. "I live above you. It's late. You need to follow building rules and hit mute on your chanting."

From inside the apartment, a husky female voice called, "It's all right, Abdi."

54

The teen sneered at Craig, then lumbered back into the apartment. A beautiful young woman took his place in the doorway. With long chestnut hair, high cheekbones, mocha skin and incandescent green eyes, she appeared quite international. Craig would later describe her to a friend as "omni-cultural." Her lavender silk robe stopped just south of her hips. The fabric parted, flashing sleek thighs. To avoid gaping, Craig stared at the woman's forehead.

"I live above in 202. My name is Craig Olduvai Heebner."

"What a fascinating middle name."

"As archeologists, my parents were deeply moved by the work of Dr. Margaret Leaky at Tanzania's Olduvai Gorge."

"I simply adore very old things. I'm Festanya Mercat. Was there something you wanted?"

"They teach now at Cal State Fullerton. My parents. That's where I'm from originally. I mean, Orange County."

Craig grimaced as a sharp pain rammed into his brain through both ears. He felt skewered by a stainless-steel lance. Staggering backwards into the first-floor hallway, Craig exhaled sharply.

An impatient note colored the voice of Festanya Mercat. "Were you collecting for something? A charity?"

Battling an urge to flee to the elevator, Craig blurted out, "I'm working on a play. We have a table reading Friday night. I really need to focus."

The brain pain diminished. Craig felt relieved. Festanya crossed her arms, leaning against the doorjamb. "Then you're the servant of your muse."

"This will be my big break. I mean, everyone in Hollywood writes screenplays based on whatever fluff is popular. But there's only a few theatrical works dealing with real issues in any emotional depth. My writing has a better chance to pop."

"Do you also direct?"

"If you want your own work done right, you'd better direct."

Festanya tilted her head. Pert. Cute. "I've certainly found that to be so."

"When you think of it, most actors need guidance. 'Stand there, say it this way.' Meat puppets, really. Though I don't approve of that term."

"Craig Olduvai Heebner, maker of art, molder of souls, minder of many things."

He loved her phrasing and the way she pronounced his name. Bit of an accent, but he couldn't place it. Crag grinned like a goof, but couldn't help himself. "It's the little overlooked things that trip you up. Anyway, I was wondering, could you please hold down the chanting? It bleeds up into my unit."

Festanya covered her mouth with long, sharp, rose-colored fingernails. "How thoughtless. We were playing a fantasy game."

"You and Abdi? He used to deliver pizzas on his skateboard. I heard he quit."

She ignored the bait. "Do you write all alone up in your apartment?"

"Lately. Going through a breakup. But it's cool."

She placed a hand against her heart. Craig wished it were his hand there as

Festanya said, "I promise we'll be the quietest of neighbors. I have to fly now, but stop by again."

Her robe shifted a final time, revealing smooth thighs. Craig's mouth hung open like a shad in a net. Finally, he croaked, "Soon."

As the door shut, Festanya said softly, "I'm right underneath you."

The aspiring writer-director stood enchanted, listening to the click and rattle of numerous locks. Of course; crime sucked in the neighborhood. Maybe that's why she kept Abdi: a big animal for defense.

Fuzzy with carnal thoughts, Craig foolishly attempted to open the door into Festanya's kitchen; along with exterior metal fire escapes and high ceilings, a second front door leading into the kitchen was part of the building's antique design.

Now, a day later, Craig felt he was right back where he'd started Thursday evening. From Festanya's apartment below rose a softer, more restrained chant. Something about "Gorgo, Mormo, thousand-faced moon, sacrifices." Well, it wasn't too bad. And tonight's table read had been a knockout. The actors had loved his dialogue. Opening a Blue Moon wheat beer, Craig removed cycling shoes and a Mac laptop from his backpack. Festanya seemed primed for more mature sexual action. Brushing his teeth before bed, he felt a stab of anxiety: hopefully, she wasn't an actress, so needy and insecure, so *Mina*. Soon, Craig drifted off to sleep, fantasizing about mocha thighs.

At some point in the early hours, he dreamed of green eyes, gleaming and sly. Air buffeted his cheeks as if he were blasting downhill during The Cool Breeze Century Ride. Beside him, Festanya's lavender silk robe snapped in the wind like a yacht pennant. Ringed with May blossoms, her chestnut hair streamed in the manner of a galloping mare's mane. An amber fragrance emanated from her. Concealed within its woody notes was a faint hint of feculence, like perfume sprayed inside a porta potty. Rose fingernails gently stroked Craig's neck, hinting at more sophisticated sensations.

Heebner awoke Saturday morning to the cries of a mourning dove on his windowsill.

He consumed a breakfast of green tea and cronuts at his laptop as he plugged in notes from last night's table read. While successful, the reading had exposed larger questions. Did the actress portraying Kellie Malcolm have the depth to sell her twin betrayals? Mina could've pulled it off. For all her cloying emotional issues, she'd possessed acting talent by the crate. But Craig had tired of her needy insecurities, and grew colder and more remote. So Mina had walked out, carting along bottomless self-pity, narcissism and the Hamilton Beach juicer. She'd also removed her sleek, yoga-tight body, dumb-charming jokes, and quiet mornings in bed beside Craig, eating Pop Tarts and checking text messages.

Throughout the day, Craig mixed writing and laundry, trooping from laptop to basement. To reach the venerable washer-dryers, he needed to pass the first-floor hallway. He experimented with pretexts for knocking on Festanya's door: *Thanks for cooling the chants? Take a walk to Starbucks?* Suppose Abdi answered? Delicate. Very delicate.

Late afternoon, and Craig carried his last basket of dried clothes up the basement stairs. After a moment's hesitation, he told himself that fortune favored the brave.

Heart pounding, he rapped on 102. Several nervous seconds passed before Festanya answered in Capri pants and a silky tank top. She examined Craig and his basket with merry, teasing eyes.

"Are you selling clothes now?"

"No, no, I was just in the basement." Before he could stammer out further inanities, he blurted, "I wanted to invite you to my play."

"How exciting." Her eyes sparkled. "Nothing religious, I hope. I've suffered badly from such things."

"Who hasn't? Still, one character discovers peace praying to Gaia Earth Mother."

"Are all performances at night?"

"Except for a few matinees. We're at the Drama-Rama Playhouse, just down on Fundament Way and Western. The exact opening night isn't set, but soon."

She made a cute sad face. "Nights are my busy time."

"Oh? Are you an actress? You could be."

"What a sweet remark. I'm involved with children and young people. Sometimes I'm so terribly overwhelmed."

Caught off guard by this unexpected admission, Craig floundered, "I'll bet it's pretty stressful."

"I wish I knew more people willing to make a difference." She sighed. "I'm sure I'd have more time for your play."

Out came the words in a mindless clot of language, "What do you need help with?"

"Delivering them to where they're supposed to go. You know how kids are."

"Sure. It's just that I don't really drive. The environment and all." For a moment, Craig thought Festanya would weep. He hated himself for not driving. "Sorry. I mean, I'd like to help."

To Craig's surprise, rose fingernails stroked his cheek. "This might sound a little woo-woo, but I believe if you ask, the universe will manifest your needs. Say you'll help me and a way will be found."

"I'd rather not commit to something, then flake out."

"Just say it. Words have power."

"Okay. I'll help you. If I can. Rehearsals and performances permitting."

"Craig Olduvai Heebner, you're so very wonderful."

Sweet endorphins flooded his brain. Craig lowered his voice. "I shouldn't say this, but Abdi tortured a dog outside last night. Someone threatened to call the cops. Just saying."

Festanya's eyes narrowed into eerie green slits that seemed to elongate, rising up to meet her temples. In a flat, toneless voice she said, "I'll speak to him."

At Craig's alarmed expression, her pique evaporated, eyes once again playful, amused. "Don't forget to fold your things before they wrinkle."

"I'm doing that now. I mean, I'll do that soon."

Dusk drifted into evening. Garments neatly folded, day's pages written, Craig relaxed with a dinner of frozen white bean sausage and kale soup. An LAPD helicopter hovered overhead for a time, then stuttered off. Craig's old college roommate texted, inviting him out for drinks. Craig passed. Instead, he sprawled on the couch, sipping craft beers and watched a new Hulu series. *For Love of Flooby* was a bold drama about a man battling bigotry and discrimination after marrying a California sea lion. A member of Craig's theater company had landed a small role as the intolerant, Bible-spouting civil servant who bans Flooby from the town pool. But Craig had trouble focusing.

Did Festanya's eyes really do that weird thing? He couldn't shake that image. Deliver kids? Were they free range? Where did Abdi the Doberman fit in? Festanya hadn't seemed freaked out over Abdi killing animals, only about the possibility of someone complaining. So many creepy questions.

Switching off the Roku box, Craig retired early. Tomorrow was a cycling day. As usual, he'd chill on Sunday, cruising the roads of Griffith Park. Dozing off, Craig wondered if Mina had found someone else.

At some point that night, Craig felt his lungs aflame. Running past apartment buildings, he pursued skateboarding Abdi, wheels clattering on the cement like a diminutive freight train. Arms pumping, Craig could neither stop nor slow down, compelled to keep a crisp pace. He was vaguely aware of moving through a gray June Gloom world without ambient noise: no trash trucks, Spotify play lists through the car stereo, or leaf blowers. No people walking, jogging, laughing. The encompassing silence pressed in like fog.

Up ahead, Abdi clattered across a street, then leapt from his skateboard. His football jersey and baggy shorts hung on him as if he'd borrowed his father's clothes. Abdi darted into a park strewn with garbage: plastic milk crates, Amazon boxes, and chest-high weeds. Craig dashed across the street, lungs heaving.

A series of jerky disconnected actions flashed before Craig's eyes—jump cuts in a film. Up ahead, Abdi halted, twirling a nylon rope with an attached, multi-prong grappling hook. (Where had that come from?) The big teen's face appeared shrunken, pinched and anemic. A fresh, bleeding suction mark covered his right cheek. Abdi released the rope like a cowhand on the open range. Craig staggered to a stop, sucking in air, watching the grappling hook sail into a stand of chickweed.

An agonized, high-pitched scream split the eerie silence.

Abdi hauled in the rope.

Something wriggling. Craig's mouth opened, spine flash frozen. Wearing a cartoon T-shirt, a five-year-old boy kicked and moaned. Blood from barbed hooks soaked SpongeBob and Squidward.

Abdi delivered a vicious kick to Craig's thigh. "Little rat; better learn to shut up."

"Wait, wait."

Abdi kicked him harder. "Pick up the kid."

Craig winced. He felt constrained, compelled to be there.

"And pull out those hooks, dickweed."

Craig shook his head 'no,' then doubled over as a fiery sensation like a burning lance skewered his eardrums, driving into his brain. Seconds passed like an afternoon with his palm pressed against a hot stove. Tears streaming, Craig Heebner blurted, "Whatever, okay, just stop."

The sudden absence of torment left him docile, passive, frightened that a wrong move would invite back the pain.

Abdi kicked him again. "Pull out the hooks."

Fumbling with the grappling hook, Craig undertook a series of clumsy, brutal actions that left the bloodstained boy howling in torment. Each wail stabbed Craig's heart like a dagger.

At some point, Craig found himself holding the bleeding boy in his arms, running once more, deeper into the park.

In a gazebo up ahead, wrapped in purple nightshade, Festanya reclined on a bench. Dressed in a short-sleeved peasant top, jeans and high-top Chuck Taylors, she appeared ready for an afternoon of shopping and lunch with friends. A rose-colored nail indicated a spot on the grass. Craig fell to his knees before her.

"I'll take that now."

Terrified, Craig removed the child's clutching hands from his shirt and handed the boy up to Festanya.

"I was forced to bring him."

"Oh? Didn't you volunteer?"

Festanya's jaw lowered, her mouth opening wider and wider. Impossibly wide.

Craig wanted to run, but couldn't rise. He wanted to look away, but his neck wouldn't turn. He wanted to avert his eyes, but they saw everything.


Sunday morning and butterflies glided on a spring breeze, passing ahead of Craig. He never noticed, circling Griffith Park in a dark bewildered funk. A coyote trotted along beneath California oaks, watching Craig roll past.

Peddling alongside the golf course, past the Autry Western Heritage Museum, wheeling by the trains in Travel Town, Craig cycled up into the hills. Other early morning riders greeted him with waves and nods. Craig ignored them.

Upon awakening ninety minutes ago, he'd sighed in relief. But waiting for his tea to boil, Craig found himself examining his clothes and shoes for grass and bloodstains. Films about dreams often provided a tell to the audience. The protagonist would discover a ticket stub, a memento, a souvenir that said, 'Your experience was real.' But he found nothing beyond memories that left him squirming in shock and fear and shame.

While his tea steeped, Craig jumped online. He searched L.A., Orange, and Ventura counties for local missing kids within the last twelve hours. A kidnapping in a custody battle up in Ventura, and a 10-year-old girl struck by a bus in South Gate. No missing boy in a SpongeBob SquarePants T-shirt.

Only the image of Festanya's jaw unhinging like a rock python.

As the grade steepened, Craig shifted to a lower gear. His parents always believed that, when in doubt, you read the literature. Craig decided he'd Google 'nightmares,' 'disturbing dreams,' 'pressure.' Get opinions on social media. Call home and snag a therapist recommendation from his parents. Cresting the hill, Heebner relaxed for the first time that morning. Too much time alone, no sex, rewrite pressure. He zipped downhill faster and faster, smiling in the breeze, whisking past the turn-off to the old zoo.

On Tuesday afternoon, Zavala listened to Craig. Wearing a U.S. Army sweatshirt and clean Dickie's work pants, the unemployed housepainter sipped a sixteen-ounce Bud. Porfiro leaned back in his recliner, watching Craig as if he were an absorbing documentary. Craig perched on the edge of a dusty hunter green couch.

Eyes ringed with dark circles, Craig continued. "So, anyway, this is still Sunday, I go online. Basically, all my friends tell me I've been working too hard, or needed better pot, or a vacation in Indonesia where there's awesome snorkeling. By afternoon, I was feeling pretty chill."

Framed family photos ringed the living room. Zavala had introduced Craig as if the subjects were present and deserving of courtesy: wife Teresa, dead of lymphoma; daughter Specialist 4 Sylvia Zavala, killed in a Ft. Lewis helicopter crash; estranged son Alfredo, administrator at Cal State Dominguez Hills, mortified by his father's backward social views and fearful of their potential damage to his career; and Chava, a happy-looking springer spaniel, suspected victim of coyotes.

Heebner sipped tap water from a plastic LA Rams cup. "Sunday night, I dreamed Abdi lanced a little girl through her bedroom window. The kid screamed like Mothra when we hauled her outside. Naturally, I end up bringing the kid to Festanya."

Scratching white, unkempt hair, the house painter nodded.

"So, Monday morning I called this psychiatrist my parents knew. She was booked until today, but recommended Pilates. Then I tried buying Cartwheels. I figured I wouldn't sleep until I talked with the therapist. But my drug guy wasn't around and I dozed off. Last night, well, more of the same."

Porfiro Zavala bowed his head.

"How come there's nothing in the news about missing kids? A text from the county. Something."

"A clever thief always robs the neighbor of a neighbor."

Craig's voice rose, teetering on the brink of cracking. "But, hey, I saw a shrink this morning. She prescribed Ambien. Pills to help me sleep. Isn't that special? I swear, man, I'll cycle in front of a trash truck before I deliver up another kid."

"You gave her your word."

"Who cares? What happened in Sonora?"

Porfiro stared at Craig.

Outside on Fundament Way, traffic raced.

Finally, Zavala sighed. "My uncle and others killed the bruja with guns and machetes. They soaked her body in gasoline and burned it to ashes. Then the priest sprinkled Holy Water on the ashes and buried them."

A bitter laugh later, Craig said, "Is that all? Wonderful. Great. Very Practical. You know, San Luis Obispo is a nice place to live. I have family up there."

60

"Sea air is good for house painters. But the bruja will find you, 'Eebner. You gave your word."

"What is all this shit about words? Words are words. You say what you need to, when you need to. It's all situational."

Zavala pressed the beer can against his forehead. "Do you believe in God?"

"What is wrong with you? Guns, machetes, now God."

"Under what power would you revoke your word to a bruja?"

"My own. The environment. The universe."

Zavala shrugged. "Festanya doesn't fear those things."

"What if I call the cops?"

"What will you tell them?"

Craig sat forward, then leaned back. He held up a hand as if marking a place for the words he was about to speak. But no sound emerged.

Porfiro Zavala continued, "And now many people know you have bad dreams. You think the police won't look on your computer?"

Craig restrained an urge to bellow at Zavala in frustration. But a sudden idea induced a bright smile. "What if we sneak into Festanya's apartment during the day and open all the drapes?"

Zavala rattled his empty beer can and frowned. "The bruja is weakest at night, when her soul travels. That is the best time. But you must approach very quiet, or she'll return to her body."

Craig said, "Too bad I don't own a machete."

Zavala sat forward in his chair. "You must kill her body. She will be trapped between worlds, or so Father Raymundo said."

"Call one of your priests. Don't they do in-home service?"

"Father Raymundo was a priest. Here they believe in politics and money from the city. They are social workers with collars."

Rising to his feet, Craig Olduvai Heebner stormed to the front door, then back to the couch, then paced the living room as if hunting a hidden exit. He fumed. "This is insane. I mean, is that it? Murder a sleeping woman?"

Zavala rubbed a gnarled, arthritic finger across his chin. "In your dreams, how does the fat boy look?"

"Skinnier now, sucker marks everywhere, more wasted every night."

"A bruja is a harsh boss. The boy is fed with sex while his life energy is drained. Then it will be your turn. How many more nights will the pizza boy last?"

Craig had a crushing sarcastic response dangling on his lips. But he held his tongue, considering Zavala's question as a car alarm sounded out on Fundament Way.

At 3:04 Wednesday morning, Craig entered the kitchen of Apartment 102. Scented candles flickered on the counter like marsh gas. In the sink, pots and pans rose in a disordered heap. A lavender potpourri atop the stove failed to mask a sickly odor of sulfur and decay, pungent as a beer fart.

Moments ago, an astonished Craig had watched a very drunk Zavala pick 102's kitchen lock. The old man used a paperclip and a tension wrench. Then, with a rubber band, Porfiro unhooked the security chain. Apparently, in the house painting trade, doors were always locked that needed opening.

But he wouldn't enter.

"I'm old. No good."

Shocked and bewildered, Craig leaned out of Festanya's kitchen and watched Porfiro meander back across the hall to 103. Opening his front door, Zavala called, "St. Michael defend you."

With a mighty slam, Porfiro Zavala shut the door.

In stocking feet, clutching a utility knife and an LED flashlight, Craig considered fleeing back to his apartment. Confused, he stood inside someone else's unit, pockets of his sweat pants stuffed with salt. Holy Water dribbled from his ears onto the shoulder of his moisture-wicking cycling jersey.

Go home. Then what? Run somewhere. And wait to fall asleep? He'd never find the nerve to return here again.

Cursing under his breath, Craig stepped back into the kitchen. He left the door open a crack. That way, he could bolt. Craig knew the layout of Apartment 102 was identical to his own apartment upstairs. At the end of the long kitchen, a right turn would bring him into the living room. Cross the living room, bearing right, then pass the front door. A hallway lay ahead. Down the hallway to the right, separate coat and linen closets; ahead to the left, a tiny bathroom; the hallway ended at the door to a single bedroom.

Passing lambent candles as well as what appeared to be a dog collar, Craig hesitated at the living room turn. Outside, wind rustled palm trees. A burst of angry Spanish rose from the alley below, probably taggers fighting over an undefiled wall.

Did Abdi's soul also travel? Wouldn't it have to? Despite the utility knife, Craig didn't think himself capable of slicing anyone. Old vampire films flashed across his mind: Festanya in her coffin in the bedroom. Abdi crouched on the sofa like Renfield, a tripwire. Craig's nerve seeped away. *Leave. Figure everything out later.*

Turning to go, Craig almost shrieked at a dark shape and a blinding light. He froze as Jack Daniel's emanations joined the kitchen aromas. A slurred voice said, "We finish this now, *vato*."

With a headband flashlight around disheveled white hair, Zavala gripped a carpenter's hammer—a combination claw hammer and hatchet. Brushing past Craig, he clumped around the corner in paint-stained work boots. Craig's knees shook. *We're rolling now.*

Scented candles twinkled about the living room like farm house lights seen from the air. Black fabric cloaked the windows. Porfiro's headlamp swept the room. Runic symbols, cryptic signs, and demonic images marred the walls. A tripod brazier stank of blood, charcoal and sulfur.

No Renfield. No sofa. A few plastic lawn chairs.

Porfiro whispered loudly, "They're in the bedroom. We have them trapped."

"Keep it down. Have you ever killed anyone?"

"Ha."

Hatchet blade cocked, the old man passed the lock-rich front door. He entered the hallway, clumping past the coat closet, then the linen closet.

"Come on, 'Eebner."

Passing the closets, blood roared in Craig's ears. An important thought squalled for his attention. "Stop a second. What are we gonna do?"

"We avenge." Porfiro sounded confident, commanding, pointing his carpenter's hammer toward the bedroom door like Cesar invading Gaul.

A skateboard crashed down onto his head.

Blood erupted from a torn scalp. Zavala fell against a wall. Abdi stepped into view from the small bathroom. His skateboard rained down a series of brutal blows onto the cringing housepainter, shattering Porfiro's headband flashlight.

Behind Craig, a closet door clicked open.

The hallway filled with the scent of amber and feculence.

Warm moistness fanned across the floodplain of Heebner's sweatpants.

Trembling, he stuck his flashlight into his waistband. Reaching into a pocket, Craig squeezed a handful of salt.

"Craig Olduvai Heebner, look at me now."

Spinning around, Craig flung the salt.

Festanya screamed when it struck, backing away, flailing her arms. In the gloomy hallway, Craig thought she might be flailing more than two appendages.

Turning back to Abdi, Craig slashed with the utility knife. The razor blade sliced through sucker marks on the teen's forearm. Blood and pus oozed out. With Craig so close, Abdi couldn't swing his skateboard. Improvising, the teen held it across his chest like a shield. Rushing forward, Abdi drove Craig backwards into a gas-heating unit.

Craig struggled, pinned as he and Abdi fought for the utility knife. But blood from Abdi's wounds made it tough to sustain a grip. Grunting, Abdi landed several knee strikes into Craig's hip and thigh. Mashed against the heating unit, Heebner felt Abdi was seconds from wresting away the knife. A high-pitched cry filled the hallway. Craig was unaware that it came from him.

The pressure against his chest and wrist eased.

The skateboard dropped onto his foot. He kicked it aside with a clatter.

Abdi staggered backwards like a drunk on an escalator.

Fumbling at something behind his head, Abdi half spun, then collapsed before the bedroom door. Blood and cerebral spinal fluid flooded his sucker-coated face and neck. Using the flashlight, Craig spied the hatchet blade of a carpenter's hammer securely lodged in Abdi's skull.

Blood streaking gnarled forehead and cheeks, Porfiro Zavala quivered on his feet. He reached out to Craig. Then the old man's eyes rolled upward. Porfiro Zavala fell to the floor like a dropped marionette.

At the same time, a dry, warm tentacle wrapped around Heebner's waist. Pressure, then Craig felt a moist erotic sensation caressing his belly. For a moment, he relaxed, allowing the tentacle to tug him gently back down the hall, away from the bodies of

Abdi and Porfiro. A warning cry bayed in Craig's mind. Panicked, he plunged the utility knife into the tentacle. But the razor blade wouldn't penetrate skin that seemed thick and tough as a monster truck tire. Craig dropped knife and flashlight, reaching again into his pockets. He smeared the sinuous organ with salt. The tentacle jerked away.

Festanya whined, "Why are you hurting me?"

Stumbling into the bathroom, Craig slammed and locked the door. Turning on the light, he sat on the toilet seat, staring at the black and white checkerboard linoleum. The skewering brain lance pushed at his ears. Scrunching up, Craig braced for crushing pain. To his surprise, no affliction followed the initial sensations. Carefully, he touched his ears. Still damp. But what happened when the Holy Water dried?

Lifting his cycling jersey, Craig discovered a bleeding, circular stomach wound the size of a bathtub stopper. Disgusted, he dabbed at the blood with wadded up toilet paper. *Poor Porfiro; a flawed mentor, but he saved me when it mattered.*

A click. Craig jumped as the doorknob twisted right, then left. He bit his bottom lip in fright. A sharp creak as the entire doorframe bowed inward. Craig felt poised on the lip of a high dive above a dry pool. Kneeling, he spread a salt barrier across the bathroom threshold. He dusted his hands and scraped his pockets bare for salt. There wasn't much.

Seconds passed.

With a reluctant groan, the wood eased back into place.

Craig fought the panic erupting inside him like water from a burst pipe. The bathroom window was familiar, featuring a crank instead of a slider. Turning the crank, he watched the outside night appear.

A voice, soft and pleading, "Craig?"

Window open, Craig discarded the screen into the bathtub. Reaching through the burglar bars, he touched early morning air. The skewering lance struck once more. This time the sensation penetrated his ears. However, its power was weak. A minor headache flared.

"Craig? You've made everything so crazy. Come out and we'll talk. I can help you in many ways."

He searched for the escape latch to the burglar bars. Then he'd drop onto the fire escape and flee to Fundament Way. Cops were always around for traffic accidents, tagging, cell phone thefts. Fingertips traced the base of the window. But if there were a lever, it was concealed under generations of paint.

Craig recalled setting his smart phone down on Porfiro's kitchen table. What had he done? Heebner yelled, "Help. Can someone help me? I'm trapped in apartment 102."

A merry laugh from the hallway, sounding like the chitter of imps. "Seriously, Craig. In this neighborhood?"

Clasping the burglar bars, Heebner shook them like a caged ape.

"That old fool across the hall lied. He wanted me, but I turned him down. Now he's using you for his stupid, idiot revenge."

Once again, Craig felt around for the escape latch.

64

In the hallway outside, footsteps receded. The sound of a door closing was followed by footsteps returning.

"Would you open the door to my bathroom please?"

Heebner froze, fingers on what was once the escape latch. But a portion was broken off, leaving only a jagged nub.

"Do you care for this old fool out here?"

Craig heard a click, then an electronic whooshing sound.

"You mean the guy Abdi killed?" Using forefinger and thumb, Craig struggled to push the metal nub of the escape latch. There wasn't much to work with. His thumb and forefinger bled.

"He still lives, but needs medical attention."

*Whoosh, hiss.* Craig realized he was hearing a vacuum cleaner. Back at the bathroom door, he discovered his salt barrier scattered. Shit.

The vacuum cleaner cut out.

Craig searched the bathroom for something to protect his bloody fingers and thumb. He needed to keep Festanya talking. "How's Abdi?"

"Fortunate to be dead. I'm sure *you* would've remembered to properly secure the kitchen door."

"Who's going to deliver your supper? Uber Eats?"

"Clever. Come out and keep me company."

In the bottom of the bathtub, underneath the window screen, Craig found a mildewed hand towel. Wrapping an edge of fabric around the lever nub, he tried yanking it open. No movement.

*Could Porfiro still live?* Uncertainty dogged him for a moment. *No. Bruja lies.*

"Craig? I can help your play. Would you like to hear?"

Checking the medicine cabinet, Craig seized a plastic bottle of nail polish remover. Wetting the towel, he rubbed acetone over the escape latch nub and called out, "Let me go and I'll take the old man to a hospital. I'll say he was robbed."

"And Abdi?"

"What if I give him a proper roll down a hill into a brushy canyon?"

"I thought you didn't drive? The environment and all?"

Had he said that? Another brain skewer, stronger this time. Craig gasped as a major migraine crushed his temples. Touching both ears, he felt only a hint of moisture. Craig said, "Suppose we call it a draw. You get a new bestie and I take out the trash and keep my mouth shut. Think it over."

Silence from the hallway. Craig felt a surge of excitement. The acetone was stripping away the old paint. Trying the lever again, Craig Heebner felt the faintest movement. But he needed more leverage.

Festanya said, "I agree to a draw. Now help me wrap Abdi in a blanket."

"Okay. Deal."

Behind Craig, wood creaked, then splintered. Peering down, he spotted a dark tentacle forcing its way into the bathroom from under the door, tip stabbing the air like a black mamba.

65

Heart thudding, Craig spied a can of shaving cream on a bathtub ledge. Placing the base of the can against the broken lever, he pushed, feeling more movement. The cranial skewering increased. Craig's eyes watered. *Oh, God, oh, God, oh, God.*

*Clack* went the escape latch.

The burglar bars swung open.

Craig hauled himself up onto the sash as a warm tentacle touched his leg. In a burst of squirming, he wriggled outside. Hopping down onto a fire escape, Craig fled apartment 102. The skewering pain lessened. Heebner clambered down a ladder, jumping the last three rungs into the alley. Breaking into a sprint, Craig blew past several figures in the shadows.

Heebner felt a wild, almost feral rush of endorphins. *I'm out.*

Rounding a corner, he bolted into Fundament Way.

How odd that everything passed by so fast and upside down.

Thus marveled Craig Olduvai Heebner, pinwheeling through the air before landing in the bike lane across the street, breaking his hip in two places.

An ambulance arrived within minutes. A police officer with an old-school buzzcut questioned a Prius driver. The man had been texting his girlfriend when some crazy guy shot in front of him. "Didn't even look both ways."

The cop's partner, a woman with crow's feet around her eyes and honey-blonde hair pulled back into a severe bun, examined Craig. Standing behind the EMTs, she noticed Heebner's bloody right forefinger and thumb.

"What happened there, bud?"

"Take me to St. Benedict's."

The officer asked an EMT, "Did that happen in the accident?"

"Maybe, but I doubt it. Hey, Carlos, let's slide the board under him."

Craig's jersey rode up as he was secured to a backboard. Crow's Feet Cop noticed an odd stomach wound the size of a bathtub stopper.

"Hey, Bud, that happen in the accident?"

"I want a crucifix and Holy Water and salt."

As the EMT wheeled Craig to the ambulance, the two cops compared notes.

Curious, they retraced Craig's steps into the alley, questioned a surly group of taggers, and found little drops of blood on the fire escape ladder. Cautiously, the two officers climbed up. Pistols at the ready, they approached the open window of Apartment 102.

# SMOKED

## GABRIELLA BALCOM

Bettie fanned the air in front of her nose with her hand and winced. Although she looked like a sweet granny with her spectacles and fluffy white hair, she didn't wear her usual smile. Rodney, sitting one table over, was smoking and the fumes drifted her way again. He'd been several tables away when he first sat and lit up, but after she'd asked him to put more distance between them, he'd come closer instead. Bettie's chest felt tight—an unsurprising symptom of her COPD and asthma. "Rodney, could you please move farther away to smoke?"

As usual, he seemed oblivious to the trappings of common courtesy. Instead of answering her or doing as she asked, he yawned, stretched in slow motion, and stared out across the Pacific. In the distance, a buoy bobbed and sunlight reflected off the ocean's choppy waves. Rodney looked at the large sign to the left which read "No Smoking. Oxygen In Use," smirked, and turned his back to Bettie. Glancing at their coworker, Bill, who was making short work of a vanilla shake, Rodney pantomimed sticking a finger down his throat. Bill frowned and shook his head, but Rodney grinned and told Bettie, "Nobody said you had to sit here."

"My new tank was being delivered." She gestured to the oxygen strapped to the back of her wheelchair. "This is where I agreed to meet the deliveryman."

"Well, you got it, so why didn't you leave? Why stay to bug me?"

"Bug you? You weren't here then. *I* came out first. You came later and began smoking, although I've told you repeatedly that your smoking's hard on me."

"Tough!" He shrugged. "If you didn't like it, you should've moved. Like they say, suck it up, Buttercup." He took a long drag on his cigarette and blew smoke toward her.

"She told you she was here first, Rodney," Janie said. Unlike Bettie, she wasn't on oxygen but she *was* a nonsmoker. "This side's nonsmoking and you know it. Lenny talked with you before."

The nursing home where they worked stood on a beautiful stretch of California coast. In order to capitalize on the ocean views, the home had two covered patios. One way off to the left was for smokers. The other to the right was for everyone else. Staff came out to relax, chat, eat, enjoy the breeze blowing in over the ocean, and occasionally feed the terns and gulls. Now and then they saw dolphins or whales in the distance. Patients walked outside or were wheeled there, including some using oxygen tanks.

Rodney screwed his face into a nasty grimace. "Waah, waah, Janie." Walking toward Bettie, he blew smoke into her face and flicked his cigarette butt onto the ground.

The smoke affected Bettie the way it always did; her chest tightened and she coughed.

Strolling away, Rodney voiced a breezy, "Bye, Felicia."

*—The Watchers' eyes blinked. They looked away.*

Janie patted Bettie's back, adopting a soothing tone. "Try to relax while I—ah, here we go! I've got your oxygen." She fit the tubing around Bettie's neck and helped position the nasal cannulas in her nostrils. "Breathe in, hon. This'll help. A good, deep breath. That's it. Good girl."

"Try to breathe nice and steady," Bill urged. "Focus on the sound of your breathing and think of something pleasant. Going fishing. The sound of waves lapping against the pier. Relaxing in the sun. You'll feel better pretty quickly."

Bettie soon reported, "The tightness eased up. Thank you, Janie. You, too, Bill."

"I say karma's real and Rodney's going to get it someday," Janie said to no one in particular. The other employees relaxing outside nodded.

"When karma does bite his butt," Bill said, "I hope it bites hard. Hey, break's over, folks."

Bettie reached for her wheels.

"Here," Janie offered. "Let me push instead of you fighting the wheelchair."

"Thank you." Bettie beamed. "You're a sweetheart." Her regular wheelchair had developed problems, and she'd been forced to revert to the old one in her garage. It was rusty and had to be hand-maneuvered. Diminished upper-body and shoulder strength from a heart attack made it hard for Bettie to propel herself.

Janie spoke to Bettie after they'd gone inside the building. "Hon, you're sixty-seven compared to my thirty-eight. You should be home relaxing, not working or having to deal with the likes of that loser, Rodney." She raised a hand to forestall Bettie's reply. "I know, I know. You've told me what happened, but it's a shame you had to return to work."

"I enjoyed retirement and volunteering," Bettie admitted, "but someone had to take Mike." Her fourteen-year old grandson had lost his parents—including Bettie's only daughter Jean—in a head-on collision a few months ago. If Bettie hadn't stepped forward, Mike would've gone into foster care. Unfortunately, having another mouth to feed, especially a tall, husky teenager either going through a growth spurt or just perpetually hungry, meant she needed more money. He ate her out of house and home —literally. She'd been a stay-at-home mom, raising her and her deceased husband's children. Eventually she took a job as a clerk, where she'd made very little. Her resulting Social Security was meager, and she often had to choose what to pay. Rent or food? Food or medicine? Medicine or electricity? Now she had Mike's needs to consider, too.

So she'd returned to work. Fortunately, she knew how to type and use computers, and she'd been ecstatic to be hired by the very place where she'd previously volunteered.

Three days later, while stopped at a traffic light, Rodney flicked his cigarette out his car window, ignoring the car beside him.

The other driver, an elderly man, had his windows down and jumped when the smoldering missile flew into his vehicle and landed between his legs. With a yell, he squirmed and managed to grab it. "Don't throw cigarettes in folks' cars!" he fussed at Rodney.

Answering with a one-finger-salute, Rodney lit another cigarette. As soon as the red light turned green, he deliberately sent the cigarette flying at the other driver. "Waah, waah, waah," he taunted, zooming away.

The elderly man must have accidentally taken his foot off his brake, because his car rolled and drifted into another lane. Other drivers saw his head vanish. "Put it in park!" someone yelled. The old man's head popped up and his car halted abruptly.

A woman pulled alongside him. "Are you okay, sir? I'll call 911 and report that jerk."

He tossed something out his window. "He threw a cigarette into my car. I'm glad I found it, but now there's a burn hole in my seat." Then he shrugged. "Don't bother calling the police, dear. I didn't get that rude fellow's license plate or even the make of his car."

"I didn't, either," she admitted. "Well, are you good or do you need help?"

"I'm good. Thank you kindly for your kindness, ma'am."

*—The Watchers did not look away.*

Forty minutes later, another man honked and yelled after Rodney, who'd sped past him, "Slow down, idiot! You're not supposed to drive like that in a school zone!"

Rodney snorted and pushed on the gas. Why should he care about some stupid kids? They probably had *real* parents who spoiled them, unlike him. His parents had abandoned him when he was little. He'd been in foster care for years before being

69

adopted, and deserved some of life's perks for being dumped. After all the time he'd waited, those perks were yet to come. How fair was that? Everyone got what they wanted *except* him!

He remembered visiting his foster-turned-adoptive mother last week. She'd turned him down flat when he'd asked for a new car, saying she couldn't afford it. He knew better. She had foster kids in her home, and that meant she got state money every month. She could've helped him if she'd *wanted* to. She was like everyone else, unwilling to help a deserving guy out!

Bitterness flooded Rodney and he ground his teeth together. He ignored the red stop sign on the bus stopped twenty yards ahead to his right and pushed down hard on his gas pedal. His car leaped forward, almost striking the children crossing in front of him. Laughing, he sped on after the bus driver yelled, "Watch out for the kids!"

—*The Watchers' eyes were cold.*

Driving to work late two days later, Rodney swerved from the left lane into the right with no warning, almost side-swiping the vehicle there. The woman, who was driving a van full of children, jerked her wheel hard to the right to avoid being struck. The road was slick with rain, and she fish-tailed into a ditch, missing an electric pole by inches.

Rodney heard crying and screams behind him but kept driving. "Whiny brats." He didn't give them another thought.

—*The Watchers' eyes narrowed, looking at one another in unspoken agreement.*

Four hours later, several employees, including Bettie and Janie, sat outside the nursing home, eating and sharing pictures of grandchildren and pets. One man spoke of his plan to take his grandkids fishing during the upcoming weekend, and how excited the kids would be to ride in a boat for the first time. Another staff member broke a piece of bread into pieces, and tossed them onto the ground nearby. Gulls dived to snatch them up. A couple of them landed and walked toward the people. Janie threw the birds some of her french fries, which were rapidly devoured.

"Man, stop being a douche," Bill griped at Rodney, who was smoking. "You know you shouldn't smoke right here. Some people can't handle it."

"So what?" Rodney shrugged. "If they don't like it, they can move." Everyone either grimaced, glanced at each other knowingly, or ignored him altogether. His eyes narrowed. How dare they whine over stupid kiddie and animal pictures but dismiss him? He'd show them, especially that insipid Bettie who'd taken *his* job. He'd applied for it first, but took an orderly position when *she* stole the one he'd wanted. The fact that he lacked typing and computer skills didn't concern him.

70

Noticing a few inches of Bettie's oxygen line lying slack on the ground, he moved near, then positioned a foot beside it. No one noticed, and he eased his foot on top, bearing down with all his weight. Leaning close to a woman—ostensibly to study her Dachshund photo—he twisted his foot right and left on the line. Lighting a cigarette, he blew smoke at Bettie, despite coworkers berating him.

She had trouble breathing within moments, and this time her oxygen didn't help.

Rodney left amidst clamoring voices. Would she drop dead and free up his job? He didn't see Janie locate the crushed hose or Bill run for a replacement.

*—The Watchers' eyes blazed.*


An hour later Rodney smoked in the nonsmoking area once more, although he'd already used up his breaks. He scowled over his failed sabotage and intended to try again.

He took a hard draw on his cigarette, and it twitched in his fingers. Blinking, he wrote that off as a trick of the light. Then it moved again, and he froze. His mouth fell open when the cigarette got bigger, and he dropped it. This had to be a trick—those dopes inside getting back at him. But how could they make a cigarette expand?

It kept growing—to three feet in length and as big around as a small dog. "I'll be rich when the tabloids hear about this," Rodney gloated aloud. His eyes widened as the cigarette bent in the middle and rose like a person standing. Two eyes stared from the top portion—was that the head?

The cigarette-person-thing soon topped six feet, taller and huskier than Rodney. Bending over him, it whispered, "I'm from the world of Karma's Watching, and I came here for *you*." Its eyes glowed an eerie green.

Rodney froze. *That can't be good,* he thought. He shot up to run away, but the being seized him as if he weighed nothing and flipped him sideways, holding him like a spear. The whimpering man stopped moving and shrank into a cigarette almost instantly.

Meanwhile, Mr. Cigarette was taking Rodney's shape.

Human Rodney would've yelled, but couldn't speak. Cigarette Rodney flicked a lighter, lit the former-man's feet on fire, then sucked on the filter, which had previously been the old Rodney's head.

Feeling searing heat in his feet, Old Rodney tried to scream but couldn't. His mouth was full of tobacco.

Cigarette Rodney drew hard on the filter and Old Rodney felt his feet withering. The physical pain faded into a numb pressure, but the panicked terror and emotional pain of knowing what was happening was excruciating. His calves burned away quickly—next, his thighs—then his hips. Old Rodney wailed soundlessly, but could do nothing. Horror filled him as his stomach burned up and the smolder moved up his chest.

71

Within seconds, Old Rodney's cigarette body was gone. Only fragments of consciousness remained, encapsulated in the filter.

Studying that very filter, New Rodney tossed it onto the ground. He positioned his right foot over it and bore down with all his weight, swiveled his foot back and forth, and ground what was left into smithereens.

New Rodney stretched, inhaled the fresh air, and enjoyed the breeze blowing on him. Looking at the ocean, he watched a dolphin leap out of the water and go back under as gulls flew overhead. Then he sauntered toward the nursing home doors. It wouldn't do to be fired his first day on the job. As bits of paper, tobacco and ash blew away behind him, he smiled and said, "Bye, Felicia."

# LET ME INTRODUCE THE DEMON INSIDE YOU

## P. F. MCGRAIL

I was five years old when they came for me.

I believed—at least in the beginning—that they took me because I was different.

But Mama explained that they took us because *we* were different, and I did not understand.

Because I had learned from an early age that I was the only one who saw them.

Before we left, there was a change in the way that people looked. Tall, thin figures stood over most of them, with ugly blood dripping down wiry, burnt arms as the demons forced every action of the people below. Sinewy limbs would turn their heads downward whenever people attempted to see what was controlling them.

No one was able to see these figures besides me.

The only thing that I understood completely was that I should never speak of them. When the uniformed man came to our house, I asked Mama about what I saw. I wanted to know why he appeared as a man at first, but when I looked closer, he became red and wheezy and hot. The creature ground his teeth together, back and forth, back and forth.

I wanted to know why he was angry. Mama silenced me, pinching my shoulder so hard that her hands shined red. I could see her wings wrapped around my body, but they trembled so.

I did not see Papa spread his wings at all. He appeared very blue and cold. I could feel his shame, but I did not understand why.

I knew better than to ask.

. . .

We packed little more than our clothes before leaving the next day. I asked Mama how long we would be gone, and she told me that it would be just a short vacation. We had never taken a vacation, and she turned green as she spoke, so I knew that she was lying. I cried and told her to tell me the truth.

That's when Papa slapped me. It was the first and last time he ever did so, and I silenced myself immediately.

He stayed blue for the rest of the day. Throughout the train ride that took us farther and farther from home, no one spoke.

When it came close to nighttime, we got off of the train and walked past a large sign. I struggled to sound out the word before asking Mama what it meant.

"What is 'Manzanar?'" I asked, breaking my hours-long silence.

Mama did not look at me when she answered. "It's an American word. It means we're home."

She was glowing bright green.


I did not understand why there were so many men with guns. I had never been allowed to play with one, no matter how fun I thought they would be.

When I looked at them closely, I was afraid of what I saw. Most appeared red, with their muscular arms bulging as they ground clawed fists around their weapons. They licked long, angry tongues around sharp, jagged teeth.

One that scared me more than the rest was a man who got shorter when I looked directly at him. He turned different shades of pink as the crowd of people walked past. Every time that he looked at a woman or a little girl, the shade of pink changed.

He stared at Mama much longer than all the rest.

That was when the pink glowed brightest.


Mama had told me that the word meant "home," but that did not make any sense. We slept in a big tent with many other strangers, so I did not understand how we could be home. Whenever I asked Papa about it, his wings drooped, and he became very blue.

He never had an answer for me.

One of the guards, a man with the name "Schuld" written on his uniform, was not like the rest. Instead of glowing red or pink, he was blue just like Papa. He was the only one with wings like my parents. But they must have been dead wings, because they dragged behind him wherever he walked. I didn't understand why this made me want to cry.

I could not ask anyone to explain why I saw people as special shapes or colors. No one else saw the world in such a way, and that made people afraid.

We're no exception to the rest of the planet's animals; scared people are the most dangerous ones.

.   .   .

In the beginning of our stay, the toilets did not have walls built around them. Everybody who walked in or out glowed much bluer than normal.

But almost everyone was blue in our new home.

The guard who became short when I looked at him spent a lot of time near the women's toilets. He was very pink when they were blue.

Papa rarely looked me in the eye at our new home. He would say "shikata ga nai" and say no more.

But while Mama wrapped her bright wings around me whenever she was near, Papa's only dragged on the ground. He turned blue more often than anyone else.

The short, pink guard once followed as the three of us walked alone between two large tents. He quietly told Papa and me to turn away from him. We immediately did as he told us, because Papa had taught me that obedience was a virtue.

Mama started crying as soon as we could not see her. I tried to look, but Papa grabbed me and turned my head toward the tall mountain that towered over the camp.

That's when Schuld, the guard with the fallen wings, appeared before us. "Verrater, what the fuck are you doing?" he shouted to the other man.

I did not understand what happened next, because Mama and Papa never spoke of it again.

They said nothing to one another for a very long time after that.

I witnessed the brightest blue light I had ever seen while I was in bed that night. Its brilliance woke me, and I struggled to discern its source.

It was my father. He was sitting on the edge of his bed, quietly sobbing into his hands.

I had never seen him cry. It made me so uncomfortable that I snuck out and left our tent, despite knowing that this was a cardinal sin.

When I emerged into the cool and endlessly windy night, I did not know where to go, so I hid in the shadows. No sooner had I disappeared than a guard emerged from around the corner.

Schuld walked past me without noticing. His wings still dragged, but no blue shined from his body that night.

The greatest changes tend to come when we think all the changing is already done.

I don't know why Mama and I were outside alone after dark that night. I do remember her wings wrapped snugly around me. Her eyes were unusually wide as she looked rapidly back and forth, and her hand gripped me so tightly that I thought she might break my tiny bones. The light around her was gray that night—far grayer than I had ever seen it.

We walked quickly, our rapid footsteps muffled in the dirt. We took a long and winding route back to our tent, which confused me.

The sudden stop confused me more. Mama hid me behind her back, enveloping my body completely within the shimmering folds of her wings.

It was all I could do to peek around and see the guard Verrater. He was smiling.

The man's hands were around Mama's wrists faster than I could comprehend. She gasped and sobbed. A part of me knew that she wanted to speak, but for some reason she could not find the words.

Part of me also knew that she wanted me to run. Far away. She wanted me to leave her behind, and never to question why.

But I remained frozen in place, as though my mind had retreated to safety and left my body to face the dark.

I saw red liquid, and I knew it came from my mother.

I didn't cry, because tears are meant to encapsulate fear and to process it. I understood then that some things are beyond comprehension or reason, and that sometimes pain exists simply of its own accord. It was how I learned to be afraid of the world, and terrified of the species that made it go round.

A golden hue blinded me. I squinted at it and saw that, for the first time, Schuld's wings were held aloft. He strode confidently toward Verrater.

There was screaming, and I was thrown to the ground.

I groped in the dark and found my mother's arm. I grasped it so hard that I expected to feel the skin erupt and spill blood beneath my grimy fingers, but I refused to relent. Her arm was limp and unmoving, and I cried and begged her to be alive as I shook her unresponsive body.

I remember hearing one more thing from Verrater. "You're going too far, Schuld! Stop!"

He said nothing more after that.

I don't know how long I held my mother. Pain distended time.

When I looked up again, I saw just one man walking out of the darkness.

He had no wings.

My heart screamed against my ribcage. I grabbed Mama's arm and pulled her, but she would not budge. I dropped the arm, dove to the ground, and covered her body with my own.

The man stepped into the moonlight.

It was Schuld. Bloody stumps protruded from both shoulders. The blood covered his hands as well.

He knelt down next to Mama, clutching her neck and chest.

He looked at me sadly.

"She's alive, kid."

Mama stirred, and my world turned upside down. The feeling was too intense for me even to recognize as happiness.

Schuld lifted her up. "It would be better if nobody knew you two were around. This... is going to be bad."

He carried her from the moonlight into the shadow. I followed, my eyes fixed on the sad, broken stumps of his back.

It was the last time that I saw either Verrater or Schuld. It took me years to understand what had happened that night.

The greatest of angels are the ones willing to shed their wings.


We left Manzanar when I was eight years old. By that time, my mother's lie had become truth: we were leaving home, because there was nothing left for us anywhere in the world. Our former house had long since been inhabited by other occupants.

The three of us were together when we left, and Papa said that was the most important thing. "Shikata ga nai," he explained confidently, and said that our lives were beginning again.

Except that wasn't entirely true. Papa glowed a steady blue that followed him from Manzanar for the rest of his life. He died in 1953, just two days after his fortieth birthday.

Mama continued to manage the landscaping company he had created. By the time I graduated from college, she was the quintessential American success story.

I continued to see the animals within people for the rest of my life, though age and experience honed my understanding of what was being shown to me.

My mother never remarried, and I was never able to quench her loneliness. I grabbed her arm and begged her to come back one more time, on August 5th, 1993.

It didn't work.

Part of me—a deep part, one so fundamental that I had not known of its existence —broke as I watched her aura of solitude finally disappear into the sterile sheets of her hospital bed.

I'm afraid of what I would see if I could step outside my body and look at myself. The ability does not work in mirrors, so I have spent a lifetime wondering how I really look.

I can imagine, though.

And I am glad for what I do not see.

Loneliness feeds fear, and fear feeds itself. It is a simple beast, and one that is much more easily nurtured than destroyed.

And fear is the worst one.

He's tall and thin, perpetually crouching over the people in his grasp. He uses bloody and sinewy hands to manipulate the limbs of unknowing men and women. Whenever they look up and risk seeing his face, he tilts their heads back to the ground and forces them onward.

When I encounter large groups, the quantity and power that he wields is overwhelming.

So I stay away from large groups.

I am simply unable to bear the fear that seizes me in those moments, and how quickly it can take control.

# GEMINI DREAMS

## ELANA GOMEL

There was a cross stuck into the road shoulder by the Motel 6 and he hesitated, uncertain whether to pull in. But his gas gauge was on low and the car—an old hybrid with its battery shot—had developed a throaty rattle like a consumptive's cough. The sky grew the color of bruises as the sun dipped toward the horizon. Anyway, it was an ordinary cross, not a double one. Perhaps it had long been there.

In the spare lobby, the receptionist stirred when he walked in. He almost left when he saw her. But then he realized she was an Unmarked; just grossly obese.

The old ballpoint tore through the paper as he filled in the registration form. Name: Arthur Chu.... Address...

He put in the Red Bluff address. It did not matter. Nobody went to Red Bluff anymore.

The receptionist counted the cash and shoved an electronic key across the counter, which was decorated with yellowing postcards of Sonoma Wine Country. Two of her nails were long and filed to a point, with freshly applied red polish; the rest were short and bitten. Well, people invented strange defenses sometimes.

In the room, he stretched out with a sigh on the creaky psychedelic-colored bed. He had always had a sneaky fondness for cheap motels, even when he could afford a Park Hyatt. Now this shabby room with its generic landscapes and neatly arranged worn towels was as close to home as he was likely to get.

From the nightstand he picked up an old brochure with the chain's motto, "We'll leave the light on for you."

But what if he needed darkness?

A familiar restlessness slithered through his body. He grabbed the remote control.

CNN and Fox News were on; most other channels were snow, though he caught a glimpse of something like swollen worms undulating beyond the jagged lines of static on NBC. On CNN, an evening news broadcast was just beginning. Arthur muted the sound and stared at the anonymous sea of faces. Iowa or Oregon, Ohio or New Jersey, it made no difference. The crowds were the same: boys and girls with a steely glint in their eyes; gaunt men and women whose devotion was secretly rotted by fear.

The Lord's Army. Anna's Army. His sister's Army.

*Kneeling on the edge of a swimming pool, the water teasing him with its turquoise glamour in the dry Californian heat. Giggling, touching the cool surface, concentric waves passing over his reflection, stretching and distorting it...*

*"Art!"*

*His mother standing on the porch, the white of her dress throwing the sun back at him in sharp slivers. He does not reply. They seldom do.*

*"Art! Where is your sister?"*

*He shrugs off the intrusion, but his reflection reacts. It rises through the shimmering layers of water and light, breaking the jeweled surface.*

The TV swarmed with faces like an aquarium with exotic fish. He regretted he had nothing to read, not even a newspaper. He pulled open a nightstand drawer and hastily slammed it shut when he saw a Bible.

Was there somebody out there writing the Book of Anna?

Of all her betrayals, this one hurt the most. She had usurped his letter: the first letter of the alphabet that rightfully belonged to him, the firstborn.

Arthur and Bertha. Their parents never explained why they had chosen these old-fashioned names. They were not big on explanations. Their father's halting English and incomprehensible Mandarin; their mother's long bouts of depression... Now Arthur regretted that he had never really talked to his father, had never asked him how he felt about his miraculous children. It was too late now. Like the rest of the things he had not done, had let slide, had run away from...

The human fish in the TV aquarium gaped mutely as the camera panned across rows and rows of them, toward the approaching presence.

A scream cut through the silence.

Arthur jumped off the bed, rushed to the window and pulled the curtain aside.

The moon the color of bone shone in the ashen sky, providing just enough illumination to see two shadows barreling around the dry swimming pool. One of them crossed the strip of light spilling from Arthur's window, and he saw a ratty T-shirt flapping on the thin adolescent body. The second, massive shadow moved into the light with a clicking sound.

He must have been a big guy once, his gut swollen by beer. Now swollen by less mundane fluids, his gut was elevated six feet above the ground on spindly jagged legs, their knees bent backwards. The belly was majestic like a zeppelin, and neither the scrawny shoulders nor the short, rudimentary arms with comb-like extremities detracted from its pre-eminence. But the head was also striking. Neckless and eyeless, covered with patches of rotting green, it bore a complex arrangement of mandibles around the gaping mouth.

A locust-man!

Arthur's hand cramped as he clutched the curtain. The locust-man's head dipped as he continued to advance on the boy who must have seen Arthur's face in the window because he started hammering on his door. The locust-man was less than a half-pool away.

Arthur recoiled and let go of the curtain. But the hammering continued. The boy had no voice left to plead with, but his gasping was audible even through the din of knocking.

The door shuddered but the lock held. The clicking grew louder.

On the TV screen the sea of faces, some of them Marked, though none as blatantly as the creature outside, glowed with fervor. The camera rose with their gazes, focusing on a veiled woman swathed in dark robes.

The veil was lifted. Arthur's lips thinned as the crowd went wild.

The knocking stopped.

Arthur threw the door open.

The boy was in the locust-man's serrated mandibles, his blood dripping onto the cracked macadam.

"Let him go!" Arthur commanded.

The creature paused as if some dim memory confused its few remaining synapses. Then it went on, stripping off the boy's clothes with its mouthparts.

The Marked could be killed, but their corpses would release the winged Elect that were even more destructive than their larvae. It was a flight of the Elect that had depopulated Red Bluff.

"Stop it!" he screamed, half-fighting the uncoiling of the power inside him. After Bertha's betrayal, he had promised himself never to use it again.

Suddenly the promise seemed childish. He let the power rise.

He had not done it for so long that he had almost forgotten the exaltation. Suddenly he was a god again, his hands dripping with the golden wine of omnipotence as he lifted them and pointed at the locust-man. The swollen belly, harboring a ready-to-hatch Elect, wobbled above Arthur's head.

He had to jump out of the way when the belly swooshed down, the chitin-covered legs folding like the struts of a plane. The mouthparts, suddenly too small to hold the struggling teenager, clicked and dripped foamy saliva.

The boy rolled away and scrambled to his feet, winded and bleeding. He stared as the locust-man shrunk like a pricked balloon. The transformation was fast: within seconds, it was the size of a dog, a cat, a rat... But it was not easy. Arthur felt as if the disappearing mass flowed into his own body, pumping it up with pain. But he kept the power focused until the locust-man was the size of a real locust. Then he let go and dropped to his knees. The boy whimpered.

"Squash it!"

With a wet squelch, the boy brought his foot down upon the creature.

Arthur pulled himself upright. The boy stared at him fearfully. Did he recognize him? Arthur had grown a short golden beard as a disguise. And in any case, the Prophetess went veiled most of the time.

A door opened across the courtyard, spilling feeble light. A fat woman waddled toward them. The receptionist.

"Marty!" she cried.

The boy ran into her embrace. Arthur stumbled toward his room. Glancing over his shoulder, he saw the receptionist stick out her long-nailed fingers toward him, warding off evil.

The live broadcast of the Prophetess' sermon was still on. He could not hear her words and he did not want to look at her. It would be too much of an acknowledgement. Picking up the remote, he thrust it back over his shoulder with his finger on the power button—and froze.

There was a mirror above the bed, reflecting the TV. A close-up of her face filled the screen, hypnotically beautiful, achingly familiar. As familiar as his own.

But it should not be.

Slowly Arthur turned to the screen. He studied the almond-shaped eyes shining with self-intoxication and the Cupid's-bow mouth spewing venom. Her perfect complexion owed nothing to makeup. He knew it well. His own skin, uncared-for in many months, was as flawless as hers. But there had been that one small blemish they had been born with: a tiny birthmark in the outer corner of the left eye. He looked back at her reflection in the mirror. There it was; an almost invisible dot on her left temple. He raised his hand, touched his own birthmark. His mirror-reversed double reproduced the gesture, touching his right temple.

The TV was still filled with her face. And there was a birthmark in the corner of her right eye.


He left the motel early in the morning, seeing none of the other guests who had made no move to help the boy last night. But what could be expected from mere humans?

Mere humans… Arthur frowned as he rummaged in the glove compartment for an old map of California. This had been one of the first cracks between him and Bertha. She had objected to what she saw as his too-easy dismissal of their kinship with the human race.

> "This is so arrogant, Art! So thoughtless! You're always saying how arrogant they are, and look at you!"
> "They have nothing to be proud of and we do!"
> "Who are 'we'?"
> "Oh, come on, Bertha! You know who we are! You and I!"
> "Yes, but what are we?"

This always silenced him. The unanswerable question. They were their parents' children, and in the global world there was nothing exceptional about the pairing of a Chinese businessman and a Californian beauty queen. Nor was the birth of fraternal twins unusual—until it had been discovered that they were not fraternal but genetically identical and yet, unaccountably, of opposite sexes. Scientists had descended upon their LA home in droves until their parents got fed up, went offline, and moved to the inconspicuous town of Red Bluff for privacy. They had enough money to pay for being forgotten. It worked so well that only a couple of transient news alerts blinked on when their mother's spiraling depression culminated in an empty bottle of sleeping pills. Afterwards, their father withdrew into obsessive worship at the ancestral altar, complete with incense-burning and gifts of fruit and red-bean cakes. The twins were relieved when he moved back to China, leaving them with a healthy trust fund to take care of their needs.

Central California had been badly hit by the Tribulations and was now all but abandoned. It suited Arthur just fine. In the first year after Bertha left, he had desperately sought human companionship. He had found it as satisfying as eating plastic fruit to assuage hunger. And then Anna's Army started to grow; rumors, fears and hopes flooded the web; the first Marked appeared; and the first Elect were hatched. His personal problems receded into insignificance as he watched, first with incredulity, then with horror, and finally with numb resignation, his sister destroying the world.

Red Bluff was on a state freeway, but he decided to take the less conspicuous Route 36 that skirted the wilderness of Shasta State Park. Major roads were often blocked, and not always by humans.

The day was perfect, sunny and bright. He searched within himself for some emotion at this belated homecoming. But he felt nothing. Home had been with Bertha. Without her, Red Bluff was neither more nor less alien than the rest of the planet.

So why was he going there? He had no answer except a vague but irresistible impulse, set into motion by the realization that Bertha's face was now, inexplicably, a mirror-reversed reflection of his own rather than the perfect likeness it used to be.

There was a chainsaw carving on the shoulder, its face long and drooping. As Arthur drove by, the carving stirred and shambled off into a thicket of manzanitas.

He slowed down in the gold-and-green twilight of the redwoods, moved by their beauty. A winged, manlike silhouette passed over his head, half-hopping, half-flying through the high branches.

The final stretch of the road wound through the tawny hills scattered with charred trees. One of the twisted trunks scrambled away, its branches flickering like a centipede's legs.

Arthur drove on.

The first of the abandoned ranches came into view. Arthur knew the family who had lived here. The twins had been contemptuous of other children, but before their mother's final descent into depression she would occasionally insist on a playdate for the sake of sociability. The boy—his name was Jake—had been smitten with Bertha, who had generously tolerated his worship.

Was Jake still alive?

The gate of the ranch hung open. Arthur pulled up in front of the porch. Most of the windows were broken.

Hopeless.

He was about to go into reverse when his ears caught a strange rustling sound in the dry grass on the side of the driveway. Locusts? Real ones for a change?

The engine idling, he peered out.

The grass erupted with a flood of tiny bodies that poured into the driveway. They were not locusts or cicadas.

They were horses.

Horses the size of a large grasshopper. They galloped along the driveway: bay, and chestnut, and roan, miniature hooves ringing on the pavement, miniature bodies extended in flight as they leaped over cracks and pebbles. Arthur grinned. This was the first Tribulation miracle that did not make him want to puke.

The horses arranged themselves in a semicircle in front of his car, their whinnying like buzzing of bees. He killed the engine and stepped out.

Arthur knelt and saw that the one of the horses had a rider. At the apex of the semi-circle stood a bay stallion as large as a gecko and seated on his back was a Lilliputian human being. In the blinding glare of the noon Arthur could not make out his features. But somehow, he knew.

Jake.

Jake loved horses. He had taught the twins to ride and they spent many afternoons on redwood trails.

"Hello, buddy!" Arthur said.

The sound coming from the rider was as delicate and ungraspable as the beating of a butterfly wing.

"It's okay," Arthur said. "I can make it right!"

He felt the soft fire of the power rising in his body and wondered how he could have kept it down for so long. It was stupid to renounce it because of Bertha. He was the elder. If she had misused her power, it was up to him to make it right.

The bay stallion and his rider began to grow.

This was a different sensation from shrinking people and objects. Shrinking was like gorging beyond the point of satiety. Enlarging things took energy out of him in a painless swoon.

Once, both had been a game—their game.

"Hey, kids, where is my necklace? C'mon, Bertha, I saw you play with it!"

A conspiratorial glance, a repressed giggle.

"Bertha, honey, would you please give it back? Mummy needs it to go to dinner."

They hated it when their mother adopted this whiny tone of voice. Look at poor little me!

"Bertha! Art!"

Rushing into the yard and there collapsing together in a heap of intertwined limbs and shared giggles. A tiny speck of gold glued with saliva to Bertha's outstretched pinky.

The sun exploded into a jagged rainbow. Arthur leaned his forehead against the car, fighting faintness. It was hard to do this without Bertha.

*And how was she doing it without him?*

He banished the question but he knew it would be back, trailing an even worse one.

*How was she doing alone things they were never able to do together?*

This had been their power in the days gone by: the power to change the size of objects, animate and inanimate. But they had never found a way to change the essence of things. Through the years of their adolescent experimentation they had shrunk SUV's and hidden them in matchboxes; they had unleashed a spider the size of a cow on their neighbor's garden; they had caused a clover-leaf intersection to vanish into a flower-bed. They tried to avoid casualties, mostly because they were afraid to draw attention to themselves. But even though they discovered no limit to their power to modify size (Arthur had been trying to talk Bertha into absconding with the Golden Gate Bridge just before she ran away), they never managed to change lead into gold, stone into water, or flesh into grass. Even a giant spider remained a spider and when shrunk back to its proper size, serenely continued to weave webs and prey on flies. Even a tiny horse remained a horse.

A high-pitched voice penetrated the hum of blood in Arthur's ears. Jake was trying to tell him something.

"Okay, okay!" Arthur said impatiently. "I'm doing it! No sweat!"

He let more power flow; Jake and his horse were growing, he could tell.

The high-pitched garble intensified into a sound of distress. Arthur opened his eyes, squinted into the glare.

The horse and the rider were now the size of a pony and a child. No, make it a pony-and-child.

They—it—were a two-headed centaur, a human torso growing from a horse's back. Jake's suppurating flesh melded into the stallion's scab-covered hide. There was nothing below his hips. The face was ravenous, parchment-like skin taut on brittle bones. The horse's head was barely more than a skull, his lips chewed into bloody tatters.

Both the man's and the horse's mouths folded into an identical plea, the two voices overlapping like a poorly tuned radio.

"Kill us!"

Arthur swallowed bile.

"Kill us!"

He remembered what he had done to the locust-man. He lifted his hand and let it fall limply. He had no power left.

He staggered into the car, turned the ignition. The Jake centaur did not move from the driveway. Arthur closed his eyes and stepped on gas.

A heavy impact jolted the car and it skewed sideways with a sickening *crunch*. Gritting his teeth, Arthur fought to keep it under control.

When he was finally on the highway, the sun shone red in his face through the splattered windshield.

Even at best of times, Red Bluff would be deserted on a scorching Saturday afternoon, downtown shops hunkering down behind lowered shutters, an occasional hopeful café displaying rows of empty tables. The people would be at home, AC on and the ceiling fans toiling away. So Arthur did not find the empty streets shocking. Rather it was their ordinariness that perturbed him. The houses looked untouched.

He pulled to the curb, procrastinating. He knew that the futility of his homecoming would soon be revealed; his house would be as empty as the rest of them. And then he would have to face the decision for which this road trip had only been a postponement and an evasion. He would have to go to the headquarters of Anna's Army in Richmond, Virginia. He would have to force his way through the barrier of her fanatical guards. Well, this was the easy part: his face would be his pass. And then he would have to confront her. Anna the Prophetess; Anna the Tribulations queen. His sister, Bertha. Changed in some mysterious, unfathomable way.

He wondered again why even thinking of their meeting gave him the shivers, while being in his hometown left him unmoved. Perhaps because this had never really been his hometown, just as this world had never been his—their—home.

A flight of starlings passed above his head and then he heard a heavy flapping in one of the courtyards.

Arthur sped through the deserted intersection and found himself in the familiar street of big Spanish-style houses with spacious front lawns and backyard pools. The lawns were dead, killed by the drought, and there were no cars, but otherwise the street was as he remembered it.

Here was his family home: cream pseudo-Mediterranean curves, a tiled roof, rose bushes along the driveway.

There was a car in the driveway and the roses were in bloom.

Before he knew it, he was running to the door. He was at the porch when the door opened and Bertha stepped toward him.

Cupping her face in his hands, he touched the birthmark again, stroked it with his fingertips, unable to get enough of the miracle of it.

The birthmark. A tiny, almost invisible blemish on the perfect face. In the corner of her left eye.


"You're hungry."

This was not a question. They always knew when the other one was hungry, thirsty or in pain.

Sitting in their family kitchen, at the familiar scrubbed pine table. The sky was pink and mauve outside as the sun dipped below the fringe of the trees. The heat had abated and she had turned off the AC.

"There's power still?"

"I have a generator. Dad's."

Yes, he remembered now, their father used to keep a generator in the basement. Dad did not trust American power companies.

He was amused to see their father's Chinese altar in its place in the living room, with their mother's picture added to the black-and-white ancestral snapshots. There was even an incense stick smoking in the holder.

"So you think Dad's still alive?"

"I think so. China has been mostly untouched."

"Why?"

She put a plate before him, filled with vegetable stew. "I grow the vegetables myself."

He was mildly surprised; they had never been interested in gardening. But the stew was excellent as he knew it would be.

She poured their favorite wine: Robert Mondavi merlot 2001.

"Because there are relatively few believers there. At least believers of the kind she needs."

He pushed the stew away. Finally, here it was, out in the open.

"Anna."


"I didn't know what to do. You wouldn't listen to me. You were happy just playing around. Like a kid in the huge sandbox the size of a world…"

"Bertha!"

He was shocked. Not listen to her! It was like not listening to himself!

She frowned. "Let me finish!"

He fell silent, his eyes on the sweetly familiar face. She hadn't changed, of course. After their eighteenth birthday, they had not aged a day, gained a pound of weight, or developed a wrinkle.

"I had to know who we were, what we were. I started having strange dreams…"

"And you didn't tell me!"

"Shut up, Art!"

This *had* changed; she had never spoken to him like this before.

"I needed to be on my own. I thought that if I were a singleton like the rest of them, I would have a better insight into myself. And I wanted to study. I knew that many mythologies have stories of divine twins."

"The Dioscuri, Castor and Pollux," he said.

This stopped her.

"So you studied this too."

He shrugged.

"I had nothing much to do after you were gone."

*Crisscrossing the country in a succession of progressively shabbier cars, living off his father's trust fund, picking up and ditching girlfriends, surfing obscure New Age sites, hunching over mythology dictionaries in public libraries, going into museums and*

*gazing at the marbles of Castor and Pollux, Helena and Clytemnestra. Finding in their*
*serene perfection a strangely soothing echo of his own.*

"So, you know the legends. The twins were the creators of this world, like Ormuzd and Ahriman in Zoroastrism. Or they were offspring of a divinity like the Greek Dioscuri, the children of Zeus."

"I'd rather be a god myself," he said with a forced attempt at levity.

She shook her head, taking it seriously.

"I don't think so. Would we have diminished ourselves so much if we really were gods? No, I think we were divine children. Or maybe just children. In another world that encloses this one."

"Encloses?"

"Art," she asked, "why is the only power that we have is the power over size?"

He shrugged. "I guess it's just the way it is. Maybe this is all that children are allowed."

"In some African mythologies, the world grew from a cosmic seed scattered by a giant cosmic tree. The Dioscuri were hatched from a tiny egg, fully grown. And what about the Big Bang? It started with a single sub-microscopic particle!"

"So? We most certainly were not hatched from an egg! Mother couldn't stand chickens!"

"But what if this entire world, our entire universe, is like an egg, a tiny seed, in another, infinitely larger, universe? And we lived in that universe? And then one day we decided—I don't know why—to penetrate this smaller universe, to become part of it?"

"And so we shrunk ourselves..." he said slowly.

"Yes! Shrunk and shrunk until we fell into the seed universe, still retaining a little of our original nature..."

"This is all just speculation!" he burst out. "And even if it's true, what difference does it make now? Or were you so wrapped up in your mythological research that you failed to notice that this world is going to hell in a handbasket! And the person responsible for this just happened to look like us! Does your cosmic egg theory have anything to say on the subject of Anna and her fucking Army of freaks?"

"Art," she said calmly, "you just mentioned the Dioscuri. Do you remember who they were?"

"My memory is quite all right, thank you!" he snapped. "Two brothers, Castor and Pollux, and..."

He stopped.

"Two sisters, Helena and Clytemnestra," she finished. "Four. There were four of us, Art."

The darkness was oppressive. There had never been many streetlights here, but the nights had always been faintly lit by the reddish glow from downtown. Now the front

87

yard seemed to be piled up with shifting moon-shadows. Sitting on the porch, Arthur was idly trying to sort them out.

*Falling through the darkness, ghostly beasts jostling and crowding him…*

No, it was not a memory, just a childhood nightmare. Even if Bertha was right and the four of them had fallen, shrinking, into the seed of another, sub-microscopic universe, he had no memory of their journey. And was it not like death? If the slate was wiped clean of his previous life, what did it count?

The four of them…

*"So where were they born, the other two?"*
*"Sheffield, UK. Anna's her real name."*
*"And the brother?"*
*"Bernie. Bernard. He was the second-born."*

Of course. Four identical twins, two mirror-pairs.

*"Who were their parents?"*
*"A Vietnamese woman and an Englishman."*

The shadows roiled and buckled; Arthur leaned forward. There was something solid there, all right!

He remembered the porch-light and clicked it on. An Elect stepped into the pool of jaundiced-yellow illumination.

He stank. The sweetish stink of baby poop. Arthur gagged. The creature's body was appalling: fibrous brown skin, whose gnarled texture made it seem he was flayed; shriveled genitals; and large drooping downy wings with pinions of sickly green. His face was covered with a membrane that was sucked in and ballooned out with each labored breath like the plastic bag on the face of a suffocation victim. And yet there was a strange and compelling vitality about him, and for the first time Arthur realized why so many willingly followed Anna, clamoring for the privilege to be Marked. The Elect looked unfinished and raw like a fetus, and like a fetus, he was brimming with promise.

They looked at each other; at least, Arthur assumed that the creature looked at him because only a mess of shifting shadows could be glimpsed through his membrane.

"Go away!" he said hoarsely.

He had seen people being torn to pieces by the Elect. The creature's apishly long arms were equipped with sharp talons.

The Elect cocked his head. Then he turned around and shambled away into the darkness.

Arthur let out a pent-up breath. So this was his sister's—his *other* sister's—creation! What was she trying to achieve?

What if there was a rational purpose behind the madness of the Tribulations? What if she was trying to recreate the denizens of their own world, to crack open the cosmic egg and let it grow and develop?

What if this had been their joint plan from the beginning?

*"How do you know so much about them?"*

*"She sought me out."*

*"Anna?"*

*"Yes."*

*"How did she know?"*

*"She remembered more than we did. At least she remembered there had been four of us. Her own parents kept a low profile and never consulted doctors about them, so nobody but themselves knew she and her brother were identical. She found an online reference to opposite-sex identical twins in California. After that, it was easy."*

*"What did she want?"*

*"She wanted me to join her."*

There was a pale pinkish glimmer on the horizon. False dawn? The color seemed wrong. A wildfire perhaps. They had been raging all over the United States for the last year.

Arthur did not know what time it was but he knew—felt—that Bertha was still sound asleep.

*"You said no, of course."*

*"Of course. I had a moment of hesitation, I admit…"*

*"You did?"*

*"She is one of us, Art! Don't you remember how lonely we always felt? And now, another one of us…"*

He had felt a yawning abyss opening under his feet when she said it. Lonely? He had never been lonely; she had always been enough for him. And now he knew that he had not been enough for her.

So this must be love, he thought ruefully. This is what his forgettable girlfriends always blabbered about. Love: when nothing is enough but you're trying to give everything.

*"We were meant to work together, the four of us. Their power is complementary to ours. We can manipulate size; they can manipulate essence. But something went wrong; what she's doing… it's crazy! So much pain, so much suffering!"*

*"You keep saying 'they' but there is only her, Anna. Where is her brother? Where is Bernard?"*

*"She consumed him."*

Even thinking about it made him nauseous. He had been enraged when Bertha discussed it calmly and lucidly, as if she were talking about a scientific challenge.

*"Remember, they can change things. It's not like she hacked him into pieces and put him in a pot. She may have transformed him into the air she breathed, into the wine she drank..."*

*"'May have'? Didn't you ask her? Didn't she boast about how she did it? Didn't you two discuss the recipe?"*

*"She didn't say and I didn't ask."*

The glow on the horizon was getting stronger. A wildfire, no doubt. Huge tracts of the forest had already been devastated. There were no redwoods left in the Big Basin State Park.

*So what? It's not my world.*

*It's the only world I know.*

*"This was the only way, she told me. She absorbed his power, added it to her own. She needed it. She could not do it on her own. And he refused to work with her."*

*"Why?"*

*"For the same reason I did."*

*Our world.* Perhaps it's a grain of sand on a beach of that other, enclosing, universe, our true home. Perhaps it is an atom or an elementary particle. But pain is not measured by volume.

*"Why didn't she try to kill you?"*

*"She still hopes I'll join her. And then... it's not easy to kill one of us. I think he let her do it. But I won't."*

Dawn was definitely breaking. Combined with the glow of the wildfire, the pale light was strong enough to see Bertha's lush roses unfurl as the automatic sprinklers came on. Arthur made his way into the kitchen, turned on the coffee-maker. On the counter was an opened package of Cheerios. He smiled. They were still starting each day with a bowl of rainbow loops just as they had done as children.

Cereals were beginning to be hard to come by. The Marked ravaged the countryside; starvation and disease followed Anna's Army. The world's financial markets had collapsed. Famine, War, Pestilence. Death.

The four of them.

*"We will fight her, Art! I was waiting for you to come back, to understand that we cannot be passive, that we have an obligation to this world! I was waiting for you to grow up!"*

*"Thanks!"*

*"Oh, come on! You know what I mean! Your power is greater than mine, but you only wanted it for play. Now you can finally see what must be done!"*

This he could.

He poured himself a cup of coffee, sat at the table.

What she did not understand was that it was not immaturity but an essential weakness in his character, an essential flaw. He knew what must be done but he had no strength to do it.

He thought with a shudder of revulsion of the locust-man he had killed; of Jake's tortured eyes and blood on the windshield; of the raw energy of the Elect. These encounters had already drained him of what little determination he had possessed. He imagined confronting armies of such creatures and shook his head. He could not do it.

For the first time, he thought—really thought—of their fourth sibling, his unknown brother, and felt a pang of pure longing. Perhaps they could have been strong together. But now there was an imbalance, a flaw. One unified was more powerful than two sundered.

If Bertha had enough determination to walk away from him, she had enough determination to fight her mirror image. She did not need him by her side, dragging her down. But she needed his power.

The coffee cup in hand, he wandered into the living room, stopped in front of his father's ancestral alter.

"Hello, Dad!" he said softly.

China was still relatively untouched—for how long?

Arthur went back to the kitchen, poured another cup for Bertha. She was waking up; he could feel her emerging from deep sleep in the bedroom above.

He put out a bowl, filled it with Cheerios. And then, standing close to the table so he would be able to jump on it, to vault the bowl's edge and then to dive into the sea of rainbow loops, he started to shrink.

# SANTA'S VILLAGE

## EVAN PURCELL

Nate felt a blast of cold air on his face. It wasn't winter yet, but they were already high enough on the mountain to feel a change of temperature. Unless it was just his imagination. "Almost there?" he asked his older brother.

Jeff ignored him.

Nate tried again. "Hey, Jeff!"

Still nothing.

When Jeff was with his girlfriend, he tended to block out the rest of the world. Well, he tended to block out Nate.

"I think your brother's talking to you," Maxine whispered loud enough for Nate to hear.

"What?" Jeff said. "I thought that was just the wind." He wrapped his arm around her narrow shoulders.

"You're so mean," she said, pulling away, and slapped him on the shoulder. Nate could tell she didn't really care about his feelings because she was laughing as she said it.

"I am not," Jeff said, and he was laughing, too.

Nate knew he was the tagalong. As soon as Maxine agreed to come along with them, Nate knew he would be the unwanted extra person. He knew that he'd be struggling to keep up with them and their long, teenager legs.

They'd been walking up the side of the mountain for the longest time, but they finally reached the top. Jeff and Maxine saw Santa's Village first because they were faster, but Nate wasn't too far behind.

"Dang," Jeff said. "This place is…"

"Creepy?" Maxine asked.

"Awesome!" he said.

Nate wasn't impressed. He knew the place had been closed for decades. He knew the rides wouldn't work and the decorations would be half-broken, but he wasn't expecting... this.

Santa's Village.

The workshop was water-damaged and boarded up. The little stone elves were all missing body parts. A human-sized gingerbread man with half a face was stuck in the dirt at their feet. Everything—every single thing in this awful place—was crumbling into nothing.

It didn't look safe.

Without realizing what he was doing, Nate grabbed onto Jeff's shirt. "I don't like it here."

Jeff shook him off. "Just give it a chance," he said. "This place is crazy."

The three of them walked through the candy cane entrance. They explored the little yellow pathway for a few minutes, but Jeff and Maxine sped up once they got to the dark cave tunnel behind the workshop.

"Jeff!" Maxine squealed. "It's the tunnel of love!"

None of the swan-shaped cars were functional anymore, but that wouldn't stop them from at least walking through it.

"Okay," Jeff agreed, his eyes lighting up. "Let's do it."

"Okay!" Nate said, trying to sound excited.

Jeff turned around, acknowledging his little brother for the first time since they got there. "This is a two-person ride," he said.

"What?"

Maxine tapped Nate on the shoulder. "It means you should probably explore another area of the park," she said.

"But..."

Jeff sighed. "Just go."

"But..." Nate said again. He knew his voice sounded whiny, but he couldn't help himself. He'd been looking forward to this stupid trip for weeks. It was bad enough that none of the rides were working. Now he had to walk around the park by himself? That wasn't what he'd planned.

"This is our alone time," Jeff said. He squeezed Maxine's hand and she kissed him on the cheek. *Alone time*. That was what Mom and Dad said when they locked the bedroom door and wouldn't let Nate into their room.

"Fine, then!" Nate said. "I'm gonna have so much fun by myself."

Jeff didn't say anything.

"So much fucking fun!" He wasn't supposed to say the f-word. That was for grown-ups. He knew that would get a rise out of Jeff.

But Jeff still didn't say anything. Instead, he half-waved at his little brother and then led Maxine in the other direction.

And Nate was alone. Totally alone.

Whatever.

He stood there for a bit, just in case Jeff changed his mind or felt guilty or something. When Jeff didn't come back, Nate mumbled the f-word one more time—just because he could—and walked toward the big Christmas tree in the center of the park.

The tree didn't move or light up or do anything special. It just sat there. Like a tree. It was behind a tall glass cage and had presents all around its bottom. Most of the glass panels were broken and dust had gotten inside. Stupid thing.

He picked up one of the presents—a little purple one—only to find it wasn't a real present at all, but a painted wooden block. It wasn't even purple all the way around, just on the side that would've been seen by the public. The rest was unpainted.

Nate suddenly got the urge—the uncontrollable urge—to smash the present into a million purple pieces. He wasn't quite strong enough for a million pieces, but he stepped on it and the rotted wood crumpled like a cardboard box. Which was okay.

He left the ruined present on the ground outside the tree's enclosure and then walked toward the snowman area. On the way, he saw a half-faced gingerbread man lying on the ground. It looked so sad—what with half a face and all—and the mushy ruined half reminded him of the present he'd just smashed. He stared into the man's fake gumdrop eye for the longest time. "Sorry," he muttered. He was apologizing for the present, and for the two times he said the f-word, and for everything, really. He was sorry that the gingerbread man had to sit there with half a face for all eternity.

But mostly, he was just sorry for himself. Maybe Jeff would find him and take him home soon.


The tunnel of love smelled like animal urine, but Jeff didn't seem to notice. He was too busy exploring the rough surfaces of Maxine's tongue with his own. She tried to say something, but he kissed her harder.

He wanted this to be a magical moment, dammit, and he knew that if he let her talk, she'd tell him that they needed to check on Nate.

Maxine's mouth was so warm. He wanted this moment to last forever, or at least the next few minutes, but she pushed him away. "We need to check on Nate," she said.

He knew it! He saw that coming, and damn the little brat for acting so defenseless all the time. Even when he wasn't around, he still ruined things.

"Five more minutes," Jeff said, and kissed her again.

"No more minutes."

"Two more minutes."

She pushed him away a second time. "Jeff," she said, "how old is your brother?"

"I don't know," he said. "Six? Ten?"

"Come on," she said. "This place has a lot of holes and rusted metal and stuff."

"Fine," he said. Together, they walked out of the tunnel of love. Once they left the darkness—and the animal urine smell—Jeff realized how weirdly quiet the whole place was. No wind. No animal noises. Nothing at all, really. "Nate!" he shouted.

No answer.

"Nate!"

Still nothing.

Jeff felt a pinprick of fear in his bellybutton area, and it started to grow. He was getting a little nervous. Christ. Why did Maxine have to talk about rusted metal and all that stuff? His little brother was a royal pain, but anything happened to the kid…

"NATE!"

It wasn't like Nate to run off like this. He was a boring little kid, scared of everything except videogames and Star Wars. He couldn't have gone too far.

Jeff walked around the snowman area and the peppermint sticks, but he didn't see anyone. Maxine followed him every step of the way, but she didn't seem too nervous. "Where'd he go?" Jeff asked.

Maxine shrugged. She was useless, too. This whole trip wasn't turning out like he'd hoped. And BAM! Jeff accidentally slammed his foot into one of the stone elves lining the path.

"Christ!" he shouted.

"Are you okay?"

"No, I'm not okay! Look at this stupid thing!" The elf was looking up at him with a giant smile and two squinty black eyes. Its suit used to be green, but most of its paint had chipped off over the years. "What are you looking at?" he asked the statue.

It didn't respond, of course.

"I said… what the hell are you looking at?"

"Come on, Jeff," Maxine said. "I think he's cute."

"Well, I think he could use a facelift." With that, Jeff picked up a rock and bashed it against the elf with all his strength. Its nose crumbled off. So did half its jaw. "See? Doesn't he look better now?"

Maxine didn't even look at the elf. "Let's go find your brother," she said.

Jeff was done listening to everybody else. He'd taken them up here to have a little fun, and he was going to have some fun, Goddammit, even if he had to do it alone. "Jeez, Max," he said, "stop being such a downer."

Maxine's face went blank, but only for a second. "I'm bringing you down? This is my fault?" she said.

As soon as the words left his mouth, he realized he'd made a mistake; his girlfriend was not the best at taking criticism.

Maxine puffed out air through her nostrils. She walked over to the elf and pushed it as hard as she could. It teetered at first, then went crashing to the ground. On impact, its head popped off.

"Are you happy?" she said, annoyance flashing across her face like a traffic light changing from yellow to red.

Before Jeff could say anything else, he saw a small figure dart behind the cottage. Apparently it didn't want to be seen, but Jeff had seen it nonetheless.

*That has to be Nate*, he thought. Nate was the only other person here, and the figure was about his size.

*Christ, if he's playing a game, so help me God…*

They followed the shadow without talking. Maxine looked a bit confused. It was clear she hadn't seen or heard anything

"Hello?" he called. "Hello?"

Nothing.

"Hello?"

And then the silence—that throbbing, powerful silence—gave way to something else. A skittering noise. It seemed to come from every direction at once, alternating between loud and quiet, loud and quiet, until Jeff felt dizzy from the noise.

He wanted Maxine to clutch at his side, to cling to him for support, but she didn't, and he kind of hated her for it.

The skittering noise crescendo, each tiny rustle converging into loud, single pair of footsteps. Footsteps that were approaching them from the darkness. At first, Jeff couldn't see the figure approaching, but he knew it was there. He knew it was small and dark—and walking directly toward them, but he didn't know what it was.

Until he saw the pointy hat. And the pointy shoes. And the black eyes that grew larger—impossibly large—as the figure approached. It looked angry. No, it looked furious.

"Uh, Jeff," Maxine whispered. She clung to his side now, but by this point he didn't even notice. He was staring at the approaching elf statue. Its movements were awkward, like a child taking its first steps. Something that was not accustomed to moving about.

Something... that shouldn't exist—but did.

"Go," Jeff whispered. "Go now."

When Maxine didn't start running, Jeff did. Sure enough, she followed. They barreled through the park, over rocks and other broken things, until they made it to the workshop.

The footsteps behind them didn't stop. They didn't run, either. Just slow, even thuds against the ground.

"Is it safe in there?" Maxine asked.

Jeff didn't answer. He gripped the rusted handle and twisted and pulled as hard as he could. He felt pieces of it—cold slivers of the metal—jab into his palm. "Open, please open," he whispered.

But it didn't. They were trapped.


After sulking around for fifteen minutes, Nate had had enough. He'd seen everything he needed to see, and it sure wasn't a lot: some concrete snowmen with missing carrot noses... a carousel that had been half-dismantled before people realized it wasn't worth anything... even a bathroom shaped like a gingerbread house. He was done.

Besides, fifteen minutes was a long enough time for Jeff to start feeling guilty about how he had treated his little brother. Head held high and hands jammed into his pockets, Nate began walking back toward the main courtyard.

He wasn't scared. He was alone, but he wasn't scared. He only thought about his brother, about what he could say to make him feel guilty for abandoning him.

When Nate passed by a maintenance shed shaped like an igloo, he heard low breathing coming from within the building through a partially open window. "Hello?" he whispered. He put his face against the glass, squinting his eyes to make out any shapes inside. It was too dusty, though. He couldn't see anything.

Well, he saw movements. Something was inside, something low to the ground. It swayed back and forth. What was it?

Nate tapped three times on the glass. "Jeff," he whispered. Then he raised his voice a little. "Jeff?"

No answer.

But the figure inside heard him because it turned around and started walking toward the dusty window.

"Jeff, are you okay?" Nate asked.

The figure shook his head no. He gestured for Nate to lean closer. He wiggled his impossibly long fingers through the air. Jeff didn't have such long fingers, but maybe had found something in the park, a costume or something, which he put on in the hopes of scaring Nate.

*This doesn't feel right*, Nate thought. His whole body was tense and his neck hairs were standing up. He felt, deep down in his bones, that something was very, very wrong.

Still… he should always listen to his big brother. He leaned closer.

The figure on the other side of the glass leaned closer, too. It raised one hand and wiped away at some of the dust.

What was it? Nate still couldn't see it clearly because there was so much dust.

The figure cocked its head.

BAM!

In a burst of sudden movement and loud shattering noises, the window broke open and the wall collapsed. Glass flew everywhere. Dust did, too. Something large and white dived at Nate. It had a spherical head and two black lumps for eyes. There was a perfect hole in the center of its face, where some small bird had made a nest.

Snowman!

The thing clawed through the air. Three twig fingers on each tree branch arm, all reaching toward Nate, digging at his shirt.

Nate felt jagged fingertips tear at his shirt. He twisted to the side, just managing to wiggle out of the snowman's grasp. It grunted like an animal.

"Jeff!" Nate shouted. "Jeff! Help me!"

There was no response. Not even an echo. Then, rising out of the silence… his brother's voice! "Nate! Nate!" It sounded far away.

The voice had come from the workshop!

Nate looked around but the snowman had disappeared. He couldn't see it anywhere. The area around that igloo was silent and still. He circled around and headed toward the workshop.

The sky grew darker. The clouds were thick and full of rain and blotted out the sun.

Nate struggled to catch his breath. "I'm… here," he whispered. But where was his brother? He looked around the corner of the workshop. Two figures—Jeff and Maxine —were standing at the door, trying to yank it open.

"We're here," Jeff said, but Nate had already seen them.

With a groan, the workshop door shifted but didn't open. There was a padlock in the way, something they hadn't noticed in their panic, and from the look of it, the damn thing had rusted shut a long time ago.

Nate ran to his brother. "Did you... Did you see that snowman?"

"Give me room," Jeff ordered. "It's gonna break soon. It'll open."

Nate trusted him. Besides, Jeff was big and strong. He played lacrosse.

*Creeeaaaaak.*

The weathered wood splintered and the clasp fell away. Jackpot! But before the door could open completely, it stopped. A foot of open space. Light spilled from the inside of the building. And slowly, an elf hobbled out. He was smaller than any of the statues they'd seen. Part of its leg had crumbled away, and it looked like a pirate with a peg leg. "'Tis the season," the elf said.

Maxine backed away.

The elf took them all in with a sweeping glance. "You know, children always get what they deserve at Christmastime."

"What does that mean?" Jeff said.

Another elf stepped out of the shadows. This one was headless. "It means payback," the creature said. God only knew where the voice came from. Perhaps from the hole in his open neck.

Nate wanted to throw up.

The headless elf pointed straight at Maxine. "Get them," he ordered.

Jeff jumped. Nate had never seen his brother this scared before. It didn't seem right.

More elves surrounded them, their movements jerky, like broken toys. Paint chips flecked off them and left trails on the ground.

There was nowhere to run. They were in the middle of an abandoned theme park on the top of a mountain. People were forbidden to come here. Hell, people were afraid to come here. And now Nate knew why.

Nate noticed Maxine nudge Jeff. It was some sort of secret boyfriend-girlfriend code. She expected him to do something, although Nate didn't know what his brother could do against so many.

He had faith in his brother, though. Whatever plan Jeff had, it would totally work. His plans always worked. Nate trusted that his big brother would take care of them. He just wished it would happen faster.

"Hey." Jeff motioned for the first elf to come forward.

It did. Its peg leg made crunching noises. In slow, deliberate movements, it tried to attack Jeff. Its fists pummeled the air. Jeff dodged it easily. He smiled, the little victory clearly going to his head.

"Be careful," Maxine warned.

"Yeah, yeah," Jeff said. He steadied himself, pulled back his own fist, and punched the elf right in its face. There was no damage done to the elf, but Jeff let out with a loud, painful scream.

Jeff's knees buckled and he collapsed onto the grassy ground. Maxine grabbed him under his armpits and tried to pull him back to his feet.

"You're okay," she said. "They're tiny."

Jeff shook his head. "They're stone!" he said. He held up his hand for her to see. It was twisted unnaturally, and there was a sharp bump under his ring finger. "I think... it's broken."

The elf pushed Maxine away. He got closer to Jeff. "You get what you deserve," he said. In a single motion, he balled up his stone fist and punched Jeff right in the face. Nate couldn't describe the sound it made, not in words, but it was a sound that echoed through his brain and wouldn't leave.

Jeff's nose and jaw shattered in a cloud of gore.

Nate's big brother, the one who was supposed to protect them all, fell backward and didn't move. Blood pooled under him.

"Please," Maxine whimpered. "Don't. Please."

They didn't listen.

"Let me go," she begged. "Take the boy, but let me go. I wasn't even supposed to be here."

The elves were upon her now and drove her to the ground. Grabbing at her. Tearing at her. Their little fingers with their sharp, irregular edges tore at her clothes, her flesh, her eyes.

"Please," Maxine howled. "I don't deserve this. I didn't do anything."

The headless elf walked to her and placed his head into her hands.

"Oh," Maxine moaned from a place deep inside her. She lowered the elf head to the ground.

The next elf—this one wearing red—limped forward. One of its legs was twisted. He held a long, metallic stick painted like a candy cane. He set the curved end to the ground and positioned himself next to the sobbing girl.

"I'm sorry," Maxine said. "I didn't mean..."

The red elf giggled. He tapped the candy cane against Maxine's temple. She was moving too much, so he put one pointy shoe on top of her head. to keep her still. He raised the candy cane high over his shoulder, like a golfer.

"Please."

Three.

Two.

One.

The red elf brought the cane down. Maxine's head made a juicy noise and was separated from her body. It flew through the air. As it hit the ground and rolled, all the elves did a little victory dance.

Nate didn't realize he'd been screaming the whole time.

. . .

Pain. Searing, unimaginable pain.

When Jeff came to, his brother and girlfriend were gone. He wiped the blood from his eyes, careful not to touch the torn, ragged gash where his nose had been.

"Nate," he croaked. "Maxine. Nate."

With a grunt, he bit back the pain and managed to sit up.

There was a red trail that started in his own crimson pool and led toward the workshop. Someone, perhaps two someones, had been dragged there.

With two fingers, Jeff reached up and touched his face. Slickness—that was the blood—and lumps—those were the twisted bone. He was mangled, probably beyond recognition.

He'd always seen himself as a good-looking guy. His jaw was strong, and his aunt always told him that his great-grandfather was a Native American, which meant he had some killer cheekbones. He rarely got zits, and the freckles along the bridge of his nose weren't particularly obtrusive.

Yeah, Jeff had been handsome.

But now he had mush for a face.

How was he possibly going to live the rest of his life like this? How could he find a girlfriend? How could he show himself in public?

Jeff coughed a little. Blood and small amounts of bile dripped out of his mouth. He didn't throw up, but he probably would've felt better if he had.

But he didn't have time to think about his own blood. His girlfriend and his brother were still out there, and there was a blood trail leading back to the workshop.

He crawled toward the building. He didn't call out anyone's name, though. He kept quiet.

There was a rosy glow coming from inside the workshop that hadn't been there before.

Using the doorframe, he was able to stand, and once on his feet, he gave the door a push. It creaked open. He was in too much pain to think of a plan, so he was just going to have to see how things played out.

On the inside, the workshop was cozy, warm, and inviting. Rows of elves happily banged away at toys on an assembly line. A Christmas tree rotated in the center of the workshop, shining its multicolored lights in all directions. And at the far end, a massive Santa Claus sat on a throne, and in his lap was Nate.

*Its* lap.

Not his.

This Santa wasn't quite human.

Just beyond them, a few of the elves were decorating Maxine's headless body as if it were a tree. They sang nonsense words. Some of them laughed. Otherwise, there was no other sound in the workshop. Even the machinery didn't make any noises.

Nate looked at Jeff, his eyes blank. He didn't seem afraid of the Santa. He seemed almost... comfortable.

Jeff motioned his younger brother to come to him.

Santa ignored him. The elves ignored him, except for one who threw a handful of glitter in his direction. The only person to acknowledge Jeff was his brother. Nate looked over and said, "I don't know."

"What do you mean you don't know? What don't you know?" He didn't even know if Nate could hear him.

"You should've protected us," Nate answered. "You should've protected Maxine."

"Yes, but I'll... I'll protect you now." His voice caught in his throat.

Nate leaned his small body against Santa's giant gut. "I don't need protecting. You guys were naughty, but I wasn't. I'm safe here."

Jeff watched the Santa as its black eyes blinked and its head swayed left and right. It looked wrong. It looked like what a toy factory's cheap copy of a human would look like.

"Nate," Jeff begged. "Come on. Come with me. Slowly."

Santa laughed, its whole belly trembling. Nate shook in its lap.

"Don't listen to bad children," Santa told Nate. It stroked his hair with one gloved hand. Jeff noticed with horror that there were little red spots on its white gloves. Blood.

"Yes, sir," Nate said.

"And you," Santa continued, "have been a good boy. You didn't hurt anyone. Not like those other two." He was talking about Jeff and Maxine, the naughty ones.

Jeff touched his face, smearing some of the blood down his cheek. "But we can leave," he protested. "I already paid my price." Like the elf he had destroyed, he'd suffered a shattered nose and a mangled chin. An eye for an eye. It should've been over.

Santa shook its head. Its shark eyes never left Nate, though.

An elf walked into the workshop. He held a smashed present in both hands. It was purple and crumpled.

Santa still stroked Nate's hair. "It looks like someone crushed one of my darlings," it said. "There's one more price to pay."

Jeff didn't understand. He didn't remember smashing any presents. He hadn't seen any presents like that anywhere. Then he saw Nate, saw the widening sense of horror spread across the younger boy's face, and he realized what his brother had done.

*Oh God!*

"We can't accept that," Santa said. He scratched the tip of his red nose. "We believe in giving what you deserve. Now, if you come clean, I will be nice. I will only crush your bottom half, not the rest. But you need to admit what you did."

Nate looked at his big brother, panic across his face.

*Crush?*

Santa gestured toward a toy-making machine in the corner of the room. It looked like a trash compactor decorated in alternating stripes of white and red. It had a hole in the top where could be lowered into the machine. It was big enough for a person to fit.

"Please," Jeff said. Blood was dripping into his mouth again. "I... Please."

"If you lower yourself inside voluntarily," Santa continued, "I will only crush you halfway." His deep, booming voice laughed. "Your little brother can leave, and come back with help if he so chooses. However, that deal is only if you admit to crushing the present."

Jeff looked at his little brother. Then the machine.

He would lower himself into the machine. He knew he would. If he survived that thing, if he could crawl out of it with his upper body still functional... what sort of life would he be able to live? He couldn't imagine. No legs. Half a face. He'd be nothing.

But he was the big brother. He had to protect Nate, even when life wasn't fair.

Wordlessly, Jeff stumbled toward the machine and climbed a small ladder until he was able to pull himself onto the top of the machine. Then he lowered his legs inside.

Santa clapped. He laughed and clapped.

"Now," Santa said to Nate.

*Now?*

Next to Nate was a large peppermint stick lever protruding from the wall.

Jeff saw the look on his little brother's face. At first, it was confusion, but that quickly morphed into a mixture of horror and queasiness. Nate was going to have to pull the lever himself. He wasn't just allowing his brother's legs to be crushed; he was actively making it happen.

Nate—eyes wide—looked straight at Jeff. Christ, he looked at Jeff for permission. He was asking Jeff to willingly sacrifice his legs so that Nate could go free. After everything...

Jeff looked away. He couldn't. He couldn't bear to look at his brother anymore.

"I, um..." Nate said.

Jeff tried not to move his lower half. Metal pieces were cutting into his legs.

Nate walked over and grabbed the candy cane lever.

"Wait," Jeff said. He couldn't do it. He couldn't go through with this. There had to be another way.

Nate looked at his big brother. He had a blank look on his face. No expression at all. "I'm so sorry," he whispered.

Then he pulled the lever.

At first, nothing happened. Then the floor beneath Nate opened up and the younger boy disappeared into darkness. The machine never started. Jeff was safe, and Nate was gone.

Jeff didn't understand. He looked at Santa for some explanation.

The elves started cackling. Like their voices, their laughter was shrill and loud. Even the broken elf head laughed.

Santa joined in, and his laughter was loud enough and deep enough to rock the entire building. When it finally stopped, he turned to look straight at Jeff. "Santa hates liars most of all," he said.

102

# CROSSROADS

## MADISON ESTES

Rust crusted the edges of the beige car door, infecting the metal springs with orange and brown granules. Thomas's biceps bulged as he jerked it open. The Camry protested with a high-pitched screech.

*Ehhhhhheeeeeeeeeeee!*

"Not this one," he said.

"The squeaking will go away with a little WD-40," Ruben replied, patting the hood like he would a dog's head.

"The squeaking won't go away until the door falls off this old piece of junk." Thomas shut the door, another shriek filling the air. "I need something bigger anyway."

The L.A. sun beat down on them as they strolled through the auction lot. As an actor, Thomas saw sunscreen as an investment in his future rather than a luxury, and so his pale skin was spared the sun's cruel wrath. Ruben was not so lucky, as the bright summer day reddened his ears and shoulders.

The police auction was far bigger than Thomas expected. They'd checked in with the front desk (the window of a broken-down prison bus), filled out paperwork, and received a bidder card and auction list. They spent the morning walking the yard, looking over each car with a fine-toothed comb. Ruben owned a junkyard and lived and breathed used cars and car parts. The Camry had been one of a dozen cars Ruben suggested that Thomas passed over.

"Yeah, wouldn't be easy to fit a car seat in there anyway," Ruben said. "You gotta think about things like that now."

Thomas scowled. "I guess." The words *As Is* floated around in his head as he passed dozens of signs reminding him all sales were final.

*No refunds*, he thought as the ultrasound flashed in his mind. *No returns. No going back.*

"It's not like we have to get one today," Thomas said. "I've got time."

When they came across the Porsche, Thomas almost passed it up. Not because of the state it was in, but because the mere fact that it was at a police auction made him suspect it was too good to be true. Thomas nudged Ruben anyway.

"What about this one?"

Ruben frowned. "A Porsche?"

"Look at the highest bid though. That's less than the Camry."

"Which means it probably won't run."

"Yeah." Thomas frowned. "But couldn't you fix it, or buy it off me for parts and make a profit?

Ruben rolled his eyes and nodded. Without hesitation, Thomas made a bid. He and Cindy had nine months to get a safe car. He would sacrifice his dream condo, new headshots, late nights at *The Echo* and *Skybar*, if he could just have this one thing, this one remnant of the life he wanted. He could face what was to come if he had the Porsche. He would make the necessary compromises of his time and money, he would give and give without end, but he would not give this up. This was for him.


"I cannot believe you came back with a Porsche." Cindy's hands were on her hips as she glared at her boyfriend.

"Hear me out."

"We need a family car."

"And we'll get one. We're both going to be working when we move to the suburbs. We're both going to need cars," he said. "And there *is* a backseat in this. It's not the greatest, it's not President of the PTA mom material, but we can squeeze a baby back there if we have to."

"Did you just hear yourself? 'Squeeze a baby back there'?" She crossed her arms.

His own arms rose in surrender. "Maybe that wasn't the best choice of words, but you get my point."

"Sure, let's just throw the baby back there with your stupid dumbbells and gym gear."

"Why put him in the backseat at all?" Thomas scratched the back of his head and gave a little shrug. "We'll just chuck him in the trunk with a baby monitor."

"You mean a cellphone. Baby monitors are so last gen."

"If he needs us, he'll text, right?"

"We're going to be great parents." She smiled, exposing the top row of her perfect teeth. He wrapped his arms around her, planting a kiss on her cheek, then on her lips. He smiled into the kiss, and for a moment, his worries washed away.


As Cindy's belly swelled, so did his anxieties. His parents were gone, not that either of them had been there for him much anyway. One pill popper and one drunk meant that he'd faced a decade of empty seats on opening nights and broken promises. It was his grandmother who really raised him, and her parenting advice to him before she passed away was, "Don't have children. It's not in our blood."

Thomas had done the best acting of his life in the past few months, pretending he felt as happy as Cindy and her parents. Sometime during the second trimester, Cindy began to show so much that every time he looked at her, all he could see was what was coming. Crying, tantrums, stress, messes, financial strain. But also glittery cards on Father's Day, hugs, teaching his son or daughter how to fake cry their way out of a ticket (Thomas had never been good at sports, and a father has to teach his child *something*). His moods flipped like a tossed coin spinning in the air. Except when he was inside the Porsche—everything was calm there.

He liked driving around the streets of L.A. like a bigshot in his car, but he truly found serenity driving outside of L.A. where there was less traffic. His foot tapped the accelerator and he passed the speed limit of 65 mph. He watched the barometer pass 70… 75… 80…

*"Don't have children."*

85…

*"It's not in our blood."*

90…

"What do you know?" Thomas said. "You raised a fucking druggie."

95…

"You weren't there for me either, you fucking bitch. No one was."

100…

Several yards ahead, he saw a woman cowering in the street. Her screams filled the air. He slammed on the brakes. His knuckles whitened as he gripped the steering wheel. The car stopped.

She was gone.

He took a shaky breath. He stepped out of the car, looking everywhere for her, even under the car. When he got back into the driver's seat, he noticed the glove compartment had opened when he hit the brakes. He found a few pieces of junk mail he'd thrown inside, and a white rag. His forehead glistened, and he felt clammy. He grasped the rag to wipe perspiration from his face. As he unfolded it, he realized it wasn't a rag at all, but a baby onesie, with dark red stains across it. A deep male laugh echoed from the backseat. Thomas dropped the onesie on the floor as he spun around to look behind him. Nothing.

He picked up the onesie *(how did that get in there?)* and tossed it in the glove compartment, then shut it. Shaken, he started the car again and headed home. When he glanced in the rearview mirror again, he nearly swerved off the road.

The seatbelts were strapped in.

Thomas bleached his hair in the bathroom. On a whim, he decided to go blonde instead of dyeing just the greys out of his hair like he usually did. As he wiped some of the dye off with old rags, it reminded him of the onesie.

As soon as he got home that night, he tried to put the whole bizarre drive out of his mind. He'd shoved the onesie in the trash and washed his hands afterwards. He didn't think it was likely, but he had to ask Cindy if she'd put the onesie there. He called and asked her about it after he finished washing his hair.

"No, I've barely been in your car," she said. "I know that's your mancave on wheels."

"Ha-ha. Very funny. I was just wondering how it got in there." He went to the garage to look at the car.

"Who knows? That's the best part about buying things secondhand. All the fun little surprises you find."

He circled the Porsche like a cop sizing up a suspect.

*Cheater* was scratched into the door.

"I have to call you back." His heart pounded. "Someone is on the other line. Could be work."

"Okay, I'm almost home anyway. See you soon."

This was just what he needed. Cindy had already been glancing over his shoulder when he was on the phone, throwing him suspicious looks whenever he mentioned going out at night. He couldn't say he blamed her. His mind hadn't been right since he saw that little plus sign on the pregnancy test. Cheating wouldn't be a huge jump considering he couldn't predict his own behavior from day to day.

The problem of course was that he wasn't having an affair, nor was he even entertaining the idea of it with anyone. He'd flirted with a few girls at the clubs, but never gave any one girl enough attention to think it meant anything. There wasn't anyone who would resort to vandalism to get back at him.

He grabbed a soft cloth and toothpaste and tried to buff the scratches out. His knees ached as he kneeled on the concrete, still buffing away when Cindy came home. He tossed the cleaning equipment in the corner and stood awkwardly when the door opened, trying to shield the word from her view.

"Hey."

"What the hell is that?"

A sigh escaped him. "Look, baby, I have no idea how this happened. I just…" He stopped when he noticed she was looking at his hair and not the car.

"Okay, Eminem. And is that toothpaste on your shirt?"

"Oh, yeah. I was just buffing the car." He turned to lean on the door, hiding the markings from her again.

She rolled her eyes. "You know, I'm starting to get a little jealous of that thing."

"Don't be silly," he said, giving her a kiss on the forehead. She took his hand and he let her lead him out of the garage. He glanced back, and the word was gone. He pulled away from her and examined the door. His finger trailed along the metal, searching for the indentions. Cindy groaned.

"Oh my gosh, really? You buffed the hell out of it. It looks great. Are you going to admire it all night?"

He shook his head. "Of course not. Let's go in."

. . .

"I miss getting carded," Thomas whined as he and Ruben left the bar.

"Don't we all?" Ruben supported Thomas as they made their way to Ruben's truck.

"Hey, did you ever want to be in a band?"

"No. The only instrument I ever took to was the triangle, and there's not a huge demand for triangle-ists. Come on now, in you go."

Ruben dropped him off a little past midnight. Thomas staggered to his front door, laughing when he rang the doorbell. He couldn't remember the last time he'd been so drunk. It was the kind of drinking he was supposed to have done in his twenties and thirties when he was hopping from place to place using parties to meet people in the business instead of enjoying himself. He felt like he'd made up for twenty years in one night.

He tried to stick his key in the hole and giggled when the door opened.

"Hi, baby. I'm drunk."

"I heard." Her tone was clipped. "Ruben let me know he was dropping you off."

He zigzagged his way to the couch. The room spun like a tilt-a-whirl. Cindy stood next to him with her arms crossed.

She looked at him, and in that moment he knew that she saw him as he really was. Not the life of the party, the B-list actor, the charmer who could talk his way into parties and out of tickets. Not the prankster or the guy with connections. She saw beneath the Porsche and the ridiculous new hair and the late-night drives and his sad need to hit every bar and club in L.A. before the baby arrived. She saw that he was a scared boy in a grown man's body—an almost forty-year-old man, for Christ's sake—and he could feel shame and embarrassment radiating off her. She shook her head and threw a blanket and pillow on their couch. He nodded, unable to meet her eyes. His stomach twisted as she continued to give him a look of disappointment, worse than anything she could have said. It was like getting caught in an affair, or having to be bailed out of jail.

"Thomas," she said, and then paused. He closed his eyes, preparing for a scolding, for her to ask him what the hell he was doing. She placed one hand on her belly and the other on his leg. "Do you hate us?"

"What? I... No," he said, placing his hand over the one she'd put on his knee. He squeezed her hand. "I love you."

"Then stop acting like your life is about to be ruined. Before it actually is."

She went into the bedroom and shut the door. The sound of the door locking echoed, as did her muffled crying.


In the morning, Cindy made pancakes and coffee and didn't mention the night before. He was grateful the Porsche was still at the bar. He didn't want to see the physical manifestation of his midlife crisis. Knowing the car was across town felt like a weight being lifted, although he didn't dwell on why he felt so much better with it gone.

107

He ditched an audition and they spent the day together. They watched television, made love, decorated the nursery, and discussed baby names. The unpleasantness of the night before was forgotten.

Ruben came over midafternoon to drive Thomas back to the bar to get his car. Thomas couldn't explain the mixed feelings stirring in him as they entered the parking lot and he saw the green Porsche sparkling in the sunlight. He'd anticipated that someone could have vandalized it overnight, but it looked like someone gave it a professional cleaning instead.

His stomach turned. Something told him not to get behind the wheel.

"Meet you back at the house?" Thomas said. "Cindy is making pot roast for dinner."

"Sure." Ruben eyed Thomas up and down. "You okay? You look pale."

"I'm fine," Thomas replied, getting out of the truck. He opened his Porsche and got in. The air felt wrong. It was heavy and solid. He rolled the window down and gasped. The drive home was bearable with the window down, but he felt inexplicably exhausted once he got home.

Ruben was already there. He was setting plates and silverware out.

"That smells really good, Cindy," Ruben said. Thomas operated on autopilot. He greeted Ruben. Sat down. Ate. Listened to their banal conversation.

"I appreciate you inviting me to dinner. You guys know I cook about as well as Gordon Ramsay fixes cars."

Cindy laughed. "That's really funny, Ruben."

*It wasn't that funny,* Thomas thought. He grimaced when she hugged Ruben goodbye after the meal was over. Their hug was a little too long for his taste.

"You're fucking him, aren't you?" he said the moment Ruben was out the door.

"What?"

He knew it was insane the moment the accusation left his mouth. He chuckled. "I'm kidding, babe."

"What's gotten into you?" she said.

An excuse was already forming in his mind, but he bit it back. Her words scared him because something had gotten into him, and she used to be the person he could talk about those things with. He bit his lip. Maybe she still was. "It's the car. I think there's something wrong with it."

"What?" she said. She couldn't understand how the car connected to what had been happening to him. He didn't understand it himself.

"Maybe, like… a carbon monoxide leak. Not enough to make me pass out or die, just enough to make me feel funny, you know? I never should have gotten a car that was sold as is anyway. I don't fix cars like Ruben."

Cindy nodded. "Have Ruben take a look at it, or just sell it." She didn't reach out to him or hold him. He took her hand. He sighed in relief when she didn't pull away. She didn't try to get closer to him either, though.

"Yeah, I should just sell it." He kissed her hand. "Everything is about to get a lot better."

She gave him a small smile and kissed his cheek. "I think so, too."


Thomas didn't offer to sell the car to Ruben, didn't want to involve him in whatever it was that was going on. He put an ad up on Craigslist and took the first bidder. Thomas would still be making a few grand in profit, but mostly he was just grateful the car would be off his hands.

As per the buyer's wishes, they met in a public place. Thomas introduced himself and shook hands with the potential buyer. He looked way too young to be buying a Porsche, probably mid-twenties, although everyone not on drugs looked younger in L.A. But Thomas didn't care to figure out the guy's financial situation. Cash was cash. He was just glad to be getting rid of the car.

"I bought this car in 'as is' condition, and that's how I'm selling it too."

"It runs, though, right?"

"Absolutely. You want to go for a test drive?"

"Sure."

Thomas hesitated. He didn't really want to get in, but he didn't trust the kid not to drive off with the car. He opened the door, got in the passenger seat, and buckled up.

The kid got in and Thomas handed him the key. The kid tried to start the car.

*Errrrrrrrraaaahhhhhhhhhhhhhhh ti ta ta ta*

*Errrrrrrrraaaahhhhhhhhhhhhhhh ti ta ta ta*

"Sorry, dude. I'm gonna have to walk away from this one," he said, getting out.

"Wait!" Thomas said, but the kid was already on his way back to the car he came in. Thomas tried to get out, but the door wouldn't open. He crawled over to the driver's seat and tried to open that door. Locked.

"Fuck," he said. He played with the buttons on the door, trying to roll down a window or unlock a door. He started beating on the window, trying to get someone's attention. The kid was already in his car, and no one else noticed him...

"Let me out. Let me out, come on."

"You don't want out of this car, Thomas. You want out of this life, and I don't blame you one bit."

Thomas spun around and looked into the backseat. A man was sitting back there in a three-piece suit, legs crossed, arms resting on the backs of the seats.

"Who the fuck are you?" Thomas yelled.

"I'm Rick Stanson, and once upon a time, I owned this car."

"Get out. Or let me out," he said. "Now."

The man chuckled. Thomas recognized it as the same laugh he'd heard during his strange drive.

"You were there," Thomas said. "When I almost had that accident."

"That was a good night. And between you and me, it wasn't an accident. At least not the first time it happened."

Thomas closed his eyes, seeing the woman's figure cowering under the headlights. He shook his head. "That really happened?

109

"Yes it did, and it was one of the best nights of my life."

Thomas's mouth dropped open.

"She deserved it," Rick said. "That homewrecking bitch ruined my life. I offered to pay for an abortion. She didn't want one. I offered to pay her rent and all her expenses, a well-kept mistress, and visit her and the child regularly. A second family. She didn't want that. I offered to let her go off on her own and raise the child and still financially support her. Do you know what she did? That whore told my wife everything, the sneaking around, the expensive gifts, the business trips that weren't business trips. She even showered her letters I wrote. She held nothing back, nothing was sacred to her. She said she did it because she wanted her child to know their siblings, that the secret had to come out, but I know she was just jealous and wanted to ruin my family so I'd be stuck with her. Well, I showed her, didn't I?"

"Jesus." Thomas closed his eyes. That woman's screams came back to him. He looked over his shoulder, expecting her to pop up and bang against the side window. He took a deep breath.

Rick went on casually. "I like to think about what she might have felt in her final moments. Fear. Defeat. Regret. I remember the feeling of her striking my front bumper. The sudden impact jolting me forward, the seatbelt yanking me back. I can still see exactly how far the car threw her.

"She didn't move after I hit her the first time, but she wasn't dead, so I drove over her again, slowly, crushing her under my wheels. I still think about her bones breaking under the weight of this car, the crevices in the rubber tires filling with blood. Her screams. Her hair stuck in the grill.

"I felt two bumps when I drove over her the second time. First I crushed her, then the car bounced and tilted a bit higher—that's when I knew I'd crushed it, that I'd turned her baby bump into an indentation."

"Stop." Thomas winced. He tried to open the door again, to no avail. As he pulled the handle harder, his grip weakened. His chest constricted. He gasped, jerking on the handle more.

"You know, they didn't replace the tires," Rick said. "Everything in the car is 'as is.' They just hosed them down. I bet if you sprayed some luminol down there, it would light up like a blue neon sign."

"Just let me out. This has nothing to do with me."

"Oh, but it does. You'll see."

The last thing Thomas saw before he passed out was Rick Stanson's beady eyes peering at him from the backseat.

Thomas awoke to children's voices blaring from the radio.

> *"The wheels on the bus go round and round,*
> *round and round, round and round*
> *The wheels on the bus go round and round*

*All through the town.*
*The people in the road go thump, thump, thump,*
*thump thump thump, thump thump thump,*
*The people in the road go thump thump thump,*
*As they fall down."*

He hummed along, dimly aware those were not the correct lyrics.

*"The bones in the bodies go crunch crunch crunch*
*crunch crunch crunch, crunch crunch crunch*
*The bones in the bodies go crunch crunch crunch—"*

His head shook. He rubbed his face, trying to wake himself.

"That's my children singing, you know." Rick grinned at him in the rearview mirror, the smile of a proud father. "I only get to hear their voices on the radio now. Do you know what that's like? An eternity away from my own children. Hell isn't hot enough for her. I hope that's where she is now. If I deserve it, so does she."

Thomas shook his head again, still dazed. Darkness was all around him. Streetlights shined from above. He must have slept for hours. It felt like the car was doing donuts even though they were parked. The singing continued.

*"The baby under the tire goes squish squish squish—"*

"Stop it!" Thomas yelled.

"I miss my children," Rick went on, ignoring his outburst. The singing died down. "My real children. Not the bastard that whore carried inside of her. Probably wasn't even mine."

Thomas choked, the air hot and heavy. He tried opening the door again. When that failed, he beat on the window.

"Let me out!"

"You have a one-track mind, don't you? You haven't even figured out why it's so hard to breathe in here."

Thomas met Rick's eyes in the rearview mirror. He turned his head and found the backseat empty. Rick continued smirking at him in the mirror.

"Can you believe that whore told my children what we did? My wife might have planned to tell them in a gentle way, but Susanne got to them first. God knows what she told them. My children hated me. I had nothing to live for after she ruined my life, so I ended it in this car. Gassed myself. But it doesn't have to be like that for you. Not all bastard children have to ruin lives."

"Cindy and the baby aren't ruining my life." He concentrated on breathing. His lungs refused to cooperate.

"Aren't they? What are you going to miss out on because of them?"

As he thought about his future, he didn't see the missed opportunities anymore. He didn't care about not having time for auditions or money for clubs. He just wanted to be there with Cindy and their baby. He wanted to let her squeeze his hand when the baby came. He wanted to hold his own flesh and blood. He wanted to know if he was having a son or a daughter.

As if reading his thoughts, Cindy's name appeared on the radio dashboard as the car called her.

"No," he whispered. "No. Please, no."

"Hello?" She sounded like she just woke up. "Thomas, where are you? I thought—"

"Cindy, call the cops! Call 9-1-1. I'm being held hostage." Thomas banged the buttons on the steering wheel, trying to end the conversation.

"Hello?" she said again. "Thomas? I can't hear you."

"Honey, hang up and call 9-1-1."

"Hello?"

"Oh baby, thank God I got ahold of you," Rick said in a voice that sounded just like Thomas. It came from the speakers. "Meet me outside of town. I'll text you the location. There's no time to explain. I need your help."

"Okay." Her voice trembled.

"No!" Thomas's protest went unacknowledged.

"And Cindy," Rick said in his perfect Thomas voice. "I love you."

"I love you too. See you soon."

The call ended. Rick, suddenly appearing in the back, crawled over the divider into the passenger seat. The car started up and rolled forward.

"You're not the only one that can act." Rick smirked. Thomas grabbed him by his suit jacket and threw him against the dashboard.

"What the hell did you do?"

"I'm saving you. You'll thank me someday."

"What have you done? What are you planning?" The car swerved as it made an abrupt right turn. Thomas fell over, still holding onto Rick's jacket.

"It's almost time," Rick said. "It's July tenth. The day you become free."

"What's so special about July tenth?"

"It was the day I became free. In my case, death was freedom. But for you, death will only be the beginning."

"This isn't happening. This isn't real."

"Oh, it's real. As real as that baby trap, as real as crushed dreams and potential. My life was over the moment Susanne went to my wife, but yours doesn't have to be. You have your whole life ahead of you. That bitch wants to take it all away. She's jealous because you have talent, real potential to do something with your life, and she'll never be anything special. She got pregnant on purpose to trap you. Most 'unplanned' pregnancies are entrapment. History is full of poor saps stuck with manipulative women because they were too good to walk away from them. You're not going to be one of them."

"If you kill her, I go to jail and my life is over."

"Nonsense. That's why we're meeting her far away. It will be quite easy to clean up a body hit in the middle of nowhere. This car cleans up after itself, in case you haven't noticed."

"Please don't do this," Thomas said. His grip weakened.

"It's already done," Rick said, a maniacal grin on his face. He went on and on about his mistress, but all Thomas could think about was Cindy, how she was almost due and she was driving out to meet him in the middle of the night, no questions asked because she was concerned about *him,* scared for *him,* because he hadn't been himself since he got the car, or even before then.

He wanted to cry. He'd failed her. He'd been failing her for a long time.

"If you don't want to watch, just go to sleep. When you wake up, this will all be over."

"No." Lightheadedness set in, threatening to knock him unconscious again. He straightened up. "You can't have her." As the words left him, he realized he misspoke. "*Them.* You can't have them."

He grabbed the wheel and yanked it to the right, steering them head first into a tree.


Cindy screamed at the top of her lungs for the second time that day. The first had been when she found her boyfriend's car smashed into a palm tree. Their last conversation played in her mind, how final it seemed, and between the contractions, she wondered if he'd driven into it on purpose to escape them.

He'd seemed so happy the past few weeks. She knew that a lot of people who committed suicide were, because they knew the end of their problems was in sight. But she hadn't thought he'd been that conflicted about parenthood. They'd made plans for the future. He wanted his child. Didn't he?

Pain shot through her abdomen, and all thoughts of the collision ended. All she could think about was the fact that she was alone. No one had expected the baby to come for another two weeks, and Thomas was supposed to be there, her parents were supposed to be there, but now she was by herself in a strange hospital bringing a fatherless child into the world.

She screamed again, and after one more aching push, her baby boy screamed with her.


Ruben came the next day, after her parents and her friends left to get some rest. Bouquets and stuffed animals covered every surface of the room. All the flowers and teddy bears made the hollow look in her eyes even more heartbreaking.

"I'm sorry, Cindy."

"Me too."

"That fucking car," Ruben said, shaking his head.

"Do you think the car malfunctioned?" She clutched the bedsheet.

He hesitated.

"I think it was a bad car," he said, his hairy plump hand resting on the bed's handrail. "He loved you. He was selling that car for you, because he was coming to his senses. It was an accident."

She nodded. After Ruben saw the baby and offered congratulations as well as more condolences for Thomas, the nurse took the baby to the nursery so Cindy could rest. When she woke up, she went to check on him. Another man was looking into the nursery, focusing on her son.

"It looks just like him," the man said.

"Who are you?"

"A man without children." He smiled sadly, looking out the window. "And now a man without a home. Without purpose."

His gaze returned to her baby. He smirked. "He'll be a handful. You keep him close, won't you? Children must be kept close. They can be taken from us at any moment."

"I want you to leave," she said. "Right now. I'm calling security."

He nodded toward her and turned to go. He walked next to the window into the blinding sunlight and vanished. She blinked, certain that her eyes were playing tricks, but did not see him walk down the hall or hear his shoes on the tile floor. He was just there, and then he wasn't.

Just like Thomas.


Insurance declared the car a total loss. Ruben bought what remained of it once it became available for salvaging and took it to his junkyard. The walls of the baling press closed in on the broken windows, the unhinged doors and crushed hood. What remained of the Porsche curled in on itself like a swatted spider's legs folding against its own body. When the machine finished compressing, it ejected the metal through the hole in the side. It was hard to believe so much devastation could come from something that could be crushed into the size of a small refrigerator. As Ruben stared at the heap of metal, he felt like he'd avenged his friend's murder, killed a killer rather than simply crushed a couple tons of metal into a compact form.

He waved away one of the approaching forklifts. The employee furrowed his eyebrows and shrugged.

"I'll take care of it myself." Ruben stared at the metal with a sense of wariness. He had a spot picked out for it, a grave he'd dug for the sole purpose of putting it to rest.

"This one's not for sale."

# THE BLACK BAND

## KOURINTHIA BURTON

I don't remember waking but suddenly I'm there, standing in the darkness of the familiar unfamiliar. The house that looks the same, but with a pulse beneath that puts me on edge. When did I fall asleep? I cannot say. The darkness is so thick here in this familiar unfamiliar place that I can feel it filling my lungs, making my limbs heavy. The silence that is an extension of the darkness hums in my ears, fooling me into believing for a moment that I am alone in this familiar unfamiliar place. But deep in my soul, in the part of me that wants only to survive, I know the truth.

I am not alone.

Distantly, the sounds of muffled movement reach my ears but my mind is dulled by the heaviness of the darkness. Finally, I realize what my ears have been screaming at me: there is someone, or something, behind the curtain-shaped darkness to my left. How I can discern shapes when no light exists I do not know, but I am able to see the living room I stand in. The front door to my right, and the window that holds unknown danger to my left. I approach it even though I do not want to; curiosity, or perhaps recklessness, leads me towards it.

I reach out mindlessly, aware of my own mortality. The darkness at the window shifts, and I pull my hand tightly to my side. I back away as the movement increases until it is nearly frantic, a stark contrast to the stillness of the familiar unfamiliar living room. I am now close enough to the door to feel the pull of escape. I wrench it open without looking back, and run for the street. I hear the sound of dark feet rushing after me.

. . .

115

Outside is dark, too, but it feels lighter somehow. I can see the familiar unfamiliar streets spanning across my vision. The feel of the Bakersfield neighborhood unknown, unrecognizable in this unreality. My legs are pumping but my body doesn't feel taxed. My lungs never burn. I feel invincible in my panic. I take a sharp right at the end of the driveway and race down the road. I hear feet rushing after me and turn to see others running the same direction. Behind them, my eyes discern a mob of shadows running after us.

The group joins me as I rush forward. Together, we turn left at the end of the street. We continue to run and run and run. Soon we burst out onto a large road. The only building in sight is a market store, its windows dark yet bright in a way I do not understand. I look around as I rush run, taking in the familiar unfamiliar surroundings. Known yet unknown, the world I remember is no longer there, just a blur in my memory.

We arrive at the market and rush through the door, securing it behind us. The place is in disarray and we're afraid to speak in case the pursuing shadows hear us.

The seven of us, no two alike in appearance, disperse to find something, though we do not know what. I walk down an aisle littered with household cleaning supplies, then turn to walk up an aisle filled with snacks, crushing chips underfoot. I turn again into the last aisle. The glass fridge doors exude coldness. There are no lights; light does not live here. Just the cold of emptiness. Of falseness. Of familiar unfamiliar.

I stop in my tracks, my chest constricted in fear. A shadow is standing in the corner facing away from me. I cannot tell if it has heard me yet, but I know we must act quickly before it hears us. Before it gets us. Before the unknown.

I tiptoe back to the front of the store where the others congregate. Through silent gestures, I communicate what I've discovered. We follow each other through instinct, unclear who is in the lead. Not that it matters in the familiar unfamiliar. Nothing matters except distance. Except escape.

Beneath the mat where the cashier would stand is a door that leads into a new kind of darkness. This one smells of dirt and moisture and coolness. Something tells me that coolness was desirable in the place I lived, in a reality somewhere else. We climb down one at a time. Once my head is finally submerged, I realize that, for the first time since I awoke in the familiar unfamiliar, I cannot see.

This darkness is total; no shapes greet my eyes, no sounds muffle my ears, and the hairs on my arms stand on end. From cold or from fear? I cannot tell. Silently we move as one, though I do not know how I know that, through the earthen tunnel. Like worms or moles or some other hidden creature that fears the sun and the heat. I exist, that is all I know. Or all think I know.

The sun is a distant memory. The golden place, the golden state in which I lived, feels more like a dream than this familiar unfamiliar. I cannot remember falling asleep or waking, but tendrils of a valley filled with cities and towns pulls at my mind. Is this familiar unfamiliar place my home? Is this cavern where I crawl on my belly part of that golden place I lived? The golden place that is familiar but unreal here, in this place where only darkness exists?

We have gone only a short distance when we hear the crash from above and behind us; the shadows have found the door. Our secret tunnel is no longer secret. We run. We run and we run, finally feeling the tax on our bodies just like the hairs on our arms; finally, a human reaction after so much inhumanity. The tunnel stretches on in an unnaturally straight line, a familiar unfamiliar cavern in the distant inky abyss. We run. We run and we run, and we never stop, we never stumble, we never trip into each other.

The rushing sound behind us is eternal. I can feel it pulsing under my skin, like a second heartbeat. We are pushed forward, almost as if the shadows chasing us are a gust of wind, and we nothing more than dandelion seeds. We run and we run in this familiar unfamiliar until I can feel the ground changing.

The incline is gradual at first, but then I register the ache in my legs and the tilt of my body. Uphill we go in the darkness. Uphill in the tunnel. Uphill but always just barely away from what follows.

Forever passes before the light appears.

I squint at it, disbelieving the light. The slender line of white against black is no more real than my own skin. It does not grow larger as we run on, uphill in the darkness with the shadows behind.

Suddenly, the light is all around us. We are in a vast field, green and bright in every direction. The hole in the ground from which we emerged like ants from a hill is unseen through the grass that surrounds us.

Still we run on, distancing ourselves from the shadows that will follow. That do follow. Uphill. In the dark. Always behind. I run and run until I stop. I must stop, though I cannot say why. I stop and I turn to face my pursuers.

Instead I see dozens, hundreds of people staggering out after me. People of all types, no two alike except a black band circling their right upper arm. Are these the shadows? These familiar unfamiliar people who follow? Are they what chased me when I awoke? My thoughts are loud yet silent, racing yet sluggish as I try to understand what is beyond understanding.

Then we hear it. Us and the Others. Those that followed after us. The sound of blades cutting through the air. I look up and see a metal ship sailing towards us. And then another and another. *These* are not familiar unfamiliar. These are something else. Something different; I know, somehow, that these are men with power. They have come to handle the situation, whatever that is and however it came to be. Us and the Others in this familiar unfamiliar green place.

I do not know how we did not see them coming before they descend upon us. I do not know and I do not know how to make myself curious. The men in the uniforms come and build. They build tents, and cordons, and barriers. They build to separate.

117

They build and build and build until everywhere is something new. No more green. Then they separate.

The ones who came with me—those without the mark—are examined, for what I cannot fathom, and moved to a different place. A place I know is safe. A place that is peaceful. Then the Others are checked—for evil perhaps, or for a soul. Again, I cannot say. They are moved aside to a place I fear. A place that is familiar but different. A place where bad things happen. I know this. In the part of me that wants only to survive, I know the truth. There is only pain.

My turn comes and they check me for the thing I fear to understand. They check me and check me again, and finally I am moved. Hands tighten on each of my arms. The place where bad things happens lies ahead, where there is only pain. I fight them but they are too strong, with strength that is familiar unfamiliar.

When I thrash, I see what I had not before: a black band circling my arm. After that, I do not fight.

I cannot.

# ONE LAST E-TICKET RIDE

## DOMINICK CANCILLA

Peter smiled when he heard he'd been laid off. His supervisor, Christina, had let him know in the nicest possible way—backstage, in private—and twenty years working full time in the happiest place on earth had leached away all but the cheeriest elements of his personality.

"Gosh, Peter," she'd said, "I really wish there was something else we could do." She sounded completely sincere, and the framed portrait of the world's most famous mouse hanging on the office wall behind her reinforced the air of gentle authority.

"That's okay!" Peter said, the same way a young Annette Funicello might have said, "Golly gee!"

Christina pushed the castle-logoed pay envelope across the desk toward him. "You've been with us a long time, and you've been a model cast member, so I won't hear of you taking any of this personally."

"Heck no!" His response made Christina grin broadly and, for a split second, Peter had the sensation of looking into a mirror.

"I'm glad to hear that. There's two weeks' severance and a letter of recommendation in there," she gestured toward the envelope with a flawlessly manicured finger.

"That's great! Thanks!" He picked up the envelope and stood, smoothing his vest and shirt in reflex.

"Why don't you go straight to wardrobe and then take the rest of the day off," Christina said, sounding like an old friend as she stood to dismiss him.

"I really appreciate that, Christina! You've been great!"

She nodded modestly and Peter walked out of the office with a spring in his step.

On the way to his locker to retrieve his "real world" clothes, Peter gave cheery Howdys to everyone he met. To a one they responded in kind. The cast commissary, waste stations, rest areas, control rooms—everything Peter passed was as familiar to him as the kitchenless efficiency apartment that swallowed a good percentage of his wages every month.

Everything seemed fresh and light, as it always did, until he'd just about reached the last corner before wardrobe. There he was suddenly overcome by the realization that for the rest of his life, as long as that might be, he would never be bathed in the happy aura of these hallowed halls again. For the first time since he signed the phone-book-thick employment agreement and received his first name badge, there was a flicker of a frown at the corners of Peter's mouth.

It felt horribly, gut-wrenchingly wrong—completely alien to the beaming, contented worker he'd become. Worse than the summer month he'd spent doing double shifts in the Sully outfit. Worse than working vomit detail on Star Tours. Worse than a month of grad nights. Worse than the nightmares of being chased down Main Street by a pantless Audio-Animatronic Abe Lincoln. For an instant, Peter felt discontented.

He didn't like it. Not one bit.

Not knowing what else to do, Peter ducked into a restroom, locked himself in a stall, and fought against rising nausea.

He shook his head, breathed deeply. "What a silly I'm being!" he said with a little laugh that rang hollow in the acoustically perfect room.

Standing, leaning against Snow-White-clean tile for support, Peter waited for everything to spring back to normal. He thought about the bright faces of young guests, filled with childlike innocence and wonder. He hummed "Whistle While You Work," tapping a foot in time. He visualized each of the princesses in canonical order. None of the tricks they'd taught him in Mickey's University worked. It was disturbing to say the least.

In the hollow where Peter's sense of self had atrophied amongst echoing aphorisms, slogans, and mottoes, a little voice spoke forbidden words.

At first, it merely reminded him of those things that he'd been instructed to forget lest they uncolor his perceptions: deaths on the Matterhorn, certain lawsuits, an old cartoon with Donald Duck in a Nazi uniform, *Song of the South,* Superstar Limo, the early days of California Adventure, Michael Eisner. While Peter's conscious mind was still fighting "verboten thoughtens," the voice breached the strongest taboo and began asking questions. He was taken completely by surprise.

If there had to be a reduction in staff, the voice asked, why had Peter been singled out for cancellation when there were others more deserving? Security cameras had twice recorded Steve after hours in "it's a small world" peeing into the fiberglass-lined river and he still had a job. Louise, upset about being transferred to Galactic Grill, had sneezed on every burger she made for an hour, but she hadn't gotten a pink paycheck. Larry and Shawnee were caught in a storeroom beneath the Haunted Mansion, him lying on the floor half out of his Prince Charming outfit, her with her Pocahontas skirt hiked up around her waist, riding the Matterhorn. They'd not only missed their shifts but mixed genres in a way Uncle Walt would never have approved, and they weren't being transferred from pure enjoyment to unemployment. How could such inequity exist in such a happy place?

120

Peter had no answer, but the little voice could not be ignored. The innocent glimmer in his eyes flickered, his rosy cheeks paled. The goofy grin that hadn't even wavered when he'd passed a kidney stone the previous year collapsed completely. It hurt in a way Peter had never hurt before.

Five-hundred acres, fifty-thousand people, and Peter was the only one slipping into a wallow of despair. He had never felt so alone in all his life.

Of course, said the little voice, you don't *have* to be alone. It was a cast member mantra that good show was paramount, but if good show created happiness and magic, then bad show…

The thought restored Peter's grin to Jafar-like force. There were so many things he could do, so many rules he could break.

Peter could point at things with just one finger. He could refuse to wave at the train. He could see litter and just leave it there on the ground. He could chew gum. But would guests even notice such little things? And if he was going to go off the rails, why not go completely off the track?

Once begun, ideas—better, stronger, ideas—for spreading the misery flooded through him. He could put real bullets in a Jungle Cruise skipper's gun. Show porno films in the Main Street Cinema. Chop down Tarzan's Treehouse. Start a riot in the Golden Horseshoe. Sink the *Mark Twain*. Streak through Club 33. Climb the Matterhorn and shave Harold. Paintball a *Star Wars* stormtrooper. Throw roadkill around Radiator Springs. Put pickle juice in the Dole Whips. Derail Casey Junior. Set Mike Fink's cabin on fire. Herd all the cats into Monsters, Inc. Annex Tom Sawyer Island. The possibilities would never end so long as there was imagination left within him.

Then an idea, grander than all the rest, took hold of Peter's mind. It wasn't the largest, or the flashiest, or the most complicated, but it was bound to be the most satisfying—and would leave the deepest scars. Spurred by inspiration, he flew from the bathroom like Tinkerbell on a mission.

Peter beelined to wardrobe and its racks of character outfits. With the afternoon parade only a short time away, nobody paid him notice as he scanned the flattened forms of anthropomorphized dogs and dust-iced Country Bears looking for the perfect identity. When his eyes settled upon the hollow head and carpeted skin of Winnie the Pooh's friend Eeyore, he felt as if every firework in the park had been sent soaring into the night sky just for him. Not so high-profile it would be missed, not so obscure it wouldn't be recognized, Eeyore was perfect.

He hefted the bundle from its resting place and hurried to the changing area.

It was a stroke of luck that Lena was getting ready for the parade when Peter reached the changing area. She was nineteen, blonde, cocoa-skinned, and voluptuous, and never wore anything under her costume in summer. Everyone else was too busy either averting their eyes from her transformation into a happy-on-the-outside-harlot-on-the-inside Roger Rabbit or trying to look like they weren't ogling every playboy's favorite bunny to pay any attention to Peter.

He had on the donkey carapace and was scooting toward the on-stage area before you could say "Piglet."

There was enough room in the enormous head that some cast members were known to keep snacks and reading material in there. The suit was baggy enough that he could wear a linebacker's padding without showing an extra bulge. Had he wanted to, Peter could have loaded up the suit with munitions and marched to any point in the park without being looked at askance before becoming Commando Eeyore and turning Fantasyland into a public relations nightmare. But he had nothing so heavy handed and suicidal in mind. Behind the donkey's frozen, artificial, over-dramatically sorrowful countenance, Peter's grin was back in full force.

There was no need for Peter to go on stage—that would be an open invitation to the usual clamor of tourist photographers, autograph-hound kiddies, and crotch-kicking teenagers that populated fur-character cast-member nightmares. Instead, he waited just offstage of Critter Country, the translucent screen of Eeyore's eye pressed to the seam between double entrance gates.

He only had to wait five minutes before he saw what he was looking for. Had it not been for his deep-seated inhibition against speaking when in costume, he would have squealed with glee.

The little boy couldn't have been more than five, if that. He was toddling about in a pair of 101 Dalmatians overalls, eyes wide with wonder at the colors and sounds all about him. In his chubby hands was a large soda container, one of the new premium ones shaped like Mickey, and he was sucking future diabetes through a straw stuck into the mouse's skull as he walked. His parents were nowhere in sight.

The little boy was a summary of everything that that the park supposedly stood for —innocence, wonder, imagination—and Peter couldn't think of a better person to drag with him down the road of despair. By the time he was done, the child's only associations with the kingdom would be of horror and violation. Peter though that was pretty neat.

When the moment was right, Peter pulled one of the gates open with a mittened hand. His timing was as perfect as Jessica Rabbit's figure. The boy was looking right at the door, but nobody else seemed to be. Peter knew he had been seen when the child's face lit up, his little mouth opening in surprise to let carbonated sugar run over his chin.

Getting down on one knee—no mean trick with the weight of a second skull—Peter held the gate open with one hand and gestured to the child with the other. The little boy didn't hesitate, but rushed into the arms of his dear friend Eeyore.

Peter hugged the child, feeling for a moment a twinge of guilt for what he was about to do. His resolve faltered like a dancing alligator trying to hold a tutued hippo aloft, then roared forth with Chernabog's strength when the little voice inside him recounted the depth of his betrayal.

He took the boy's hand, stood, and swung the gate shut.

From there, Peter had intended to take the boy to a little place he knew, a corner beneath the train tracks where they could remain alone for as long as was necessary, and where the child's screams would be swallowed by the yells of Splash Mountain. All of that had to be set aside when, through the shrinking slit of the closing gate, Peter saw a pair of security officers pointing his way and speaking into their lapels.

Park security was as omnipresent as it was efficient. No cast member knew just how many officers were on duty at any given time, how many of them were in the guise of tourists or were keeping tabs on events through the pen-sized cameras in facades, vehicles, faux parcels, and bulky hairdos throughout the park. If one of them had seen Peter entice the child offstage, then he had only minutes to do what he'd planned.

Peter gave up the idea of walking hand and hand with the child as if the youngster was lost. Instead he scooped the boy up and ran as fast as his size-sixteen donkey feet would carry him toward the nearest backstage restroom. The boy laughed and giggled with glee, dropping his soda to clutch his rug-skinned friend in a crucifixion-wide hug.

There was a bit of a bang as Peter burst into the bathroom, slamming the door against the wall, but it upset the boy not at all. He felt no fear, safe in Eeyore's arms, just as Peter had once felt nestled in the embrace of the world's most beloved corporation. They barreled across the room into a wheelchair-accessible stall, stopping only when Peter belatedly put on the brakes and slid face first into the wall. "Whoops!" he mouthed, still not daring to speak.

As gently as haste would allow, Peter lowered the boy to the floor and pried the child's hands from his fur. That done, he closed and latched the stall door. There was no telling how long they had before security tracked him down, and Peter only hoped that he would have a chance to deliver the poison apple from the bitter, bubbling cauldron within him.

When Peter turned back from securing the stall, he saw that the boy was standing where he had been set, waiting more patiently than he would have for one of his own parents. He beamed up at Peter, head tilted back so far that the highest points on his body were a pair of rosy cheeks.

Peter gave a little wave; the child tried to respond in kind, holding up a hand spreadfinger-fist-spreadfinger-fist. For the second time, the cricket of Peter's conscience chirped at him—the kid was incredibly cute.

From outside the bathroom a gruff voice called, "I think he went this way." The beat of dress shoes against pavement pounded quickly closer. It was now or never; Peter thrust his hesitation aside. Forcing his voice through a lifetime of conditioning, Peter spoke.

"Hi chum!" he said, sounding as Eeyorey as he could manage. "Wanna see something neat?"

The boy nodded deeply, his eyes somehow growing even brighter.

"Look't this!" Peter said, and he raised his hands.

At some point the bathroom door crashed open and security agents rushed in, but Peter didn't notice. He was captivated by the expression on the child's face. At first it was Christmas-morning joy, childlike anticipation of gifts unimagined. There was a shift toward pure curiosity as Peter's hands reached higher, with a final plunge into slack-jawed shock and disbelief at the sight of sad, sullen Eeyore, beloved by children world round, lifting off his own head.

The sound of the stall's door being torn from its hinges by 250 pounds of no-nonsense hired muscle was lost in the piercing shriek of a horrified pre-kindergartner.

"See, kid! I'm just some guy!" Peter said, grinning, happy as a Mouseketeer on Guest Star Day.

"*No!*" the security agent yelled, throwing his body between the headless donkey and the gaping innocent.

"My God, what have you done!" a second agent cried, grabbing Peter's arm and dragging him out of the room.

Peter's contented smile grew even more broad in the afterglow of his terrorist act. He kept smiling as they hauled him through the tunnels beneath the park, even giggled as they approached Mickey's University in the castle's bowels where a cast-member reeducation cell awaited him. It had turned out to be a pretty darned neat day after all.

# MELICIOUS MALADIES

## N. M. BROWN

*"Feeling down? Have a sinister sweet tooth? I have just the solution, Melicious Maladies! One of California's hidden gems! Over on the corner of Brigantine and Salado; open every Monday through Friday, eleven to four."*

A woman's smile froze onscreen.

Melange Joilee appeared perfect to the average eye. Men loved the sultry bit of bayou that she brought to the California coast. She was a gorgeous woman, about twenty-eight if I had to guess. In the commercial, she stood behind a vast assortment of cupcakes. Her olive skin had a glow about it, complimented by large, dark doe eyes and a wide smile. Makeup wasn't necessary for this one, and she knew it.

The cupcakes looked damned amazing! My mouth watered every time the commercial came on, and I hated sweets. Arrays of pastel frosted jewels, each topped lovingly with fluffs of buttercream. Grandma's Coconut was advertised as the cupcake of the month, adorned with sugar pearls.

There's a sinister type of nursery rhyme some of the local kids came up with. *"If you go to Melange's Tuesdays at half past five, after you leave... someone you hate might stop being alive."* Juvenile, but catchy. Call me curious, morbid. Hell, you can even call me crazy if you want, but I *had* to know what went on there.

With a wad of cash in my pocket, I waited outside the back door at exactly 5:30 that evening. The legends didn't extend to protocol. Did I knock a certain amount of times? Was there a passcode? Would there even be anyone here at all? My thought process was interrupted by a burly man coming out of the back door to take out the trash.

"Oh! Uh... excuse me, this is going to sound silly but, may I come inside?" I asked the man tentatively.

"Closed." He grunted, without meeting my eyes.

Sometimes persistence is key in these types of situations, so I tried a different approach. "Yeah. I know, I just uh… I wanted to order from the menu in the back."

He didn't look up or stop what he was doing, almost as if he hadn't heard my question at all. His hulking frame lumbered past me on the way back from the dumpster and walked back inside, leaving the back door slightly ajar.

In my mind, there could be two reasons for this. Option one: he'd gone inside to fetch more garbage, and left it open for convenience. Option two; he left it open as an unspoken invitation for me to come inside.

So, I went inside and eagerly studied the menu.

- Lavender: For Eternal Rest — $499.99
- Pina Colada: For an Insatiable Thirst for Alcohol — $274.99
- Mocha Lotta: Speed Up Internal Life Clock — $333.33
- Pistachio Matcha: Financial Ruin and Insanity — $699.99
- Vanilla Crème: You Were Never Born; Invisible to Your Loved Ones — $199.99
- Banana Quinoa: Weight Altering (+/- whipped cream) — $109.99
- Death By Chocolate: Self Explanatory — $999.99 + mortal sin

Mortal sin? Never mind that, the prices were exorbitant! Who in their right mind would *ever* pay more than five… okay, *ten* dollars at *most* for a single cupcake?

I set the menu down, spun on my heels to exit the way I entered.

But an empty wall stood where the entrance had been mere moments ago.

*What the Devil? How?* I frantically rubbed at my eyes, but nothing changed. My head spun at an endless circle of blank walls. My heart began to race. I slowed my breathing to steady my mind.

A woman emerged from a hidden corner of the room. The same wide smile I'd seen on television rested on her gorgeous face.

"Bonsoir! What were you lookin' to buy?"

"Uh… I wasn't really wanting to buy anything. honestly. I just heard about this place and wanted to see it for myself. Not to be rude, but even if I did intend to purchase, these prices are completely unreasonable. It's a wonder anyone buys anything from that list at all."

She shook her head at this, her smile never faltering. "Ahh, don't you worry about them, cher. Dese are a bargain, really. Tell me, mon ami, can a price ever be put on permanently changing someone's life? In some cases, ending it completely? Mouri!" She snapped her delicate fingers. "Poof, like dat; gone!"

My mouth fell open. An incredulous look burned in my eyes despite myself. "Bullshit! That's not possible. What, do you put poison in them? Sinisterly sweet death traps? This is nuts. Let me out. How can you do this? I don't understand. Don't you feel bad for those people? I'm sure some of them are innocent."

Melange waved her hands through the air dismissively. "People have der reasons, and evil will find its way, with or without my help. I offah something da real World don't: protection… safety. No one will believe in killa cupcakes." She let out a chuckle that sounded like tinkling bells. "Analysis of my baked goods reveal nothing other than standard ingredients available in any other bakery around heah. Don'tchu have any enemies, mon cher? Any scars that haunt your soul inflicted by those who suffer no consequences?"

Unbidden, my ex-fiancé came straight to mind. She broke my heart, and cleaned out my bank account along with half of our business.

The name escaped into the air. "Abigail. What about the banana one? How does that work with the whipped cream and the effects?"

"The person who eats our banana quinoa will have drastic changes to their weight. If you want a bigga belly, you gotta get da whip. If you want dem to waste away to bones, get it without da whip. No difference to the price eitha way."

This was ridiculous. Even if people did deserve such fates, it wasn't up to us to give it to them. If everyone was a karma god, the world would be enveloped in madness.

Even so, I took the money out of my pocket and handed it to her. She handed me the boxed cupcake in exchange: banana quinoa with extra whipped cream. *This better not be some kind of sick trick*, I thought. In my mind though, I couldn't think of a more deserving person for this than Abby.

My truck pulled into the parking lot of our old apartment, to which I still had a key. Her Mazda wasn't there, so I took the opportunity to let myself inside. I slipped the box into her fridge with a note on top with her name on it, and went so far as to sign it with her new boyfriend's name.

My heart wants to say that I never went back to Melicious Maladies again, but it isn't true.

Over the next year, I bought almost every cupcake on her list. Though I at first convinced myself that it all had to be a farce, I could no longer argue with the results when, a month later, I saw Abby.

Daily errands took me on a route close to our old complex. As I passed by, I saw the parking area was swarmed with ambulances and EMTs. Abby and I lived in that apartment together for quite a few years, and I knew most everyone that lived there. So, I pulled into the lot and got out to see what was going on and make sure no one I knew was hurt or worse.

The crowd parted like the Red Sea to make way for the stretcher. That's what I saw her. Her skin was a canvas of rippled dents and bulges. Stretch marks covered her body like twisted scars. Some were stretched so tight that they ripped open, revealing oozing sores rimmed with infection. I could almost smell almonds in the breeze. You know how infection smells? The pus-filled smell of a bandage as you take it off to throw it away, the wound on the cat's leg that won't heal, that kind of stuff.

Her face was monstrously wide, folds swallowing an oxygen line hooked to a tank. I ran as fast as I could to get to her, but the ambulance was faster. Right before the doors closed, I saw them work the defibrillator, jiggling flesh with jolts to the chest.

That vision haunted me for weeks. It was with me in my waking hours and tormented me to sleep at night. Nightmares of when we were together and would make love. Her face growing wider until the skin started to rip. Her body growing larger; crushing my bones underneath her. Most of the time I woke up before she exploded, but not always.

So, after all of that turmoil, I swore to myself that *never*, under any circumstance, would I go back to Mel's. Abby haunted me. Her face as she was wheeled into the ambulance. The sight of the body that once fit so perfectly under my own, now expanded to the point of ruin.

Things changed when I got the call two months later that my two-year-old nephew, Landon, was dead. My brother-in-law, Allen, was drunk at the wheel. They crashed on the way to my sister's house. Allen walked away without a scratch to drink another day, while Landon's body lay twisted, broken beyond repair. If the bastard would have put him in his car seat, he might have had a chance.

Of course, the police investigated. but Allen faced no charges. My sister was destroyed beyond recognition, along with the rest of our family. Her spirit was lost to her five-year-old daughter, now her only living child.

After a night of binge drinking, wrong on many levels, an idea came to me. If Allen wanted to drink, I'd help him drink. My only fear was that the limited availability menu at Melicious Maladies might not be there anymore. But there was only one way to know.

Melange was still there, happy to take my money and as Creole as ever. Our second encounter didn't take as long as the first. The door didn't disappear, either. The Pina Colada cupcake was boxed and stamped with her signature double M monogram, then released into the world, determined to find its target. I wouldn't let it down.

The corner market had a special on roses for an upcoming holiday. I bought three white ones to deliver alongside the cupcake. A mourning gift for a friend to brighten their son-less life. Poetic and appropriate, in my opinion.

Allen's wiry frame sprang up from his porch chair when my truck pulled into his yard. A look of surprised anger sat on his worn face. My hands were raised in a gesture of peace, one of which was holding the box. The other held the roses. We sat down and I asked him to have a drink with me and open the box.

His face drooped and his bloodshot eyes were further exacerbated by fresh tears. Allen went on to tell me how Landon loved cupcakes and how he wished he could share it with him. I almost felt bad for a second, until I saw the ease with which he tossed back his glass of Dewer's. The message was sent, the cupcake was eaten; it was time for me to leave. I paused on my way out the door to glance at him; knowing this would be the last time I truly saw him.

He didn't show up to work a few days. The police came after another employee placed a citizen's check call. Sure enough, Allen was dead, face down in his own sick on the floor. And no one thought twice about it.

Remember earlier, when I told you about Abby and how she took off with my business as well as my heart? As it turns out, the new boyfriend I mentioned was actually her husband. Unbeknownst to me, they'd gotten married a little less than a month before I delivered her cupcake. He had his hooks in my business as well now as a result of her death.

The shareholders voted me out under his command. No one's loyal when they know a pay raise is on the line. Employees I've had for years were among the first to marinate in his oily personality. My first boss used to say that all is fair in love, war... and *business*. What a crock.

One thing I can say is that I was offered an extremely generous severance package. One that I fully intended to put to good use. Seven hundred dollars out of ten thousand is nothing to be able to watch someone you hate fail. It killed me to sink the company that I started, but it wasn't mine anymore, was it?

So, it was time for another trip to the cupcake shop. Three visits in just over a year's time now. I comically wished that she had a punch card; buy three, get one free.

I didn't stick around to see this one through. It was too risky. All efforts had to be made to put as much distance between myself and the company as possible. Word does travel, though, and fast too. Before long, former employees were ringing my phone off of the hook about how the new boss was driving the company into the ground. I faked agreement and feigned helplessness through the wicked smile on my lips.

The lavender one was easy. My gran was suffering from dementia, along with stage three lung cancer. The thought of killing her didn't sit well with me. I wasn't a monster; I loved Gran. But the sight of her suffering so much was torture. I couldn't imagine what she went through every minute of every day. Struggling not to drown with every breath, her only form of sustenance coming from tubed liquids.

Not on that day, though. Tears made their way down the creases in her face as I sat with her. Her mind just active enough to be scared and aware of the pain she was in. I combed her hair and showed her old pictures. I told her life's story to her as if it were a fairy tale, talking until well after her tears stopped.

I placed my grandfather's wedding ring in her hand just as I left the room, tears streaming down my own face to match her own. The nurses called me the next morning to let me know that she was found unresponsive, but alive. There were faint wisps of cake crumbs found at the corners of her lips; her labored breaths smelled of lavender. Gran wouldn't ever have to fight to take another breath again. A machine did it for her now. She would go on as long as it did.

The next cupcake on the list certainly took some time. My heart felt certain that Melange was done with me. That time of my life seemed so far away for a moment.

Sandra and I bumped into each other in an odd but not uncommon way: a fender bender. She had tapped my car due to not stopping at a stop sign. The second she stepped out of her car, my insurance info flew disappeared from recollection, probably due to blood loss if I'm honest. She was gorgeous! Something about her captivated me. I found myself having fantasies I hadn't had since my early twenties. Lust completely had me by the balls here, pardon the phrase.

It was like a kick to the gut to find out she was barely eighteen years old. Thirty-seven is no senior citizen, but compared to eighteen? It was way out of my level of acceptability. If I'm old enough to be your Dad, I don't need to be banging you. But with Sandra, I could not and would not resist. She felt the same way too. As wrong as it felt, I needed to have her.

The Mocha Lotta cupcake was an easy three hundred dollars to spend if it meant I got to have *her*. On my way home from the shop, I dropped by Sandra's work and delivered it to her. I told her to eat it on her break, and that I remember that she said she loved coffee *(a lie)*.

I was afraid that the cupcake would alter her body and not her mind. We moved in together after a bit, and I watched her as closely as possible. Things were fine for months! Then we started noticing little changes. Her hair would thin a little more than normal after she washed and brushed it. The prescription at her eye doctor's office had to be strengthened. Her ears became less sensitive to tone and pitch. It wasn't until her yearly gynecological visit that we were informed something was wrong with her on the inside. Her egg count was drastically low, lower than a perimenopausal woman. I didn't have the heart to tell her what I had done, even after we married. I still haven't, even to this day.

Someone transferred into Sandra's company. The new woman stole my wife's lime-light, creativity, and promotion. The things we do for love, power, and greed. My sweet bride welcomed her new boss and offered to celebrate her new position with a vanilla crème cupcake. I tried to refuse. I told her she was out of her mind. But she didn't have much time left, thanks to me. I had to do something to atone for that.

Sandra claimed to understand what it meant to feed that cupcake to the newcomer, but I don't think she really could have ever absorbed the implications of her actions.

After just ten days, her rival's body plummeted down seven stories onto a car parked below just as Sandra was coming back from lunch. My wife saw the entire thing, and knew she somehow had a hand in it.

Which brings us to the present. I haven't been back to the cupcake shop for over two years now. Sandra requires the assistance of a walker and is completely blind. Not even twenty years of age, and with all of the ailments of someone who's seventy-five.

She insisted on we celebrating my birthday today, one of the last ones left of my thirties. A large, ornately decorated cake rested in the middle of our kitchen table. Candles peppered the top of it, though there wasn't enough room on top to hold all thirty-eight. My smiling wife sat next to an empty pulled out chair, beckoning me to join her.

We sat and ate cake, my love and I. It was the absolute best I've ever tasted in all of my life. The moisture and decadence of the chocolate was too complex to properly describe.

But my third piece revealed something most horrific to me. Under my slice, in the faintest of calligraphy, I saw an all too familiar monogram: *MM.* The corner of a note peeked out from under the opened box:

**Melicious Maladies After Hours Service:**
**Now Making and Delivering CAKES!**

# THE PALE TENANT

## EDWARD KARPP

I will tell you right from the start that I cannot match my uncle, Joseph S. Grant, by measure of wealth or fame or stature. After all, he was the top silent Western star from 1915 to 1918. I have two things over him, however. One is that I am alive, and the second is that I am his next of kin, his heir. I am Henry Grant, a humble steel worker and the great man's eldest nephew, though I only met him once when I was ten years old. My parents took me out West to visit him at Grant Canyon, the ranch he was building in the mountains north of Los Angeles. The unfinished, dust-blown, worker-filled property was chaotic and frightening to me, nearly as frightening as the craggy man on the movie screen forever pointing revolvers at the audience. I hadn't a clue, of course, that I would inherit that rambling Spanish Colonial Revival property after he succumbed to pneumonia, having outlived two wives and three elder brothers, including my father.

When I was notified about the inheritance, I first attempted to determine the sale value, only to be informed by Uncle Joseph's attorney via a series of letters and one expensive telephone conversation that the property was unlikely to sell, given the state of the economy in 1935. Due to my unfortunate lack of employment and prospects, my wife Anna, my twelve-year-old daughter Patricia, and I packed up our belongings to take full advantage of the mansion I had inherited.

The railway fare of almost three hundred dollars was covered by my uncle's bequest. During the four days of the train voyage, life seemed open to endless possibilities as we crossed the country to California, to occupy a movie star's mansion, no less. The luxury of meal service on the train and the passing vistas outside the window— tree-shrouded hills and valleys in the East, golden fields in the Midwest, rough mountains in the West—only made it more clear day by day that our station in life was rising.

When we reached the train station north of Los Angeles, Uncle Joseph's attorney, a heavy-set man with red hair named Alistair Marcus, had a car waiting to drive us the three miles to Grant Canyon, past stone-pillared gates and up a winding hill lined with palm and eucalyptus.

The car stopped at the top of the hill, near the foot of the steps leading to the main house. "I'll give your family a tour of the home," Mr. Marcus said, "and then we'll discuss the living arrangements."

The tour took fifteen minutes, enough time to show us the two servants' rooms and the film screening room on the lower floor, the four bedrooms on the upper floor, the kitchen, and the enormous living room filled with memorabilia that might have been from Uncle Joseph's Western movies, or from the real American West. Mr. Marcus had us sit on sofas in the living room so he could explain the living arrangements. My uncle's will, it seemed, included an unusual requirement. "Mr. Grant had an agreement with his tenant, which continues in perpetuity. The tenant may come and go as he pleases, and the will requires your family and guests to respect his privacy and not to engage in conversation."

Upon hearing this, my first question involved the rooms we saw downstairs, all of which were tidy and appeared unlived-in. Anna had a more direct question: "Who is this tenant?"

"Mr. Grant and the gentleman worked together in the films and felt he owed the man a debt." He coughed and seemed embarrassed. "His name is not in any of the documents."

After Mr. Marcus left, Anna and I discussed this substantial complication while Patricia explored the grounds. I was of the opinion that we could live in the house temporarily while we worked on selling the estate, but Anna, always practical, pointed out that this mystery tenant would make it all but impossible to find a buyer. We had no choice but to move our belongings into the house and collect more information about the situation.

"I saw the tenant," Patricia said when she returned at sunset from her explorations. She described a tall, willowy man wearing a black business suit and no hat, hands clasped behind him as he stood at the top of a rise staring down at a grove of eucalyptus trees. She had watched him from across the empty swimming pool behind the main building. "He didn't move," she told us. "I think he's a ghost."

I told her the idea was nonsense, not least because of the way she'd described him, casting a long shadow, hair tousled by the light breeze. My wife shook her head disdainfully as we continued to converse about the matter.

No, the tenant was not a ghost, though I would not argue if you said he haunted the main house. During our first week at Grant Canyon, we heard him moving about his quarters, whose exact location I am embarrassed to admit I could not locate. The tenant's footfalls seemed to originate from different parts of the house, though always downstairs. The servants' quarters were empty, their slight furnishings accumulating a layer of dust. I concluded that his bedroom must be underneath Patricia's bedroom at the back of the house, and that the entrance must be hidden in a corridor I had yet to locate.

I casually explored the lower story several times during that first week, but the fact that the rear of the lower story was set into the hillside made it difficult to understand how extensive the building might be, and where a hidden or obscure entrance might be placed. On one occasion, I located a suspicious door halfway along the downstairs hall. When I pried it open, it revealed nothing but a broom closet occupied by two spiders that crept back into the shadows when exposed to light. Something moved, clanging in the bucket on the floor. A rat started climbing up the wall of the bucket, dragging the innards of some poor animal behind. I slammed the door shut. Then I realized I wasn't halfway down the hall at all. I was standing at the end of the hall, boxed in by cramped plaster walls that I swear had not been there before. I turned around quickly and hurried upstairs.

I myself saw the tenant for the first time on the Saturday of our first week, having decided to fix up Uncle Joseph's screening room, unused for years due to my uncle's long illness. I descended the staircase that morning and entered the eighteen-seat screening room, crossing underneath the projector window at the back, intending to go inside the projection booth to check on the condition of the equipment. But the door was stuck. I waited a few moments for my eyes to adjust to the dimness in the theater, after which I saw the tenant sitting in a front row seat, still as could be. The black curtains covering the screen were closed, so he was looking at nothing but darkness.

I was startled that I was not alone, but I said loudly, "Hello." I'm not certain if I had forgotten Mr. Marcus' entreaty not to interact with the tenant, or if I was simply frustrated with the awkwardness of the situation. In either case, the tenant did not respond to my greeting.

I stepped down one level. Even in the dimness, I could tell that his thinning hair was white as fresh snow. I cleared my throat. "Sir, excuse me, but I feel I must introduce myself."

I took a step closer and started to reach out for a handshake.

He began to turn his head.


I typed "He began to turn his head" and struck the period key. The words fell near the bottom of the page, so I pulled it out of the typewriter. My habit at the end of the day is to leave the page in the typewriter, making it easier to continue the next day, but it seemed the right time for Karen to read the pages. I found her at the dining room table grading workbooks—finishing the week's grading was her Friday night ritual. The pile was almost finished, so I paced around the apartment until she was done. I ended up staring out the window over the couch at my own reflection, and behind it the blue nighttime glow of the swimming pool down in the apartment courtyard.

Karen took the pages to the couch. A minute later—it didn't surprise me anymore how quickly she read—she said, "I'm not sure. Is anyone interested in Westerns anymore?"

I felt defensive, but Karen was always direct with me, and almost always right. "It's really a haunting, not a Western."

"A silent Western actor? Remember, *Gunsmoke* was cancelled in 1975. That was five years ago. I haven't seen a Western movie in a long time." She glanced up from the pages and saw the expression on my face. "I'm sorry, Mike. But it has potential. I know where it's coming from. I think you should get to the haunting more quickly and skip some of the Western stuff."

I nodded. It was all connected, in my mind if not on the page.

"And don't even think of hurting the little girl," she warned.

"Don't worry. I would never harm a child, not even in a story." Exhausted from my job interview today, I cracked open Keith's bedroom door to check on him—fast asleep with his stuffed bear, a gentle breath lifting his chest—before I headed to the master bedroom three paces away. Karen stayed in the living room watching TV, the volume low, her way of diluting the stress of the classroom, and the stress of supporting the three of us.

I climbed into bed. *I know where it's coming from*, she'd said, and she did know part of it. My father and I had visited Joseph S. Grant's mansion last year, soon after Keith and Karen and I moved to the San Fernando Valley. Dad had wanted to visit the mansion for decades, more for the Western paintings and memorabilia on display than because of Grant, though the actor had been popular when my dad was in grade school. Dad had impressed the tour guide with his knowledge of Grant's movies and those of his contemporaries like D. W. Griffith and Mary Pickford, who had attended many parties at the mansion in its heyday. Dad even bought a souvenir, a bronze replica of one of Grant's diamondback-pattern boots on a stand, a boot that now sat on top of the bookshelf in our living room. Dad remembered the Westerns like he'd seen them yesterday, yet some days he barely remembered my mother or me. After the trip, he seemed to shrink into himself. Two months later, he didn't even remember the movies. Three months later, he was dead.

Karen didn't know the other part, the part about the dreams that had started after my father's funeral. Dreams of a cold plaster house with doorless rooms full of dressmaker dummies wearing cowboy hats. Dreams of hallways ending in rough, dripping rock with veins of quartz that began to pulse. Dreams of a huge hairless beast hunched on all fours, its eye sockets black and empty, a film projector poking from a hole in the center of its forehead and pouring flickering light onto the stucco wall, projecting monochrome images of scalpings and throat slashing and gunshot after gunshot. The pale tenant was in those dreams, just out of sight, thin enough to hide behind the dummies, between the frames of the Western bloodshed projected onto the walls. Watching me.

I recalled what I'd seen out of the corner of my eye this morning after Karen went to work, the glimpse of a tall pale man reaching for Keith's doorknob. Nothing was there when I turned my head. I put it out of my mind.

I fell asleep trying to work the half-remembered dreams into my story. Perfect sentences came together but drifted into jumbles of words, and then the sun was streaming through the curtains and Karen was asleep next to me. I slipped out of bed and padded to my desk in the corner of the living room, typed the first sentence that came into my head as quietly as I could.


I don't know what that sentence is, the first sentence that came into Mike's head. It's important. The tenant is there on the page, his page, turning his head to confront Henry Grant. What does Mike have Henry see? The words are cold on my MacBook screen. The acid smells inside Starbucks make it hard to think here, but the rain pounding against the windows won't let me leave.

The tenant grows. It takes time. He builds his nest in shreds of story. People forget. He comes back stronger. Brings others like the projector-thing. That's just the start.

The door opens to let a man and woman into the Starbucks. Spatters of rain hit my keyboard. There is nothing behind the entering couple, but the lighter patches of gray mist seem to move like figures approaching the door, figures at least two stories tall.

I dry the keyboard with my sleeve. Hit command-S. Visualize the tenant in his weakest form, a gaunt, elderly man with no color or vitality, dressed all in black. That was how I first saw him before the divorce, on the Cub Scout trip to William S. Hart Mansion in Newhall, north of Los Angeles and less than twenty miles from home. None of the scouts knew who Hart was, but my son Jack and I drove out there that morning with the troop to see the sad little petting zoo with the Beware of Rattlesnakes signs, the buffalo grazing on brown grass, and the big old house the silent Western actor had left to the county as a museum.

The scouts were bored with the tour, Jack most of all. Our troop filed through the house along with three or four families. The scouts complained it was just an old house. I felt a little sick looking at the paintings and sculptures that all depicted violence, twisted men and twisted horses falling forever into the dust. When we went outside to see the stables, the boys started running despite the guides' warnings. Jack's friend Austin tripped and cut himself on barbed wire hidden under a pile of leaves. While the adults' attention was on the boy, the others dispersed around the grounds. I realized Jack was one of the troublemakers and looked for him, my feet crunching through dead leaves as I rounded the corner of the stable.

They were there in the shadow of the stucco building, Jack sitting in the dirt with a look of panic on his face, his hand clutching a rock. The old man stood over Jack, turning his head toward me. Not colorless, really; just a pale old man with sunken eyes, wearing a black jacket and a black cowboy hat. No expression at all on his face.

I yelled, I remember that, and I remember Jack crawling backward through the dirt and leaves. Then suddenly Jack was leaning against the wall, his head down, and I was beside him clenching my fists, my right fist bleeding, both fists aching as if I'd been punching something over and over. The man was gone. Sheriffs closed the museum and searched for hours, we filed reports, Jack grew more volatile month by month, everything was my fault.

The tenant came back to me first in dreams, which medication barely dulled. When

I realized he was more than just a dream, that he was trying to climb out, it was too late. Maybe the medication helped by making the dreams indistinct. Maybe it did the opposite. I saw the man's reflection in the pond at the park next to Jack's old elementary school. Just his reflection in the water, nobody there to cast it. This was after the divorce, after Jack was gone. I stayed away from ponds and mirrors after that, but it didn't help. He would be there from time to time when I walked around corners, just like at the Hart mansion, growing paler each time, and taller.

At this point, the only way to keep him away is to write, to trap him behind layers of fiction, put him in Grant Canyon, a fictionalized Hart mansion. I think—I hope—the Western imagery will help to cage him in a genre nobody thinks about anymore, a dim reflection of a time nobody remembers, fiction trivializing mass murder and genocide, a time better forgotten. The tenant is a parasite, feeding on the same empty, violent fantasies exploited by the movies. If he stays there in his shallowest, weakest form, wallowing in meaningless nostalgia, then there might be a chance.

When the rain lessens, I'll print out the story and go back to Hart Mansion to scatter the pages around and prove he's meaningless, trapped within fiction inside fiction. I don't know what else to do.

I take a deep breath and type.


"His eyes were dark and his skin was more than just pale." The words sat on the page. Maybe Karen was right and nobody would ever see this. But I wanted to write it, if only for me. I continued to type, more nervous writing about the tenant in the bright Saturday sunlight than I had been in the dark last night. The words were there, not quite flowing, but I finished three pages before I heard Karen in the kitchen making eggs.

I left the page in the typewriter and went to the kitchen to kiss my wife, holding her for a few extra seconds. When I went to check on Keith I paused before opening the door, wondered what I would do if the tenant were inside leaning over the bed. But when I opened the door Keith was alone, sitting up in bed reading his chapter book, the one I'd started reading to him before bedtime three weeks ago, the one he was reading now on his own.

After breakfast, Keith and I took a ten-minute walk to the playground while Karen went shopping for groceries and school supplies. I watched Keith rock back and forth on a metal horse with a spring for a body, though he was too big for the ride, until a classmate arrived and they chased each other around the playground. I nodded at the classmate's mother, then realized that the man standing a few paces behind her wearing a dark suit, here in the bright Sherman Oaks sunlight, was the tenant, looking straight at Keith with dark, sunken eyes.

I ran to Keith and told him we had to leave, raising my voice at his protests. I didn't look at the tenant as I took Keith's hand less gently than I intended and pulled him along. Was the tenant following? I waited until we were two blocks from the park before I released Keith's hand and glanced back. We were the only people on the sidewalk.

We reached the apartment before Karen got home. The irrationality of seeing the man in broad daylight suggested an irrational solution: return the souvenir boot to Grant's mansion. After all, the dreams had started when we'd brought it back from my parents' house after the funeral. While Keith watched a cartoon on TV, I paced around the apartment waiting for Karen. If we'd owned two cars, I would have taken Keith to the mansion immediately, but it wasn't long before I heard her key in the lock. I helped her with the groceries while explaining that I needed to return to Grant's house for research for my story, that I wanted the two of them to come with me because it would be educational. She wouldn't understand if I told her I didn't want them to be alone.

There was little traffic and we reached the mansion just after one o'clock. I couldn't remember the mansion's or its owner's name as we drove, just that it only had one syllable. The sign was obscured by bushes but I knew the way. We parked and climbed out of the car. I hung my camera around my neck and reached under the seat where I'd stuffed the boot inside a grocery bag. Karen asked why I'd brought that back and I said something about photographing it on the mansion grounds.

At the beginning of the tour, I set the bag down near an open utility closet off the foyer. I took some photos of the foyer and the living room, then I walked away from the bag as if I'd simply forgotten it. Nobody noticed. As the tour continued through the halls and past the bedrooms and out around the stables, I grew certain the bag would turn up in the car or the apartment, but when we circled back to the foyer it was still sitting by the closet, the souvenir still inside.

I didn't know what to expect as we drove home. I felt no sense of relief; my heart was beating as hard as it had on the drive up the hill. Karen left Keith and me at the apartment because she wanted to drop my film off at the drug store and she needed to go to the bank, and it would give me a chance to finish my story. Keith read his chapter book, sitting on the couch where I could see him. I sat down at the typewriter. The family would stand together and banish the stranger and live a happy life.

At least the story I was writing could have a conclusion.


His eyes were dark and his skin was more than just pale. It was colorless. The screening room appeared even blacker by contrast. The man's visage made me shiver, and I admit I recoiled from him. He opened his mouth and spoke quietly, saying something like "know you are eating," but I was already walking to the exit, startled and embarrassed, certain Mr. Marcus' warnings were, at the very least, good advice.

I found Anna in the kitchen. I was anxious to share my encounter with her, but when I convinced her to sit down with me at the table, I was surprised to see Patricia enter the room from the back door, her hands trembling and her hair unkempt. To my astonishment, she told us she had just seen the tenant. He had accosted her outside by grabbing her shoulders and pushing her down to the ground, but she had managed to escape.

Furious, I thrust open the back door and tramped around the stables to the clearing with the empty pool. A strong wind came up, scattering gray husks of eucalyptus bark across my path. I saw nobody on the grounds, but I could no longer consider this tenant an ordinary person so I called out, "Show yourself!"

I turned, startled by a tree branch cracking in the wind. Anna and Patricia stood back at the stable wall. Anna's expression was angry. She wrapped one arm around Patricia's shoulder. I saw their eyes widen and I turned around again, and suddenly the tenant was standing on the other side of the empty swimming pool, his back to me.

I circled the hole in the ground. I am not proud to say I intended to overpower this elderly man. No other option came to mind. I touched his shoulder and the sensation was not unlike touching a refrigerated coil in a meat-packing house. Startled, I could do nothing as the tenant turned and began pushing me backward. He appeared inches taller than he had less than an hour earlier. His face looked as white and expressionless as it had in the screening room, though the wisps of hair were rising and undulating in the wind. My left foot slid over the edge of the pool so I leaned forward with a desperate effort, to no effect.

I fell into the hole.

Perhaps my recollection of the events to follow were affected by the force of my fall on the back of my head and my neck, barely cushioned by the thick mat of leaves. Though my vision was slightly blurred, I could see a scuffle up above the rim of the pool, and Anna swinging a square-bladed shovel. Then the tenant was standing over me in the pool, the ankles of his black diamondback-pattern boots covered in leaves. I struggled unsuccessfully to climb to my feet as he knelt down beside me to whisper in a voice no different from the rustling of the leaves.

His words made no sense. "I took her," he said with a trace of a grin on his lips, and I realized that, somehow, Patricia's body was lying in the pool not far from me, completely still, and that Anna was kneeling above us on the edge, her hands covering her face. I refused to believe the liquid seeping down the wall of the pool was blood, my daughter's blood.

I shook my head, unable to understand. He looked at something far past me and spoke slowly as if explaining something to a child. His whispered words made even less sense than before, as if they were directed at someone other than me. "I took them. The son, the father, the daughter. You could not protect them. Your boy Keith is next."

My vision remained blurry but I saw him vanishing down into the leaves, his outspread hands dripping black liquid. Though I will never be certain that it was not just the sound of rustling leaves, I believe I heard the tenant say, "I know you are reading. I will be with you soon."

# DO YOU WANNA PLAY, MOMMY?

## CINDAR HARRELL

When my family went to Los Angeles to visit some friends, I insisted that we go to the doll shop. The shop was for a Japanese toy company that specializes in beautiful resin ball jointed dolls. They only have one store in the United States, and it's in L.A. I had always longed to own one of those dolls, so big and beautiful. It was the only thing I wanted to do in California, even over going to Disneyland. My mom was reluctant just because of how expensive they were, but in the end, she agreed. Each doll is crafted to the buyer's specifications so no two dolls are alike. When they are ready, they have a special ceremony to "welcome" your new doll into your family. Like a birthday.

When I opened the door of the store to pick up my doll, the room was dim. When we came to order her, it had been much brighter.

"Ah, hello! You are just in time for the ceremony!" the store manager said as he appeared from the back room. "Please, come right this way." He motioned for us to follow him into the back.

"But what about the shop? What if other customers come in?" my mom asked hesitantly.

"It's no problem. We always close down for the ceremony. This is something special just for you," he said pointing at me. I smiled, excitement welling up inside me.

There was a table set up in the back, candles around a beautiful box decorated with red roses. The box was open and I could just barely make out my doll sleeping inside. The storekeeper gestured for my parents to sit in two chairs at the back of the room. There was a cushion on the floor in front of the table. This was my spot. I knelt and waited to be given my doll.

"Now, this is a very special doll. You created her, gave her a character, a story. You gave her life, now it is up to you to maintain it. You have to take care of her. Do you understand?"

I nodded. "Yes."

He smiled.

I thought he would give her to me then, but he didn't. Instead, he walked out of the room and closed the door, taking away what little artificial light had been in the small room.

My parents made protests, but I didn't hear exactly what they were saying; my focus was on my doll.

She moved.

The candle light flickered across her pale resin skin, dancing. Her dress, a deep crimson satin, shifted. Raven hair fluttered in the nonexistent breeze.

I held my breath.

The lights went out.

A laugh belonging to a little girl echoed in the quiet room.

"Do you wanna play, mommy?" A voice whispered in my ear. I gasped.

Pain shot through my chest and a scream died in my throat. A flash of light illuminated a set of ice blue glass eyes right in front of me.

I couldn't breathe. I held my hands to my chest and felt something sticking out of my flesh. A knife? No. It was her hand. She pulled her jointed hand back, nails perfectly sculpted into points, now dripping red. My blood.

"Thank you for giving me this body, mommy. I promise I'll take good care of it."

I felt lightheaded and closed my eyes.

*Why, dolly?*

The lights came back on.

"What happened? Where did he go? I knew we never should have agreed to this," Mom said. "Are you all right?" she asked, turning towards me.

I smiled. "Of course." Cradling my new dolly in my arms, I started walking to the door.

"Where are you going? Are you ready to go already?" Dad asked.

I turned to look at him. "Why not? I got what I came for."

Once we were back in the car, I noticed mom looking at my doll in the rearview mirror. "Isn't she beautiful?" I smiled. "Do you wanna play, Mommy?"

# A COLD & LONELY EVIL

## DUANE BRADLEY

Getting your ass whupped by a redneck is bad enough for a regular person, but when you're famous, it's worse.

When you're a stand-up comic turned actor-director, when you've worked with big names and made a dozen films, when you've won awards and graced magazine covers and been linked to some of the most glamorous women in the world, losing a fight to someone named Zeke is about as humiliating as it gets.

In my defense, my mind was on other things. The African-American Film Critics Association and the Black Film Critics Circle had just showered me with awards for my movie *Neighborhood Threat*, a body swap horror picture where rich white folks transferred their souls into the bodies of poor black folks to give themselves a shot at immortality. Everyone thought I was Making A Statement and wanted to reward my good intentions, so who was I to tell them my movie was basically *The Mephisto Waltz* with a racial twist?

The critics quit kissing my ass shortly after midnight and I was searching for my car keys when Zeke jumped me in the parking lot. I've been in my share of fights (on film anyway) but nobody had hit me in the head for at least six months. So when Zeke appeared, I wasn't ready and went down like a sack of potatoes. That's my statement and I'm sticking to it.

If you've never woken up in the back of a '00 Aztek with nothing except a spare tire and some moldy newspapers for company, I don't recommend it. Especially if you're coming to terms with having your ass handed to you by a fella with prison tattoos and missing teeth. I also do not recommend giving in to self-pity and going on a crying jag while covered in mildewing copies of the *Los Angeles Daily News*.

This wasn't rock bottom, by the way. I didn't know it yet, but this was just the next rung down on a ladder that descended straight into Beelzebub's living room.

It's amazing how a long ride in a dirty trunk can alter your perspective. In the space of a few hours, I went from kidding myself that I was going to break some heads the moment they popped the trunk to admitting that there were probably several other guys as well as Zeke and they all had shooters while I didn't. I didn't know where they were taking me or what the hell Zeke had in mind, but it probably didn't involve a nice meal and a mariachi band.

The car finally groaned to a halt. The driver set the brake and killed the engine. Then, for the first time I heard Zeke's voice.

"When does it get light around here?"

"When the sun comes up," someone said.

"No fucking shit, Dick Tracy. You got an ETA on that?"

"Couple hours yet. Why?"

"It's a full moon tonight. I don't like being out in the sticks when it's a full moon."

Doors slammed. The trunk popped open.

Two shotguns filled the space, and behind the shotguns were two goons with tattoos and ripped T-shirts, Central Casting's idea of how a redneck might look. Behind the goons stood Zeke, not armed as far as I could see, but clearly enjoying himself. A smug grin was smeared across his face like lipstick.

"*Hola*, Rudy," Zeke said. He pronounced it *hole-arr*. "Fellas, say howdy to Rudy Ray Washington. Back home in Hollywood, he's the hottest ticket in town right now. Out there, he can name his price and do just about anything he wants. Hell, I bet he even gets to tell white people what to do. Give it up for Rudy, boys."

The goons clearly weren't fans. They stared straight ahead, shotguns raised, saying nothing.

"You don't mind if we take up some of your valuable time do you, Rudy? I mean, you're not working at the moment, are you?"

"Have your people call my people," I said.

"Ho ho, he's funny. He's lying in my trunk with a shotgun in his face and he's funny. Let's get him on his feet and see how funny he really is."

The goons reached inside and brought me out. We were in an empty tarmacadam lot. It was dark and there was a bad smell on the air, the kind you get from a motel that rents rooms by the hour.

I staggered across the macadam to the room and thought about shouting for help, but decided it probably wasn't such a good idea. These guys likely knew the motel owner, who I doubted was on the side of the angels.

Drawing the curtains, Zeke pulled the couch into the middle of the room and pushed me onto it.

"Okay," he said, "cards on the table. From now on, your ass belongs to me. Got the deed right here, see? It says do what I say or I'm gonna shove my foot so far north that Rudy Jr. is gonna feel it."

"I don't know you," I said, "but I'll tell you this much. Today, you got lucky. Any other day, I could whup a grizzly bear in a fair fight."

"That right?"

"I've got witnesses."

"Well, goddamn, I never would've thought. This is really messing up your head, isn't it? Getting clobbered by a white boy, I mean."

"Stranger things have happened."

"Like what?"

"Your mother fucked your father."

"You should see my mother," he said. "Mention her again and I'll kill you."

"Why don't you just say your piece and leave me at the nearest bus stop? I've got better things to do, and you've got a probation meeting in a few hours."

Zeke actually chuckled at that.

"Yeah, I heard you were funny," he said. "Heard your movies are a real hoot. I wouldn't know, I don't watch black propaganda films."

"Prefer *Barney the Purple Dinosaur*, huh?"

"It's easier to sit through. None of that shit white liberals want to hear, like how we should allow the races to mix. They think you do that, you're gonna end up in a utopia. Doesn't work like that. Once you mix the races, you're counting down to white genocide."

"I'm more of a *The Banana Splits* guy myself."

"You people don't find white civilization comfortable, that's your problem. Every time we tell you to follow the rules, you howl about being oppressed. We say walk down the sidewalk, not down the middle of the street, you scream oppression. We say stick to our standards of punctuality, you complain about victimization."

I didn't say anything. I had an image of seven-year-old Zeke sitting a test and giving up after five minutes because math was hard and drawing pictures was fun. He'd gone through school like that and when as an adult he realized he'd never earn decent money, somebody told him it was the fault of minorities and Zeke believed it.

"Victims, my ass," Zeke said. "You can't even follow our age of consent laws."

"There's a point to this, right?"

"Oh, there's a point alright, *amigo*. There is definitely a point. I know how you all love to portray whites as lazy and stupid, but that's not the truth. We're smart. We're educated. We've been working on... hey, Charlie, what's that word again?"

"Regenerate," Goon One said.

"Regenerate, right. We've got a serum that attacks a body's bad cells and *regenerates* them into good cells. When you inject it into a black fella, it turns him into a white fella."

I stared at Zeke. He didn't look like he was kidding.

"We'll be the first people to do this," he said, "and it's gonna make us famous."

"No doubt about that."

"And rich."

"Unlikely."

"What do you think?"

I glanced back at Zeke. He still wasn't kidding.

I looked at the goons. They weren't kidding either.

"I think you're full of shit," I said.

"That's what I thought you'd say." He nodded to the goons. "Time for a demo."

Four arms pinned me to the couch. Zeke fished a hypo out of his pocket and held it up for me to see.

"You might feel a little prick," he said.

"Story of your life."

"C'mon, it won't hurt a bit." He thought for a moment and said, "Well, maybe just a bit."

The goons held my arms from behind but my legs were free, so when Zeke was close enough, I lashed out. I got him a good one between the legs and as he bent double, he tried to administer the injection while falling forward.

It didn't work.

Zeke was aiming for my neck, but one of the goons had an arm there and Zeke's aim was off. When the needle broke skin on the goon's upper arm, the guy screamed like a girl, jumped backwards and, losing his footing, fell flat on his ass.

He hit the floor, *whump*, and instead of groaning and starting to get up, he began screaming and lashing out. He pulled the needle out and it sailed across the room.

Zeke called "Charlie?" a few times but Charlie wasn't home; he was coughing and spluttering and about ready to go into convulsions. With his eyes squeezed shut and his mouth open wide enough to reveal a full set of yellow gnashers, Ol' Charlie sure looked like he'd seen better days.

Curled into a fetal position with his head moving back and forth, he might've been a dog dreaming about chasing rabbits. This went on a while longer. Then the spasms became twitches and eventually stopped. Charlie lay very still and looked very dead.

Zeke watched all this with folded arms and a disappointed expression. I didn't know the exact relationship between him and Charlie, but Zeke looked like he was mentally composing some bullshit excuse to Charlie's next of kin.

Goon Two, whose name turned out to be Marvin, knelt over Charlie and felt for a pulse.

"Well?" Zeke said.

"You want the good news first?"

"What's the good news?"

"He didn't shit his pants."

"What's the bad news?"

"He's fucking dead."

Zeke was quiet for a spell. He started pacing.

Eventually, he looked at me and said, "This is your fault."

"That's right, blame the other guy," I said. "That always works for you, doesn't it?

"I vote we waste him," Marvin said.

"I second the motion," Zeke said.

Marvin raised the shotgun. "Motion carried," he said.

He racked the shotgun, looked like he meant business, then something caught his eye. When I realized what it was, I thought Marvin did well to maintain his composure.

144

Charlie was back on his feet.

He stood up to his full height and looked at Marvin, who was rock calm and steady. Maybe he was trying to figure out if he was hallucinating. He wasn't, but he didn't realize it until Charlie leaned over and sank his teeth into Marvin's throat.

Marvin staggered backwards, blood spraying from the wound, and when he slammed into the wall, the shotgun discharged. Marvin's left foot disappeared in a red mist and down he went.

Charlie made a beeline for Zeke, who squealed and dodged to the left. He collided with me, then grabbed my shirt and hurled me in front of Charlie.

I tripped and fell, landing in front Charlie. Charlie reached down, roughly brought me to my feet, then stared at me for five seconds that felt more like five minutes. To say I wasn't expecting what happened next is a major understatement.

Instead of doing what I expected, which involved redecorating the room in arterial red, Charlie clapped me on the shoulder and walked past me, making another beeline for Zeke.

"What the fuck was that?" Zeke said.

"You turned his bad cells into good cells," I said. "He only attacks racists now."

Grabbing the shotgun, Zeke hit Charlie in the face several times. One, two, three and down he went.

"Who you calling racist?" Zeke said. "I'm a human and civil rights advocate with an emphasis on the Caucasian demographic, goddamn it." He opened his mouth to say something more, but Charlie grabbed his foot. Zeke squealed again and started kicking him, but Charlie was having none of it and pulled him down to the floor. I watched them wrestle awhile longer, then walked outside.

The sun was coming up over the hills and it looked like it was going to be a pretty day. As I crossed the lot to Zeke's car, I looked around and took in all the things I hadn't noticed earlier. The motel was every bit as cheap and shabby as I'd expected, and on the edge of the lot was a wooden board that instead of displaying For Sale notices and such was covered with paraphernalia from a group calling itself the American White Knights.

In amongst the flyers for Unite the Right rallies were pamphlets that said anti-racist was code for anti-white because only white countries were being forced to accept unlimited immigrants and were expected to become mixed race. At the bottom of the board was a drawing that showed one figure stomping another above the words GOOD NIGHT ANTI-WHITE.

"There a problem here?"

I turned and saw an old man unlocking the front office. He was sad-eyed and humorless, with a belly that pushed against his T-shirt. ONE MILLION BATTERED WOMEN IN AMERICA AND I'VE BEEN EATING MINE PLAIN, the shirt proclaimed.

"No problem," I said. "I was just leaving. Are you the manager?"

He nodded.

145

"There was a noise coming from one of the cabins. You might want to check it out."

"Don't tell me what I should do," he said, and disappeared inside the office.

I walked back to the Aztek. Zeke, true to his nature, had left the keys in the ignition and a stroke book on the seat. I tossed the book and had the engine running when the manager reappeared and strode purposefully towards the cabins, which was the last thing I saw before I drove away.

# THEDA AND ME

## LORNA WOOD

I didn't so much mind moving out of the house; I'd only been rattling around in it anyway, since my wife died fifteen years ago. But over forty-odd years of screenwriting, I'd accumulated a lot of what I call "memorabilia" and my daughter Vita calls "junk."

Lord knows I tried to take care of my junk when Vita asked me to. But it's not as easy as it sounds. It wasn't until Theda's photo literally leaped out at me—springing from the envelope with Mother's 1918 letter about the flu—that I realized all the time I'd been mooning over old scripts and reviews, I'd only and always been searching for that photo, seeking and at the same time dreading the spirit that has haunted so much of my life. Mother hadn't sent it, of course. Theda wasn't the kind of girl you tell Mother about. Vita must have tucked the picture into the envelope during one of her cleanup campaigns.

I'm ashamed to say that faced with the choice of rereading Mother's last letter to me or poring over the picture, I chose the picture. But Mother hadn't written anything remarkable in the letter—she couldn't have known the flu would take her so soon, and only thought of warning me against it. Theda, on the other hand... perhaps I should have said the picture chose me.

It was a glossy studio publicity shot, showing Theda as "Lena the leopard tamer." Brazenly she faced the camera, clad in flimsy strips of leopard skin. Her thick, wavy black hair hung around her face, only partially restrained by a jeweled barrette on one side. In her right hand she held a whip, in her left a cigarette in a long black holder. Gazing through the silver wreaths of smoke, her dark, kohl-lined eyes were veiled in feral inscrutability.

Immediately I was drawn back to my early days, when Hollywood and I were young, and anything seemed possible. I saw her again, standing on the curving staircase of her Beverly Hills Spanish colonial, welcoming her guests with an imperious wave of one chiffon-draped arm and her customary invitation: *"Bienvenue,* ladies and gentlemen. Pick your poison." And I saw myself, a greenhorn drawn like a moth to her flame, carrying that picture around in my wallet.

Nobody seemed to know anything about her, though lots of people thought they did. "Theda LaMorte" was clearly a stage name, and her faint foreign accent was hard to place. Some people swore they'd seen her lose her temper in Brooklynese, and others said they knew for a fact she was part French, Russian, Indian, Chinese, or Creole. Even her marital status was anyone's guess. Some said she was widowed, others said divorced, and still others claimed she was secretly married to some foreign prince or ultra-respectable millionaire who could only see her on the QT.

Naturally her age was a closely guarded secret. She might have been anywhere between thirty and forty, but I didn't care. In my early twenties, I imagined an affair with an older woman would be thrillingly educational. Looking into her eyes in the photo, I sought to penetrate the timeless mysteries of existence: love, sex, and the purpose of my own puny struggles.

But those cat eyes gave me nothing, even in person. The more fascinated I became, the more I floundered out of my depth. She wasn't kidding when she invited us to pick our poison. Her place was liberty hall—stocked with everything from absinthe to heroin. But for me (and many others) the most dangerous addiction was Theda herself.

My career wasn't exactly taking off. Theda's parties were loose affairs that required no direct invitation, only a connection with someone who knew about them. At first, I went not only to be near her but to get my name out there, make some contacts. If nothing else, I thought, I could pick up some juicy news items for the gossip columns. Theda didn't disappoint—she never did. I became intrigued by the number of mysterious fatalities she was somehow mixed up with—though nothing was ever definite or provable. There was the radiant young ingénue Eva Gibbs, for instance. Everyone was scandalized when she died at twenty of a heroin overdose. But no one ever came forward to verify the rumors that Evie was carrying on a passionate affair with Theda under Mr. Gibbs' very nose (their house overlooked Theda's), or that Theda may well have supplied the fatal dose.

I did know for certain that a dealer who frequented her parties supplied handsome young Edward Montjoy (née Howard Hickson) with cocaine. But he died in his bungalow from stab wounds, and nobody ever figured out which of a dozen women he had loved and left did it. Theda wasn't one of the suspects—she had been on tour selling war bonds at the time of his murder.

But everyone heard how she opened her home and her heart to child star Lottie McPhee when the sixteen-year-old ran away from her fiendish stage mother. At one of Theda's parties, Lottie, already a notable drinker, first encountered the charming, thirtyish Montjoy, and both she and her mother made open threats on his life when he refused to marry her. Only after her suicide was it revealed that she had been forced to abort their child to preserve her pure image.

Hoping to mine this vein of scandal, I fortified myself with Dutch courage and approached Theda one night. She was surrounded by admirers of both sexes and all ages, all talking and laughing. Everyone was smoking and sipping a new cocktail she had invented. I stood near her, on the edge of the circle, smiling at the jokes I could hear and keeping my hands busy with my own cigarette and cocktail.

There was an anxious edge to the talk. Even back then, Hollywood was obsessed with youth. The actors and actresses in the group all had their diet and beauty tips to trade. Plastic surgery was new, and the risks were much debated. On this occasion, Jane Knowles (known as "America's mother" to casting agents) shuddered and let out her cigarette smoke with a gasp at the mere mention of the subject. "Please don't talk about it! Too terrifying." Lowering her voice, she continued, "You know what happened to Lucy Tucker."

Everybody knew. A child star still playing dimpled little girls in her early twenties, Lucy had been severely burned in a freak accident with a poorly ventilated fire. She survived, but her dimples and career did not. Influenced by sympathetic friends, including Theda, Lucy underwent reconstructive surgery, only to die from effects of the anesthesia.

There was an awkward pause at Jane's allusion to a scandal connected with our hostess. Jane's husband, an acidly witty gay director, broke it. "If I were you, my dear," he remarked, stubbing out his Turkish cigarette, "I should not count myself too safe. Even a mud bath can kill if you go into it packed to the gills with booze and pills."

There was general laughter, except from Jane, who only forced a smile. Then Aram Gregorian, a handsome Armenian refugee whose tailoring skills were in high demand, leered and said, "It's all very well to fix the face, but what about the body? These girls must understand. They cannot lie around eating sweets all day and expect the costume magically to contain their figures!"

"No indeed," Theda agreed. She lifted up her arm so that her diaphanous sleeve fell back to her shoulder, revealing the substantial muscle of her tanned arms. I sipped my drink, thinking of Amazons and *National Geographic*. "It's good to be strong," she said. Lowering her arm, she brought her cigarette holder to her lips, inhaling with deep relish.

"All very well for you, Theda," piped up a petite young woman I didn't know. "Your parts call for it. But I've just been cast as a starving beggar girl—again. If I gain even five pounds, I really will be starving and begging. So what's everybody's secret figure saver? Spill."

"Never have children," said Jane, at once.

"America's mother has spoken," pronounced her husband, to general laughter.

Then everyone had recommendations, from smoking to enemas to patent nostrums. Jane Knowles enthusiastically praised the occasional tapeworm pill, but in the end, most agreed with her ectomorph husband that cocaine was just as effective and much more fun.

I seized my opportunity. Adroitly turning so as to wedge myself into their circle, I raised my glass in a toast. "Hear, hear!" Before anyone else could collar the conversation, I turned to our hostess, who was giving me an amused smile. "But please tell us

149

your own opinion, Miss LaMorte. What do you recommend against the ravages of time?"

She threw her head back and laughed, her latest lungful of smoke issuing from the black cave of her mouth in an aromatic pall. Her admirers hushed, hanging on her words. At last she said, in a husky murmur, "I picked my poison long ago, my dears, and I invite you all to try it—but there will be few takers, I think. It is simply this: to brush so close to death that the world seems as false as a movie set." She paused and looked around. They waited for more, silent and motionless.

"That's it, friends," she said, releasing them from her spell with a wave of her cigarette. "Embrace danger. Then, and only then, you will be truly alive."

The awkward silence in the circle was filled in with party noises—indistinct talking and laughing, "The Alcoholic Blues" wafting from the jazz combo in the corner. Finally, Jane Knowles broke the tension with her horsey laugh, the petite actress gave a squeal and a little shiver and went in search of a refill, and Jane's husband lifted his glass and said, "Really, Theda, it's a shame the pictures can't talk. Half your talents are going to waste." Downing his drink, he took his wife's arm and ambled off toward his dealer.

One by one the others found reasons to leave until at last only Theda and I remained. I was excited. Something was about to happen, I sensed—something much bigger than an item in the gossip columns, though if I played my cards right, I might come away with that too. I remained casually at Theda's side, thinking with disdain of those lesser, departed mortals, too craven to take up the gauntlet she had thrown down. I, Frank Hartwell, would show her the stuff I was made of.

Unloading her glass on a passing tray, she suddenly grasped my jaw with her free hand and looked into my eyes. "I like you, kid," she said. "You got courage."

Just as abruptly, she released me. "So, you want to risk everything?" An amused smile played around her generous mouth.

I downed my drink. My throat felt dry suddenly. "Yes," I said, trying to sound bold, though my voice came out as a croak.

She appraised me, sucking her cigarette down to a nub in the holder. She let the smoke trickle out, narrowing her eyes against it. "You ever ride in a Bugatti?"

I almost dropped my glass. "You got a Bugatti? How? Where?" I gabbled, losing every shred of dignity. I had to stub out my cigarette in a nearby ashtray while I regained my composure.

When I straightened, she was still giving me that smile, which seemed to promise so much. "Come with me, Frank Hartwell," she said.

Resisting the urge to ask how she knew my name, I followed her down dim hallways, past curious domestic help, to a door opening into a courtyard. The garage was a modest brick building in the same Spanish colonial style as the house. It had large wooden double doors, and she let go of my hand to tug them open.

Before I could offer to help, she was standing in the doorway. A slight breeze stirred the folds of her gown and lifted her hair. "Welcome to Ali Baba's cave," she said, sweeping her arm toward the dark opening behind her.

I followed her in. She must have hit the lights, because I was suddenly dazzled, and not only by the brightness. There, in the middle of a newly poured cement floor, gleamed a sleek, silver torpedo of a car.

"It's a prototype," she said.

Everything felt like a dream, even the vaguely Russian way she rolled the "r" in "prototype." I approached and ran my fingers over the glossy finish and the ridged openings designed to ventilate the engine sleeping inches from my hand. "How fast?" I asked, in a reverent whisper.

Her face came close to mine, and I closed my eyes, breathing in French perfume, Turkish tobacco, and her own musky, animal smell. When she kissed me, the world fell away. I was under her spell, and could only brace against the car as she stoked my desire.

At last she drew back. Laying her cigarette holder on a shelf, she picked up two pairs of goggles and tossed one to me. "You'll need these."

We put them on. "Now," she said. "Turn the crank."

The engine roared almost as soon as I touched the lever. We smoked one more cigarette, waiting for the oil to warm, but the engine was too loud for conversation. Finally, I followed Theda around to the passenger side, and she extended an arm to me. I stared at it a second, unable to believe she was letting me drive this poem of an automobile, but recollecting myself, I supported her as she climbed lightly over the side of the cockpit and folded herself into her place. There was hardly even room for two. Her right arm, flung out behind my shoulders when I sat in the right-hand driver's seat, rested on the car's tail.

The engine seemed straining to test its power as I maneuvered out of the garage, into the courtyard, the drive, and the road. At last, shifting into higher gear, I sent the car leaping forward before settling it into a humming, popping flow of energy.

The drive was not conventionally romantic. Although we were so tightly wedged in the cockpit, we were separated by the gearbox, which quickly got hot, as did the floorboards by the foot pedals. Then again, between delicately operating the pedals, which felt like toothpicks to my American-man-sized feet, and hauling lustily on the steering wheel, not to mention maneuvering the outside shift lever, my limbs were fully occupied. Theda too was busy. It was especially important that she keep an eye on the fuel pressure. Our only physical contact was her outstretched arm behind me.

Yet psychologically, the two of us immediately meshed with the car and each other. We gave ourselves up to its demands, to the relentless roar and the hot, brimstone fumes of the engine, even to the stinging sand and debris the car threw into our faces. As we gained speed, the bumps and turns made Theda fly off her seat alarmingly, but I was so intensely occupied with the steering wheel that I couldn't even throw a protective arm out. Later, when I relaxed enough to turn my head in her direction, I saw that though she gripped the side of the car with her free hand, she was smiling into the bugs and grit.

We drove out along the freshly paved roads of the canyons. I wasn't entirely familiar with them, but I got along by following the headlight beams and Theda's occasional gestures. The car was exquisitely responsive, executing turns with precision, leaping up hills at a touch of the gas. I was its master, but at the same time, hurtling along on a rush of fuel-tainted air, bouncing and swaying between the hot gearbox and the low scuttle of the cockpit, I knew I was a hair's breadth from destruction. Theda was right—I did feel truly alive.

Near the top of a long ridge, we came to a straightaway carved into the crumbling canyon wall. To the left sheer rock loomed over us; to the right, a few low-growing bushes camouflaged a steep drop down to the stretch of palm-lined road that had brought us here. I was just coming to grips with the thought that one large rock could hurl me into the void when I felt Theda's hand tighten again on my shoulder. "Faster, Frank," she shouted, above the engine and the hot, rushing wind.

Ahead of us the lights picked out a clear stretch of road. There was no way to know what lay beyond in the darkness, but everything conspired to impel me forward—my need to prove myself, my desire for this fearless woman, my quest to transcend the myriad disappointments of my young adulthood. Above all, I was caught up in the moment—the three of us, her, me, the tube of metal streaking through the night, fused in a race toward destiny. I shifted gears again.

The Bugatti ate up the ground like a ravening beast. I clung grimly to the steering wheel. The soles of my shoes were so hot I worried they might melt, but I was determined to ride this tiger. I knew that Theda was right. After this, if I survived, nothing in life would ever be the same. The speedometer climbed from sixty to eighty in seconds. After that I couldn't tear my eyes from the road to look. All I knew was the roaring, stinking hell of the car, and Theda, her hand tight on my shoulder, her hair loose and streaming behind her in the night.

Then, out of the darkness, came the curve. A narrowing bend of the road disappeared around the sharp end of the rock wall, and ahead, beyond the bend, was a blackness even the lights of the car could not penetrate. Yet I was so drunk with speed and desire that even then my mind could not free itself from the insane mechanism of the car. My whole focus was on forcing my right arm, frozen in stiff terror, to move from the wheel to the shift lever.

Trapped in a fool's nightmare of slowed-down time and deluded attempts at logic, I downshifted and prepared to turn, a maneuver that, even at our belatedly decreasing speed, would bring swift, certain destruction. But at the last possible instant, as the darkness beyond the turn sprang forward to swallow us, my foot, acting on its own, found the brake toothpick. Instantly immobilized, the wheels locked and the car began to skid.

"Yes!" Theda shouted—but as we rapidly neared the turn and my hands remained frozen to the wheel, she yelled, "Steer!" and, when that failed, reached over with her strong left arm and wrenched the wheel. "Now steer!" she commanded again, as we slid impossibly into the turn.

The car's light, compact design made it amazingly maneuverable, even with the brakes on. The rear wheels drifted dangerously toward the void—and the next moment we were around the bend.

All I had to do was release the brake and steer out of the skid, but I failed. Seeing our trajectory and my paralysis, Theda tried to help again, but the wheel was stubborn, she was at a bad angle, and probably my grip hindered her. Also, my foot, still operating independently, refused to leave the brake. At least she managed to prevent our colliding nose first with the canyon wall on the left. Instead there was a hideous scraping and screeching and a bright spray of sparks, followed by a sickening jolt and the sound of the axel buckling as the front left-hand side of the car, now moving at a considerably reduced speed, hit an outcropping of rock.

My forehead collided with the windshield, which rose like the rack of a music stand behind the steering wheel. But I struck it at an angle, so that though I was stunned and felt blood trickling over my right eye, I did not lose consciousness. I heard the engine cough and die, and at the same time saw the lights go out.

Theda's side had no windshield. I flung off my goggles, prepared to help her, but evidently she had fared better than I, because she was standing on the seat, towering over me. The other side of the car was too close to the rock wall for her to exit that way.

"Get out," she said, her voice like a steel blade. I scrambled out as best I could.

She waved away my efforts to help her down and leaped lightly onto the road. I wanted to offer to pay for the damage, but my throat was dry and tight, and we both knew I couldn't afford it. "Where are you going?" was all I could manage as Theda stalked indifferently away into the darkness ahead.

She turned back and pointed behind her to a light off to the side of the road. "I'll go up to Saul Hayman's place," she said. "They'll take care of me and the car. But I don't think you'd be welcome. They don't like nobodies."

She turned her back on me, then thought better of it and faced me once more. "Frank. I like you, so I'm giving you some advice. Stop playing games with me. Get away from here, get a job, find a nice girl, be happy. I don't matter as much as you think."

She turned again and began walking toward the producer's mansion. Still shaking, I lit a cigarette and watched until she disappeared into the darkness, leaving me alone with the wrecked car—a metaphor for all my hopes and dreams.


Eventually I took her advice. Oddly enough, it was only after I gave up on fame and glory that my dreams started to come true.

I got a job doing the crime beat on a newspaper in a town south of Los Angeles. Although it seemed like a sleepy little community on the surface, Prohibition changed all that, and I covered some pretty colorful stories—bootlegging, corrupt city officials, even a gangland shootout. In the process, I met a warm Italian lady, Maria, who was willing to take a gamble on a scruffy reporter. We got married, had Vita, and lived in happy poverty over her father's restaurant, where we had first met.

I'd like to say I forgot all about Theda, but that wouldn't be true. The trauma and humiliation of that night never quite left me. I was haunted by dreams of car wrecks and tall sorceresses controlling me against my will. Once or twice I even thought I caught a glimpse of Theda rubbernecking at the gorier crime scenes I covered, but it seemed unlikely she'd be slumming so far from Hollywood. I lumped these sightings in with my nightmares, chalking the lot up to my unsettled mind, and tried to cope by throwing myself into work and family.

By the time the talkies came in, a couple of my news stories had garnered national attention, and I'd had some hardboiled fiction published as well. A friend of mine from the old days showed one of my efforts to a producer, who liked it, and the rest, as they say, is history. Hollywood was desperate for people who could write colorful dialogue, and I fit the bill.

Of course it crossed my mind that I might see Theda socially again, but just around the time we moved to Hollywood, she retired. Her melodramatic gestures were unfashionable in the new style of the talkies, and her sexpot allure raised alarm as the forces of censorship began rumbling toward the Production Code.

She kept her mystery alive to the end, though. No one knew where or precisely when she had gone. The wildest rumors came during the war years. She was variously said to be spying, possibly as a double agent, for all the Axis powers except Japan. A British actor I knew who had fled Singapore swore Theda had been trapped there and likely confined in a POW camp.


After the war, for many years I thought of Theda only in passing. I didn't even dream about her anymore. When I wasn't working, I was busy watching Vita grow up. Eventually she became a physical therapist, sensibly rejecting Hollywood glitz.

Then one day there was a small headline in *Variety* and the major newspapers: "Vamp of the Silent Screen, Six Others Dead in Fatal Crash." A small plane Theda had been in crashed in the mountains. She remained mysterious even in death. To this day her date of birth has a question mark next to it, her birthplace remains "unknown," and her profession is listed only as "silent film vamp." Reading of her death, I felt a pang for the object of my youthful obsession, but at least there could be no further speculation about her supposed supernatural powers. I was confident that my involvement with her had ended.


In the seventies, another chapter of my life closed when Hollywood dropped me as abruptly as, decades ago, it had embraced me. My scripts were "square," no longer "where it was at." Nobody "dug" them, and the Oscars fobbed me off with a Lifetime Achievement Award.

Still, I thought, I had Maria. We enjoyed puttering and traveling. One night, however, Maria had trouble keeping her balance when she walked. I drove her over to the emergency room at Cedars-Sinai, but after checking her over they said she probably just had a bad migraine and sent us home.

I tucked her into bed and got her a cup of tea. I remember she was especially vivacious, imagining all the therapeutic "tortures" Vita would dream up for her if she couldn't walk right. She insisted her head didn't hurt a bit. She felt "odd," she said, but it was nothing a good night's sleep wouldn't cure.

"Just hold me, Frank," she said, so I did. She went to sleep quietly, and eventually so did I.

In the middle of the night, I thought I woke up because I had thrown an arm out to Maria's side of the bed and found it empty. It took a second for my eyes to adjust to the dim light, and then I cried out in fright.

Theda was standing over the space where Maria should have been—the old Theda of the old, wild days, dressed in her buckskin costume for *Hiawatha*. Her hair was bound into braids in an unconvincing attempt to make her look "Indian," and makeup darkened her face. She carried a bow and quiver and wore the stern, wise look Hollywood deemed appropriate for "good Indians."

"*Shh!*" she said, putting a finger to her lips. "There's nothing to be afraid of. I'm not hunting *you*." She turned away.

I leaped out of bed and followed her, shouting the kind of stock things I would never put in a script: "Why are you here? Where's Maria? What have you done with her? You're supposed to be dead!"

In the doorway I stumbled over my wife's lifeless form and, as I later came to believe, awoke from my nightmare. By the time I remembered to look for Theda, she was gone. According to the doctor, Maria had a massive stroke, which ER had misdiagnosed in its early stages. "Don't worry," he said. "She probably never knew what hit her."

## OCEAN BREEZE, SANTA MONICA, OCT. 28, 1980

Vita was right: this place is not so bad, as nursing homes go. All the usual amenities, only nicer because I'm lucky enough to have some money. The ocean view is inspiring —it's comforting to connect with the infinite vista of water stretching away to the horizon while you contemplate your own passage toward the great beyond.

Something interesting: one of the nurses is Mary LaMorte. I noticed the resemblance right away, and she confirmed Theda was her maternal grandmother. Of course I didn't ask her how she ended up with the LaMorte surname. But I never even heard Theda had a child, much less a child out of wedlock. You'd think that would have merited at least a tiny notice. And then her daughter the same, though no one would take any notice if she wasn't famous. I'm not one to judge, much less visit the parents' sins on their children. Just found it curious.

Luckily, Nurse LaMorte is not much like Theda, apart from looks, so I'm not troubled by the connection. She was all business while taking my vitals, though I couldn't help wondering if she ever lets all that wild hair down the way Theda used to.

NOV. 22

Life has mostly settled into a routine here. In the mornings I write this journal and a few odds and ends, like my account of Theda, for my amusement. In the afternoons I read the paper, do the crossword, play bridge, and write letters. Vita visits every weekend.

There is a fair amount of interference from the quacks and their nurses, of course. For the most part, I'm resigned to it, but I may have to lodge a complaint against Mary LaMorte. She keeps invading my suite in the middle of the night to check me. I don't think this is standard procedure for a healthy inmate here. To be honest, the only reason I haven't complained already is that when she checks my blood pressure during the day, she smells good, like flowers, not antiseptic, and she has a pleasant way of brushing her breasts against me every now and then. You wouldn't deny a few moments of pleasure to an old widower, would you?


NOV. 26

Reconnected with an old acquaintance, Sarah Shulman. That wasn't her stage name—America knew her as Mary Lee Adams, if they knew her at all. She mainly played waifs in the silents, and never the lead. I wouldn't have recognized her, but she remembered me, all right. She's thinner than ever—as fragile as a bird—and seems to live mainly in the past, poor soul.

I was having coffee in the sunroom when she came over to my table. Ocean Breeze is emptying out for Thanksgiving, so she was the only other resident there midmorning. I could tell she was a little lonely, and I didn't have the heart to turn her away. Besides, as people from your youth start dropping off, you become fond of the ones that are left, even if you weren't close before. You have a shared past with them, a bond that gets rarer with each passing day.

So we got chatting. I soon realized that she must have been the young woman at Theda's the night of the accident who asked about weight-loss methods. Like so many others, she'd retired when the talkies came—just settled down and got married—but she kept up with her Hollywood friends, so after we'd gone over our families and where we planned to spend the holiday, we talked about our mutual acquaintance.

Almost immediately, she brought up Theda's granddaughter. Lowering her coffee cup, she cocked her head, looked at me with her bright, birdlike eyes, and asked me what I thought of Nurse LaMorte.

I could see why she'd left acting—her ploy was transparent. She was concerned about Mary and wanted to find out if I was concerned as well. I said something about Nurse LaMorte being a little "overzealous," and Sarah was off.

"Overzealous!" she exclaimed. She reached over and tapped my knee. "I suppose you call trying to put a pillow over my face 'overzealous.'" She spoke in hushed tones, and her brown eyes were wide. "What's more, I saw her going into Anna Petrov's

room, and the next day—" her bird claw hand traced the path of a rolling gurney—
"the very next morning, gone."

Seeing I still hesitated, incredulous, she held up her hands, palms out, to forestall
objections. "Oh, don't think I expect anyone to believe one old lady. But *you've* seen
enough of Nurse LaMorte to be disturbed. Maybe others have too." She leaned forward
conspiratorially again. "I'm going to find out who they are, and then we'll go together
and make a complaint. You in?"

I smiled, thinking this scene was a great parody of the gangster scripts I used to
write, but I assured Sarah that I would back her up with my own experience and would
be on my guard in the meantime.

"Thank you," she said, wringing my hand. "Shalom."

"Shalom," I said. I watched as she pushed herself out of her chair with her stick-
like arms and trundled determinedly away with her walker.


DEC. 1

Wonderful Thanksgiving weekend with Vita, her husband, and the grandkids, but
returned to some sad news. Sarah passed away peacefully at her son's home sometime
after Thanksgiving dinner. At least that puts Nurse LaMorte in the clear. Probably
Sarah's suffocation story was just a bad dream.


DEC. 2

Suddenly I understand so many things. Vita would say, "What took you so long?"

Last night I went to sleep thinking about Sarah and Nurse LaMorte and Theda and
the old days. I was dreaming about an earthquake when I woke to find Nurse LaMorte
sitting down next to me on the bed.

Her hair flowed over her shoulders the way Theda's used to, and her nurse's
uniform was unbuttoned suggestively. She took my hand and slid it inside her bra. I felt
the soft warmth of her breast against my palm. "Come on, Frank," she said, in Theda's
throaty, seductive tones. "We both know it's no fun to be old. Let me take away your
troubles."

I'd fantasized about just such a moment, of course, but now I struggled. This felt all
wrong, and not just because Sarah had warned me. I felt again the same engulfing
terror I had dreamed so often. My mind replayed the car careening toward the cliff,
nothing ahead but certain destruction.

I'm not as strong as I used to be. I freed my hand, but I couldn't budge her as she
leaned over me, her body weighing me down, the flowery scent of her perfume dulling
my wits. Perhaps she sensed a core of determination in my struggles, I don't know, but
suddenly she seemed to relent. She sat up and buttoned her dress. I could only lie there,
looking up at her, gulping air like a drowning man.

"It's all right," she said (and now a touch of Theda's unplaceable accent crept into

157

her speech). "When you are ready, I will fold you in my arms, and you will find your heart's desire."

I got no sleep when she was gone. Not wanting to risk meeting Nurse LaMorte, I waited until the day nurses were on duty and made a complaint to one of them right away. Lizzy Flagler is a nice young woman who talks about her kids a lot and laughs at my jokes. She was concerned at how pale and shaken I looked, and indignant that a fellow nurse had besmirched her profession. As I recounted what had happened, her mouth made a thinner and thinner line.

When I finished, she burst out, "I'm so sorry, Frank. I don't blame you for being upset. Are you all right? You look pale."

She made me sit down and gave me a cup of coffee while she went to check the records. But in just a few minutes she returned and sat down next to me. "I'm sorry, Frank, but no Mary LaMorte has ever worked here. I checked."

Of course, then she was insufferably concerned, and I had to make an appointment with the head quack to appease her. I hid my own agitation as best I could so as not to alarm her any more than I already had. The whole episode must have been a bad dream, I insisted.

As soon as I could get away, I came back here, to the sunroom looking out over the ocean where Sarah and I had our talk. I'm surprised myself at how calm and clear I feel now. Oh, not about "reality." At my age it's not so surprising that whatever grip I once had over *that* slippery concept is failing. I have less understanding than ever of who Theda really was or is.

But I know she was right when she told me to forget about her, that she wasn't as important as I thought. Sure, I never really gave up trying to conquer her, to show her I could "really live" in my own way. We're all like silent movie stars: little lumps of star-dust, flickering across the screen in transient bids for immortality. But mostly I didn't live my life for that. I lived it for Maria and Vita and the grandkids. For all the things we touched and felt and saw and tasted together; for the kind of love that gets so old sometimes you think maybe it's gone, but it never is; and for all the memories and things you wish you could share when it really is over.

I need to call Vita and the kids today and remind them I love them, even if they think it's embarrassing. Before too long, I'll be too tired to struggle with Nurse LaMorte anymore. I'll reach out to her, and she'll fold me in her arms. It's simple. Nothing to be afraid of. In that moment, when she gratifies my heart's desire, the projector will snap off, and the house will go dark for the last time.

# A MURDER OF CROWS

## C. C. RAVEN

*"It's a good day*
*when I wake up vertical*
*and I ride my convertible*
*along the Monterey Bay.*
*It's a Good Day!"*

At the pinnacle of the Monterey peninsula lies the quiet, seemingly idyllic village we call Pacific Grove, the last hometown. The seaside village, a town of redwoods and cypress trees and the Monterey Pine, and a charming Victorian town in its own right, is host and home to not only humans, but to clusters of Monarch butterflies overwintering on the eucalyptus trees, a herd of reindeer (no, plain deer), antlered stags strutting by like so many Donners and Blitzens, families of raccoons skittering along tall Monterey pine branches in play, red foxes (vixen showing their pups around the local golf course), and a peaceful little cemetery, El Carmelo, with a murder of crows. Not a literal murder, of course, but the equivalent of a gaggle of geese or a scurry of squirrels.

This little murder of crows consists of about twenty birds, particular to Pacific Grove due to white feather stripes on their wings. The leader of the murder has three feather stripes on his wings. I dubbed him "Sergeant." The first time I saw him, he was riding on the back of a stag who had roses tangled in its antlers, the residue of a morning's breakfast on the graves of the cemetery.

The rest of the crows have single white feather stripes on their wings, like "privates," and I've fattened them all on a steady diet of raw peanuts, which they have learned to catch quite aerobatically, in so doing demonstrating both individual styles and unique athletic abilities.

They have developed a game I call "Drop the Peanut," similar in some ways to soccer or rugby, where the "referee" flies up high with a peanut and drops it down below. The rest of the murder fly along from one end of the cemetery to the other, cawing in Morse crow and planning their strategy. Thus, the game begins. They swoop upside down and sideways, diving like falcons and trying to "catch the peanut."

In another sort of game, the whole flock will take to the air, following my red convertible Mustang like a bunch of black kites, around the cemetery and along the ocean by our Lighthouse at Point Pinos, catching tossed peanuts all along the way. This can be a little disconcerting to tourists unexpectedly coming upon the sight of twenty crows following a red Mustang. They point. They photograph. And sometimes they duck for cover.

One such day, I was parked by the ocean across from the lighthouse. The whole murder of crows was sitting opposite, along the picket fence by the lighthouse, waiting for peanuts. Sergeant, who literally "keeps the rest in line" along the fence, sat in the number one spot and let no others pass. He gabbled and squawked at them to keep the proper pecking order.

That particular day, a tourist on his new bike came riding by. Seeing the crowd of crows lined up, he tried to scare them off, waving his arms and shouting loudly, as he passed by.

I decided to make a quick U-turn and follow a bit behind the biker. I was soon joined by a large black cloud, hovering ominously above.

Alarmed, the biker began to ride as fast as he could to escape the menacing crows, but we followed him closely for a ways, until the biker took shelter under some cypress trees. But then the crows promptly landed all over the cypresses above, creating a rather Hitchcockian moment of terror for the biker.

We finally took pity and all departed, leaving one puzzled tourist to wonder about the murderous crows of Pacific Grove!

# HOW CANALS ARE TAUGHT TO EAT

## SYDNEY MEEKER

No one should have introduced water to California's Central Valley.

Everyone who has ever lived there was tricked into believing that things could live there, that the earth itself did not despise their presence and the water they brought with them. They should've noticed the dark water in the summer, spreading from grapevine to grapevine, long tan rows of ruts slowly filling with that deeply unpleasant water. Even the eucalyptus and the cottonwoods bend away from it; even the living things that know the earth better than we do tremble in its presence.

There are no rivers in the Central Valley, only a spider's web of canals through these wide plains where no one should live. Every twelve or fourteen country blocks there's a pool, clear and clean and chlorinated. The bees and the people all flock to them in the summertime, fighting one another for use of any given watering hole. Even the bees know to avoid the canals.

"Rafael knew the water better than anyone," little Gabriela told her Papi. "He was the best swimmer in the world. He went swimming every day, always, at school and at home." With her little hands, she grabbed at the edge of his shirt, imploring him to listen. She had been taught to honor the word of her father and mother, but this time she couldn't accept it. "It's impossible. You're lying. He couldn't have drowned."

Her mother straightened clothes hangers for a living, as there were no houses to clean in the valley—only trailers. Her father drove trucks larger than those trailers. Rafael, Gabriela's older brother, was her world: a lush, vibrant, welcoming world that the central valley earth beneath her feet denied her. For all eight years she'd been alive, she watched her brother's form as he walked the mile and a half in the dry heat to a pool so generously offered up by their neighbors. Every evening, he'd return when night arrived all in his swim clothes, and in his room stood trophy after regional swim trophy.

To her, he was like a fish, so she sometimes called him *Pez*. She knew, more sincerely than anything, that fish simply do not drown on accident. Every question she asked pained her mother dearly, deeply, but she needed them answered. In their yard—a barren plot of dirt where nothing could grow—lay wire after wire of straightened hanger. Another fell on top of the pile as her mother straightened it, like a log onto a lumber pile. "Mija, your brother is gone. He knew he shouldn't swim in the canals, and yet he did. There are grates under there, things get stuck in there." She couldn't say it plainly. "There's too much pressure and it's too hard to get back out."

"Except that he could swim past anything! If he's really dead, why can't I see him? Is he in the ground with Pacific already?" Pacific was another, long-dead fish, named for the nearest body of water several hour's drive away. The matter was simple to Gabriela: if Pacific died and could be buried, then why not her brother?

"I told you, things get stuck down there. No one can go down there or they'll get stuck, too." Her voice, even in the dry heat, was a wave of calm in the face of immense tragedy.

"If he really died, why can't we drain the canal and get the body?"

"We would need help from the police, and you know we can't call the police, mijita. He's going to have to stay under there." Her hands moved rhythmically over the wire. With her calm came an aura of responsibility and deep-seated guilt. She had known, when she arrived in the Central Valley, when she hoped to raise children in the area, that the canals were just as hungry as the people. "You stay away from the water, no matter how hot it is. Tell me you understand, mijita."

"I understand," Gabriela replied. The little girl thought she knew better than her mother. In her worn-down sandals, she ran to American and Chestnut, where the Washington Colony Canal intersected two roads. The dark water lay still; she had been warned countless times that there was a deadly current beneath. She tossed a rock or two in, then a eucalyptus leaf. It swirled down beneath the bridge. After she instinctively looked both ways (there were no cars for miles), she ran across to track the leaf.

When it didn't surface, she narrowed her eyes. Why had her brother swam here? There was something she didn't know, something that other people weren't telling her. No one wanted to tell her.

So she set to find out for herself. She scoured her school library, and finding nothing, went to the public library. The libraries—and schools, and pools—were all part of the trick; people should not live there. The earth knew it, the trees knew it, the water enforced it. But no one told the child, and she did not understand the discoveries she made.

From books and newspapers, she discovered that child after child had drowned in that canal grate since it was put in some thirty years prior. But that was no cause for conversation—every canal grate had claimed someone's kid, someone's pet, someone's cousin. How else is the canal expected to eat?

But she thought she knew better. Slowly, she pulled one wire away from her mother's pile every day. She made a chain, one hanger looped and twisted over the other, until she couldn't carry the bundle without a wagon. She gathered graham crackers, juice, aguita, *pan,* and a water jug. *Only the important food,* she thought. She threw the chain, the food, and a disposable underwater camera she stole from her uncle into her little red wagon and was off before her parents woke.

Spangled with hoofprints and the occasional worker's boot, the path along the canals saw little wind and still displayed her brother's footprints in the sand. She found the journey much easier than the first time she took it, especially with the addition of well-timed snack breaks. *Maybe I'll make this trip every day,* she thought. *Maybe I can be just as good a swimmer as he is, and then I won't need a chain to swim in a canal.*

She arrived at American and Chestnut just as trucks were taking to the roads. It was already hot; heatwaves shimmered along the asphalt and the vineyards. The poles at the end of the grapevine rows made for a sturdy place to wrap her hanger-wire chain. As she looped it around herself, she considered what she might see: a body held in place by the force of water. If she could get pictures, and come back out, then she could convince her parents to retrieve him and bury him. *If I don't find him in there,* she thought, *then everyone's been lying to me.*

Set aside, her sandals left little imprints on the roadside. It burned her soles to remain on the hot sand, so she slipped along the edge of the canal, kicking up thick clouds of dust. She poked at the water with her foot—it was cold several inches in, but its skin was already warm. Her eyes shut, she dipped her head under, and then back up, always keeping a tight grasp on her chain.

After briefly submerging the camera, and making sure it was on, she dove under. Dirt and specks of eucalyptus and grape leaves floated in the water, leaving her with barely a foot of visibility. The water pulled her toward the grate, but she held tight to her mother's chain.

She came up for air one last time before plunging in again, this time ready to at least make it to the grate. The water shoved her into the dark maw and suddenly the oppressive sunlight was gone; no light for her, or for the camera. Despite the push of the water she held tight, careful to always be a few pulls away from air.

For a moment, she couldn't tell if she were upside down or right-side up, and she reached out to grab hold of something, anything, other than the chain. She hit the grate suddenly, spewing bubbles from her mouth. In the black liquid she reached out her hand and found the grate. She couldn't even see it, but she recognized the material in her palm by touch. Her mind showed her unconscious recollections of the touch; pulling pieces off ham at Thanksgiving, a stolen wing from a Super Bowl party, a decayed mouse in the grapevine. She knew this touch—it was unmistakably bone. Yet the bone-grate seemed somehow different than other bones she'd touched—it had a slippery film over it, not quite like algae or moss, but like something familiar. Something she knew. Something she had touched every day.

In the cold dark, she remembered putting her tongue against her new teeth, too big for her mouth. She remembered biting into a snow cone, the way her teeth grated against the neon-colored slush. That was the sensation—the layer of spittle over her teeth. As she felt along the grate, fascinated and frightened all at once, there was a tiny movement in the water. The water shifted, the darkness pushing her closer and closer to the long, crisscrossed bones. Between the numbing, cold pressure against her skin and the water's white-noise burbling, she was in a kind of deprivation chamber, unclear of whether she could believe even her own sense of touch. When the bone-grate began to shake, she lost any doubt of what she was touching. The only thing she could feel then was panic and terror, unable to understand what was happening to her. She let out a long soundless scream, spewing only bubbles into the dark cavern.

If someone had been watching her—and nobody was—they would've seen the chain pulled so hard that it nearly tugged the grapevine pole loose from the earth. They would've seen the hanger-wire chain shudder and shiver, sending out quivering ripples along the black water's surface. They would've seen a flourish of bubbles break the surface of the water, the hanger-wire snap with a loud metallic resonance, and a disposable camera float away downstream. But no one did—there was no one for miles.

And the canals would keep it that way.

# THE LAST ROYAL

## GABRIEL VALJAN

The most reclusive Hollywood starlet since Garbo had picked him, Tara de Clare acquiesced to give William Symonds the interview.

The invitation came not by email, social media, or over the phone; it arrived by snail mail. Ms. de Clare disliked computers and cell phones. She neither owned those modern devices nor believed in them.

Bill returned from lunch to find the staff waiting, gathered around his desk, the 4x5 envelope propped up against his monitor, the sender's initials in Parisian font on the back of the envelope exposed to him. He rather enjoyed his moment since he was a junior-varsity scrub in the eyes of the office crowd, the last of the newsroom tribe in a town that ate and discarded celebrity and commoner alike.

With the Academy Award presenter's slow stare into his audience and even slower tearing of the envelope, he extracted the piece of paper inside. The crowd edged forward. He quickly scanned what she had written in India ink with a fountain pen. He admired the distinctive penmanship before refolding and slipping the note back into the envelope.

"What does it say?" one colleague said. "Is it a Yes or No?" another asked.

"A Yes." They cheered.

"Conditions?" the editor demanded.

"No photographers. No recording devices."

The crowd booed and dispersed. A solo assignment for him, all the glory.

Twenty-eight-year-old Tara de Clare was Hollywood royalty, the last of her kind with the name, cachet, and pedigree that rivaled the Barrymores or Fondas. Her family was Old Hollywood, harking back to a time when women had both written and directed films before the immigrant boys had muscled in and taken over the desert town. The De Clares were not native Angeleños; they hailed from New England stock and claimed that members of one branch of the family tree had been hanged in the Salem witch trials.

She had selected him. Her latest film was to premiere in six weeks, and he had the exclusive, the scoop. His article would be above the fold.


On the appointed day, minutes early, the driver dropped him off in front. He pressed the button on the intercom. A sepulchral voice answered and Bill stated his name and purpose. After the buzz, the gate opened just enough for him to walk through it. Sideways.

Her house in the Hollywood Hills was secluded, an austere villa with tinted glass and a terra cotta tile roof. He walked up the long black driveway, which terminated in a horseshoe in front of the main door, as if the entrance and exit were a snake eating its own tail.

He had not detected any movement behind the blinds on the way up, and he noticed that not one weed spoiled any of her greenery, although it seemed so politically incorrect that she would have a Negro jockey in equestrian pants and jacket, a deer slayer cap on his head, on her lawn.

The door opened just as he was about to knock. "Mr. William Symonds, I presume."

A butler, as tall, serious, and ancient as Alfred from the original *Batman* series, stood there in a tuxedo. He offered his hand, which confused Bill.

"Your jacket, sir."

Bill shifted the pad of paper under one arm to work each arm and shoulder free of his blazer. He reached for the pen clipped inside his breast pocket, but Alfred had taken the garment and folded it over his arm.

"Per madam's instructions, I assume that you do not have any recording devices on your person."

"I do not."

Bill didn't know why he felt compelled not to use contractions. "The invitation did not stipulate No pen and No paper. What am I supposed to use?"

"I trust you are in full possession of your faculties. I'd advise you to use them. If medieval troubadours could recite romances from memory, I don't see why you can't do the same with a simple interview. This way, please."

The long walk proved there was more house than Bill had surmised. He passed room after room. Artwork lined the main hallway. The heavy wooden frames would kill a man if they fell during an earthquake. Alfred led a slow train, so Bill peeked inside one room. Antique silver frames and photographs. He recognized the photographers: George Hurrell, Sid Avery, and Max Autrey. He caught up to Alfred, his steps as fast as a cat burglar, in time for them to mount a steep staircase.

Alfred rapped on a closed door once they summited.

"Any advice?" Bill asked.

"It is not appropriate to my station to give advice, sir."

"You do know we are in the twentieth-first century? Help a guy out."

"If you insist, then I recommend the following in this order: manners above all things; wit within good taste; no sarcasm or profanity and, under no circumstance, flatter her. The lady's intellect is the razor's edge, a far sharper one than you or I will ever possess over several lifetimes. If that will be all, sir, I would suggest that you do not keep her waiting."

In other words, Tara de Clare possessed Hemingway's built-in bullshit detector.

Bill went in. Two empty chairs awaited him. The table was next to a railing that overlooked a garden. He looked around. No one. He heard her voice. Confused, he searched again. Nothing. The voice again, this time from behind.

"You can tell a lot about a man when he walks into a room, more so when he is in unfamiliar territory."

Tara de Clare stood there. All of five-foot three, a full head and shoulders shorter than Bill, and about forty pounds less. Small, deceptively delicate, she looked tenacious as a flower that could survive long desert nights and the Santa Ana winds. Dressed in white linen, Tara talked as she walked around him.

"The unexpected reveals three things. Character. Vulnerability. Adaptability."

She extended her hand. She expected him to take it and kiss the back of it. He did. He pulled out her chair for her. She looked over her shoulder as a way of thanking him. He asked her if he could sit down. She nodded.

At twenty-eight, Tara de Clare appeared and acted very retro. A deeper shade of blonde hair was parted to the side, a Thirties-style curl thrown across her forehead, and her eyebrows were tweezed into a thin line. Tara possessed the De Clare family cheekbones and hypnotic eyes. Then that voice.

"I am Tara de Clare. You are William Symonds."

"You're one mysterious lady."

"Hardly, Mr. Symonds. Reserved and private, yes, but not an enigma, I can assure you. You have to draw the proverbial line in the sand in this town, with the paparazzi and all."

He tried not to stare at her lips, her perfect skin. He looked away.

"Those bougainvillea down there." She peered over the railing.

"What about them?"

"They're like ivy, except with thorns. They show up where you least expect them, which makes them a nuisance and difficult to tame in your garden; they'll climb and crowd the face of a building until there's nothing left of it."

"Not unlike the press or public, unless you establish boundaries."

"A man for metaphors. I've read your column. You must think I'm like the bougainvillea because my family name is synonymous with ambition and overcoming everything in its path. Or perhaps, you think I have thorns."

She let out a relaxed laugh. Nice teeth, natural, and not pristine or perfect like the ones found on the plastic beauties the studios minted. He chose to remain silent, and let her think what she wanted.

"I think I like you, William. May I call you Bill?" He nodded. "See here, Bill, there's the old canard in this town that when people stop talking about you is when you should start to worry. My thinking runs contrarian to the adage."

Her fingers tapped the table. Perhaps she craved a cigarette.

"I'm no diva," she said. "I'm paid well to do a job I love, and I do it to the best of my abilities. I can't rest on my family name. Sure, people will have things to say about me, not so nice things, but I have two words for such people, and I think you know what those two words would be."

"I have no doubt. Shall we talk about your new film?"

"Not yet. I'd like to get to know you better. Consider it foreplay, which is a lot more fun than the main event." Bill hadn't expected that, and it must've showed because she said, "The arched eyebrow is cliched. Don't act so shocked."

"Surprised, not shocked. You're a candid woman."

"And you're not that much older than I, and I'm sure that you've heard worse, or are those virgin ears stapled to your head?"

Bill just smiled. The best interviews were when the subject talked content. His job became similar to a gardener's: give the material direction and some shape so there is no ramble to the rose. Tara was some rose: pretty to look at, and nice to smell. He couldn't place the perfume.

"It's Casma Caswell-Massey. The perfume, if you were wondering," she said. "Bet you didn't you know ESP runs in my family?"

"Thought that was a legend. Color for the trade magazines for the fans."

"Don't be so quick to dismiss it," she said. "My grandmother took great pride in the fact that Houdini couldn't debunk her. She had the gift from a young age. She predicted his death. Not many people know that. Did you?"

"I've heard some of the family lore, but not that particular nugget."

"Golly, she was quite the bucket, with moxie, too."

Bill gave thought to what he'd tell the editor, if Tara de Clare didn't discuss the film. He figured he could steer her into a conversation about it, if he dug into family history. Get the story from that angle, he thought. She was fresh, vibrant, and odd in her own way. Who used words like golly and moxie these days? Tara, who acted in front of the screen before she was wearing a bra, was not linked to any scandals, nor had she done one stint in rehab and little to nothing was known about her sex life; rather remarkable for a woman from a family that had both closets and skeletons to spare. There was also that De Clare predilection of retiring early from the screen.

"I have heard of your grandmother's escapades and your mother's adventures, romantic and otherwise," he said.

This was the direction he would take with her. He saw the light in her eyes, and she had this most adorable dimple in her chin. He pressed forward.

"I'm sorry to hear about your mother's passing."

"What can you do? We all have to die sometime. Dying is part of the job description. My mother took the shortcut, the expressway, even by De Clare standards. Know why we kept the funeral private and out of the public eye?"

"No idea."

"Debauchery and decadence are a sensational lede for any newspaper, I suppose, but it doesn't look pretty in the casket. That whole James Dean's saying of 'Live Fast, Die Young, and Leave a Beautiful Corpse' is utter tripe. Do you know which movie he lifted that line from?"

"*Knock on Any Door* with John Derek and Humphrey Bogart. Nicholas Ray, 1949, though the credit should go to a letter the *Riverside Daily Press* ran in 1920."

"A newspaper? Why, Mr. Symonds, you've impressed me."

A door opened. Alfred appeared with a silver tray, two champagne flutes on it. He walked with a muscular determination, determined those glasses would still have bubbles in them when they arrived at the table. Tara and Bill, like the mistress and lord of the manor, stopped talking. Alfred said something to her in French and she responded with what sounded like an order for some food.

"I forgot you attended the Lycée Français de Los Angeles."

"Twelve years, not counting preschool. You are a man who has done his research. I'm certain you are aware of the other family tradition. Mother insisted on the Grand Tour before university, so I would never do anything so vulgar as Spring Break in Palm Springs. She may have had her problems, but you'd never catch her in an uncompromising photograph, or wearing a thong. Please, let's enjoy some of our champagne before we have some hors d'oeuvres."

They clinked and tilted glasses. In the breathless air the scent of honeysuckle drifted into the room. The cold champagne tickled his nose. She drank it like a seasoned pro, in appreciation of its effervescence, its clean, dry taste.

Alfred returned with another tray. The bubbly made Bill think of champagne paper and that made him think of the bougainvillea beneath him, how the red leaves resembled delicate tissue paper. Alfred set down a dish between them. He identified the items on lace doilies in French without any translation, before he refreshed the flutes of champagne.

"You admire the bougainvillea, don't you?"

"Was I obvious, or is it the family ESP?"

"You like to tease, but you also have manners. I like that. My butler gave you great advice. Dare I ask what else he told you?"

Another thing. He must be transparent, he thought.

"I don't betray something said in confidence."

"And loyal. Touché."

Tara pressed the flute of champagne against her cheek. She held the glass stem as if it were her scepter. A small silver bracelet encircled her wrist.

"You've almost got that Jimmy Stewart aw-shucks humility down pat," she said. "This 'I don't betray confidences' is a rather ingenious way to draw me out. Sure you're not more than a journalist?"

Bill tried not to slurp the mousse purée of something-or-other off the curled spoon. "Not trying to lure you into anything," he said. "I've left it to your discretion as to what we'll discuss. As for my line of work, journalism provides a decent living. You like performing and I like writing."

"With every shiny penny, there's always a tarnished side."

"Depends on whether you live clean, or you hide dirt well. All a matter of intelligence, observation, and ingenuity."

"Or influence, money, and power," she said.

"Or heredity, environment, and discipline. Your family history is filled with alcoholism, drugs, mental instability, and crazy affairs, and yet it's wild with staggering accomplishments. Emmys, Oscars, and the like."

She rotated her champagne. "What about you, Bill? Do you hide secrets well?"

"I'm one generation away from farm country. I live the dull life."

She took that sip. She was quiet for a moment, those pale eyes serious now. "Which is why I picked you—not for the dull part, but for your integrity, if such a thing exists these days."

"Jaded, are we?" He offered her the last of the hors d'oeuvres. She pushed her plate forward. He placed it on her plate for her.

"Jaded, no; cautious, yes. I have a house full of secrets; it goes with the name, with the legacy, with the honorific of 'Hollywood royalty.'" Bill's fingers rested on the base of his own glass. Her hand reached across the table. She laid her fingers on his and asked, "You don't seem interested in your champagne. May I finish it?"

"You are the hostess."

"You wouldn't find it rude... or too intimate?"

Bill moved the glass in front of her. "I'll trade it for a secret."

"Only if you don't print it. Promise?" She smiled. "You could save it for your memoirs."

"Autobiographies and memoirs are self-indulgent, and often written by an unreliable narrator, but I promise."

She dragged his champagne flute slowly across the tablecloth. Nice hands, nails with French tips, and no hint of time in the California sun. Her bracelet sparkled like a shard of glass.

"This bracelet was a gift. My grandmother was close friends with Carole Lombard."

Bill answered with the usual epithets such as 'Gable and Lombard,' 'screwball-comedy actress' and 'killed in a plane crash in '42.'"

"Carole died on a bitter cold January night." Tara said it with a shiver. "So my grandmother told me, and she said it was the saddest day of her life. Journalists then spared the public the gruesome details. I saw photographs of Carole's body before it was wrapped up in a blanket. Papers said Eddie Mannix identified her body, but the truth is he found it." Tara tried to redirect the mood of the conversation with a bright smile. "My grandmother and Carole knocked around together. Talk about complete opposites, the two of them. Grandmother was somewhat guarded, standoffish, while Carole was funny and free with the profanity. The Profane Angel is what they called her; the woman could curse up a storm. Did you know that Carole had a terrible car accident when she was younger, almost bled to death?"

Bill shook his head. He had known, but pretended not to.

"Few people know this but Carole's face was full of scars. Glass from the windshield, especially here." Tara pointed to the side of her left eye. "You had to look for it, but the cameramen... those men knew how to hide it. Old Hollywood may've been factory of illusions, when the studio system kept stars in servitude, but there was a foundation of respect. Shutterbugs today wouldn't obscure the sight of FDR's braces these days; they'd spin a fable, or maybe you think I'm sentimental?"

"I think you're a realist. Now, you promised me a secret."

"My grandmother had an imperfection, one I've inherited." Tara pointed to her nose. "Look close and you'll see that my nose is crooked. Carole had taught her a trick with makeup. Draw a straight line down the middle and blend the makeup until the flaw disappears. There's one secret for you."

Tara glanced over the railing. "Carole took care of a lot of 'little people.' That's what she called them, not that she meant it in a derogatory way. She valued loyalty and helped people when they were down on their luck. Carole had a great, big heart; she was a good friend, and it's a shame that she was so damn impatient to get on that plane that night. Sorry, I usually don't cuss." She fluttered her hands in front of her face. "Twenty-two lives were lost on Flight 3; fifteen of them were members of the U.S. Army Air Corps."

Bill saw the wet orb of a tear on each of her eyes as she gave him her De Clare profile. Again, enraptured, Tara seemed so caught up in an anecdote of family history that he had no doubt that here was an actress who could take either the tragedy of a fiery crash into a mountain or something as mundane as ordering French appetizers and make it an Oscar-worthy scene.

"Sorry. My grandmother and I spent a lot of time together. I heard all her stories."

"Thank you for trusting me with that."

"Would you mind if we continued this conversation later? I'm unwell and wish to lie down. You can stay; or, if you prefer, we could resume the interview at a later date."

"I would like to stay, if you don't mind."

"Not at all. I'll have a drink brought out to you. Feel free to look around."

Bill got up to pull the chair out for her. He glanced down and the strap of her dress gave way just enough for him to see a port stain birthmark the shape of a heart on her right shoulder. He had thought it was a tattoo at first, but the margins were too irregular.

"You're quite the darling, so patient and forgiving," she said.

Bill was no leading man; she led this dance. She had put both hands on his arms and leaned in and gave him the Continental kiss, lips on one cheek and then the other.


Alfred came into the parlor downstairs with an Old Fashioned. He said it was the family recipe, using a touch of maple syrup instead of simple sugar. The old man departed as he arrived: slowly, and with earnest concentration.

The room was Art Deco, with geometric zigzags. Southern California sunlight through the brazen tinted glass had not bleached out any of the wallpaper, the dark wood in the room, or the red in the area rug. All the leather seating suggested an expectation of tobacco, of cigars men smoked in the room for decades, but there was none of that. The room was empty, warm, and inviting. The rug reminded him of the birthmark he had seen.

Though the masculine drink glazed his thinking, he had the pioneer's urge to explore the first floor. The library held first editions of Hemingway, an inscribed *Great Gatsby*. A weathered *Main Street* rested next to the Dos Passos trilogy. His fingers fanned the spines of the foreign books. He pulled one out here and there, but he didn't understand the titles, although he recognized some iconic names, only because films had been made from the novels.

He walked from one end of the room to the other, taking in the photographs that he had seen earlier and savoring the back note of bourbon as he admired the display. He stood before a Mack Sennett Bathing Beauty. The woman was no De Clare, but the portrait was an early example of the cheesecake pose. He squinted and noticed the scratched last name of Evans with the encircled c for copyright and L.A above it.

The Hurrell and Autrey glamour portraits didn't fail to impress him. He could see the resemblance, the De Clare features in black and white photographs. Only one photograph there intimated the faulty nose, but the lighting was so exquisite, and the De Clare women so ethereal and angelic in the composition, that to indicate a flaw would have been sacrilege.

There was the Lombard bracelet.

Finished with his drink, Bill didn't want to abandon it just anywhere. He kept it as he searched for more photographs of Tara's mother. Of all the De Clares, she was the riddle. Biographers said she died from a drug interaction between painkillers and her daily champagne fix. Nobody knew for sure because no death certificate was filed. No memorial service either. It was straight into the mausoleum wall in Glendale with the rest of the De Clares.

He thought he'd returned to the door to the room where met Tara earlier. Solid oak, dark and varnished. The wood had sucked in the finish and kept the shine trapped within. All the doors were like a gameshow choice. Each door showed little light and no movement through the bottom space between the wood and the flooring. He grabbed hold of a doorknob and made the decisive twist.

More pictures. Odd, he thought, seeing a pleasant still of Tara's great-grandmother wearing the same silver bracelet. The pose was so Edwardian, so proper. The etched date said 1915 and the name 'Lois Weber' next to the De Clare matriarch. He examined the image, got his nose close to the glass, but it was too blurry, too faded from exposure to sunlight behind the wrong type of picture-glass. He thought he was mistaken: a silver bracelet had to be a common trinket in her day.

He toured the room. Hairstyles changed; poses did not. Women wore wide-brimmed hats, heads turned to reveal their best side, or they gazed into the camera with dreamy eyes. The De Clare eyes were intent, purposeful, and challenging. Tara's grandmother possessed the eyes of a femme fatale, the siren call to the other side of the train tracks, yet sophisticated enough to mix with the high-society types after she hid the victim's body.

There was the nose. He saw it in all the photographs now: the facial feature handed down from great-grandmother to grandmother, and grandmother to mother and to Tara herself. Genetics. He would never have noticed the De Clare nose at all had Tara not shared Lombard's makeup secret.

He had thought of Lombard, and there she was with Tara's grandmother in front of him in crisp black and white. This was no glamour shot. Lombard sat in front of the vanity mirror with her brush. The open mouth and tossed-back head implied Lombard had just told a joke, perhaps a blue one that concerned Gable's big ears. Tara's grandmother glanced over her shoulder at the photographer in a strapless dress, the crookedness in her nose already camouflaged. Those nice teeth, those lips; but wait, he couldn't believe it—the birthmark on the right shoulder.

He pulled his head back and then moved in close. He had no magnifying glass, but the shape was obvious, unequivocal: a dark heart. He scanned the walls fast. He visited another photograph of her grandmother; he found it again. He was mistaken. He stepped back shocked and disoriented to discover it was Tara's great-grandmother. He verified the date: 1910.

Bill walked from photograph to photograph reading dates. He wanted to catch that butterfly of a birthmark.

He revisited the Lombard picture. No date. "Hold on," he said. He put the empty glass for the Old Fashioned down. He had to think.

"Carole died in January in a plane crash, in 1942." He examined the photograph. "Lombard was thirty-three when she died." He leaned in to scrutinize the bracelet and butterfly. "Tara said it was a gift."

The door opened. Alfred.

"There you are, sir. Would you care for another Old Fashioned?"

"No, thank you," Bill said and walked over to the abandoned glass. He placed it on the man's silver tray. "May I ask you a question about a photograph in this room?"

"I'm afraid I'm not conversant with every photograph in this room."

"What about this one here? It's Lombard in front of her vanity."

"What do you wish to know?"

"What year was this picture taken?"

The man raised a pale hand riddled with age spots and large blue veins to his forehead as if to agitate his grey matter for computations. "That picture was taken some years before Ms. Lombard had become Mrs. Gable."

Bill had no idea when Lombard had married Gable.

"If you can't tell me the year, then tell me how old Tara's grandmother is in the photograph. An approximation will do."

The man's milky eyes contemplated the picture once more. "It's unwise for men to guess a woman's age."

"I said a guess would suffice."

"Twenty-eight, more or less."

Bill walked over to the great-grandmother's picture. "And how old is she here?"

"I couldn't say."

"I'd say not a day over thirty. There isn't a picture in this house of a woman a day over thirty."

"If you say so, sir. Would you care for another cocktail?"

"No," Bill said and watched the man turn like an arthritic turret gun. He aimed for the door. "One last question. You must have been here when Tara's mother died."

"I was in the De Clare employ, yes."

"Did you see her body?" The old man shook his head. "Did anybody see the body?"

Bill heard a new voice. "What is the meaning of this?"

"I shall excuse myself, Ma'am," the butler said. Tara held the door open for the man and closed it with a soft click when he passed through the portal. She rested the back of her head against the door. "I wish you could have left things alone. You had so much promise. I thought you were different."

"I think I'll find my coat and leave Hotel California. No need to worry yourself one bit. I don't plan to breathe a word of this, whatever this is, to anybody."

She had sad eyes now. She stepped forward, froze, and then turned and opened the door for him. "We'll talk soon. I know what you are thinking."

"Don't count on it."

Bill stormed down the stairs. He didn't care about the article. He stopped at the bottom of the staircase, looked left and then right. "I want my coat, my pen and pad. I want the hell out of this place."

He opened several doors in search of a closet for his things. He found none. He stalked into majestic rooms under watchful eyes in numerous frames until he arrived at a small back room, a modest servant's kitchen, to find Alfred at a small table. He was enjoying a pot of tea; his teacup lifted up from the saucer, blowing soft, measured breaths to diminish the heat.

"There you are."

"Here I am," the old man answered.

"I'm sorry if I've made a racket coming down the stairs. I was upset."

"It's understandable."

Bill heard the delicate snort of hot tea. Breaktime ushered in the use of contractions.

"Where is my jacket? I want to leave."

"Understandable, sir."

"Look, you don't have to get up. Just tell me where you put it and I'll show myself out."

The man held his teacup, stared ahead without a word or any sense of acknowledgement. Bill was about to repeat himself when the man spoke.

"I'm afraid that's not possible, sir."

"Fine. I'll leave without my jacket. Keep the damn pen and paper. There, I violated one of your sacred rules. I cursed."

"Given the circumstances, it's perfectly reasonable."

Bill narrowed his eyes in suspicion. "I don't know what your deal is, but—"

"There is no deal. You are here to stay."

"Stay? Are you nuts?" Bill sighed. "Never mind that. All this time I've been here, I never caught your name."

Bill heard the teacup land in the circle on the saucer. The man rose, faced him and straightened his tuxedo front, with all the dignity of a veteran soldier.

"My name is William, your predecessor. I hope you enjoy your stay."

# CONFLAGRATION

## RICHARD BEAUCHAMP

To this day, the therapist that Gus and I were advised to see calls it a stress-induced group hallucination. A small part of myself wants to believe her. It was sure as shit stressful, being surrounded by literal walls of flame, the inside of your suit reaching a hundred something degrees, the roar of all-consuming fire screaming in your ears when your squad mates weren't yelling commands at you over their shoulders. Conditions to which we had been subjected too for hours on end, *we* being one of the many squadrons called on that day to beat back one of the worst wildfires in fifty years. For a while I was willing to entertain the notion that me and my colleagues, some of the best firemen in the state of California and all mentally sound, could have temporarily lost our minds and all seen the same things that weren't actually there. Yet when I close my eyes at night, trying to find temporary oblivion in sleep, I see it. The thing which makes my pink, burned skin crawl with horror and fear.

It's hard to talk about the things I've seen with anyone, which I guess is part of the reason why I'm writing it down. Everyone has this flowery romantic depiction of fire fighters. We're the brave, brass-balled heroes who fight the fires, save the day, and get all the glory. When you try and tell someone you have PTSD from being a fire fighter, you tend to get that look. These people don't think about the fact that a disturbing amount of the fires I've been called to fight weren't always put out in time. I've been an unwilling witness to so many exhibitions of human destruction.

I had been a firefighter for ten years prior to the Angel's Pass incident that nearly broke my mind. I saw my first dead body a year into the job. Apartment fire. We got there just in time to stop the whole complex from being burned, but three units were a total loss. Once the blaze was extinguished, we went about clearing out the three units, and in the first one we had discovered the cause of the fire, and who had started it. Ignition point was the oven in a small one-bedroom studio apartment, reduced to ash, walls blackened, the stove open. Sitting sprawled to a charred lazy boy, the flesh melted into the exposed metal springs of the chair, was a body almost completely charred over. The face still had some cooked skin on it, a few patches of glazed brown hide around the whitish gleam of skull. Sticking out of the charred arm, which hung down to the side, was a blackened metal syringe tip, the adjoining plastic tube and plunger a hardened melted mass on the floor. Heroin overdose. Then we had gone into the bedroom, where someone had found the charred metal skeleton of a baby pen, and the small, blackened mass that lay curled up in its center.

Once our station was called to help assist on a high-rise blaze, a twenty-story hotel called Isle Mystique located in Oakland. Freshly built by a contractor who had skimped on the design because, as we would later learn, he had called in a few favors from a good friend who happened to be a city inspector. As a result of that, the half assed installed extinguisher system put in had failed critically when one of the units caught fire on the tenth floor. Turned out to be a bad circuit that threw some sparks next to exposed insulation. What should have been an easily extinguished quirk of architecture had turned into a full-on blaze when our trucks rolled up to throw water, and I had noticed a few crimson streaks on the ground where people had jumped from the windows trying to escape. As we hooked up to the nearest hydrant and waited for the hose to get pressurized, I saw someone ablaze hurl themselves out over the deck of the room they were trapped in, a human comet that went streaking to the ground with a thud I felt in my bones.

The fall wasn't bad enough to kill her, but you couldn't tell by looking at the body. Someone had immediately doused her in water, but by then it was too late. The fatty epidermal layer of her skin had been burned away in most places, leaving splotchy pink patches that faded into twitching exposed muscle tissue. Her eyeballs had exploded, the two sockets a gluey mess of hollowed-out gore, the skull smashed and leaking cooked brains onto the hot California asphalt. Her legs were a broken ruin beneath her, the gleam of white bone poking through shiny cooked skin like an overcooked bratwurst stabbed by a skewer.

I only reflect on these horrors because it's important to show that I was no stranger to death and trauma by the time the wildfires began cooking the state alive. Even during those previous horrible scenes of human suffering, I did not witness anything paranormal or extraordinary while on duty, or suffer breaks from reality.


It was in August when we got called out. Small scrub fires had been popping all over the state that year because of the record-breaking drought, but luckily the winds had never been strong and the fires either died out or were quickly contained with strategically placed fire barriers. Then Angel's Pass, a section of heavily wooded hills in the southeast part of the Sonora mountains, caught fire. They could never figure out the original ignition point of the fire, as Angel's Pass is in one of the most

177

remote parts of the state, and in that brutally hot summer very few people were hiking.

Along with that is the fact that Angel's Pass sat atop a state-protected Mojave burial ground, and people caught trespassing on the historical site were usually fined heavily. But something or someone must have started it, because within four hours, the blaze was fanning out in all directions, moving five feet a minute. Five upscale subdivisions flanked the nearest borders of the forest. Those neat and close together colonial styled neighborhoods for the upper-class white-collar families went up like tinderboxes, much to the pleasure of the hipsters and yuppies who complained about bay area gentrification.

It soon became clear that this was going to be a big one, and with the total loss of those luxury neighborhoods, including ten people already claimed, the governor had declared a state of emergency. Calls were made across the state for some of the best, strongest firefighting teams from each active station to join up and help fight the blaze. It was inevitable I would get picked, being six-four and two hundred and fifty pounds of Samoan muscle, my nick name was "Big Lu" because I towered above the rest of the guys in my squad. Me, and two other people—Gus Ellison and Jerry Fitzpatrick—were chosen because of our experience, physical endurance, and strength. Although all the guys wanted to volunteer, we needed at least half the station in working capacity in case they were needed in our station's jurisdiction, which happened to be thirty miles from where the blaze was eating through million-dollar homes, protected forests and everything in between.

The one-hour drive took three because we had to meander our way through the wave of evacuees fleeing the blaze. We were still some ten miles away from the rally point for our first skirmish with the blaze, but it looked like literal hell on earth from the highway. The normally bright summer sun was obscured by an obsidian haze of smoke; the orange cinders and embers rose into the sky like burning stars threatening to bring the sky down with it. I could see the few ethereal bodies of the airplanes flying through the smoke, being called in to do water drops on a few areas, but those did little good. The heat was incredible with a blaze that size, and the water simply boiled into steam before it had a chance to douse the flames they were aimed at.

We had to pilot our large engine around stopped cars and people wearing respirators and shirts around their heads. I had slipped my own mask on before getting out of the engine, the air smelling of burnt everything. Eventually we saw the sign and clearing for EMT's and fire fighters. We took a dirt fire road that snaked up through the valley. We passed several water tank trucks; due to the remote location, no hydrants or stationary water sources were around. We were waved on by men wearing respirators to the left, and followed another dirt path. We barely had room to pull over to let the ambulance pass that came from the direction we were headed in, it's siren lights obscured by the smoke. Eventually we came to a spot where a lone tank truck sat, and we assumed that was our cue to get out. I guessed right when I walked over to the lip of the ridge and saw the steady wall of flame that came marching towards us. I remember how hypnotic it was, staring at that massive dancing orange and yellow body through the shimmering heat waves. The way the trees quite literally burst into flames before the fire even reached them, the intense heat spontaneously combusting the bone-dry pine and scrub bush like it was soaked in kerosene.

"Lumou, quit sightseeing and move your ass!" Gus called. But even then I paused in my duties, because I thought I saw something. A tall, slim figure, almost as tall as the pine trees, that seemed to be made of flame, walking along the fire's edge. Like a child's primitive stick figure blown up to a massive scale and comprised entirely of fire. It seemed to glide along the edge, arms outstretched, almost... *frolicking.* The way you would see a beautiful woman frolicking through a field of flowers for one of those cheesy commercials. Graceful, at ease.

"Lu! You gone fuckin deaf? We gotta soak this whole slope before that shit gets a chance to cross the road. Come on!" Jerry yelled. I did a double take towards our parked truck. Gus and Jerry were both uncoiling the connector hose, the two volunteer truck drivers, whose names I never caught, helping Jerry drag it over to the valve on the water tank. I took another quick glance back at the firewall, but lost site of the figure in the blaze, which seemed to have encroached another ten feet in the short time it took me to look at my colleagues. I ran over, and got the generator going on the truck to build the water pressure up. Once the hose was connected and pressure was established, we started soaking the bank directly below us, taking care not to slip down the sandy embankment towards the few remaining unburned acres.

I scanned the burning horizon fervently as I directed the hose out in a wide fan, walking to the left as I went, trying to create a wet barrier as long as I could before the hose ran out or the fire snuck up on us. I thought I could see movement to the far right, where the tree line disappeared around the curve of a small mountain. Then I heard a thunderous roar, and instinctively ducked as one of the modified DC-10's roared by overhead, a bright red cascade of fire retardant blooming from its belly as it did a close pass of the eastern firewall, close to where I thought I'd seen the fire specter.

Twenty minutes into our efforts, a man wearing goggles, a respirator, and a water-soaked hoodie came flying down the dirt road, nearly colliding with Gus and Jerry, who were in the middle of the road guiding the hose along as I walked, making sure it didn't get kinked. He slid to a stop five feet from Jerry.

"We got an emergency!" the man began. I flipped the pressure release on the hose, shutting it off for a second.

"You take a look around? Half the damn state is an emergency," Jerry shouted through his respirator.

"We got a park ranger stranded two miles from here at a ranger's station. Got a broken leg and he's losing his shit over the CB. Fire is almost on him. Who's the strongest sonofabitch of you three?"

They all pointed to me, and I shrugged, looking at Gus. He nodded.

"Go on, big Lu. Go be a hero. Enough people have died already. We got it from here," he said, taking the sputtering hose from my hands.

"Come on! We gotta haul ass if we're gonna beat this thing." The driver said. I quickly grabbed the first aid kit and a fire blanket from the truck, then climbed on back of the ATV, the suspension groaning with my added bulk.

In what seemed like a blur of heat, motion and burning trees, we arrived at a narrow trail. In the distance off to our left, perhaps some two hundred feet into the forest we saw the ranger's station, which was actually a fire watchtower. Some fifty feet beyond that was the wall of the blaze; this side of the mountain was already nearly consumed. Without a word I jumped off the four-wheeler before he even came to a complete stop, and ran headlong into the blazing void. I could see the ranger; he was halfway down the tower, sprawled out in a heap on the steps. Must have fallen trying to flee.

As I drew closer to the tower, I began to hear a peculiar sound over the roar of the fire and my own beating heart. A rhythmic thumping, like an army marching in step or the mighty thump of a tribal band's bass drums. Powerful enough to make the ground shake. I hesitated in my sprint, looking to my left. My gaze fixated upon the sight that still haunts my dreams.

Propelled by long spindly legs that ascended into a round fireball of an abdomen, from which jutted five or six limbs that I guess could be called arms, the entity bore down on the tower like a wide receiver sprinting towards the goal line. It was nearly as tall as the ranger station, and as it drew closer, I could see that it had a head. There were two coal black eyes perched atop the stubby head, like someone born without a neck. If it had a mouth, I did not see it. It didn't appear to have any substance to it, no charred skin or bone structure visible through its burning limbs. I don't know whether to call it a demon, a god, a creature, or a monster. All I know was that it moved with singular purpose.

I had halted completely when I saw it run into the tower. In a sudden eruption the body dematerialized into a fireball as it seemed to go through the tower, and instantly the structure was ablaze. I ran forward, but the heat had stopped me some forty feet from the base of the tower. I watched as the ranger rolled down the stairs wildly, I could faintly hear his screams over the dull roar of the fire, and then watched with helpless horror as he crawled through the gap of safety rail between the stairs and fell two stories to the ground. He began to moan and writhe on the forest floor, and managed to extinguish part of his body in the fall. I put the fire blanket around me, trying to get as close as I could to perhaps drag the man to safety. But at forty feet the pain was just unbearable; I could feel my skin broiling and my head grow foggy and delirious as heat stroke threatened to debilitate me. Then I smelled burning hair as my humble mustache and nose hairs started to singe. I took one squinting glance at the ranger, who had managed to crawl forward a small amount before dying.

His face was a blistering, charred mass of vague flesh as his skin began to melt from the indirect heat, much like an oven broiling steaks. He reached out one hand, bright pink and oozing blood at his fingertips, bits of burnt leaves and dirt embedded in the raw, cooked flesh as he tried to drag himself across the ground. His polyester and rayon ranger's uniform had melted to his body, bubbling up instead of burning away like cotton. He opened his blackened mouth to scream, and that's when I saw his head twitch, little explosions sending bits of white shards out of his mouth as his molars exploded, a phenomenon I had heard about but had never actually witnessed. His eyes, which were already bulging out of his head in a ridiculous parody of shocked surprise burst, the insides running and steaming down his face like half cooked egg whites.

I had to peel myself away from the horror as the fire started to surround me. I could hear the driver of the ATV shouting for me and I turned to run. The flames were on either side and threatening to surround me if I didn't get to the roadway in time. I ran, my lungs burning as they inhaled hot, smoky air. I somehow managed to make it to the road, nearly collapsing before I got to the four-wheeler. The driver grabbed me and steadied my large mass as I sat down heavily on the rear edge of the seat.

"Take me back to my squadron," I remembered saying, and held on to him as he floored it, trying to escape the heat and outrun the blaze. That's when I lost consciousness.


I was awakened by Gus, who was looming over me. There was an oxygen mask on my face. I was lying on the ground, confused as to where I was. It felt like I was inside a furnace.

"Jesus, man. I thought we almost lost you." His face was pouring sweat; all color had drained from it. "Come on, get up, we need you. No time for a hospital. We gotta get the hell out of here!" he yelled as Jerry appeared. Both of them pulled me to my feet with a grunt of effort. The ATV driver was gone. We were somewhere along the dirt road. The fire blazed on either side of us. I stood unsteadily on my feet, and saw that the tank truck was ahead of us, still married to our fire truck via the connector hose.

"Where are the others?" I asked stupidly.

"The drivers had to be evaced out, got heat stroke. We need help disconnecting the hose so we can scram," he said. I noticed that a couple gallons of water had leaked from the hose connector, and the dirt road had transformed into a small mud pit where the fire engine was. As me and Jerry walked over to the tank truck, I heard it, that familiar thudding. I froze up, and turned around. Through the tops of the trees I could make out fast movement.

"Man, we've been hearing that damn thumping all day. What *is* that?" Jerry asked, looking around.

"We need to go, right now." I ran over and quickly began twisting off the connector valve. A spray of hot water shot out as the remaining fluid from the hose flowed out the empty end, soaking my pants. I ran back over to the truck, quickly reeling in the connector hose while Jerry and Gus reeled in the main hose. The thumping grew closer, and I could see the form coming through the burning trees.

I screamed at them. "Get the truck going! Fucking demon or something!" was all I could think to say, and either the expression on my face or the lack of color in my normally dark skin must of scared Gus, because he stopped reeling in the hose, looking over his shoulder to see the impossible form running through the trees. With ten feet of hose still hanging off, a sacrilegious act among trained fire fighters, he ran into the driver's cab. The throaty roar of the diesel engine coming to life spoke over the thumping percussive tattoo. Jerry stood mesmerized at the thirty-foot form growing up from the wall of flames like the devil himself, knocking over burning trees like they were saplings and approaching us.

"Jerry, come on!" I screamed, running up the side of the truck's cab. Unlike some of the other fire trucks on call that day, ours carried a chemical retardant which was disbursed via a hydraulic nozzle station perched atop the truck like a gunner's turret. This was due to our station's proximity to the commuter air strips located a few miles southeast of Santa Cruz. I prayed the reservoir of chemical foam was full. Luckily, it was. The truck started moving, the whole frame shuddering as Gus tried to maneuver the big fire engine through the mud pit and heavily rutted road. I watched as Jerry stood like a deer in the headlights, his vacuous gaze following the fire behemoth. It reached the road, bursting out through the tree line just as the truck crawled its way out of the mud pit and all six wheels found traction. The engine roared like a metallic beast as Gus floored it, and I watched helplessly as the thing bore down on Jerry. He didn't move as the being, a horrifying monstrosity that so resembled a hastily drawn spider on two legs, shot out one thin burning pilon of an arm. Blazing, ethereal appendages like fingers disappeared into Jerry's midsection.

It was an almost instantaneous thing. I would hazard maybe a second after the thing speared Jerry, he exploded. It was if he'd decided to ingest a couple sticks of dynamite and light the fuse on the way down. I ducked as a burning piece of his arm came flying at me, the cauterized stump hitting me in the face and leaving the circular scar I still have today on my left cheek. Burning chunks of Jerry came raining down, and the smell of boiling blood and burnt polyester uniform cut through the smoke.

Then it was charging at the truck, long skinny legs propelling it forward with ease. Understanding I was about to die a horrible death, I depressed the pressure release button and aimed the tapered mouth of the nozzle at its midsection. For a moment nothing happened. Then a small sputter of white foam shot out. I almost wanted to laugh because of how ridiculous this all was. I was about to fight a giant paranormal fire creature using chemical retardant meant for putting out jet fuel fires, and the damn thing didn't even work. For a split second I thought I might be going crazy, until I felt the heat radiating off the being like it was the surface of the sun. I cringed back, but didn't keep my hand off the nozzle. Right as the thing reached out one long arm towards the truck, a beautiful white jet of PhostrEx agent arced out of the nozzle, right into the midriff of the hellish being.

Things happened very rapidly then. I remember the way the foam quickly expanded, the way it's supposed to in order to snuff out the fuel source. The thing collapsed in on itself, the limbs losing substance and falling like a collapsing camp fire. I aimed the nozzle up to increase the arc as the truck sped away, rounding a corner in the fire trail. Then I saw as the thoroughly covered mass blossomed in one giant foamy mushroom cloud before the second explosion happened. I don't remember much except a white flash, which was bright enough to burn a small hole in my left cornea. I was knocked unconscious from the blast, and according the Gus it felt like the shockwave from an atom bomb had hit the truck. He had to fight to keep it from flying off the road.

When I woke up again, I was in the hospital, being treated for a concussion and second-degree burns on my arms and face, with a small black hole in my vision where the cones and rods had fried.

It was one of the deadliest wildfires of the century. Thousands of acres ablaze, hundreds of homes destroyed. The whole ordeal took a month for the final cinders to be extinguished. Eighty people perished, twenty of them firefighters. It was upon psychiatric evaluation at the hospital that I was recommended to go see a therapist after doctors heard me ranting and raving about demons getting Jerry while I was under sedation. Gus didn't see as much as I did, but he corroborated my story about the fire entity, and on the department's orders, we both had to attend at least eight cognitive behavioral therapy sessions.

What I haven't told my therapist is that in my downtime, while I sat at home, body half bandaged and looking like a Hawaiian Freddy Kruger, I began reading articles on the internet about the fires. One thing led to another, and I eventually ended up on the personal blog of a reporter who was there when the blaze first erupted. She had managed to snap a few blurry photos of something moving through the wild fires. DEMONS OF THE MOJAVE? Was the headline of the article.

I have since done my research, hours of reading through anthropology and historical texts about the Mojave people in the area, and discovering the elemental gods that they, along with many other tribes across the nation, worshipped and feared. Johanna was the god of wrath, a fierce, unforgiving deity who took the form of the sun, and punished those cowardly warriors who refused to fight, as well as those that practiced the black magic of their region. If what I saw was in fact an ancient native American god, what did that make me? A god killer? I don't know. All I know is that I'm done fighting fires. I've seen enough burned bodies and felt enough heat to know what hell is like if I ever go there.

# BEACH BOY

## DAVID DANIEL

*Windwhipped white curtains bellying into the room of his dreaming stir him... storm coming. Half-formed in the cinemas of the subconscious the thought flickers out of focus, fogging, white... Waking now... dream gone.*

Rolf Benedict opened his eyes. Rising was a labor. A chore. Had to be done though. Everything else grew from the initial act of moving from the prone to the perpendicular. As with most things, however, it was far easier to think than to do, and so Benedict lay there in the sheets and, for an attenuating moment, remembered his youth when, living in this very house, he would rise summer days before dawn and stand for an instant on the cool wood floor, blinking, ahead of his mother slamming windows against the wind and scolding, and then be out on his bicycle, awake in the remotest capillaries of himself, pumping with wild glee through the still-dreaming streets. He had never needed an alarm clock then, nor did he now, unfailingly snapping awake seconds before his bedside clock radio could wake him. One of the bitterly few blessings of old age was you woke early. On the red ink side of the ledger, the column was long: perfidious memory, stiff joints, a quirky bladder, rheumy eyes, and a body so slow to mend that every little ding and dent left its mark. But his memory was sharp, yes. And back then, those cool childhood mornings—

The radio clicked on: a fragment of news, a body found somewhere, mutilation, murder... He shut the radio off, should just unplug the damn thing, but he liked it at night when sleep proved elusive, and to ease him into unconsciousness he listened to *Coast to Coast*, people from the heartland phoning in with fantastic stories of alien abductions, crop circles, strange conspiracies. He lay back, tried to re-immerse himself in the stream of consciousness, but youth and its memories had eddied past and were gone, as was whatever he had just been dreaming. Wincing, he pushed up to sitting, swung one leg then the other out of bed, set his feet on the cool floor.

In the dresser mirror, in the pale concealing milk of foggy dawn, it was possible to miss the erosion of the years, still possible to discern the relative firmness of muscles underneath loose skin, which at eighty-four, adjusting for the decades, put him in a league with the bodybuilders and shapely young people who populated the beach in the later hours of the day. He doubted that many of them, with their bulked shoulders and rippled torsos, would fare any better than he had when they were his age. Most would have long abandoned the rigors of conditioning, overtaken by the demands of making a living, maintaining families, defining and defending some tenuous sense of identity in an uncertain world. They, like most people, would soften into the general populace of couch potatoes, feeble beings putting in their days. Not for nothing had he spent nearly forty years working in life insurance, first in Chicago as a sales agent, then out here in Santa Barbara, where he'd done the work of (though without the degree or the pay of) an actuary. He knew the charts. Most people would never live to see his age.

Still, it was small consolation to consider what would befall *them*. It was, after all, *his* corpus that stood there before the glass, the growing light revealing more: sagging, blotched skin, shoulders that wanted to slope and a neck eager to droop forward. With effort he squared himself, tucked his chin, and in doing so cast his gaze at the trophies that lined the shelves of the room: silver cups and plaques and medals for bicycling, tennis, running, and surfing, even one for boxing, all hard won. They were dusty now, dulled with time, serving merely as reminders of what he once had accomplished, once had been.

The kitchen smelled faintly of bleach. Opening the refrigerator, he took the solid mass from the freezer compartment, unzipped the plastic storage bag, and plunked a part of the contents into the blender, along with some brewer's yeast, flaxseed oil, and coconut sugar for a bit of sweetening, then poked the button. The machine ground and churned the mass into liquid the color of plums, nasty to the tongue, but drinking it gave him heart for the workout. At the sink he rinsed the blender jar and glass. Beyond the window, in the tiny backyard, were dishtowels and rags, bleached bone white hung limp, ghosts in the ground fog. He was rattling along the coast road in his old car, the sun bleeding up from the ocean fog, when—

*Curtains bellying into a room*

—he pulled loose a strand of last night's dream.

It was familiar. One he sometimes had in childhood... the billowing white cotton and the storm coming, which sometimes was his dad coming up the stairs after a night out on the booze. It was in those years when young Rolf would ride his bike in the predawn, speeding along the shore road, out of the house, away from the old man. The old man who had baited him: "pencil neck" and "weakling" and, (something which he never even understood until many years later) "the best of you got wiped off on the sheets." Rolf's mother, who had always doted on him (hadn't she dressed him in frilly smocks until he was five, kept his hair uncut in blond ringlets?), would offer weak protest, but never enough, and the storm would spill.

The old man was an insurance agent, working long hours on straight commission. He made a show of success by driving a new automobile every year, always a Plymouth Fury (when a more economical car would have done, Rolf's mother said). But the old man never achieved the wealth he pursued, letting, instead, everything build to a slow wrath. In his younger years he had been a solider (not a very good one as it turned out; he was given a bad conduct discharge); later in life he sometimes took to wearing his faded uniform to downtown bars and picking fights. One night he had picked the wrong bar and the wrong people. Health complications from the beating contributed to his death six months later. The life insurance salesman had no life insurance. Rolf was fourteen at the time.

His mother had resumed her doting, probably hoping she was comforting, but to Rolf she had merely seemed weak and pathetic; though perhaps that was her design after all. Rolf had turned increasingly to his own needs and care, anyhow, and then, as if freed from her own double yoke, his mother had left him with her sister and gone east. Aunt Hannah, unmarried, moved into the small house and took over. But Aunt Hannah wasn't bad. Anyway, he had his habit of riding out early, going to the beach and his jungle.

It was still early, as Rolf Benedict liked it. Businesses along the coast road (surf shops, fast-food restaurants, bars) were still night-shuttered, abandoned-looking, like barges run aground in asphalt. The beach parking lot was empty. There were new bathhouses, bright blue plastic barrels for trash, freshly painted lifeguard towers rising from the sand. The occasional ravages of a storm, shifting sand and breaching sea walls, or a fire moving down from the hills, changed the topography, but the beach was little different from when he was ten and then fifteen, those mornings when he would rise and jump on his bicycle and ride out among the rows of tiny whitewashed houses with red tile roofs that had never been so mum as then, concealing the secrets of all who had ever lived and worked and died within them, and he, oblivious, flush in the certainty that he was going to live forever. Long ago, long ago.

From the car trunk he retrieved the nylon daypack, inside which were a water bottle, a pair of three-pound HeavyHands dumbbells, swim goggles, a rubber cap, and a white towel. He didn't bother with sunscreen; what was the point? Anyway, he'd be gone from the beach before the sun got high. Fitting the daypack on, he locked the car and walked to the end of the paved lot and entered the low dunes.

He took the path—more like a groove in the deep sand—sludging past where the beach tipped downward to his left into the dense jungle of vegetation and wild grasses. It was sometimes a trysting ground for lovers; always had been, apparently, for he had memory of his mother warning him against all that, though he had played in it happily enough. It was also a bower of death, where at least three dead bodies had been found in the past dozen years or so; and then, only recently, a fourth. He slowed already slow steps to peer into the tangles of foliage, branches festooned with the bright flame of flowering vines, though the colors were muted in the dissipating fog. In the shadowing light he imagined he saw movement. Likely, it was birds at this hour; still, he was acutely conscious of living things in there. He picked up his pace, feeling the surge of his heart. He was thinking again of those days of youth. Memory slowed with age, but thoughts still sprang to mind as random, as evanescent as ever. The sand deepened and his steps grew stodgy. At the rise of the last dune before the beach sloped down to the sea, he paused and could not help but glance back at the jungle again, and again he imagined something moving in there, swarming.

He had lived most of his life along this area of coast, but it wasn't as if he had never gotten away. Military service had taken him places. As had marriage. Eleanor had been a Chicagoan, from a large and close-knit Irish Catholic family, and to make her happy in their early years together he found work there, became one of the gray minions who toiled in an office in the vast hive by the lake. It had not been a joy, but he had done it for Eleanor. Then she died.

He came back home, away from the cold and the flatness of the land, back to the contours of coastal California, to the ocean and the house, his aunt Hannah having died long since. Always, however, wherever he was, he kept fit. Running, biking, lifting barbells long before it became a fad, practiced first in the backyards and garages of the houses of friends and later at army bases in the South. The earliest and best of those friends had been Bob Everett, whom everyone in school called "Atlas" because of his physique. It was Bob Everett who had first taught him about reps and sets and the training effect.

There were other workout partners over time, though just as often he exercised alone, content with his own thoughts and the rhythm of his breath and heartbeat. His most recent training buddy had been Carl, a fifty-year old sales representative for Lexus. Carl had hung in there for several months of workouts along the beach, determined to lose his winter girth; then he stopped coming, hadn't shown up at all this week. It often was that way. People began with eager intentions, but some vital component was missing. Was it will? Ambition? Possibly, simply, what they lacked was vanity. Whatever the case, they quit coming back.

People liked the *idea* of being fit, but not the work involved. How many television commercials did one see: GET FIRM IN 3 DAYS WITHOUT EXERCISE! Or magazines at the supermarket checkout: EAT ALL YOU WANT AND LOSE POUNDS AS YOU SLEEP? Claims as ludicrous as those made about alien abductions and grand conspiracies on the late-night radio program Rolf listened to for entertainment.

He had never wavered. More than seventy years. A "fetish" is how he had long considered his exercising, a term someone had once applied, inexactly but admiringly, saying something like, "Fitness is almost a fetish with you, Rolf," and though strictly speaking it wasn't that—there was some sexual component linked to that word—he'd liked it enough to have kept it.

"Sorry I'm late," Carl said one time early in their exercise friendship, the same morning he arrived when Rolf was already stretching and Carl revealed with a flushed pride that his new wife was twenty-five years younger than he. Rolf, smiling, understood.

"Are you married, Rolf?" Carl asked.

"Once, a long time ago. I'm a widower."

There had never been a second time. Eleanor was gone and that was sad, but life was simpler this way. *His* life was simpler. Habits grew ingrained. Friends let him down.


At the water's edge, reading the tide, he set down the daypack, removed his sneakers, pulled on the rubber cap and swim goggles, and waded in. With the seawater clutching coldly at knees and shriveling privates, he gauged the gentle rollers for a moment, then cupped several brisk handfuls to his face. Bracing, he surged forward, surfaced, and began to swim out. When he got beyond where the waves broke, he turned and began to stroke parallel to the shore. He kept up the exertions for several long, slow back-and-forth circuits of breath and blood and body, then finally he body-surfed in, and in a long, hanging moment he had a floating sensation of youth, of soaring on his bike on early mornings, his father's rage and mother's scolding little more than murmurs of wind in a seashell.

On shore he toweled off, then put his sneakers back on. From the pack he got his HeavyHands, only three pounds apiece but they felt twice that after a long slow mile on the sand.

In high school, he and Bob Everett had poured coffee cans and gallon paint cans full of concrete, joined them with four-foot lengths of pipe and had barbells. They lifted under the backyard palm trees and spent hours high jumping over a bamboo pole hung between two upright 2X4s, confecting dreams of Olympic glory. Sometimes, after a workout, they would sneak into Bob's dad's liquor cabinet and toast their athletic prowess with little Dixie cups of blackberry brandy. There existed a Polaroid snapshot (he had a recollection of it curling dustily somewhere among the trophies and medals) in which he and Bob Everett stand grinning into sunshine, each with an arm flung companionably around the other's shoulder, outer arms raised in a biceps flex. "Like a pair of young Adonises," Mrs. Everett had smilingly called them. He'd liked Mrs. Everett, who was small and dark-haired and pretty, unlike his own mother had been. Mrs. Everett took the photograph, two snaps, one for each of them. Then Bob, jovial and teasing, said, "Pick my mom up! Go ahead, pick her up." After some encouragement from both of them, he had. She was petite and he had lifted her—one arm hooked under her knees, the other under her back, a standard muscle man pose: holding her in his arms before him. She was wearing white shorts and a red top that left her tanned shoulders and lower back exposed (a halter top, he came to understand later). As he held her (Bob peering through the Polaroid's viewfinder), Rolf was aware of Mrs. Everett's heartbeat against his arm, a quick throb, and he tried to pray away the intruder that was pushing at the front of his trunks. It was faintly visible in the damp snapshot that Bob pulled from the camera and gave him, unnoticed, apparently, by Bob and Mrs.

Everett; not by Aunt Hannah, however, when a month later she found the print in his bedroom. "What's this?" she confronted him.

He dismissed the photograph as fun, something playful, but she was unyielding. "That's the road to real trouble, boy," she warned darkly and confiscated the picture.

His friendship with Bob Everett came to an abrupt end when Bob braced him after school a few days later. "You had my mother's *picture* under your *mat*tress?" Aunt Hannah had evidently phoned the woman. "You're *sick*, you know it! You're a perverted *freak*." Rolf didn't bother to protest that it hadn't been under the mattress; it was part of a display on his windowsill, along with seashells and bright pebbles and the feathers of shore birds: a shrine to beauty.


Olympic glory didn't come. Life did. Reality. Darkness. The intrusions of this and that. Though there were adventures enough, and women and good times. And Bob... he later died, seventeen years old, motorcycle accident.

In the way that memory leads to memory, Rolf found himself thinking about the Greenbergs, good-looking blond brothers, identical twins who had seemed to live on the tennis courts across town by the high school, playing morning to night against each other in singles, but at doubles always a team. It became Rolf's goal to best them, which he did eventually, in singles, though never in doubles. Gone now, both of them, heart attack one of them (Barry?); the other, he wasn't sure. He understood why people died when they did, and surprisingly often it was as a result of some miscalculation they made, some dangerous habit. Statistics bore this out.

Run completed, he drank water and then took his time stretching. Sun had burned off the fog and the morning light was rich now, warm on his shoulders. The young people would begin arriving in an hour or so, showing up after a night of whatever it was they did: gummy-eyed and loose-limbed in spandex and bikini tops, bronzed skin stained with tattoos and agleam with tanning oil: men and women flush with the heedless confidence of youth. Even in the face all the dangers of his early life, hadn't Rolf felt that same confidence when, the far-flung reaches of night and dreaming exhausted, he would waken and ride out and listen to the Raleigh 3-speed speaking to him in the *click-click* of gear changes and the soft *tic tic tic* of coasting? Ah, but his was not a generation who could remain heedless long, what with the political and social upheavals, and the dislocations that tended to follow.

With his daypack he began the trek back to the parking lot. In the distance, made dizzy by the reflection of sun on the sand, the skeletal form of a life guard tower glowed whitely. No one on duty yet. As he started up the sandy groove between dunes that would take him to his car, he glanced again at the jungle, on his right now. It was surprisingly dense for all its rising out of mere sand. Even with the fog gone and the sun higher, not very much light fell in there. It was a secret place, full of yearning somehow, and again he imagined swarming darkness in there, ghostly, like some unlived part of himself. He shivered.

At the top of the trail, he drank the last of the water and walked over to a blue barrel to deposit the empty plastic bottle. The barrel was half-full of rubbish and in it was a crisp and yellowing page of newspaper, partially legible. BRUTAL SLA. The rest was torn off. He dropped the plastic bottle on top.

In the parking lot two suntanned young lifeguards were standing in their zippered white sweat shirts and orange trunks, chatting with the young beach cop who patrolled the area. The three of them stood together in the idle, self-contained attitude of youth. They paid Rolf no attention.

At his car, he unlocked the trunk, dropping in the daypack. It made a soft clang and he moved aside a bleached white towel. Underneath lay some old newspapers whose headlines read: SECOND BODY FOUND. POLICE SEEK CLUES. GRISLY DISCOVERY. Tabloid tales of unsolved murders, hearts carved from chest cavities. The most recent page read: AREA AUTO SALES REP MISSING. Beneath the papers were a roll of duct tape, handcuffs, and the stainless-steel gleam of a surgical saw. He shut the trunk.

As Rolf drove away, the young beach cop barely looked up from opening a striped beach umbrella over a lawn chair alongside a yellow barricade, acknowledging Rolf with the barest nod: an old beach jock in a worn-out sedan. Rolf Benedict rode past, smiling. He had the same feeling he had experienced all of his life following a work-out, a feeling like no other. Calm, clean, in control. He would go home now to the cool quiet of his small house, where in the backyard bleached towels and rags would be bellying white in the wind, like mysterious semaphores of no discernable meaning. He would shower and then blend another shake of the red stuff that would put life back into him. For just a moment, as he reached the parking lot exit, he paused and drew a deep, cleansing breath. Off to the left, like a mirage, the small beach jungle shimmered, and beyond it the Pacific rolled, sun-spangled and curling in in perfect regularity and precision, ever changing, never changed.

# ROSA CASTILLA

## JEAN ANKER

As we rounded the bend, peeking through the mist, I could see several whitewashed structures in various states of decay juxtaposed against the deep green foliage that covered the surrounding hillside. We were nearing the Rosa Castilla, an old California ranch Darlene said was haunted.

"What a lovely place," I said, hoping it was something we could all agree on.

"No wonder the ghosts don't want to leave," mumbled Toni under her breath.

"We get it, Toni," I whispered. "You don't believe in ghosts or haunted houses."

"And I'm entitled to my beliefs, aren't I?" she replied, "I also don't think all this talk about death and haunts is good for Paulette."

I nodded, thinking she was entitled to her beliefs but that it didn't mean she could be rude to Darlene, even if she was worried about Paulette, who had just finished her last round of chemo.

As if on cue, Darlene remarked again what a perfect day it was for encountering the Lady in Black.

"Of course, she *would* be wearing black," quipped Toni. "If I ever come back as a ghost, I'm definitely wearing pink!"

I couldn't wait to get out of the car. As we approached the rusty iron gate and a dilapidated sign that said, "Welcome to Rancho Rosa Castilla," I only hoped we weren't too late for the last tour.

"This is going to be so fun," promised Darlene. Paulette nodded her head in agreement.

"It looks deserted," declared Toni, emitting her usual aura of negativity.

Noticing an old Cadillac at the end of the parking lot, I said, "There must be somebody here."

We piled out of Darlene's Jeep and walked until we saw a hut with a sign that said

191

Visitor Center. We were about to enter when we saw someone walking towards us. The late afternoon fog made it difficult to determine whether it was a man or a woman, especially since the person was wearing a slouchy cowboy hat and riding boots. But as she drew nearer, I could see a long blond braid hanging over their shoulder. On her khaki jacket was a badge that said Docent.

"I'm Maxine," she said in a soft, low-pitched voice. She pushed back the braid and adjusted her cowboy hat with her gloved hand, then said she had been ready to leave, but turned around when she saw us.

As she led us down the pathway towards the stables, she told us the first owner, Don Hidalgo Vasquez, had named the estate Rosa Castilla because of the abundance of wild roses growing by the stream that flowed through the property. Already, I was grateful we had a guide to lead us around the expansive estate.

After giving us a tour of the barn, Maxine led us up a stone path, then stopped midsentence and bowed her head before beckoning us to enter the main foyer of the house. The moment wasn't lost on Darlene and Paulette, who quickly bowed their heads as well. Toni rolled her eyes and mumbled, "I suppose Darlene's praying we'll see a ghost."

As our tour continued, Maxine told us that after his first wife's death, Don Hidalgo had taken a young bride, Maria Louisa, who was not satisfied with her elderly husband despite his wealth. As we stood across from Maria's sitting room, we listened to a tale about the brutal murder of a young ranch hand, reported to be Maria's lover. He was found with a kitchen knife lodged between his shoulder blades.

"Nobody was ever charged with the murder, but Don Hidalgo's eldest daughter with his first wife Elena sent to a convent in Mexico," Maxine added as we entered the white-washed chapel on the lower floor of the main house.

As we stood near the large crucifix with its anguished Christ, surrounded by faded paintings of saints, Maxine continued her tales of grief and woe. Seventeen children had been born to Don Hidalgo and his first wife Elena, but only seven had survived childhood. Elena had bled to death with the delivery of her stillborn son, who was buried next to her in the rose garden.

In a hushed tone, Maxine then informed us that mother and child had been seen many times wandering the grounds.

"So, she's the ghost known as The Lady in Black?" prompted Darlene as we stood looking into the children's nursery, where a cradle in the corner appeared to be holding a live infant. I felt myself shiver and was relieved to see it was only a doll.

"That's correct," answered our guide in a voice that was barely audible. "But Maria Louisa also often plays the piano in the music room."

"Are you serious?" Toni demanded. "You mean to say that you hear actual piano music being played by a dead woman?"

Maxine looked pointedly at Toni and replied, "If you are here at the right time, you will hear it too."

But Toni remained unconvinced.

"When is the best time to be here for a sighting?" demanded Darlene.

"It could happen at any time," Maxine replied. "You just never know."

As our tour came to an end, we entered the large walled garden adjacent to the edge of the vineyard. After pointing out some of the medicinal plants, our guide stopped in front of a beautiful bush with deep crimson flowers.

"This was Lady Elena's favorite plant" She pointed to a shrub with open faced flowers. "See how *dark* the petals are? The color is very rare. According to legend, after she was buried here, the petals changed from pale pink to the color of *blood*."

"She was buried here?" I asked.

"Yes," replied Maxine. "Until they moved her body to the cemetery." Then, despite the prickly stem, she deftly broke off one of the dark red rosebuds and handed it to Toni. "For you, my dear," she said softly.

Darlene's mouth opened briefly. I sensed that she was about to demand her own flower, but it was clear that Maxine was only giving out one, and she had specifically chosen Toni.

After bidding Maxine goodbye, we headed towards the parking lot. But since Paulette was famished and Toni had had the foresight to bring snacks and a thermos, we sat down at one of the picnic tables.

"That was interesting," said Toni, "but I guess the ghosts are taking the day off."

"But didn't you *feel* the energy?" said Darlene. "Especially in the nursery. Paulette and I both thought the cradle was rocking."

"Yeah, whatever," said Toni. Then we noticed that Paulette was wandering away from the picnic area.

"Paulette," I called out. "Come eat, it's getting late."

"Look here," she said, full of excitement. As she walked towards us, I could see she was holding an old glass jar. "I found it in the dirt. It's perfect to put Toni's rose in." She gently picked up the flower that was lying next to Toni and placed it in her newly found vase. "It even has a little rose on it."

"You can have the flower and the jar, Paulette, since it means so much to you," Toni offered. "I certainly couldn't care less."

Obviously pleased, Paulette filled the vase with water and placed the wild rose in the middle of our picnic table.

An hour later, we'd left the ranch behind and had driven nearly to the bottom of the hill when Paulette suddenly cried out. "Toni! Did you pick up my flower?"

"Why would I?" demanded Toni. "I gave it to you!"

"Don't *you* have it, Paulette?" asked Darlene.

"I thought I handed it to Toni when I put my jacket on." Paulette sounded panic-stricken.

Toni was annoyed, but Paulette was jubilant when Darlene turned the car around and headed back to Rosa de Castilla. Unfortunately, by the time we drove back up, the gate was already closed. Toni immediately began berating Paulette and insisting she had been the last one to hold the flower.

While they were arguing, I scouted around in the dusky light and noticed that although the car couldn't go any further, there was an opening in the fence that I could easily walk through. I could cut across the pathway that led to the vine-covered trellis along the vineyard, go to the parking lot, and retrieve the flower. I figured if I moved quickly, I would be back before the sun went completely down.

"I'll go with you," said Darlene.

"Not in those shoes." I pointed to her strappy sandals. The truth was, not only could I do it faster on my own, the last thing I needed was to listen to Darlene talk about how she could feel the presence of the spirit world. Toni with her short legs would only slow me down, and I wouldn't even consider Paulette.

Cautiously, I slipped through opening in the fence and headed down the path towards the trellis. It was a little further than I had anticipated and I soon became aware of the silence and the unfolding darkness. Clutching my phone in my cold hand, I decided to break into an easy jog until I reached the parking area. I had been running for a few minutes when I turned around and realized I couldn't see the lights from the car anymore. *It's because of the fog*, I told myself as I headed past the vineyard towards one of the archways.

When I reached the parking lot, the old Cadillac was still there. Feeling relieved that Maxine was still on the premises, I walked over to where our car had been parked and looked at the ground. Although the light was fading, I felt certain I would be able to find the red rosebud in the glass jar, but I didn't see it.

Giving up on the parking lot, I walked over to the picnic tables just in case Paulette had been mistaken. Feeling a little uneasy as the last shreds of daylight began slipping away, I was relieved when my cellphone rang. It was Darlene.

I tried to answer, but couldn't; though I still had power, I could neither take the call or return it. I debated whether I should try to find Maxine, but decided it would be better to go back before it became completely dark. Besides, she might not like the fact that I had basically broken into the place by slipping through the fence.

As a last-ditch effort, I walked over to the Cadillac, thinking that maybe Paulette had wandered that direction. It was then that I saw that both of the tires on the far side were completely collapsed into the gravely dirt and the back window was broken out. The old car clearly could not have been driven for a very long time.

I tried to remain calm, but something about being all alone next to that old dilapidated Cadillac gave me the jitters. As I turned to run, I slipped on loose gravel and fell to the ground. I cringed when my hand landed on what I thought was a dead animal. But it wasn't an animal at all; it was a long blond braid of hair, identical to the one that fell over Maxine's shoulder. I tossed it away from me like it was a rattlesnake, got up, and began to run in earnest.

Nearly out of breath, I ran past the vineyard, searching for the trellis that led to the opening in the fence. It was almost completely dark and there were barely any stars. My eyes were having trouble adjusting. I tried to use my cellphone for light, but it was dead. The air seemed to grow heavier and I thought I felt a sense of decay all around me. I imagined that the ground had been trampled by hundreds of feet, and all those people had met their maker. My heart thudded and I struggled to catch my breath. As I sensed the steady beat of death and loss, I felt almost paralyzed.

In my nostrils swirled the odor of musty white linen. I tried to convince myself that the cold metallic taste of fear was just my own imagination. Suddenly, there was the sound of a baby crying in the distance. *It must be a bird, just a bird,* I told myself. As the cries grew louder, I realized I had no idea which direction the fence was. I stopped walking and tried to get my bearings in the darkness. Finally, the cries began to subside. The ensuing silence was almost unbearable. Through the windy breeze I heard the distinct sound of a piano playing, a furious music that might have been coming from the depths of hell.

"Help me! Somebody help me!" I screamed into the night, afraid to go any further, terrified at the thought of what might come next. I was totally confused and not even sure which direction I had come from. After a moment the piano music ceased, and the only sound I heard was my own breathing. Then I felt a strong but gentle force pushing me towards a path that seemed to have appeared from out of nowhere. I made no resistance, and dared not look back as I gave myself up to the darkness.

Unsure whether it was minutes or hours later, I was suddenly aware of lights and a figure standing by the fence. I breathed a sigh of relief realizing it was Toni, and the lights were from the car. "Are you okay?" she shouted. "I was almost ready to slip through the fence myself and start looking for you."

"I'm fine," I lied, not wanting to give away too many details of what happened. Toni would tease me; Darlene would want to go ghost-hunting, and it might upset Paulette.

On the way home I said little. Paulette sadly came to realize that the flower was gone. Darlene insisted that something mysterious had made my phone go dead. All the while, Toni smugly assured me that nothing out of the ordinary had happened.

A few weeks after our visit to Rosa Castilla, I received a phone call from Toni's ex-husband. He told me that she had collapsed at work and had been rushed to emergency the previous day. At the hospital I was told she had some sort of blood clot and her outlook was grim.

Seeing my dearest friend in a deep coma and clinging for life was almost more than I could bear. Then I noticed something on the table by her hospital bed. I let out a small gasp and called for the nurse.

"Where did *this* come from? "I said, touching the glass jar. In it was a dark flower identical to the one Maxine had given her.

But nobody, including Toni's ex-husband, knew who brought the flower.

The following day Paulette, Darlene and I were all standing at Toni's bedside. "It's definitely the jar and the flower we got that day," confirmed Paulette. "Look at the rose etched in the glass. I don't even think you can find a jar like that anymore."

"It must have been Maxine," said Darlene.

"*Maxine the docent*?" I said. "How would she even know that Toni was in the hospital?"

I looked at the flower and the jar. It had to be the same one Paulette had lost. The bud was now in bloom, and it looked like another bud was breaking through the stem.

I knew right then that I needed to find answers.

It turned out that the Rosa Castilla Docent Society had no knowledge of a docent named Maxine. The only Maxine they had ever heard of was the horse-loving wife of the citrus millionaire who owned the place in the 1920s.

"But obviously, she's been dead for over fifty years," the woman on the phone added.

As for the jar with the distinctive rose etched in the glass, it was used for honey when the property still had several hundred beehives, long before the war.

I took it all in very calmly. I decided not to mention it to the others; now that Toni was on life support, we had more important things to think about.

The day after Toni died, Paulette, Darlene and I were helping to plan her memorial service when her eldest son brought in the jar and the still blooming rose.

"This was by my mom's bed, but there wasn't card," he said. "I guess we should invite the lady who gave it to her to the memorial."

"Who was she?" I asked, even though I dreaded her answer.

"I never met her, but the night nurse told me she thought it was a woman in a cowboy hat. I figured one of you guys would know her."

"I told you it had to be Maxine," responded Darlene.

It was all I could do to keep from slapping her. But then the lights flickered, and for the briefest instant, I saw Maxine watching us through the living room window.

"Maybe she will be there after all." I said.

# INDUSTRIAL BREEDING PROCESS

## TREVOR NEWTON

"I'm telling you, Juan." Hank paused and gulped down the remainder of his beer, then motioned to the bartender for a refill. "If the Pelicans win the championship this year, I'll cut off my fucking foot. This is a Lakers year, plain and simple. We got Lebron now. The other teams may as well throw the towel in as soon as the season kicks off."

Juan's eyes shifted from Hank to a table behind him repeatedly. "Yeah, maybe."

"Maybe? Where's your loyalty? All I hear from that birdbrain at the office is how they got that kid from North Carolina. What's his name? I can't remember, but it sounds like a fucking medical cream for my hemorrhoids."

Juan shifted his eyes back to Hank and chuckled lightly, not knowing anything he'd just said. "Yeah, I don't know. We'll see, I—"

"What the hell do you keep looking back there for?" Hank twisted backwards and his chair creaked under his enormous weight. "Ooooh, I see. Swapping eye kisses with the brunette, huh? Not my type, looks like she hasn't seen the sun since God said 'Let there be light,' but, hey, I'll get outta your hair."

"You don't have to rush off, I'm sorry. I didn't mean to ignore you, Hank."

"Forget about it," Hank said. He strained to stand up, grunting loud enough to garner attention from the other bar patrons. Lighting a cigarette, he patted Juan on the shoulder. "I'll see you on Monday. Don't forget, we got a meeting with that new ketchup company outta San Benito."

"Of course," Juan said. "See you on Monday."

*"Hey, Matt! Put whatever we had on my tab, huh? Even Juan's fruity drinks!"*

A cold sweat broke out on Juan's forehead and down his back from embarrassment, but a cute laugh from across the bar made him forget all about it.

. . .

He was only half awake, caught somewhere between consciousness and dream state. He moved his hands across the opposite side of the bed. She was no longer there, but the warmth from her body lingered in the sheets.

Now, with the sun barely beginning to peek through the blinds, fragments of the previous night shifted through his mind. Seeing her at the bar and making eye contact while Hank went on about sports, aching for him to leave and feeling guilty when he finally did. Her beauty multiplied when he finally worked up the courage to walk over. Cascading dark hair that illuminated against her pale skin, minimalistic makeup, blue eyes.

Briefly, he sat down at her table. Her accompanying friend excused herself and said her goodbyes. Truth be told, Juan hadn't even noticed her. Surroundings seemed irrelevant, almost invisible. Even as two grown men shouted obscenities at each other and exchanged fists at the bar, he found himself too enamored to care.

Before long, they were cruising down Pacific Coast Highway in his ruby red Corvette with the top down. She laughed at every little thing he said, massaging his leg through the entirety of the ride.

"I have a place on the beach," Juan said with a smile. "Del Monte." He coughed and rubbed his nose with a nervous twitch. In that moment, he wondered when he'd last done something like this. Surely decades ago, when he and his ex-wife were still dating.

"This nice car and—"

"It's a Corvette."

"Right, a Corvette." She smiled. "*And* a place on the beach? You must have an exciting job."

"I don't suppose you'd believe me if I said I was some sort of secret agent?" He hoped the question would be dropped. There was nothing fruitful or moderately interesting about the true answer: he slaved away in an office all day with numbers, occasionally leaving its mundane boundaries to interview clients (business owners or representatives) for an out-of-business accounting service. He could tell her the truth and end the inevitable silence with something along the lines of: *it's not much, but it has its moments.* But why bother?

Boring her was the last thing he wanted to do.


Before he could even slide the key into the front door, they were pressed against each other, tasting one another and moaning with desperate pleasure. The door swung open as he blindly unlocked it, and they ripped at their clothing while he led the way to the bedroom.

Sitting on the edge of the bed, he kissed her bare stomach and made circles with his tongue. He ran his uncalloused hands up the coolness of her back while she ran fingers through his thinning hair.

She gently pushed him away, motioning to the master bathroom. "I'll only be a second."

He could feel his cock uncomfortably pressing against the crotch inseam of his pants. As he kicked off his shoes and pulled down his pants, he swore he heard a *buzz* sound from the bathroom. His stomach swirled uneasily and he felt frozen in an unknown fear. He couldn't place why he felt this way. He wanted to call out and ask what she was doing, but his mouth seemed unable to cooperate with his brain.

*Stop being ridiculous,* he thought. *Maybe she's using your electric razor or something.* Deep down, he knew those two sounds did not coincide.

Massaging his cock so its stiffness would not falter, he finally called out for her to hurry up, hoping he sounded more playful than demanding.

Only wearing panties, the moonlight through the window turned her skin a snow white as she inched toward the bed. They locked for a kissing embrace, but he'd had enough of that. He pushed her down onto the bed, and soon her legs were spread and the saliva from his tongue was mixing with the essence of her quivering sex.

He couldn't help but notice she was unshaven, not that he minded, but the origin of that noise still pestered him. He pushed the thought from his mind, internally scoffing that he could let something so insignificant invade his mind during a moment of pure euphoria.

When he finally plunged into her moist warmth, he thought he would release instantly. He relaxed his legs and hindered his movements, but her dissatisfaction was evident. She wasn't interested in being made love to, she wanted to be fucked. He picked up the pace and plunged all the way in with every muscle at his disposal, but her expression of disappointment showed no signs of wavering. His back broke out with that familiar cold sweat and Juan thought for sure his cock would go soft from sheer humiliation. Then she took control. Pushing him onto his back with an incredible amount of strength, she straddled him and began pumping away before he was even comfortable. He was mortified by the limits his age seemed to impose on him.

She moaned and smiled at him, displaying an immense amount of fulfillment. He would rather be on top, in control and pleasing her himself, but as her moans became louder, his mind became quieter. He relaxed his legs and kept his breaths deep, waiting for a signal that she was about to cum. After ten minutes of relentlessness, she announced it with authority. Tensing his legs and gritting his teeth, Juan grabbed a cheek of her ass in each hand, ready to explode inside her. As their orgasms aligned, she dug her nails into his shoulder.

Something wasn't right.

He seemed caught within the orgasm, pressure building where a release should be fluttering. Suddenly she laughed wildly, pressing hard against his chest. Her wide grin parted unnaturally, cracking as her jaw dislocated. A black open-ended needle, pulsing with green veins, burrowed up her throat and lurched into his neck, piercing through his skin. Sharp pain shot through his urethra and as the pain became unbearable, his vision faded to black.


Squirming, rippling waves underneath his skin brought him fully awake. His entire

199

body felt as if it was slightly vibrating and internally itching. As he tried to sit up, a blast of pain in his pelvis took him back down. He threw back the covers. His cock was red and swollen, inflamed. A thick, yellow liquid dripped from the head and the aroma of infection caused his eyes to water. He touched his shaft and pain electrified his entire body.

Burrowing, burning agony encased his organs and as he screamed, maggots fell from his mouth and nostrils.

The *buzz* sound came from the doorway which led to the hall. She was standing there, her single eye sockets now a cluster of thousands. Transparent, veiny black wings prominently descended to her calves.

Juan tried to scream again, but with the maggots clogging his throat, only inaudible gags surfaced.

*"Just relax,"* she said. *"You'll make a great dad."*

# IT COMES TO DRINK

## JUSTIN HUNTER

Gary grabbed a gallon jug of water from the bed of his truck, sat directly down on the ground, and tilted the jug back, taking long gulps of the sun warmed water. Gary's skin prickled at the heat radiating off the 90s Ford, but the truck provided the only shade around. The sun was almost at its zenith. Even thinking about looking anywhere above the Sierra Mountain Range made his eyes hurt. He took drink after long drink, begging his wizened skin to start leaking sweat. Gary knew that if he got to work right away without getting used to the heat, he might as well keel over now and be done with it. He pulled at the loose skin on his right arm and let it flap back weakly in somewhat the same shape before he pulled. His skin felt like dried kiwi rind. It looked like old paper. Not matter how much water he drank, it never seemed to be enough. He rinsed his mouth out with water and spit into the greedy, arid soil.

There was a small pile of materials lying next to him. The makings of a small dry-wash machine he'd fashioned himself. Every now and then he would look around, as if he was waiting for someone that he didn't want to arrive. Gary stood up and put the water back into the truck cab through the open driver's side window. He turned and bent to gather materials.

"Hello," Gary said. "You sharing my shade?"

A tortoise was lying on top of a leather bag that held some of Gary's hand tools. Gary leaned back against the truck and smiled at the creature, who looked at him with the normal tortoise sleepy gaze. Gary put his hands in his pockets and waited. He could get into some serious trouble for messing with the protected animal here in Randsburg. He'd heard that they would even piss themselves so badly when scared that they would dehydrate and die. He definitely didn't want that. Especially since he wasn't supposed to be where he was.

Gary rolled into Randsburg a few months ago. The area was your run-of-the-mill

California mining ghost town. There used to be a lot of gold here. Well, maybe not so much, but enough to keep men like him around since the gold rush days. Randsburg had a gas station and a general store and not much else. There was a motel that basically begged him to take a room, but there wasn't any money for that. Gary never had much money, which was okay with him. But the years hadn't been kind to him and a long life of living off the land had broken him down enough that he'd thought about settling down with as much of a nest egg as he could. When that ran out, he would probably just step in front of a passing tour bus and end it all.

When Gary came to Randsburg, he had an old RV that he'd owned since the 80s when his mother died and left it to him in her will. He found another old timer who lived there and traded the RV for the truck and free use of the man's scrap materials and shop for a couple weeks. In that time, he fashioned the dry-wash and now here he was in the desert. The plan was to wash some of the tailings from the old mine and get enough money to live on. He could mine enough gold for food and just spend the rest of his life right here. It wasn't a bad idea, he thought. Many had it a lot worse than he did.

The tailings he was mining weren't his to mine. They belonged to some corporation somewhere who owned the land and paid some second-rate miners to run the tailings. He didn't like what the men would do if they found him out there. Probably shoot him or something worse. It wasn't like there was a police force worth mentioning anywhere around there. The Wild West was still alive and well in parts of the desert. There were a lot of holes in the ground filled with the bodies of people who died over gold. Still, Gary figured that he could stay out of the company's way and if he was careful, they would never know that he was here. His dry wash was small and he didn't want to take a fortune of gold. He just wanted enough for food and drink. Just enough to stay alive for another day.

The tortoise finally pulled its bulk off Gary's tool satchel and moved off toward the mountains in a straight line that belied some intention of direction. Gary looked off in the direction the reptile was moving and didn't see what the animal was heading toward. He shook his revelry away. His sweat was coming freely now and he could swear he saw it steaming off his arms from the burgeoning heat. There wasn't time to daydream. There was mining to do.

Gary knelt down, his knee joints audibly popping as he did so. He took wrenches out of his leather bag and began putting his dry wash plant together. When all said and done, the machine only went up to waist and was about a hundred pounds all told. He could lug it around to test the ground at his leisure. He looked out over the pile of tailings near his truck and mentally mapped out a grid from where he would take his samples. He dragged the dry wash over to the center of where he planned on starting and began to dig. He dropped small shovelfuls of dirt into the machine's hopper and worked a foot pump that shook out much of the dirt and removed the larger tailing rocks. He would set the sifted sample aside for later panning. Then he would start on another hole. It was tedious work, but he figured it would save him a lot of worthless panning if he found a pretty good streak that the original miners missed.

The sun was setting over the Sierra Nevadas. Gary felt like a sponge that was all wrung out. He had plenty of water on hand, but whenever he took a drink it felt like his body was a sieve and it would come pouring out of him until he felt as dry as a sunburnt corn husk. He'd dug thirty test holes in all. As he stood next to his truck, he gazed upon the rectangular grid of holes. His dry wash plant hummed along as it shook the dirt free from the rocks. He still had many pans to clean out and test. He knew it would take him all night, and as much as he burned during the day, he would have the opposite problem when the sun was gone from the sky. He could already feel the goosepimples rising on his arms as a cool breeze began to carry away the dust and heat of the day.

Gary picked up five pans of dry washed rock and took them down to a small pond a couple of hundred yards down from where he was testing. The pond was made from some runoff from the hired workers' wash plant. It was a small breach in their wall from their wash pool they pumped in. The water was muddy, but it would serve his needs enough to clean out what he'd dug and see if there was anything worth pursuing.

Gary stopped fifty yards from the pool. Something was already there.

Gary wasn't too sure of what he was looking at. The light of the setting sun was in his eyes and his brain was fried from working in the heat all day. For a moment he thought what he saw was a total mirage, but it was no trick of his mind. The thing made it to the edge of the pool and bent directly from the waist, plunging its head in to the water and taking loud slurps as it drank its fill. Gary knew of no man who could bend like that. It drank for a few moments and then folded upward to a standing position, moving with the fluidity of a cobra. It looked around and then walked back the way it came. Gary watched it until it was out of sight. He took a step toward the pool, but he didn't feel safe anymore. He was no longer alone. He walked quickly back to his truck, looking over his shoulder every few steps, silently cursing every time he made a sound above the soft scratching of sand beneath his feet. He made it to his truck, turned off his dry wash and got inside the truck's cab. He locked the doors and let the front seat fall backwards. Then he stared out into the night from the driver's seat of his truck until he fell asleep. Every moment he was awake he thought the creature would appear at the window. He prayed for daylight.


Gary woke up. His eyes squinting from the bright glare of the sun. He sat up. His shirt sucked wetly against the seat. He put his hand to his forehead and rubbed, letting out a little groan. He reached over and picked up his canteen, emptying the contents into his eager mouth. Gary gave the canteen a gentle slap on the end. A few extra droplets went into his mouth. He tossed the canteen back onto the driver's seat and looked around the cab of the truck. He picked up the canteen again and gave it a shake, already knowing it was empty. He looked out the window for a full minute, scanning the horizon. He got out of the truck and went over to his dry washer. Gary began cursing as he realized he left it on all night, and it was out of gas.

"What a waste," He said, kicking the ground. He walked back to the truck, took a five-gallon plastic gas tank, and filled up the dry washer. He emptied the rocks in the hopper and put a new load in. The machine began to chug and shake. Gary brought the gas can back and picked up his canteen from the truck. He closed the door and faced off in the direction of the runoff pool. He wiped a dry hand over his brow. It came back dripping with sweat. He pulled at his shirt. It was getting stiff from the drying sweat.

He walked toward the pond, eyes darting around at almost every step. He made it to a small hill of tailings and stopped. By the pond was the creature. Its body looked all black. Gary couldn't tell if it was wearing clothing or not, but in the daylight, he could discern what looked like spikes jutting from its back.

It was bent over again at the waist and drinking. Gary crouched down in the dirt. He put his body flat on the earth, ignoring the searing pain of the hot ground on through his clothes.

The creature stood up to its full height and turned in his direction. Gary didn't think it could see him, but the creature didn't move. It just stared toward him, unmoving. It was long and lean, the body almost twice the height of a normal man. In contrast, the face looked like a white mask, standing out starkly against the ebony of its skin.

"Not a man," Gary whispered. "Not a man."

After a long time, the creature turned and walked away from the pool, toward what Gary thought was the main mining camp. Gary waited while it moved, and almost stood up to get water when the creature turned back and sat down in the shade of a small, haggard tree.

Gary knew that if he hadn't seen the creature drinking then he wouldn't know it was watching the water. He would have walked right up into its line of sight. The thought made Gary swallow, a dry and hollow attempt that hurt his throat. He put his hand to his head and began rubbing again. He waited until a few dark spots left his vision before crawling backwards, away from the pool and its guardian. Gary crawled about a hundred yards before he felt comfortable enough to stand and return to his truck. He dumped the tailings on the ground and put the pans into the back of the truck. He took apart his dry wash machine and loaded that in as well. All the while his head was on a swivel. His movements were hurried yet careful, lest he make too much noise. He got into his loaded truck and turned the key. There was a clicking sound and then nothing. He tried again and the clicking sound was fainter this time. He looked out over his hood and noticed it was unlatched, laying higher than it normally would. It was like he didn't close it hard enough after doing an oil change.

Gary got out of the truck and opened the hood. Something had severed his battery cables. Holes punctured the hoses of the truck like someone had poked it with a spike. His serpentine belt was cut, but some of the others were okay. It looked like something damaged his truck without exactly knowing what they were doing, so they trashed it like middle school vandals.

He closed the hood and looked out down the dirt road. Fifty miles out from town. Gary put his hand over his stomach. He didn't think he could walk that far. Not without water. Gary turned back in the direction of the pool and the mining crew. He figured he would have to go there and get help. They wouldn't be happy knowing what he was doing out here, but it was the best thing he could think of.

Except between there and here was that creature.

He would have to skirt the pool and the creature and get to the mining camp before his body gave up from dehydration. Gary gazed up at the sun. It wouldn't take long in this heat. That was for sure.

"It comes to drink."

The voice was like sandpaper scraping across violin strings. Gary tried to turn his head and saw the face of the creature only inches away from his own. Its eyes were splotchy white orbs sunk deep within its skull. Its lipless mouth stretched open in an endless smile. Long, thin teeth bunched together in its mouth like a cluster of razor grass. It was hairless, with skin so black that it would be nearly invisible in the darkness. It smelled like fish left out in the sun to rot.

It reached out a three fingered hand and pointed in the direction of the water.

"It comes to drink," the creature said again.

Gary began walking.

He went walking toward the water.

# SHADOW MAN

## FRED WIEHE

Blackness engulfed him. Despair embraced him. The stench of rotting vegetation, mold, and decaying flesh clung to him. Lost in memories of the dead and thoughts of the dying, he reveled in the cries for mercy and the pain-riddled screams that only he could hear. As if rising from the depths of Hell itself, he ascended the rickety wooden staircase. He was but a shadow. But with him, he carried death.

Somewhere in the house, a stair creaked. Emily woke with a start. A door opened and closed. Not loudly, with a bang, but softly. Still, it was the unmistakable sounds of a squeaky hinge, followed by a doorknob bolt clicking back into the hole of a strike plate.

Next to her, Brooke slept soundly. Undisturbed. Oblivious of any sounds in the night. Dark hair covered half her pretty face. A soft snore emanated from her slightly parted lips.

She thought of waking Brooke but didn't. Instead, she sat very still, cocked her head, and listened.

A floorboard creaked in the hallway.

She pushed red bangs from her eyes, held her breath, and waited. Again, she thought of waking Brooke. Again, she didn't. Mostly because she knew Brooke would only make light of her, roll over, and go back to sleep. She loved her, but Brooke could be dismissive at times, thinking her flighty and overly imaginative.

When all remained quiet, she too began to think her imagination was working overtime. Climbing out of bed, she planned to have a look for herself. She slipped on a robe and slippers, grabbed her phone for the flashlight app, and tiptoed to the door. It

206

opened without a squeak. She let the door stand open a crack to avoid the click of the doorknob bolt. In the dark hallway, she stood very still, listening. The only sound was her own breath and beating heart. Both seemed oddly loud and erratic in her ears.

She switched on the flashlight app. The door to the small bathroom opposite the bedroom stood open. She stepped in and turned on the light. Nothing and no one hid there, not even behind the shower curtain. Back out in the hallway, she shone the light down the short hallway toward the living room.

Nothing but shadows greeted her.

Tiptoeing to the living room, she pulled her robe tighter to ward off the growing chill. Why was it so much colder the farther she ventured from the bedroom? Half Moon Bay was cold in October at night, but usually not this cold. She could see her breath. She had grown up in Michigan, and this felt more like wintertime there.

She swept the light across the living room. Except for furniture, it too was occupied only by shadows. The front door was closed. She crept to it. Tried the doorknob. Locked. Just as she thought; she remembered locking it.

Turning away, she left the living room for the small, open kitchen. Nothing and no one hid there, either. Her eyes and the flashlight beam both came to rest on the closed door to the basement. The house was small, only a cottage really, and this was the only other door. It was closed like the front door. But, unlike the front door, this one had no lock. Still, there was no outside entrance. The only way into the basement was by this door, which meant coming through the front door. That meant someone had to have already been down there.

Her breath and heart now ran a race. They were neck and neck, speeding toward panic. Sweat clung to her T-shirt under the robe, even as she pulled the robe tighter to ward off the growing chill. Clouds of fog escaped her lips.

Should she wake Brooke?

She took a deep, hitched breath.

No. She needed to find the courage to investigate by herself. It was probably nothing anyway. No one was down there. It was just the house settling. They'd only lived here less than two weeks and were still getting used to it and its sounds. Every house had its unique noises. And if it did turn out to be nothing, she didn't want Brooke to know. Brooke would tease her incessantly.

After tiptoeing to the door, she quietly opened it. Blackness greeted her. A frigid draft swept up the stairs. A rotting stench rode on that breeze. She didn't remember the basement stinking like this when they moved in. She didn't remember the cold draft either. Crinkling her nose, she fumbled for the light switch on the wall. One bare bulb at the bottom of the stairs illuminated the basement in a sickly yellow glow. Turning off the flashlight app, she slid her cell in a robe pocket.

The top step creaked underfoot. She froze at the sound, not wanting to give herself away if anyone was down there. But there was no avoiding it; she could only be as quiet as the old stairs allowed. She took another step and another, the stairs creaking underfoot with each step.

At the bottom, she scanned the small, square room. Shadows lived everywhere, in every corner and nook. The cement floor was dirty and old tools—hammers, screwdrivers, saws, and tools she couldn't readily name—littered an old workbench pushed against the wall, as well as an array of metal shelves, all left behind by the previous tenant.

But there was no sign of anyone.

She crinkled her nose again at the prevailing stench. It seemed an odd combination of mold, rotting food, and something else she couldn't readily identify. A shiver shot up her spine, and she pulled the robe tight around her like a protective cocoon. White plumes of condensation blew out in front of her with each panted breath. She didn't understand how it could be so cold or what could be making that horrible odor, but it was obvious no one was in the basement—it wasn't big enough to hide anywhere—so she turned to leave.

With one foot on the bottom step, she was plunged into darkness. The door at the top of the stairs slammed shut. Panic swelled in her throat, choking her. Biting down on her lip, she stifled a scream. That was the last thing she wanted to do—scream. Immediately, she tasted blood. She fumbled in her robe pocket for her cellphone, but when she pulled it out, it tumbled to the floor and was lost in the surrounding black.

"Shit, shit, shit…"

With one hand on the railing, she quickly guided herself up to the door, the stairs creaking underfoot as she frantically climbed. But the door wouldn't open. That was impossible, though; there was no lock on this door. She tried the door again. It wouldn't budge. She tried the light switch. Nothing happened.

That was it. It was time not to care what Brooke thought.

With tears in her eyes, she pounded on the door. "Brooke! Brooke!"

But even after several minutes, Brooke didn't come to rescue her. Resigned, she sat on the top step, back resting against the door. She knew she should go back downstairs to retrieve her phone. It would give her light, and she could call Brooke's cell. But the thought of going back down terrified her. So, she sat there, knees pulled to her chin, sobbing and shivering, choking on the stench, unable to move.

And that's just how Brooke found her the next morning when she opened the basement door. "What the hell?" she hunkered down. "Emily, honey?"

Emily moaned. She raised her head and looked around, bleary eyed and confused. "What? Where am I?"

"You're sitting at the top of the basement stairs, silly."

"Huh?" Emily blinked rapidly and ran a hand across her face, then through her short, red hair.

"What were you doing?" Brooke reached out and touched Emily's arms. "What were you thinking?" She helped Emily to her feet. "Were you down there all night?"

"I heard a noise." Emily choked back a sob as her memory focused. "I went downstairs, and the…" She wiped away tears. "… the door slammed shut and locked."

Brooke took Emily into her arms and held her. "That door doesn't have a lock, honey. You could've gotten out anytime."

Emily pushed away. "Then it was jammed. I couldn't get out. I pounded on the door and yelled for you, but you never came."

Brooke snickered.

Emily's eyes narrowed. "Don't laugh."

"I'm sorry." Brook stifled herself. "But you were never locked in. I just opened the door with no problem."

"It was locked, dammit," Emily insisted. "And it smells awful down there, like someone died."

"Okay, okay," Brooke tried to placate her. "Let's go down and take a look."

Emily trembled at the thought.

Brooke flipped the switch at the top of the stairs. The bare bulb at the bottom of those stairs glowed a diseased-looking yellow.

"The light," Emily mumbled.

"What about it?"

"It went out when the door slammed and wouldn't come back on no matter how many times I flipped the switch."

Brooke shrugged. "It's on now."

Emily eyed her partner. If she didn't know better, she would've thought Brooke was trying to drive her crazy.

"Come on, let's go down and have a look." Brooke started down the stairs.

Emily faltered. The last thing she wanted was to go back down there. And for some reason, she didn't trust Brooke. She had no reason *not* to trust her. She loved her. But still she couldn't shake the uneasy, dark feeling in the pit of her stomach that nagged at her not to.

Brooke stopped halfway down and looked over her shoulder, up the stairs. She smiled. "Come on, honey. There's nothing to be scared of down here."

Taking a deep breath, Emily descended the stairs, following Brooke into the small room.

"I don't smell anything too bad." Brooke sniffed. "Maybe it's a bit stuffy and moldy, but that's all."

Emily didn't smell anything like the stench last night either, which just frustrated her even more. First the door wasn't locked but wouldn't open, then the light turned on even when it wouldn't last night, and now the smell was gone. Maybe she *was* crazy.

She eyed her partner.

Or maybe Brooke just wanted her to think she was crazy. Why hadn't Brooke come to help her when she pounded on the door and cried out?

"Is that your phone?" Brooke reached down and plucked the cell off the dirty floor. She brushed the dust and dirt away.

"I dropped it last night," Emily admitted.

Brooke shook her head. "You could've called me. My cell was on the nightstand next to me."

Emily stiffened. "It was dark. The light wouldn't turn back on."

Brooke bit her lower lip and nodded. "Sure… right." She handed the phone back.

"Let's go back upstairs and forget about this whole episode. There's nothing down here except junk that needs to be cleared out. Nothing to be scared about." She headed back upstairs.

Emily took one last look around, her frustration growing, then followed.

"I'm heading for the beach." Brooke smiled. "Want to come."

Emily shook her head.

"Are you sure? It's a lovely morning. Just the kind of morning we dreamed of back home on winter nights. It's why we moved to California. Come with me."

"No."

Brooke nodded. She approached Emily, took her by the hands, and kissed her tenderly on the lips. "I love you."

Emily didn't respond. She couldn't shake the apprehensive feeling that Brooke was somehow responsible for last night. And even if she wasn't, she hadn't been very sympathetic to what happened.

"You need to let this go," Brooke whispered. "You promised you'd try to not be so... *sensitive* about everything."

Emily gave a half-hearted smile. "I'll try. You go. Have fun."

Brooke smiled back and turned to leave. At the front door, before leaving, she turned back to Emily. "I *do* love you."

Emily smiled. Her apprehension eased, if only a bit. "Love you, too."

While Brooke was gone, Emily sat at the kitchen table with her laptop. There was something odd about Brooke's attitude, something she couldn't shake. There was something odd about the house they shared too. They rented the place at Brooke's insistence, but she never shared her partner's love of the house, never felt comfortable. Now, after last night, she wondered about the place and its history. She'd always considered herself intuitive, not clairvoyant or anything but empathetic to her surroundings. She felt things... *deeply*. And this house felt more and more oppressive to her each day, darkening her thoughts, her soul.

Not able to shake that feeling, sure she would find something ominous in the house's history, she Googled her new address in Half Moon Bay. Public records only told her estimated worth, square footage, acreage, number of bedrooms and baths—one of each. Nothing interesting. Other links just took her to realtor sites, which listed the house as *off the market*. Then she came across a reference to the address in an old news article dated September 1996. The resident at the time, Frank Gardner, was a person of interest in what was known as the *Shadow Murders*. The article didn't specify whether he was a suspect or a potential witness, however. It did say that he was missing and asked for the public's help in locating him.

She had never heard of the *Shadow Murders*, but then in 1996 she was only twelve and lived in Michigan.

Quickly, she clicked on a related link that gave more information about the murders. In a span of five years, from 1991-1996, eight women were tortured and murdered in the Bay Area. In each case, the victims' eyes were cut out and their faces were flayed, the skin taken as trophies by the killer. And in each case, in place of the eyes and faces, the killer had left a note that read, *She is now but a shadow of herself.* Profilers and psychologists all had differing theories on what the note meant, but no one truly knew except the killer. Working on an anonymous tip, the FBI raided a house located in Half Moon Bay on Coast Road.

She did a double take on the address. "Shit…" Her breath came out with that word. She hadn't even realized she'd been holding it.

It was their house, hers and Brooke's.

"Shit, shit, shit…"

They had found the eyes and faces preserved in glass jars in the basement's workshop. An APB was put out on Frank Gardner, but he had slipped away into the shadows and was never found. No one could be sure if he was truly the killer, but the murders stopped with his disappearance.

She closed the laptop and stared into nothingness. Her heartrate slowed until she thought it might stop altogether. Her breathing was shallow, almost nonexistent. She didn't move. The air was heavy, oppressive.

When Brooke opened the front door and entered, life began again.

Emily started. Her heart jumpstarted. She took a deep breath and slowly exhaled.

Brooke came into the kitchen. "The day is glorious." She came to Emily, stood behind her, bent down and kissed her on the cheek. "You should've come."

Emily opened the laptop. "Did you know about this?"

"What?"

"The Shadow Murders."

Brooke froze. She read the computer screen. Without answering, she walked to the refrigerator and pulled out a bottled water.

"You did." Emily gasped. "You knew and didn't tell me?"

Brooke opened the water. Took a sip. "Of course I knew. The realtor had to disclose it. I didn't tell you because it didn't matter, and it would've upset you for no reason."

Emily snorted. "No reason? A serial killer lived in this house. That's no reason?"

"It was never proven he was the killer."

"They found his trophies. Eyes and faces in glass jars."

Brooke capped her water. She went to Emily and hunkered before her. "Look, it's one reason the rent was so affordable. We couldn't afford to live in this area otherwise, and I knew this is where you wanted to be."

Emily stiffened. "Don't put this on me. Don't make it my fault we live in a serial killer's home. You made the choice without consulting me." She stood and pushed past Brooke, leaving her hunkered there on the floor.

That night, they went to bed mad. Normally, they fell asleep in each other's arms, many nights after making love. Tonight, they lay on their sides, backs to each other, an angry silence like a wall between them.

Emily woke in the middle of the night to a loud noise. She sat up. Her breath caught in her throat. Next to her, the bed was empty. Brooke was gone. Another noise echoed, the sound of metal.

She slipped out of bed. Forgetting her cell phone and not bothering with slippers or a robe, she crept from the room in only a T-shirt and underwear. She tiptoed down the hallway, stopping in the living room. The temperature plummeted. Her breath escaped in plumes of white condensation. Gooseflesh scampered up and down her arms and legs, across her scalp. Even so, she continued to follow the noises to the kitchen. There, she stopped.

The basement door stood open like a gaping wound. The sickly yellow light shone up the stairs and glowed in the open doorway. It was not inviting.

She went to it anyway. At the top of the stairs she hesitated. Hand trembling, she reached for the railing. She shivered at its icy touch. That same rotting stench prevalent the night before wafted up the stairs.

The noises below continued. It sounded as if someone were rummaging through the tools stored on the workbench.

With the stealth of a cat, she descended into the basement, halting her advance only after feeling the cold cement floor on the bottoms of her feet.

Brooke stood in front of the workbench with her back to her, moving tools around as if looking for a specific one.

"Brooke," Emily muttered.

Brooke spun around, dark hair a tangled mane around her face, eyes wild. She held a paring knife in a trembling hand. "I heard voices." Her own voice sounded thick and heavy. "And I smelled that God-awful stench." Her breath blew out in front of her with every word. She shivered. Then, she stepped toward Emily, brandishing the knife.

Emily gasped and took two steps backward. "Brooke, stop... put down the knife."

Brooke looked at the paring knife in her hand, scrutinizing it as if unaware before now that she even had it.

Emily took another two steps back, toward the metal shelves full of tools.

Brooke shook her head, tangled mane flying. "No, no, you don't understand. I heard strange voices." She advanced on Emily. "You don't understand."

"Brooke, stop!" Emily reached behind her. She felt the wooden handle and the heft of a hammer.

Brooke kept advancing, brandishing the knife.

Emily screamed as she swung the hammer, hitting her lover in the head with a sickening *thump*.

Brooke spun on impact and dropped to the floor.

"Shit!"

Emily dropped the bloody, hair-matted hammer. It clunked onto the cement floor. She dropped to her knees, staring down at the bloody gash on the side of Brooke's head, at the blood oozing out onto the floor. Tears streamed down her cheeks and sobs choked her throat even as she reached for the paring knife beside Brooke's broken body. As if in a fugue state, she used the knife to cut out Brooke's eyes. She placed the eyes on the floor next to her and stared into the empty, black sockets. Next, with a deftness of skill she didn't know she had, she used the knife to flay Brooke's beautiful white skin.

"She is now but a shadow of herself," she murmured, repeating it over and over as she worked on Brooke's face.


Unbeknownst to Emily, he knelt by her side, the stench of rotting vegetation, mold, and decaying flesh clinging to him. *He* was but a shadow. But with him, he carried death.

# THE LOST CABIN

## MARIANNE REESE

The string of bells bounced against the glass, announcing Trent's entrance into Hank's General Store.

The elderly man behind the counter looked up from the small shelf he was constructing and nodded at Trent. "Can I help ya, son?"

"I'm just gathering some supplies for an excursion." Trent looked about. "Is this the only store in town?"

"Depends on whatcha looking for. Stampedes is down the road." He pointed with his screwdriver at the window toward another building. "Sells clothing, boots, and such. The store don't look like much, but they's got some quality goods. This here store sells 'bout everything else. Groceries over there, tools an' gear at that end, some clothes an' touristy junk back there." He twisted hard with the screwdriver, securing one side of the shelf. "We don't get many tourists round here, but I keep a bit of product on hand just in case." He turned over the shelf and tightened the screws on the other side. "And if you need ta be mailin' something, I act as the post office. We ain't got an official post office in this town. Have to go to Trinity. I take the trip twice a week for mailin' packages and such." He righted the shelf and shook it to test its sturdiness. Content with the outcome, he placed the small shelf at the end of the counter.

"Okay, thanks. I'll take a look around."

"Name's Hank, if'n ya need anything," he said as he arranged boxes of lip balm, gum, and mints on the shelf.

"Thanks."

Trent walked up and down each aisle, looking for a few specific items as well as nothing in particular. For such a small store, the selection of staples Hank carried was impressive.

"Where ya' heading?" Hank eyed the items Trent laid on the counter.

Trent nodded toward the scenic mountain scape of the Trinity Alps through the frame of the store's window. "In search of some fabled ruins."

Hank turned to look out the window. He raised a brow as his gaze returned to Trent. "Wouldn't be meanin' that ol' lost cabin, would ya? The cabin people's been searchin' years for near Caribou Lake?"

Trent noticed how Hank referenced the cabin. "That's the one. Laust's cabin."

Hank tilted his head and pursed his lips. "You takin' anyone with ya?"

Trent smirked. "I tried to get my buddy to go, but he chickened out. Said he valued his life too much. Me, on the other hand, I'm not one to pass up an adventure."

Hank nodded. "Your friend's the smart one." He jerked his thumb over his shoulder toward the scenery behind him. "Too many folks have gone in search of that cabin and ain't never returned. Matter 'fact, young man like ya'self went lookin' for it just a few days ago now. Ain't been heard from since."

"Ha. Well, I don't plan on becoming one of those statistics." Trent tried and failed to mask the amusement in his voice. He wondered if Hank was concocting the story to frighten him.

"Take this." Hank handed Trent a business card. "It's the number to the sheriff, if'n you get yourself in trouble up there. Best of luck ta ya, son."

Trent pocketed the card then extended his hand. "Name's Trent."

Hank shook his hand. "Nice ta meet ya. If'n ya make it back, stop on in an' let me know whatcha found."

"Deal." Before leaving, Trent paid for his items and arranged them in his pack.

As he drove off, he looked in his rearview mirror and noticed Hank watching him through the doorway. A concerned look covered his face.


Dusk had fallen on the third night before determination rewarded Trent with his find. A fortress of trees hid a dilapidated cabin that the legendary Ben Laust had built against a granite mountainside. The cabin was farther from Caribou Lake than Trent anticipated. Without his compass and the crude map he had taken from his great-grandpa's journal, he was sure he never would have found the cabin, as Laust hid it well.

The floorboards creaked as he pushed open the door and stepped through the threshold. Trent paused, detecting a low hum that emitted from somewhere within the cabin. He cocked his head, trying to decipher the sound and its location.

"Hello?" He wasn't expecting a reply, as the cabin looked long abandoned except for the faint noise… and a faint light shining from an open door at the end of the dark hallway.

The back of Trent's neck prickled as he approached the door. It hung askew from one hinge. A smell permeated through the opening, assaulting Trent's nostrils. The odor triggered a curiosity he could not ignore. Abandoning his search of the main level, he inched down the long, narrow stairwell carved from the granite shelf where Laust had built the cabin. Four steps down, he stopped midstride and stared at a message etched into the wall. He traced his fingers over the letters as he whispered

215

them aloud: "Can you keep a secret?" The words spun webs in his mind as he wondered as their meaning.

As he continued down the steps, his eyes darted from side to side, searching for more writings, but found none. His mind told him he should call the sheriff, but curiosity overrode his power to reason. Nearing the bottom, he covered his nose in the crook of his arm as the stench of decay thickened.

The dust-encrusted lightbulb at the top of the steps did little to illuminate the cave-like basement that greeted him as he reached the last step. The hairs on his arms spiked with goosebumps as an invisible cloud of cool air surrounded him. An overwhelming feeling of being watched invaded his senses. He squinted his eyes to adjust his vision, to no avail. He could no longer hear the humming sound and wondered if it was a generator of sorts powering the light above. How else would there be electricity in a cabin tucked this far into the wilderness? *Something* powered the light, which meant someone had to be here—somewhere in this rundown cabin. With trembling fingers, he fumbled for his flashlight in his pack. Clicking it on, he stiffened as he moved the beam of light around the room. In a ghostly dance, shadows stretched and danced from chunks of sinewy matter that stuck to the granite walls.

*What the heck had happened down here?* There was no body, but the smell of death told him something had died in this basement. Something had been killed. Was it an animal? Was this a hunter's cabin? This wasn't what he was expecting to find when he set out on his excursion in search of the fabled cabin.

A thin, dark stream that snaked alongside where he stood caught his attention. With the beam of his flashlight, he followed it to what looked like a pile of desecrated entrails. He covered his mouth with his hand and winced in disgust at the sight of congealing liquid that oozed from the putrid mass. The thick liquid flowed in a slow roll to a cluster of holes bored into the center of the floor. He hadn't noticed that the ground sloped toward the uncovered drain.

He turned his gaze from the gore, and his heart skipped a beat at the sight of a boot leaning cockeyed against the wall. Trying to avoid the chunks of matter that littered the floor, he inched closer for a better look. A sickening feeling churned in his stomach as he trained his light on the boot. The boot, once tan, was marred with dark spots and ripped apart at the ankle. A shiver crept along Trent's spine as he recognized the brand, a popular one for men his age, as that of the pair he was wearing. Could this boot belong to the guy Hank had mentioned—the one who was missing?

Trent caught sight of a pipe protruding from the wall several feet above where the boot rested. The pipe's dark channel took on an ominous look, as years of neglect were evident by its jagged edges. With apprehension, he peered in the pipe as he shined his light into the opening. The hole sloped upward for nearly a foot before disappearing at a bend that angled toward the cabin's main level. Trent placed his bare hand in front of the hole, feeling for airflow. Nothing. He curled his fingers into his palm and noticed his fist was about the same size as the pipe's opening. He turned his fist to and fro, contemplating the pipe's purpose.

A thick wetness fell from above and splattered on his wrist. "Shit!" He jerked his hand, shaking off the gunk. Lifting his gaze, he risked a look at the ceiling. Bits of meat hung, like gelatinous icicles, directly above his head. He sidestepped out of target range, not wanting to fall victim again.

From the corner of his eyes, he noticed a dot of red light high on the wall barely visible behind a square of smoke-colored glass. He shined the flashlight on the square. "Is that... a camera? What the hell?"

Trent pulled his cellphone from his pack's side pocket. It was time to call the sheriff. He willed himself to stay calm as his thumb print unlocked his phone to the home screen. His stomach plummeted. No signal.

*Clink... Clink... Clink.*

Trent whipped his head around and beamed the flashlight toward the pipe. Something was rolling through it, the sound echoing as it banged along the pipe's siding. He could hear it through the wall.

*Clink... Clink.*

He fell back, nearly dropping his flashlight but holding tight to his phone, as a metal ball shot from the pipe. It hit the floor with a *clang*, bounced awkwardly then rolled between Trent's feet.

The grenade's explosion was silent beyond the craggy basement walls where the cabin's secret stayed safe with Trent.

# SOUL TOLL ON THE BAY

## GREG TURLOCK

I should have known better.

Today had been like any other Monday: work was work, customers were grumpy and my fellow workers had left their minds at home, buried deep in their weekend trips to Muir Woods or Fisherman's Wharf.

Then it happened: "Mumble, mumble, mumble." I was riding the crowded BART home when my mind was being drowned by the thoughts of others. It was as if fifty people were conversing, rambling and complaining simultaneously—to me.

"Mumble—what? Grumble—what? Hummity, hummity, hum!" The thing was, I couldn't shut them off or even make sense of what they were saying.

I cupped my hands over my ears, hoping to drown out the stampede of thoughts. Heartbeats pounded my skull like a medieval drum. I stared at the floor and began to count the rivets. But with each count, I heard a new voice. Sometimes the voices painted an image—a rape, a murder, a kid in trouble. It wasn't pretty.

Rivulets of sweat gathered near my temples and dripped to the floor. I felt my eyes bulge out like a snake, anticipating the move of its next victim. The train lurched to a stop in Oakland and *he* got on.

Our eyes met immediately. He was a man of the cloth—unshaven, unkempt but with a virgin-white collar and bible held snugly to his chest. His probing eyes pierced through his spectacles and came to rest on me. "He sent you, didn't he? We have been expecting you."

I looked away and continued counting rivets in the floor. "I don't know what you're talking about Father." The thoughts kept rumbling through my mind like a roller coaster on a collision course with reality. I could taste bile as my stomach churned.

"I can help you, my son. Obviously, you're being tormented by the demon himself!" I didn't know whether to punch him or throw up on his shoes.

"Look, preacher, leave me be. I can't concentrate—I'm losing my mind."

"Of course, my son. Your sins are tormenting your scarred soul." He took out a small vial of holy water from his lapel pocket. "Do you want to confess?"

It took every ounce of energy I had to lift my head and make eye contact with him. I didn't like what I saw. His pupils were blacker than original sin itself, a crazed glaze lurking in the guise of a fanatic demon worshipper.

"You know what, Father? You're the one who should confess." I yanked the holy water from his trembling hands and splashed it in his face. He screamed like a chained prisoner from Alcatraz as the water turned to acid and burrowed deep into his eyes. It dripped down his cheeks, plowing a furrow of charred flesh to his jaw. His eyelids hung in shreds, his screams transformed into voices of the damned:

"The voices you hear, are yours on this day
For you are my son, in darkness you'll stay."


"Is this him?"

"Yes, Doctor. The police took him to Saint Francis Memorial and then brought him here—something about a disturbance on the BART. All he talks about are the voices."

"Voices, hmm? Let's have a look. Hello, son. My name is Doctor Beel Zebub. I'm here to help you."

I felt a needle prick my skin, and the cool, silky-smooth feeling of something flowing through my veins. I felt a wave of euphoria sweep over me. It brought me to a place that I didn't want to be.

I could hear *his* voice.

I couldn't have picked a worse time to open my eyes. The cardiac arrest was instantaneous.

My soul was his…

# ROCK 'N' ROLL EATS ITS CHILDREN

## JON BLACK

Kyle reviewed the chapter's final lines.

*Nothing better illustrates this venue's significance as a cultural touchstone than the phrase "Fillmore-era." In serving as shorthand for an entire era, it is unique among American music venues.*

Satisfied, he clicked "print." He had always preferred hardcopy for editing. After stapling the pages together, the finished Fillmore chapter went on top of the others: the Casbah, Cuckoo's Nest, Eve's After Dark, Madam Wong's, the Mint, the Roxy, Troubadour, Trout's, Whisky A Go-Go, and so on. Back to the Gold Rush dancehalls. All the chapters were there. Except one.

He regarded them with pride. This project was Kyle's shot at doing something credible. Something that mattered. It was his chance to break out of a steady but low-paying stream of concert and album reviews into actual music journalism.

His phone vibrated with an incoming text. *What's up with Taya?*

Kyle sighed. Taya, the project's photographer, was talented. One of LA's top concert photographers, she'd brave a violent mosh pit or 300-pound security guard to get the perfect shot. Unfortunately, she was also, well, "capricious" was a kind word. Kyle wondered what she had done now. If Skylar was texting him about it at 3 a.m., it couldn't be good.

*Don't know. What do you mean?* he replied.

*Too long to explain. Come by tomorrow*, Skylar responded.

Kyle wasn't a night owl. The dream had woken him again. The same one that first came a month ago and returned with increasing frequency. Kyle waded through a wide, warm, shallow body of water as he searched for something. Searched for, but dreaded finding. He always woke before locating whatever it was.

Exhausted from completing the chapter, Kyle slept soundly.

He called Taya the next morning, hoping to head off Skylar's problem. Irritatingly, his call went straight to voicemail. Texting also yielded no response. Her social media showed nothing more recent than selfies from a backyard South LA punk show the previous week.

After lunch, Kyle drove to Skylar's Los Feliz office, located above a struggling mom 'n' pop drycleaner just off Vermont Avenue. Framed concert handbills on the wall and a Martin guitar in one corner testified to the professional musician she had once been. Along the way, Skylar Starr reinvented herself, making a living by conceiving, managing, and executing crowd-funded media projects. Her office said she did pretty well for herself.

Skylar contracted Kyle to be the writer for her current project, a pictorial history of great California music venues, past and present. Taya, of course, was the photographer. There was an editor somewhere. Denver maybe? Rounding out the team was Hien, her long-suffering personal assistant.

As always, Skylar radiated intensity. Today, a frown accented her fierce, if attractive, features. Periodically, she ran her hands over the long black hair she invariably wore up. Kyle cringed. He had learned to recognize the gesture as a sign of intense displeasure.

Never one for small talk, Skylar got straight to her point. "Taya's ghosted. I haven't heard from her in a week. Her phone goes straight to voicemail. She's not answering texts. She's hasn't updated any of her social media."

Kyle knew all that but didn't think confirming it would improve his boss's mood. "What was she doing last time you heard from her?"

"She was supposed to be driving to the Salton Sea to take photos of your damn Renewal Room." Skylar answered. Kyle heard the air-quotes around "supposed."

"She's flighty," he acknowledged wearily, "and she's high-strung. Maybe she burned out?"

"She might have," Skylar admitted. "Rock 'n' roll eats its children. You know that as well as I do."

"What do you want me to do?" he asked, unsure he wanted the answer. "Track down Taya?"

"Too late for that. We're on a tight schedule. You're not Taya, but you're a decent enough photographer. Go down and get those shots. I need them by the end of the week."

As Kyle prepared to balk, Skylar raised an eyebrow. "In this city, you don't want a reputation for not being a team player," she warned. "Plus, you're the one who insisted on including the Renewal Room in the book in the first place."

Kyle acquiesced with a sigh. "I'll leave tonight."

As he got up, Skylar grew conciliatory. "Kyle, we both know you're perfect for this project. It's the chance you've waited for to show what you can really do. How great it would be if you got a photography credit, too?"

After the meeting, Kyle dropped by Taya's apartment. Her roommates hadn't seen her for a week, but didn't seem concerned. He wasn't surprised that Taya failed to leave contact information.

Back at his place, replaying their conversation in his mind, Kyle considered telling Skylar what she could do with herself. The book would survive being pushed back until the Taya situation was sorted. Grabbing his phone, he thought better of it. He wanted the book done as badly as Skylar did. Plus, she was right, he had put the Renewal Room on their radar.

After allowing both the afternoon traffic and unseasonable summer heat to subside, he rolled out of LA on the 10 in his '67 Pontiac Bonneville. Kyle had never been into cars... until he purchased one that was a small piece of music history. He bought the Bonneville from the financially distressed former bassist of the Holsters, a San Diego group that explored a catchy, radio-friendly brand of country-influenced rock years before anyone had heard of the Eagles. The group, and its ride up the charts, had come to an end in that Pontiac. Somewhere out near Needles, highway patrol officers had discovered an eight-ball of coke on the seat after a high-speed chase.

Leaving city lights behind, the car radio found a new-wave program worthy of KROQ's glory days: Animotion, Gleaming Spires, The Little Girls, Humans, Missing Persons, The Motels, Oingo Boingo, Romeo Void, Stan Ridgeway, and it just kept going. Songs started running together in Kyle's mind as his thoughts drifted to the strange manner in which the Renewal Room first came to his attention.

In his constant quest for musical memorabilia, Kyle had cultivated an octogenarian Boyle Heights native with a secondhand shop on East 1st. It was no Eagle Rock or Echo Park vintage store, with the good stuff already picked-over or marked up. It was a junk shop, plain and simple. He'd found some rare gems there and Old Linden made sure to set aside anything he thought Kyle might like.

"Got something for you, kiddo," Linden croaked during Kyle's visit last month, handing him a two-tone concert poster, its edges curled with age.

*Sheri & The Skylarks*
*Eddie Cochran*
*Maddox Brothers & Rose*
*April 21ˢᵗ, 1954—The Renewal Room*

Kyle had never heard of the Renewal Room. And it caught his eye that Sheri & The Skylarks, obscure if talented rockers, had top billing over rockabilly golden boy Eddie Cochran. Linden wanted $20 for the poster. Giving him $40, Kyle knew he was still cheating the old man.

Back home, Kyle dived into online research. The Renewal Room had been a nightclub someplace called Renovaro Beach on the Salton Sea. As to the act's billing on the poster, research reminded Kyle that Cochran had just begun his too-brief career in '54. Perhaps more tellingly, he discovered the Renewal Room's owner was none other than Sheri... of Sheri & The Skylarks.

Digging deeper, Kyle's appetite was whetted by a dozen black and white photos scattered across the net, plus one scanned handbill. The Renewal Room had been no dusty roadhouse. It was a swank establishment flourishing during the Salton Sea's brief brush with glamor and affluence during the '50s and early '60s.

One photograph showed an exterior that was nondescript, save for chrome double doors. Each was set with a large circular window and etched with an odd, almost Deco, insignia. Other photos revealed an elegantly apportioned interior, also awash with chrome. Its marble dancefloor, elaborate bandstand, leather couches, high-backed chairs, and long drapes gathered to Doric columns testified the establishment hadn't courted riffraff.

But it was the musicians who had traveled through the Renewal Room that inspired Kyle to include it in the book. The venue would be his hook for the piece which made his reputation. Pictures showed homegrown California rock, rockabilly, and country virtuosos. The handbill, headlined by Martin and Davis, testified the Rat Pack had been through. A blurry image on a T-bone Walker fan site revealed the bluesman strumming his Gibson on one of the Renewal Room's leather couches. Another photo, he was certain, showed Ivory Joe Hunter tickling the keys of a baby grand.

Of course, there were several photos of Sheri & The Skylarks. Even in grainy black and white, Sheri's strong features, penetrating gaze, and long, dark, curled hair were compelling.

The Renewal Room had followed the Salton Sea's descent into obscurity. Kyle found no reference to when the club closed. A photo of its ravaged exterior, posted to an urban explorer website about Salton Sea ruins, confirmed its doors had shut for good. The shot revealed broken windows, much of the doors' chrome gone, what remained was faded and scratched.

A couple sites referenced a book, *First Stars: Evolution of the California Sound 1946-1966*, published by the University of California Press. Kyle shuddered at the prospect of slogging through what gave every indication of being someone's thesis-turned-publication. Still, its chapter on Sheri & The Skylarks discussed the Renewal Room. Using his alumni borrowing privileges, he had obtained a copy from the UC system library before leaving town.

Near Indio, Kyle left the 10 and turned south onto Highway 86. Hosting the Coachella festival, Indio became the global center of music journalism for a week each April. And was a musical dead zone the remainder of the year.

Though the car traveled in quite the wrong direction, its radio slipped into a Bakersfield mood. As the Bonneville's headlights cut through the darkness, illuminating strips of barren landscape on either side of the blacktop, Haggard sung about turning 21 in prison, Buck Owens was under her spell again, and Joe Maphis crooned about dim lights, thick smoke, and loud music.

Serendipitously, it was followed by the rambunctious proto-rock of Sheri & The Skylarks.

Sheri, from everything Kyle knew, was a musical puzzle. As talented as she was enigmatic. Raised in the San Joaquin Valley, she was surrounded by musical traditions carried by Dust Bowl refugees from the prairies of Oklahoma and Texas. Sheri quickly mastered the rough, energetic country stylings popular in local honkytonks.

When the sounds of rock and rockabilly reached the West Coast, she transformed from honkytonk angel to rock 'n' roll queen. Assembling a new band, the Skylarks, Sheri barnstormed through California's earliest rock clubs and released several regionally-popular sides on the local Crest and Specialty labels. Though they influenced many better-known rockers, including Eddie Cochran, Sheri & The Skylarks ended in obscurity. Some would say, in tragedy.

Merging onto Highway 111 and approaching the Salton Sea, Kyle rolled through North Shore, Bertram, Bombay Beach, and Pope. Lights shone from maybe one building in five. Inky silhouettes against the starry night, the vacant buildings reminded him of giant teeth.

A few miles after Pope, a figure appeared in the dark road. Logically, Kyle knew, he had no time to notice details. Taya must have been on his brain. He swore the figure wore a broomstick skirt and had the photographer's distinctive long, braided hair. As Kyle made a panicked, clumsy swerve into the other lane, the figure disappeared. Not darted into the darkness. Just blinked out of existence.

Kyle straightened the Pontiac and cursed at himself. He had been driving too long. He was too tired. In the empty darkness, his mind conjured phantoms.

The red and blue lights exploding in the rearview mirror, however, were all too real. Kyle cursed again. Of course he had to swerve like that in front of what was probably the only cop between Indio and El Centro. A run-in with small town law enforcement wasn't what his evening needed.

He pulled the Bonneville to the road's side, the aging Police Interceptor following behind him. Approaching the car, the officer scanned the Bonneville's interior with his flashlight baton.

Kyle rolled down his window. Tall, with a ginger mustache, and wide-brimmed hat, the policeman was a caricature. And he was wearing sunglasses. At 1:00 in the morning, he was wearing mirror shades. This did nothing to improve Kyle's attitude toward the exchange about to occur.

"License and insurance," the officer demanded. He examined the documents before returning his attention to Kyle. "Mr. Acevedo, I pulled you over because you were weaving back there."

"I'm sorry officer, I saw something in the road." It was as close to the truth as Kyle wanted to come.

The officer asked if he had been drinking or using narcotics. Kyle responded in the negative. Considering Kyle's response for a moment, his face softened. "You a little tired, son?"

"Yeah, I am."

"It happens pretty easily on this stretch," he acknowledged, handing back Kyle's documents. "Tell you what, there's a motel a couple miles up in Renovaro Beach. Nothing fancy, but it will do. Failing that, pull your car off the road and get some sleep."

"Thank you. I'll make it to Renovaro. That's where I was headed anyway."

"Have a good night and be safe," the officer said before returning to his car.

Relieved, Kyle coaxed the Bonneville back onto the blacktop. Between dodging the phantom figure and being pulled over, adrenaline kept him wide awake the rest of the way.

He barely made out the faded "Welcome to Renovaro Beach" sign as the Pontiac rushed past. By night, the community offered few signs of habitation, looking even more ill-favored than the other towns he'd traveled through. A lonely security light provided the only hint a decrepit service station wasn't permanently shuttered. There was some kind of 24-hour diner. Another faded sign took him south on Palms Avenue toward the water.

Sitting on the beach, the Boca Inn motor court was obviously another relic of the Salton Sea's glory days. Its large, bright, neon sign was in sharp contrast with the rest of the establishment. Built in an L-shape, one wing appeared to have been boarded-up and closed for decades. Even the other wing left Kyle wondering how often it saw use. Between them was a glass-fronted office where a smaller neon "vacancy" sign flickered weakly.

Opening his car door, a wall of torrid air hit Kyle. The artificial, and accidental, inland sea's odor was so briny and ichthyic it almost overpowered him. *Better get used it to it*, Kyle told himself.

Inside the motel office, the Salton Sea's aromas were replaced by the smells of mildew and stale cigarette smoke. Carpet and upholstery, once the height of early '60s fashion, had grown faded and dowdy. On the walls, yellowed photos showed sportsmen enjoying themselves on the water. A laminated sign proclaimed "Insured by Smith & Wesson."

After Kyle rang the bell on the desk, the proprietor emerged from a rear door. She could have been anything from a hard thirty to a soft sixty. Her hair and traces of lipstick were carrot colored. A nightgown concealed, barely, an ample bust.

She regarded Kyle appraisingly. Extinguishing her cigarette in a crowded ashtray, she smiled. "What can I do for you, sweetheart?"

"Do you have a room for the night?"

"As many as you want," she replied with friendly sarcasm. "Just one night?"

"I think so."

"If you decide you want to stay longer, just let me know." When she quoted the price, Kyle made her repeat it to ensure he heard correctly. He doubted there was a cheaper room in the state. Signing the guest register and taking his metal room key, he felt as if he'd stepped back in time.

"Ice machine is next to the office," she explained. "The AC is quirky, but if you kick it hard enough, it'll work. Let me know if you need anything else."

Kyle wondered if her emphasis on "anything" was only in his imagination.

The room wasn't as bad as he expected. It smelled only faintly of smoke, the bedding had been replaced within the past decade, and the AC worked after the first kick, rattling terribly. He'd had worse apartments.

Though he should have expected no Wi-Fi, it came as an unpleasant surprise. After sending Skylar a text confirming his arrival, he sank into a deep sleep.


Kyle was back in the water. Its heavy warmth pressed ominously against him. Wading along, occasionally ducking beneath the waves, his fingertips searched the sandy bottom. On the distant beach, he was aware of darkened buildings, dim lights, and the faint din of people. Submerging one more time, he grimaced as his fingers brushed against something firm.


Kyle woke. Sunlight poured in around the privacy curtain's edges. He had kicked his blankets and sheets to the floor. A sour taste cloyed in his mouth. His body shouted that it was sore, dehydrated, and very hungry. After showering and dressing, he walked up Palms Avenue toward the main road. Passing what remained of the trees which had once given the road its name, now just gray-white skeletal trunks baked by years of sun and scoured by years of windblown sand, Kyle reached the diner he'd spotted last night.

Blue paint peeled from the cinderblock structure, its wide-paned windows caked with dust and brine. A utilitarian sign proclaimed "24 Hr. Diner." It was the dry-erase board out front that grabbed Kyle's attention. *Breakfast Special: poached eggs w/ lox, hazelnuts, and strawberries.*

"The special. Is that for real?" he asked the lone server.

She nodded.

"Special and an orange juice, please."

He settled into a booth, its cracked vinyl seat less than comfortable. The diner's inside was cleaner than its outside, but only just. The sparse clientele was an odd mix of short-haul truckers, CalEPA employees, and idiosyncratic locals. Its décor was folk-art, including a disturbing pastel interpretation of Goya's *Saturn Devouring His Son*.

With a wan smile, the server placed Kyle's meal in front of him.

The special was exactly as described. And it was delicious. As pleased as he was mystified, Kyle vigorously tucked in to his food.

Leaving the diner, he reflected that, by daylight, Renovaro Beach's desolation was picturesque rather than ominous. Across 111, atop a low rise, sat an abandoned wooden church. Its design spoke of an antiquity atypical for the region. After photographing the Renewal Room, perhaps he could get some shots of the church as well.

Kyle knew where to look for the Renewal Room. Street signs, clinging to Renavaro Beach's former glories, still proclaimed the road Boardwalk Boulevard. Walking parallel to the shoreline, aside from a few graffiti-covered concrete pylons, it was clear the eponymous boardwalk had long ago disappeared.

Having seen pictures, it was easy to spot the building. But the Renewal Room's decline continued in the decade since the ruined photo posted online. Sections of the wall had crumbled, revealing the studs, drywall, and insulation beneath. The gorgeous chrome doors were gone, replaced by a large piece of plywood with a red and white "No Trespassing" sign. Curiously, the plywood had been tagged in spray paint with the same symbol once adorning the club's doors.

He took a few photos on his digital camera before walking around the building's outside. In back, Kyle found the remains of a wooden deck which once stretched out over the water. The skeleton of a gazebo still loomed over the desolation. Those hadn't been in any of the photos. It was a small discovery, but a discovery nonetheless. Kyle took more photos. He hoped the shots of dead fish strewn around the ruined gazebo were poignant.

The club's rear doors were also replaced with plywood. Here, however, explorers, transients, and scavengers had done their work. One corner was loose enough that, crouching, Kyle wriggled inside.

Empty windows and holes in the roof provided dim illumination. Here, too, years had ravaged the Renewal Room. Its chrome had vanished, as had the chairs. Wooden frames and rotted stuffing were all that remained of fine couches skinned of their leather. Successive layers of graffiti covered Doric columns, once a pristine white. The old bandstand, long ago graced by legendary artists, was a wreck.

Though many tiles were missing, and those remaining were in bad shape, the marble floor was mostly intact. It had been inlaid with the same distinctive sign as on the front doors, another feature not documented elsewhere.

Taking photos, Kyle found the Renewal Room retained a spectral charm. For all its decay, he could easily visualize the club as it had once been. Almost hear the music and the anonymous babble of patrons. Losing track of time, Kyle discovered he had taken over one hundred photos inside the venue.

Surely, that was enough. Yet Kyle felt the urge to linger. On the other hand, there was the "No Trespassing" sign. The Salton Sea wasn't a wise place to tarry, uninvited, on someone's property. After running through a mental checklist to ensure he'd taken all the shots he'd need, Kyle shimmed back outside.

His encounter with Renewal Room left him drained. Temping as it was, he decided against checking out the church. He just wanted to get back to LA.

Instead of its usual rough purr, only impotent grinding came from the Bonneville's engine. Uttering some choice words, Kyle got out and popped the hood. Whatever the problem might be, it wasn't any of the things he had learned to troubleshoot since acquiring a classic car. With additional colorful commentary, Kyle hiked to the aging service station. It looked like the kind of place that might have a mechanic on duty.

And it did. Unfortunately, it was open only on alternate days. Today, of course, was not one of them. Kyle made some quick calculations. Towing the Bonneville to LA and repairing it there would be more expensive than staying an extra day in Renovaro Beach and having their mechanic look at it tomorrow.

The Boca Inn's proprietor was reading a magazine and smoking a cigarette as he entered the office.

"It turns out I need to stay another night." He smiled.

"Okay." Either he had imagined her flirtation or daylight cured her interest. Her demeanor was curt to the point of unpleasant. Fixing a skeptical stare on Kyle, asking for payment she demanded he re-sign the guest register. Not wanting to antagonize her, he politely handed over cash and signed the register. More awake and alert than last night, this time he noted the signature above his.

Taya had been here after all. Somehow, knowing she came this far before flaking out made it worse. For all he knew, she already had the photos and this trip was unnecessary. He would definitely have words with her when she turned up again.

Returning his gear to the hotel room, he texted Skylar an update.

*Sucks,* she replied. *Remember to keep receipts.*

Reflecting on what to do with an extra day in Renavaro Beach, Kyle realized he could visit the church after all.

Walking across the empty Highway 111 to the top of the rise, Kyle noticed a small cemetery abutting the church. Erosion long ago rendered its sandstone monuments illegible. If the church had ever known paint, the elements had likewise stripped that away. Its naked wood was sickly gray in color.

Unlike other Salton Sea ruins Kyle had encountered, the church was at least unmolested by people. The walls sported no graffiti and every filthy pane in its narrow, sharply arched windows remained unbroken.

Forcing his way inside, Kyle pressed against one of the massive double doors. Its heaviness gave the illusion of resistance, a trick of the mind making it seem as if something pushed back against his effort.

Entering the church was like walking into a furnace. Grimy windows let in light but trapped heat. Decades of oppressive temperatures had warped the wood inside, giving the impression that the sanctuary had been designed in accordance with some unearthly geometry. Years of heat had sweated resin out of the wood, crystalizing like spittle from some giant beast.

Any furnishings had long vanished; only the rows of pews and a simple pinewood pulpit remained in place. On the pulpit's front, in place of the expected cross, Kyle was surprised to see the same strange sigil from Renewal Room's doors and floor. He wondered if the congregation that once worshipped here had been less than orthodox.

It was an unpleasant environment. As if the hot, stale air wasn't bad enough, the shadows and warped wood gave Kyle the impression someone was behind him, looming over his shoulder. After taking a few photos, he was glad to leave. Compared with the sanctuary, the normal Salton Sea heat came as a relief.

Unsettled by his visit to the erstwhile church and realizing it had been a long time since breakfast, Kyle revisited the diner. He was only half-surprised to find the dinner special was chile relleno stuffed with queso adobo, polenta crumble, pulled pork, and fresh cilantro.

The server, the same one from breakfast, reacted to Kyle's return with a neutral stare.

"A special and an iced tea," he announced, returning to the booth where he'd sat earlier.

Other than bringing his food, she ignored him, even after he thanked her. It was unsettling, especially following his treatment at the hotel. But the meal, every bit as remarkable as breakfast, went a long way to improving his mood.

Afterward, Kyle noticed a gray van in the diner's lot, parked so as to be clearly visible from the highway. In front of the van, a wide assortment of objects was displayed on blankets. A hand-lettered cardboard sign proclaimed *The Happy Drifter: Vintage Stuff—Handmade Jewelry—Secondhand Goods.*

Curiosity piqued, Kyle approached. The roadside emporium's skinny, thickly-bearded proprietor rested in a lawn chair, head shaded by an oversized sombrero, an open tallboy clutched in one hand.

"How's it going?" Kyle asked.

"Just another day," he replied in a strong, pleasant tone. Bright blue eyes shone from a weathered face dominated by the man's dense, dark beard. "See anything you like, let me know. I feel like making a deal."

Kyle glanced over a blanket of homemade jewelry and another of used electronics and appliances before focusing on one piled with books. The selection was haphazard, fiction and nonfiction covering many genres, themes, and publication dates. He zeroed in on several issues of *BAM*, all bundled neatly together with string. For two decades, the 'zine had been *the* publication for keeping a pulse on Bay Area music. They would be a great professional resource… and a lot of fun to read.

"How much do you want for these?" Kyle handed them over.

Wetting his index finger, the Happy Drifter counted the 'zines. "Twelve issues. Ten dollars work for you?"

It was a steal. In LA or San Francisco, the same collection would cost at least $100 from anybody who knew what they were doing. While the Drifter was counting, Kyle spotted a well-worn history of the Salton Sea. It might be useful background for his chapter about the Renewal Room.

"What about this?" he asked.

"You've got a fine eye, my friend. Four dollars?"

Kyle couldn't respond immediately. On another blanket, alongside the used electronics and appliances, a red Leica grabbed his attention. The high-end camera was an anomaly among the rejects. It was also identical to the one Taya used. Examining the wares more carefully, he spotted a thumb-sized piece of lapis wrapped with copper wire. The pendant was as distinctive to Taya as the red Leica. Even in the heat, Kyle shivered.

Stammering awkwardly through the rest of the transaction, Kyle clutched his book and magazines and walked quickly away.

The Renovaro Beach Police Department was a singlewide trailer covered by a free-standing corrugated aluminum roof to keep the direct sunlight off. Parked in front was a familiar-looking Police Interceptor.

Its inside was as Spartan as the outside. Maps and a few mugshots were pinned to the walls' cheap wooden paneling. A venerable coffeemaker sputtered in one corner. Behind a cluttered desk sat the officer who had pulled him over last night, casually strumming an acoustic guitar.

"Hello again. Mr. Acevado, isn't it?"

Kyle nodded.

"You look awake now." He studied Kyle for a moment. "Maybe you look a bit too awake. What can I do for you?"

Kyle poured out the story of the missing photographer who was the reason behind his visit to Renovaro Beach… and how he found two items belonging to Taya among the Happy Drifter's wares.

The officer frowned. "Sal's eccentric, maybe even a bit 'touched' as they say. But, other than public intoxication, he's never made trouble." He paused. "Still. I need to check this out. And when I'm done, we need to talk about your missing photographer. You want to wait here? Or do you want me to find you at the Boca Inn afterward?"

"I'll stay here."

Setting the guitar down, the policeman rose, grabbed his hat, and put on his sidearm. Leaving the station, he turned back to Kyle. "Make yourself at home. There's coffee, of a sort."

Hearing the Interceptor roar away, Kyle settled into a threadbare chair. Looking around, he noticed a door labeled "Bathroom and Cell."

With nothing else to occupy him, he reached for his recently acquired book. It had been published in 1994, a time when the Salton Sea's fortunes were turning from bad to worse. Checking the index, he flipped directly to the section about Renovaro Beach.

*This site is unusual for hosting two different communities over its history. Before Renovaro Beach, there was Renewal, a small religious settlement occupying the same location.*

*Renewal was established in 1906, the year after engineers from the California Development Corporation accidently created the 350 square mile Salton Sea while attempting to redirect water from the Colorado River. Viewing the inland sea as a divine portent, a religious movement called the Temple of Renewal relocated here from their original community deep in the Santa Monica Mountains.*

An old photo showed the church that Kyle had visited just a few hours earlier. Beyond, a haphazard collection of crude cabins, lean-tos, and shacks stretched to the shoreline.

*The Temple's insular and clannish nature means little information is available about them. The few secondhand accounts which have been preserved suggest the group believed in bodily immortality in this world and conducted rituals centered on an esoteric interpretation of communion.*

*In 1935, Renewal and its entire population were wiped out by a flash flood.*

The church's location on higher ground, Kyle realized, explained its survival.

The area's later history proved unremarkable. When the Salton Sea boom began, the site where Renewal once stood was tapped by local entrepreneurs for new development. Rechristened as Renovaro Beach, its first buildings were erected in 1953. At its peak, it boasted a marina, public beach, six hotels, and a variety of clubs and restaurants, crowned by the Renewal Room. Decline set in during the 1970s, with floods in '76 and '77 striking near fatal blows.

The officer returned, taking a moment to situate himself behind the desk. "I got a statement from Sal," he began. "He says he bought the camera and some jewelry off a couple who came through yesterday. At this point, I have no reason to doubt him, but I'm going to follow up." He removed his hat and wiped his brow. "First, though, we need to get a missing person report out on this lady-friend of yours."

Kyle told him everything he knew about Taya. As they talked, he learned the officer was the sole employee of the Renovaro Beach police department. "I'd call myself 'chief,'" he chuckled, "but I wouldn't have anybody to order around."

Passing the diner on his way to the hotel, Kyle noticed that the van had gone. He considered returning to the station and letting the officer know. In the heat, that seemed awfully far away. He'd mention it when they spoke next.

Back at the hotel, Kyle turned both locks on his door and latched the security chain. He had no intention of leaving the room before morning.

Phone in hand, he tried distracting himself online. Its small screen wouldn't allow him to forget the strangeness all around. Instead, he took *First Stars: Evolution of the California Sound* from his bag. He was glad he'd gone through the hassle of checking it out from the UC system library before departing LA. Holding the book close to his face and shutting out the world, Kyle relaxed just a bit as he read the entry for Sheri & The Skylarks.

*Born Cheryl Pantano in 1931, her original country act was called Cheryl & The Cowboys. Jumping to rock, she rebranded herself "Sheri" and jettisoned all the Cowboys except Tina Wood, backup singer and Pantano's childhood friend. She also remained linked romantically with Cowboys guitarist, Sam Couchman.*

The author gave props to the Skylarks as full partners in the act's success:

*At a time when female drummers were rare, Jessie Mae Jones was a rhythm powerhouse. A rumored lascivious streak to the percussionist prompted behind-the-hand comments about "Yes, you may" Jones. Also flouting convention was Delia Miller on standing bass. Tom Salinger's rich tenor voice complimented Pantano's strong alto. Guitarist Jimmy "Irish" Nell laid down fluid licks in country, rock, or rockabilly.*

*Opening the Renewal Room in 1954, Sheri provided a forum for up and coming artists like Cochran. By booking high profile touring acts, she also lent musical credibility to the upstart Salton Sea.*

*The group's transformation from rising stars to obscure legends began in 1965, when Pantano experienced a series of personal losses. Her parents were killed in auto accident. Couchman died from a burst appendix. Wood overdosed on barbiturates. Sheri never recovered. She made no further recordings and her live performances quickly dwindled to nothing. The following year, she disappeared from the public eye. Nothing is known about her later life. No death certificate has ever been found.*

If still living, Kyle calculated, Pantano would be almost ninety. Against the odds, but certainly not impossible. The Renewal Room, the book declared, had declined with Sheri's career, closing its doors by the end of the 1960s. Setting the book aside, he closed his eyes. Sleep came with surprising ease.

Kyle woke with alarm. As his limbic system screamed danger, he knew instinctively that someone had tried the doorknob. Bolting from his bed, Kyle crept to the door and gazed through the peephole. He saw only a fish-eyed view of the parking lot. Empty, save for the incapacitated Bonneville.

Perhaps he had imagined it, but Kyle wouldn't take any chances. After pushing his dresser against the door, he packed everything and got dressed—ready to exit at a moment's notice. With nothing to do but wait, he reclined on the bed. To keep anxiety at bay, Kyle resumed reading.

*For many years, Pantano's origins were contentious. Some sources indicated her family were "Okies" while others suggested native Californians. Documents recently uncovered in Fresno County reveal elements of truth to both.*

*She did grow up in the San Joaquin Valley, where her family mixed well with recent arrivals fleeing the Dust Bowl. They were an important musical influence as well as highlighting her chameleon-like ability to blend and change her image. Pantano, however, was born in California, in a now defunct Imperial County community named Renewal.*

Exhausted, Kyle drifted asleep.


Again, he searched beneath the waves for something he dreaded to find. Surfacing for air, Kyle beheld electric lights illuminating the crowd which watched him from a distant deck. Boisterous music sounded as figures danced around a brightly lit gazebo. Diving into the water once more, his fingers wrapped around something curved and solid. Emerging, he clutched a human skull, its surface marred by long, deep scratches.

Kyle struggled to stay afloat as he screamed.


Kyle awoke on a cot. He was in a jail cell, with the red-mustached policeman looking at him from the other side the bars.

"What am I doing here?"

"You're not under arrest, if that's what you mean. You're in there as a precaution," the policeman began, before explaining that Kyle showed up at the station during the night, ranting about dead bodies in the water down by "that old club." After telling his tale, Kyle apparently passed out.

"I spent a couple hours wading through that God-forsaken soup and didn't find anything." The officer didn't look or sound pleased.

Kyle couldn't remember any of it.

"Look," the policeman said, "I'm not sure if you're on something or you're having some sort of episode, or what. I don't think you've got bad intentions, but you might be a danger to others. You're definitely a danger to yourself. I called the last number in your phone. Ms. Starr is driving down to get you. Until then, I'm keeping you where you are."

Hours later, Skylar entered the cell with the officer. Given her usual temperament, Kyle was surprised. Not only did she refrain from making her telltale gesture of displeasure, running hands over her worn-up black hair, she actually smiled at him.

"You take it from here?" the policeman asked.

Skylar nodded before turning to Kyle. "Okay, cowboy, let's get you home."

Exiting the station, hairs stood on the back of his neck. Amid the clutter on the officer's desk were parts from a car engine. They certainly looked as if they could be from an old 455 V-8. Precisely the kind of engine sitting in his currently inert Bonneville.

Outside, panic overtook him. Again, he shook in the sultry air. "We need to get out here now, Skylar," he said. "Forget my car. Forget my stuff."

"Kyle, what's going on?"

Walking to her car, he told Skylar about the engine parts. Then he rushed through an erratic account of the events befalling him since arriving in Renovaro Beach.

She took his hand, giving him a sweet, almost patronizing, smile. "Kyle, the officer's right. Something's happened to you. How can you be sure those parts are from your car? Half the cars around here don't look like they'd move. And, yes, I'm concerned about Taya, too. But isn't it more likely she flaked out than that she got killed by some drifter? The Salton Sea does strange things to people. Don't let it get to you."

Skylar's words and touch reassured him. He realized how he must sound. No, he couldn't be sure the parts were from his Bonneville. No, it wasn't likely something gruesome had happened to Taya. Yes, Renovaro Beach was a weird place. Alone, dancing with the ghosts of the past, maybe he had gone a little loco.

"Okay," he said with a smile he didn't quite mean. "Let's get my stuff and get the hell out of here."

At the hotel, they loaded his bags into Skylar's MINI. "As long as we're here," she said, "Let's see this Renewal Room I've heard so much about."

Kyle stared at her like she had lost her mind.

"Come on, we'll be in and out in two minutes." As Kyle prepared to protest, Skylar added, "I drove all the way here to get you. It's the least you can do."

"Okay, two minutes."

He insisted they park to the Renewal Room's side. There, her car was unlikely to be spotted by anyone concerned about trespassers. Around back, Kyle led Skylar past the plywood barrier into the club.

They weren't alone in the dimness. The policeman was there. So was the hotel owner. And the waitress. And the drifter.

"What the hell?" before Kyle finished the sentence, the officer pinned his wrists, slapping cuffs over them.

Turning to Skylar, he was shocked by her lack of surprise, her expression of expectation. She moved away from him, joining the others. Letting down her hair, with black curls falling around her face, Skylar bore a remarkable resemblance to Sheri Pantano.

"You're her granddaughter!" Kyle exclaimed.

They all laughed.

"No. Sheri never had children. I never had children, I mean. Kyle... I *am* Sheri."

He dismissed her words as madness. Then he noticed the others. And recalled photos of the Skylarks. They all matched. The hotel's proprietor looked like Jessie Mae Jones. The woman from the diner, Delia Miller. The Happy Drifter, without this beard, was the spitting image of Tom Salinger. Hadn't the officer even referred to him as "Sal?" And the policeman himself? Jimmy "Irish" Nell.

Which was crazier? What Skylar claimed? Or that, coincidently, these five people were all dead ringers for the Skylarks?

After wrestling Kyle to the floor, Jimmy Nell positioned him atop the symbol inlaid into its marble.

"I was born right here, Kyle. Back in '31," said Skylar. Or was it Sheri? "My parents were with the Temple of Renewal. Daddy started feeling guilty and told some outsiders about what went on here. They got a posse together, rode into Renewal, and killed everyone but our family. Then they burned it all. Except the church. They were afraid to go there because of what they thought they saw inside."

She stared feverishly into the distance, as if replaying it all in her mind. "They said it was a flood that killed them all. And the lie got told so many times it might as well be true. My family and I? We were spared. But we were also marked. We saw how the outsiders looked at us. Daddy thought, if we stayed, sooner or later an 'accident' would happen to us. Just like one had happened to Renewal. He moved us up to the San Joaquin Valley and we just blended in with the Okies."

As the others frenziedly tore away Kyle's clothing, Skylar stroked his hair. "My folks worked hard to put the Temple behind them. I think they almost succeeded, except for those nights they woke up screaming. It was easier for us kids. It was all like a dream. Then, in '65, everyone I loved died. I decided I wasn't ever going to die. When everyone at Temple got slaughtered, I was just a little girl. But I remembered enough of the ritual to revive it. I initiated the rest of the band, too. Our communion works, Kyle. It keeps flesh and blood young forever. But it also takes flesh and blood to work."

The five formed a circle around him, her standing over his head. "Sorry it has to end this way, Kyle. But I told you at the beginning. I told Taya, too. Rock 'n' roll eats its children."

Kyle screamed as rows of needle-like teeth erupted from the gums of Skylar and her band. When they began tearing through his flesh, Kyle couldn't scream any louder. No matter how much he wanted to.


Excerpt from *Great California Venues, Past and Present*, copyright 2019:

*This book is dedicated to writer Kyle Acevedo and photographer Taya Vanderlaren, both of whom vanished during its completion. Fans of California music owe them a special debt for rediscovering Renovaro Beach's Renewal Room. Hopefully, their work will inspire new generations of fans to visit that fascinating location.*

— SKYLAR STARR

# FRY MACHETE'S MONSTERS, MUNCHIES, AND MAYHEM

## STUART CONOVER

"So, when I'm in California, I like to take a load off and have a good time. If I'm at the beach, I want to get something quick and easy. What's easier than a food truck when you are just looking to kick back your feet and soak in the rays? Not much!

"If you've got a taste for something a little different than your standard dogs or may not be quite of the human persuasion... I want to introduce you to the 'The Cryptoid Truck' which has been serving the hunger of all types all day and all night. It opened a couple years ago by two of the most unlikely of friends and they have cornered the market on this ghoulishly fun and original take on finger foods.

"With a mobile meat wagon and a tolerant attitude, they've been able to dominate the late-night scene. At least for those brave enough among the living, dead, undead, dying, and even some merfolk to keep things fair across the board. You can find a little of everything here in this rolling sliver of SoCal and it's all coming up right now on "Monsters, Munchies, and Mayhem."

The camera cut and Fry Machete sighed as he leaned against his 1996 Lamborghini Diablo and lifted his sunglass to rub his weary eyes. He might feasibly live forever at this rate, but thirteen seasons of crossing the country showcasing food joints for the fiendish wore thin, even on him. One would have to make a deal with the devil to find this much success and keep ratings up after so many years. Or, if not the Devil, maybe a deal with the next best Evil God out there available on short notice.

Of course, any deal like that would come at a price as Fry knew all too well. He had a job to do, though, and not sucking up to the audience at the other end of the cameras. No. His real job involved slaying some of the monsters that lay in plain sight among the human populace and fed off them. The information came in packets he had mysteriously been receiving since he had started hosting the show. The ones that linked together murders which had been committed by the nightmares made real. The ones kept secret from the public and, per his latest batch of information, death was sticking to The Cryptoid like white on rice.

Looking at his reflection Fry slowly slid the shades back over his eyes. They were rimmed with almost the same color red as his short spiky hair. He couldn't sleep from the hunger, again, but the last thing he needed was the studio to think he was on drugs. Again.

The Nom Network might not be able to fire him, but they could make his life a living Hell if they so choose to.

While he had been on the wrong side of substance abuse in the past, that was when he was trying to hide from starving all the time. He had no plans to spend another six months getting clean from a drug he was no longer on. These days he was just hungry.

All he wanted was a snack and his stomach rumbled in encouragement, but that was one craving he wasn't willing to satisfy. Not again.

Just as his frustration kicked in, Fry's assistant bounced up. Her overly positive nature and unlimited surplus of energy had him convinced that she wasn't human. At least not purely human. He couldn't ask, though, HR policies and whatnot. The last thing he wanted was a lawsuit on his hands.

Discrimination against nonhumans was a hot ticket for the blood-sucking lawyers these days. Hell, it was even worse than sexual harassment. Whoever had thought it had been a good idea to let vampires have equal rights in the legal system had really ruined it for everyone else.

God, how he hated them all.

Sighing, he threw on a smile as Karen opened her mouth and still couldn't help but wonder what creature could be so wickedly happy all the time. Better yet, who he had pissed off at the network to be stuck with her.

"So, Boss, I think you're going to really like this one," she said. "I was just talking to the chef and not only do they cook everything in pure lard, but the rumors are it's human fat!"

"Humans are animals," he muttered, though she steamrolled on. Maybe she hadn't heard or was just completely ignoring him.

"Of course, they won't say what kind, but you can imply the Hell out of it. Inspections being what they are, they couldn't do that without labeling it, but it'd be a great sound bite or two for the show."

Fry did everything in his power to keep the smile plastered on his face for her as his stomach did somersaults. Ratings. It always came down to ratings. That was her job, though. It was just hard to focus on that with the rising need to feed.

"That's great Karen, I'm sure to use that. What were the specials today that I needed to bring up?"

She looked down at her clipboard, blonde bangs covering her eyes and Fry swore she still watched him.

"It looks like some spicy deep-fried eel kabobs called The Electric Eel. You'll try a mystery dish known only as The Teasing Tentacle. It's a squid tentacle stuffed with their secret recipe. Finally, you'll have some garlic-crusted crustacean on a stick. They call it From Another World for the different flavor that pops in your mouth with each bite. Though, if there's time, they also want you to talk about the Deep-Sea Challenge eating contest that they have."

"Does it look like things have gotten bad enough that we're going to talk about food eating contests?"

A fire burned in his eyes, barely concealed by his sunglasses as he pointed a finger at her.

"I'm not that desperate for ratings."

"Sir, I was just thinking—"

"NO!" he cut her off. "It's bad enough that we're still doing this traveling road-show. I'm not going to cheapen it even more with that innate drivel. There are already other shows on another network for that crap."

"Yes, sir." She bit her lower lip and turned to go. "Oh, and you're expected inside in three minutes."

Shit. He was going to hear about that little outburst from the studio. Any time he outright disagreed with Karen, he heard from them. At least he hadn't let out his little digs on another network's show in public. Or, even worse, on film.

Sighing, Fry readjusted his shades, put on a saccharin smile, and walked up to the back door of the truck. He hated filming in these things. Hot and cramped as is, imagine adding extra lighting, a cameraman, and Fry's enlarged gut. No one could truly be happy during shoots in food trucks. Hell, half the kitchens they were in were too small.

Not even thirty seconds passed before his forehead was beaded with sweat.

*Just wonderful. This is shaping up to be an absolutely fantastic night. I can't wait to see how much better it can get.*

Fry had just finished filming in Chicago, and he hadn't yet adjusted back to the stark contrast in temperature. Things were quite different from the Still-in-Winter-Spring and the 70-degree nights here at home. The Windy City had always had bad winters, but ever since global warming had really kicked in the winters of the Midwest seemed to last forever.

Not only that, but the snow made that much harder when there was a killer on the loose.

Fry had no idea why the suckers still lived there. What kind of an idiot would put up with the cold when there was still plenty of places who considered fifty degrees a cold winter?

Two men were prepping food for the cameras for filler shots on the show. The chefs had the same uncomfortable posture of everyone who ended up on Triple M and didn't look naturally laid back while cooking. They were trying too hard. Everyone wanted to be Fry.

At least he wasn't going to have to coach these two that much for the camera.

The chefs were both showing off and Fry finally cleared his throat to get their attention.

They looked up and excitement broke out on one of their faces while the other didn't look as if he knew how to be excited. Clearly, he knew which one spoke to the customers. He wondered which of these two fresh-faced looking pups was in charge.

"Fry!" the younger of the two shouted out. Of course, with so many nonhumans out in public, age became too difficult to guess anymore.

Fry stuck out his hand to shake theirs. He wanted to see if he could tell by touch if they were human or not.

"Johnny Applegate," the first said while vigorously pumping his fist.

The second man slowly wiped off his hand before reaching out with a little too firm of a grip and a smile that didn't quite reach his eyes.

"Dakota," Mr. Personality said simply before looking away.

"Like the state?" Fry prodded and forced himself to not wince as Dakota's grip tightened to where it almost crushed his hand.

This one didn't feel human no matter how well he had the appearance down. Maybe Fry had found the killer he was looking for.

"Yes, just like that." the grip finally loosened and gave one last solid squeeze before letting go. Dakota glanced up for a second before looking away. Fry couldn't read his expression.

Fae weren't that strong, and vampires avoided open flames. Perhaps he was a shifter of some type. Fry needed to know exactly what kind of monster Dakota was before he could take him down. Oh, and if he was responsible for the rash of recent customer deaths. Fry couldn't just go out and kill one of them for not being human, no matter how much he might want to.

That would make him no better than they were.

"So, fellas." The smile crept out of Fry's voice. "What exactly do we have going on?"

Applegate immediately jumped in, his gaze bouncing back and forth between Fry and the camera. A far too fake of a smile was plastered on his face and the words were coming out of his mouth at a mile a minute.

"Whoa, whoa, whoa, home slice." Fry held up his hands. "You're going to have to slow your roll just a second there."

So much for not having to coach either of these two to look good on camera.

"The smile and enthusiasm are great but, while one of my friends may always want you to kick it up a notch, you still need to act natural. Act human." He paused and looked at Dakota, "Do you talk to your customers that fast?"

Applegate clearly understood and calmed down so the two could develop a rhythm. That let Fry's mind wander. He would have to find out what species Dakota was and get him away from the cameras before he made his move.

Fry probably wouldn't get anything done before they finished shooting the episode.

With a few takes on the first dish now on film, it was time to switch things up and get a pre-commercial attention grabber in.

"I've got to tell you, those Electric Eels were off the hook. When we come back, I'm going to share some Garlicky Crustacean on a stick with these gentlemen, and we'll be finishing things up later with the mysterious Teasing Tentacle." He oozed the last three words out in a suggestive tone and raise of an eyebrow. "It's all coming up when we return to Monsters, Munchies, and Mayhem."

"Cut!"

"'Scuse me for a second, fellas. It's hotter than Hell in here." Fry walked off. he had started to figure out a plan to get Dakota to out himself.

Clearly, Dakota wouldn't be in the kitchen if there was something in it that could hurt or expose him. Fry had a plan figured out for that, though. A potent dose that mixed silver, sulfur, sriracha, and mayo. Not enough to injure someone, but more than enough when taken together to expose most of the nonhumans out there for the monsters they really were.

Making sure no one was paying close attention to him, Fry slid a capsule out of his car and debated grabbing a weapon, too. The enclosed room in the food truck could work to his advantage, though. Most of the cooking items could double as a weapon in a pinch.

He walked back to the food truck there was a huge smile dripping off Fry's face. His pulse quickened as he knew that he was nearing in on his target. He often felt that in another life he would have been a natural born hunter.

Or serial killer.

He buried that thought.

Fry kept telling himself that the killing wasn't for pleasure.

He had to do it.

Not just as revenge for what had been given to him, for what had been taken in return, but because lives were at stake.

He didn't understand the bargain that had been struck until it was far too late. All he knew is that the monsters had to pay. Especially those that were hurting innocent humans.


Striding into the truck, his pulse was racing as he tried to decide how to get the tablet into something Dakota ate. And a way to get some of the creature's blood.

Though it looked like that last part wasn't going to be a problem.

Fry almost laughed when he saw Dakota tightly holding his hand while Applegate scrambled to get a first aid kit open.

Fry noticed it was a small cut but deep enough to see that the blood was a dark crimson. Natural. This wasn't the blood of a shifter. Besides, if that's what Dakota was, he'd be healing already.

"It's not too serious to pass up being on the show, I hope," Dakota said, watching the crew as they finished bandaging Chef's finger.

"Oh, absolutely not!" Applegate cut in. "As quiet as he's being tonight, this is all

Dakota has been able to talk about for the past month. Ever since we found out we'd be on the show."

Fry was puzzled. That didn't seem like the man before him, or how a killer, would react. Still, Fry was sure that whoever was committing the murders was related to this food truck. Perhaps it was one of the patrons?

Fry looked out into the sea of faces for those waiting for food and his stomach growled. He tried to tell himself it was from the futility of investigating in the day he had here, and not from the hunger that gnawed at him.

Like it or not, he needed to feed before he lost control.

"Well, if you are all bandaged up, we'd better get going," Fry stated. "You've got regulars to feed and we've got a show to film."

Fry considered dosing all the food going out, but he didn't have enough pills with him for that. Besides, there could be any number of paying customers in attendance that weren't human, and he couldn't risk losing the cover of his show for hunting the dangerous ones.

The chefs were halfway through talking about the various shrimp, lobster, and crab that could end up on the daily special when, finally, Dakota poured himself a glass of water. While Fry felt growing doubts about Dakota being anything other than human, he had a chance to figure it out now.

Fry moved in closer, pretending to get a better view of the crab which was being cooked in his honor. He turned back to give the camera one of his trademark looks showing how sneaky he was being. In doing so, he made it look like he accidentally knocked Dakota's glass over.

"Well, that has me caught red-handed." Fry held up a pair of the crab's claws and raised his eyebrows." He bent down and picked up the glass before his mark had a chance. "Let me get that for you, home slice."

It was now or never.

Fry turned away and crushed the capsule into the cup as he started filling it with water.

Smiling, he handed Dakota the new glass of water and tried not to flinch as the man's fingers brushed against his. The quiet man was far too nervous around him and it showed while he thanked him profusely for the water. Could he know that his reign of terror was close to coming to an end?

Fry took a step back and prepared for a reaction when Dakota took a big swig.

Only none came.

Fry's heart dropped. He had been so sure of himself.

Dakota wasn't one of the creatures. Fry had to keep the frustration out of his voice so that the real murderer would not suspect something was off.

"Now, what everyone wants to know is a bit more about your signature dish, The Teasing Tentacle."

"Well, this is a specialty of my own creation," Applegate said from behind him. "It's a little something I worked out that no one can get enough of!"

Fry swung around just as a tray full of pre-cut tentacles floating in a liquid was being pulled out from a fridge.

"The secret is in the marinade," the young man continued.

Fry stuck his finger in it and put it to his mouth before Applegate could stop him.

"Hmm... it tastes like soy sauce, basil, and..." he trailed off, raising an eyebrow and pulling at his goatee. "I'm actually not sure on the rest."

"Well, that's what makes it a secret recipe." Applegate tried to mimic the sly look that Fry gave the cameras. "And if I told you, I'd have to kill you."

They both laughed though Fry suddenly felt uneasy. Had he been targeting the wrong chef this entire time?

His train of thought was abruptly cut off as his unease faded to the background. His stomach truly rumbled, and Applegate laughed.

"Don't worry, Fry, this'll be ready soon to fill that appetite of yours."

All Fry could do was smile and nod. The hunger had blossomed to new depths and he was using all his willpower to keep it in check.

"What can I say," Fry said through clenched teeth. "Your food just leaves me wanting more."

"Why don't you try the real thing and quit wasting time on just the sauce?" Applegate asked.

Still playing to the camera, Fry was on autopilot as he took one of the tentacles on a stick being offered to him and heartily took a bite. This kind of food would never take the hunger away, but sometimes when he jammed enough down it could alleviate his urges.

"Mmm... this is—" he paused to lick off his fingers and knowing that was a mistake the second his flesh touched his lips, "—a totally fresh take on squid."

His stomach grumbled so loudly he worried that the camera would pick it up. He clutched his stomach with one free hand to force himself to not double over.

Whatever was in the marinade was setting off his need to fill his belly.

He had to get out of here, away from these people, and the cameras before he did something stupid. "Cut!" He got out of the truck before bursting into a sprint, Applegate's laughter trailing behind him.

"Fry! What the Hell?" Karen yelled after him, the bouncy enthusiasm in her voice nonexistent for once.

Out of habit, he ran towards his car. On the way, he realized that he was in no condition to drive and switched direction towards the beach. While being a celebrity allowed for certain eccentric actions, this probably wasn't one of them. Fry could feel the camera phones of everyone who had pulled up to see Fry interviewing their favorite food truck trained on him.

Fry knew that he had to get away, but the beach stretched indefinitely in front of him.

Suddenly the pain became unbearable and he pitched forward. He could hear someone approaching him across the sand.

"Stay back!" he rasped. "You have to..."

The pain came in waves and forced him down. He could smell the scent of the sauce in the air. Applegate must have come for him and if he was going to go down in public for what he was, Fry didn't care who the killer was if he could take the bastard with him.

Snarling, he rose to his feet and pounced on the man standing over him.

Through a dim haze, part of him recognized that it was Dakota he had pushed to the ground before his teeth sank into the man's flesh. That rational part of his mind could only observe. He mostly shut down while the hunger overtook him.

Fry tried not to watch as he tore into the man. He couldn't close his eyes to the life that he was taking but pulled himself back from it and let the hunger take over. In fact, he became so disconnected that he wasn't aware of the cameras that were filming or the people watching.

All that mattered was the meat. Each and every savory bite of flesh that he tore off. The true price for his pain, the unstoppable hunger that he had allowed to build once again would finally be his undoing. As Dakota's life blood gurgled out with his last breath, Fry licked his lips. His mind was awash with the fear of what was about to happen and the hatred he felt for those who had made him this way.

Shakily, Fry got to his feet and turned around. Before him stood Applegate, the camera crew, and Karen, who was on the phone. Probably with the police.

"Yes sir, we've got it all on camera," she bubbled. "No, there shouldn't be any problems getting him to agree."

In his mind, Fry knew that he would be lucky if he went to prison for this. Non-humans found guilty of murder ended up taking a long walk off a short pier.

Karen hung up and bounced up to him before handing him a towel.

"Clean yourself off while we take care of this. I want you presentable when we talk about your new show."

He took the towel and looked on in confusion as Applegate took an envelope from Karen and one of the cameramen started dragging Dakota's body back to the truck.

"New show?" He wasn't sure what to make of it. "What's going on?"

"First off, get that tone out of your voice. After this little stunt of yours on camera, I just got bumped up from your assistant to your executive producer." Karen smiled wickedly. "Next, we're about to announce, 'Fry's Foodie Fights.' A new show where for the first half of each episode you go around the country checking out and participating in food contests or eating competitions. In the second half, you will host public events that pit foodies in the area against each other."

Fry glared at her with teeth clenched. The smile that crossed her face was inhuman in the sadistic satisfaction she clearly felt at this turn of events.

"Oh, don't give me that look. This is where the money is, and we all know how far you're willing to go to earn another buck and have your face on TV." She paused. "We're also going to have to talk about your little side project and hunger issues. The first is going to be stopping, as the studio feels that you've been too sloppy with your work, while the second... well, the second is why I now own you."

Fry fell to the beach, the sand working its way into his clothes and he didn't even care. As the spring breeze warmed his skin the waves slowly rolling onto the beach carried away his last hope of ever going back to a normal life. With those hopes went any chance for revenge against those who had turned him into one of the monsters he despised.

"The studio might have wanted to lower monster killing to help their shows be accepted," Karen said. "But these days, it's all about the bottom line."

# THE CACTUS

## PATRICK CANNING

The Cadillac DeVille, a new '75 model, colored a cactus white then red as it raced by at a good clip.

Glancing in his driver's side mirror, Steven saw the three-pronged plant disappear back into the desert's darkness. There had been a cactus just like it outside the living room window of the house he'd grown up in. Mother would play piano, every day, just for him, while he sat and looked at the cactus.

The piano playing on the DeVille's 8-track cassette was good, but not nearly as good as Mother's.

"Good and evil," said a voice behind Steven. "Racket if I ever heard one."

Louis.

Louis stretched lazily across the backseat of the big sedan, unbuttoning his black rodeo shirt with a groan. "Lord Almighty, this heat. Can we at least listen to some different music? Don't know why I need to keep askin'…"

"And I don't know why I need to keep telling you," came the reply from the front passenger seat. "Steven's driving, so he picks the music."

Robert.

With his tight crew cut, black-frame glasses, and white, short-sleeved dress shirt, you'd think Robert had just stepped out of NASA mission control. But the three men were a long way from Houston. They were a long way from anywhere really. California was big, and so was its desert.

"No harm in askin', is there, fairy boy?" Louis drawled in Robert's direction.

Robert adjusted his glasses in irritation. "I just don't know why you have to be so rude about it. I really don't."

"Don't start." Steven's dark-ringed eyes were bottom-lit by the glow of the speedometer. His head was shaved, his face stubbled. The body under his gray undershirt was wiry but muscular. Even allowing the twenty years that had passed, he bore almost no resemblance to the apple-cheeked boy in the photo dangling from the rearview mirror: smiling proudly next to Mother's piano in his Sunday Best, cactus faintly visible in the background.

Now he was roaming the countryside with two men Mother never would've approved of. Good-for-nothings, she'd have called them. Steven may not have had the bravado of Louis or the smarts of Robert, but he was the decision maker, the king. King of the losers maybe, but a king just the same.

He lowered his window to spit and invited a furnace blast of air that cleared the sweat gathering on his jawline.

"Lord Almighty! At least keep the window shut," Louis complained from the backseat. "Anyway, what I was saying is that mo-rality, so-called, is a waste of time. It's all perspective at the end of the day, so why put any stock in how another person *thinks* you should act? Excepting your boss or old lady, of course."

Robert rolled his eyes. "Next we're gonna hear about the virtues of Nixon."

"We'll look back on this time in disgrace," Louis snapped. "This country should've supported its President! Now we're stuck with a weak-willed hillbilly."

"You voted for Ford!"

"I voted for *Nixon*! Woulda cast a separate ballot for vice president if they allowed it, which they damn well should."

"How would that even work, Louis? It's shocking to me you're allowed to vote at all. I keep saying they should have an I.Q. standard."

"So smart, aren't ya, Robert? Smart brain and a smart lip. I'll bust that smart lip wide open you keep it up."

"Always *straight* to violence with you—"

"*ENOUGH*." Steven squeezed his eyes shut and the car momentarily drifted into the other lane. Neither of the other men protested; it had been over an hour since they'd passed another car.

Steven opened his eyes, got back into his lane, and tried to enjoy the piano.

"Can we *please* switch up the music?" Louis asked with over the top politeness.

"Why don't we just change it," Robert said tiredly.

"Fine." Steven ejected the 8-track.

All he wanted was to listen to the piano, to think of Mother. Like always, that was apparently too much to ask.

His fingers scrolled the tuner through a forest of static until it finally picked up a news report.

"*—n Dooley escaped from Barstow Psychiatric Hospital after killing two attendants with an improvised knife. Dooley is also suspected in the murder of a third Barstow resident, identity yet to be released, killed soon after the escape—*"

"No. I'm sorry." Steven pushed the 8-track back in and sighed with relief as the charming piano melody resumed. A pressure valve opened in his skull; he could breathe again, think again. "News reports are just police blotters these days, they never have anything good to talk about."

"See but that's what I'm saying," Louis leaned forward, resting his forearm on the seatback like a friendly neighbor. He slicked the pomade sweat oozing down his forehead back into his jet-black hair and wiped his hand on Robert's shoulder. "Take that psychopath the radio just mentioned. May be, he's a real devil, or may be, he had good reason to gut those guards."

"Oh, that's rich." Robert brushed fitfully at the stain on his shoulder. "I would just *love* to hear the justification for why those men deserved to be murdered."

"How do we know they weren't mistreatin' him? Maybe he was jailed innocent in the first place. Same for that third person got killed. No tellin' what they put the fella through. All in how you look at it."

Robert gave up on the setting stain and sighed. "Well it's very clear how *you* look at it, Louis. And I must say I find it quite disturbing."

Steven refused to join the other two on their well-worn track of argument. Louis and Robert disagreed on everything. Which bubble gum flavor to buy. Which state had the best fly fishing. Which team should've won the World Series. And they were both in it for the combat, sometimes even switching positions in the middle of an argument. Louis pushed Robert's buttons and Robert let him, sending them around and around until Steven was ready to scream.

But he was trying to be better.

He concentrated on the dashes of yellow being inhaled by the Caddie's white hood, on the oven-baked air rushing through his open window, on the pleasant piano dancing through the car's high-quality speakers.

The music calmed him down. It always had.

He'd been angry as a child. Bad even. But Father had died and left them a good deal of money, so young Steven had received a lot of treatment for his moods: fancy doctors, fancy tests, fancy medicines. In the end, only Mother's piano had helped.

The windshield's endless scroll of cactus and sand was suddenly invaded by something new.

"Look at that," Steven said.

Louis and Robert stopped arguing as Steven brought the Cadillac to a stop behind a weathered blue pickup, sitting half on the road with its hood propped up.

There was no sign of movement, just the drift of dust they'd been pulling through the desert that fell softly across the back of the truck like a dirty rain.

Louis blew a raspberry and flopped back down onto the bench seat. "An empty truck. Whoop-dee shit. Let's keep going."

"Someone might need our help," Robert said.

"Then why don't you go and ask, *Robert?*"

Robert looked anxiously at the truck, then busied himself by cleaning his glasses.

Steven looked back and forth between them. Mother was right. Good-for-nothings.

"Christ, I'll do it. You two are completely worthless sometimes."

He flung open the door and stepped out into desert air, each breath a bite of a stale biscuit. His legs were stiff from the long drive and a healthy fear of the unknown. The Cadillac's headlights spot lit the truck. Steven followed his shadow up the rear bumper and peeked carefully into the bed: a rusty shovelhead and some cinderblocks.

He moved on to the cab, which was similarly sparse: a few roadmaps and balled-up candy wrappers littering the dash.

Up at the front fender, he carefully laid a hand on the exposed engine block.

"Engine's hot," he announced as he climbed back into the safety of the Cadillac. "Someone was driving that thing not too long ago."

"Oh, come on," Louis said, finger-combing his greasy hair. "Whole damn desert's set on broil. Truck could've been there for days."

"It'd be warm, not hot," Robert protested. "The sun's been set for hours."

Steven jerked the DeVille's handle down to drive and they shuddered back onto the road. "Well we didn't pass anyone, so either they wandered off into the desert, which you'd have to be crazy to do—"

"Or he's somewhere up ahead," Robert finished. "Which means he came from the same direction we did. Barstow. *Barstow*." His voice was shrill.

"So what?" Robert yawned.

"The mental hospital was in Barstow, you moron. The news report? The escaped murderer?"

"Oooooh," Louis tickled his fingers against Robert's ear.

"Knock it off, Louis," Steven said. "And Robert, don't you get hysterical."

"But the news report said he stole someone's truck," Robert whined.

"It said vehicle," Louis corrected.

"A truck's a vehicle last time I checked."

"*Last time I checked*," Louis mocked.

"Shut up," Steven warned, and the men fell silent.

He twisted the steering wheel just to feel something solid, his sweaty hands drawing a squeak from the ring of red leather. Whenever Louis got hysterical, Steven's imagination took the imagined horror and ran with it. But not this time. He was trying to be better.

Steven drove in silence, letting the 8-track's piano curl around his mind until the roadway bleached white and the dashes of yellow charred black. Miles turned to octaves; an infinite keyboard stretched to the horizon—

*A hitchhiker filled the headlights.*

Steven slammed bare foot on the brakes and jerked the steering wheel. The Cadillac pitched around in a full circle before coming to a rocking rest.

"Holy shit," Louis said. "Did we hit him?"

"No," Steven panted, his mind stinging from the sudden splash of adrenaline. "At least I don't think we did."

"Steven, please keep going," Robert begged, looking nervously in his side mirror.

Steven was about to listen, when a hand fell on his shoulder.

"Hold on a tick," Louis said. "Let's say the fella on the roadside back there is the fella they're lookin' for. Likely there's some kinda re-ward."

"The reward is a prison shank between the ribs," said Robert.

248

Louis ignored him. "C'mon, Steven. Even with Robert's yellow belly, we got the bastard outnumbered three to one. And I'm the one that's gonna be sharin' my seat, so my vote counts for double."

"But I count the votes," Steven said flatly. He tried to wipe the sweat from his face but his undershirt was soaked-through.

What kind of person almost hit a man and just drove away? A good-for-nothing, that's who. He was better than that.

"Louis is right," Steven announced. "If it's the fugitive, we could score a big payday. And if he's just some poor schmuck that ran out of gas, we'll have done our good deed for the week. Just let me do the talking, you two put people on edge."

"You're putting our lives in the hands of fate," Robert complained.

Louis nodded out the back window. "Here comes fate now."

A man shuffled out of the darkness and into the cherry-glow of the DeVille's tail lights. He stood outside Robert's window and knocked on the glass.

Robert slunk down in his seat and shut his eyes.

"For Christ's sake, Robert." Steven lowered the power window. "Howdy, mister. You okay?"

The man was wearing a brown vest over a white undershirt. Jeans. Long hair and a beard.

Steven swallowed nervously. There were lots of motorcycle gangs in this part of the state, and even three on one wouldn't be good enough if the guy was a Hell's Angel.

"Close call back there, man," the stranger laughed as he leaned on the doorframe. He brushed aside strands of dirty hair to reveal youthful eyes and big smile. His arms were thin and his chest was sunken. No tattoos anywhere.

This guy wasn't a Hell's Angel. He wasn't even a Heck's Angel. He was a hippie, as harmless as they could've hoped for.

Steven considered mentioning the escaped convict but stopped himself at the last second. Maybe the real hippie was dead back in Barstow and this dude was wearing his clothes and smile. "Looks like we're headed the same way if you wanna hop in back."

"Far out, man. My dogs are barking."

The stranger threw open the back passenger door and collapsed onto the red seat, immediately filling the car with the smells of body odor and skunky weed. Louis slid all the way behind Steven, the scowl on his face suggesting no interest in getting chummy with their fragrant new friend.

"Ohhhhh, man," the stranger moaned. "Can't tell you how good it feels to sit down. Hope you don't mind if I stretch out a little." He put his hands behind his head. The pits of his undershirt matched the yellow daisy patches on his vest.

Steven got the car back up to speed while keeping a close eye on the rearview mirror.

"Yeah, go ahead make yourself comfortable," Louis grumbled as the stranger flipped off his shoes.

"Louis," Steven said calmly.

"My name's Warren," the stranger said, running his hands across the car's red

249

upholstery. "And hot damn, man, is this a Cadillac? Hell of a lot nicer than what I was driving."

"Blue pickup?" Steven asked.

"You saw it, huh? Yeah, haven't had it long. Damn thing picked just about the worst spot in the world to crap out on me. Bad timing too."

"How's that?" Steven asked.

"Well," the stranger began coyly. "Truth be told, I'm sort of avoiding the law at the moment."

Robert's eyes went wide behind his thick glasses. Steven gestured for him to stay calm.

"Probably one pig in the whole desert," the stranger went on. "But it'd be just my luck to get rolled by some wayward highway patrolman, y'know? When I broke down, I figured I'd try and hump it on foot to the next service station. I'd been walkin' for an hour or two when you showed up."

"What kind of trouble you in with the law?" Steven asked.

"Oh, nothing special. I butt heads with the capital-M Man from time to time. Grass and whatever else they can think to pin on me. I'm not such a bad guy once you get to know me." He yawned broadly. "Any chance you got something a little stronger than piano? Been a hell of a day."

"Yeah, sure," Steven said, grinding his teeth. He popped out the 8-track. The FM station that had played the news report had gone back to music: a coarse, brass instrumental with no piano. It was rude and grating. Perverse. Good-for-nothing.

"Yeah, that's better," the stranger mumbled as he burrowed comfortably into his corner of the backseat. "Hell of a day, man, hell of a day." The eyelids behind the matted strands of hair drooped, then closed. Before long, he was snoring.

Louis leaned forward. "Told ya, didn't I? We got him. Trouble with the law? Ha! I'll bet, you murder spree maniac! We got the looney dead to rights, boys! Imagine the re-ward for a triple homicide."

"That's assuming he doesn't add three more," Robert whispered. "What do we do now?"

"Drive him to the law!" Louis said.

"First things first." Steven interrupted. "We tie him up."

"With what?" Robert asked.

Steven pulled at the shoelace-thick string that threaded along the elastic of his pants. The arrogant horns on the radio were digging into his brain like razor blades but he had to focus. Music preferences took a backseat when there was a killer in yours.

He handed the string to Robert. "You tie his wrists. Louis, you be ready if he tries to fight."

"Oh, I'll be ready," Louis cracked his knuckles. "You just keep us nice and steady so our guest's slumber isn't disturbed. And just in case things really go sideways…"

He dropped a tape-wrapped blade into Steven's lap.

"*Where did you get that*?" Robert hissed.

"Always keep one on me just in case. Looks like this is one of those cases. You just worry about the hogtie and I'll be ready to slug him one. Stevie, you're our insurance. You ready?"

All Steven wanted was to hear Mother's piano. It was so much better than Robert and Louis bickering, better than news that only reported nasty people doing nasty things, better than the garbage music demanded by a good-for-nothing who'd wasted no time in making himself at home in Mother's car.

"Ready."

Robert and Louis nodded to each other and moved slowly toward the stranger.

Steven kept his eyes on the road. He drove around a small pot hole, shaking the car for just an instant.

Robert whimpered.

"H-he's waking up."

"Finish the damn knot, Robert," Louis spat.

Bitter adrenaline flooded back into Steven's brain. He crushed the gas pedal in a manic spasm and the Cadillac veered dangerously toward the edge of the road.

"What the hell?" the stranger shouted.

"He's too strong!" Louis shrieked as the sounds of a struggle grew louder. *"Knife him, Steven! Knife him now!"*

Steven reached back with the tape-wrapped blade and jabbed blindly at the stranger's corner. He felt warm blood spill onto his hand and forearm. Someone was screaming. He stabbed again and again until the steering wheel spun from his grip and the car veered across the shoulder. The Cadillac's hood buried into a berm of sand that ate the headlights, plunging the desert back into perfect dark.


"Lemme make sure nobody's in trouble." Carol Anne Sr. clicked off her seatbelt and got out of the station wagon. "You stay here, Sweetie."

Carol Anne Jr. sipped loudly through the straw in her can of Diet Pepsi as her mom got out and walked toward the car up ahead. Somebody had driven it right into the sand. The sun was only just rising now. Maybe they hadn't been able to see.

The slurping got louder as she sucked up the last of the soda. The loud sound was her favorite part, especially since it covered up the man on the radio reporting the morning news. News was always so boring.

Carol Anne Sr. reached the back window of the white car and cupped her hands on the glass. She let out a strange scream and fell back onto the road. Then she screamed some more and scrambled backwards on her hands and knees to get away from the car.

Carol Anne Jr. stopped slurping.

The man on the radio read his news loud and clear.

*"... leaving the Wildcats with another ninth-inning loss. More now on the morning's top story of fugitive Steven Dooley, who escaped from Barstow Psychiatric Hospital approximately twelve hours ago. Dooley killed two guards and a third individual authorities have now identified as Patricia Dooley, the suspect's mother. Dooley was last seen fleeing Barstow in the deceased's white Cadillac DeVille."*

. . .

"Just like that man in Yuma," Robert moaned. "And those poor girls in Blythe before that. Now a hitchhiker. Your plans always get us into trouble, Louis."

"I had him pinned down just fine," Louis said. "All you had to do was tie him up and we'd have it made right now."

Steven let them argue.

It wasn't their fault.

It was Mother's.

She knew her playing kept him calm and she'd stopped anyway. "Fourteen years is enough," she'd screamed. "Fourteen years of playing the piano all god damn day! I can't do it anymore, Steven. I won't do it anymore!"

Then she'd smashed the instrument to bits while he cowered in the corner. He couldn't watch her do it, couldn't watch her kill the piano. He focused on the cactus through the window instead, listening to the voices in his head get louder.

When he ran away, the voices came with. To Yuma. To Blythe. And back home. He told mother what he'd done. And what did she do? She told on him. She told the law what he'd done. She was the one who'd stopped playing the piano, but he was the one who had to go away to the building with soft walls and drooling neighbors.

Ten years. Steven stayed there for ten years. Ten years without Mother. Ten years without piano. And when he had to hear it again, the voices suggested he visit Mother. He listened.

"Don't feel too bad," Louis punched Robert lightly on the shoulder. "Remember what we talked about last night. It's all perspective. We did what we had to do and other folks won't ever understand, so why bother trying to explain? I say we forget the whole thing ever happened, just like Yuma and Blythe. What do you think, Steven?"

Steven thought for a long while, then smiled.

"Not a lot of towns out here, but the ones there are mostly have bars." He nodded at the sun-warming horizon where distant buildings grew larger with each step. "One of those bars is bound to have a piano."

And the three of them walked on, chatting happily as they passed through the three-pronged shadow of a lone cactus.

# ROADS

## MERCURY

I was happy to leave the crazy traffic of Los Angeles. Bumper-to-bumper cars all trying to get ahead of each other; no courtesy at all. I turned up my phone, which was connected to my grey Prius and blasted my music. I used Maps to navigate my way up North, but I had done this a few times now and things were getting familiar. A few more miles, and the offramp would be approaching. I rolled down the windows some and let the cool evening breeze in. It was still early enough that no one needed headlights yet.

Bobbing my head to the music, I noticed another grey Prius come flying up from a lane over to my right. I waited several moments, then put my blinkers on and got over as well. I tapped my hands on the steering wheel. I had three hours to go. The first rest stop, and I was going to fill up on gas and take a leak. My ass hurt from sitting for four hours already. Road trips were fun till you realized how stressful it was to drive through traffic all damn day.

I looked at my phone to see my exit and noticed my Maps begin to load continuously.

"Fuck, just what I need," I said. "Thank you, T-Mobile."

I recognized my exit and turned, pulling off of the freeway behind the other grey Prius. My Maps stopped loading and flashed the words "Signal Not Found." I rolled my eyes and just hoped the way North would be muscle memory by now. Most of the way was pretty easy: a long stretch that took you around mountains and through a segment of forest. Immediately, we were on a two-way highway, heading towards the first set of giant hills.

The Prius in front of me picked up speed as we reached the base of the hills and took the turning road a bit too fast for my comfort. I watched the car disappear around

253

the bend. I chose this moment to flick on my headlights. It would be dark soon, and I didn't feel like struggling to see the road as the light waned.

I switched the song on my iPod and turned the heater on, feet only, sitting back and relaxing as I drove. The road was significantly less busy than the freeway. The cars in front of me had pulled up far enough that I could only see their taillights. I looked out over to my left. The road dropped off some yards away and down below was a small town by the sea, surround by tall trees and woodland.

From behind me, two headlights suddenly shined into my sideview mirrors, making me squint and shield my eyes. I could tell by their height and brightness that they belonged to a semitruck.

"There goes my night vision."

I sped up a bit, trying to put some distance between us. I checked the time. Almost six thirty. Twenty more minutes and it would be fully dark. The next rest area wasn't for a several miles. I was still making good time.

Lights shined into my rearview mirror and I squinted again. The truck had caught up once more but I hadn't slowed down; it had sped up.

"All right, already. Fine, just go."

I checked for oncoming traffic then put on my lights, pulling to the left and slowing down so they could pass. The truck sped up and as he reached me, I heard the voice of a man.

"You motherfucker! Hey!" they shouted.

I turned my music down then leaned over, confused. I looked out of my partially rolled-down window briefly to see a middle-aged man, scruffy face and sun-tanned skin scowling down from the cabin of his truck. He stuck his hand out his window and flicked me off. Great. I sped up.

The trucker increased his sped, keeping up with me. We were flying down the highway and I was in the wrong lane. Headlights flashed ahead and a surge of fear shot through me. I laid on my horn but the truck driver didn't budge.

"What the hell is your problem?" I screamed, throwing on my brakes.

I slowed down enough to get behind the truck and let the car in the other lane pass by without incident. However, ahead of me, the trucker was throwing on his brakes. I slammed mine and came to a steady halt. My heart was racing. What in the world was going on? I began to turn my wheel, taking that moment to try and get ahead. But the trucker was already getting out and as I tried to pass, he jumped in front of my car, slamming his hands on the hood.

My mouth was dry as I stared into his dark eyes, full of rage. I didn't understand. Do I get out the car? Do I run him over? Where the fuck was highway patrol when you needed them?

"You think you can cut me off, huh?" the trucker yelled. "You cut me off at the highway!"

What? I shook my head and waved my hands to signal I didn't I didn't know what he was talking about. The man slammed his hands on the hood of my car again.

"Dumbass grey Prius think you can fuck with anyone!" he shouted.

Grey Prius? My stomach sank and I remembered the other grey Prius that shot ahead of me. I was certain I didn't cut this guy off. I took in a deep breath. He was mistaken. I took another breath and collected myself. We could work it out. I unbuckled myself and got out, putting my hands up in a friendly manner. I tried to smile. The man immediately stood up straight and balled his fists up.

"Easy," I said. "I didn't cut you off. I think it was the other Prius that passed me."

The man looked at me.

"Bullshit," he said.

"No, really. There was another grey Prius. I saw it."

The man's eyes seemed to darken even more. He bared his teeth in a furious fit. "Right," he said. "Scared motherfucker afraid to admit it. I'll give you something to get scared about."

The trucker reached behind his back and came away with a gun. A jet-black gun, gleaming in my headlights. I felt myself freeze, and my head suddenly felt light. He walked towards me. On instinct I moved back, frantically grabbing for my car door, but the trucker had his gun raised.

"Don't move, motherfucker, or I'll blow your brains out!" he yelled.

What the hell was happening? I didn't know what to do. I panicked. I climbed in my car and the man rushed me. I closed my door and went for the gearshift, but the trucker reached through my partially open window and slammed the cold, hard metal of his gun against my head. I saw stars; my head and ears rung. He hit me again, catching me on my left eye. I cried out and felt the blood and swelling begin. I scrambled towards my right and caught a glimpse of my phone, noticing my Maps had finally loaded.

"Get out of the car," the trucker said. "Get out of the fucking car!"

There was nowhere to go. Where was everyone? These roads weren't as crowded as near the city. That's why I was alone. I hated traffic.

The car door opened and hands grabbed at my shirt, dragging me out of the Prius. I flailed and felt a scream bubble up from my chest. This was happening. This was really happening. I opened my mouth to release the terror that filled me only to have the trucker bust the front of my mouth and teeth with the butt of his gun. I tasted and saw my blood spilling out of my mouth. I groaned and whimpered, tears blurring my vision.

"St-stop. I swear—"

"Swear what? Huh?" the trucker yelled in my face.

"Please, it wasn't—"

He hit me again, this time with his fist. I dropped to the ground, covering my head as he began to punch and kick me. He looked like he weighed fifty pounds more than I did, and I felt it in my ribs as he kicked me in the torso, knocking the wind from my lungs. I felt like I couldn't breathe. When was he going to shoot me? Would they find my body out on the road, my brains drying on the pavement? Would my family miss me?

"Look at me," he said. "Look at me, cocksucker."

The trucker grabbed me by the head and turned it so that I was looking up. I

255

couldn't see out of my swollen left eye. The man pressed the barrel of his gun against my forehead then spit right into my blood-soaked face. I flinched and he laughed. He held my head for a moment, fingers gripping my skull so tight, I thought it would burst like a watermelon.

"Dumbass, Prius-driving asshole," he said then shoved me away, hard enough my head hit my car door.

I curled up, waiting to be shot or for the beatings to begin again, but all I heard was the crunch of boots then the sound of a door closing. I listened as the wheels of his truck pulled off and his roaring engine became nothing but a purr in the distance.

I stayed on the ground, crying. A couple of cars passed me on the side of the road. One honked at me for lying there, obstructing their path. It was dark now and the only light I had was the moon and my headlights.

I finally got up, half blind and missing teeth. I clambered to my feet, coughing and spitting blood all over my shirt. I got into my car and felt around till I found an old rag. It was black and dirty because I used it for wiping my car windows. I pressed it to my mouth anyhow and shut my car door. I looked at my phone and thought about calling the cops. I hadn't even got a license plate number, much less the guy's name.

Suddenly overwhelmed, I slammed my fist against the steering wheel, screaming and crying in pain. My music was playing softly in the background. Grabbing my phone, I noticed Maps was still open and my ETA had lengthened by thirty minutes. I cut the music off and sat in the silence of my hybrid car, its engine silent and still. I placed one hand on the wheel, trembling.

Then I put my car in drive and headed for the nearest rest stop.

# SHE BY THE SEA

## TAMIKA THOMPSON

She sat alone on the strip of sandy beach. Her shorts, men's denim that she'd gotten from an unattended dumpster before trash day, came to her knees. Her tank top was black and pasted to her skin by sweat and salty seawater. The shore-side restaurant next door, with its glass-enclosed patio and thatched-roof bar, had closed at four because no one drove that far north on the Pacific Coast Highway for food on a Tuesday. She didn't like the long and official name "the Pacific Coast Highway." It didn't feel like a highway, more like a wide road along the ocean filled with burger joints, surf shops, and drug rehabs. And, anyway, the locals called it PCH.

She captured a bass in a net and speared the spotted fish with her knife, savoring the pungent smell of fresh caught food. Thanks to Daddy's tutelage, she had perfected the art of the fillet. Salt gathered on her flesh as she used only ocean water to clean the fish because bottled water made it taste like crap. She descaled by stripping away from her stomach and slicing along the dorsal fin from head to tail. She removed the skin and threw the fish on a makeshift fire atop some rocks, leaves, and twigs. She never used gloves.

She rinsed her fillet knife in a cut-in-half plastic milk jug filled with seawater, wiped it with a clean cloth, and wrapped it in two fresh pieces of paper towel. She then slid that inside of a gallon-sized freezer-storage sack, and tucked the pack deep inside her bag where no one could get to it easily. She moved to a spot just below a grassy cliff. She had been robbed of ones, fives, and reefer before. She'd be damned if she'd let someone get to her knives.

Mostly, no one bothered her. She typically bathed by waiting for the waves to come in, wash over, and cleanse her. That's how she relieved her bowels and bladder, too. Earlier, she'd brushed her teeth in a Chevron station bathroom. Food was another story. She was five feet nine inches and weighed a hundred ten pounds so she traveled light, relying on faith and fate to feed her. Her protection was that switchblade—which Daddy had given her for fishing the summer before he left for good—and his fillet knife.

She remembered Daddy's voice, and the way it dropped when he told her about the monster in the sea. Her distant memory was pretty good, and she could mostly remember things that happened last week, last month, and last year, but that recent memory was weak and at risk of fleeing with a bottle of whiskey or a hit of smack. She figured she'd been near the sea for a while, though she couldn't remember how she'd come to live near the waves.

Or, come to think of it, she could. Daddy telling her about the sea creature. That was it. That's what had led her to the ocean. Daddy had been from Detroit. He had seen the *Creature from the Black Lagoon* when it premiered in 1952. Or was it 1953? No, 1954. That was it. He'd seen it several times with 3D glasses at a downtown theatre and then again several more times at his neighborhood cinema, where the image was flat. Both versions were in black and white, he'd told her.

She'd never seen the motion picture but felt as if she had because Daddy talked about the Gill-man as he was putting her to bed, or roasting s'mores with her, or building a campfire, or when they were raking leaves together. He even told her the story when they went fishing in his canoe on Lake Superior. The idea of the scaly prehistoric beast, physically somewhere between a sea and land animal, always made the corners of her eyes and the middle of her nose wet, and, when she was really young, she'd cover her ears because she didn't want to hear how the thing had grabbed the movie's leading lady and taken her to its lair.

"That ol' Gill-man was misunderstood," Daddy said. "He looked hideous to a bunch of folks who were the real hideous ones. They mistook his simple desire for bloodthirst. And anyway, aren't we all a bit more bloodthirsty than we should be?"

A therapist once told her that Daddy's obsession with the film's details had been unhealthy. That it was unusual to recite this sort of story to a young kid every night for much of her childhood. It's funny what seems normal until under scrutiny by an outsider. In her youth, she developed a hatred for sea animals that found her spearing anything that swam in water—bass, catfish, sea lions, crabs, and once, in Hawaii, she'd even gotten a shark that swam too close to her boat.

The therapist wanted her to watch the picture once and for all to break the spell that Daddy had put her under and to stop obsessing over and killing fish herself. Instead, she went off her medication and stopped seeing the therapist. It was about six months later that she came to the sea.


After dinner, she put the fire out and went into the ocean for her evening bath. The water was cold on her chest. The air, fresh. The waves roared and sea foam snaked over her fingers as the tide went back out. The moon was full so when the water rushed in again, it was closer to her backpack than she was comfortable with. From a trash bin, she'd snagged an untouched six-inch submarine sandwich, and she didn't want the meal to wash away. That would be her dinner tomorrow. But the ocean seemed to have its own mind, and, in the evenings, swallowed the things in its path that it had been observing all day. Who could fight it? The ocean wanted what it wanted. The roar of the waves was its voice, and the swell, like a pair of hands, touched the things that lay before it.

With the water no longer on the shore, a large shape appeared on the sand twenty feet in front of her. Perhaps it was a seal, hurt or dead. It wasn't moving.

Matted and dripping, she stood and shivered as she stepped forward. She could make out a hand and a wrist with a shiny watch, white sneakers, and a jersey top with a large number eight in the center. When she leaned down to get a better look, she found the right cheek was bloody and bloated, the forehead was distended, and the chin was swollen to the size of a kiwi.

She took the watch, gold with a row of diamonds for the hour and minute hands. His skin was like rubber as she slipped it off. His leather wallet was still in the pocket of his shorts with thirteen hundred dollars, his American Express card, and California driver's license inside. He was smiling in the photo. His address was in Anaheim. His name seemed to be the largest thing on his identification. It was a familiar name. A famous name. She blinked. Had she read that correctly? Was it really him? She looked around in disbelief and then back at the name. Her breath caught in her throat and she gasped at the realization—not of the body, but of whom it had been. It couldn't be. It just couldn't be. But apparently it was.

He was Kip Longfellow, of the Anaheim Arrows. The greatest power forward since Larry Bird. Worth seventy million dollars easily and with his own shoe. Everyone knew that he and his wife lived in a compound in Roper Estates. That's why he'd been hired to do all of the cell phone and laptop ads, because he had a trustworthy smile and a squeaky-clean image. The sportscasters called him "All American Kip." His slogan for ComTel was, "I can always call. So answer."

But then he'd tried something else, that Kip. He'd started his own marijuana-growing business legally in one of the first weed states. Tabloids said he often brought that product out to California because he was trying to get set up for retirement and wanted to expand out of the state he'd started in. If there had have been bullet holes in him, she could have chalked his murder up to a gang turf war or a mob hit. Maybe he'd pissed off the wrong S.O.B. But the bite marks were something else. The teeth marks on his arms and the gashes in his clothes looked like they came from an animal. Coyote? Large dog? She was shivering, and it wasn't from the cold. She thought of Gill-man. She'd seen a lot of deadly shit in her day—mangled bodies after car accidents, mutilated dogs, discarded newborns—but ripped away flesh was the sort of thing that made a person look over her shoulder. And she did just that again. The palm trees swayed and a few cars filed along PCH, but she was still alone.

She took the cash. She tossed the wallet into the ocean. What could have happened to make someone want to kill such a beloved and wonderful guy? Actually, poppycock. Public image was mostly imagination. No one knew this kid but him. His wife probably didn't even know his truths.

She scrambled up the beach, snatched up her backpack, and dropped the watch and cash securely inside. She took out her knives just in case the killer was around and watching her. Who knew how much she could get for the watch? It might be worth a fortune. When she glanced back at the spot where Kip lay on the beach, he was gone, though no waves had come in since she'd stepped away. She walked back down there. She stood in the spot where he'd lain in a bloody and mangled mess, and looked up and down the beach, but there was no one who could have taken his body away. She knelt down to touch the sand where he'd been. It was damp and cold, but bore no indentations. Had she imagined him? She wasn't one to hallucinate. She opened her backpack to see if she'd really just put his things in there. She had. She had seen correctly. He had been there.

Her relief didn't last long because a figure appeared at the surface of the water as the wave came back in. It was probably Kip's body being thrown about by the force of the surf. Only something began to slither toward her in the shadows of the water under its own power, and that couldn't have been Kip. It was about the size of Kip, but Kip was dead. He couldn't be moving toward her.

She held her breath as if she were seconds from drowning, felt its scales as it stalked up the water and brushed against her right shin. Its eyes were black, its mouth open as if it were about to take a bite of her. She should be running and screaming, but she'd imagined Gill-man so many times and thought of it just before she fell asleep, and dreamed of it at night, that even though it was dangerous, it was familiar. She leaned back on her elbows, and let it come closer. Closer until it was almost nose-to-nose with her and its rancid deep-sea smell rushed up her nostrils. She let out that breath, hoping that it hadn't been her last. Curious, exhilarated and frightened, she raised her blades, and, before the scale-filled creature could brush against her skin for a second time, before it could get its human-shaped scaly hands on her, she speared it in the chest once, twice, three times, then turned and left it where it lay. She'd finally conquered the Gill-man, and without having to watch the movie. Fun thought, it was, but, in reality, she had probably just killed a large gator. *Do gators frequent the Pacific?* She cleaned the blood off the knife by dipping it in the saltwater and dried it on a sweatshirt in her backpack.

Her bag felt lighter as she tossed it onto her shoulder, her muscles were stronger as if the cash had given her energy, and, when she got to the dumpster at the edge of the beach, she tossed the sandwich inside. She stepped onto PCH watching cars whiz by, the wind blowing her damp hair around her ears and cheeks. Did those drivers know the change that had just occurred for her? Did her face betray some sign of what she'd seen? Of what she'd done? What exactly had she done? She was happy to have the money and to have killed the thing from her bad dreams, but that poor guy. She paused when she got to the other side of the road. She couldn't do anything for him. What was done was done.

She headed north on PCH in search of a decent meal in a sit-down restaurant. Fifteen minutes into her walk, she passed Rudy's Surf Shop and Supplies. Rudy sold boards, wetsuits, and a lot of trail mix, jerky, and beer.

"What's shakin', Colleen? Haven't seen you in a minute, for real. Wanna keep your tab open?" Rudy always let her spend imaginary money on an imaginary tab, no more than five dollars a day. She'd never been able to pay him and he'd never asked. Because he was so generous, and she enjoyed staring into his hazel eyes in that chiseled surf-boy face, she used the credit sparingly.

"You know I don't want any handouts. Put me to work, Rudy."

"And you know I keep costs down by doing everything my damn self. What can I do for you?"

She purchased a pack of Virginia Slims, Grandmother's favorite, to keep her warm on the walk. She told him everything that she'd just seen, leaving off the part about taking the watch and the cash, though she handed him a crisp bill from her bag not realizing that this might raise suspicions.

"A twenty? Where'd you get this?" He stretched out the bill, held it to the light, and scrutinized it as if she'd handed him a hundred. His face became bunched with concern. This was the problem with good people. They were often too honest.

"Call the cops. Tell 'em what I told you."

"A down-on-her-luck black woman finds a dead white millionaire athlete. I can see the headlines now. That ain't gon' work out for you at all. And this story sounds made up. Kip Longfellow? He just scored twenty-eight points against Cleveland on Sunday. You trying to set somebody up? Get back at somebody?"

"Just tell them a white customer told you. A man—"

He raised a brow and didn't look as if he were going to make the call.

"Trust me, Rudy. I might be a fool, but I know what I saw. Anyway, keep the change."


The television above the steak and alehouse's bar was tuned to the national news, and, before she could order a drink in that dimly lit restaurant, Kip's face was already plastered across the screen with the "happening now" banner above it. His sweet face looked nothing like that swollen and bloody mess she had seen. The media had found out so quickly. Was it because Rudy had called? What exactly had he told them? Had he mentioned her?

The program switched between images of Kip as a boy, smiling while holding up a trophy after winning in a youth basketball league, Kip smiling as he walked across the stage at his college graduation and shook the university president's hand, Kip smiling as he posed beside his lace- and-tulle-covered bride, Kip smiling on draft day as he put the Arrows cap on his head. Kip's smile. His damn smile. It was the smile that started the throbbing in her chest. The money was heavy and thick against her thigh in the pocket of her shorts, and the wad seemed to be throbbing too. Could others sense the vibration?

She drank the ice water sitting in front of her to wet her dry throat. She was disheveled, yes, but her clothes were dry now and she sat in a corner near the kitchen where only the wait staff could see her. When she returned the glass to the table, the waiter walked over to take her order, but she'd been so lost in thought about Kip on that screen and the money in her pocket and Kip's damn smile that the waiter asking, "What would you like?" startled her, and she knocked the glass across the table, with the water and ice creating a puddle near the empty plate.

She ordered quickly and returned to her viewing of the television screen. Apparently, the paparazzi moved faster than the police because they were already parked outside Kip's home. There was no audio on the television so she read the closed captioning. It said, "No leads yet on who might have committed the stabbing, but there will be a homicide investigation."

Stabbing? He hadn't been stabbed. She hadn't seen one stab mark on him. She knew what a stab mark looked like. They formed thin lines on the flesh, almost as if someone had drawn them in crimson ink. She'd been stabbed before with a box cutter by another drifter who thought she was trying to take an EBT card he'd lucked up on. Kip hadn't been stabbed. And why didn't they mention the bite marks? Something had bitten him. But what if she hadn't seen clearly? Could those have been stabs instead of bite marks?

Her belly was full, but she couldn't enjoy it because her stomach was bloated, with acid churning and rising up her chest. She returned to the beach to see the body. Surely he had been bitten, but she just needed to see it again, in person. Police tape, fire trucks, and ambulances jammed up the shore. A crowd had parked on PCH and walked to the sand barefoot, with their hooded sweatshirts drawn tightly on heads hung low. Folks hugged one another, wrapped their arms around the shoulders of the person next to them, many drying their eyes and noses on their sleeves. The ambulance drove away as soon as she arrived as if Kip sensed her there and wanted nothing to do with her.

Was it wrong to steal from a dead man? It wasn't like he could use the money, and he had had so much of it to begin with.

"Did you see what happened?" She stared into the face of a teenager with a tattoo of an eagle on his neck and a pierced upper lip. Surely the teen would know what happened. Teens thought they knew everything.

"No. Just heard Kip Longfellow came to the beach to meditate and was stabbed to death down there by some homeless lady. They say she robbed him. Got it all on surveillance video."

The teen pointed to that shore-side restaurant next door, with its glass-enclosed patio and thatched-roof bar. The one that had closed at four because no one drove that far north on the Pacific Coast Highway for food on a Tuesday.

The world was upside down during the week that she staggered the sixty or so miles from the beach to Anaheim. She barely ate. She couldn't sleep. A drifter offered her a hit of blow and she couldn't bring herself to try it. There was no way she had imagined those bite marks. No way she had mistaken his stab wounds for bites. No way that when she'd stabbed the Gill-man she had really stabbed Kip. He was much taller and stronger than her anyway. If she would have raised a knife to a man that big, he likely would have flicked it away with a swat of his gargantuan hand. Anyway, the order of events was all wrong. He had been dead when she'd found him.

When she reached Anaheim, she scoped out a residential street with drifters pulling things from the trash, and she discarded the watch in a garbage bin.

She arrived at the gate of Kip's home the day that everyone was away for his funeral. She removed the cash from her backpack. She counted it. She had eleven hundred dollars left, all in wrinkled and knotted twenties and hundreds. She wrapped it in the plastic bag that she usually kept her knife in and laid the cash beside a stone-covered archway just inside the iron gates. She stared at the money as she backed away. Tears gathered in her eyes. She was walking away from easy meals and nights at a motel when the weather got too cold. She was walking away from help, a respite, and a much-needed break. Just as she rounded the corner and headed back north, a twenty-deep line of black limousines, Bentleys, and Mercedes Benzes snaked toward the home in a slow and sad procession.


To say that she had no home really wasn't true. She had a tent at the base of a pier, far enough from the ocean to not get caught in the rising tide, and hidden enough to protect her from the sun when it was high and hot. The only things she had to worry about was another drifter coming along and stealing her shit, scavengers rummaging through her found clothes, books, seasonings, and photographs of her parents, birds eating what food she could gather, and, worst of all, cops.

Cops would make her move. Cops would confiscate her tent, bringing her to the door of starvation to save up money for another one. Cops would shove her with their clubs or the heel of their shoe, anything to avoid touching her with their hands. They would do this when she was at her lowest and had nothing to numb her hunger.

But the tent was home. She returned there now that she had rid herself of all that tied her to Kip. She had bought herself one last meal on him—pastrami and fries. Her stomach was full and she actually cracked a smile when the breeze floated in to her. It wouldn't be a hot night at all, and it wouldn't get too cold either. This was wonderful sleeping weather. She dozed in the middle of a library copy of *The Old Man and the Sea*. Her flashlight's battery eventually died, but the moon was high and showing off so her tent was still well lit. It was about then that she heard the voice.

"I can always call, so answer." The voice belonged to a man. She sat up and grabbed her switchblade because the person sounded as if he were close. Unzipping the flap and easing her head out, she checked to the left and right, but nothing was out there except the wind, moonlight, and waves. It was so bright that she could see as clearly now as she could at dawn. She craned her neck to listen.

There were no footsteps in the sand. No shadows of anyone who might be walking nearby. The tide seemed to be closer to her than it usually was at this time of night, but the water never made it up to her distant spot near the parking lot. She returned to her tent, zipped it, and lay down for sleep. Only she couldn't now.

Her heart was pumping as if she'd just gone for a run. A chill passed through her bones, and she could feel fear creep up her chest to her throat.

"Answer," the voice said again.

It sounded like Kip, only he sounded angry, sinister. The words came from his slogan, but the tone was not like his slogan at all. What exactly had he been doing out there near the water? The teen had said he'd been meditating, but she wasn't buying it. A guy like that would have an entourage, an agent, bodyguards. No one had robbed him, obviously. And there was no way that he had robbed anyone else. And there had been those bite marks that no one seemed to be aware of but her. Maybe it hadn't been about his drug business. Maybe he had been out buying drugs. Heroin. Or crack. Nah. They're so easy for the rich to get without having to go on their own to score. But they had found his car on PCH, so he'd driven himself there.

She wished that she'd never been on that strip of beach. She wished that she'd never seen him or heard of him. She wished that she hadn't watched the news report or talked to the teen who said that Kip had been stabbed by a homeless lady, and all caught on video. Maybe that was the part that she had imagined. That's it. The bite marks and the Gill-man that she stabbed had been real, and the news reports and the kid on the beach who told her that Kip had been killed by a homeless lady—those were not real. Those other things had just been her guilty conscience playing tricks on her.

"I can always call."

She unzipped the tent's flap again.

"Who's there?"

The tide had come in dangerously close to her. It was only a few feet away now. Forgetting the voice, she rushed out, threw her clothes and books and seasonings and photographs into a sand-filled duffel bag, and was seconds from taking down her tent when she blinked and saw that the tide was several dozen yards away still.

Her confusion and fear had heightened her awareness and put her in touch with her exhaustion and hunger so, not knowing what else to do, she had some of the bread she'd taken from the basket at dinner. She had about seven rolls, and it was that crusty Italian kind. She ate and wondered why she was drawn to the water this way. She knew how to float, and she could even hold her breath while fully submerged, but putting those things together to actually swim had eluded her.

After falling asleep again, she felt water lapping against her toes. When she woke and opened her eyes, it was still dark. She sat and ocean water rushed in through a small gash in her tent, soaking her clothes, bread, photographs, matches, and books.

"I can always call," the voice said. She stood and tried to lift her backpack before it got wet, but the fabric floor shifted under her feet. The water was getting higher and the tent was floating now, knocking her back. She fell against the side and then landed on her back on top of her now-underwater sleeping bag. She reached for the zipper as she came to her knees. The water was at her chest now. The zipper would not budge.

"I think that's her tent over there." That was Rudy's voice.

"Stay back. We'll go down." Sounded like a man's voice. Neither of those people sounded like Kip.

"I can always call."

"Help me!" She wanted the real voices to save her from the not-real voice, but which were real and which were imagined?

She still couldn't unzip the flap even though she had a good grip on it.

"I'm her friend. I want to be the one to tell her. I don't want her to be upset with me." That was Rudy again.

"We said, 'stay back.'"

"Help!" Enough of their arguing. Whoever "they" were, "they" sounded authoritative like the police. Had Rudy brought them there to save her from the voice? She just needed for them to get her out of her godforsaken tent.

"So answer." That was Kip. As the water pulled the tent over the sand and toward the ocean, she found her knife again. She tore a gash into the side of her home. She saw him. It. The gill-man from her nightmares. The creature that she'd imagined when Daddy had told her those stories all those years ago—it was pulling her toward the ocean.

"Hey. You fucker!" She raised the blade.

"Colleen! Don't!"

Gill-man stopped tugging her. It gripped the sides of her tent, reaching its lizard-like hand through the hole she'd created, brushing against her thigh as it grabbed the photographs of her parents that floated in front of her. Then it turned her tent on the side where the hole was and gave her one final push toward the black horizon.

Booted feet ran through the shallow ocean towards her, splashing her face with icy water. Rudy yelled, "Colleen! It's okay. You will be fine. I had no choice. You have to believe me, Colleen. Don't run. Don't resist! You need help."

Of course she needed help. The Gill-man was attacking her. Thank God Rudy could see that now too. The water filled the tent, washing over her as she slashed at the remains of the cloth and at the creature and at anything that her blade could make contact with. Several schools of fish, large and small, saltwater and freshwater, surrounded her—bass, catfish, sea lions, crabs, and a shark. Some of those fish were not indigenous to the Pacific, but that was all right. She slashed at them too. Then the water took her. It wanted what it wanted. It filled her nostrils and ears and she destroyed the cloth around her, and yelled, "You will not win!" just as the water's hand covered her eyes and snatched her away.

# THE CUTTING ROOM

## JEFF SEEMAN

"It's called *The Cutting Room*."

Through bloodshot eyes, producer Hal Blechman looked across his cluttered desk at the latest screenwriter desperately trying to seduce him with a pitch. In this case it was a tall kid in his twenties, dressed entirely in black, dark hair and eyes, with a pale, expressionless countenance and an unnervingly intense gaze. *Norman something*, Blechman thought. *Cinder? Schneider? Something like that.*

"It's a horror about a psychotic killer," the kid continued. "Only it takes place in Hollywood. And the killer's a screenwriter."

"Uh-huh," said Blechman. How many pitches had he already heard this morning? Six? Seven? Shit, would this day never end?

"See, he's been struggling to make it in Hollywood. And finally he snaps. And he exacts his revenge on all the studio execs and development execs and producers and agents and managers who've pissed all over him."

"Uh-huh," Blechman repeated.

"Only it's not a straight horror. It's kind of broad. More like a horror-comedy."

Blechman sat up. "Like *Scary Movie*?"

"No, that wasn't a horror movie. That was a *parody* of a horror movie."

Blechman looked at him blankly. "And what's this?"

"This is an actual horror. Only with comedic elements. It's more like a self-referential pastiche paying tribute to the genre."

"A what?"

"What I mean is, it's not so much a parody as a... a satire."

Blechman cringed. "Satire is what closes on Saturday night, kid. You ever hear that? Sam Goldwyn said that."

"Actually, I believe it was George S. Kauf—"

"Look, you seem like a nice kid, so let me level with you. That movie never gets made. You know why? No producer's going to finance a movie about producers getting offed. You see what I'm saying?"

"It's just a... a satire. A satire on Hollywood. I just thought..."

"That's your problem, kid. You think too much. *Satire. Self-referential...* whatever the fuck you called it. No one wants that. You know what people want? Huh?"

Blechman leaned back and tapped the poster hanging on the wall behind him, a garish montage of explosions, guns, speeding cars, and screaming, half-naked women. The title emblazoned across the bottom was *Citizen Kane 2: The Revenge.*

"Uh... yes, I noticed that when I came in."

"*Kane 2*, baby! That's our next big hit. You ever hear of the original?"

"*Citizen Kane*? Of course."

"Of course. Of course, he says. That's the beauty. Everyone's heard of it, but no one's seen it."

"Actually, I'm pretty sure millions of people—"

"Which is great for us. Means we can do whatever we want with the property. I finally screened the original last week. Nothing to work with there. God awful boring. Damn thing's not even in color. Do you know it starts off with a newsreel? It's like a movie inside a movie. And then the lights come up and we're in a different movie. What the fuck is that? Confused the hell out of me."

"Uh... not really sure what to say here."

"Anyway, so we get to start from scratch. Completely reinvent the franchise."

"The franchise?"

Blechman leaned forward, warming to his subject. "See, Kane dies at the end of the first one. So in this one, he comes back. He's a zombie, see? And he can't rest in peace until he gets his sled back."

"His sled?"

"Yeah, it's from the original. The whole stupid picture ends up being about this fucking sled. Anyway, Kane can't rest until he gets his sled. And he kills everyone who stands in his way. Now honestly, does that sound like a great picture or what?"

"Honestly? It sounds... awful."

"What? Fuck you."

"You asked for my opinion."

"What the fuck do you know? You know how many pictures I've produced? How many hits I've had? How many years I've been in this business?"

"You just asked me—"

Blechman grabbed the Academy Award from the bookcase behind him and slammed it on the desk.

"That's an Oscar, you snot-nosed punk! A goddamn Oscar! 1972! Best Assistant Gaffer to the Second Assistant Director, motherfucker! What do you say to *that?*"

And what Norman Snyder said to that was to stand, pick up the weighty statuette, and bring it down on Hal Blechman's head. Again. And again. And again. Until his head cracked open like an overripe melon, and blood and brains rained down on top of

*Death Fist 5000* and *Love Is So Funny* and *Vampire Robots From Hell* and all the other unread spec scripts that littered the top of Blechman's desk.

Norman stood for several long moments, dispassionately looking down at the bleeding corpse. Finally, he walked around behind Blechman's chair, where Blechman had hung his jacket, and unclipped the dead man's studio lot badge from the breast pocket.

Located in Culver City, the Warnamount Studios backlot was a 100-acre labyrinth of offices, sound stages, exterior sets, and various other buildings that housed everything from costumes and props to post-production services and screening rooms. The layout had probably made sense to someone somewhere at some distant point in the past, but to present-day visitors it invariably seemed a random jumble of sets and buildings, some in use, others deserted. And although a badge was required to gain access to the premises, once on the grounds a visitor had free rein to go virtually anywhere he wanted.

So Norman strolled about the premises, investigating, wandering past row upon row of nondescript gray buildings, then through a Western ghost town of 1850, then past a line of modern-day shops and restaurants, then through a deserted Manhattan in the 1930's, then past more rows of gray buildings, periodically trying the random doorknob here and there to see if one would open.

And so it was that, after roughly half an hour of exploring, Norman successfully opened the door of Building G19, one of the small, gray office buildings on the Warnamount backlot, and stepped inside. He walked up and down the hallways of the mostly deserted building until he found an unoccupied office with a decent view and a comfortable chair. And that, Norman decided, was his office. He fished some Warnamount stationery out of a desk drawer, found an old fax machine at the end of one of the hallways, and sent a press release to *Variety* and *The Hollywood Reporter* announcing his new position: he was now a development executive with an office at Warnamount.

It was just a matter of days before query letters began pouring in from screenwriters trying to nab his interest in one project or another. *Now I'll finally find out what it's like*, he thought. *Now I'll finally see what it feels like to be on the other side of the desk.* Norman set up some pitch meetings.

The first meeting was with a nervous, balding man with bad skin.

"Hundreds of thousands of people died when the U.S. dropped atomic bombs on Japan at the end of World War II," said the man seriously. "This is the story of their pain and devastation. Only with singing and dancing. It's called *Nagasaki Nights*. It's for people who are concerned about nuclear annihilation, but who also love musicals."

Norman stared at him for several long moments.

And then removed a ten-inch butcher knife from his desk drawer and stabbed him in the face.

Next was a bookish woman in her forties. "*Recipe For Love* is a classic feel-good boy-meets-girl romantic comedy," she practically cooed. "Only she's a professional chef. And he's a cannibal."

Norman split her chest open with an axe.

Then there was an effeminate young man with a nose ring. "It's called *Lube Job.* Two robots arrive on earth and must keep their forbidden love secret from their intergalactic overlord. It's *Brokeback Mountain* meets *Transformers.*"

Norman threw him into a wood chipper.

"It's what happens when a famous Mexican painter meets a rampaging serial killer. It's called *Frida vs. Jason.*"

Norman took a meat cleaver to her jugular.

"It's *The Sound of Music*, but with prostitutes."

Norman took his head off with a chainsaw.

By the end of the morning, Norman was exhausted and decided to stroll over to the studio commissary for lunch. The commissary looked like any other cafeteria anywhere in the world, except for the plethora of people in costumes. Cowboys, Indians, soldiers, uniformed cops, intergalactic storm troopers—all wandered about holding their orange cafeteria trays in front of them, swapping stories about the morning's shoot and trying to decide between the cheeseburger special and the tuna surprise.

At the salad bar, Norman saw a strikingly beautiful brunette with high cheekbones and large, almond-shaped eyes. She looked him up and down disdainfully.

"You're covered in blood."

"Corn syrup."

"Looks real."

"Thank you."

The woman paid for her salad and found her way to an empty table. Norman followed her.

"I noticed you're sitting alone," he said. "May I join you?"

She glared at him as if he'd just taken a dump on her croutons. "Are you above-the-line or below-the-line?" she demanded.

"Excuse me?"

"Are you above-the-line talent or below-the-line? Because if you're below-the-line, I can't be seen with you. It's bad for my career." She turned her attention back to her arugula.

Norman studied her carefully. *An axe*, he decided. *Definitely an axe.*

That evening, Norman stood in the shadows of the studio parking lot as the woman made her way to her car. And as she drove through the gates and eased her red Mustang into the perennial traffic on the 405, Norman followed close behind.

It was dark by the time she arrived home, a small apartment complex in Van Nuys. Norman watched as she unlocked the door to her first-floor apartment and entered. Thunder rumbled and rain began to fall as the light in her apartment window switched on. Norman opened the trunk of his car and removed the axe.

He walked slowly towards the door, the rain falling more steadily now, the axe dangling at his side, gravel lightly crunching beneath his feet. Standing beneath a solitary light, he tried the doorknob. The door opened a crack, secured only by eight inches of chain. One swipe of the axe split the chain from the door frame and Norman was inside.

He walked slowly through the small, dimly-lit apartment, following the sound of running water that emanated from within. Slowly through the modestly furnished living room and into the darkened bedroom, littered with discarded clothing. Norman stood silently before the bathroom door, listening to the sound of the running water and of the woman softly humming, the door open just a crack, throwing a sliver of light across the room.

The nude woman spun around as Norman threw open the door, her face a mask of shock and horror. The beginning of a bloodcurdling scream was just escaping from her throat as Norman raised the axe high above his head and, in one quick motion, brought it down on—

"Is that it?"

"I think that's it."

"We can't do anything with that."

"I know."

"There's no fucking ending."

"I know, I know."

"Sherm, turn up the goddamn lights!"

The lights in the screening room rose as producers Joel Weisberg and Sheila Kaufman rubbed their eyes.

"That's two hours of my life I'll never get back," said Joel. "Did we finance that piece of shit?"

"Don't know," said Sheila. "We don't even have a record of the project. Sherm found a bunch of unmarked canisters in the back of the storeroom. No indication what they were. Figured we might as well take a look." She shook her head. "Maybe we can fix it in the cutting room?"

"Fix what? Can't create a third act out of thin air."

"No," she agreed.

Joel sipped from his half-empty cup of coffee, long gone cold, and grimaced. "Besides, it's got other problems. The tone's all wrong. It's too gruesome for a comedy and too wacky for a horror."

"No way to market it."

"Exactly. And the comedy's way too heavy-handed. That whole bit with the producer at the beginning? Yeah, okay, the producer's a schmuck. We get it. But he doesn't know from *Citizen Kane*? That's just stupid. Nobody's going to make *Citizen Kane 2*, for Christ's sake. The humor's too broad by a mile."

"Still," said Sheila, her eyes narrowing, "horror's an easy sell on the foreign market. And they won't even get the jokes."

Joel considered her words. "Valid point," he conceded.

"Why don't I at least have Ed take a look tomorrow? Maybe he can find some way to salvage it."

"Knock yourself out," said Joel. "I'm heading home."

They left the screening room and walked towards their offices, down a long hallway decorated with the obligatory framed posters advertising various features they'd released over the years.

"I actually thought that actress at the end was pretty good," said Sheila. "Seen her in some other low-budget stuff."

"Yeah, Veronica something-or-other. Never thought much of her before."

"Want to hear something strange? I swear I've heard one of those pitches. That Nagasaki musical thing? I'm sure I've read that log line. How's that for weird?"

"Serious?"

"It might even be in that batch of spec scripts you took home with you."

"Well shit, *that* gives me something to look forward to."

Driving west on the 10, Joel replayed the last few scenes of the picture in his mind. *Veronica Reynolds*, he thought. *That was her name.* He'd heard she was difficult to work with, a real ball-buster. Still, he had to admit, she'd given a convincing performance. She was beautiful, she had screen presence. And clearly she was willing to do full frontal. A great combination.

Lately, Joel had been devoting almost all his time and energy to his latest project, *Casablanca 2: Vichy France Strikes Back!* He'd been struggling with the casting, however, particularly the part of Ilsa, Rick's long-lost love who, in this version, was a space alien. Perhaps Veronica Reynolds was just the actress he'd been looking for. As he pulled into the driveway of his Malibu home, he resolved to call her agent first thing in the morning.

The following morning, lounging poolside, Joel placed a call to Ted Kiel, Veronica's agent. Kiel told him he was no longer repping Veronica due to what he delicately described as "personality differences." He didn't think she currently had representation, but he offered to give Joel her home number, which Joel gratefully accepted.

Joel punched the number into his cell phone. A man answered.

"Yes?" came a gruff voice.

"Can I speak to Veronica Reynolds?"

"Who's calling?"

"Joel Weisberg."

"You a friend of hers?"

"No, a producer. Who's this?"

"Detective Larry Doyle. Homicide. I'm afraid Ms. Reynolds is dead."

Joel sat up. "Dead? When?"

"Last night," said the detective. "Most likely between 8:00 and 10:00."

*Between 8:00 and 10:00? That was when he and Sheila had screened the picture.* Joel felt a chill rush through his body.

"Was she...? She wasn't killed with an axe, was she?" The words were out of his mouth before he could stop them.

271

"How the hell did you know that?" the detective demanded. "Mr. Weisberg, where are you? I want you to immediately—"

Joel hung up. *What the hell was going on?*

He rushed inside to his office and began tearing through a tower of unread spec scripts, glancing at the title pages. There it was, just as Sheila had said. *Nagasaki Nights.* Some idiot had actually written that. Joel dialed the number of the writer listed on the bottom of the page. A woman answered.

"Hello?"

"Can I talk to Jerome Stelzer?"

"He's not here. Who is this?"

"Joel Weisberg. I'm a producer."

"Are you the one he met with last night?"

"Last night? No."

"He had a pitch meeting with someone from Warnamount last night."

"A pitch meeting at night?"

"At 9:00. We both thought it was so bizarre. But Jerome went and I haven't heard from him since. I keep calling his cell, but there's no answer. I called the police. This isn't like him at all. He—"

*9:00. That's probably when he and Sheila had been watching that scene.*

Joel hung up. His mind was spinning now. *This is crazy. This makes no sense.* The movie seemed to have depicted events that actually occurred last night—and at the very same time that he and Sheila had been watching them. *What the fuck?*

Joel's heart began racing and he broke into a cold sweat. The events in the movie had taken place over the course of several days. But like a dream that seems to go on a long time yet really only lasts a few seconds, the movie appeared to somehow collapse time, depicting events that were actually happening at the exact moment they unfolded on screen. *Depicting* events? Or *causing* them? Joel shuddered. How long had those canisters been sitting in the back of the storeroom unnoticed? Would anyone have been killed if he and Sheila hadn't watched the movie last night? It was as if the very screening of the picture had caused the murders depicted in it to happen. *But that's insane. That's not possible. Is it?*

Trembling, Joel dialed Sheila's cell. She answered from her car. His words spilled out in a rush.

"VictoriaReynoldswasmurderedlastnightwithanaxeatthesametimewewatchedithappeninthemovieandtheguywiththeNagasakipitchactuallyhadameetingwith—"

"Whoa, whoa," said Sheila. "Slow the fuck down, Eminem. I can't make out a word you're saying."

Joel took a breath. "Victoria Reynolds is dead."

"Who?"

"The actress. From last night's movie. I think the movie's... dangerous somehow."

"What? I can't... only... driving through Laurel Canyon... reception... sucks..."

"Sheila? Are you there?"

272

"Going to… with Ed… screening room… Ed said… maybe… meeting… screen… movie again…"

"No! Sheila, don't screen the movie!"

"… can't hear… losing… have to meet… show Ed… talk to you…"

"Sheila, whatever you do, do *not* screen that movie again! Sheila? Sheila?"

The connection was lost.

Joel jumped in his Porsche and took off for the screening room in West Hollywood, a hundred questions flooding his mind. Who was Norman Snyder? Was he really just a disgruntled screenwriter? Had he made the movie himself? And if not him, who? How had it ended up in the back of their storeroom? And, more importantly, how was it doing what it seemed to be doing?

Joel battled his way through the traffic on the PCH and the 10, followed by the inevitable crawl down La Cienega. It was a full ninety minutes later before he finally burst through the door of the screening room, sweating, panting, and on the verge of hysteria.

Sheila and Ed were already seated and watching the picture. Sheila turned to him with a confused look.

"It's not the same movie," she said.

"What?" said Joel. "What do you mean?"

"Must be some mix-up with the reels," said Ed.

"It's the same character," said Sheila. "The same killer. But it's a totally different story. Like a sequel. The victims are all different."

"No!" said Joel. "God, no!"

"Hey!" said Ed. "Look!"

They turned to look up at the screen.

And there, displayed on the screen, were the three of them in the screening room, looking up at another screen. And on that screen, there they were again, looking up at yet another screen. A movie within a movie within a movie within a movie. And on and on and on into infinity.

"What the hell?" said Ed.

"Is this a joke?" said Sheila. "Is there a camera in here?"

"Oh, shit," said Joel.

And the characters on the screens repeated their words, only with a two-second delay between each movie, creating a weird rippling echo of voices that went on forever.

And then suddenly everything was drowned out by the roar of a motor. And Norman Snyder—huge, towering, dressed in black from head to toe, his face a white snarling mask of death—stepped onto the movie screens and into the screening room, a whirring chainsaw in his hands.

What followed next was pandemonium. Ed was immediately cut down where he stood as Norman sliced through him, sending blood and bone and entrails splattering across the room. Joel and Sheila sprinted for the door, only to find it locked shut. They pounded on it with all their might, screaming and clawing like animals, to no avail.

Until suddenly Joel turned to find the bottom half of Sheila's body had been ripped out from under her. The realization seemed to hit both of them at the same moment and they looked at each other in shock for the split-second before the top half of her torso collapsed to the floor in a pile of gore.

And then Joel felt an intense pain in the back of his head. And everything faded to black.

When he regained consciousness, he found himself seated in one of the aisle seats, bound securely with duct tape.

"Time to wake up," said Norman, towering over him. "Intermission is over." His words echoed over and over on the screens behind him.

"What... what are you going to do with me?" asked Joel.

Norman grinned sadistically. "Well, I was going to force you to watch all fifteen hours of *Berlin Alexanderplatz*. But I think I'll be merciful and just torture you to death instead." He gestured to the screen behind him. "And you get to watch it all on the big screen."

"No. Please." Joel shut his eyes.

"Oh, no. But you *have* to watch."

Norman pinched Joel's right eyelid between his thumb and forefinger, and with a ten-inch butcher knife, proceeded to slice the eyelid off. Joel screamed in pain as the blood poured down his face.

"No struggling now. Only half done," said Norman.

Joel felt his left eyelid being pinched and then, again, the sting of the blade.

"Very *Un Chien Andalou*, don't you think?" said Norman, as Joel's screams echoed into infinity.

"And now it's time for some movie trivia. Because everyone loves movie trivia, don't they?" Norman pulled out a pair of pruning shears and placed the little finger of Joel's right hand between the blades. "And you know all about movies. So this should be easy for you, shouldn't it?"

"Please," Joel pleaded, "please just let me go."

"Question one: What two movies are generally credited with beginning the French New Wave?"

"The French—? What are you—? Please! Please let me go!"

"What two movies are generally credited with beginning the French New Wave?" Norman demanded.

"I don't—I don't know! Please!"

*Snap*. Pain shot through Joel's hand as his finger snapped off in a spurt of blood. He screamed and watched in horror as the scene unfolded on the screen in front of him, over and over and over.

"Wrong. The correct answer is Truffaut's *400 Blows* and Godard's *Breathless*. Question two: What film, now considered a classic, was booed when it premiered at the 1960 Cannes Film Festival?"

"Oh, God! Please! Please!"

*Snap*.

"Wrong. The correct answer is Antonioni's *L'Avventura*. Question 3…"

"Sherm!" Joel screamed at the top of his lungs. "Sherm, wherever you are, turn off the goddamn projector! Sherm! In God's name! Turn off the fucking projector!"


"Is that it?"

"Guess so."

"I kind of liked it."

"I thought it sucked."

Bob Hertzel and Ray Sternberg sat in Bob's office watching the now-blank video screen.

"No end credits," said Bob.

"Very *avant garde*," said Ray.

"No markings on the DVD, either. Where'd we get this thing?"

"Must have been mailed to us. I assume he's looking for distribution. Contact info must have gotten separated from the DVD. Should I track it down?"

"Don't bother. I don't want to distribute the piece of shit anyway."

"No? I kind of liked the whole circular, self-referential thing."

"Seen it. Charlie Kaufman meets Wes Craven. Big fucking deal. You hungry?"

Bob pushed the button on the intercom. "Cheryl, can you order us some lunch?" Silence. "Cheryl?"

"Hey, it's not over yet," said Ray.

And the screen showed Bob's outer office, where Norman Snyder was slitting Cheryl's throat from ear to ear.

"What the fuck?"

They both turned as the office door opened.

# STRAY

## SCOTT HARPER

Otis Crumb crouched low by the roadside, keeping his head down while the Santa Ana winds kicked up warm swirls of desert dust around him. His long, greasy hair hung down in clumps over haunted blue eyes, his skin so white it practically glowed in the surrounding darkness. Otis's nocturnal vision allowed him to see clearly in the darkness. His uncanny hearing had picked up the sound of an approaching motorcycle that was still several miles away. He calmly girded himself for action as the vehicle approached and its sole occupant came into view.

Otis sprang up from behind a small ridge of sand and launched himself at the biker. He smashed into the vehicle's side and sent both himself and the driver careening over the crest of the road. They landed hard in the sand, but Otis was back on his feet almost instantaneously, scrambling spider-like over to the fallen biker.

The man was stunned, but not out of action. Otis noted a long mane of black hair spilling out from under a crimson bandana, an unshaven chin, and jailhouse lightning bolt tattoos covering the man's neck. His keen sense of smell detected both Jack Daniels and marijuana on the biker's breath. As the man stood, Otis was impressed at his size: the biker was nearly seven feet tall with close to three hundred pounds of weight-trained bulk. The black vest he wore did little to conceal massive slabs of chemically-enhanced muscle. The big man appeared confused at first, perhaps wondering who could be so stupid as to jump on him. Then bewilderment turned into testosterone-fueled anger as he looked more closely at the small, innocuous man who had assaulted him. The giant reached into a black leather sheath concealed underneath his vest and withdrew a large hunting blade, brandishing its keen, serrated edges menacingly in Otis's face.

"Keep the hell back, ya' freakin' albino!" the biker screeched hysterically, his voice filled with fury, spittle flying from his cracked, wind-chapped lips. Otis assumed such

276

theatrics would usually terrify a normal person; of course, Otis had never been "normal," and, as of one month ago, he had ceased to be a "person." He took a step in the biker's direction.

The large man attempted a quick thrust at Otis's midsection, only to have his wrist encircled in a vise-grip that bruised his flesh. He struggled frantically to break free, amazed at his attacker's strength.

Otis was barely over five feet in height, his body reed-thin and ghostly pale. Yet his unearthly strength made the big man's struggles seem like those of a fitful child. With a flick of the wrist, Otis casually broke the man's massive forearm, jagged bone jutting from the skin. The biker sagged to his knees, on the verge of passing out, but Otis brought him back to reality with a vicious backhand slap to the jaw. Blood and broken teeth showered from the big man's shattered mouth, while snot poured from his hairy nostrils.

"Wake up, chuckles, you can't miss this," Otis crooned into the shaken man's face. Then he smiled, unsheathing fanged teeth. Since his recent transformation, Otis had noticed a new viciousness surfacing inside him. He wasn't comfortable with it, but it seemed to overtake him every time he fed. He assumed the ferocity just came with the new dentures, a type of package deal.

Otis tore out the biker's throat and gorged himself on the arterial spray, relishing in the adrenaline-spiked blood. He had never been a bright man, but he had watched a late-night horror flick or two in his time. He knew that the *strigoi* were usually detected by the telltale twin fang marks left on the victim's throat. Therefore, no throat, no marks—no problem.

He felt the warmth gradually leave the biker's body and begin to fill the empty coldness inside him. New vitality and strength sang through his muscles and sinews. He almost felt alive again.

Otis quickly sifted through the dead man's pockets, withdrawing a wad of cash from the biker's blue jeans. He momentarily eyed the remnants of his meal with a moderate degree of self-satisfaction before transforming, bat-like leather membranes shooting from his wrists to attach on his hamstrings. His clothing faded out of existence into the air around him. He took flight.


Winging his way back from the desert to the motel room in Long Beach where he spent most of his days, Otis contemplated his new existence. He'd been born dirt-poor and spent the majority of his adult years wandering from one low-wage job to another, a journey that had taken him practically across the entire country. None of it had prepared him in the least for the demands of undead existence.

If he could have re-lived his life, he would have at least read *Dracula* once. It was while wandering along the coast in California one month ago in search of work that an inhumanly strong attacker had reached out and pulled him down the proverbial deserted alley. Otis had struggled valiantly against his puissant attacker, trying to escape to the nearby beach and at one point succeeding in drawing blood by biting one of his assailant's hands. Before his own lifeblood was vacuumed out from twin holes in his jugular, Otis saw his murderer's furrowed red eyes. Sand and dust covered the majority of an outdated three-piece suit, as well as brittle locks of jet-grey hair. The ashen skin of the man's face was wrinkled like alligator leather, so dry that it was actually flaking off in the wind as they struggled. Massive, bushy-white eyebrows met over the man's hawk-like nose, which in turn rested on an unkempt moustache. Otis's last human memories were of dying in the hands of Methuselah. Three nights later, he wiggled his way out of the sand and attempted to begin a new "life."

Otis concluded that one benefit of his new condition was that working was no longer a necessity. The victims who provided him his nightly sustenance also forfeited whatever valuable possessions they had on them at the time of their demise. The money he'd taken from the biker tonight (most likely obtained from the sale of meth-amphetamine, judging from the white crystalline-laced packets in the dead man's vest pockets) would take care of the motel rent for the next month. Eventually, if he picked the right prey, Otis believed he might work his way up to his own mansion. Maybe even a castle someday.

At one time, living as a thief would have disgusted him. He had been raised in a home where the Protestant work ethic was deeply ingrained, where one's own self-esteem was derived in large measure from the contributions one made to helping the family. The fact that his recent criminal exploits no longer bothered what remained of his conscience gave him pause. Perhaps, he reasoned, the exigencies of his new existence forced him to act in ways that were at odds with his previous moral standards. And since he limited his nocturnal attacks to mostly parolees from the local state correctional institute and other such riffraff, Otis concluded that he might, in a strange way, actually be working toward the betterment of society.

A block from his residence, Otis assumed human form and landed in a nearby alley, his clothing coalescing from the night air around him. Otis believed that, in whatever eldritch domain the *strigoi* had originated in, there must have been just a touch of dark magic involved in their creation: whatever clothing he had on at the time of shape-change mystically returned when he shed that form.

Otis entered the dingy complex and walked up the flight of dilapidated stairs that led to the second floor. He ran into the motel manager, Mr. Dubrava, in the walkway. Dubrava was a large, gruff, old-world type with a thick Russian accent, oily hair, and an unseemly belly that draped over his too-tight pants. Usually unshaven and under-dressed, he typically reeked of onions and garlic. Otis had learned from painful experience to keep his distance.

Otis had overheard other tenants speak of Dubrava in hushed whispers, barely able to conceal their fear. Back in his native country, Dubrava had apparently been a man of some importance, somehow vaguely connected to the Russian mafia. He'd been some type of enforcer, well-versed in making his enemies disappear. Otis imagined that, in his prime, Dubrava might have cut quite an imposing figure with his size. Now he was definitely over the hill, weighed down by years of alcohol and calorie abuse. On occasion, Otis had seen young men who spoke in a foreign language enter Dubrava's first floor office, so he imagined the landlord might still have some connections with the local underworld. It mattered little to Otis now. No human could intimidate him.

"There is blood on your shirt," the man muttered, pointing at Otis's T-shirt.

Otis looked down at the front of his shirt and noted some tiny red stains, reminders of his meal from earlier in the evening.

"Must have cut myself," he lied. He quickly found his room key and opened the door. He was about to close it when Dubrava inserted his foot between the door and the wall.

"There is a rancid smell in your room, no?" Dubrava accused. "Maybe you forget to take out trash? Or maybe you keep body hidden inside somewhere, eh?" Dubrava's tone was flat and emotionless.

Otis was in no mood to deal with the Russian. He applied a fraction of his new strength to force Dubrava's foot out and close the door.

"We talk some time, maybe soon," Dubrava said loudly into the closed door. He walked down the stairs, each one in turn groaning under his substantial weight.

Otis picked up Dubrava's last comment, but he chose to ignore it. The stench of decay Dubrava had mentioned assaulted his nose, smelling like a combination of rotted fruit and fresh feces. Flies buzzed around his small room. The stink seemed to originate from his bed. He discarded his shoes and clothes and hopped into bed, noting as he did so that his mattress was uncomfortably stiff and lumpy. Otis twisted and turned, attempting to get comfortable. Since his recent resurrection, he had experienced insomnia. He felt greatly fatigued every morning with the onset of daylight, but could never seem to fall into a deep sleep. He would phase in and out of consciousness, plagued by persistent nightmares. He closed his eyes and proceeded to drift into a fitful slumber.


Otis awoke to the smell of blood.

He catapulted himself out of bed and almost fell. He found Mr. Dubrava laid out on the floor next to the bed, pale as a sheet, his head twisted around one hundred and eight degrees. Blood dripped from his open mouth out onto the floor. The corpse's hand gripped a thick stake of lacquered wood over three feet in length. A discarded mallet lay nearby. Above Dubrava, leaning next to a heavily-curtained window, was a brown-haired man of moderate height and build, dressed in an expensive black suit and tie. His arms were casually folded across his chest, while a mischievous smile played on the corners of his rosy lips. Though he appeared to be in his early thirties, his dark eyes radiated a confidence that reflected wisdom beyond his years. Otis's hyper-senses alerted him that the intruder wasn't breathing, and didn't have a heartbeat.

"Our first meeting and already you are in my debt, child," the stranger intoned, sounding amusedly irked.

"For what?" Otis squeaked, doing his best to sound defiant and in control. His fangs erupted defensively, but inside he was shaken, not knowing what to make of all this confusion or how to deal with it.

"Pop those back where they belong, young one, or I shall remove them myself!"

The newcomer's eyes blazed crimson and Otis immediately felt about as threatening as a small puppy. His fangs receded and he took an involuntary step back.

"Good. Now, where were we? Oh, yes, that wretched stench? How can you stand it?"

The man moved with unnatural grace and speed across to Otis's bed and flung the grimy mattress aside, scattering flies. Resting on the box springs was the black, bloated body of a woman. Maggots crawled from her open mouth and eye sockets, and her throat had been torn out. She looked like she had died screaming. Dark, viscous fluids stained the bottom of the mattress.

"The proverbial corpse under the motel bed! An urban myth, proven fact! Congratulations, young one. Hah, your brain is obviously not firing on all cylinders."

Otis did not remember the girl, but he assumed he had fed on her in one of his less lucid moments.

The man then walked over to where Dubrava lay and palmed the stake, his eyes still fixed on Otis. "You, sir, owe me your existence. Your friend here discovered your true nature and decided to remove you from his list of tenants. Permanently." He smiled, his irises slowly losing their red glow as his mood calmed.

Otis eyed the stake. "Would that have worked?" he somberly asked. Otis had been in no hurry to put the legendary immortality of the *strigoi* to the test since his resurrection.

"I assure you, they work quite well. Any weapon of wood can cause temporary immobility if it penetrates the heart while we sleep during the day. Nasty thing— hawthorn, it appears." The cultured *strigoi* shifted his eyes to the stake and closed his hand, grinding the thick wood into splinters with incredible ease. Otis noted the sharp, finely-manicured nails attached to each finger.

The man turned his attention back to Otis. "I'm not surprised that you aren't aware of your new limitations. There was no one there for you when you awoke that first night, was there?"

"I don't know what you mean."

"The false death. We all endure it to become what we are. Your sire abandoned you to the night without instruction. Look at you. You're closer to the final death than you realize. I take it you've been having difficulty sleeping, no?"

Otis bobbed his head cautiously in agreement, not sure where the other *strigoi* was heading with the conversation.

"Can't say I'm surprised, sleeping on that corpse like you were. We cannot prosper without soil from our native land. It is one of our limitations. There are others. We can chronicle those later. For now, we have matters which must be addressed. Your feeding habits are… shall we say, less than discreet. The victims you have littered over the city have become fodder for the news media. You've become somewhat of a *cause celebre*: the press has labeled you an 'Angel of Vengeance,' extracting justice from those the penal system is no longer able or willing to punish. However, we both know your intentions are less than lofty.

"No traces of feeding can be left or we attract unwanted attention. Such attention can prove fatal. Fortunately for you, I arrived just in time." He gestured at Dubrava's limp corpse. "He had not completely forgotten his old-world roots. Most people dismiss us as the stuff of myth and legend. Still, we need not be so obvious in our dining patterns; in fact, we need not even kill."

The newcomer crossed his wrists behind his back and began to walk slowly toward Otis. "Listen to my little story, friend, for I believe that you and I have much in common, much in common indeed." His gaze pinioned the young *strigoi*. "Quite some time ago, I was a solicitor, one of some renown, back on the isles."

Otis looked perplexed.

"Real estate, my good man, back in Britain, the United Kingdom as it were. I was young, handsome, innocent... even engaged to be married. It's all in that damned Stoker book. Anyway, a certain ancient Walachian nobleman contacted my employer at the time, Mr. Hawkins. Hawkins sent me off to the famed Land-Beyond-the-Forest to finalize the purchase of an estate in London. The rest, as they say, is history."

Otis continued to look confounded, his forehead wrinkled in confusion.

The stranger continued. "The book Stoker wrote is basically true, but Victorian society could never have tolerated the actual ending. It wasn't acceptable then for the villain—and worse yet, a foreigner!—to triumph, even if those he 'victimized' eventually came to accept his gifts and appreciate their richness. I never needed fear losing my Mina, as that bloody Dutchman Van Helsing would have had us all believe at the time; in fact, I'll now enjoy her company for as long as I so desire.

"The old count was never the devious strategist the Dutchman made him out to be. He just wanted to 'live' again, away from the forests and wolves and inbred townsfolk. He wanted to be part of the new century, not a relic of the past. In his own time, he was considered a hero by his people, a protector of the faith. Standards were different then; behavior that modern men label barbaric was in those days a necessity of existence. Times change, people change, even we change, at least on the inside.

"My friend the count is not what he used to be. The knife wounds inflicted by the Dutchman and his friends corrupted his blood, infected it with grave mold, turning it into little more than ichor. His blood became your blood, and now your brain is addled too. Imagine, sleeping with a rotting corpse under your mattress! You are *strigoi,* not some ghoul! Like him, I imagine, your mind comes and goes, periods of lucidity mixed in with absentmindedness and plain obliviousness. Six centuries of existence have taken their toll on him; sometimes he forgets what and who he is. He left us recently while we were visiting Los Angeles, just up and fled in the middle of the day. Now I have to find him and bring him home. A people cannot be without their king. You were unfortunate enough to cross his path during one of his less lucid periods."

The elder *strigoi* paused momentarily. Otis was not sure who this so-called "king" was, but he was not in a hurry to make his acquaintance again.

"Oh, don't worry, we'll catch up with him," the other continued. "Fortunately, an exchange of blood must occur in addition to the bite for the corpse to revive. I've had some difficulty separating your trail from his, destroying or concealing all those mangled corpses you two have left behind. Lots of bodies under beds, if you will. You have so much to learn. Think of this new life as a beginning. It has plenty of advantages, and if you play your cards correctly, you just might be around to savor them for a long, long time. Anyway, enough for now. We've got to get moving. This neighborhood is like a maze; I have no idea where I parked the car."

He walked over to the window and began to pull apart the thick curtains that covered it.

Otis screamed in mortal terror, shielding his face with his hands and backing away in a crab-like scuttle. "No, the sun, don't let it in!"

The other *strigoi* laughed. "Oh, child, you watch too many movies. Sunlight weakens us and limits our powers, but it will not kill you. Look!" He proceeded to tear the drapes down, letting the early morning light flood into the little room. Otis winced, gagged once, but was shocked when, after several seconds, he did not begin to burn. He looked at his new benefactor in stunned disbelief.

"I'll teach you more as we go along, my new friend. For now, call me Jonathan." With that, the elder *strigoi* grasped Otis' clawed hand in his own and led him out of the room.

# THE HULDUR

## LAWRENCE BERRY

The Nighthawk Estate was located in Contra Costa Country, on the rising slopes of Mount Diablo. The sprawling mansion covered most of Devil Mesa. Hidden Lake occupied the rest of the rise of land. It was a dry country of red earth and sandstone formations, the still blue water bright in the afternoon light. The desolate house rose out of the wasteland ahead like a black thorn.

"Why is the house painted that color? It's atmospheric as heck, but we're in a desert," Lucy said to Perry Erpelding, location scout for *Among The Dead*. Lucy was an assistant producer. The alleged haunted house had to pass her scrutiny before it went further up the food chain.

"Maybe Elias Nighthawk liked the color. I don't know. It didn't come up in my research."

Lucy put her hand on the passenger window. It was hot to the touch. Beyond it the landscape they passed through rippled with heat. "Not the smartest choice."

Tara Nicks laughed, sitting beside her, for the last hour silent as a sphinx.

Before Perry could answer, Lucy asked, "And why is that funny, Tara?"

"Nighthawk was a diabolist. I imagine he liked the heat." Tara gave Lucy a wry smile.

Lucy found Tara's attempts at humor out of synch with the show. "You put that in the working script—he was a warlock who sought his own hell? You write like a college drama major."

Tara glanced over at her, her gaze impossibly direct and challenging. She had large green eyes in a pale face and the blackest hair. Despite her gothic looks, and the undeniable depth of her knowledge of the paranormal, Lucy seldom found Tara worthwhile. Personally, she detested the woman. It was like trying to warm to an Egyptian asp, tattooed with hieroglyphics from The Book of The Dead.

Perry cleared his throat, disturbed by the acrimony between the two women. He'd been on the road for a month before he found the house. Things just got better from there. His searches turned up the Nighthawk atrocities, a kind of occult slaughter, and learned that the people in the closest towns avoided even driving by the Nighthawk estate. This was a solid find if Lucy and Tara didn't erupt into open warfare. "The lake cools the house. It's fed by an underground aquifer and the water is quite cold. Isn't that right, Edgar?"

The Trustee stirred, a thin old man perched between the two tense women. "Elias Nighthawk was a contrary man. It's in County zoning ordinance that any house on a prominence has to blend into the surrounding landscape, but he wanted his black pearl. That's what he called his monstrosity of a mansion."

Perry was right about the cooling effect of the lake. Lucy felt the July heat fading away as they gained elevation, the crisp scent of open water filtering through the air conditioning of Perry's Suburban.

A final S-curve and they reached their destination, the long house three stories high and massive in size. A flight of stairs twenty feet wide led to an imposing oak door, intricate statues of a great mass of small rat-like creatures guarding each side of the entry.

Lucy avoided the marble rodents, taking care as she went up the broad steps.

Perry let them in with a cordial gesture, taking the keys from Edgar after the trustee tried three times, his hands shaking too much to work the lock.

Edgar was disturbed by his show of frailty and turned to Tara. "Young Perry has told me you're a research assistant for *Among the Dead*, but what does a research assistant do, Miss Tara?"

"I have a degree in occult sciences from an Academy in Paris. I work in the command van while Nick and Eddie investigate the houses—so add techie and actress to my titles."

"You're an actress on the television show?" Edgar asked, clearly impressed.

"She does voiceovers, mostly," Lucy said, answering for Tara. "Sometimes we show her weird face to add a corpse-like effect and get some spectral atmosphere going. She's the best thing we have next to a dead body."

Perry stepped back so Edgar could lead them through the great room to a sweeping staircase. The enormous chamber was filled with dark furniture and in its center was an amazing collection of crystal balls, each on a sandstone pedestal, glowing where a few rays of sunshine leaked through the plantation shutters.

They went up to the second-floor landing, minute noises following them—tiny creaking whispers, scurrying small feet, an infinitesimal crash as some small item in the crowded room fell over.

Lucy put these down to house sounds. No domicile was ever silent, and it was good news for the show. This way they wouldn't have to layer in any atmospheric effects.

284

They passed a large portrait painting and Edgar gestured vaguely. "This would be Elias Nighthawk and his vicious little beasts."

Nighthawk was tall, thin, saturnine, sitting in a velvet chair petting one of the animals that adorned the steps. Lucy shivered as she walked close enough to really study the image. There was another of the small beasts on the chair back, not far from the man's neck.

"What are these things?" Lucy asked. While the animals were the size of a small rodent, their paws seemed to act almost as hands, the individual claws like stunted fingers. The heads were oversized and they had intelligent, feral eyes. The animal Nighthawk was petting was misshapen and unnaturally large.

Edgar paused before the painting. "He showed them to me a few times. Actually called the little monsters to him like household cats. I know he fed them raw beef and seemed affectionate when they were around. Nighthawk was not a warm man and affection didn't come naturally. He didn't say what they were and I didn't ask."

"They're Huldur, native to India where they are quite prized," Tara said.

Lucy had read quite a number of occult works as part of her position on the show, and she remembered seeing something like them in an ancient book Tara had brought in called *Mors Bestia*, a collection of animals sacred to the dark gods of legend. They sure weren't from India, that was malarkey. These things were something he'd called up to serve him. In that moment, Lucy believed in everything they were here to see—that Nighthawk had engaged in human sacrifice, that he had attained wisdom denied to most sane men, and that he'd domesticated a great evil for his own purposes. Perry had at last found a good haunted house. Maybe the best one so far.


"It's a vanity painting. Let's not put too much stock in it," Perry said, trying to urge Lucy forward. She finally began to move, Tara not needing any encouragement, thank God. Tara scared Perry.

A few more steps and Perry unlocked double stained-glass doors, the leaded-glass showing ravens tearing apart a carrion deer.

"Paranormal reality shows can be deadly dull," Tara said, in what had become a prolonged silence. "The viewers find me interesting. And pale skin is what's in."

"Uh-huh," Lucy said sarcastically. Tara really was a bitch today.

Perry handed them each a flashlight and together they illuminated a study, the walls lined with books. There was a huge pentagram branded into the oak floor, and in its center stood a primitive stone altar, the obsidian-like stone veined with some bright metal. He went around lighting pyramidal candles.

"That's copper in the sacrificial stone," Perry said. "The stone itself is granite and iron ore."

"Nighthawk claimed it to be an asteroid he found in the desert. Discovering the altar is what began everything that happened." Tara turned her flashlight off, her emerald eyes seeming to glow in the dim light.

"You mean the sacrifices," Lucy said.

"Possession by a demonic darkness," Tara added, as if that explained the murders.

As they came closer Lucy could see that the top of the altar was green with tarnish from the blood. Enough had spilled that it had run down the sides filigreeing the rock with thick runnels of rust.

"Elias Nighthawk would have gotten away with it if one of the crew he hired to kidnap children and virgin women hadn't spilled the goods," Lucy said. "Even then, the lazy Sheriff happened to drive out when he was trying to stick a ceremonial knife into the eighth victim and she was screaming her head off."

Tara turned her green eyes toward Lucy, glowing like jade embers. "Worried, Lucy?"

Perry looked from Tara to Lucy, confusion making him frown. "Why should Lucy be worried?"

"Our Lucy is a virgin. She gave this fact up in a game of truth or dare at a cast party last week."

Lucy colored. "It's not a crime waiting for marriage."

"Of course not, it's only proper" Perry said, turning at a skipping sound that seemed to be following them—but, of course, nothing was there but shadows. "Edgar has had exterminators out, but they haven't found a thing and nothing has touched their poisons."

"I told you, Mr. Perry, these aren't rats and I did that just to please you. These skipping noises are his pets. Nighthawk may be dead, but *they* haven't gone anywhere. I was his attorney when he was alive and he showed me the nursery he'd raised, nesting them in the caves beneath the house. They're still down there, eating God knows what."

"The Huldur are a myth," Lucy said with a sniff, finally remembering the details she'd come across in her reading. "The only people that believe in them are the Welsh."

"Believing isn't a choice in this house," Edgar said dryly. "I shouldn't have come out here. This house is no place for an old man."

"Let's turn out our lights," Tara said. She stood in a shadow and would have been invisible if not for her glowing domino of a face and luminous green eyes.

Lucy and Perry followed her example, doing it for the good of the show, and they stood in midnight ink. Where the room had seemed stale and foul before, now Lucy felt an intangible flow of substance brush against her ankle and made a sound of panic, switching her light back on.

"Did you feel that?" she asked Perry.

"Maybe something small, darting past us."

Tara gave Lucy another look of disdain. "You want to find real haunted houses and when you do, the flimsy things you call nerves give way." She turned to Edgar, who had a penlight switched on, checking the floor all around him. "You said there's a crypt? Let's see the old warlock in his decaying glory."

"It's in the basement, but I don't advise going down there. It's too close to Windrun, the cave Nighthawk cut into when he began breeding the Huldur."

"Even better. The place where all the boogies live."

Elias Nighthawk's ebony coffin lay on a bier of polished redwood, the crypt showing leakage from Hidden Lake; water dripped in the vast charnel, uncertainly lit by oddly arranged sconces holding thick candles, some of them sparking from the wetness. Judging by its size, Lucy guessed that the burial chamber contained most of the dead members of the Nighthawk family. Lucy didn't trust Tara to do the research. She was lazy and poorly organized. In her studies there didn't seem to be a trace of morality in Nighthawk's heritage. His grandfather traveled to Europe to fight with the Nazis. Earlier ancestors reportedly preyed on the local Indian tribes, sacrificing any they could trap to the nameless gods the Nighthawk clan worshipped. They'd been exiled from one state after another until they came to the wilderness of California, building a black house on a red mesa, Hidden Lake mirroring it like an obsidian obelisk smuggled away from the tombs on the West Bank.

Lucy went up to the coffin, surprised to find it had a window over Nighthawk's face. He'd been interred face down. The glass had lines of copper in it and Lucy touched the pane, immediately drawing her hand away. The coffin seemed to respond to her fingers, and there was a grinding sound as some unseen lever released.

"What did you do?" Perry asked. "We're here to look, not meddle with the grave articles."

"She's awakened the sorcerer if our luck has entirely left us," Edgar answered. "I never believed the evil in that man would find the rest that comes to good people."

"I just touched the glass," Lucy explained as gears moved and cogs shifted on their pins.

Tara found the panic and pandemonium comical and laughed her strange, musical, deep laugh. "The granddaughter was never found. She lived here with him while he was sacrificing the people his men kidnapped, and the police want her. Maybe she's come back and that's her we hear, scampering about this old ruin."

A hatch opened in the coffin and a mound of small creatures tumbled to the dusty floor. Perry turned his flashlight toward them and gave a cry of disgust. They had humanoid faces and arms, but the bodies and fast legs of a rat.

"He was buried with vermin?" Perry asked, his voice filled with disgust.

"Huldur are supernatural beings that can move between the worlds. They aren't rats." Tara inhaled deeply. "God, I love the rotten stench of a crypt."

"Keep back away from them!" Edgar half-shouted. "There's no telling what they can do." He tried to back quickly up, barely moving.

"What other worlds?" Lucy asked, moving to stand beside the niter-encrusted wall. Tara had never finished a sentence in her entire life.

"The living and the dead, each to each, until there's linkage and one melts into the other."

The Huldur flooded around Edgar, Perry and Lucy, leaving silver talismans on their feet, their claws scraping blood from their skins.

"Open the damned box," Tara said, stepping away from the others. There was a tone of command in her voice and it seemed to be directed at the creatures. "Turn him!"

It took Lucy a moment to realize that Tara was really speaking to the Huldur—and that *they were listening to her.* All she wanted to do was run and her feet felt nailed to the stone pavers.

The coffin lid opened as a mass of Huldur swarmed around the silver catch and the tiny animals dived inside, flipping the body over. There was a long knife in Nighthawk's dead hand, the blade made of copper, inscribed with runes that seemed not just centuries, but millennia old.

"Walk over and take the knife," Tara said, staring at Perry.

Perry made sounds of fear and distress as his feet began to move, carrying him to the oblong box. Fighting with all the strength he had, he resisted Tara's indomitable will. Before long the weapon was in his hand, his chest heaving with effort. He stared at the blade in shock.

"Now cut your throat and feed Granddad the blood."

Perry leaned over the coffin with a strangled cry of dismay and sliced his throat open in one deep cut, his arteries pouring blood on Nighthawk's dead and withered chest.

Lucy tried to run, she tried to scream, but the talismans on her feet held her in place and her voice was a dry rattle. Edgar reached out and patted her wrist. He'd been so quiet she'd forgotten about him. Looking at Edgar now, she could see naked terror draining his features of blood and a horrid expression of resignation. It was as if he'd expected this nightmare to encompass them all.

Perry fell to the floor, still jetting blood. The Huldur moved on him in a pack, dragging him away into the recesses of the tomb, moving rocks aside and slipping away into a hole seemingly gnawed into the wall tiles.

"Don't try and run," Tara said, stroking Lucy's hair. "The Huldur have denied that to you, but yes, I'm Jasmine Nighthawk and I'm here to raise the dead. There are rules to true magic and I had to be invited in after Edgar had the house exorcised, but who would do it? And why? Your show provided an answer to those questions."

Perry's blood soaked into the corpse like a sponge and the dead man moved, a twitch of long-forgotten muscles driven by dead nerves.

"Dear God," Edgar moaned. "I knew I shouldn't have come. The priest said he'd put the house to rest."

"There is no God of man in the Nighthawk household. You aren't much, Mr. Wyatt, but I'll see to your offenses when I finish with little Lucy."

"You can't do this," Lucy said, raising her arms to fight the taller woman.

"It takes two to raise the dead," Tara said, pushing Lucy's hands down to her side. "A man's blood to feed the body and a virgin to bring new life. It's about time to finish the feeding. Are you ready, Lucy?"

The Huldur were returning to the chamber, silver eyes glowing to match Tara's lambent brilliance. Abruptly, Edgar put his hand to his chest and issued a great groan as he slumped to the glowing red tiles.

"You've killed him," Lucy said, unrestrained panic raising the hair on her arms.

"A waste of good blood, but there should be plenty in you." Tara shoved Lucy toward the coffin and she took her first unwilling step toward Elias Nighthawk's grave.

# SOUTH COMMAND

## J. P. FLORES

KILGORE COUNTY SHERIFF'S DEPARTMENT

South Command

Special Problems Project:

DIVISIONAL DIRECTIVE: #025-038

Effective immediately, in accordance with the recently passed Assembly Bill on "The Reconditioning," (AB-647) all Non-Living Animate individuals, (NLA's) will no longer be described by the term "Zombies." Every identifiable NLA will be marked and tagged and will be afforded every right as any natural born citizen of the United States of America.

They paired me up with Patrol Officer Sherry "Dingleberry" Montoya and we worked the Styler-Boggs district, in the South Command. It was mostly middle-income homes but it also covered a portion of the inner city as you got closer to the central business area.

I liked Dingleberry. She was a dark-haired Latina with bright white teeth and easy with a smile. She pulled her hair up in a bun of maximum density that sat on top of her head.

'Sherry-Sherry Dingleberry' earned her nickname in the police academy when she accidentally tased someone in the testicles during a training exercise. No one dared laugh as the instructor, a no-nonsense police sergeant in his fifties, screamed and danced in pain which only caused Dingleberry to panic and send another jolt of electricity through the lower appendage of our teacher. Later she earned our respect because during PT we had wrestling bouts after our runs and almost everyone who went up against her got folded in knots even though she was small and petite.

As she drove, I reached in the back seat of the police car and pulled a brand new bright colored shirt out of a large cardboard box.

"There's got to be about a hundred of these in here," I said.

"That's why we're going to the feeding hub," she said. "I figure we can find most of them there."

The Rotters, brainless and void as they were, gravitated to their regular food source every day. There must have been seventy or more making their way to the center of town. Some limping, some crawling, and some walking very well. Not one of them caring or understanding that the law had granted them citizenship with legal standings and rights.

"How many of these are ours?"

"Fifty-three, and I think I see one now," Dingles said, turning the car right on Carondelet street.

A lone Rotter stood on the sidewalk facing the wall of a building. "Hey," Dingles yelled out, but it was busy pawing at the wall and gurgling. He kept trying to scoop food from the image on a poster of spaghetti. It was a bad one and he looked to be about thirty when the virus got him. The right side of his face was just exposed skull, the corresponding eye socket nothing but a black hole. His other eye was passable but completely gray. Most of his jaw was still intact, but his lips were gone and he was forever grinning at the world through jagged teeth. Dingles slipped a pair of blue latex gloves on and gently pulled him away from the wall. "No, sweetie," she said. "That's not real food. The good stuff is that way. But, hold on a second." She held him still and nodded to me.

I took a photo of the new citizen and the recognition software in the unit did its work with a bell tone. A name appeared over the image of the Rotter. "Jonathan Sampson," I read off the camera viewer. "He's on our list."

I found the shirt with the name emblazoned across the chest in metallic letters. It was dyed bright orange, made of light Kevlar, and there were two quarter-sized metal discs on the front of the shirt and four on the back.

"By the powers vested in me by the County of Kilgore, I hereby deem you born again as Mister Jonathan Sampson."

After Dingles slipped the shirt over the undead freak, I passed the tagging device over each disc. A regular person would have screamed in pain as they fused to skin and bone, but Jonathan Sampson only growled and smacked his teeth, looking over his shoulder at the spaghetti.

In the academy, Doctor Carol Moss said that 'Non-Living Animates' really don't need to eat anything. It's just that they are wired that way. She called it 'vestigial survival instincts' and her own system of reconditioning altered their murderous behavior. Instead of looking for brains to eat out of people's heads, the NLAs wandered around aimlessly until the appointed feeding time. Then, like Koi in a pond, they gravitated to where they knew food was going to be. Once inside the feeding hub they were allowed thirty seconds to scoop up a slop composed of chopped up hotdogs and grape juice with both hands while the sound of people screaming in horror was played over a loudspeaker. It satisfied them, sometimes for two to three days at a time, and it kept them docile and manageable.

"One less Rotter to tag," I said as Dingles pointed him in the direction of the feeding station.

"Really? David," she said to me, "if we can't use the Z-word, do you really think 'Rotters' is okay?"

I looked at her and smirked. "I'll get the next one."

"Yeah, you will."

We drove around the residential district waiting for the facial recognition camera mounted on our car to alert us to the next Rotter that required tagging, but it was still early afternoon and the NLAs were probably still loitering about the food. We drove around looking for actual police work to do.

"I got a DUI," I said, "Blew a one-four and a one-five. Captain calls me in and says that in the interest of acclimating me to the cultural diversity of the unique County of Kilgore, I am being reassigned to the South Command for a period of one year. Bullshit, right?"

"I guess," Dingles said.

"And I didn't know we had to live here while assigned here."

"Yup."

"So, what did you do to get here?"

"When you're a cop you find what you're good at," she said, chopping off the sentence like she didn't want to talk about it anymore.

"What does that mean?"

"I chose South Command."

"It's dead here, Dingles. I want to catch bad guys, not scabies. Maybe if we corralled all the Rotters and locked them up in a big building, people would move back and South Command would be like a real city."

Dingles looked at me with a resting bitch face that would have killed Medusa.

"Sorry. NLAs."

Fortunately, the alert tone on our computer terminal went on and a grid map of the area appeared on the screen with a blinking dot.

One of the NLAs on our list was nearby.

"Over there," Dingles said, bringing the car around to the opposite curb.

The Rotter was a female making her way down the street. Dried food remnants were in her hair. She was nude and her dehydrated skin hung on her bones like a bathrobe on a clothes hanger. The bright orange T-shirt we were going to give her would be a great fashion improvement.

Her face was sunken over her skull. Her eyes were pretty much intact and, unlike Jonathan Sampson, she still had lips.

I slipped my gloves on and nudged her to a stop. Dingles snapped her photo as I held on to her.

Instinctively, the NLA resisted my grasp. That wasn't uncommon amongst the first generation of reconditioned ones.

"Gonna have to tag this for a re-up," I said.

"Amanda Silvio," Dingles said reading the screen. "I think I went to school with her."

"Number twenty-three on the list," I said.

I let go of her and fished through the T-shirt box in the back seat of the car. While I turned my back, the NLA went forward and lunged at Dingleberry who deflected a swipe of the bony hand just in time.

The NLA swung again and Dingles stumbled back, falling to the sidewalk.

I unholstered my taser and flipped the switch to arm it. Tasers shot out volts of electricity to incapacitate a combative suspect and weren't meant to be used on NLA's since they felt no pain. Still, I had it in my hand and I fired it. The double-pronged weapon shot one into the NLA's chest. The other deflected off of her exposed clavicle and lodged in the side of her head just above her ear.

Simultaneously it shot out a five second jolt of electricity. Dingles pushed Amanda away from her and we both watched the NLA convulse for a full five seconds.

"Did she scratch you?"

"No, thank God! But can you pay a little more attention to what you're supposed to be doing?"

"I didn't think she would go all 'level three' on you."

"No, you just didn't think," Dingles said.

"Sherry?"

The voice sounded raspy but it was clear. It came from Amanda the NLA, who had stopped convulsing.

We both stared at her as she looked back and forth between us.

"What is going on?" she said, panic creeping into her voice.

Neither of us could think of any words as Amanda looked down at her hands, at the peeling skin and exposed bones. She looked down at her naked, dehydrated chest and then she touched an exposed rib.

"What is this? What happened to me?" she cried. She touched her face, felt the dry leathery skin, touched the sunken flesh around her eyeballs and then turned and looked at her reflection in the window. "Oh my God! Sherry! What is this? What is going on?"

And then she screamed and Dingles grabbed her by the shoulders.

"Amanda!" Dingles said looking into the orbs in her eye sockets, "Listen to me! We're going to help you!"

"How? How are you going to help me? I'm a freaking monster!" she said.

"There are people that know about these things!" Dingles said as the Rotter pulled out of Dingle's grasp and tried to run away. But her knees collapsed and she fell.

"Amanda!" Dingles cried, helping the NLA back to her feet. "Amanda!" But there was nothing left. The blank stare on what was left of her face was gone. She growled once and then she stopped moving.

Dingles grabbed my taser, lifted it to Amanda's head and fired it off again.

Nothing happened.

"She's dead," Dingles said.

"You mean, again?"


"It was a tiny remnant of cognition, like the last few drops from a thermos caught in the recessed lining of the container. The jolt jarred it loose and for a brief moment she was Amanda Silvio again, pre-virus Amanda," Doctor Moss said.

The Doctor was thinner than I remember from the academy, and she looked almost like an NLA herself, except with good skin and clothes.

"I suspect it must have been a shock to the subject, but what you've discovered could be our gateway into finding exactly what it was that caused the epidemic. If we could get a glimpse into their last memories, we might find some answers."

"She was terrified," Dingles said. "Do you intend to put them all through that?"

"Certainly not all of them."

"It doesn't seem right, Ma'am," Dingles said.

"No, it doesn't. But it's important for our future."

We had four more hours in our shift and Dingles was silent for most of it.

"They were people once," she said. "Yeah, that sucks," I said, "But I don't want what happened to them to happen to me."

We tagged five more NLA's and we were done. The weekend was here, and I planned to spend it miles from Kilgore County, hopping bars and dancing with college girls a mere hour's drive away in San Francisco. I invited her along since several of us who graduated from the Academy together were making it a road trip. But she said she had a prior commitment with her family.

The next day, before I left, I got a call from her.

"Changed your mind?"

"Can you stop by my place?" she asked.

"You okay, Dingles?"

"Yeah, it'll be quick."

When I got to her house, the front door was open and the strong odor of sandalwood incense met me on the porch.

"It was a mistake telling Doctor Moss," Dingles said. "You saw Amanda. She was normal for a moment and she was terrified. How would you feel if it had been you? Waking up from a coma to find out you're a monster?"

"I don't know, Dingles."

"I mean, that would be pretty bad, right?"

"I guess. You asked me here to discuss NLAs?"

"I don't know what to do." Her cheeks glistened with tears and she sat on the edge of her couch, staring out the glass sliding door of her apartment. A department-issued taser was in her hand. "I can't tell you how many times I wished for just one more moment. One more chance to say 'I love you'."

It was then I saw two NLAs shuffling back and forth in the small enclosed patio. It was a man and a woman that were probably in their fifties when the virus caught them. As Rotters go they were pretty well preserved, but they both had sunken faces and the pervading stink of mummified roadkill.

"You can't keep Rot-NLAs in your home, Dingles," I said.

She looked at me and I looked at the weapon in her hand. "Just one more chance, Dave. But how do I explain it in a few fleeting moments, and then tell them thanks for giving me life and for raising me and for all the sacrifices and then tell them not to be afraid, that they'll be at peace, and then say goodbye and that I love them? How do I do it while they're freaking out?"

"Why did you call me, Sherry?" I asked her.

"I need you to do it for me."

"I don't know what you're talking about," I said, but I did and I was hoping she wouldn't go through with it if I forced her to say it aloud.

"There's only one way to do this." She opened the sliding glass door.

She led the female—her mother, I presumed—into the living room and then closed the sliding door again. "Okay," she said handing me the taser. "I removed the prong cartridge. Just apply direct contact right at her temple. Same spot as Amanda."

"Sherry, I didn't agree to this."

She faced the Rotter and held it by its wrists. "Do it now."

"Sherry!"

"Just do it!"

I did it.

As the electricity cackled at the Rotter's head, Dingles watched, waiting for a sign of recognition.

"Maybe it doesn't work all the time," I said and then the Rotter spoke.

"What are you doing home?" Dingle's mother said, her protruding eyes fixed on her. Without answering, Dingles grabbed her in a tight embrace.

"Oh, my! What's gotten into you?" the Rotter said. "Are you having a tough day, Sher?"

"I'm okay, Ma. It's my birthday, remember?"

"Is it?" her mother said as she hugged Dingles back.

"Thanks Ma," Sherry said, her voice cracking. "I love you."

"You're acting very strangely, honey."

"I'm so sorry."

Her mother's grasp loosened, weight dropping as her knees collapsed, sending her to the floor in a heap.

Dingles' mother lay unmoving on the carpet.

"I'm sorry, Ma," Dingles said through her tears. She opened the sliding door and went outside.

We did the same with her father, but when he snapped into awareness, she told him to close his eyes for a surprise. He did it with a grin of exposed and discolored teeth. Dingles hugged him and told him she loved him.

"Love you more than Oreos," he said, then went silent and dropped.

I helped her place their bodies at the curb and covered them with a blanket. I called the NLA service Department and offered to stay until they came to pick them up for disposal.

She looked at me, her eyes red with tears and she smiled through them.

"I'm good," she said, and meant it.

# THE ONE THING I CAN NEVER TELL JULIE

## LAURA BLACKWELL

One cool Tuesday evening in June, Julie and I walked into Three Little Knittens to find Marie-Grace arranging Filipino bakery cookies, ever so carefully, with a napkin-wrapped hand. Across the room, nerdy Bill hunched awkwardly over four knitting needles and a swath of red-orange wool. He gave us an unaccustomed grin. On the edge of the chair next to him, dividing wide-eyed attention between Bill's handiwork and Marie-Grace's cookie mosaic, perched a thin woman.

The new person looked so unassuming, so innocuous, my eyes slid away from her. She had a blank, unwrinkled face, and I think her hair was a dull brown. I remember that she wore an ill-fitting gray dress, with no coat or even a scarf to take the edge off the ocean breeze that chilled San Francisco's Outer Richmond District. Her hands lay slack in her lap.

Another knitting-circle regular, Svitlana, sailed in and shut the door with enough force to make its glass pane shudder. "It's cold," she said sternly. "Why you call this summer, I will never understand." She strode over to sit next to Bill's guest, who he introduced as "my girlfriend, Tracey."

Bill, whose hairline was retreating as if it feared his big glasses, with a romantic involvement? Julie and I would have something to talk about later. We talked about everything: our jobs, my dates, her fertility problems. We'd been best friends since college, and thought we would be forever.

A half-dozen more regulars had trickled in by the time Marie-Grace took her place on a tall stool. She selected a ball of gray wool and began knitting without a pattern.

Bill gave Tracey a ball of yellow acrylic yarn and asked what she'd like to knit, but she offered no opinion.

"Crochet is easier for a beginner," Svitlana asserted. "Tracey and I will make a scarf." She crocheted several inches of chain stitch, then handed hook and yarn to Tracey. "That will get you started."

Tracey held the hook like half a chopstick set and twiddled it in the yarn. Julie took the open seat next to Bill, and I sat on her other side. The lacy shawl Julie was making shimmered as it caught the light.

"Do you have a new chapter?" Julie asked. Bill had suckered her into reading his fantasy novel-in-progress; she was too sweet to say no.

"Not this week. I've been working on the appendices." He proudly brandished his needles, dangling a mess of wool. "Thanks to this knitting circle, I've made five ceremonial beards this month. It's giving me a lot of insight into dwarven society."

Bill called himself "an inveterate world-builder." When he and Julie discussed *The Five Fates of Caltibranzia,* I got very involved in my knitting.

Everybody in the circle was pleasant, but I wasn't there for them. I wasn't even there for knitting so much as because Julie asked me. I'd do anything for Julie. When she and Min-jae got married, I wore a floor-length lavender dress and carried smelly lilies.

"Tracey and I met at a writers' workshop," Bill told Julie. "Well, I was there for the workshop. She was browsing in the store."

"Do you like to read fantasy?" Julie asked, smiling the careful, encouraging smile you give a shy child.

"No," answered Tracey in a toneless voice. "I just like to see what people are making."

I thought Tracey was the most forgettable person I'd ever met, but I wasn't given the option of forgetting her. She showed up with Bill at Three Little Knittens the next week, and the week after that, with Svitlana's discarded J hook and the same ball of yellow yarn.

"You've made no progress at all," Svitlana fussed one evening. "What's wrong?"

"It's good when you do it, but I can't." Tracey's shoulders drooped.

"You'll get it," said Marie-Grace. "It just takes practice." She brought something gray from behind the register. "Tracey, since you're becoming a regular, I've made you a gift. If you like, I'll teach you how to make another two, so you'll have Three Little Knittens of your own."

Tracey accepted the toy with an expressionless "thank you," turning it over in her hands as if searching for loose yarn. There was none, of course; Marie-Grace had made dozens, and they were seamless as molded clay.

Usually there was more exclamation over the kittens, but Bill had conversational plans for Tracey and Julie. "Did the revised appendices help? I didn't want to overburden you, but the political tensions changed when I realized that Queen Mellith died of the poison and not the stab wounds, and now the gnomes' language uses glottal stops as possessives."

Knitting a coffee-cup sleeve was a thousand times more interesting than hearing about Bill's novel. I tuned him out.

Throughout the session, Svitlana tsked over Tracey's shoulder. Finally, she grabbed the hook and yarn from her and crocheted several stitches. "Like that, see?" She handed them back to Tracey with a joke. "I may have to give you lessons."

Tracey's face lit like a paper lantern. "Yes, please."

Bill and Tracey showed up at Three Little Knittens every Tuesday, him with a new ceremonial beard and her with the same project. Julie made admiring comments about the progress she was making, but Tracey always said, "Svitlana did that part."

Tracey was growing on people. She never volunteered anything about herself, but she listened to everyone else's ups and downs, and she gave compliments from time to time. And she dutifully worked her crochet hook in and out of the yarny rectangle, though she never had anything to show for it.

Still, Julie worried. "Tracey's so thin," Julie whispered as she brushed her shoe-soles on the welcome mat outside Three Little Knittens one evening. "Her body, her hair... even her skin looks thin. Do you think she eats enough?"

"I don't know." I glanced through the door-glass. "Don't you think her face looks fuller than it used to?"

Tracey was already in her usual place, yellow yarn in her lap and Bill at her side. Svitlana sat on Tracey's other side, knitting a red glove with green chevrons. It was September, and the circle was crafting for the holidays. Everybody but Julie, knitting a granny-square baby afghan for a co-worker, and Tracey, fruitlessly poking a crochet hook at the increasingly grubby yellow yarn.

"These cookies with the nuts are so good!" enthused Julie. "Let me bring you some, Tracey."

"I don't want sweets," said Tracey.

"You are a strange woman," said Svitlana with an indulgent shake of her blonde head. She watched Tracey struggle with her yarn for a second, then set down the glove. "Let me help you." As she took the mess from Tracey, the hook dropped out and clattered to the floor. Tracey dove for it like a cormorant for a fish, and pressed it into Svitlana's hand. Svitlana accepted it and made a few more stitches. "Like that. See? Do you need me to finish the row? Of course. Turn, and chain three..."

When Marie-Grace unplugged the water heater, Julie packed up her granny squares, stroking them wistfully. She was taking Clomid and some weird herbal supplements, desperate to have a baby with Min-Jae. As I marked my spot on the ornament I was making, a black bowling-pin shape that would someday be a penguin, Bill called us aside.

"Julie? Nicole? Can I talk to you?" He hovered tentatively by the door.

"Sure. What's up?"

"I'll be just outside," he called to Tracey, who was still tangling yarn around a crochet hook.

Once the three of us were on the sidewalk, I checked around for wandering junkies —the neighborhood's gone downhill in the past few years—while Julie studied the dark circles beneath Bill's eyes with concern. "Are you coming down with something?" she asked.

"Me? I'm fine. Well, maybe dividing my energies too much." He took a deep breath. "It's time to buckle down on the writing. I found a critique group that meets on Tuesdays, so…" He trailed off.

"We'll miss you," said Julie, "but I'm glad you'll be spending more time on your book."

Bill laughed. "Sometimes I think there's more of me in Caltibranzia than there is in my body. I've been living part of my life there since I was in middle school." Then his face got serious again, anxious eyes peering from the depths of his thick lenses. "Thing is, Tracey's still enjoying the circle. She's learning a lot from Svitlana, but I worry about her getting back to our apartment. Could you please look out for Tracey? Make sure she gets on her bus?"

My eyebrows shot up before I could stop them. "You live together?"

"She moved in months ago," he said as if he couldn't believe his luck. "Almost the day we met."

"That's great!" Julie said with a big smile. "Of course we'll keep an eye out for her."

I couldn't congratulate Bill on getting saddled with Tracey, but sometimes being quiet near Julie let me pass for being as nice as her.

Early the next afternoon, I was dragging through the balance sheet when my cell phone rang with the arpeggio ringtone I'd assigned to Julie. Normally she would just text during work hours.

"Nicole, I'm sorry, but…" She sounded stuffy, like she'd been crying. "I just found out and there may not be much time."

"What's wrong? Are you okay?" I started closing out the programs on my desktop.

"It's Svitlana. She collapsed late last night. Marie-Grace is at the hospital, and it doesn't sound good at all."

"Oh my God." I'd seen Svitlana almost every week for three years. She was a part of Three Little Knittens, solid as the fixtures and reliable as Marie-Grace.

"I'm leaving work now, so—"

"I'll meet you in the lobby of your building and get us an Uber car."

The driver was a handsome Asian-American with a radiant smile, but I didn't make chitchat. Julie's knitting needles were already clicking when I sat down, and they didn't stop until we pulled up to the tall, boxy beigeness of UCSF Moffitt Hospital.

Svitlana was in the ICU, so only two people could see her at once. Her parents were in with her when we got there. Her barrel-chested husband was pacing the waiting room, while relatives and half the knitting circle squirmed in the hard seats.

Julie went straight to him. "Vitaliy, we just heard. How is she?"

"They're calling it multi-organ failure." Vitaliy enunciated the phrase with distaste. "But why would her organs fail? Svitlana is never sick."

"She did seem subdued lately," said Julie, casting her eyes downward. She twisted her fingers together, probably missing the comfort of yarn and needles. "I didn't think anything of it."

"Well, she was losing weight," said Vitaliy. "She was pleased. But I could see she was tired. I told her not to be silly."

I hadn't noticed the weight loss—Svitlana kept her coat on—but she had seemed run-down. I should have known something was up.

Vitaliy and one of Svitlana's sisters were in the room when an electronic alarm sounded. Nurses came charging through, and I heard Vitaliy shouting. Then there was silence.

Tears ran down Julie's face, but her fingers kept moving. When I handed her a tissue, she dropped her knitting, flung her arms around me, and sobbed on my shoulder. My eyes stung.

Across the room, Marie-Grace was crying, too. So were Svitlana's relatives, pulled together in a knot of shared misery.

Sitting upright in a plastic chair, head back and eyes closed, Tracey pulled the yellow yarn to unravel the last few stitches of the crocheted rectangle.

Marie-Grace spent a minute talking with the relatives in a low voice, telling them how highly we thought of Svitlana, how sorry we were. Everyone was gracious, but it was obvious we couldn't stay.

Outside, the wind whipped at our hair and teased a piece of yarn from Julie's usually tidy knitting bag.

"We should get a drink," Marie-Grace said suddenly. "Svitlana liked a drink."

The closest bar had the dark wood paneling of a former English pub and the maybe-tiki-maybe-Mexican decorations that helped sell umbrella drinks. The bartender chivalrously checked the birthdates on our IDs—except Tracey's. She didn't have one on her.

"Don't you carry a driver's license?" asked Julie. "Or a state ID?"

"I don't have anything like that." Tracey's voice had an unaccustomed lilt that sounded mocking.

"We'll see you next week, Tracey," said Marie-Grace firmly. "We're going to toast Svitlana's memory."

Tracey turned and walked away with a spring in her step. After shifting from foot to foot, Bill mumbled an apology and lurched after her. I gave them the side-eye, but everybody else seemed too numb to notice.

"Tracey and Bill," mused Marie-Grace. "Good for her. Bill's a nice man. Steady. Blondes do get their pick, don't they?"

"Tracey's not blonde," I said, startled.

"It looks like she started getting it highlighted recently," said Marie-Grace. "A good job, too—very natural-looking."

I opened my mouth to protest that there was no way that Tracey, who didn't even get professional haircuts, was springing for highlights. But I realized I'd rather not talk about her.

The next Tuesday, Julie told me over tamales at Tommy's that she and Min-Jae were expecting a baby in May. We toasted with margaritas—hers a lime slushy, mine the real deal—and we talked about nothing else until we walked into Three Little Knittens. Then we tabled the subject. Julie hadn't told her boss yet, so she wasn't going to tell anyone but me.

My happiness soured when Tracey bounced, bright-eyed, through the door. Marie-Grace was right; her hair was dishwater-blonde. Her clothes draped better, like on a person instead of a hanger. That night, though, she didn't have her tangle of yellow yarn.

Julie sat on my right side, practically glowing. For Julie, I would make an effort. I nodded to the chair on my left. "Want to help me sew this penguin together?"

Tracey took the seat eagerly. "Can you show me?"

I had forgotten my tapestry needles, but I kept a sharp needle in the mending kit in my purse. I showed her how to stitch the wings to the body. "I'll knit him a scarf while you do that," I told her.

Ten minutes later, the scarf was done and Tracey had only prodded the penguin.

"I'll take that." Irritated, I grabbed the penguin too roughly, and the needle pushed deep into Tracey's thumb. "God, I'm so sorry." Horrified, I dropped the penguin into Tracey's lap and fished a clean tissue out of my purse.

"I'm fine," said Tracey, pulling the needle out. I pressed the tissue against the wound. Tracey didn't resist.

"Are you bleeding?" asked Marie-Grace, unfazed. "I can get a Band-Aid and some disinfectant."

The tissue came away sodden but unstained. Clear, thick liquid welled out of the puncture. Not serum. Not blood.

Tracey's eyes met mine, and it was like facing down an animal. Worse. There was something like camouflage to those eyes. There was no color to put on a driver's license.

The penguin and the needle fell to the floor as Tracey stood up. She walked out without a word, leaving the door ajar.

I told Julie about it at the bus stop.

"Poor Tracey. She really is different," said Julie. "It's a good thing she has Bill. She must have been lonely."

Being an introvert, I have a clear understanding of shy versus quiet and lonely versus alone. I never thought Tracey looked lonely so much as needy. Now, just thinking about her made me tired.

That Sunday afternoon, the arpeggio ringtone trilled as I was steeping a mug of lemon tea and settling in to binge-watch *Orange is the New Black*. "Did you see that email from Bill?" Julie asked. "I'm not sure what to make of it."

I checked my email. "Hang on a sec."

*I'm writing to you because you two were so welcoming to Tracey and me. I asked her about the knitting circle, and it came out that she doesn't want to go anymore. I think losing Svitlana affected her more than we knew. I said I was sure you'd take her under your wing(s), but Tracey says it's okay.*

*We're doing great. This came up because I'm trying to get Tracey to join my writing group. She doesn't write, but she's a very encouraging critiquer.*

*The shop doesn't have email listed on its site (maybe someone should mention that to Marie-Grace), so if you could let people know, I'd really appreciate it.*

*Bill*

"I don't think Bill is one for subterfuge," I said. "I'm guessing Tracey didn't complain about me sticking her with the needle."

"That was what I thought, too. If she didn't mention it, she must be fine. Maybe it wasn't as bad a jab as you thought?"

"Maybe." I suspected that Tracey's reasons had less to do with pain or personal epiphany than with fear of exposure. Whatever she was, she was not a normal human being.

But seeing neither Tracey nor Bill at Three Little Knittens, I stopped thinking about them. By mid-November, I had nearly forgotten what Tracey looked like, and I wouldn't have tried to remember if Marie-Grace hadn't given us the news.

It was a turbulent time of year for a knitting circle, with many regulars out for travel and parties, and newbies coming in for help on projects they shouldn't have attempted. Marie-Grace sat down empty-handed and said, "I'm sorry to be the bearer of bad news. Some of you will remember Bill, who used to attend this circle. Bill has passed away."

I heard one voice squeak "What?" and another demand "How?" I knitted relentlessly without looking down. Julie's trick: keeping my hands busy made me feel more in control.

"It's not clear what happened," Marie-Grace said. "He missed two days of work before a coworker went to his apartment. The neighbors hadn't seen him, and there was… a smell, so they called the police."

"Is Tracey all right?" Julie asked.

"The police haven't been able to locate Tracey. Bill's sister told the police that he and Tracey came here. Does anyone know how to find her?"

Marie-Grace's gaze traveled the circle, but met with only blank faces and regret. Nobody knew Tracey from anywhere else. No one even knew her last name.

As the store cleared that night, Marie-Grace asked Julie to stay a moment. "It wasn't just the police who came by," said Marie-Grace. "Bill's sister asked me for the Caltibranzia files. She said they were gone from his computer. She tried a recovery program, but it couldn't even locate the files. Do you have any of them, by any chance?"

Julie looked stricken. "They disappeared from my Dropbox last week. I thought Bill's writing group had inspired him to make revisions."

Marie-Grace furrowed her brow. "I can't picture Bill deleting his book."

"I can't, either," said Julie softly. "It was his life's work."

At the bus stop, Julie said, "I hope Tracey is okay."

"The whole thing is suspicious as hell." I was surprised that Julie had any doubts. "Think about Svitlana, too."

"I am. Poor Tracey, losing the two people she's closest to. You don't think she had anything to do with it, do you?" Julie's eyes filled with tears. "I couldn't live with knowing I sat next to a killer every Tuesday for months."

"Of course not," I lied. Whatever Tracey was, whatever she did to Svitlana and Bill, she was gone. I wasn't going to upset Julie's delicate pregnancy. She could believe what she needed to believe.

A week later, I hopped onto the 38 after work, lucked into a seat, and pulled out my knitting needles. I had started a blanket for Julie and Min-Jae's baby. They didn't want to find out the sex, so I was using variegated pastel yarn. I could finish the layette set in pink or blue when the baby was born.

The bus wasn't that full. When I felt somebody standing too close, I glanced to the side, and my heart sank.

"Who's that for?" Tracey asked.

"Julie," I snapped without thinking. Then I looked up and realized what I'd done.

The gaze that held mine wasn't human, but it wasn't unintelligent. Tracey had been to enough knitting circles to know that a pink-and-blue square was going to be a baby blanket.

I could swear Tracey's hairline was further back than it used to be. She grinned wolfishly, and her fingers twitched.

Not a wolf. A parasite.

I felt a rush of cold stiffen my hands. Could there be such a thing as a parasite that ate creativity? One that could draw nourishment from an ever-changing fantasy world or a never-completed scarf? That kind of animal wouldn't be interested in finished works, like expertly-knitted amigurumi. And maybe the host would die when it was done.

In my mind's eye, I saw Tracey's trancelike expression as she unraveled the last of the yellow yarn, as she unraveled Svitlana's life. Did she nibble Bill's epic word by word, or did she gulp it down file by file? Did he feel himself dying? Did he beg her for help as his body shut down?

She looked too pleased that Julie was gestating a hard-won fetus.

I could give Tracey CalTrain fare to Mountain View and tell her to go entrench herself at some startup, but even if she left, would she stay away? I couldn't chance it.

I chose my words with care. Lies were inventions; Tracey might be able to spot them. "I'm turning over a project in my head. Would you meet me later to go over it?"

"What kind of project?"

"I want it to be a surprise."

The sky was dark and starless when I arrived at the ocean-side trail. It was high in the cliffs, and the air knifed cold through my work clothes. I walked fast, knowing the park had closed at sunset.

Tracey was already at the lookout point, shapeless as a rock outcropping.

"Come this way to see," I told her, walking to the guardrail. I could hear a dog barking on Ocean Beach, and the wind stirring the eucalyptus trees all around. A bonfire blazed by the water, some distance away.

Tracey stepped up to the white-painted rail. "Where is it?"

I didn't answer. I just drove the knitting needle into her chest.

If creative energy was her food, perhaps a creative tool could be her destruction.

Her face didn't change, and she didn't fight. Even when Tracey's chest was riddled with holes, the thick liquid on the knitting needle remained clear. Not serum. Not blood.

When Tracey's breath grew unsteady, I pushed her over the railing. I heard her crash against the rocks as she fell. It was too dark to see all the way down, and I didn't stay.

Ocean Beach is notorious for its riptides. I checked the news for weeks, but I never saw an article about a Jane Doe found on the rocks or in the water.

I don't know what I've become. If a tapeworm took on human form, would it be a murderer, or just a parasite? And if a person killed a parasite that looked human, would she be a murderer, or just an exterminator?

Julie can tell there's something wrong, a distance in the awkward conversational lulls and the increasing lag between messages. But she's busy, too, her time and attention directed toward the perfect little boy she gave birth to last month. He has Min-jae's features and Julie's smile.

She probably thinks parenthood has driven a wedge into our friendship. Although it twists my gut to see the hurt in Julie's eyes, I hope she always thinks that.

# L.A. WHEN IT BLEEDS

## SARAH CANNAVO

Claire Haining stood stricken in the empty room, trembling as reality and uncertainty ran together and blurred. Then a horrified, heartrending scream clawed its way up her throat and burst free, bleeding into sobs as she fell to her knees. Ribbons of her red hair clung to her tear-streaked cheeks and her back bowed as she held her head in her hands, as though the weight of the fracturing mind within was too much to bear.

And the director called "Cut!" and stood, his chair groaning in relief at the release from his bulk, the deserted living room became a bustling set, and Claire Haining climbed to her feet and, beaming, brushing her hair back from her face, turned back into Kayla Cassidy, the up-and-coming star making her big-screen debut in the psychological thriller *Edge of Reason*, director Scooter Fleming's self-proclaimed passion project.

But passion never promised smooth sailing, in this case especially. From the start of shooting, the production had been plagued by malfunctions of equipment that had moments before worked perfectly, the mysterious destruction of footage, and damage to sets that was just as unexplained. Rumors flew early and often that the whole thing would be scrapped to save the studio more hassle. Whenever questioned, though, Fleming just mopped the brow beneath his baseball cap and proclaimed the problems "small fires," easily extinguished. In the middle of some rewrites, though, the screenwriter, Paul Mann, had driven off the studio lot late one night and crashed his car on Sunset Boulevard, his death a harder fire to contain.

Which was why local writer Mickey Grant was now on-set, watching Fleming alternately bellow orders at the scurrying crew and heap praise on Kayla Cassidy— which her acting definitely deserved, Mickey thought, even if Fleming was directing his words more at her admirable rack. The talent Mickey had seen in raw footage of her was a large part of the reason he'd agreed to finish the rewrites for *Edge of Reason* when normally he avoided Hollywood's inner workings in the same way he avoided his more bitter exes.

Well, that and the fact that his agent was starting to sniff around for another novel, and he hoped doing *something* would pacify Annabeth for a bit. The former sounded nobler than the latter, though.

"Whaddya think, Kali?" the incubus asked, dropping his crumpled copy of the script into his lap. "The movie biz as glamorous from the inside as it looks on the outside?"

Beside him, his short, tan best friend Kallista Winters snorted and tossed her long, dark brown hair back. "If I wanted glamour, I wouldn't be hanging out with *you.*"

"Cold, woman." Mickey crossed his long legs, dark jeans rustling. "I'll have you know I can be quite classy when I have to."

"Giving your girlfriend the first snort of the coke isn't class, Mickey."

"Says you."

Kali rolled her light brown eyes, but fondly. Supernatural sex demon or not, laid-back Mickey had a genuinely good heart, despite the snark he'd spun into an art form and the jagged realities he captured in his writing. He looked like a man in his late forties, white-skinned, tall body still muscled and lean, with thick dark brown hair typically rumpled—overall he had a rumpled look to him; as Frank, Dean, and Bing might have put it, he looked like an unmade bed—albeit a bed he'd just rushed from because somebody's boyfriend or husband had come home early. Like other incubi, he subsisted on sexual energy; unlike many others, he never coerced the countless women he drew in with his mental abilities, nor drained them to death, or even to a noticeable point, and they typically walked away as pleased as he.

Now he spotted Fleming heading towards him, short ponytail bouncing and a bit of something caught in his short basement-dweller beard. "Oh, shit," Mickey muttered, forcing a smile and bracing himself for the inevitable shoulder-slap, which nearly knocked him from the chair when it came.

"It's great, isn't it, Mick?" Fleming said, surveying the set like a king.

"Oh, it's awesome, Scoot," Mickey said, and Kali choked a laugh off behind her hand. "But, um, does the therapist really have to turn out to be one of Claire's hallucinations? It just feels so clichéd at this point, you know?"

"Oh, no, no, no, that's got to stay." The director looked like Mickey had just suggested lopping his dick off for the fun of it. "It's a vital part of Claire's journey. I love what you've done to the script so far, Mickey, but this has to stay how it is."

Mickey smiled pleasantly. "What exactly did you hire me for, then, if I can't make changes the script needs? Because if it was just to jack me off, I know a few hookers who could do a much better job than this."

Fleming's face flushed crimson. A cold sheen dropped down in his eyes, and Mickey glimpsed the hardness that lurked beneath his outer amiability, famous for flaring when he was crossed even slightly. Mickey stared back, uncowed. "It stays," he spat, and swept away.

Mickey shook his head. "There's something seriously fucked about a grown man who calls himself Scooter."

"Agreed." Kali hopped up. "Wanna pillage craft services?"

"Hell yes."

Mickey's mouth was stuffed with shrimp when behind him he heard the voice, haunting in heartbreak and happiness. "So you're the guy putting words in my mouth."

Mickey quickly swallowed and turned, managing not to choke. "That's me." He tossed Kayla Cassidy an easy smile. "And that's probably the least offensive thing I've ever been accused of."

Kayla laughed. Beside them, Kali knew where this was headed, and as the pair flirted, she surveyed the set herself, half-hearing as Kayla informed Mickey she wasn't needed for the next few scenes. Then she pressed her body to his, all heat and eagerness, and invited him back to her trailer.

Mickey tapped Kali's shoulder, his other arm around Kayla's lush waist. "Hey, Short Stack. You gonna be pissed if I ditch you for a bit?"

A few feet away, a blonde woman—studio security, by the uniform, evidently on break—stood, and when her eye caught Kali's she smiled invitingly. Kali waved Mickey off and smoothed out her strappy black top. "Go. Mama'll be just fine right here."

"Yeah, I'll bet."

A simple printed sign taped to Kayla's trailer door bore her name, belying the space inside, which was better than most places Mickey had lived in; the studio was betting hard on their new star. "Make yourself comfortable, Mickey," Kayla said, disappearing into some dim part of the interior, and Mickey lounged on the low blue sofa. When she spoke again, her voice was slightly muffled. "You like Led Zeppelin?"

"Lady, you're ensorcelling me," Mickey called back as *Houses of the Holy* spilled from hidden speakers. He heard Kayla pad back in, glanced up, and found her winding a lock of fiery hair around her finger, bare but for a catlike smile.

"Yep," he said. "Definitely ensorcelled."

She straddled his lap and he leaned up and kissed her; as their mouths moved his hands met her warm, smooth skin and he felt her need like a heartbeat, pulsing as rapidly and deeply as his own. "Shit, maybe Hollywood isn't so bad after all," he said, freeing his mouth a moment.

Her hand found his zipper. "It has its moments," she agreed, and together they tumbled under.

He was inside her and she was riding him when the pounding started on the door, shouts erupting in tandem. "Oh, Jesus *Christ*." Mickey dropped his head back in disbelief.

Kayla paused. "Wait, isn't that your friend?"

It was, and there was urgency in Kali's throaty voice as she shouted. "Mickey, get some goddamn pants on and get the *hell* out here! *Now!*"

Mickey exhaled, irritated. "Something better be on fire."

. . .

The flames snapped and snarled, roving over the row of buildings standing in for a city street on set, leapt through windows and licked the dark brickwork; tongues of orange and blood-red reared towards the pure blue sky as if raging against another perfect L.A. day, and as sheets of fire billowed and roared black smoke spilled oil-like through the searing air.

Cast and crew clustered a safe distance back as sirens screamed ever-nearer; Scooter stood spitting jagged fragments of disbelief studded sharply with profanity close to Gillian Anderson and Dennis Quaid, Claire's parents in the film, both looking like they'd rather be in the burning building than listening any longer. Kali, Mickey, and Kayla skidded to a stop in the crowd, Mickey still hopping into his shoes and Kayla belting her silky robe tight.

"Nobody's *in* there, right?" Kayla asked, wide-eyed, and Kali shook her head.

"How'd it start?" Mickey said as around them people jostled for the best cell-phone shot, pointing, gaping, exclaiming.

Kali shrugged wildly. "Nobody knows. They were setting up for a street shot and Clive Standen smelled smoke, somebody screamed, and all of a sudden there was just this *fire... Look* at this shit!" she said as another window burst, scattering smoke and glass.

What struck Mickey was a sense of the surreality embedded in studio sets like these, worlds within their world, the disconcerting drift of displacement—how, though just outside the studio gates were streets lined with palm trees and a brief drive brought you to the Pacific Ocean, you stood at the same time on a street in New York City, watching it burn.

He glanced down to comment on this to Kali, but his gaze caught instead on the cell phone footage she was capturing. Across the screen a shadow whipped, writhing dark in the furnace-heart of the flames—a vaguely human form, but elongated, featureless, slipping away quick as a snake.

"Wait, wait, what was that?" Mickey's hand shot to Kali's shoulder; he looked at the real fire, but if anything had been there, it was gone, and a cold bolt pierced Mickey's chest.

"What was what?" Kali hadn't seen anything, and when Mickey made her play the video back, pause it, the dark shape in the flames was blurrier, less formed, more possibly smoke. But Mickey couldn't shake the sense that something had been there, and Kali's brow creased when she looked up at him.

"I don't like that look," she said. "Time to panic?"

"Not sure yet," Mickey said, senses shifting. Meanwhile, the crowd was being corralled even farther away, Scooter snagging crew members and giving new orders. Mickey shrugged as he and Kali bled back into the pulsing flow of work resuming, pulled a cigarette from the pack in his pocket, lit it, and brought it to his lips. "Anyway," he said, "the show must go on," and his words turned to smoke in the air.

*Accidental* was the official consensus. Stray sparks and faulty wiring had started the fire, though even the marshal wasn't any more specific than that. The pall that had hung over the production from the start descended further; cast and crew muttered about bad luck, and tabloids and bloggers screamed it over footage of the burning set.

But the all-clear had come, so cameras rolled again, and a week later Jessie Watkins, Kayla's stunt double, smiled and waved from the sixth-story window she was about to plummet from as her harness was buckled, checked and rechecked and Fleming rearranged the cameraman's positions with the precision of a surgeon and vicious intensity of an interior decorator. The scene was a nightmare sequence in which Claire dreamt her husband Brett, played by Clive Standen, pushed her from their bedroom window, and another camera had been rigged up on a high wire to catch the descent while Jessie herself wore a body cam so the audience would experience Claire's terrifying fall for themselves—"be pulled right down with her," as Fleming put it, grinning with dark glee.

Mickey's own easy grin was for Kayla as she passed by with Margot Robbie, who played Claire's hallucinatory therapist Dr. Emilia Getz. "You're still hitting that?" Kali asked as Kayla waved and winked back, red hair rolling like a wave over her shoulders. "Lucky bastard."

"What about you and Officer Hot Stuff?" Mickey asked, remembering sensing Kali's desire for the blonde security guard, and that it definitely hadn't been one-sided.

Kali attempted to smooth her hair out. "Pam? Dude, where do you think I was for the past half hour?"

Mickey held out his fist and she bumped it, both grinning in satisfaction. Each of their love lives was a winding, tangled thing full of stops, starts, knots that topped nooses and those that marked lasting bonds, and through the ups and downs of their respective searches each was the other's constant, there to support or smack sense into them as needed.

*"Quiet on the set!"*

Fleming's bellow cleaved the air and all bustle died quickly away, the gazes of those gathered rising to the mock-brownstone where Jessie stood on her mark at the window, waiting for her cue. The hush held a sense of expectancy—that surrealism again, like a spell being laid—and excitement, and even Mickey felt it; strip away the power trips and back-room bullshit, and it turned out there was still magic left in moviemaking after all.

The edict "No flash photography" was cried to the crowd—*Under pain of death,* Mickey figured; no doubt anyone Fleming caught leaking footage would never be seen again, either on set or by friends and family—and once he was satisfied his orders were being followed, Fleming resumed his canvas-backed throne and called *"Action!"*

Jessie was supposed to go headfirst through the trick glass of the window and fall several stories before the harness pulled her up short—the moment when, in the movie, Claire would wake from the nightmare—and the stunt's first moments were flawless. Glass exploded in a jagged froth as Jessie burst through, she and the shards seeming to hang suspended midair for a single stretched second before she dropped, hair streaming wildly behind her like a streak of blood on a wound.

But halfway down the safety line jerked as if, impossibly, someone had yanked it back, and as she tumbled, she tangled in it and swung back, whipping with sickening speed into the front of the building. A crack echoed as she collided with the dark stone, cutting off her scream, and in the silence that followed she hung limp in the harness, unnaturally still. Her head tipped at a crooked angle on her neck, blood dripped from the corner of her mouth, and her body bobbed like a pendulum, like a puppet someone had forgotten to put away, eyes staring sightlessly at the sky.

It all unfurled in less than a minute, like film fed too fast into a whirring projector, and for a moment no one moved, no one breathed, no one seemed to believe, a dark-mirror inversion of the anticipation that had suffused the set before the leap.

And then somebody screamed and the silence shattered, panic erupting in its place. Set medics swarmed, but they could have taken their sweet time and it wouldn't have made a speck of difference to Jessie. As the dead woman dangled before them Kali gripped Mickey's arm, rigid with shock, her white-tipped nails carving crescent furrows into his flesh, and repeated "Oh my God—oh my fucking *God,* Mickey!" her pitch rising and voice cracking with the snap and scratch of a skipping record.

Mickey barely felt the sting, numb with the same disbelief and wondering if Kali's cries were solely for the stunt gone wrong, or if she'd seen the same thing he had: a black, bone-thin figure framed in the broken window's maw, elongated fingers slithering from the safety line before it bled away in the blink of an eye back into the shadows of the set.


Production shut down, but two days after Jessie's death cast and crew gathered on-set for an informal memorial, wearing black armbands and laying flowers and flickering candles around a framed photo of the stuntwoman smiling and kneeling next to a black dog—her dog Licorice, according to another stuntman. Jessie had been twenty-seven years old.

Press lurked nearby, snapping what photos they could and dropping cluster bombs of questions about the apparent accident and the movie's future, hoping to hit someone who'd answer. When Fleming arrived, they swarmed, slavering for news; he shouldered through and shouted for someone to "get those vultures out of here!" looking every inch the indignant mourner, even having deigned to don a black cap for the occasion.

But with the cameras gone, as people spoke and sobbed, Fleming looked more irritated than grieved. Kali nudged Mickey at one point, gestured with a jerk of her head and a wide-eyed WTF look, and Mickey looked over, saw Fleming wringing his cap in white-knuckled hands—Mickey could almost hear the man's bones grinding like teeth beneath his skin, smell the smoke from his simmering impatience, and behind his dark sunglasses Mickey grimaced in disgust.

Nor were Mickey and Kali the only ones to notice. Beside Mickey Kayla fumed, and Pam, arms crossed, kept an acid glare on Fleming. Gestures and murmurs made the round among the crowd, but if Fleming noticed, he didn't seem to care.

After the speeches had been made, the memorial broke up into smaller groups and conversations—some tearful, some lighter with laughter, most a mix of the two—and several flasks were pulled out and passed around. Mickey lit a cigarette and watched Fleming and a suited studio spook talk nearby, Fleming's expression and gestures growing colder and more tense by the minute.

"What, were we not mourning fast enough for him?" Pam asked, curling her arm around Kali's waist.

"Are you kidding? He's pissed," Kayla said. "Jessie's death wasn't in his script, and it's screwing with his plans for his masterpiece. Yesterday I overheard him arguing with somebody on the phone about how much filming time he's losing with the set shut down—I'd bet my contract that's what he and Mr. Pinstripe are discussing right now."

"All right, now that's fucked," Kali said. "A woman just *died*, for God's sake."

Mickey tipped ash from his cigarette's glowing tip. "There's dedication to your craft and there's douchebaggery, and he's just pissed on that line. You want to put blood, sweat, and tears into your work, fine, but they should be your own."

In an ideal world, anyway, but this insular land of light and shadow wasn't one; it was Fleming's, shot for shot, and he wouldn't give up his hold no matter the offscreen horrors his determination wrought or how high they piled up—after all, Pharaoh didn't halt construction on his pyramids when a few slaves fell under the stone they hewed. Each movie Fleming made was his baby, his beast, and he would keep feeding this one until they were both satisfied, never mind what it was they were glutting on.

But what was he really feeding?

Kali's eyes met Mickey's and she knew he was thinking of the shadow. She hadn't stopped thinking of it either; it mingled in her mind with the waking nightmare of watching Jessie die. First in the fire, then at the stunt... Jessie's body cam hadn't caught anything; the other footage was reportedly distorted, a black mass whipping through the background but at the wrong angle to be the shadow of a fleeing saboteur —besides which, anyone up there would have been seen.

*Anyone human, anyway,* thought Kali, who'd often gotten too close for comfort to the supernatural since meeting Mickey and knew well now that coincidences like the shadow appearing first at the fire, then the stunt, were usually anything but.

Even if that were true here, too, though, it couldn't be proved; anyone attempting it would sound like Claire Haining, confusing reality with the insidious instability simmering in her skull. So as soon as he could Fleming would start shooting again, unaware of what he might be inviting.

Of course, Kali reflected, watching Fleming and the studio rep shake hands, Fleming beaming now with the friendly grin the Devil might wear having clinched a soul he'd been craving, even if he *did* know, it probably wouldn't stop him.


"I *know* how it sounds, Brett," Kayla said, eyes shining wetly under the set lights, voice shivering like a loose plank in a rope bridge. "But I thought you of all people..." She broke off, biting her scarlet-glossed lip, and looked away, everything about her radiating the rawness of an exposed nerve.

"Claire…" Clive Standen drew Kayla close and held her, but as he continued his lines the cameraman signaled to Fleming, shaking his head.

"*Cut!*" Fleming called.

Clive and Kayla broke apart, looking drained; it was far from the day's first take. Fleming stood, slapping his cap down on his chair. "What now?" he demanded, leaning down to look at the monitor.

"There's something wrong with the picture," the cameraman said, replaying the last minute of footage; the picture abruptly pixelated, corrupting the actors' faces into cracked, grotesque masks, and when it cleared a smear of black stretched and wavered in the background—one of the actors' shadows, Fleming thought, brow furrowing, and then the picture cleared completely, the camera functioning fine once again.

"We have to reshoot." The words were wrenched from Fleming like rotted teeth. "All right, everybody, we're going again! Stu, check the lights; I think there's something wrong with the angle near Kayla."

Stu, one of the lighting crew, nodded and mounted the scaffolding of the soundstage, where they were shooting a scene in Claire and Brett's chic living room. As Stu moved along adjusting the overhead lights Mickey jogged up to Fleming, clutching the notes he'd scribbled in his script, and kept up as Fleming strode across the soundstage.

"Got a sec, Cecil B. DeMille?" he asked, holding up the script.

Fleming pinched the bridge of his nose, eyes squeezed shut. "What now, Grant?"

Mickey flipped through the script to his notes. "Here, the scene in the department store—I think you can cut the hallucination. By this point it's repetitive, and it doesn't really add anything. If we have Claire talk to somebody, we can still convey how afraid, how fragile, she is, while adding to her character. I wrote a few lines, here…"

Fleming scanned Mickey's scrawl and nodded slowly. "All right. I'll have new pages made up and we can try this out." He looked at Mickey. "You know, you're good when you're not being an asshole."

"Bet that hurt to say." Mickey noticed Stu on the scaffolding, talking on his headset as he worked the lights. "What's going on?"

Fleming's face clouded. "There was a problem with the shot. Too much shadow in the background. We have to reset and go again."

Mickey froze. Fleming's muttered tirade about more lost time went unheard, and the stirrings of sexual hunger Mickey had been hoping to satisfy with a quick trip with Kayla to her trailer died away, darker senses popping up in their place. "Shadow?"

"How's that look, Pat?" Stu said into his headset, looking down into the faux living room below.

Pat Evanger, another crew member, studied the scene. "Looks good, Stu," her voice crackled back, but then she glanced up and frowned. "Stu? Who's up there with you?"

"What?" Stu looked around, confused. "Nobody. Why?"

The shadow peeled itself out of the mass of them in the scaffolding, rising snake-like behind Stu, looming for a moment before it latched on. Stu struggled and twisted, catching the eye of people below and setting off a barrage of horrified exclamations.

"Who the hell is that?"

"Oh my God, *Stu!*"

"Somebody go *up* there!"

The sound of their chorus caught Mickey's attention; one look and he bolted, leaving Fleming behind. No doubt few felt or saw him as he wove through the crowd; incubi were faster and stronger than humans by far. But even so, Mickey—and the humans who'd climbed the scaffolding in an attempt to help—arrived too late as Stu flipped over the railing and plummeted, smashing right into the Hainings' stylish glass coffee table. His punctured body lay twitching fishlike among the shards for several moments and then stilled, blood pooling scarlet from a thousand wounds.

And though there was nowhere to go, every way off the scaffolding blocked by people who'd come up to grab the assailant, they'd somehow managed to vanish.

"Poor Stu," Kali said when Mickey called and told her what happened. Currently behind the counter of the Leather & Lace, the adult store where she worked, Kali knew her boss, Heather, would flay her alive if she caught her taking a personal call on shift —even though the aisles of vibrators and edible panties were currently empty of customers—but had figured Mickey wasn't calling from the set to shoot the breeze and risked answering. "Why does this shit always happen around you, Mickey?"

"No idea. You know I'm a lover, not a fighter. But it's pretty clear somebody doesn't want this movie made."

"And they're using, what, black magic to stop it?" Kali leaned on the counter. "Dude seems pretty damn desperate."

"And we both know what a turn-off that is," Mickey said. "But it could explain the escalation in bad luck, at least, from equipment failure and lost footage to—" He paused. "Fuck me."

"I'll assume that's meant metaphorically," Kali said dryly. "What're you thinking?"

"Paul Mann, the original screenwriter. Maybe his accident wasn't one—maybe he was the first human victim of the curse." Mickey's mind raced, remembering the shadow's propensity to appear on-camera. "If there's any security footage from the night he died, it might show us something."

"Great, Master Detective." Kali drummed her manicured nails on the counter. "You know somebody with access to that footage?"

"No." Mickey grinned. "But you do."

Pam and Kali met Mickey that night at a café a few blocks from the studio. A laptop glowed faintly on the table as he took the seat across from them. "I'm still not sure why you want to see this," Pam said, cueing up the footage she'd managed to discreetly copy at the end of her shift. "The cops looked it over and couldn't find anything. They said Paul just had an accident."

"Just like Jessie and Stu," Mickey said, grinning grimly.

At first the black-and-white footage, of the main studio gate, capturing all comings and goings, showed nothing unusual—even, it seemed, when Paul Mann's silver BMW, rendered a grainy gray on-film, pulled up and paused while the night guard raised the gate arm. Paul waved, thanks or goodnight, and exited to his grisly off-screen demise.

"Wait, baby, go back." Kali touched Pam's hand, starting the same moment Mickey did. "A couple seconds—there."

Played at normal speed, it didn't look like much, just a flicker of darkness, there and gone. But played frame by frame it took shape, though it lingered only a moment, easy enough to miss. Mickey paused the footage and the trip stared at the screen; Kali clapped her hand to her mouth and Pam murmured, "What the *hell...?*"

Crouched low in Paul Mann's backseat was the shadow.

"Well, that settles that," Kali said.

Pam pointed. "What *is* that?"

"A somewhat-physical manifestation of black magic, most likely a curse someone's working against the movie, though we don't know who or why," Mickey said.

"Black ma..." Pam's mouth worked for a moment, bow lips loosing only a shaft of silence. "You're shitting me." She studied the friends' faces. "Oh my God, you're not."

Kali patted her shoulder. "Trust me, babe, you never really get used to it."

Mickey decided, at the look on Pam's face, to hold off on disclosing his own super-nature for the moment. As she stared at the steam coming off her coffee, as if waiting for it to take shape and attack her, he pulled a flask from his faded jeans pocket and shook it. "Need something stronger?"

Pam grabbed it gratefully, took several impressive gulps, and passed it back. "So... what? You two investigate this kind of stuff?"

Mickey shrugged. "We don't go chasing it, if that's what you mean. It just seems to fall into our laps—like a drunk stripper, but not nearly as fun."

"Ignore him." Kali looked at Mickey. "You know what this means, don't you?"

"Neither Scooter-boy nor the studio will be willing to scrap the movie because a writer and a sex-shop clerk tell them someone's laid a hex on their asses, so the attacks on the filming will continue and, no doubt, keep escalating, so more innocent people are gonna wind up hurt and/or dead?"

"Well, yeah, that, but it also means your alcoholic whore-ass only got this job because black magic killed the guy who had it first."

Mickey considered this. "Well. Tits."

"I want to laugh," Kali said, "but I know I shouldn't."

"Thanks for the sensitivity," Mickey said, sarcastically toasting her with his flask. "My bruised ego appreciates it."

"Um, could I have another sip of that?" Pam asked faintly.

. . .

"Look, guys, I know this shoot hasn't exactly been smooth sailing," Fleming said a day later, and Mickey waited for any diabetics on-set to go into insulin shock at that sugar-coating. "And all that's happened is terrible—tragic." His voice gave a pitch-perfect quaver, then strengthened. "But I don't buy the bullshit some people are trying to sell, that this production is jinxed, or doomed, or whatever else they're saying. You make your own luck, and we're making this damn movie. Who's with me?"

On cue he paused for applause. Nobody obliged but his assistant, a replacement for his previous, long-time one, who'd quit unexpectedly just before production started. Her flurried claps quickly petered out when no one else in the small crowd joined in. Mickey sensed the momentary writhings of Fleming's irritation, and the director finished, "But if any of you want to leave the production, I understand."

Some had evidently taken Fleming's offer up before he made it; looking around, Mickey found quite a few faces missing, but knew they'd be replaced in no time, new grips and PAs culled from the ranks of Hollywood hopefuls looking for any way onto a set, even one purported jinxed, so desperate to make their mark they didn't care if it was in their own blood.

*Cannon fodder,* Mickey thought.

Kayla stepped up beside Fleming; she compelled their attention in a way he hadn't, and said as she pulled her sunglasses off, "I, for one, am staying. We've all been hit hard by these tragedies, but we can't let all this darkness tear us apart; we should pull together and finish this film in spite of it, if only to honor the memories of those who put so much into it."

It was in the same vein as what Fleming had said after Paul Mann's death, but this time visibly genuine and therefore garnering the emotional return the original had fished for and failed to hook. As those gathered clapped Kayla blushed, and her eyes met Mickey's; he stopped clapping to whistle, and she smiled back at him.

"They don't need me right now," she said, coming up to him as the crowd dispersed, her sultry grin growing as Mickey's hands slid to her hips, "but I was wondering if maybe you did."

"Always," Mickey said. "Just give me five minutes to talk to Scooter Spielberg over there and I'll meet you in your trailer, okay?"

Kayla mock-pouted, and Mickey's mind flooded with what she envisioned them doing, as rich and vivid as if she was in his arms already. "Two minutes," he amended, tearing himself away and jogging after Fleming. "Give me two minutes."

"Aw, don't sell yourself short, Grant, I'm sure you can manage a bit longer than that," Kayla called after him. He turned around briefly to bow and, smiling, she started for her trailer.

Outside it she paused, pulled her phone from her pocket, snapped a few selfies to kill time until Mickey showed, and scrolled through to pick one to post. She called it connecting with fans, her agent called it branding, *but whatever,* Kayla thought; there were palm trees in her photos now, and that wasn't anything she'd ever had back home.

None looked quite right. She deleted them and set up for another, but as she flashed her best peace sign and smile something black swirled behind her in the shot, against the white side of her trailer. *Huh?* She half-turned, lowering her phone. "Hey, is somebody the—"

The shadow ripped itself from the trailer side, opaque, moving with a horrible liquid ripple and a silence so complete it tore at Kayla's ears. Featureless, it grew, tall but skeletally thin, and reached for her with grotesquely long-fingered hands; the sight of them stretching towards her snapped Kayla from her shock, but as she made to scream the shadow's hand covered her mouth—*clung* to it, with a tar-like consistency —and stifled her as it shoved her to the ground.

Mickey was half-hard as he neared Kayla's trailer, but his tumescence retreated when he picked up the adrenaline of terror rather than sex, so strong it stung. Cursing, he bolted for the trailer door, but something skittered out from the other side of the trailer as if kicked—Kayla's phone, screen black, cracked.

"Shit," Mickey said, changing direction.

He found Kayla flat on the ground—struggling, but to no avail. The shadow crouched beside her, smothering her; her chest heaved and she clawed at the shadow but couldn't seem to grasp it, and for the first time close to it Mickey saw the energy flickering around its flowing edges like an image on a screen, pulsing with power.

"*Shit,*" he repeated.

The shadow's head snapped up at the sound, and Kayla's panicked eyes rolled and saw Mickey, spurred him; everything else slipped away, and he lunged.

Incubi could dreamwalk, could reach into the minds and souls of humans; energies evanescent to other beings were substantial to them, and so when Mickey reached the shadow, he collided with it, ripping it off Kayla and rolling with it across the ground. The shadow's energy crackled and charged like a current beneath Mickey's skin, and as his own surged to resist it—thank God he'd been so well-fed recently—he knew his spirit side had to be flashing in and out of view. *Wonder what Kayla'll make of that.*

*If we both manage to survive.*

They came to a stop, Mickey on top, and suddenly his senses were choked by, of all, things, surprise flooding from the shadow—no, he had time enough to realize, not from it but whoever was casting it, coming across the magical connection, surprise that somebody was somehow fighting back.

But before Mickey could yank on this thread, trace it back to its source, the shadow shoved Mickey off and vanished. Body aching, muscles strung tight, Mickey pushed himself upright, his relief tempered by the certainty he felt that he hadn't won anything except a brief respite.

"Someone's using black magic to attack the production." Kayla stared at Mickey, blanket wrapped tight around her shoulders.

Mickey nodded. "Yep."

"And you could fight that... *thing* off because you're an incubus, which is why your face got all..." She waved vaguely in front of her own.

Mickey nodded again. "Yep."

Kayla sat silent, considering. They were in her trailer, Kayla's hair still damp from the shower where she'd tried to scrub the feel of the shadow from her skin and a bottle of whiskey half-empty on the table, Mickey sitting close to Kayla on the couch, carefully watching her reaction. After a minute she burst out, "Why *me*?"

"My guess?" Mickey said. "Because someone couldn't get the shoot shut down, even once they'd started killing people. So they decided to take it a step further and pick a victim who'd have more impact. And you were pretty vocal today about keeping things going, so..." Mickey shrugged gently. "They picked you."

Kayla laughed shakily. "Whatever happened to posting horrible things on gossip blogs?"

"Not nearly dramatic enough."

Kayla's smile seemed steadier this time, and then she looked at Mickey. "An incubus. That's like a sex vampire, isn't it?"

He chuckled. "Kind of. Lilin's the technical term, but sex demon works for casual use."

Something seemed to strike her. "Is that how, when we hooked up, you knew to do that thing with your tongue, when you...?"

"One of the perks of being an unholy creature who lives on sexual ecstasy," Mickey admitted, grinning. "I can sense needs and desires, what'll attract and please humans— although I tend to shut that sense down when I don't need it, otherwise I'd be constantly bombarded with every kink in L.A."

Kayla laughed. "Now *that's* terrifying."

Mickey smiled. Kayla leaned in, rested her head on his shoulder, murmured, "Thanks for saving me, Mickey."

He wrapped his arm around her, kissed the top of her head. "Of course." For a minute they were silent, then Mickey said, "I know it's a lot to take in, Kayla—I know how weird this shit must seem. And if it's too much for you, I want you to know I understand, and I don't blame you."

"Fuck that." She looked at him, eyes gleaming. "I'm not walking away, from this movie or you."

Mickey stroked her hair. "Even with the incubus thing?"

"Baby, it's L.A." Kayla rolled her eyes. "I've seen weirder shit."


"'Lo, 'tis a gala night,'" Mickey said, lifting a glass of champagne from the tray of a passing server and surveying the wrap party's glittering guests.

Kali bumped him with her hip, little black dress rustling. "Knock it off. You know I get nervous when you start quoting Poe."

"Sorry, Short Stack." Mickey bumped her back. "But I think we can lighten up a bit now that the damn movie's finally done."

Fleming's ginger beard grew patchy in the last weeks, as if he'd begun pulling it out; the crew's nerves had been strung so tight it'd seemed Eric Clapton could've wailed out "Cocaine" on them; Gillian Anderson stormed off set saying she "didn't need this shit" and was barely talked into coming back; but the movie was finished without a rise in the real-life body count, and Fleming was throwing the wrap party at his mansion in the Hills, the king's castle crowded with grateful peasants celebrating both the film being finished and, only half-jokingly, their own survival.

So there was an air of abandon, relief, to the gathering, bubbling like the free-flowing champagne. For now, guests mingled in the mansion's gleaming rooms or on the light-wrapped deck, but later *Edge of Reason* would have a private premiere in the mansion's screening room—if, Mickey figured, anybody stayed awake through the self-congratulatory speech Fleming would surely give first, as trademark as his baseball cap.

*There's not enough blow in the world,* Mickey thought, but he and Kali headed off to search for some anyway.

It turned out to be a memorable speech, in the end. Fleming stood, black-tie-attired and ballcapped, beaming, in front of the blank gray screen, and the angle of lighting threw his shadow larger-than-life across it. After his opening comments he raised his arms, spread them wide, godlike, and called the main cast up with him. Kayla, wearing a red dress she seemed poured into, murmured something to Margot Robbie and blew the audience a kiss, grinning like a kid on Christmas.

"Great cast, am I right?" Fleming clapped. "I'm telling you, I couldn't ask for better people to bring my vision to life. And though my friend Paul isn't with us any longer, I know he would have appreciated the work Mickey Grant put in to make sure the script was the best it could be."

Kali nudged Mickey as she and Kayla led the clapping; Mickey hid his face behind his leather jacket. Fleming continued, "Behind every great film, there's a vision, and not to stroke my own ego, but the moment I conceived this movie I knew I had something brilliant on my hands, and—"

The audience waited. His mouth worked, but soundlessly; Kali went cold and grabbed Mickey's arm as before their eyes Fleming's shadow grew against the screen. Before anyone could react, it peeled free and swooped down on Fleming, and as if it were a razor a long gash slashed itself open across his face. Blood gouted onto Dennis Quaid. Fleming stumbled, screaming, bleeding, nearly knocking over Clive Standen.

But the shadow wasn't done. As people panicked, trampling each other trying to flee, it whipped around Fleming again and again, ripping and rending; blood sprayed scarlet onto the screen and his screams grew higher-pitched in pain.

"Come on." Mickey grabbed Kali's arm, on his feet. He'd reached out again, senses latched onto the shadow, and this time was flooded not with surprise but pure black-hearted hate and rage from the conjurer; this time he'd traced the shadow to its source.

Kali's heels clicked as she hurried after him. "Where?"

"Upstairs. The killer's here."


A voice—muffled, rhythmic—was audible through the door Mickey was drawn to; it broke off when the door burst open and Mickey and Kali rushed into the room, staring at the scene set there.

The bed had been shoved aside, and in the cleared central space of the room a circle had been drawn, four feet wide and studded with black candles and glistening symbols. Screams, oddly thin, still echoed in the air—coming, the pair saw, from a laptop on a table beside the circle, the screen showing the scarlet horror downstairs. A camera, the conjurer must've hidden a camera somewhere in the screening room so he could watch his shadow's handiwork as he cast the spell...

In the circle's center was the conjurer himself.

"Really?" Mickey drew up short. "Gotta be honest, I was expecting a little more Aleister Crowley, a little less Wizards of Beverly Hills."

The conjurer glared. He had disheveled blond hair, uneven ears, a prep-school student's face and jeans he'd probably bought faded. All he needed, Kali thought, was an earpiece and a latte—and then it struck her she'd seen him before.

"Hold up, motherfucker. I know who you are—you're Scooter's old assistant. Brian Malcolm," she said. Mickey looked at her. "What? Heather left a tabloid lying around and I flipped through it."

"But you quit," Mickey said to Brian, who flushed apoplectically.

"Of *course* I quit!" he said. "How could I keep working for that egomaniacal asshole after what he did to me?"

"Well, I know where this is going." Mickey rolled his eyes.

"*Edge of Reason* was *my* idea!" Brian screamed. "I took it to Fleming and asked for his help getting it made, and he stole it for himself."

"And there it is." Mickey shook his head. "Brian, that's clichéd even for L.A."

"Dude, that's just sad," Kali agreed.

As Brian's rant rolled on, he didn't seem to notice the friends were inching further into the room; his own drama was all-consuming. "I couldn't do anything about it—Fleming threatened to destroy my life if I went to the studio, and everyone in Hollywood might hate him, but he's still powerful enough to do it. I knew that, so I quit—I couldn't just stand by and watch him fuck my dream up. So—" he gave a cold crooked grin— "I decided to get back at him my own way."

"Magical murder. Naturally." Mickey's eyes flicked to the laptop. Fleming was still alive, but covered with countless cuts, his screams far fainter, and the shadow struck still.

Brian shook his head. "I didn't want to kill anyone at first. I wanted to destroy Fleming by destroying the movie, but no matter what my shadow did, they kept filming. So I thought *one* death might stop it. *One.* But no matter who got hurt, who *died,* he didn't stop. He just... didn't... stop." He ground his fists into the sides of his head, teeth gritted.

Mickey's hand brushed Kali's. He traced a circle on it, stroked across it, and Kali had learned enough of magic to know what he meant: Brian was safe in the circle, but if he stepped out, it was open season. "So you came here tonight," Kali said, to keep Brian distracted. "Did your act onsite for once."

Brian's eyes were lightless, red-rimmed, his smile hollow. "Every great drama needs a grand finale, and I wanted to be here to see my greatest work unfold."

Kali snorted. "Now who's the egomaniac?"

Mickey moved then, running not at Brian but the laptop and camera. Brian's expression contorted in horror at the thought of missing the denouement of his master-piece, and desperately lunged after Mickey—and, as he did, crossed out of the circle.

Mickey tumbled out of the way. Onscreen the shadow vanished. A moment later it appeared in the room; Brian, realizing his mistake, leapt for the circle's sanctuary, but too late: the shadow hooked him, hawklike, and he just had time to scream before it enveloped him completely and both of them disappeared.

They left a grim memento, though: frozen on the fallen laptop's screen was a still shot of Brian Malcolm's face twisted in a tortured scream, the only thing visible in the black mass swirling around it.


Kayla rushed into Mickey's arms when he and Kali came downstairs and he held her, felt her trembling. Kali's phone was choked with frantic messages from Pam; appar-ently the chaos had made the news already. Outside the mansion police lights strobed the night; inside Fleming, dead of shock and blood loss, lay covered in a sheet soaked cherry-red.

"Can't wait to see how they spin this," Mickey said, lighting a cigarette.

"What do you think happens to the movie now?" Kayla asked as Kali rejoined them on the sidewalk, pocketing her phone, having reassured Pam she was fine.

"Hopefully, they burn it," Mickey said as Fleming's covered body was wheeled into a silent ambulance. A low warm wind moaned, carrying the smoke of Mickey's cigarette away into the night. "Annabeth should be happy, though; I think I'll be sticking to novels for a bit after this."

"What's the matter, Grant?" Kali said. "The movie biz not as glamorous from the inside as it looks on the outside?"

"I've had all the Hollywood insanity I can handle for a while," Mickey said, and the ambulance's doors slammed shut and it drove off, past the reporters already gath-ering outside the mansion, clamoring for blood.

# CALIFORNIA DOUBLING

## DJ TYRER

"Are you sure the African rainforest has quite so many redwoods in it?" I asked as I tried to detach my skirt from the branch of a shrub.

When I arrived in Hollywood, well, I guess I was naive. I'd imagined moviemaking to be different, more glamorous, less false. An *art*. But, here, I was in a forest of Californian redwoods, pretending I was somewhere in the Congo, with a bush for a restroom. Not at all what I'd expected.

"If it was good enough for *Jurassic Park*," said Joe, the director, "it's good enough for *Jungle Fever*. I mean, it's not like anyone ever notices California doubling."

"If you say so." I was eager to get on. The woods were full of bugs and poison oak, and I was sick of the restroom arrangements. The sooner we got back to LA, the better.

"Ready... and action!"

I went through the scene for the seventh time. That was something else I hadn't realized before I came here: just how long it could take to shoot a short scene and the number of takes it demanded. It was exhausting!

"And, cut! Great! Take five."

"About time," I muttered, and headed over to the picnic table for a cup of vile coffee in a plastic cup and a lifeless pastrami sandwich. My 'co-star' Bud slumped down in a lawn chair.

Steve, the cameraman, came over and started hitting on me, which was enough to make me announce I needed another rest break.

Steve swore and shouted after me, "Is there something wrong with you?"

I flicked him the finger and headed off into the trees.

I finished the coffee and crushed the cup. I wished I hadn't brought it with me, having nowhere to put it.

The problem with a forest, when you aren't used to the woods, is that one part looks much the same as another unless you're paying attention, and I wasn't. I heard Joe calling my name, but when I turned around to go back, I realized I wasn't certain where I was. Still, all I had to do was go in a straight line, right? Except it's never that simple: you move around trees and, when those trees are redwoods, that can really turn you about so that a straight line is neither possible nor necessarily the way you want to go.

Joe's voice seemed to fade away to nothing and I was starting to feel nervous.

"Guys? Guys, where are you?" I called, but there was no reply—I could feel my face growing numb, my breath coming in shallow gasps. I wished I had a paper bag.

It was then that the woods changed. Up until then, the forest had been, well, a forest. You know what I mean? One step up from a park, nothing threatening, where the worst you have to worry about is being stung or bitten by bugs. But, suddenly, it seemed darker and denser. Overbearing. I shivered and continued to fight to control my breathing.

"Guys, please!" There was still no answering call. The forest was eerily silent. It felt as if I were miles from anyone.

I had no idea how I was going to get back to the others or find my way out of the woods.

I began to wonder: Was I safe? Weren't forests full of all sorts of critters? Like bears, wolves, and mountain lions—did you get those in California? I couldn't remember. I'd read in a newspaper that some guy had spotted Bigfoot in the woods somewhere around here. Not that I believed in Bigfoot. Not really. I wished it didn't seem so likely to be lurking in the shadows between the trees.

My breaths were starting to come more regularly and, while I still felt a little dizzy, I no longer felt as if I were about to die. If I could keep calm, I could find my way. I pressed on.

That was when I realized how pants and a sensible pair of shoes would be much more practical for traipsing about in the woods, let alone in the Congo. I didn't care how Joe justified his plot; it was a ridiculous outfit. My feet were sore, my skirt kept snagging on branches, and I was absolutely sick of the forest and seriously rethinking my plans to become a movie star.

There was a sound of movement from the brush ahead of me. I paused and listened. Yes, there it was.

"Guys, is that you?" I asked, then wondered if I should've kept silent; what if it was a mountain lion?

Then something pushed through the plant growth. It was human-shaped, on two legs, yet somehow, I could tell it wasn't a person. A bear? No, too lithe. It had to be Bigfoot!

But it wasn't Bigfoot; it wasn't as tall and not at all hairy. As it pushed its way out into view, I saw it had a sort of scaly, pebbly skin and a long-snouted head.

It was a man-shaped lizard.

I laughed a jittery laugh. "Very funny, guys. Very funny."

Steve had to be nearby, filming me. They'd set me up. Probably, it was Joe's way of slipping a twist into his film and turning it into B-movie horror. He'd probably hoped I'd shriek in terror for a verisimilitude his low budget couldn't buy.

The lizardman cocked its head, looked at me quizzically, and blinked.

"Okay, guys," I mumbled, my certainty draining away. I'd expected Joe to shout "Cut!" and appear laughing, but the forest was still silent. With a prank, you expect someone to jump out and laugh. The longer I looked at the lizardman, the less it looked like a man in a cheap rubber suit and the more it looked like a lizard that had somehow contrived to stand up on its hind legs and develop hands.

I shivered and wished I knew which way to run.

It couldn't be real, could it? I'd seen a site online that claimed there were things like this in a hidden city beneath the streets of LA, and supposed native legends of their cave cities, but that was sheer garbage, typical 'net nonsense, surely. So, why did one of them appear to be standing in front of me?

It opened its mouth and coughed a sound.

I turned and ran; I'd clearly seen into its throat. That was no costume.

I thought I heard it running after me, crashing past plants, but I didn't look back.

Suddenly, the ground disappeared from beneath my feet and I found myself falling down a slope to a stream.

I landed with a splash and wasted no time in scrambling to my feet. My skirt was heavy with water and clinging awkwardly to my legs. There was no way I was going to make it up the other steep bank, so I headed in what I hoped was the direction it flowed.

There was a splash behind me and I didn't need to look back to know it had followed me down.

I was breathing heavily, my heart hammering and my leg muscles burning as I struggled to run.

Suddenly, I heard Joe calling my name again, distant but undeniable. I shouted out.

He called back, I answered him and, a moment later, he appeared atop the bank.

"Where have you been?" he shouted. Then, he saw what was behind me and cried, "What the hell is that?"

"Help me!" I screamed.

"Come on," he replied, crouching down and extending an arm.

I ran to him and grabbed his arm. He seized my shoulder with his other hand and hauled me up the muddy bank.

"Run!" I shouted.

He asked again what it was, but I didn't have the breath to answer him.

We stumbled back into the clearing, where Steve was standing at the picnic table pouring himself a coffee. There was no sign of Bud.

"Oh, there you—what's up?" he asked as he turned. "What's wrong?"

I couldn't answer, but fell to my knees gasping. Joe ran over to the equipment bags and began rifling through one.

"Dude, you're scaring me," Steve said, then dropped his coffee when Joe turned around and began loading bullets into a large revolver. "Dude!"

For a moment, I was surprised to see the gun, then remembered he'd said something about it, 'just in case' we ran into dangerous wildlife. A lizardman certainly counted, as far as I was concerned.

"What's going on?" demanded Steve, voice rising.

Joe turned and pointed. "That!"

Steve and I both turned. The lizardman was standing at the edge of the clearing. Steve swore and I managed to stumble back onto my feet.

Joe raised the gun and fired.

The lizardman jerked and toppled backwards in a spray of reddish-black blood.

"What the hell was that?" Steve gasped.

"That's what I want to know," said Joe, looking at me.

I shrugged. "I don't know. I thought it was you playing a prank."

Steve swore. "You don't think…"

Joe crossed over to it and nudged it with his foot, then crouched beside it. He stood with a relieved sigh.

"It's real. The damn thing's real."

"We have to leave," I said, crossing to where I'd left my slacks and vest. I pulled off the dress, not caring if they were looking or not, and put them on.

"It's dead," said Joe. "You don't think there're more out there?"

"I don't know—and I don't want to find out. Are you coming?"

"She's got a point," said Steve. Then, he swore again and pointed. Another lizardman had appeared.

Joe raised his gun and shot it dead.

A third one hurled itself out from among the trees at Joe and fastened its jaws on his throat. Joe let out a gurgling cry and I heard the gun discharge again as he fell.

I screamed and ran. Steve was just behind me.

Then, I heard him cry out in pain and crash to the ground. I glanced back: Two lizardmen had pinned Steve down and were tearing into his flesh with their jaws.

I kept running. I know it's horribly selfish, but I prayed that killing Steve would distract them long enough for me to escape.

Luckily, the trail we'd taken to the site wasn't too hard to follow and, finally, I reached the track where Joe had parked the 4×4. Of course, it was then I realized he was the one with the keys.

I'd picked up my cell phone when I'd changed, but there was no signal, so I set off down the track. At least I knew I was headed the right way. I just had to hope the lizardmen weren't following me, as I wasn't able to go very fast. Steve and Joe were dead, I knew it. I wondered what had happened to Bud. Had they got him when he headed off for a rest break, or had he managed to get away? I hoped so; he was an okay guy.

Every so often, when I stopped to catch my breath, I'd try my cell phone and, finally, I had a signal. I dialed 9-1-1 and was put through to a Park Ranger who drove out to collect me.

After I'd been taken to a ranger station, they went out to look for the others. They located where we'd been filming and found the gun and the blood, but no sign of the others or the dead lizardmen. They began to question what had happened up there. Had Joe shot the others in a rage over creative differences? I guess that sounds plausible out here.

Naturally, as the only survivor, their attention turned to me and, I guess, the truth was doing me no favors. After all, nobody believes in crazy stuff like that. But, what else could I say?

Still, my court-appointed defender says he's confident the fact only Joe's finger-prints are on the gun and the fact there was no blood on me or other forensic evidence to connect me to the deaths will show sufficient reasonable doubt to get me off. I just wish I didn't see doubt in his eyes when I try to explain what really happened.

I'm not mad. I really saw them. There are lizardmen out there. Believe me.

# THE DEAD ROAD

## KEVIN JONES

Even though it was past eleven p.m., it was still murderously hot in the high deserts of Southern California. When Jerry stepped though the entrance of the all-night truck stop, the first thing that he noticed was that it was only moderately cooler inside than it had been out in the parking lot. The interior of the greasy spoon was nearly empty. The only people in evidence were a lone trucker sitting at the counter, and a hard-looking waitress who might have been attractive about a decade ago. Jerry took a seat a few stools down from the trucker.

The waitress walked toward him. She had peroxide-blonde hair and wore a pink and white uniform with a nametag on it that read *Annie*. She smiled, revealing a mouthful of nicotine-stained teeth. "What can I get for you, sweetheart?"

Jerry grinned back at her, trying to appear friendlier than he felt; after being lost for what had seemed like an eternity on the pitch-black desert highway, his mood was shot. "I think I'll have a coke and a slice of pie."

"What kind of pie?"

Jerry shrugged. "Doesn't matter, really. Whatever's fresh, I guess."

Once the waitress left to prepare his order, Jerry turned to the trucker. "Can you help me out? I'm trying to get to Lancaster to see my sister, but I think I'm all turned around. I'd really appreciate it if you could point me in the right direction."

After swallowing a mouthful of mashed potatoes and gravy, the heavyset trucker muttered, "You ain't kidding about being lost, friend. You've gone about a hundred miles in the wrong direction."

Jerry smiled sheepishly as he pulled a map from his pocket. "Damn, I was afraid of that." He pointed at an old county road that crossed the desert. "So it looks like if I backtrack to this road, it'll take me near Lancaster."

The trucker glanced down at the map and chuckled. "You mean the Dead Road? I

327

wouldn't go there if I was you. I'd drive back to the interstate and head north. Eventually you'll make it to Lancaster."

Jerry scrutinized the map again. "But the interstate is much further out of my way. This road here will shave at least eighty miles off of my trip."

When he didn't answer, Jerry looked up from the map. The trucker was gone. A wad of bills sat on the counter next to his half-eaten meal. Jerry turned in his seat just in time to catch a glimpse of him as he hurried out the door towards his big rig.

Annie returned with Jerry's soda and dessert. Her face was a mask of concern. "You must not be from around here, sweetie, or you would have heard of the Dead Road."

Jerry swallowed nervously. "I'm not. I'm from Colorado. I'm down here visiting my sister. She just recently finalized her divorce from her deadbeat husband and bought a new house in Lancaster. I thought I'd use up some of my vacation time and help her get the place set up. But what's all this talk about the Dead Road?"

The waitress's voice lowered to a whisper. "Nobody around here even likes to talk about the Dead Road, but I'll tell you so I don't have to read about how something terrible happened to you in tomorrow's paper. That road is bad with a capital B. There's been over a hundred fatal car crashes on it since the late forties."

Jerry smiled; he had always loved a good urban legend, and he had a feeling he was about to hear a real whopper. "Okay, I'll bite. What's wrong with the Dead Road?"

Annie's face grew grim. "There's nothing funny about any of this. It's as serious as a heart attack. It started a few years after World War II. There was this hot shot fighter ace named Major Fogel and he was testing out this experimental jet at Edward's Air Force Base. The brass hats said the plane was safe and ready for testing. Only it wasn't. He went up in a huge fireball that spread all over that shortcut you want to take. Ever since Major Fogel died, almost anyone who tries to drive down that stretch of road crashes and has to be scooped up with a shovel by the Highway Patrol. People say that it's the Major's phantom plane that swoops down out of the sky and runs people clean off of the road. But I haven't told you the worst part of all of this." The waitress paused for dramatic effect. She leaned closer to Jerry before continuing, "The folks that have been killed on the Dead Road? Their restless spirits wander the desert at night. I know I've seen 'em more than once when I'm driving home from work in the wee hours of the morning. Hell, almost all of the people who live around here have had a run in with the ghosts. Sometimes the dead show up at people's houses in the middle of night and bang on their doors, begging for help before they vanish into the darkness. The spirits seem like they're drawn to people who talk about them, so most locals never speak about the Dead Road. Hell, most people won't even say its name out loud."

Jerry didn't buy a word of the waitress's colorful story, but he kept his voice neutral. "Well, thanks for the heads up. I'll be sure to keep clear of the Dead Road."

Annie could obviously tell that he didn't believe her. She grimaced as she turned away and headed towards the kitchen. Jerry hurriedly ate his peach pie, then threw down more than enough money to pay for his food before he slipped out of the diner. While he unlocked his car, he took a moment to survey his surroundings. Besides the diner, he could only see a few scattered homes here and there. Everything else was just dirt and rocks. Jerry had never visited California before, but this desolate landscape had not been what he had expected. He mumbled to himself, "Why couldn't my sister have bought a house by the beach or next to Disneyland?"

He pulled out of the parking lot and backtracked down the highway. A few minutes later, he reached the fork in the road. If he kept going straight, he would wind up back on the freeway and eventually make it to Lancaster. But if he took the left path, he would reach his sister's place in half the time. He glanced down at his wristwatch. It was already after midnight. "To hell with it," he said. "I'm not going to let a ghost story scare me away." He turned onto the Dead Road.

After traveling for several minutes down the lonely old highway, he chuckled nervously to himself and thought, *Might as well be on the dark side of the moon. There's not a single structure or light for as far as the eye can see.*

Up ahead something started to come into view. At first it looked like a small red flame. Then out of nowhere, the entire area was lit up like the Fourth of July. Dozens of road flares covered the blacktop. To the side of the highway was an overturned station wagon. Parked next to the wreckage was a highway patrol cruiser, lights flashing rhythmically. Jerry did a double take as he drove past the accident. The patrol car was practically an antique. It looked like something out of an old movie from the fifties.

Jerry stuck his head out the window as he started to hear a rumble in the sky. It sounded like a jet engine bearing down. When he popped his head back inside, he slammed on the brakes; the wrecked station wagon, the highway patrol car and flares had vanished. The only thing he could now see in his rearview mirror was darkness.

Sweat started to pour down his face as the terrible roar of the jet engine grew closer and closer. Then the night sky was brilliantly lit up by a huge fireball. The boom that followed was so violent that it nearly burst Jerry's eardrums. Debris and burning jet fuel rained down onto the highway. Jerry quickly did a U-turn and then jammed his foot as hard as he could on the gas pedal. As his old clunker sped down the Dead Road, a grin spread across his face; just up ahead was the fork in the road.

Then a column of fire and smoke shot up from the blacktop. Out of the flames came a man dressed in a burning flight suit and helmet. The specter ran straight at his car, howling like a damned soul. The steering wheel leapt from Jerry's hands as the car skidded off the road. He slammed on the brakes with all of his might, but nothing could stop his car from cart wheeling into the jagged rocks and sun baked earth that surrounded the Dead Road.


Annie looked up as she heard someone enter the diner. It was the young man who had been looking for directions a few hours ago. "What's the matter, honey? Did you get lost again?"

He did not answer as sat at the same stool that he had before.

"Can I get you some coffee or something?"

The young man did not reply. His skin was paler than it had been earlier in the

329

evening. His eyes darted around the empty diner in a furtive way that gave him the look of a cornered animal.

"Are you all right? Do you need me to call someone for you?"

Finally, he tried to speak, but no sound emerged from his mouth. He looked like a character on a TV that had been muted. Then something happened that would remain with Annie until her dying day: he started to fade before her eyes. Within seconds, nothing remained of the lost motorist.

A tear trickled down Annie's cheek. She knew only too well what had happened to that nice young man. The Dead Road had claimed another victim.

# ANGEL REPUBLIC

## MATHEUS GAMARRA

"So, where are you from again, Mr. Gaglianone?"

"For fuck's sake, Mr. Momte, I've already said I'm from California! How hard to understand is that?"

"You be careful with your tone. We're not joking here. Wait for me here…" The officer stood up and left the room, going straight to the coffee machine where he grabbed a cup, then put Canadian sugar inside it. The hot, soft flavor would help to calm his nerves, and keep him awake. He needed to sleep so badly. Almost fell on the damn interrogation table several times.

"Are you sure you can handle him?" said Laiara, his supervisor, while texting something on her smartphone. She had asked him the same question several times that day, but he kept refusing to answer. Until that point.

"No, Chief. Not anymore. Just thinking about his case gives me a headache! What the fuck is this California he keeps talking about?"

"He says it's in America, right?"

"Yes. But that state doesn't exist." Paul Momte brought up a map of the United States through Bing and showed it to his boss. "See? When I showed him this map, he said California is here, but all we have there is water."

"Wait, maybe he's talking about Angel Republic and has a mental disease or something."

"Angel Republic? That's in the middle of Pacific."

"I know, but the landmass was once part of the Americas. Just try it, okay? It's the closest thing to a lead we got." Paul sighed and re-entered the room. He looked into the face of the man who had caused him trouble for the last five hours. Gaglianone was as confused, angry and scared as he was.

"H-here, have a look at this." Momte exhibited a map of the world on his phone, and pointed his finger towards Angel Republic. He was about to ask a question, when the man proclaimed:

"Yeah, yeah, that's California. That's where I live. But why is it in the middle of the sea?"

"Because that's not California. That's Angel Republic. But explain to me, where did you get those documents with the name California on it? And how the hell did you get into France with that *blue* USA passport?"

"That's a normal passport, what's wrong with it?"

"That is not a real American passport. This is." Paul showed Gaglianone a photo of a red-and-green passport with the symbol of a Turkey and the letters "CSA."

"Okay, you've got to be kidding me. Is this a fucking TV or YouTube prank? Seriously? Are there cameras somewhere?" Although clearly pissed, the stranger was trying to simulate a smile.


Mr. Gaglianone was still next to an interrogation table, but this room was far more respectable than the last one. Cameras were on the table, there were one-way mirrors all around him, and two suited men wearing sunglasses sat across from him. One of them glanced at a tablet, then looked at the stranger.

"So, California, eh? That's the name from where you are?" he asked.

"Yes. Yes, it is."

"That isn't funny at all, Mr. Gaglianone. You understand California is just a myth, right? We'll give you a chance to drop this pathetic theater and explain to us who the hell you are and how you got into France so we can properly deport you. Otherwise, we'll be forced to lock you up until we figure it out by ourselves."

"What? I'm not joking! Do you think I'm crazy? Why the hell would I waste your time with fraud? California! The home of Los Angeles, San Francisco, and Sacramento! Of motherfucking Hollywood!"

One of the agents took a deep breath.

"California, like Atlantis, Hy-Brazil or El Dorado, is a fictional island created by Spanish dumbasses in the sixteenth century. It has never existed. They simply mistook the Tijuana Peninsula for an island. The landmass you're referring to broke off from the mainland more than nine million years ago."

"Wait... The San Andreas Fault... Before I woke up in the airplane... Now I remember, there were earthquakes and massive ravines... And I fell into the abyss..."

"Sir, nothing you're saying makes any sense at all. We will be obliged to get you evaluated."

"No, no! I need... I... I... What's the name of that island the airport officer mentioned? Angel Republic? Can you deport me there? Maybe I can find some answers there..."

"Calm down, sir. Explain what happened. How did you get on that airplane?"

"I live in San Francisco with my family, my wife Nancy and my daughter Anne. It's a city in California. I was coming home from work on the twelfth of July. I believe

332

it was ten o'clock. I was coming early that day because I had a sudden nosebleed and a headache. But then the earthquake started. A hole opened under my car, and I fell. I woke up immediately inside the airplane. I don't know what the fuck happened. I just want to go home."

"Mr. Gaglianone, please wait." The agents quickly left the room and went to their supervisor, who was watching everything from behind a one-way mirror.

"Boss, he seems to be telling the truth. That doesn't mean his truth is real. We should send him to a psychiatric hospital," one of the suited men said.

"The ambassador to Angel Republic just got in touch. They have his records there. He's been missing since the events of the twelfth of July. We're arranging his return."

"But he forged his passport, sir. How did he even board that airplane?"

"I don't have any idea, but this is none of our business. We just have to send him home and worry about things that actually matter."


Andrew Gaglianone entered the embassy and sighed in relief when he saw the state flag hanging on the wall. He expected to see the familiar bear and the words *California Republic*. But it was all wrong. Instead, the flag read *Angel Republic*. Upon it was a weird green-robed angel holding a lamp in his hands.

"Mr. Gaglianone, I had been waiting for you!" Hector Evans, the Angel Republic ambassador, strode forward.

"Thanks, I guess. I'm very confused. The people here are insane, they say California isn't in the US and—"

The ambassador interrupted him. "Yes, yes, the police informed me of your condition. As an Angelian, you'll be guaranteed access to psychological help as soon as you arrive at the main territory. Follow me to my office. Quickly, please; I have an appointment soon."

"Oh... Ok." Gaglianone followed the diplomat through the refined yet curiously empty embassy corridors until they reached an office. Both men sat down. Hector opened a binder, taking a file out.

"Sir, can you confirm to me you are Andrey Gaglianone, cook, thirty-three years old, father of twin boys and husband of the chemistry teacher Samantha Gaglianone, forty-four years old?"

"*What*? My name is Andrew. My children are twin sisters! What kind of files are these?"

"Calm down, Andrey. I'm quite sure this is you." The ambassador slid the file across the desk to his unwanted guest. It did have Mr. Gaglianone's photo.

"What the fuck? B-but I'm..."

"Sir, I understand you're going through something, but your family wants to see you. You've been missing since the last flood two months ago." Gaglianone began to argue, but the other man interrupted him. "Sir, I have a lot of things to do and not a lot of patience. Just tell me, how did you end up here?"

"Here? Where is here? France, right?"

"France is up the border. We're in Taured. Please, Mr. Gaglianone, sign the document already. I can't get you home until you do."

"Oh, damn this. With the treatment I received from the locals I suppose I can't stay here, either." He grabbed the pen and signed.

"You signed Andrew... Well, your mental health is not my business. I'll just briefly clarify the situation for you: You are an Angel Republic citizen. You've been missing for some weeks. Your family looked for you everywhere. You somehow ended up in France, and then Taured, remembering your life incorrectly." The diplomat looked at his phone. "Your transport is here. I'll escort you to the cab." He got up and gestured for the citizen to follow.

"I'll get there by car?" Gaglianone asked as the duo walked to the entrance.

"No. By train. The cab is your transport to the train station. Here is your ticket. You'll arrive tomorrow afternoon. Your family will be waiting for you," the ambassador said as a black taxi stopped in front of the building. Gaglianone took the ticket and entered the car, so confused that he forgot to say goodbye to his host.


"Is Father going to take much longer, Mother?" asked one of the twins. The bench wasn't exactly uncomfortable, but the station was extremely cold. There were small ponds of water forming all around due to the intense rain.

"No, offspring. Just one or three more minutes," the mother answered, hugging both children to protect them from the cold.

A few minutes later, a train came out from the underwater tunnel and a small group of people exited into the station.

*"WELCOME TO LOST ANGEL"* boomed a voice from overhead speakers. The last one to get off the train was Gaglianone.

"Father!" Both children ran up and hugged him. The woman came after them, noticeably worried.

"Where have you been, Husband? How did you end up in Europe?"

"Fuck, there's been a misunderstanding, I..." Gaglianone looked at her. She was nearly identical to his wife, but paler and thinner. "Lisa? What happened to you?"

"What happened to *you*, Husband? You have been missing for months! Don't you know how I worried about you? How the offspring worried about you?"

He took a look at the twins. They looked exactly like his daughters, only male. Maybe the ambassador was right after all. Maybe he *was* misremembering. Maybe he was crazy. Maybe he had always been from Angel Republic after all.

"Husband, the state has arranged a psychiatric evaluation for you tomorrow. But come now. The offspring have waited to eat with their father all day." The woman kissed him and led the way through the station out to the parking lot.

The entire way home, Gaglianone couldn't stop looking at his surroundings. The place was like if Los Angeles had been built in New Orleans and then submerged in a swamp. There were ponds of water everywhere, and the place was notably underdeveloped, with some streets illuminated only by torches. Most buildings in the area were made of wood, but he saw skyscrapers on the horizon, too—identical to the ones he knew, though significantly dirtier.

On the horizon, he saw mountains. On one, giant letters formed the word "HYYPERSWAMP." Behind the letters, a giant, green-robed angel statue mounted on a bear watched over the city.

"Lisa, what *is* that monstrosity?" He pointed at the angel.

"Have you forgot everything already? That's the Light Bearer, the angel that guided the settlers to our magnificent island in Angelian Mythology. Husband, you really do need that evaluation."

"Oh… Yes, I'm sorry. I'm having a hard time remembering things correctly." He shut his mouth until the car stopped in front of a two-story Victorian house, clearly old and decaying. His true house was similar, but with a modern, comfortable design.

"This is our house, right?" Gaglianone asked.

His wife approached, and whispered: "Yes. Listen. I'll explain this once for you because of your… illness, Husband, but you must remember. Her name is Augusta. Don't refer to the houses as houses. In Angel Republic, our houses are alive. Since you disappeared, things inside have gone missing, and the electrical systems have been failing. It's usual when family members leave their home suddenly. It's a reaction from the house's soul. Now that you're back, Augusta will give back our old things, or perhaps new things to replace the disappeared ones. If you find things that weren't there before, it's a gift from the house, so don't be afraid. If you show fear, it'll annoy her and she'll stop compensating us. Also, don't acknowledge Augusta's existence, even if you see her physically walking around, and never speak to her."

"Did you become insane while I was away, Lisa? This doesn't make any sense!" he shouted.

"Don't disrespect Angelian traditions, Andrey. Even if you don't believe in them anymore." She entered the house followed by the twins, and then her husband.


"Well, Patient, how has your first month back home been? I hope—" Dr. Edgar Ronaway's speech was interrupted by a clap of loud thunder. He ignored it and tried to focus on his patient, even with the office lights flickering and the ceiling drips flooding the room.

"It's hard to get used to all this water. I can't recall the last time I was in a truly dry place. This is nothing like real California."

"Andrey, your wife told me you always liked water. At least before the… disappearance. You are upset by your actual situation, but trust me, so is your wife. She contacted me recently. She barely recognizes you. Your offspring are frightened by your new behavior."

"New behavior? I constantly try to wake up myself. Every night! At first, I thought I was misremembering things or this was all an elaborate prank, but… this isn't. I wish so badly it was. I feel like I'm stealing someone else's life. I look at our family portraits on the house's walls. It's me there, but I don't see me. Like I'm looking at another person. I don't remember wearing those clothes. Don't remember having this house. Hell, I don't remember having twin boys! I had daughters. And I didn't call them 'offspring.' I called them by their names. Anne and Nicole. My name isn't even Andrey. It's Andrew."

"Andrey, I understand it's hard to accept who you are. But even if you come from another dimension, there's no way to go back. You can only go forward from now on. Accept your life. Being stubborn won't help."

"It's not stubbornness, Dr. Ronaway, it's fear. I can't understand what happened. How I ended up here. And what will happen next. I can't be who you want me to be. My job in this goddamned isle is to be a cook. But I'm not a cook. I can barely cook properly. I'm an engineer. It's not going to be long before they fire me again. I have a family that I barely know, and I don't even know how I'll be able to sustain them! I just... I just want to go home..." He broke down in tears. Drops fell from his eyes straight into the pools of badly illuminated rainwater on the floor.

"Home. Home is gone, Patient, if it ever was at all. There's no going back. I hate to be harsh, but crying about how you miss your fantasies will not help you. If you wish to stay alive, you must adapt and overcome. Have you been taking the Risperidone injections I prescribed?"

Thunder roared, and all the lights finally went out.

"Wait! That's it! I fell in a ravine just before I woke up in that airplane. Maybe I died. Maybe... I need to seek spiritual help!"

"Patient, spiritual help can be useful, but it will just alienate you if you keep believing in that supposed past life. It didn't happen. It's all in your head. You need to realize it and overcome those thoughts, or our talks and medicines will be useless. If you keep wanting to believe, nothing will help those hallucinations. Don't believe them. They are not real."

"Thank you, Mr. Ronaway! I'll be back here next week." Gaglianone left the office. As soon as he heard the door close, he saw, in a dark corner of the flooded waiting room, a pair of strange eyes watching him. From that figure, an uncanny voice emanated:

"You miss home, Gaglianone. But there's no home to be missed. You miss California, but there's no California to be missed. You miss your old life, but there's no life to be missed. You don't miss death, but she misses you."

Gaglianone halted immediately and prepared to run away back to his doctor's room. Then the eyes closed, and the figure disappeared.


"It was hard to find this place. Finally, a Catholic Church." Gaglianone walked across the dark worn-out wooden floor of the church. The old priest looked at his unexpected guest.

"It's been so long since anyone but me entered this place. Thought I was the last Catholic in Angel Republic. But I don't recognize you, my son. What's your name?"

"Andrew... I mean, Andrey. Andrey Gaglianone."

"Andrey. Well, welcome, Andrey. If you want anything, I'm at your disposal. But don't get too comfortable. The church is closing in two months. The Vatican won't pay the bills for a church with no followers."

"What? There are no Catholics here?"

"Most Angelians worship the Light Bearer and other bizarre, folkloric entities. Some of them turned to Christianity when our missionaries finally reached the isle in the nineteenth century, but the native religions are so influential that even the most powerful religious organization in the world couldn't convert them. Do you need assistance?"

"Yes. No. I mean, I don't know if I can even be assisted. I think I died and went to another dimension or to hell or purgatory. I don't know what happened to me. I was driving and fell off a cliff, and then suddenly was on a flight from France to Taured. I went from interrogation to interrogation until I ended up here." Gaglianone sat down in one of the church's dusty benches.

"I've never heard of anything like that, Andrey. Maybe it's a test from Him. But I don't think so. God gives us liberty to sin and face consequences from the sin. Unless he wants to test how faithful you really are, taking you where Catholicism is dead. Angel Republic belongs to the Light Bearer."

"But… Will you stay here? I feel like I can trust you. More than my family, work colleagues or therapist."

"No. I'm going back to the Confederacy in a few months. I miss home. And I have to live with the shame of failing my mission."

"Can you help me, still? At least while you're here. Please, I also miss my home."

"I'll see what I can do. Come back in a few days. I'll be here."


Gaglianone entered his home in a careful manner, so the water wouldn't invade it. He removed his rain boots and his coat and proceeded to the house's bathroom, ready to take a hot shower.

"Where have you been, Husband?" Lisa said, looking at him from the corridor.

"I went to pray after I meet with the doctor. Didn't think you would notice I was half an hour late."

"Come with me, please." She walked to the kitchen. He followed reluctantly. Under the sink, a massive hole was filling the floor with the muddy water from the garden. Almost all of the plates were shattered, the fridge broken, and all food their food floated on the water. On the ceiling, a massive swarm of insects was eating the wood and infiltrating the walls.

"What the fuck? Who did this, Lisa? You? The kids? Why haven't you messaged me, for fuck's sake?"

"You're not Andrey. You were right all along. The house is trying to give us a message. There's an intruder living with us."

"Oh, sure there is! And he made a fucking hole in our wall! Lisa, we need to close

337

this thing and call an exterminator! Why haven't you done this yet? Did you even call the cops? Someone carved a hole in our kitchen, Lisa!"

"You really aren't Andrey Gaglianone. I don't know who or what you are, but you are not him. My husband is still missing."

"Guess what, I don't know who you are, either! You're all fucking insane on this island!" Gaglianone was pissed now. He stormed away from the kitchen, accessed the bathroom, locked the door, and removed his clothes in order to shower. He turned the water on and went under it. The heat calmed him down and comforted his soul, a respite from the wet, cold day.

Suddenly, the locked bathroom door opened and a pale woman with black eyes full of tears entered, carrying a long dagger.

"*Lisa! Help!*" He grabbed the first thing he saw, which happened to be a towel, and threw it at the bizarre woman. It made no difference, and she came closer, raising her blade.

"*Lisa! LISA!*" He tried to run away, but slipped and fell to the floor.

"Leave. You don't belong here. Your wrong presence deforms me. Leave before I kill you," she whispered. Suddenly, a wave of dark-green light flooded the toilet, and the woman disappeared on the blink of an eye.

Lisa entered the room, with a green lamp on her hand and a kitchen-knife on the other one.

"I'm sorry. You were right all along, Husb... Stranger. Augusta never did anything like that, and I've lived here for seventeen years. I'll pack your things. Wait for me outside the house. Your presence is corrupting her. You're not safe here anymore."


The pale moonlight reflected in the cold puddles of water all along the street. Mr. Gaglianone looked at his own reflection, created by a nearby yellow street lamp. His almost-wife had already given him two bags with some of his things. Not all of them, because they belonged to the other "him." She had given him a few Angelian dollars for his troubles, and said farewell. He felt the tears falling down his cheeks. At first, he feared he would never get back home. Then he feared he'd never get used to his new home. And now he saw he wasn't accepted anymore in either of them. For no reason at all.

Dark clouds covered the moon, and rain started falling again. A bolt of lightning struck the power lines, and every light on the street disappeared. Not that anybody cared; they were all used to the darkness.

The tears on his face fell and united with the street's muddy water. The downpour started once again. Thunder roared above him. Nothing in sight but the sound of water and the smell of mud. And then Gaglianone closed his eyes and fell to the ground.

*"'You're living it up at the Hotel California...'"*

As soon as he heard The Eagles playing in distance, Gaglianone got up. He was completely full of sand and wet, but not from rainwater. It was sweat. On the horizon he saw nothing but sand, cactuses, and a few mountains on the horizon. It wasn't night, but the sun was almost gone, and the sky had become a mix of orange and purple. He looked around, searching for the origin of the song. There was a large building with several spotlights in front of it. All doors were open, as if the place was about to receive huge crowds, but there wasn't a living soul in there. It looked like a place where a famous band was about to perform to thousands of people, except neither the band nor the public came.

Gaglianone entered the building, a bit confused, but not knowing what else he could do. It wasn't hard finding the way to the main stage. The place was entirely empty, but there was a man sitting on a chair in the middle of the proscenium. It wasn't hard to recognize the person. It was himself, but wearing the clothes of the Light Bearer, and playing a flute in the rhythm of Hotel California.

He stopped playing the flute and proclaimed, "Death looms over California, my dear myself."

"What? So California does exist? Where I was this whole time? Where am I right now?"

"Does it matter? The Light Bearer will lead California to the ocean. Soon, it will not exist anymore in your reality."

"Oh... The earthquakes... Will California become an island? That's what you're saying?"

"I don't speak. I'm inside you, Andrew. I can't tell you something that you already know. I'm just using my light to show you what you know but can't see."

"I've been stuck in a reality that isn't mine for a month! If your reason to exist is to guide me, why don't you fucking do it?"

"I'm merely living manifestation from your thoughts, Andrew. On this island, reality flows in a different manner. You know that. The only way to find reason in the wreckage of a madman's mind is to join an asylum."

"So the only way I can go back home, or at least find out where I am..."

"Is by embracing who you are now."


Lisa woke up with the bedroom door opening. There was Andrey Gaglianone, carrying his bags in his hands.

"I'm ready to be myself again. For the first time after almost four months."


Gaglianone had barely arrived home from work when his doorbell rang. Without hesitation, he opened it, even though he was still wearing his cook uniform.

"Mr. Gaglianone, I've been trying to call you for quite a long time. I am leaving for Virginia in three days, but I felt like I needed to hand you what I found before I go."

"How did you find me?" Gaglianone asked. He had already forgotten that two months ago he had visited the Catholic Church.

"I searched your name on and found out you work at a restaurant. From there, it wasn't hard to locate your house. Your case really intrigued me, and I understand your reasons for possibly not wanting to find out more about it. But with what I discovered, well... you need to know this. Can I come in?"

"Of course, Priest." Andrey guided his unexpected guest to the living room. The priest opened his suitcase and removed a seemingly very old book:

### Combating Heresy on the Mythology of Hyyperswamp

"See, this book was written by an Irish missionary called John Parlor in the early nineteenth century. The letters weren't there yet, but the city of Lost Angel had already existed for some time, and the Light Bearer statue had already been in its place for a few centuries."

"Yes. What you're saying is common knowledge."

"Keep listening. In 1876, a great flood drowned most of the island, destroying an exceptionally high number of buildings, houses and historical sites. One of the most affected ones was the Angelian Folklore Museum. Nothing from it survived, but Parlor transcribed much of the information for the book. You see, there's a ritual called *Replacement*, in which the subject can make a deal with the Light Bearer to get transported to a new life. The individual gets replaced with another version of himself in their own reality, and in exchange leaves for a better one."

"So, you're saying the real Andrey..."

"Has replaced you with him. See, for the ritual to be completed, one has to kill both him and his other reality counterpart. Kill another version of himself from another dimension."

"But I wasn't killed. I died in an earthquake. And even if I didn't, how would he kill someone from another dimension?"

"There's actually one way, according to the Angelian tales. It's a ritual called *Multi-Harm*. The subject must offer the Light Bearer something in exchange for harming someone. Usually, pain and suffering on a massive level. It can be yours, or from other people. What I'm saying is, this is how you ended up in Lost Angel. Your predecessor caused massive pain to someone, killed himself, and successfully exchanged himself with you."

"He disappeared two months before I arrived. In a flood."

"Your restaurant provides food for the crew from the Main Pumping Station, doesn't it? The one that malfunctioned and caused the flood three months ago."

"Oh... Oh my God..." Gaglianone stood up in pure horror.

"Your predecessor probably poisoned or drugged the water."

"This means that unless I make the same ritual, I'm not going back home?"

"The thing is, the pact is already signed. It wasn't you who did it, but another version of you. And that version is not less you than yourself. According to Parlor, both the exchanger and the exchanged are the same person, but in different layers of reality. And it's a dark ritual. What I mean is, you're already doomed. Your soul was sold."

340

"But he's not me! This is unfair! We probably don't even share the same soul!"

"No, you don't. But you have the same essence. And this essence allowed him to use you for his own purposes."

"How can I find the Light Bearer?"

"No, Mr. Gaglianone. This is wrong. I'm leaving for Virginia. I was ordered by the Vatican to take care of a freed slave refugee in Virginia. Come with me. Devout your life to God, and he shall save you from damnation. Staying on this cursed island will drive you insane."

"Priest, I have already accepted who I am now. It took me a long time to see, but fighting reality won't change it. I am Andrey Gaglianone now. Husband of Lisa Gaglianone, father of twin boys."

"You have freedom to decide your fate. But the door is still open. My plane leaves in three days, so if you change your mind, you can come."


Mr. Gaglianone entered the muddy cave with Lisa's green lamp in his hand. It took a bit of reading and asking around local churches, but he found it. North to the city of San Frederico, a beach connected to a cave complex supposedly marked the place where the first settlers arrived, guided by the Light Bearer. The beach was called Stinson Beach, but it and the caves were parts of the Arriving Angel Natural Reserve. A few indigenous tribes from the original colonization still inhabited the place.

As he progressed through the dark and wet cave, his green light revealed dozens of primitive paintings on the walls. Most depicted the Light Bearer or the ocean. Gaglianone kept walking, feeling the temperature getting colder and colder as he continued into the cavern. The stone became more and more refined, composed of marble and gold. The art became beautiful mosaics telling the history of the early days of Angel Republic. He was no longer stepping on rocks and mud, but on stairs made of bricks and copper.

Not long after, Mr. Gaglianone was in the ruins of an ancient underground city, full of buildings and structures dating back to ages before the birth of Christ. An enormous statue of the Light Bearer mounted on a bear was in the main square, carrying a sign in a language long forgotten. He advanced through the city entrance, looking at the huge port linked to an underground river that had connected the city to the surface so many centuries ago. Most buildings were now in pieces, and some regions of the city were clearly flooded or buried on the rocks.

"You're back, huh?"

Gaglianone looked back. An old man wearing a white robe full of green and blue symbols exited the ruins of one of the buildings. He had no eyes, but he carried a green lamp on his hands.

"Are you the Light Bearer? I've been looking for you."

"No. Sadly, I'm not. But I know how you can reach him. Come with me, I'll prepare an herbal tea for us." Even without seeing, the old man knew the way perfectly to a wooden shack in the middle of the city, protected from potential flooding with a primitive pumping system. Around the house, there were several gardens of mush-rooms and fungus, with two other eyeless white-robed monks working on them.

"I sense your smell, Andrey. But it's different now. You're the new Andrey, yes?" A remarkably deep voice said from within the wooden walls.

As the duo approached the house, the door opened, revealing a naked fat man covered in burns. He had no eyes, either. In fact, he didn't have most of his face. Some regions of it were pure bone. Gaglianone fought a desire to flee in terror.

"This new version of Andrey wants to meet with the Light Bearer. I don't know his motives, but I assume he wants revenge on the original Andrey," the guide said.

"No. I don't want revenge. I just want to go back home. Or at least find out why he did this to me," Gaglianone explained.

"Receptionist, prepare the herbal tea. Mr. Gaglianone, please come in with me." He following the old man into the shack.

The place was clearly very, very old. There were some bunk beds in there, and a table carved on the stone next to a cauldron. As both men approached the table, more hooded monks brought wooden chairs for them to sit.

The receptionist approached the cauldron and poured herbs in it, and soon a good smelling yet somehow profane fragrance filled the room.

"Is that a tea or a soup?" Gaglianone asked.

"It depends on who you ask. Is the light the light or the lack of darkness? Is the darkness the darkness or the lack of light? Or both? Soup, tea, doesn't matter. It's the only way to make you see the Light Bearer." As the naked man spoke, other eyeless men came into the house carrying green lamps and chanting.

"So, I was right. The previous Andrey did come to you. And he did seal a deal with the Light Bearer," Andrew said.

"Yes. But don't ask us those questions. Ask the Light Bearer," the naked one said.

"Sir, your tea is ready." The receptionist submerged an empty fish can in the mixture and removed it. The liquid was completely green. It smelled good, but looked dangerous.

"Am I supposed to drink this?"

"If you want to meet the Light Bearer, yes."

Gaglianone took a deep breath and swallowed it all in one gulp. It was marvelous. And terrible. And darkness.


"What the..." Andrew got up from the floor. He was terribly dizzy. Somehow, he was not in the underground wooden shack anymore. He was again in the middle of Lost Angel, seeing the Light Bearer statue and the Hyyperswamp letters on the horizon. His house was there, too, but completely destroyed. The floor was flooded, and hundreds of mangled bodies floated around him... including Lisa and the twin boys.

The statue eyes began to glow green, and its torch now a beautiful green flame.

"*Welcome, Andrew Gaglianone.*" The deep and alien voice came from inside the

342

statue. Not as though the statue itself was alive, but as though it were the microphone for something much greater.

"Light Bearer, I came to offer you my soul and life in this reality, plus the souls of any innocents you require, in exchange for me to go back to my original world."

"*It can be done. But you know the consequences of such actions?*"

"Yes. I know the consequences. And am ready to face them."

"*Our deal is then done. But know, Andrey, that even in California, you won't forget Angel Republic. More and more earthquakes will shatter the land. Soon, I shall guide yet another version of Angel Republic to the ocean. And that version is yours.*"


"So, what changed your mind? I'm so glad you left a possible sinful life to live for our lord," the priest asked. He took a sip of soda and settled into his seat. Even though the airplane was completely full of people, the chairs were very comfortable.

"That's the thing, Father. I haven't changed my mind. And I'm going back home now," Gaglianone said as he opened his handbag and removed a revolver.

# NIGHT IN WILLOW WASH

## CRAIG DEUTSCHE

"Are you ready to order?" The waitress was pleasant and offered coffee even before I asked. I'd been to the Crowbar Café many times, but was a bit surprised to see a new cook in the kitchen at the back of the room. The girl who had asked seemed familiar, but I wasn't sure. I knew the menu without even looking, and as I was alone, I took a stool at the counter. This was the Crowbar Café in Shoshone California.

"Do you have sourdough toast?" I asked. When she nodded "yes," I placed the rest of my order: the one egg breakfast with sausage and toast. I pushed the small cream pitcher off to the side. I needed black coffee to wake up after a poor night's sleep, and I was trying to make sense of those last those eight hours.

I often come to the desert to get away from the stresses that go with living in Los Angeles. Instead of a city of auto traffic, robocalls, and trash mail, this small town in eastern California provides a refuge. The silence, dark skies, and open vistas restore me. And I value the people here who seem to be in no hurry and who are not obsessed with national politics or Hollywood scandals. We can talk about birds migrating, habitat restoration projects in the marsh, and the opening of a brew pub in nearby Tecopa. It is a blessing. This was another of these trips, and with one exception, it had been all I might have wanted. It was that exception that preoccupied me.

I never take a room in a motel if there is a way to avoid it. If I wanted a roof over my head, I could have stayed home. As always, I had found some open land and slept out on the ground. Even a tent would have been confining, and I used only a ground cloth, a thin pad, and a sleeping bag. Instead of following a small dirt road into the hills behind Shoshone, this time I drove several miles east past a hot springs resort and then south. The road descended along one of the small washes near the Amargosa River. At its end I left my car to walk half a mile farther. My only concession to the weather was to put my gear at the very side of the wash under some over-

344

hanging reeds. If the sky were clear, there could be a heavy dew, but with branches overhead, my sleeping bag would be no worse than damp. It was already dark when I settled in, and after reading for an hour by headlamp, I closed up my bag and fell asleep.

It must have been several hours later when I woke, and I'm not even sure what had roused me. A third-quarter moon was peeking through a scattering of clouds that had gathered in the past few hours. The light was very odd, and where it reached the far side of the wash, a faint reflection came off the sand. Farther along, there was a low fog, and the opposite bank seemed to shimmer and then fade in the haze. For a moment, moonlight fell on the bushes beside me, and then a cloud cast me into a shadow. The fact that it was October and less than a week till Halloween must have shaped my consciousness.

When I had arrived at this place earlier in the evening, a gentle breeze had been blowing up the canyon. The sound of rustling leaves had been soothing, but now the air was motionless, and the tiny frogs that had been calling were silent. Even the highway that might have been heard in the distance, made no sound. I'm not sure why I didn't try to go back to sleep; it was as if I was expecting something to happen. At first, I wasn't sure, but then after a few moments, I could hear a scraping noise farther up the wash, then silence, then the sound again. A weak light, certainly a headlamp, moved among the tamarisk and then vanished. When I heard the sound again, it was closer. A cloud had covered the moon, and with the light turned off, the unknown person was invisible. I might have wished for moonlight to help me see, but I'll admit to being glad that I was not visible myself. Next, although it was faint, there was a distinct voice and then a second voice. In the dark, two people were somewhere walking, shuffling, and picking their way along the rocks and sand of the stream bed. They spoke only in whispers. The deeper voice said something, and the second voice replied: "This doesn't seem right. Are you sure...?"

The first voice, the deeper voice, was now a bit louder. "Keep going. We can't be seen, and we'll be fine." The voices stopped, and as the clouds shifted, two shapes appeared off in the fog. They stood pointing first one way and then another. One of them swept his light along the bushes and over the far bank. In my sleeping bag under the reeds, I surely must have held my breath. Then the footsteps continued, and I saw the pair slowly moving on down the wash. After ten minutes, it was again silent, and when the moon came out, the wash was as it had been in the early evening. I needed a long time to fall asleep, and it seemed only minutes till the first light of morning appeared in the east.

I had been lost in these thoughts but was brought back to the present when I heard the waitress ask, "Cream or sugar?" She was speaking to a fellow who had taken another stool at the counter. His tan uniform and shoulder patch identified him as a deputy sheriff of Inyo County. His elbows were on the counter, and he was holding his coffee cup with both hands, apparently to warm them. His shirt had come loose on one side, and his pant legs and shoes were covered with dust. He shook his head and made some excuse for not hearing her at first. It would be sugar, and then he ordered orange juice and a short stack with syrup. The waitress refilled his coffee. The name on his shirt read "Milton."

I could not help myself and commented, "It looks as if you've been out last night. I hope you're paid for extra duty." I was trying to be pleasant.

His only reaction was a slight tilt of his head and the words, "Yes, out with my buddy, but at least he's off now and on his way home."

I suggested, "It must have been an emergency to bring you out at night."

To this, he gave half a smile. "Yes and no. At least it turned out well." I raised my eyebrows and tried to suggest that he go on. The events must have bothered him because he began talking. It was as if he needed to get something off his shoulders. Essentially his story was as follows.

Yesterday he had been notified of an escape from the prison at Jean, Nevada, only a short distance across the state line. Two inmates in different parts of the prison had been missing at the evening count. One of the inmates had been under careful guard in the more secure part of the prison. The other was a newer and much younger fellow in general confinement. It had been a clever and well-planned escape. The older prisoner had been convicted years ago for auto theft, but this time he was in for murder. It was a notably violent death, a drug deal gone bad, and the victim had to be identified from the pieces found in a supermarket dumpster in Pahrump. The deputy shook his head. "He was absolutely crazy. He should've been in the high-security mental facility out in Ely."

The waitress brought my eggs, and for a minute the conversation lagged. Ketchup was already in front of me. A parade of motorcycles went past on the highway in front of the café. Although I could only hear them, the roar suggested big Harleys on their way north to Death Valley National Park. I had to suspect that half of their machines cost more than my old Mitsubishi ever did. While I wondered about the rest of the story, another deputy came in the door and looked around. The fellow next to me smiled and said, "Hi, Ben. Glad to see you. I'll check you in, and then I go off duty, thank God."

The waitress arrived with Milton's order, and he moved over to the table where Ben was sitting. She brought a second coffee, and the two began talking quietly. Ben was a new hire, and had not yet been informed about the events of the night. "All they told me from the briefing was that two prisoners had escaped from Jean, and that you had been out somewhere on the search."

Milton was quieter, and I had some difficulty hearing his response. "Yes, the two of us spent a hell of a night out in Willow Wash. It seems that when the Kelson murder had been committed three years ago, the perpetrator had been finally tracked and apprehended at a small, hidden camp in the upper end of that wash. The Nevada State Troopers believed the camp might be a destination for the pair, and because this was near Tecopa, they asked our department for help. It was all rather a mess getting the facts straight."

Another motorcycle went by outside the café, and so without exact words, I could only gather the sense of what they said next. Apparently, Milton and his partner, Jeff, spent hours working their way through the brush to reach the camp. Milton indicated a torn cuff on one of his pant legs and said, "It was a hell of a place to find."

"But you did find it?" Ben asked.

By now my coffee was cold, but I pretended to drink it slowly and read the advertising on the back side of the menu. Milton went on.

"We drove to the wash and stopped where the road ended. There was another car parked, and it seemed that we might be on the track. From there we walked and searched. You have no idea how deceptive the ground is in the dark... and the desert thorns are just nasty. We did our best to be quiet, because the two fugitives were certainly armed. No sense giving them a free target. Ultimately we did find the camp, but there was nothing there."

If these words had come from Heaven, they could not have been more welcome to me. Everything made sense, and I knew who had passed my camp during the night.

It was time for me to pay my bill, but the waitress was busy with others who had come into the café and were sitting at nearby tables: a couple in motorcycle leathers, two young people in tie-dyed Tee shirts, and a family of four in a farther corner. The two children were coloring the paper placemats with the outlines of a stagecoach and a horseman alongside. I assumed that the story had been finished, but Milton had still more to say. He was certainly tired, and he spoke slowly.

"The camp, if you could call it that, was in a tiny alcove on a side bank. There was a mound of brush in front but nothing inside... well, yes, a few rusted tin cans and the remnants of a fire ring. With just our headlamps, we couldn't be sure if anyone had been there recently... but all the same, it was a wild goose chase. We followed orders and had to be sure that nothing was missed. By sunrise we had searched the entire Upper Willow Wash, and then went back down to where we left the cruiser. God knows where those two went, but it wasn't here."

I looked over and saw a shadow go over could the deputy's face. His expression was one of visible relief as he said, "I'm just as glad that we didn't find that pair in the dark."

The room began to spin around me, and the hum of the refrigerator grew louder and louder. I could see the moon shadows of the wash moving through my mind. I had spent the night camped in the Lower Willow wash farther downstream. The deputies had never been past my camp.

# DOWNTOWN SAN DIEGO

## WILL SWANSON

It's so beautiful down in San Diego. It's a great place for people to see when touring the land of beautiful beaches and warm water. You can spend all day observing nature and enjoying a perfect climate, providing you avoid the traffic that plagues the area.

The old streets of downtown seem so inviting with their gas lit lamps, a warm peaceful glow that invites you to think about the good times you've had and the wonderful memories others must have other the past century, but that would not include those of the infamous Adelaide Brown.

In 1874, the streets of San Diego were definitely less populated and a whole lot dustier than they are today, but when Adelaide arrived there, she couldn't have been happier; she finally had a lead on her brother's whereabouts. He was here somewhere.

He had left the eastern seaboard four years prior, searching for his future. He wanted to step out from the family name and show that he had the gumption to succeed. He would be a self-made man.

He had gone out west as a man who knew iron and ships. He didn't like to be out in the ocean much, but he enjoyed building them, designing them, and walking around in their unfinished hulls, inspecting for cracks or fissures—his specialty.

He wrote letters as he traveled west. His sister was always glad to hear of his progress as she took over the family business at home. When it came to safes, lock boxes, and anything that could be made of the highest quality steel, her family was the best; Brown and Co. were who you wanted if money was no object. It was her brother who learned everything. Generations of skills and family secrets ended up working through not only his hands, but how he thought about the metal.

He made it to San Diego safely and managed to get hired on at a local company that built trains. It wasn't where he'd hoped to start, but it was something, and it provided a contact that would prove priceless.

Randall met William Wirt Winchester as he was standing in the engine of a quiet train a few tracks over from the rails where active trains flew past. A man came up to see the very same thing he had: an engine that had been designed and built to be beautiful. Whether it would be as fast as the designer had hoped was never to be known; the project was never finished. But it was the great machine that brought them together.

They both stared at it, Randall from inside, William from the exterior.

"It's amazing..." Randall breathed, not knowing the other man was standing out there.

"Yes, on that we agree," William replied, scaring the young man inside.

It was a moment that started a very profitable career for them both: The man who knew steel better than anyone in the area, and a man who needed the best steel for a company that relied solely on the quality of metalworks.

Randall wrote his sister a few times as things became exciting for him. He was being contracted all over the area for anything that required exceptional skills in dealing with steels and alloys. His connection with Winchester had opened all of the doors; he had more work than he ever hoped he would, and saw things he never thought possible.

But he also earned a sizeable following of men that resented his knowledge and otherworldly connection to metal.

Given the small population and the wild lands not far beyond the city limits, Adelaide started to worry. Randall, however, considered it nothing but petty jealousy. He knew no man would cross him. Winchester and all of the other men he worked for valued him too highly to let anything happen. He was watched over. He knew it, and his enemies knew it.

But as his letters back home dwindled and then died out completely, his sister was far from assured of his safety.

She reached out to Winchester to find out about her brother, but the letters were never answered. She slowly grew suspicious. Randall had sent home engravings, trinkets, and marked pieces from the Winchester factory along with his letters so she could see the factory's technology. So she knew that Randall did in fact have a bond with this man, that this man needed him, and that he was part of the genius that the company was known for. That made her wonder just how much credit her brother's name would steal if anyone else knew how important he was to Winchester's success.

Four long years passed. They were too much for her; she needed to find him. She hoped he was alive. She *needed* him to be alive.

Her trip to San Diego had been smooth and eventless. But the closer she came, the more she knew something was wrong. She had no proof, but she sensed, somehow, that he was in trouble. She cursed herself for waiting too long.

"Why, no, Miss Adelaide. We haven't seen him in weeks," Sarah Winchester, William's wife, told her when she met her at the door. She made no mention of the unanswered letters, and showed no hostility or even questionable wording that suggested she either knew the answer to, or was offended by, Adelaide's questions. "He worked for my husband frequently, but he told us of a large ship that needed his atten-

349

tion further south, down in San Diego at the port. He said that he must attend to it, but would return as soon as he could."

"We haven't seen him since." William seemingly appeared out of nowhere. "I am not concerned that he hasn't yet returned. It is a very large ship, and revolutionary. I have never seen him as excited as he was that day."

Adelaide thanked them for their hospitality and help in locating Randall, but she refused their offer to stay. She couldn't delay her quest any longer; her spirit would not let her rest until she found her brother.

She arrived in San Diego with the name of the ship's grantor. He would know everyone involved in the construction of the ship, and he would know where to find them. He would surely know her brother.

Edmund Gage was connected to everything in southern California, yet no one knew him from Adam on the streets of this city or any other. He was the man that made things happen. He never accepted any credit, never signed the deeds, never showed up in any press. But he was always there, always involved.

"I am sorry, Miss Adelaide. He hasn't been at the shipyard for two weeks. I thought he'd given up after he discovered the seams would not hold. He was distraught, you see. He kept drawing diagrams and writing out theories, but they all ended up crumpled or burned the next morning…"

He was being honest with her; of that she had no doubt.

"Was the foreman embarrassed by what he found?"

"No, Mister McKay was very fond of Randall. His discoveries about the hull made the newer ships faster and stronger. It was all due to your brother."

"Is Mister McKay still working on this ship?"

"No. He returned back east and took on another project at my insistence. His reputation wasn't tarnished by that ship; it wasn't his own design. He took over for another."

"What happened to the other man?"

"He hanged himself." Gage looked down, saddened. "He couldn't bear the damage to his pride."

"Would he have blamed my brother?"

"No. He was deceased before your brother ever came here."

There was nothing left to discuss, so Adelaide gave the appropriate pleasantries, then made her way to her hotel. She could do no more for the night.

She woke after a restless night; though exhausted, she had been far too worried to sleep.

That morning, Edmund Gage introduced her to a young man. "This is Josh McCreedy. He worked with your brother, and was his friend. He knew him better than anybody else. He can help you around the city, and show you the places Randall frequented."

This was yet another example of Edmund's generous help. Adelaide knew it was because he felt sympathy for her.

"He is completely at your disposal," Edmund continued. "So am I."

McCreedy had rough hands, his skin tarnished from the dust and shavings of raw steel. But this was nothing new to her; half the men she had ever known, including her those in her family, looked like McCreedy. In her experience, the exterior rarely matched the man inside, and such was the case with Josh. She found him gentle, kind, and rather intelligent, too.

He made some small talk, enough to avoid awkward silences, but casual enough to keep her comfortable; he was, after all, very aware of the boundaries a man should keep.

He took her to the bar where he and Randall went—or more accurately, where he used to go to find Randall.

"He used to sit here?" Adelaide narrowed in on a table at the window. "He liked to look out that window, didn't he?"

"How did you know that?"

"The view. See that bridge out there, those steel girders…" She pointed towards the skyline. "And that water tower there."

McCreedy nodded yes. She met his eyes for a moment, then averted her gaze.

"The craftsmanship of both the bridge and water tower is tremendous. One must be strong yet flexible. The other must be watertight and able to withstand earthquakes and weather." Her voice strengthened "He had admiration for both. He was trying to apply it to the ship, trying to find enough… the right inspiration."

She sat there looking through her brother's eyes, and understood his desire to be there in the bar. But still, she felt nothing that explained his sudden disappearance.

"How was he? Before he disappeared?" She looked at McCreedy, who seemed reluctant to answer that question "Did he change?"

"He did begin to act irrationally. He spoke to himself…" He stopped suddenly, a look of fear spreading across his face. "I can take you to the ship."

He spoke with such trepidation that the mere mention of the ship made her fear for her own wellbeing. But she decided she would not rest until she found out what had happened to her brother. Until she *found* her brother.


Adelaide and McCreedy arrived at the boat yard after a few detours, mostly places that Randall frequented. He ate here, bought drafting supplies there, liked to walk there. Adelaide suspected McCreedy was stalling to avoid actually getting to the boat, but after much insistence on her part, they went to the shipyard. McCreedy's pale skin and flushed face explained more than his words ever could. He did not want to be there.

"It's the boat in slip thirty-two." He pointed down the dock.

"I thought my brother said it wasn't seaworthy?"

"It's not. It's on skids. Only the bottom few feet are in the water." Though he spoke with respect for her, he absolutely refused to go any further. "I will wait for you here."

She didn't try to dissuade him; there was no way he was going to change his mind. She had been around ships, multi-ton machinery, large casting plants and loud metal working facilities. She had no fear of going alone, and with her nerves so raw she pitied anyone that might try to tell her she couldn't be there.

She counted off the slip numbers as she walked. She didn't know what to expect, but the air seemed heavier here, the clouds darker. Even the warmth of the sun started to fade, growing worse with every step.

Finally, she saw the ship. It was magnificent. She understood why her brother would toil over it. It needed to be set free. It was a swan that needed to fly. She stood on the wooden decking looking in. The steps were only twenty feet away. She could climb into it easily. There was no one around to stop her. But she could not get her feet to move. Something was wrong.

"Adelaide," she told herself, "steel your nerves. Go." With that, she convinced herself to move, into climbing the step up and then descending the seventeen feet into the unfinished hull.

She saw the smooth steel of the hull, and the area where the welding had faltered. The seams that had so concerned her brother were polished to a shine. As she reached out to touch it, she immediately realized that it must have been her brother's hands that had polished it so.

"Go away." A voice emanated from somewhere in the ship, a familiar voice.

She turned to listen. Nothing. So she reached out again and felt the smoothness of the steel under her palm.

"GO AWAY!" Air rushed past her. The voice much louder, coming from everywhere at once. It even seemed to be passing through her

*That voice.* It reminded her of her father, but the pitch was more like her brother's.

"*GO AWAY!*" This time she not only heard it, but *felt* it coming through the metal. It wasn't a man standing somewhere nearby, it wasn't an echo elsewhere in the hull. It came from the depths of the ocean. It was pain of the steel.

She felt it again. The rush of air was thick and heavy, blowing her off balance and demolishing her confidence and strength. She started to fall when she felt a man's hand grab her firmly. Then a second hand took her by the other side. She was hoisted quickly up the stairs and rushed away up the wood planking.

It wasn't until she was sitting on the gateway to the docks that she realized that it had been McCreedy. He sat beside her. She looked around slowly. There were no other people nearby, and the sun had gone low into the sky. It was almost night.

"How long have I been sitting here?" she asked.

"Maybe twenty minutes."

"But it's almost night…"

McCreedy looked around and nodded in agreement.

"Who helped you lift me out of there?"

"I was the only one there, ma'am." He looked at her oddly. "I was worried, and came to look for you. I saw no one else… heard the voice when I got near the ship. I heard it talking to you."

He said no more. He had heard that voice before, and knew it was no human that spoke. He knew that it had been Randall who brought that voice alive, and that it was not something that was supposed to exist in this world.

"Where did that voice come from?"

He turned his head to the side and closed his eyes. "Let me take you away from here. It's not a good place for you."

She nodded and held her hand up for him to take. She was done with this for today; she was no longer well, and she was keenly aware of that fact.


They walked away together. McCreedy held her hand, to help her balance more than anything. As there was no one around, neither he nor Adelaide found it inappropriate. They spoke of nothing. They had both experienced something that unsettled them; his experience had occurred weeks earlier and scared him to his very core. He'd left that metal coffin, swearing he would never go back. But for her, he had made the exception.

Adelaide was still reeling from the loss of time, the psychological blow from that voice, and her brother's connection to it all.

She finally broke the silence. "Did he ever speak of that voice?"

"He talked with it. He only talked to himself in the beginning. We paid little attention. He was always mumbling to himself, figuring things out on his own, working out the details, and then he'd come to us with a plan." McCreedy looked behind them. He felt like they were being followed, but dismissed it as an effect from the haunting from the ship. "It was only a few days before we all left that we started to hear the voice answer him back. At first, we thought there was someone else. When we discovered there wasn't anyone else, we put it down to being an echo. But then the voice started to get louder, started to answer him, to threaten him…"

The gas lamps guiding them back to her hotel started to flicker, and a man stepped out of the shadows as they passed the patent office, approaching them slowly.

"Randall!" Adelaide recognized him instantly even with his unkempt hair, soot-covered face, and ragged, dirty clothes.

"Go away." He spoke it as though in a dream. But as he lifted his eyes to her face, he spoke again. The words came out with more venom "*Go away.*"

Adelaide realized he wasn't ordering her; he was mimicking the words from the hull, right down to the tone and pitch.

She took a few steps toward him. McCreedy stayed near her, just in case.

She saw that Randall's hands were blistered deeply, not from heat but from what seemed to be a chemical burn. His face was deeply blackened by the powder that came from working on heavy machinery—the fine steel powder that will tarnish every crack no matter how small. If she had not known him, and were it not for the metallic stench coming off him, she might have assumed he'd stepped out of a coal mine.

"Randall, it's me, Adelaide." She looked into his eyes and gently took his hands in hers. "It's your sister."

"Go away," he mumbled.

"Randall…" She began to cry. He was so badly hurt, ruined inside.

"I knew you were still here!" A man's voice came out of the shadows. He burst from the darkness, running full speed at Randall with a large knife drawn.

Adelaide pulled her hands from her brother's, but had no time to get out of the way.

The knife was coming for her chest when Randall suddenly seemed to wake. He knocked her out of the way at the last moment, taking the knife into his ribs. Then he grabbed the attacker and lifted him off his feet, swinging him away from Adelaide.

Randall shoved him into a light pole with such force the man's neck broke. The steel pole bent under the impact.

"You will harm no more," Randall gasped.

McCreedy rushed over and helped Adelaide to her feet as Randall looked back at her. He saw the lights flickering around them, heard the buildup of pressure in the tubes that fed the light. His eyes were aglow with memories, brilliant and bright. He raised a hand, a motion that simultaneously reached for her and warded her off.

Adelaide wanted to run to him, but McCreedy understood Randall's gesture and would not let her approach.

"Adelaide." Randall spoke her name with love and fondness, and right then she knew he remembered her.

Then came a *pop* as the gas tube finally burst behind him. McCreedy spun her away from the light, from her brother, positioning himself so that he shielded her. Then the light exploded.

The street lit up with such brilliance it looked like sunrise.

"Randall!" She tried to get out of McCreedy's arms, but he would not let her, no matter how she struggled. Flaming pieces of metal landed all around them. One hit McCreedy in the back, another in the legs, but he would not budge.

"Randall!" She twisted and managed to catch a glimpse of her brother between the McCreedy's arm and body. The metallic dust covering her brother's body ignited and burned white hot. Red mist following soon after, encircling him and growing until he was no longer there, disappeared into the flames.

The gas line roared, producing a fountain of flame where her brother had stood only seconds before.

She finally managed to escape McCreedy's grip as the flames dwindled down and his own pain overcame the adrenaline. Adelaide watched as the red afterglow disappeared and the normal flames drew crowds of people who had been awakened by the explosion.

She wept for her brother, but knew that she would be much worse off herself had it not been for the brave man kneeling on the ground nearby. The clothes on his back had burnt away. The skin beneath was both bloody and blistered.

"Let's get you to a hospital." She helped him up as gently as possible. He nodded slightly and leaned against her. As they hobbled toward the hospital, she heard Edmund's voice echoing in her head. *"He will look out for you…"*

. . .

The people that gathered saw the blackened corpse of the man on the ground as the flames disappeared, leaving only a dim red glow from the remaining gas lamps. They couldn't tell who he was in the darkness.

"I'm glad to see you're well!" Edmund had heard of the explosion, but had waited almost a week before coming in to see McCreedy. He'd first made sure that Adelaide was taken care of. Although she came to see McCreedy daily, Edmund had followed the doctor's recommendation that McCreedy refrain from any additional company until he had healed. "I've taken care of all the expenses for your hospital stay, as well as the work you've missed. You have your choice of projects as soon as you feel up to it... but no hurry."

"Thank you." McCreedy sat up. Though in a great deal of pain, he could move, as long as he was careful not to tear the bandages or stitches. "Who was the man that attacked her?"

"John Sebastian." He handed the paperwork to Adelaide, who held it out for McCreedy to see. "He was the man who procured the metal for the ship... and for the lights along the walk."

"The steel was bad," she said quietly. "Cheapened with weak alloys. The ship's design wasn't at fault. It was the metal."

"And the street lights?" Edmund was surprised by her knowledge of the metals. He knew Randall had been quite gifted. Maybe it was in their blood.

"The same cheap, weak steel." She looked out the window. McCreedy took her hand. She smiled slightly.

"I still don't quite understand what happened to Randall's body." Edmund had heard Adelaide's explanation, that he had disappeared into the air like a ghost. She even described the metal burns and the gas bubble, and the brilliance of the blast. But the other man, although burned to a crisp, was there. His body still existed.

"He's..." McCreedy hesitated; whether due to internal or external pain, it was hard to tell. "He's here."

Edmund looked at him, wondering whether or not he was still on some sort of hallucinogen. Adelaide just sat there, holding his hand.

Finally, McCreedy smiled at Adelaide. "I need to get some more sleep." He closed his eyes and mumbled, "I'll show you tomorrow evening..."

Edmund left the room and waited for Adelaide out in the hall. He didn't understand what was going on. He knew that Randall had died, but McCreedy's strange words and Adelaide's lack of reaction brought up more questions than answers.

"I don't want to upset you." Edmund was very polite as he walked down the hallway with Adelaide. "But why does he think Randall is still alive, and you don't?"

"I won't bother trying to explain with words." She looked towards the sunset as they stepped out of the building. "Give me an hour, and I'll let you see for yourself."

355

"Can I take you to dinner while we wait?"

She nodded.


As they ate, Edmund tried to understand what had happened with the metal, how Adelaide knew about it, and how Randall discovered it. She explained her and Randall's upbringing and knowledge, and how her brother's notes pointed out things that shouldn't have been happening with the ship's design.

"He'd figured it out, but he was looking for a way around it. He loved that ship. It was going to be his shining star once it sailed." She looked at Edmund as a deep sadness overcame her. "He was going to come home after it was at sea and prove to me and our family that he had made it, that he had excelled. He was a master craftsman on a level with all of our family, but he had done it on his own. He had made it."

"And now he won't have that chance." Edmund understood her pain now: The knowledge that Randall had been so close to achieving everything, only to have it taken away by a criminal. It wasn't fair. It wasn't right.

She looked outside and saw that the sun had almost completely dipped below the horizon. It was time to go.

Edmund didn't have to be told. He paid the check and they left the restaurant without another word to each other.


She led him down to the streets where Randall had last lived. The sidewalk they stood on was the closest to the marina, nearest the ship and only a block away from where he died.

"I brought Edmund with me. He knows," she spoke into the air.

Edmund stood next to her, wondering what this was all about. He looked around, half-expecting to see Randall walk out from behind a street lamp, or approach from the shadowy area that was just out of reach of the gas light's glow.

As he watched, he noticed the lighting seemed to be changing. Maybe it was just his eyes adjusting, he thought. But then Adelaide nudged his hand and pointed to the nearest lamp. It had changed from a warm yellow glow to tangerine, then to red as they watched.

Edmund checked the other lamps both in front and back of them. None of those seemed affected.

"What's happening?" he asked, frightened.

"He's still here." She smiled at the lamp as it brightened and then faded, the red eventually disappearing and the yellow glow coming back. "He bound himself to that ship. He can't let go of it."

"How do you know this?"

"Because he's my brother." And with that she turned to Edmund, her voice stronger, more commanding. "I would like to stay here in San Diego until the ship can be fixed, until the right materials are in place and it can finally travel as it was meant

356

to. I'll need your help arranging people and permits, but I will supply the knowledge and the foreman."

Edmund already knew who she had in mind. "McCreedy."

"Yes. He has assured me that because he knows the situation now, he'll be able to continue." She looked out at the dark waters, at the ship waiting to be finished so it could fulfill its destiny. "Will you help me?"

He nodded, and with that he recommitted to not only Adelaide, but to Randall's destiny.


Adelaide and McCreedy were married within the year, the ship set out on its maiden voyage in only two. She could often be seen talking to the air on nights when all was either going very well, or when they had hit a stumbling point. The lights would glow and change color as she spoke. She knew she was accepting her own fate by staying, but she gladly went along with it.

The day word arrived that the ship had arrived in Asia was the day she decided to say goodbye. She and McCreedy had fulfilled their promise to her brother, and now it was time to begin their own lives.

Edmund was there for them at every turn, departing only a month before they did when he had decided to move back east for more opportunities, as well as to reunite with the fiancée that waited for him in New York.


"It made it," Adelaide said as she sat upon a bench the city had dedicated to her brother. The metal was smooth under her arm, the quality impeccable. The street lights and everything else that had been built with the compromised steel had been replaced. The safety of the public and the integrity of the city had been restored thanks to her actions and her brother's findings. The mayor was grateful. But when he tried to applaud her, she refused it with great humility. Then she went to the docks to see her brother.

"I am leaving now. Josh and I have married, as you know, and we are going to start our own family." She watched as the light grew red. He was happy for her; she knew that. "I love you..."

She left, and never returned to San Diego, the city where her brother had made his name, the city that he watched over, the city he still looks after even to this day.

Don't believe me? Spend some evenings in downtown San Diego. The lights will glow red even for you... eventually.

# DON'T PICK THE ORANGES

## JOHN KUJAWSKI

There were some strict rules I had to follow when I was in the backyard. This was at my grandparent's house in California. They had a yard that was fenced in and I wasn't to open the metal door to let anything in. I also wasn't supposed to pick any oranges off the tree.

I was tempted not to follow orders back when I was a kid. I was eight years old and curious about life. If something was forbidden, it appealed to me. The whole neighborhood tended to stir my imagination as it was; everything was green and the trees didn't look like ones I had seen in the Midwest. This was Grand Terrace, a quiet part of California that made an impression on me.

Playing in the backyard was one of my favorite parts of the visit when I was in town. I'd be back there alone, happy that I wasn't at school around the teachers and the other kids. At times I thought of ways I could deal with them when I got back home. It always seemed that they should pay for their unfriendliness.

The next-door neighbor my grandparents had was said to be a cruel and hateful woman. I never saw much of her, but at times I could hear her. I think she was on the other side of the fence and she'd often yell out in the kind of language I was never supposed to use but sometimes did.

On this particular day, I wasn't sure what I had heard, but I didn't think it was a person. My guess was it was someone's pet. I knew it wasn't coming from the orange tree or anywhere near it. Whatever it was had been staying outside of the yard. I wondered if it was the neighbor's pet dog and perhaps the woman had hurt its feelings. It sounded sad or wounded. Maybe a cruel kid like the ones I went to school with had gotten near it and caused harm. I was worried.

I did what I wasn't supposed to do and I went to the gate. I unlatched the door and opened it and right away something ran into the yard. At first it went past me, but then it froze, eyes locked on mine. I could tell it wasn't a dog. I sensed it might be some type of a wolf but I don't think was what it was, either. It was a strange grey color that I'd never seen before, and the animal looked sick. Its eyes were red and it was almost as big as I was. I was afraid it was planning on attacking me. It kept staring at me, and drooling.

There was only one thing in the yard that qualified as food. I walked over to the tree and then I picked an orange. I knew I was doing something I shouldn't but I went through with it anyway. I tossed it to the animal, and the thing ate it in one gulp. The animal seemed more like a monster than anything else. I was shaking at the thought of it coming near me.

The next thing I knew, it fell over sideways. It looked like it had fallen asleep. I walked over to it, feeling sick. The sight of the thing was so unsettling I didn't want to see it anymore, but the creature wasn't moving nor breathing. Upon closer inspection, I realized it had died.

I had only tried to satisfy its hunger by giving it the orange, but that one piece of fruit had killed it. I stood still for a while wondering what to. Finally, I went back and closed the gate. As I locked it back up, I looked over at the tree. The oranges were beautiful. I knew I didn't have to tell anyone that I had picked one, and I could always say the dead beast in the yard had jumped the fence.

The only other thing I knew I had to do on that visit to the yard was to pick a couple oranges and hide them. I knew I wanted to take them home.

After all, the kids at school acted like hateful animals, and I'm sure they wouldn't hesitate to steal a couple oranges from me to eat if they saw I had them.

# SOMEWHERE SHORT OF PARADISE

## TROY SEATE

"It's a world of danger where mortals struggle in defiance of the dark," some spaced-out dude once advised. I already knew that because of my previous occupation. Over the years, I had gone on drugs and gone off them. I had witnessed terrible sights and created others. I'd seen the faces of other mercenaries. They could walk and talk and go through the motions, drifting from one assignment to the next, but there was nothing behind their eyes, nothing that mattered. I had reached a time in my life when I could tell anyone who desired my services to take a flying fuck at a rolling donut. Still, if I'd foreseen the future, I suppose I would have turned my jalopy around and never crossed the bridge into the little California coastal town of Seven Fold.

Far from the glitz of L.A. and the culture of San Francisco, it was barely a dot on the map, a place taken little notice of, hardly a paradise, but just the kind of place I had been looking for. It sat against surrounding water—land's end for sure. The buildings huddled close to each other as if for warmth. I liked the look of it in its small-town-America way and believed it to be a place where people grew old together; where a newcomer, if benign enough, could successfully escape from the world, a peaceful little hamlet at the edge of nowhere in which to disappear. I wasn't the kind of man to chew on regret. Sometimes you succeeded, sometimes you failed, but burying my past was exactly what I wanted, a place to push unpleasant recollections from my mind.

Seven Fold's population was no more than seven thousand. It had only one way in and out, across a bridge. I found a low-pressure job in a hardware store. My boss, Castle was his name, was reluctant to take on someone from the outside, but he was getting up in years and could use the help. "I'll take you on if you're sure you want to stay. I can't imagine what Seven Fold could offer a forty-ish man with half his life ahead of him, Bob."

"At the edge of nowhere works for me," I told him. He didn't ask any more questions.

I rented a small apartment over a drugstore. It wasn't much, but I didn't need much, no cozy little nest, just a place to sleep when I could. It was decorated in *Better Homes and Gardens* horrible with thrift store furniture. The rug should have been thrown away years ago, and probably had been, but material things didn't matter. I arranged a sofa where I could watch TV and keep an eye on the approach to the walk-up without being seen. Old habits die hard.

Anyone who took notice of me wouldn't see the history behind my eyes or the body scars. They would only see a rugged man amazingly sturdy for his journey into middle age, and that was a good thing. My workdays were a breeze, but it struck me odd that the store closed before sunset every day. In fact, all the stores in town closed before sunset. That's when I started to notice what was different about the people of Seven Fold. I'd expected residents to hand out cracker-barrel philosophy in the hot spots like the barbershop and store where I worked, but an unnaturally subdued atmosphere hung in the air. People were affable enough if approached, but their expressions seemed to hold something more. In such a small town, I would've thought everyone would know one another by name and make meaningless small talk, but most of them kept to themselves, barely smiling, and their faces twisted with something resembling fear.

On strolls after dark, it seemed strange that I passed no one on the sidewalk. The movie theater was already closed. Even the drugstore was nothing more than another dark doorway on the long street. The nice little town, so quiet and peaceful, had an underbelly of sadness as people almost jolted to their homes at dusk as if running from something.

During my second week of employment, I bade my boss goodnight around six o'clock. A cold rain began as I climbed into my rusty shoebox of a car and headed for my apartment. A few blocks from the hardware store, my rust-bucket died. I could swear at the disloyal piece of shit until doomsday, but it refused to rattle back to life. As I stepped out, the freezing drizzle hit me like a snow ball in the face. Walking the rest of the way was going to suck big time.

Feeling like a drenched rat, I came to an intersection in the middle of town. Across the street I could see Miss Townsend closing up her bread shop while her son Tommy played in icy puddles on the sidewalk. As she finished locking doors, she noticed her son had expanded his water world to a dark alley between her store and an adjoining building. She made haste to gather up Tommy, but something went wrong, very wrong.

With an inhuman screech, a terrifying hulk unlike anything I'd seen in this world leapt from the alley and snatched little Tommy off his feet, leaving nothing but a wet boot behind. The reptilian creature then bounded to the top of an adjacent one-story building, carrying his small victim closely against his body. The image was reminiscent of some assembly-line 1950's Hollywood sci-fi flick without the blast of a soundtrack, but in living color. Dumbfounded, Miss Townsend ran back into her bread shop and turned off the lights. I hadn't escaped a combative world after all.

The creature spotted me. A feral grin showed sharp teeth as the beast clutched the boy ever tighter and disappeared into the darkness. I ran across the street toward the bread shop. I rattled the door. "Go away," Miss Townsend shouted. The streets were deathly still. I retraced my steps past my dead chariot and beyond, back to the hardware store. Its lights seemed reassuring. The only thing I could hear was my slushy footsteps and the pounding of my heart pumping what felt like a thousand beats per minute. I stopped in front of the glass doors and pounded furiously with fists now tightened into frozen coils. Castle opened up.

Tired and frozen, my mouth felt like silly putty. "Holy shit!" I stammered.

"What's up with you, Bob?" Castle asked, his face showing aggravation.

"Something took Miss Townsend's kid. We have to call someone," I warbled, reliving the gruesome event.

Castle's face went pale, but not with fear. He was withholding something from me. He suddenly grabbed my collar and damned near hoisted me off my feet. "Did it follow you here?" he said, spitting his words in my face.

"What?" I asked, confused.

"They own this town. We are like cows in a slaughterhouse." Castle's eyes bulged, his declaration almost bringing him to tears.

"What are they?" I asked, struggling to breathe.

"They're not human. They feed on our flesh, our blood. Why did you come back here? You've put me in great danger." He abruptly let go of my lapels, his balding pate darkening to mottled red and purple.

It was hard to tell if total darkness had conquered the day with the overcast sky and the falling sleet. But as quickly as I had come, Castle grabbed his coat. "I'd take you with me, but… Don't go out again. Stay here in the store till morning." He left through the rear door without another word. I heard his Ford fire up and fly out from the alleyway like a police car tearing down the main drag of some hick town.

"What the fuck?" I made my way to the front counter to call the police when I saw him—a man standing on the corner, cradling what looked like a small child in his arms. I couldn't stand the idea of two souls standing helpless in the rain with that thing running around.

I went to the front door and called to the pair. "Please come in out of the weather."

The man looked in my direction and started to walk toward the door with his bundle. A street lamp blinked on above him, casting a spotlight over the pair. The sight sent a shockwave down my spine. A winter chill embraced me like an ice cream brain-freeze.

With another gliding step, the figure came into sharper focus. It wasn't a man at all. Rather it was one of those creatures, now just a few feet from the door. I conjured every ilk of monster from fables, folklore, and those created around campfires, but this thing beyond the glass was new to my imagined creature's encyclopedia—a hybrid. Its features were clear: pointy ears, yellow-green eyes, and a body covered in scales and hair. It was indeed carrying a child, little Tommy, in fact.

The creature's eyes met mine. I watched in sickening horror as the inhuman thing's lips pulled back from the rows of sharp teeth. A slow carnivorous, rumbling came from its throat. Then the monstrosity, simultaneously reptilian and wolf-like, bit into the child's neck. He tore a large chunk of Tommy's flesh from his body in one bloody pull and fed even as he continued to walk toward me. Holding the morsel in his jaws, the hellishly large and aware eyes remained locked with mine, the gaze seeming to say, "You're next."

I backed away and sprawled into a tool rack. My instincts took over, and I relocked the door. The creature stood at the window and took another bite out of the poor child's body in a Halloween horror of gore. A sharp stab of mingled revulsion and deep sympathy hit me in the gut.

Choking down the better part of the boy's abdomen, the monster leered through the window with something that resembled a canine's bloody smile. A piece of tattered shirt dangled from its jaw. The arrogance of it turned me stone cold with sadness for the child who had become dinner.

Here was death, the lynchpin of my former life, bubbling up once more. I checked the backdoor, then hurried to the store's clearance aisle to arm myself. There wasn't much except for a double-headed ax I hoped could take care of anything in one swift, decisive chop.

When I again looked out the front of the store, the creature was gone. The only thing left was a red splat of blood on the wet glass. *The town belongs to them.* Castle's phrase sped through my mind. I'd not felt terror for a long time, but wasn't ashamed of it now. It wasn't every day you witnessed something straight from hell. Either that or I was in some mental hospital hallucinating all of this. Did people ever really outgrow their fears? I didn't believe so, and now something out of a particularly creative nightmare had stolen and eaten a child.

I curled up behind the front counter and clutched the ax handle tightly. I didn't carry a cellphone; it was too much a part of my previous life, so I set the counter phone next to me and dialed 911 two or three times before realizing the line was dead. The storm or cold or who-knows-what had knocked out the service. Didn't matter anyway. Didn't change my precarious position. The first thing in the morning I planned to head for the Seven Fold police station. I was too exhausted to rest, but I finally drifted away to that nowhere called sleep.


Horrific images filled my troubled sleep through the darkened hours. I'd hoped the visions had all been nightmares, but knew better. I awoke in the store feeling as though I had aged a decade overnight. My hands were cramped and painful as I released the ax handle for the first time since clutching it to my breast the night before. Daylight had returned, so I set the ax on the counter and headed for the door thinking about only one thing—the police.

Blood was still on the glass, but there were no chunks of little Tommy on the sidewalk. The creature had devoured every morsel, I supposed. I carefully left the building and made my way down what seemed to be an endless strip of road, passing my still-stranded heap of a car. The day was overcast and gloomy, but the streets were drying. The town was coming alive. Its residents appeared ignorant of the events that had taken place the night before. I looked at Townsend's Bread Shop and wondered if it would ever open again.

I made my way to the town center, my heart racing in anticipation of telling my story until something else caught my attention, something I hadn't noticed during my few weeks in town. It was a bulletin board littered with dozens of pictures, some dating back to the early nineties. Twenty years of bloodshed, and no saviors for the missing souls of Seven Fold. A cold realization hit me about my new home. It wasn't quite the peaceful little town I'd hoped for.

*They own this town.* The phrase stuck in my mind. Chances were there was no place to turn. I didn't know if the police would help, or perhaps lead the creature straight to me. Should I take the risk in confiding to the cops, I wondered? Shit, maybe the FBI, or the CIA…?

I headed for the police station. I had to find out what reaction my story would elicit.

"I'm Robert Clark. I want to report a murder," I informed the duty officer at the front desk.

The man looked at me wearily. "You're the new guy in town, right?"

"Fairly new."

"Hang on."

The officer left for a moment. When he reappeared, another guy waved me back to his office. It was filled with the smell of too many dead cigarettes.

"Sheriff Cumberland," the man said. He offered me a seat then sat down at his desk, rocked back in his rickety wooden chair, and locked his fingers together on his stomach. "What exactly did you see, Mr. Clark?"

I described the horrible scene in detail. The sheriff's face showed neither concern nor amazement, only curiosity. When I was finished, he said, "Ugly motherfuckers, aren't they?"

"Are you kidding me? I asked incredulously.

"Does this look like a comedy club?"

"That's it?" I asked incredulously.

The detective sighed. "No, that's not it, and it's certainly no joke, but it's more involved than just losing a citizen. Someone disappears. Sometimes someone sees something like you did, but that's not the end of it, not by a long shot." The cop offered me a cigarette. When I declined, he took one himself and lit up. He inhaled deeply and exhaled in satisfied pleasure before continuing his narrative as if recording a documentary. "Ever hear of cryptids, particularly the Beast of Busco?"

"Not hardly."

"I hear tell something showed up in Indiana of all places a while back, something reptilian, similar to what we've got here."

"And?"

"And, a few days will go by, then Tommy will show up again like nothing ever happened."

"What? You lost me."

"I'm saying these creatures somehow absorb their victims, kind of like in that movie, *The Thing* with Kirk Russell, only this ain't Tinseltown."

"Then there's more than one?"

"Oh yeah. They devour someone, and then that someone shows up later like nothing has ever happened. Now, when Tommy comes back the same, what's Miss Townsend going to do? She's going to act like nothing happened and be thankful she got him back."

Cumberland gave me a moment to digest the story.

"Maybe he'll disappear again someday and the thing that became him will come back to get someone else, or maybe it'll just stay, going on like momma's little boy. We've got several of them walking around town now that have come back just as normal as a regular bowel movement. They still have their personalities, too. Not like in *Invasion of the Body Snatchers* where everybody turns into a robot."

Cumberland seemed to be up on his monster movieology. "So the monsters become human," I stated. "They replicate a person like in *The Thing*?"

"Yup, but the people who were taken don't stay around forever."

"So they eventually disappear again."

"Many of the earlier ones have."

"Then returning as a human doesn't last forever?"

"Guess not."

I wondered about Cumberland's background. "Why hasn't everyone moved away?"

"In case those beasts are unique to the town, the populace has agreed to keep it here. Plus, it's hard as hell to accept the impossible, to believe it's real. Especially when you see the victim acting as normal as the day is long." A pause for a long drag on his cigarette. "When I was a teenager, a man was chewed apart and eaten in the presence of several witnesses. The creature got away, of course, and about a week later, ole John shows up at his house as if he had just gone out to collect the morning paper. Well, the man who was sheriff at the time took it upon himself to dispatch ole John with extreme prejudice. Knowing he wasn't really John, he shot him between the eyes right in John's front yard. Guess what happened?"

"Monster retribution?"

"Darn tootin'. Another big-toothed son-of-a-bitch showed up and ate the sheriff before the sun rose the next morning. And guess what else? The sheriff never made a return engagement. So now we have a picture of Tommy to put up on our memorial board in town, just so we don't lose track."

That explained why this sheriff was so blasé about my encounter, afraid of disappearing himself. "So where do they come from? Where do they hide?"

365

Cumberland shrugged. "Other than a little blood, we've never found a trace. Might fly in on a space ship for all we know."

"In spite of what I saw last night, you'll excuse me if I can't quite swallow all this business. I think the best thing for me to do is turn in my resignation at the hardware store, pack my bag, and forget everything I've seen and heard."

I watched as wariness creep into the sheriff's eyes. He shifted uncomfortably in his chair. "That's not so simple now that you saw what you saw. We can't let someone who's witnessed an event go off and tell the world about it. The last thing we need is reporters and media types descending on Seven Fold, something for the rag mags to latch onto. Who knows how the creatures might react? It could be a bloodbath. They might feed on outsiders and go back to their cities, spread and multiply like a deadly virus."

"So people lock themselves inside houses, while outside, a monstrous evil lurks." I could visualize the headline: *Creature eats citizens, spit them out, and sends them home.* "Am I free to go?"

"You know the old line: Just don't leave town." Cumberland's face became as expressionless as uncarved stone. "You chose to come to our friendly confines to escape whatever past you might've had. You've made your bed, so you have to lie in it with the rest of us, as they say."

"No serial killers or cult leaders California is notorious for. Just a hungry monster that shows up, snatches, and dashes, stage left," I offered before leaving Cumberland to his plume of smoke and his smile which was as genuine as a three-dollar bill. Studying the bulletin board filled with photographs, I'd hoped dates had been attached to determine if there was a pattern to the disappearances. "Every so often," was all I'd gotten out of the sheriff. These creatures weren't supernatural, I felt sure, which meant they could be killed. I'd tried to escape my past life by coming to Seven Fold, but how could I run from this? The town was caught between fear and an unholy status-quo, an acceptable level of loss, a marriage consummated in blood. It might not be my fight, but who was better equipped to break the hold on a town held captive? The victims might come back, but at the price of suffering the fate I'd witnessed? Fuck that.

Robert Clark hadn't always been my name. In my past line of work, it had been easy to play the hunter. Maybe I'd even taken pleasure in stalking prey and outmaneuvering a target, never wondering about how long *I* might survive. I'd never thought about guilt or innocence, just about survival, kill or be killed. Now, my life had turned from that dark corner in an attempt to make a fresh start. Coming here was like walking across a bridge from a violent world I'd burned behind me until the night before.

Could fate have placed me here, a person least likely to panic at the sight of a fearsome foe? Maybe I could accomplish what no other outsider could. Maybe this was a way to salvage a handful of redemption from the life I'd left behind on the other side of the Seven Fold Bridge. Maybe...

. . .

People love drama and conflict, but normally prefer it on their television sets rather than in their streets. In Seven Fold, the drama was alive, well, and active. A month passed since Tommy had been the big-toothed creature's main course. He'd returned to the loving arms of his mother a few days after the event, and like all the others, he showed no wear and tear, as good as new. I made a point of talking to the kid, not to discuss that night, but to see if he showed behavior I thought unusual. I ruffled Tommy's hair and gave him a peppermint candy. He looked like every other tow-headed kid around town except for one thing. I didn't get a good look at his face when it was being crunched between the monster's jaws, but there was something about Tommy's eyes, a yellowish ring around the pupils, barely noticeable, that convinced me the townspeople were deluding themselves.

I recalled the advice of another soldier-of-fortune back in the day. "Never trust anyone until you've looked into their eyes, mate. Remember, the eyes."

And there was something more, something deep and profound in the kid's expression, something other than emotion. What I saw in Tommy's face was distant and murky, something alien, but it was his eyes that sealed the deal. As he skipped away, I looked into a display window in the building next to me. Clothed dummies with their blank-eyed expressions stared at me, a look not unlike many Seven Fold inhabitants. From then on, I tried to look into everyone's eyes.

I stayed at my job. Castle never mentioned what happened on that terrible night in front of his store, so I let it slide. Maybe there wasn't a nest of creatures like the sheriff seemed to believe. He claimed no one had ever seen two at a time. Maybe there was only one that somehow absorbed people and then crapped them out as little clones of themselves like disposable children with some unknown expiration date that returned them to their master.

I grew to know my adopted town, as strange as it was. By day, even though people functioned, they wore haunted faces. They ate lunch at downtown restaurants, took in matinee movies, and showed brief flashes of normalcy. But after dark, the streets were abandoned. That's when I came on duty. No one asked me to do this, but stealth was in my blood.

Main Street ran between two rows of low brick buildings. The stores closed at twilight. Only sparsely placed streetlamps radiated dull circles of yellowish light in the darkness luring moths from their hiding places and creating a thousand wild shadows. Not even the blue neon light from a bar window shone to lure customers. My jalopy was running again, but I patrolled the downtown area on foot while wondering what might be watching. Several weeks passed, but the evening I'd been waiting for finally arrived. A breeze stirred up little dust devils of trash and swayed a traffic light on Main Street. It plastered a candy wrapper against one of my trouser legs, the one that concealed an automatic weapon. A block away, a young man and his girlfriend saw me and crossed to the streets opposite side. Did they fear me as much as a human-eating monster? They were taking a huge risk being out, but they were young and apparently foolish. It was hard to remember being young and innocent, if I ever was. They scurried up the street and climbed into a parked car.

"Get the hell out of here," I shouted unpleasantly. They drove away. Maybe I'd saved them from being gator bait, or maybe I hadn't.

Minutes passed as slowly as the pages of a boring novel. I was about to call it a night when the wind stopped. It became as still as death, waiting for the act to follow this quiet prologue. A thin mist rose above the pavement as something moved: a fleeting shadow across the sidewalk. It was cast from above, from the roof behind where I was standing. A sickly-sweet odor descended. Then I heard an ominous sound. A snarl, coming from overhead. I looked up and found myself staring into two carnivorous eyes peering over the edge of the building where I stood. The rest of its face appeared, its jaws snapping with teeth the size of a crocodile's. One scaly arm swooped down. I hit the deck and rolled, barely dodging its clawed reach.

With my knees bent, I unholstered my weapon. If this turned into a lost cause, I'd decided to blow my brains out before letting this thing turn me into a devoured Stepford wife.

As the monstrous form leaped from its perch, I fired a large-caliber, semi-automatic pistol into its mouth. A few serrated teeth shattered as it descended to the street, dazed but not done. I fired into one eye. That shot stopped the beast long enough for me to pull a hunting knife strapped to my other leg and lunge at my target. It sprung forward and would have sunk its remaining teeth into my face had I not managed to shove the mouth upward with my forearm, reacting like the well-oiled killing machine I'd once been. With my head against the monster's throat so it couldn't chomp my head, I drove the knife deep. An unearthly and fearsome sound ripped through the night. Even as the creature's arms closed around me, tearing at my back, I continued to plunge the knife into the scaly, hairy chest until the thing's arms stopped flailing at me. With my last ounce of strength, I raised the pistol in my other hand, put it to the side of the monster's head, and pulled the trigger a third time.

The monster and I fell to the ground together. Yellow ooze leaked out of its mouth. I disengaged from the creature that was no less fearsome in death. My wounds throbbed in sync with the pounding of my heart. I halfway expected the abomination to dematerialize like in a B monster movie, but it lay next to me like an extinct prehistoric beast.

In spite of the three shots and the howls, no one came to investigate. A full moon now covered the street with a satin glow. Night air rushed over me like a cold tongue. No one would come till daylight, when Seven Fold could once again fake it as a peaceful little town. My fleeting sense of accomplishment faded as I rested my back against cold brick. I started to doze when I heard new sounds. They crackled like insects scurrying about. I stopped breathing for a moment, wondering if a hundred little monsters were being produced out of the dead hulk next to me. Then I understood. Rigor mortis, hurried along by the night temperatures, was rearranging the thing.

I sat next to the creature all night and was there still as the sun rose. I looked at the yawning emptiness of the street in either direction. A faint drip—what passed for the creature's blood—ran from the sidewalk into the gutter. People finally began to filter out of their hideaways to the street. A small crowd formed creating a semicircle in front of the building. Their faces turned as pale as cream cheese when they saw the rapidly deteriorating creature near me. I might have expected someone to say, "We're free at last!" or something similar, but there were only slight murmurings and I knew why. I knew the killing of the creature could have side effects. Would the replacement people disappear with its death? If there *were* more than one, would they come for revenge like they had with Seven Fold's former sheriff?

In due time, the current sheriff arrived. Cumberland pushed his way through the lookie-loos and stood as silently as the rest of the crowd.

"I'm the one it didn't get," was all I had to say.


By day, anyone from the outside wouldn't be able to tell Seven Fold from any other little town. People still had to make a living. They drove cars, sat in the coffee shop, looked at their watches, and went about their business. The night was a different story. The sounds from a television or radio, or a traffic light clicking through its cycle was all there was to hear, except for the shuffling of my feet on a sidewalk. I remained in Seven Fold. I believed I had to. Already my former boss, Castle, had quit coming to his hardware store. He wasn't to be seen anywhere, in fact. The nightmare wasn't over, not by a long shot. It hadn't taken hand-to-hand combat with a fantasy-like creature to haunt my dreams. I had been confronting monsters that waited for me from the time I'd been a mercenary.

There was more. As a hired combatant, when an assignment was completed, you were always glad others were dead instead of you. I truly believed I was supposed to die in a double-cross on my last official assignment. Maybe I did. Maybe I'm dead and just haven't figured it out yet. That makes as much sense as protecting the streets of a small town from monsters.

The creature's death had not brought total joy to Mudville. The people had dealt with the issue of monsters in their midst until I showed up and took action. They had engaged in an unbelievable status quo until I upset the apple cart, forcing the town to deal more directly with difficult issues. Shame on me. Would the citizens be angry for what I'd done and retaliate, or be in more fear than ever from the creatures' response at losing one of their own?

That answer I cannot provide, because most of the citizenry slunk back into their former shells without speaking of the event. Cumberland and I removed the carcass and buried it outside of town. I stood vigil over the fresh grave for several nights, just in case, and slept with one eye open when above the drug store, leery of humans as well as creatures.

Still, I had a debt to pay, to the town as well as for past transgressions. Shortly after the incident, two returned people whose pictures were still affixed to the bulletin board re-disappeared. The families of the other replacement people were in a quiet panic of losing what passed for their loved ones. Miss Townsend tried to smuggle little Tommy out of town, but now there were volunteer guards at the bridge checking who came and who went.

Whether I wanted my latest job or not, I will deal with whatever might transpire next. I'm in a small town on a small planet in a small universe, but I have a chance to do something positive rather than continue as a mercenary who left nothing but scars on the world's skin. This time, it's to protect people rather than destroy them. I'm a man who had never fit anywhere perfectly, a real Lone Ranger, but this time I can live with my actions as long as I never forget to look into the eyes.

# THE UNHEARD SOUND ON DEARDROFF ROAD

## CHLOE BECKETT

"Wally. *Wally.* Wally, get the fuck over here."

She jerked on the leash and the pudgy dachshund mutt popped up from his investigation of coyote scat, as if this was the first he was hearing her.

"Move your ass, dog!"

She tapped him lightly on the butt until he finally got up to a reasonable walking pace. She got almost a full minute of walking in before he stopped short again.

"Seriously, Wally, I *need* to get some exercise. My back is killing me. No. More. Sniffs."

But Wally wasn't sniffing. He was tugging backward on the leash, his ears strained back and his eyes filled with panic.

*Oh. We're here again.*

Every time they reached this section of the road, Wally refused to continue. He would tug backwards, ears back and eyes wide, flinging his head around abruptly as if he heard something loud.

"What is it, bud?"

She tugged a little forward but he wouldn't budge. His nailed scraped against the asphalt as he looked up at Jess imploringly.

Begrudgingly, she complied. In the six years she'd had the dog, she had never seen him act like this. Yet every time they walked the road, same thing.

*I wish you'd just go just a* little *bit further, bud.*

Jess loved walking along the acres of walnut orchards and farmhouses, and it was the closest thing to a safe place to walk that she could find. They'd only been in the new house a week, but had already learned that the meth heads in the country took driving conventions very casually. Staying on your side of the road seemed to be optional, at best.

She was happy to be back in the Sierras, though. After less than a year in the Bay, Jess and her soon-to-be husband were dying to get back under the pines.

Granted, Railroad Flat was quite a bit further into the pines than the town she grew up in. But the house had been so much cheaper than the ones closer to town, and they figured the less people and more mountains, the better. Of course, Paul's mom had been haranguing them with fears of bears and tweakers, but Jess assured her that both preferred to keep to themselves. And if they didn't, she always had her Kimber pepper spray pistol.


"He did it again!"

"What, seriously? What a punk," said Paul as he set down a box helpfully labeled 'Random Shit.'

"Yeah, so weird. He can obviously hear something that freaks him out, but I can't tell what it is for the life of me. Hi, girlies," she added, reaching down to pet their two other dogs. Even with their triple leash, she still hadn't gotten used to walking Paul's hyperactive rat terriers with her lazy mini-hound.

Paul shook his head and looked around the room. "Got almost all the kitchen stuff unpacked, but the bedroom's total insanity."

"Ugh," said Jess, as she flopped onto the couch.

"It's okay, we don't have to do any more tonight. Did the walk help your back at all?"

"Not really, since the dummy dog cut it off so fast."

"Fuckin' Wally. Well, fuck it, I'm tired too. I'll roll us up a fatty and we'll call it a day."

"Yesss. Yes, please."


BAM BAM BAM BAM.

Jess woke up in a delirious confusion that quickly turned to panic.

BAM BAM BAM.

"What the fuck is that??" she whispered furiously to Paul.

Paul didn't answer as he fumbled for his glasses and began pulling on random clothes scattered on their bedroom floor.

BAM BAM BAM BAM BAM BAM BAM.

Paul was rounding the corner to the front door, reaching for the shotgun they hadn't gotten around to mounting, but *had* managed to load.

"WHO'S THERE?" Paul shouted.

BAM BAM BAM BAM.

*"WHO'S THERE?"*

"Sheriff!" came a strained voice from behind the door.

Paul and Jess exchanged a quick look. Why hadn't he just said that to begin with? What time was it, anyway?

Jess glanced at the oven clock—2:36 AM.

Paul ran to the door, but stopped to check the peephole before setting the shotgun down.

"Shit," he muttered, and wrenched open the front door.

"There's a fire. You need to leave immediately!"

"What? Where? Where do we go?"

"Toward Deardroff Road," he called as he sprinted back to his car. "*Get out now.*"

Paul shut the door in a daze. He looked up at Jess, his face pale with panic and confusion.

"He sounded scared. Fuck. It must be close. Which way is Deardroff, anyway? Fuck, fuck, fuck."

"I think it's where I walk—either way, let's just get across the river."

They both stood paralyzed for a moment.

"Dogs and meds," said Jess, crashing back into reality.

"Right," said Paul. He starting grabbing their prescriptions from the cabinet, toppling bottles as he searched for a bag. "What about our birth certificates and stuff?"

"Let's just go. Dogs, dogs, dogs," she called as she slipped on some shoes and grabbed her keys.

"Ummm... keys, phone, wallet. Keys, phone, wallet?"

"Right, good call. You ready?"

Paul was looking frantically from left to right for things to grab. Jess looked up at him sternly.

"Babe. Let's just get out of here. Now."

They started for the door.

"Shit, leashes!" Jess called. Paul snagged their triple leash and ran out after her.


"Are you sure it's this way?" Paul was spinning.

"No. But the river's only a few minutes away, let's just get across it."

They began speeding down the tumultuous, snaking highway.

"Shit. I hope this is the right way. Can you see anything?" asked Jess.

Paul craned his head backward. "Holy. Fuck. I see it. It's right by the house. Holy fucking shit."

The flames had already consumed acres of pines and were dancing maniacally a hundred feet in the air. They zoomed toward the sign for Deardroff Rd.

"Yes—YES! It is this way!" Jess cried.

The dogs began to whine excitedly. Almost immediately, they descended into mad yelping and growling, cowering in fear in the back seat.

"Dogs, dogs! Chill, chill, chill, chill, chill," pleaded Jess.

Their wailing had escalated into utter insanity. Wally's shrieking yips had become so intense that he sounded like a fire alarm.

"*DOGS*," Paul bellowed, and swung around to glare at the crazed animals.

He gasped abruptly, and then began to shriek uncontrollably.

"Paul? Paul! What is it? Are we okay?"

Paul ripped at his hair with one hand and pounded the other into the side of his head. He was screaming and sobbing wildly.

"Paul? Baby, what is it?"

Jess pulled her eyes off the slithering road for an instant to look behind her.

Flames, erupting into the night sky. They cackled and twisted, performing their glowing recital.

*But what was that dark patch—how is it twisting too?—those stars don't look right —that twinkle isn't of fire, but of eyes—dark, glittering eyes—impossible—was that an eruption of flames?—how could it be, that unearthly color—that impossible form— climbing, twisting—escaping?—black matted muscles leading to—what, claws?—must be branches—must be a cloud of smoke—but—that mouth—that wretched, gaping mouth—hallowed out of the night into nothingness—laughing—the corners jiggling as if cajoled by puppeteers—that unholy grin erupting in—what?—what was that sound?*

Insane, demonic, silent laughter. The human psyche unable to comprehend anything so revolting and ungodly. Her ears throbbed as the vile creature clawed out of the flaming trees, its vicious grimace widening to the stars it grasped for.


They awoke the next morning bedraggled and sore, crumpled into the front seats of their car. It took Jess a few weary blinks to remember that they had parked in the alley behind the community park in town. A young woman was walking her two boys to the playground, discreetly and suspiciously eyeing them, no doubt wondering if they were homeless or hungover.

Jess looked over and saw Paul already awake, reclined in the passenger seat looking up at the ceiling with a blank expression.

"Morning, babe," she said, rousing him from his torpor.

He looked over at her, his eyes strained, and said nothing.

Jess lowered her gaze. "So it wasn't a dream."

Paul remained silent as he slowly studied her face. She gave him a weak smile.

Wally began an almost inaudible growl from the back seat. Jess' eyes widened in terror, her ears burning with maniacal, unheard laughter.

# THE NOWHERE PLACE

## JASON MARC HARRIS

"Climb the mountains and get their good tidings. Nature's peace will flow into you as sunshine flows into trees. The winds will blow their own freshness into you, and the storms their energy, while cares will drop away from you like the leaves of Autumn."

— JOHN MUIR'S THE MOUNTAINS OF CALIFORNIA

The second night in the ranch house, something kept Amy Dranner from feeling comfortable in her own home. Not just sharp unease because her husband remained missing, nor her disoriented malaise because of the move from city to country. After all, she loved changing leaves of black oaks, dogwood, and bigleaf maples uninterrupted by lawns and traffic.

She parted the closed drapes and stared out at the midnight world. How she prized October sky. Just the previous night, she had taken Ray, her thirteen-year-old son, to the star party where amateur astronomers plopped shiny tripods upon basalt.

A tall man in overalls and cowboy boots had helped Ray. "Look at Cepheus. And there, the bluish blob, that's the ancient universe where things start to disappear. This year it's brighter than ever. Stars coming right. Just in time for the Harvest King festival. That's me this year. Great honor really."

Ray didn't cringe—so intent was he at seeing the galactic marvel of the bluish-red jets of Gyulbudaghian's Nebula—when the man patted him on the back with a three-fingered hand.

"Lost two fingers to a woodchipper, working at Pillar Ranch." He gave Amy, who *did* cringe, a bright smile and stomped his stars-and-stripes cowboy boots in a little jig.

375

Embarrassed, Amy hurried home after Ray had a few more looks at the sky.

The unease that crept under Amy's skin wasn't regret for an impulsive relocation. Amy moved to Modoc County for several reasons. It was the last place the credit card company told her Bruce had made purchases. He'd bought rope and a battery-powered lantern at the hardware store, and he'd refueled at the Likely gas station. Then he disappeared. Frantic calls to police and private detectives gained no answers.

What torture it had been for her in March to watch flowers bud on San Jose orchard trees and still not know where Bruce could possibly be. Panic shifted to weeping nights, then subsided into sorrowful resentment tinged with the muted anxiety of perpetual uncertainty. Six months later, although the pain had dulled, it waxed again as the leaves in Northern California jaundiced to yellow and darkened to frostbite-red.

Trees scorched the sky.

Their drive to the scoured lava plains passed distant volcanic sentinels. Mt. Lassen's blocky beige-and-gray domed summit and Brokeoff Mountain's chocolate-colored shattered slabs prompted Ray to say he wouldn't be surprised "if a pterodactyl swooped out of a crater and grabbed our car. That's what we get for moving to bumble-fuck nowhere." Amy chided him for swearing. But she savored his laughter, even though bitter and sarcastic. The boy had spunk.

He didn't smile much anymore. Ray missed his father, probably worse than she did.

Amy came to Modoc County not only to hunt for the truth of what Bruce had done on those trips of historical fieldwork, but to give Ray a new taste of life. Yes, it was disruptive to take him from the friends he had known and to start the school year a month late, but junior high was always chaotic, and up the highway at Alturas Middle School he would have a healthier life.

As she fingered the drapes' rough olive cretonne, she acknowledged self-interest, the appetite of all things in the universe. She sought escape from traffic, crime, and stress of the Bay Area. She'd enjoy investments that her parents had left behind. She had more money because of Bruce's disappearance; his fieldwork sometimes drained their bank accounts. She was also glad to have found a nursing job at the Modoc Convalescent Home. Even without Bruce, Ray would still be well-provided for.

Amy had planned to divorce Bruce as revenge for neglect, but she certainly hadn't stopped caring about him. She still wondered whether his disappearance was tied to mental illness, foul play, or an affair. Some country dishwater blonde who gave a good blowjob? A Modoc maiden with chocolate hair and bronze skin?

She had expected loneliness, but it was the feeling of a presence—not an absence—that woke her that second night in Modoc County. She gasped and clutched at the empty air. She got up from bed, turned on the light, and breathed deeply—reassuring herself nothing sat on her chest, no asthma besieged her lungs. Loneliness had not driven her from deep sleep to walk downstairs across the living room and to the drapes.

Whatever had disturbed her sleep, it wasn't merely ululating coyotes out in sage-brush or groaning creaks of loose floorboards. Despite the light of her deceased mother's lamp—

writhing with gilded ivy, zesty satyrs, and coy nymphs—Ray snored adolescent dreams above in the next room. Manzanita and juniper did a number on his allergies. Immune, she savored vanilla scents of Jeffrey pine planks that upheld her six-foot volleyball-player frame without a tremor wherever she walked in the house.

An owl hooted in its hunt for rodents. Peering through the narrow opening of drapes out the window at the sliver of moon, Amy fit words to her fear.

She dreaded that she was watched by something that might do her harm.

It was foolish, of course. This ranch house sprawled on three acres of property, seven miles from the nearest town, and that was the paltry population of seventy-two of Likely, which was another twenty miles from the three-thousand-person metropolis of Alturas.

Yet, something in darkness knew her.

Having hiked and camped from the Rockies to the Everglades, Amy was not only an avowed feminist but pagan nature-lover. The wild was not to be feared. Nature was her mother.

She swept back the drapes, revealing starlit lava plains and scrabbly manzanitas, branches sinuous as the hair of a decapitated gorgon. Scattered on ridges stood shaggy pines, spindly poplars, and—on the downward slopes—quaking aspen, leaves shuffling in the rippling night breeze along the unnamed creek that slithered towards the RV Park and golf course to the west.

Yelps from the coyotes punctuated the chirps of crickets, and occasional owl hoots harmonized this night music on the Modoc plateau.

Crackling by the side of the house made Amy start and freeze. Something stalked over gravel past the window. Crab-like pincers forked out of the top of a large animal. Amy exhaled with relief, recognizing a buck with a dozen points: if not the king of the forest, at least a duke of sagebrush-steppes. A favor granted her by the Lord of the Wild Hunt? She, Amy Dranner, not merely a registered nurse, but a druidess, chose well to come to the wilds.

Something gave a gurgling cry. A flash of white with a rack of twisted horns raced past her window, pursuing the deer, which had bolted into the night, out of sight and into silence.

Amy could have sworn that the horned figure running past her was bipedal.

Shaken, Amy closed the drapes. Neither rutting buck, wildcat nor coyote would have made that guttural sound. Had a bugling elk chased off a buck? That explanation was what she chose to sleep with as she padded upstairs and dozed till dawn.


"Did you sleep well?"

"Yeah, fine." Ray took a swig of orange juice and a few spoonfuls of cereal.

"I met an interesting woman yesterday at the market. Mrs. Pillar. Remember that nice astronomer with the hurt hand who had worked for her?"

"Yeah, he was cool with that telescope."

"Mrs. Pillar invited me to tea this afternoon. She has a dear friend whom she took out of the Modoc Convalescent Home, a huge woman whom she's going to give home-

377

care for, and Mrs. Pillar asked for me to take a look at her. I don't know how she'll get on. This big woman is really gaga. I mean, that's what they told me at work. She does have nice cherrywood hair and the brightest turquoise eyes, but she's also old and lost. Anyway, I'll get to see that ranch. I'll tell you all about it when you come home. We're having ourselves some adventures!"

"Yippee ki-yay." Ray clunked down his empty glass and sucked in his orange-stung lips.

"So, tell me what your friends are like at school."

Ray peeled down his lip and stuck his finger below his teeth. "Just as hick as a kid could want. They gave me some chewing tobacco. Wintergreen. It's better than a Lifesaver."

"Tell me you're kidding." Amy Dranner's appalled face satisfied her son's sneer.

Ray shrugged and shuffled his dusty Converse shoes. "It was gross. The other kids dared me. Said I was a city-pussy if I couldn't do chew."

Amy counseled Ray in the usual manner about peer-pressure. His gaze grew vacant as he finished his orange juice.

"If I listen to your lecture, I'm going to miss the bus."


The bus stopped in front of Pillar Ranch. Ray always had several minutes to wait with the other boys and girls without adult supervision.

"It's the Frisco-kid!" A big red-headed kid, Jack Malley, flanked by shorter boys, pointed at Ray as he approached the bus-stop.

"San Jose." Ray watched Jack narrow his eyes.

"Bunch of fags there too?" Jack flapped his hands to make some pantomime mockery whose exact meaning got lost somewhere between the hostile conception and the absurd rendition.

Ray frowned, blood rushing to his head, and wondered how well Jack could take a punch to the stomach and what interest the bully might pay him back if Ray dared.

"Jack wants to know that because he really likes other boys." Ed, the bulky Modoc boy whom no one dared called fat, spoke before Ray's scowl brought trouble to all of them.

"You shut up, Ed." Jack waved Ed away.

"Going to make me?" Ed took a step towards Jack.

Jack stood his ground. "You got a problem with me now because of Frisco?"

"Give Ray a break, man. He's new."

Jack folded his arms. "Tell you bitches what. Halloween night, Ray here shows us he's not a San Francisco-nabisco pansy. Let's meet after school at the Nowhere Place."

"Not cool," Ed said.

"Wait, what's the 'Nowhere Place'?" Ray looked at Ed's wide eyes. What scared him?

"Oooh," Jack danced around and jerked his eyebrows up and down. "He wants to know. Are you tough enough to find out?"

378

"It's where my ancestors did a ghost dance to get the invaders to leave," Ed said.

"Raised up some weird spirits is what it did," Jack said. "Ghosts that freaked Ed and all his people from ever going back there, and will scare the shit out of you, Frisco-boy."

Ray clenched his fists and frowned at Jack. "I'm not afraid of whatever it is."


While a storm brewed, Amy waited in a purple suede chair in the study while Mrs. Pillar made tea in the kitchen. In the guest bedroom, Huldre Capps occasionally moaned with the wind. Amy had checked on her; the woman's turquoise eyes had looked shrewdly upon her, though she said nothing but groaned like a dumb animal. Amy explained to Mrs. Pillar that she was concerned that it might be a stomach tumor or swollen spleen that caused Huldre's belly to protrude. Mrs. Pillar smiled. "Huldre is just pregnant again. Happens every Harvest Festival when the stars are right. Wouldn't be much meaning in the festival without her rising to the occasion, heh. Don't worry about her." Mrs. Pillar shuffled to the kitchen, leaving Amy to shake her head at her hostess's strange sense of humor.

Whether it was lack of sleep or the occasional pain pill Amy snatched from patients, dizziness spun her into a trance. Light had changed in the living room—perhaps due to the thunderstorm that rumbled and flickered outside—and objects gained an undefinable property.

The bookshelf in front of Amy had grown. There was now a ninth shelf, when earlier she had counted eight. She got up to investigate.

She rubbed her right thumb against the rough bindings of the books on the new shelf. Most titles and authors were unknown to her, such as Ludvig Prinn's *De Vermis Mysteriis*, Comte D'Erlette's *Cultes de Goules*, and the Duchess of Cambria's *Mother of Black Skies*. However, Amy recognized John Dee's translation of *Al Azif*, entitled the *Necronomicon*, from Ray's roleplaying interests, while *Grimoirum Verum* and *Goetia* were two of Bruce's medieval books on demonology. Clearly, Mrs. Pillar shared Bruce's historical interests in old books about the supernatural.

She flipped through the pages of *The Mother of Black Skies*. Perhaps because the book had been written in English rather than Latin or Arabic—as well as penned by a woman rather than a man—Amy thought it might be more congenial than the others. The epigraph on the title page had a rhythm and meaning that intrigued her: "Iä! Shub-Niggurath! The Black Goat with the Thousand Young has a Mother, Iä! Iä! Slagikul-gakoth! Mother of Black Skies! Watchful star-king of time's harvest, Iä! Tawil-at-U'mr. Key and Gate. Yog-Sothoth!"

Upon discovering pictures of shadows bending down from constellations marked by glyphs and accompanied by magical incantations demanding sacrifice—"let the child be fed eight days and not an hour more, for the ninth belongs to Slagikul-gakoth"—she threw the book back on the shelf and staggered backwards to plunk down in the purple suede chair.

When lightning flashed again, Amy stared at the rebounding waterfall of rain.

The interior light had changed again. The dizziness abated, and when Amy checked the bookcase, she counted eight shelves. The ninth had vanished.

"Dear? Are you alright?" Mrs. Pillar called from the kitchen.

"I'm fine! Just dropped a book." Amy pressed her palm against her eyelids and looked again. Eight shelves. No signs of strange titles. The strain of too many night-shifts at Modoc Convalescent Home? Too much caffeine? Too much Ambien and red wine on weekends?

When Mrs. Pillar set tea and crumpets down upon the end table, she pointed out the window to the lightning. The blue tinge beneath her index fingernail made Amy wonder how long before this old woman would herself be carted away to the hospital, for clearly she was suffering hypoxia. Perhaps something from deep within the earth afflicted them both.

Volcanic vapors? Infernal Caverns sprawled beneath these lava plains, ridges, and peaks. Amy imagined lava tubes riddled with maggoty monsters feasting on tree roots and crawling from toilets. She pecked at the strawberry crumpet with its rosy flecks of sugared flesh.

"What were you reading, my dear?" Amy hadn't even heard the shuffle of Mrs. Pillar's sandaled feet. Mrs. Pillar glanced at the bookcases, then at Amy's lap—laden with a crumpet on her napkin—the empty sofa, the end table devoid of books, and at the bookcases again.

"Only a silly dream. I nodded off and thought I saw another shelf in that beautiful antique."

Mrs. Pillar's Caribbean-sea-blue eyes did not blink as she listened. "There are windows, and there are doors."

"Excuse me?" Amy wondered if her hostess were partly deaf.

Mrs. Pillar's eyes finally blinked and narrowed, but her smile widened. She rested her wrinkled hand on Amy's bare shoulder. The touch of frayed rubber bands. "Your husband sat in this same chair."

Amy stopped mid-bite. "You knew Bruce?""With my library, he stayed busy looking for old Snake and Modoc war documents. Especially the battle of Infernal Caverns. See this journal? By a soldier. One of his favorites!"

Amy took the journal from Mrs. Pillar.

"He showed me your picture," Mrs. Pillar continued. "I didn't want to intrude earlier in your personal business, but yes, he missed you. He planned to come home after he'd finished more work. Ah, he was so wonderfully fascinated with our history. And why not? I'm from an ancient family. Go ahead. Take the journal home."

"Thank you so much. I'll bring it back soon."

"Of course you will. No one steals from me."

Journal in hand, Amy followed Mrs. Pillar to the front door. She was eager for fresh air.

Outside a murmuration of migrating starlings tunneled through the air in a synchro-nized flurry, dipping down to the fields of the Pillar ranch then fluttering up towards the trees, each individual bird an atom of movement in the amorphous darkness.

"It's such a wonder, isn't it?" Mrs. Pillar said. "Like the young souls I marshal for the Harvest pageant."

"How do they do it? The starlings, I mean—coordinate like that in flight?"

"How do our thoughts suspend themselves within the void?"

"I can see why you and my husband would have gotten along. He was quite the philosopher, too."

"It wasn't me he gravitated toward, my dear. It was Huldre Capps. She's the home wrecker. No Harvest King can resist the Harvest Queen."

"Oh." Amy shifted her jaw into a lop-sided half-smile. More of Mrs. Pillar's strange talk and jokes. The corpulent and demented old woman who muttered and hissed in the back room could never have tempted anyone. It was as absurd as saying that she'd gotten pregnant.

"There are pictures of last year's festival if you'd like to look. When you get home and flip through the journal, you'll see photos that I kept."

"That's so kind of you."

"Male folk always wander, Mrs. Dranner. We can only herd them to the right places. There are windows and doors. You have looked through a window, but your husband walked through a door. He grew Him. Huldre grows Her. We rejoice in what will be born from the harvest of darkness."

And with that cryptic comment, Mrs. Pillar closed the door behind her.


The edges of the journal had flecks of white mold, so Amy put on the thin but firm latex gloves she used to wash dishes. She turned the pages quickly, eager to get past this task. It felt like digging up her husband from some mildewy grave.

The words of course were not his, but that of a soldier, a certain Benjamin Brattle who had been a sergeant serving under General Crook at the battle of the Infernal Caverns in 1867. Crook was famous locally for the defeat of an alliance of Paiute, Pit, and Modocs who had dared to attack white settlers with their own stolen ammunition. The natives hid in the caverns. The afternoon of her arrival in Modoc County, Amy had visited the Fort Crook museum and read General Crook's famous words: "I never wanted dynamite so bad as I did when we first took the fort and heard the diabolical, defiant yells from down in the rocks." But the general had no dynamite to blast them out. While the soldiers attempted to starve them out, many natives evaded capture because they sneaked out a secret passage, which General Crook later discovered. The caves were lava tubes forming a network deep into the land. It was no surprise that the enemy had found an egress the soldiers hadn't anticipated.

*Oct. 15th 1867*

*We've gone on to search more of the caverns now that the rebellious Indians departed. General Crook is notorious in the press for his comment about the Indians, but it wasn't just the way they were hiding. He wanted to blast that smell out of those tunnels. Nothing from the Indians themselves, but something seeping up from deeper within the earth. If it weren't for the smell, General Crook says we might have found China or El Dorado by now. There are secrets here, he boasted, like that strange mound in Oklahoma, which might "hold gold for men bold enough to find it." Doc Hudson told him everyone went insane or disappeared who went into that mound. Hudson says it's the gases that come up from the bowels of the earth and that bullets can't save our respiratory systems.*

*The General gave his loudest "pshaw," and said the Indians didn't die from gas poisoning, but lead balls and iron sabers. "But you should help lead us then, Doc. Warn us of any symptoms of gas poisoning."*

*Doc Hudson agreed. A first-rate fellow.*

*Oct. 17*

*Doc Hudson came racing out of that deeper tunnel, claiming he saw glowing stalactites like enormous teeth, the sight of which would make us all shake in our boots at night for dreams of crocodiles. Yet when we followed him down, that whole side of the cavern with stalactites was nowhere to be seen. "Clearly some hallucinatory effects here," Doc Hudson mumbled. "Something here beyond sulphur." The General laughed but grew sober indeed when Doc started vomiting blood.*

*Oct. 19*

*Doc Hudson's health has improved, but he's foggy. The General decided rather than store munitions in those tunnels, to abandon the place altogether. He agrees now with Doc Hudson about why the Paiute and others did not use these deeper tunnels that grow fouler in stench the further they go. "There's something wrong about them for*

*sure. Maybe it's gas, maybe it's something else. The glow could be a metallic poison." The General says we should finish up our business and depart within a week.*

*Oct. 27*

*This morning we found The White Man. Jenkins pulled him out of the tunnels after pursuing a noise that the General said sounded like the bugling of an elk. But why would a beast like an elk be underground? Turns out it was this White Man with a mighty crown of antlers dug into his head. Now, this captive isn't white in any European sense of the word. He's like someone fed him chalk all his life, or he never saw a lick of sunlight. Maybe both.*

*Doc Hudson feared the cholera at first, but the White Man walked like he was healthy enough until we knocked him good in the kneecaps.*

*Here's strange business. The antlers must have been there so long, no one could tug them out of his scalp to prove it was just some stupid Indian-style get-up. It's as though an elder of his people, whoever exactly they are, poked those horns in his head the day he crawled out of a bleached devil-goat.*

*He's also got charred marks all over his belly. Doc says it's ancient writing, and he wanted the man to speak it, but The White Man just makes sounds like he's had his tongue cut. This wasn't the case, for though he answered no questions, he had an intact tongue—not even a tongue tie, Doc checked—when he spat at the General, who directly threatened him with a knife.*

*The White Man's cackles were chilling. He had no fear of the knife. We all wanted him dead, but there's something so repulsive about touching him with anything of ours. Jenkins wondered aloud if he'd bleed red, or if some corrosive slime might spill out and ruin that knife forever.*

*Even Doc Hudson wanted to fill the White Man with lead, but the General said, "let's leave well enough alone." We left him tied up on the obsidian tunnel floor, and we made our retreat.*

Reading of the cruelty of these soldiers and the mysterious nature of their prisoner made Amy feel queasy. She thought of her second night in her house, and of the deer that had vanished—pursued by something white, with horns of its own. Could she have seen some modern-day reenactment of an ancient hunting ritual? No wonder her husband was fascinated with this place and its strange history.

Clearly, the soldiers' minds had gone screwy from sulfuric fumes. Mt. Lassen had erupted four decades later in 1915. That would explain a lot. The mind was just another vulnerable organ, subject to chemically-induced madness. Amy's work with old addicts had certainly proven that truth.

*Oct. 31*

*Martha will be dressing the children up in costume today. No masks of Halloween can equal the face of that White Man as he shrieked when we walked away two days ago. This evening after sunset there was a scream that sounded much like his, followed by many more. The General suggested coyotes, but it was Doc Hudson who urged us to get ready to fight. That man has a sixth-sense: a mass of those White Men rushed up and paraded around our campfire like lunatics.*

*We loaded up and were ready to fire. Our horses whinnied, and then some great tree must have fallen in the forest. A huge crash. The White Men got on all fours and scampered in that direction. Another tree fell. Maybe they had another group of them busy with a ritual of knocking the trees down?*

*We shot after them. If we hit any or not, I don't know. None made a single sound out in the dark, and the men were too afraid to move. We'll wait till morning.*

*Nov. 2*

*I couldn't write yesterday because we all marched as fast as we could. The horses had been ripped up—but not by bullets, teeth, or knives. Not a single body of those Whites did we find. Doc Hudson says a dozen men have been taken sick and may die of fever. We won't all make it out of these mountains.*

*Nov. 5*

*I've got the fever. It's strange. I don't complain of headache so much as a foggy feeling and the dreams. Dreams of twisting tunnels and curling night skies. Something heavy, smelling of sulphur and worse, always sags above me. I wake and see my tent has become darker after I dream.*

*Something knocks down the trees. It shrieks at the sky. I am too tired to write. Shadows steal my breath.*

*Martha, I might not make it home. Not even to Fort Hollenbush.*

Amy turned the pages of the journal, but they were empty except for an envelope with the photographs that Mrs. Pillar had spoken of.

What was her surprise and pain when she looked at the photos closely and saw Bruce not only wearing antlers, but holding hands with a beautiful young woman with cherrywood hair and turquoise eyes like Huldre Capps! Most likely a granddaughter, if it were even possible that an ogress like that could have such a beautiful relative.

Amy determined to confront Mrs. Pillar about the pictures and the mystery woman on Halloween Night before the pageant at the school.


On Halloween Day, Ray ate even less than usual, but his mother didn't worry; she was too preoccupied with facing Mrs. Pillar about the strange pictures.

"You're not going in costume, honey?"

"No. That stuff is for kids."

Ray shrugged off his mother's kiss on top of his mousse-spiked hair.


After enduring taunts from Jack throughout the day, Ray could barely wait for the day to end and hike with the other boys out past the other side of Devil's Backbone and down to the Nowhere Place where ghosts allegedly lingered.

He'd seen scarier-looking tunnel entrances and caves in his travels with his parents, but the stakes with coyote carcasses and stringy dreamcatchers hanging from them certainly added a disturbing presence to the dry ring of grass that preceded the onyx aperture into the underground.

Don't do it," Ed said.

"I'm not afraid," Ray said.

"Yes, you are!" Jack hollered and did his head-shaking jumping "scaredy-cat" dance.

Ray crossed the bleached dry circle, past the dwarfish Juniper whose octopod roots had somehow found pathways to water and fertile earth despite the generally smooth basalt floor.

The boys stopped their noise and stared as Ray took a few steps into the tunnel.

Ray looked back and saw the fascination in their faces. He tried not to notice the alarm that crinkled up Ed's forehead as his friend motioned him back.

Ray shook his head. "I've already gone further than you chicken-shits, but once I go in a ways more and come out, then we'll know who the nobodies are in this nowhere place!"

384

His words made garbled echoes, but neither ghosts nor boys jeered.
Something nauseating blew in a cool wind from the cave.
Ray gritted his teeth, resolved to throw-up later.


Amy knocked, but Mrs. Pillar was not at home. Either she had left for the Harvest Pageant, or sought help for storm damage. A wall had crumbled where Huldre Capps slept. No trees had fallen by the house, but a series of increasingly larger asymmetrical indentations pitted the backyard towards the ridge beyond, denuded on top due to fallen trees and erosion—as if a landslide had gone uphill rather than downhill.

Amy opened the door to speak with the invalid, Huldre Capps, but her room was unoccupied except for buzzing flies.

Mrs. Pillar's sandals stood empty by the door. Had she gone barefoot out into the night? No, Mrs. Pillar must have taken Huldre to a hospital for treatment after the storm.

Bedclothes were tumbled on the floor, and there was puddling wetness as though an incontinent invalid had an accident. Or perhaps a pregnant woman's water had broken?

Amy shook away the thought.

Then she saw the stars-and-stripes cowboy boot caught within the blankets. She lifted up the covers with her shoe, revealing the fly-spotted, bleached-white flesh of the amateur astronomer torn asunder at the hips, with broken pieces of white antlers poking out from his head.

Amy shook and vomited upon the floor.


After a few uneventful steps over slick yellow and red leaves around the bend of the tunnel, Ray grew confident there was nothing strange around. Behind him he could see a reassuring stream of dust motes. He took a few more steps inside.

In a haze of silver light stood someone bent over and wearing his father's green sweater.

"Dad? Is that you? You've been going here all this time?" Ray came closer, more excited than scared, reaching out and almost touched not a sweater, but shining green robes.

Nor was the color of the robe the dark green plaid his father often wore while studying at his desk; that too had just been a trick of light.

Ray stepped back, sneakers crunching withered leaves and scraping basalt pebbles.

The air grew cold.

The robes dimmed to gray, undulating strangely as if things moved within. These undulations quivered more rapidly when Ray spoke again.

"What are you, the grim reaper?" His voice grew shrill, and he clutched the butterfly knife in his pocket.

"You dream." The words curled the dead leaves in wisps but were neither sound nor new thought—ripples through Ray's mind, memories recalled at the instant.

385

"Where did you come from? Where's my father?"

"I have always been here. Your father has always been with me."

A visible aura of darkness twisted around the robes. This inky splotch moved like rebounding raindrops upon wind-blown puddles; it opened in dimples of silver and black.

Out of one indentation, a human face of molten silver emerged.

Ray's heart thumped, but the metallic mask, features clenched in stern misery, crumbled into darkness and sank back amid an endless progression of rotating glyphs that flashed on top of the swollen robes. Marks like ancient pictographs representing animals—or a lost alphabet or perhaps alien algebra—flowed out of the darkness and circulated in its billowing robes.

Ray knew that evanescent face of misery was his father's, but there was no consolation in seeing that horrid silver mask. He knocked his knuckles together till they stung and ached. This was not a nightmare from which he could wake.

He backed away from the veiled undulating shape with its moving glyphs, some of them quite recognizable, such as rattlesnakes and buffalo. The others? Misshapen and monstrous. Kaleidoscopes of wings, proboscises, tentacles, and claws. Some glyphs were stars and planets; a comet streaked over the rising head of Argentinosaurus. Perplexed beneath a pyramidal moon, an orangutan scratched its head. These images—and many more—flashed, circulated, and faded through the robes.

Ray hurried past old leaves, mysteriously drained of their autumn colors, as he rushed back the way he'd come where dust motes floated.

But darkness followed. "You have always been here."

"No. No. I'll just go and tell my friends that I didn't see anything. Nothing at all."

The swirl of darkness riffled Ray's hair. Leaves began to circle at Ray's feet. Rocks stirred and oozed in irregular orbits around him.

"You will not leave."

"This is crazy. I've got to go. I've got to go!" Ray lurched away from the strange vision and tried to run, but could not pass the circling chunks of basalt.

The undulating figure moved closer to him. Not with discernible locomotion, but in shuddering gaps of perception—like the impression of stuttering leaps of a jumping spider or the strobe-light sequence of a mummy rising out of its coffin at a haunted house in a theme park; a staccato progression of imperceptible change only recognized by the mind after the fact.

Ray fumbled with his butterfly knife, pulling it from his pocket and flipping the handles apart to reveal the blade. The vastness of the thing before him also split asunder. Its robes parted. From billows of darkness, floating slime of iridescent bubbles filled the cavern.

The moving wall of rock had vanished.

Free at last, Ray ran towards where sunlight had remained a beacon for the outdoors.

But he saw charcoal darkness and ruby stars both above and below. The spaces in between these glowing nebulae were great shadows drifting closer to him from distant depths.

Beyond those caverns, many centuries, epochs, ages, long strange eons, twisted spiraling galaxies into knots. There Ray would dwell as his mind emptied among suffocating globules into a hungry oblivion deep in dark void perpetually shrouded from sight.


After calling the police, Amy raced from Mrs. Pillar's ranch to the school to rescue Ray from whatever madness the insane matron had planned for the pageant. But she was far too late.

*He grew Him. Huldre grows Her. We rejoice in what will be born from the harvest of darkness.* Mrs. Pillar's words came back to Amy, and she shivered.

Huldre Capps had indeed given birth, for the stars had been right.

Yet Amy had little idea of the full truth of what had crawled from Huldre's miraculous womb and made the children of the school pay the debts their families owed to gods that reigned far above the high plateau beneath clear dark skies.

Driving across sprawling lava plains, Amy saw a shockwave knock down the trees like matchsticks. Had Mt. Lassen again begun to erupt? It was a suitable apocalypse to join the horror of what she had seen there, rent upon the floor at the ranch.

Neither volcanic ash plume nor atomic mushroom cloud greeted Amy on the horizon. Instead, though the sky was clear and the sun overhead, a great shadow spread towards her. It was as though a mountain range stood between her and the sun.

The air grew cold.

She turned on the radio, searching for news. She tapped her phone, careful not to swerve as the road wound on. Her answers were only static and frozen apps.

After all her driving, she seemed no closer to her destination.

The sun faded to a brown dot.

Amy pulled over and dialed 9-1-1. Desperate. Frantic. In a fever.

Then a car appeared, driving over the ridge towards her. Same model of white Saab as her own.

And then another car. Again, a white Saab. And yet another. And another.

She stared at these phantom cars. She saw—as if viewing a flip-book—a series of images of herself swerving along the road, gripping her phone, pressing buttons on the radio.

Now they were stopping. Now she was getting out. Now she was turning and driving both directions. The black asphalt flowed a milky white and silver blur of paint and chrome.

Then, the air hummed without cars as Amy Dranner fell out of time altogether.

Yellow leaves blew in looping eddies across that empty stretch of lonely highway.

# MY GRANDPA'S BEST FRIEND

## ALANNA ROBERTSON-WEBB

The hunting cabin located in the wooded farmland outside of Fresno, California, was just as I remembered it. It was tiny, hardly bigger than a tool shed, and after a year of neglect dust now coated every surface. I hadn't been there in almost ten years, not since the last time I went hunting with my grandfather, Sebastian. I had been so terrified by the creature we saw in the woods that I hadn't wanted to return, and my parents just assumed I was too bored to want to spend two weeks with a boring old man. Gramps still came to visit us, but thankfully we never went to visit him.

When Gramps passed away a year ago, he left the cabin, and the thirty acres surrounding it, to his only remaining grandchild. At twenty years old, I had never expected to set foot on the rural mountainside again, much less inherit it, but a bad breakup had left me the decision of moving either into the cabin, or into my parent's basement. The choice had almost been hard to make.

The local newspaper, the *Fresno Bee*, had claimed that Gramps died of a bear attack while out chopping firewood behind his cabin. I didn't buy that story, though, and even as I pulled my beat-up old Ford into the unpaved driveway, I had my hand on my gun. The old Remington might not do much to the creature roaming those woods, but it made me feel better. I hadn't seen the thing in a decade, but if it was still around then I would be prepared this time.

Several hours later I was unpacked, and the cabin was decently clean. All of the utilities were hooked up, and the refrigerator was stocked. I had taken the week off work so that I could adjust to my new lifestyle, and I was planning on just relaxing for the next few days. My first night and day passed uneventfully, but by the second night, things were getting a little weird.

I had spent enough time in the country as a child to be familiar with creatures like raccoons, skunks, bears, and other mammals, but the freshly-made claw marks on the sides of the cabin weren't anything I recognized. I woke up on my third morning to the gouges, and I was pretty unnerved. They were too large to belong to any small critters, too high up to be from coyotes, and too wide to be from a mountain lion or bear. In this neck of the woods, that ruled out everything logical.

As I studied the claw marks, I wondered how I could have slept through them being made. They definitely hadn't been there when I first arrived, and the fresh marks stood out in a bright contrast to the weathered wood of the cabin walls. I supposed a human could have made them with a knife, but I didn't have neighbors for miles. Who would be skulking around out there just to prank me? It didn't make any sense.

It crossed my mind that my ex might have done it just to freak me out, but Sandra lived almost fifty miles away and didn't have the address for the cabin in the first place. I don't use social media enough to bother listing my new address, and we didn't have friends in common or anything anyway. I eventually shrugged to myself, deciding to let it go. I knew that worrying about it wouldn't help, but that afternoon I found myself driving the ten miles into town and buying some motion-activated flood lights and a motion-sensing camera.

Two more nights passed, and each morning I woke up to the claw marks getting closer and closer to the cabin door. As much I wanted to believe that it was a stupid prank, I had to admit to myself that the evidence was overwhelmingly against that idea. The flood lights would turn on, and the camera would snap, but all I ever saw in the photos was an empty yard. I had even tried to set up a video on my phone, but all it managed to capture was a vague blur of movement at the edge of the screen.

I had had enough. On the fifth night I went outside, gun in hand, and settled comfortably on the porch steps. There was no noise, no sound to indicate that the usual nocturnal critters were up and about. I shut all of the lights off, and waited for the creature that I knew would come. Hours passed, and as one a.m. rolled around, I snapped myself out of a doze. I could hear something moving quietly out by the edge of the woods where a figure was skulking around, its features hidden in shadows.

As the creature drew closer, I rubbed his eyes in disbelief. It was Sebastian, my supposedly dead grandpa. The unclothed figure paused mid-step, its head slowly turning to face me after hearing me gasp in shock. Gramps looked sickly, with skin pale and visible ribs. He was bald now, his once Santa-like beard and hair gone.

"Gramps?"

I could hear the quiver in my voice, and my hands were shaking from terror. The gun had fallen to my lap, nearly forgotten in the intensity of seeing my presumably dead grandfather. I had been so convinced that the antlered creature I saw years ago had killed Sebastian that I had never once considered that my grandfather might still be alive.

"Gramps, what're you doing? Come home!"

Tears were streaming down my cheeks. I didn't care what my grandfather had been doing or why he was out there. All I cared about was that he was alive. I just wanted to hug him again.

"Runnnnn, stupid boy, it's commmming!"

Sebastian's voice barely sounded human. His warning came out as an almost reptilian hiss, and before I could respond, Gramps was bounding into the woods on all fours. He was gone in the blink of an eye, the bushes hardly swaying where he had passed through. The woods remained as eerily silent as they had been, even though my grandfather's retreat should have made a large amount of noise.

Not a second later, a low growl came from behind me, the sound reverberating off the cabin walls. A massive creature, the one from my memory, approached from around the side of the cabin. Within seconds it became clear to me that it wasn't a human or an animal, unless someone was wearing an amazing costume. The creature was every bit as surreal as I remembered it. Long, pale limbs sprouted from an emaciated torso, and the ivory deer skull shined in what little moonlight managed to bleed through the clouds. It was wearing ragged old buckskin leggings, and had beads around its neck.

I couldn't see any eyes, but I knew without a doubt that it was staring directly at me. I think it was a Wendigo or Skinwalker, though the difference between the two types of monsters was always a bit beyond me. Before I could take in any more detail the thing began to laugh, a guttural sound that echoed in my head hauntingly. It was laughing so hard that it nearly doubled over, and I realized that its limbs were able to wrap around its body twice. I raised the gun and fired several shots at it point-blank, the bullets lodging firmly into the creature's neck and torso.

The being looked down at its new piercings, and it began to dig out the bullets at an unhurried pace. It dropped them onto the ground like a child plucking flower petals, and it seemed to sigh in irritation as it dug out the last one.

"Why must humans always do this?"

It spoke in such perfect English that I was dumbfounded. What was going on? What did the creature want? Had Gramps known about this horrendous thing? My head began to ache with the strain of trying to figure it out, so I turned my attention back to the monster. The bullets clearly hadn't done more than annoy it, and I half expected it to lunge for me.

"No forthcoming apology, hummm?"

It was still staring at me, its foot tapping impatiently as it waited. It shouldn't sound so human. I tried to say something, but my voice came out as more of a strangled squeak than my usual baritone.

"Well, I suppose that shall do. Now, get along inside before that evil little denizen comes loping back."

I just stood there. I tried to will my feet to move, but I was so scared that my bladder give out instead. Warm pee ran down the side of my leg, and for just a second my mortification overruled my terror.

"Oh, really now, urination? Truly? Have you not conquered your base instincts beyond this primitive farce?"

"I, I-I…"

"It is not all about you, you know! Sebastian was a dear friend of mine, and one would think you would offer condolences instead of shooting me like a barbarian!"

"You're a m-m-monster…"

"Ah, of course. Your simple little mind should be able to comprehend this more familiar form a bit better."

Suddenly the horrifying creature was gone, and in its place stood Sebastian's best friend Rufus. Rufus had been around as long as I could remember, and had always been a kind old man. He supposedly lived on the other side of the mountain, even though I had never actually seen any houses over there when Gramps and I would hunt. Rufus just always sort of appeared out of nowhere, usually startling us so badly that we had almost shot him a few times.

"There, boy, this better for ya?"

I merely nodded, still not trusting my voice. This was just a nightmare. I fruitlessly tried to convince myself that I must have dozed off on the porch, and that I could probably wake myself up if I tried hard enough. I began pinching my exposed skin mercilessly, a bruise forming after a few rough grabs. Rufus was watching me, his head cocked to the side questioningly.

"What in tarnation are you doing, whippersnapper?"

"I've gotta wake myself up!"

"Sorry to break it to ya, kid, but this ain't no dream. Now get yer hide on inside 'fore that thing that looks like yer grandpappy comes back and guts ya. The scratch marks on trees and cabins are it claiming territory, but if it gets close enough to ya to mark your face, you're dinner."

I was shaking so hard from fear that I could barely move my limbs, but I managed to navigate the steps. I'm not entirely sure why I obeyed the creature, but seeing it morph into a familiar face was easier to deal with than the knowledge that it was probably about to eviscerate me with every step. I needed some semblance of normalcy, so I went about my usual pre-bedtime routine.

I mindlessly made sure all the doors and windows were locked, then I took a hot shower to help relax and clean myself up. I crawled into bed after, my adrenaline finally calming down. Now I was just in pure shock, and I noticed that I was repetitively reassuring myself that I would wake up and everything would be normal. Too bad even getting this written down hasn't manage to convince me that things are okay.

Rufus said there were scratches on the trees outside too, so in the next few days I'm going into the woods to find out just how far they extend. I have more questions than answers, but maybe I can at least find out more about Rufus, like if he really does have a cabin nearby. I need to learn about what I'm dealing with, and I can't do that if I just keep cowering in my grandpa's cabin.

I'm bringing my gun and buying a few more in town before I go in there.

# EVERY DAY IS A PARADE

## CHARLIE DAVENPORT

Peter lay still in the early morning hours, feeling the press of the coming three-hundred and sixty-five days and the relative chill of winter nipping around the edges of his covers. The advice one of Shelby's friends had given him when he'd arrived in California ran through his head.

"Two years," a gregarious fellow named Gabriel had said, sort of respective of nothing as they sat on lawn chairs sipping away on Tecate and various other beers Peter had never encountered before. There were streamers overhead, and a decimated piñata dangled from the basketball hoop, battered from the assaults by Gabriel's children. Stretched out over all of it was a store-bought printed banner that proclaimed, "Welcome Back Shell," topped with an exclamation mark. Handwritten in black marker was the tag, "and Welcome Pete!" Peter had felt it was a nice addition.

"Two years for what?" he had asked.

"To assimilate," Gabriel had said, though in the state he had been in at that time, reached through equal parts tequila and Negro Modelo, the words had sneaked past his lips sounding more like *similate*, "and feel like SoCal is, you know, *home*."

Though on reflection Gabriel was a native Californian that had never left Los Angeles County, so perhaps his opinion on the matter should have been taken with a little skepticism. Peter still hadn't quite fallen into the rhythms of the place. He felt a little odd wearing shorts in October, and his New England accent still proved to be a source of profound amusement to far too many people. The cashier at the Vons up the street had actually asked him to repeat the classic soft "ar" sound words, such as "car" and "yard," before she would hand him his change.

Peter did not expect that he'd ever quite 'similate' but there was nowhere else he'd consider home. It was where Shelby was, and that, wherever that might be, would always be where he belonged. Their first date back in DC had lasted eight hours;

covering everything from her youth in Northern California to her research at the university and, most importantly, her very definite plans of what to do in case of the zombie apocalypse.

In the weeks that followed, Peter discovered that life had been divided neatly into two periods of time. The time with Shelby, and the time away from her. Within a month they were living together, and when she'd announced a job opportunity had come up in California, Peter didn't debate for even a moment. Less than a week later he'd successfully gotten his request for a transfer to the California branch of Bellator Corp approved with a speed that was unheard of in the firm's history.

He looked out their window on Wrigley Lane. Ordinarily the sky above his home, workplace or anywhere he could reach with two or three hours' worth of driving was the same featureless pale blue, but after half a decade of drought, El Nino had come back and brought the first honest rain that Peter had known in this place. For a week there were actual clouds above, and they had been dark and full. Today, however, they seemed to be held back at a respectful distance above the town. It was, after all, parade day.

Their son Henry lay still on the tiny screen of his baby monitor. Peter watched for a while until he could see the screen start to brighten; daylight was still approaching. In the distance, he fancied he could hear the various stage of preparation for the festivities. Nothing definite, just the wind carrying the occasional bang of a drum or a snippet of a voice being broadcast over speakers. He picked up the TV remote; this day and its event were coming no matter what. The NBC affiliate was broadcasting with their perennial hosts sitting in a booth above the route, their practiced smiles plastered tightly to their faces. He watched as the first float came into the camera's view. Poesies, river reeds, and other vegetation made a collection of fanciful scenes that flowed from jungle to peaked castle. In between the floats, riders moved from scene to scene by way of slides placed between them and cavorted with all manner of bizarre multi-limbed creatures while improbable aircraft and spaceships bounced overheard.

The tradition of the parade had been started by people like him, transplants that wanted to flaunt the warm paradise they lived in to those they'd left behind in the frigid East. It had been held in every New Year's Day since 1890, unless it fell on a Sunday. Locals said that the founders had made a nodding agreement with the Almighty when the floats rolled out that first day. They would never hold it on a Sunday, and for His part, God would never let it rain on the procession. Looking at the horizon with the line of rolling black held at bay, Peter could almost believe it. He heard their bedroom door open and his wife appeared a moment later.

"Henry?" she inquired.

By way of an answer, he held the monitor in his hand up and as on cue their son let out a comically loud snore. His wife's face broke into a grin above her puffy eyes.

"So cute," she said adoringly. "Did you make tea?"

"Not yet," Peter replied.

Shelly gave him a disapproving look. "You know the rules, Mr. Sandow. You wake up first, you make the tea. At least get the water started."

393

"Sorry, Dr. Sandow. I don't know what I could have been thinking."

"Useless." She smiled and shuffled towards the kitchen.

"Happy New Year," Peter called after his wife.

Her head and shoulders appeared at the door. "Shhhhh." She pressed her index finger to her lips, then withdrew it to point at Henry's door. "Happy New Year, honey," she said with a smile.

A small wail came from the screen and Henry's room simultaneously, announcing that their little boy was ready to join the rest of the world.

"I got him," Peter said as he got up from the couch.

"Yeah, you do," his wife called from the kitchen, being quiet no longer a concern.

They got Henry changed, fed, and then dressed. His propensity to sling formula and jammy toast around made it madness to try it any other way. His wife made waffles, while Peter prepared mimosas for them to sip and marinated steaks that would be placed on the grill. Periodically, they would check in on the parade's progress, seeing marching bands and well-groomed horses weave their way down Colorado Boulevard between the floats.

They'd yet to go to see the parade themselves, at least not the one during the day. Anybody wanting a reasonably good live view either had to be part of the media coverage, or had to have slept out on the sidewalk the night before. After the parade was over, the floats would be parked at a local highs school's parking lot, admission would be charged and folks could view all the care and craft that went into putting these wonders together up close. Peter and Shelby had talked of taking Henry to see them there when he'd be old enough to remember it, but that was years away.

After everyone had gotten an eyeful of the blossom-strewn works of art, they'd be gathered up into a convoy. The greenery would be tied down, with a skeleton crew doing various tasks to keep the floats together as they were driven several miles to the stadium; where they'd be taken apart. Stripped of their finery and rendered nothing more than bare wire frames. It was what Shelby called the nighttime show.

The first year that they'd lived on Wrigley, they'd celebrated the New Year much as they would do this year. They cooked, watched the parade, and did a fair bit of day drinking while they did. The days of carousing and imbibing like it was a task had passed them by and Peter suspected now that Harry was with them, there was a very good chance they'd soon start skipping staying up until midnight, as well. Indeed, the prior evening's festivities had consisted of him watching a rerun of Family Guy while Shelby slept on the couch beside him. When he roused her to let her know it was midnight and perhaps they should mark the moment with a kiss or something, she'd muttered something and then trundled off to bed without another clear word passing her lips. But that evening, that first New Year in their own home, Shelby had stuck her head up against their great bay window and slightly wide eyed gestured for Peter to follow her outside.

Most of their neighbors were already gathered, watching the floats pass by, slowly chugging along down the main road. Standing there, you could watch the gray shapes approach and have their remaining glory revealed in the wavering pools cast by the sodium streetlights overhead. A stripped-down, spontaneous encore of performance. A great and secret show that only the locals knew about. Standing there in the chill of that evening, he'd occasionally look at his neighbors, a group of people that did not generally interact with one another and each time he'd catch someone's eye, they would smile at each other and nod in a companionable way. No one spoke, no one hollered. There was a kind of reverence to this. Dozens of the floats passed by and occasionally the riders, those maintaining these temporary vehicles those last few miles, would look up from their labors and wave. They watched until the last in the convoy, a bizarre little scene depicting various prehistoric creatures crawling out of the La Brea Pits, faded into the darkness. Shelby was standing in front of him so he could wrap his arms around her and together they silently said good night to their neighbors as all retreated into their homes.

That night when they'd settled into bed, Peter had felt sleepy, heavy in that delightful way you get sometimes before a really good night's rest. The day had been peaceful, the night sort of magical. He slid over to his wife and buried his head in her hair and breathed deeply of her shampoo as he drifted off.

After a time, he found himself without explanation, no longer in his bedroom or the formless nothing of sleep but instead out on the corner of Colorado Boulevard. Above him, the sky was clear and cloudless. He became aware by degrees that he was not alone on the street. People of every age and hue had formed rough lines on both sides of the boulevard. They all wore the same vacant, rigid smiles secured to their faces. Peter could smell that they reeked of rotting flowers. As one they turned their heads, their eyes wide with some indiscernible emotion. For a terrible moment Peter was certain they were staring at him, but following their gaze, his eyes fell on something on the distant horizon. A speck along the curve of the Earth, tiny as a drop of blood trickling its way down a pricked finger.

He stood with the gathered crowd of cardboard people, unable to look away from that far-off thing. Soon he could feel the approach in his chest known. He began to make out the distinct individuals that comprised the front of the column and watched as each, in perfect time with their fellows, raised one leg and brought it down with a brutal crack against the asphalt, only to repeat it a moment later. With each strike Peter, could make out more details. They wore uniforms. Drab grey with brass ornaments flashing from the chest and shoulders, they made Peter think of military cadets or... a marching band.

Indeed, each of the figures held an instrument of some kind in front of them or hoisted on their shoulders. Peter could hear the music they made, or at least it was something like music. Cymbals crashed and drums banged at odd, arrhythmic intervals. Horns of every description blared shrill warnings to no one in horrendous counterpoint to the synchronicity of the march.

Every few feet, one of the marchers would tear themselves free from the crowd and post along the route, blocking the mass of humanity that had gathered to watch from coming any closer. They wore the same static, idiot leer as they crowd around Peter, but their eyes burned with an unnatural intensity that spoke only of simple hatred.

395

After hundreds or thousands of them passed by Peter, he saw a single float making progress down the street. A simple flatbed with wire frames rising from it, covered only in patches by wilted or rotting flowers. A small collection of people milled around them. Some were elderly. Others looked to be in the prime of their lives. Some held children in their arms. No one looked happy or sad, exactly; their eyes just moved languidly from one side of the route to the next with no particular interest. They did not speak to each other, did not even seem aware of each other. Well, except for the two that rode at the front of the float. One was a young woman dressed as though she'd just come from the gym, likely a senior in high school or a college freshman in her first semester. There was something wrong with her.

Her posture looked stooped, broken somehow. Her face was strained with the tremendous effort it must have taken for her to simply stand. Each jostle of the decaying platform brought a fresh expression of agony to her young face. Her hand rested on the shoulder of an elderly man seated in an old wooden chair, as much out of the need for support as any sign of affection it might have meant to impart. The elderly gentlemen—Peter privately named him the Grand Marshal of this procession— vacantly scanned the crowd as he waved to them, but received no recognition except their ever-present toothy grins. Periodically his eyes would roll to the back of his head. He wore an ornate crown that pulled with such a weight on him that his necked lolled to the side. Was it made of… thorns?

The young woman tapped the Marshal on his shoulder, pointing downward as they passed Peter. The old man allowed gravity to snap his head toward Peter. Over the cacophony, he heard a voice as old as time say,

"Hello."

Then he was awake. He sputtered around for a moment while the dream slowly bled away from him. He calmed down and began taking in the world around him: his own bedroom. He became aware of the complete blurred stillness of it. There was a small hitching noise that he could not at first identify. He heard like it was coming to him through cotton, and his surroundings refused to come into clear view. He blinked his eyes furiously and found that they were filled with salty tears. Had he woken up crying? Shelby woke up and over his stuttering breath, asked him what was wrong. Peter had no words to describe it, except he'd had a nightmare. His wife cradled him then and slowly ran her fingers over his brow until he drifted off to sleep. When he awoke again, he'd largely forgotten about the disturbing interlude. After all, there were bills to pay, birthdays to remember, and in February of that year Shelby announced that their family was to grow by one. With the press of everyday life and impending father-hood, there was no time to dwell on a single night of poor rest. That is, until one night while watching the news, Peter rubbing Shelby's shoulders, they came across the sad story of Cynthia Anne Ryder.

The story itself was not remarkable. Most people will sadly hear a version of it at least once a year or more. A local teenager on their way back from a party tries to run the stoplight, just enough alcohol buzzing through their system, and never sees the truck that had the green. According to the report, she'd told her parents she was meeting up with some friends after soccer practice. Ms. Ryder's body was thrown from the vehicle, and she expired at the scene. Both Shelby and Peter had remarked on the news item with the offhanded and directionless sympathy that anyone has upon hearing of such things.

However, the next day while sitting at his desk Peter thought about the story and felt a need, a sharp and suddenly pressing need, to put a face to the name Cynthia Anne Ryder.

Peter Googled her name and came across a few LinkedIn and Facebook profile results. People looking for new employment opportunities, a young lady in Idaho that had won a county spelling bee the previous April, but after a bit of sifting he came across the Cynthia Anne he was looking for on the local station's website. He scanned the article. Good student. Taught soccer at a summer camp for underprivileged youth. A wonderful big sister to her nine-year-old brother.

None of these or any of the other assorted specifics about her life set off any sort of bells for Peter, but when he'd seen her photo there'd be a tickle at the back of his mind. Just a little something familiar to the slope of her nose and the shape of her eyes.

*Where do I know her from?* Peter wondered the rest of the day. At meetings and in casual conversation it gnawed at him every moment until he laid his head down that night. When his head touched the pillow, he smelled Shelby's shampoo and for the first time since that day so early in the year, he remembered the parade. He was able to put Cynthia's face to the shattered form of the girl on the float in the nightmare scape. He recalled the old man, the Grand Marshal. He wanted to sit up, to do something about this. Though what that was going to be, he had no idea. Besides, it was already too late. He felt himself slipping into sleep as though sliding irreversibly down a long tunnel. When he emerged from the other side, he was along the parade route again and the float was drawing close. There was no sign of the young woman in her gym gear who would never see her first semester of college. Cynthia Anne Ryder had shuffled off this life; the parade had moved her along.

Peter saw the others still riding with the Marshal, their eyes drowsily scraping the crowd they passed. There was someone else standing by the Marshal now, a dark-skinned man with a severe military style to his manner. His face was smoothly shaven and placid, his eye full of canny wariness, looking out at the crowd with the same intensity he'd leveled during staff meetings back in DC. Unlike Cynthia Ryder, Peter recognized this man right away. He had worked with him for the better part of five years and while they hadn't been friends, they'd certainly liked each other enough to ask how their weekends had gone. Peter would ask how the wife and kids were, and Clarence Wise would ask how his "gal was getting along." He looked just as Peter remembered him. That is until he turned his head. That simply motion allowed Peter full view of his old coworker's face and the ghastly wounds that had decimated most of it. The lower part of Wise's jaw had been pulped by some terrific force and it had traveled up past his left eye and exploded out the top of his head, making his cranium appear to be some kind of gory improvised funnel. This grotesque parody of his friend looked right at Peter and recognition lit in his

397

remaining eye. He saw Wise's mouth attempt to form some kind of word as he bent toward the Marshal's ear.

"Hello," the Grand Marshal's voice said, and in the infinite weariness that resided in it, there was also a hint of familiarity. Peter was an old friend coming to visit, someone that the Marshal expected to see again.

After waking, when he'd had time to gather himself, Peter started making calls back to every number he still had in his phone for the DC office, but it being a Saturday there were no answers until he tried Kenny Brydon's number.

"Hello, Bellator Corp, this is Kenny Brydon. How may I help you, sir or ma'am?" The Jersey accent by way of a twenty-two year stay in Maryland clanged across the line.

"Hey Kenny, it's Peter Sandow." It had been two years, and though he'd been in the cubicle opposite Kenny for a very long time, he had no expectations that he'd be remembered.

"Pete!" the boisterous voice proclaimed. At fifty-seven, Kenny was filled with a bounding, aggressive optimism that could be just what you needed to hear in the middle of the week or the most grating thing on a Monday morning. "Is it you blowing up every phone in the office? You forget what day it was?"

"No, I was hoping to catch anyone really. I'm trying to get ahold of Clarence Wise. Had a question I thought he could answer."

Kenny sighed deeply. "Not likely."

Peter felt cold.

"Rumor is, yesterday Clarence got up early, made breakfast for his kids, then told his wife he was headed out to the garage to get something out of the car or something like that. After an hour or so she went looking for him."

He could already picture Clarence walking down the perfectly-shoveled path from his house with his head hung low, but moving with the same purposeful stride he'd always had.

"She found him and the note he'd written, apologizing for the mess." Kenny shuffled the papers on his desk loudly enough for Peter to hear them in California.

"Jesus, did it say why?" Peter did not want to ask how. He was certain he already knew.

"Don't know, but I doubt it. He wasn't the type to complain." An edge of admiration was present in Kenny's voice.

Peter struggled through a few more minutes of question and answer with Kenny, but in the end none of it lodged too deeply in his memory. Clarence Wise was dead, by his own hand, and Peter had known.

It would follow that pattern again and again. A relative he hadn't seen in years died of a heart attack while jogging. A drunk killed a neighbor's child because they just refused to go home. On the evening news, a family of four died in an avalanche in Colorado. Each one in turn Peter would see taking their place alongside the Grand Marshal.

There was never enough time to do anything about it. No appointed time was ever given. No address. No set of instructions that led him to the right place at the right time. It seemed he was simply to nightly bear witness to the parade and its passengers. There were times in the early morning hours, tears burning his eyes for the umpteenth time, that he considered joining Clarence. But there were still bills to pay, and he had a family to support. He had a nine to five job with the increasing responsibilities that came from climbing the corporate ladder, and he was balancing all of that with a toddler sprinting around the house trying to find any gaps in the babyproofing measures he and Shelby had taken. So his nights, filled with unease and terror as they were, slowly became just another fact of his life. Somehow, he managed the day to day miracle of not simply cracking from the strain.

At the start of October, his branch manager, Mr. Rivers, called him to the fourth floor where senior management resided to discuss a project that he'd been working on for the company. The lower floors were all open concept space. Cubicles with dividers so low that you could see all your co-workers at once, facilitating collaboration—or that was the idea, anyway. When the elevator door slid open Peter noted that the managers had more traditional offices, granting them such luxuries as walls and doors. Arriving at Rivers's door, Peter knocked and was asked to come in.

Mr. Rivers sat comfortably behind his overlarge and imposing desk. He was a neatly-attired man of indeterminate middle-age, wearing a double-breasted suit that was a few years out of style. His double chin and earnest attempt at a combover did not detract from his air of authority. Another man with a full head of stark white hair sat in front of Rivers, but made no move to turn around as Peter approached.

"Ah, Peter. Please have a seat." Rivers rose slightly and gestured at the chair next to the white-haired man. "Do you know Tom Bedford?"

Peter had heard the name and had seen pictures on the company's website. Mr. Bedford, the director of West Coast development. Mr. Bedford presenting to the shareholders. Mr. Bedford meeting with regulatory officials in DC. Mr. Bedford biking down the 101 on a charity ride he organized every year, sponsored by Bellator, of course.

"I don't believe we've met before." The man in his casual polo shirt exuded a virility Peter suspected that he might never achieve in his own lifetime. Bedford stood and, smiling, offered Peter his hand. "Hello. Tom Bedford, and I've been hearing…"

The rest of what he said was difficult to hear as the blood pounded in Peter's ears. *Hello.* The word he'd said to Peter almost every night that year. Every night as he wore that Godawful crown on his head and his rictus face turned up towards the sky. His eyes flashing white as if in mid-seizure. *Hello.*

Standing before Peter in Mr. River's office was Tom Bedford, head of West Coast development for Bellator Corp.

Stand before Peter in Mr. River's office was the Grand Marshal of the parade.

The meeting carried on for a while. Peter responded to their questions and offered projections for completion. At the end of their time, seemingly pleased with the results, Bedford excused himself as he had another appointment and thanked Peter for his time. As an afterthought, he told Peter that he was certain they'd meet again. Peter successfully fought the urge to shriek in the man's face. It was Friday, after all, and near enough five o'clock to go home.

He stayed up late that night, desperate to avoid sleep. But after a number of beers to fight the rising panic, his eyelids announced their resignation to their fate and slid down eyes as he sat on the couch.

He was out on the corner of Colorado Boulevard on a clear and cloudless day. The crowd gathered, the band struck up the music, and the parade's column moved down its appointed path. At last the float, the one he had seen so many times drew near, and Peter saw that Tom Bedford alone rode it. Without the weight of the others to balance it, the thing bucked and rattled like a rickshaw and only emphasized the horrible gesticulations of Bedford's form. It groaned to a halt in front of Peter. The music stopped. The marchers were gone. The murmur of the crowd ceased. Peter looked around and saw he was alone with the Marshal on the route. With absolute certainty, Peter thought, *It's me now. It's my turn.*

He thought about Shelby finding his corpse on the couch in the morning. Thought about her raising Henry alone and he wept and kept weeping until he heard the Marshal croak out a single word.

"Goodbye."

And with that Peter was awake on his couch, feeling the edge of a nasty hangover approaching.

Upon opening his work computer the following Monday, he saw an email in his inbox with the title, *A loss in the Bellator family.*

"It is with sadness that we must tell you that last Sunday Tom Bedford suffered a dreadful crash on his bicycle, and though all efforts were made, his injuries were too severe for him to recover."

The scuttlebutt around the office was that it seemed an insignificant accident. Another rider had drifted to close to Bedford and in his attempts to avoid the crash had fallen head first off the trail into some brambles. The jovial man had laughed at the scratches from the thorns and simply taken some aspirin when he'd gotten home to combat the ache in his head. He'd drawn up a chair at his kitchen table, an old man sitting in a simple wooden chair, and told his wife that whatever she was cooking for dinner smelled great. Mrs. Bedford was confused by this comment as it was ten o'clock and nothing was in the oven. A moment later, Tom Bedford, a man in phenomenal shape for his mid-fifties, fell off the chair and began writhing on his kitchen floor.

In the weeks and months that followed, Peter did not dream. Not of the parade or anything at all. He was grateful for the absolute simplicity of shutting his eyes and finding nothing waiting to greet him. The whole thing receded and seemed more of a fevered notion he once had than a memory of real events.

Halloween came and went. Thanksgiving followed. Then Christmas, and before he knew it New Year's Day was almost upon them. When it arrived, its presence was announced by their son Henry knocking at their door and bellowing with his adorable lisp that it was time to get up. That day, they sat and watched and clapped along with Henry at everything that tickled his fancy, from the riders on their majestic horses to the marching bands to, of course, the floats themselves. Shelby at one point, when Henry's excitement seemed that he might burst at any minute, leaned over to her husband and whispered that she couldn't wait until tonight to see what Henry thought of the nighttime show.

The following night, they gathered with their neighbors as they had the year before and watched as the wondrous fabrications were transported past their street and out into the night. Peter stood next to Shelby with Aidan in his arms, listening to every delighted "oh" that came out of his son, and for the first time since his last dream wondered if he might see the parade one more time that night.

That night, with Henry and Aiden tucked safely in their crib, Peter lay next to his wife with his eyes fixed on the darkened ceiling above him. Again, he did not want to sleep, fearing that this period had been a lull, the eye of some storm that had been waiting to toss him from shore to shore again. He fretted and turned for hours while Shelby snored heavily next to him, but it was in the early hours of that January morning, his head heavy with fog and half formed plans, that he drifted off.

The crowd welcomed him back as one of their own, and the band nodded their recognition as they passed. Peter stood impassively, letting the event simply wash over him, and watched the float rattle into view. On it he saw a fresh gaggle of the young and the old. The healthy and the sick. The deserving and the tragic. One by one, they would announce themselves to him and then go on their final way. For some reason, for no reason. Peter supposed it didn't matter.

With a muted interest he saw that someone new—a woman—sat in the chair at the front of the float. It made sense, of course. Bedford was gone; he had given up his place of honor and joined the rest in whatever place they went over the other horizon when their time had come. Peter leaned forward and could see that the once-beautiful woman's sun-kissed skin and brown eyes were ravaged by disease, something that she did not even know she had yet. Probably wouldn't know for another year. Something that was slowly turning her into a poor imitation of the vibrant thing she'd once been. In the waking world, his fists balled up by his side and he began driving them in to the mattress repeatedly. In a tiny voice that was more like his son's than his own, he wailed, "No."

Peter knew her long before she passed by him. Remembered meeting her on some random evening two thousand miles away from where they lived now. Knew her long before she waved. He could almost smell the hospital room where they'd held their son together for the first time. Knew her long before she said, "Hello."

As he watched Shelby pull away from him for the first time that year, Peter knew what Mrs. Bedford must have felt after the paramedics came for her husband. Knew what Clarence Wise's wife had felt when she saw what depression had done to her one and only. What Cynthia Ryder's little brother and parents had felt the morning after. What Henry would feel as he grew and the slivered memories of his mother would slip away from him.

Peter felt alone.

And the parade carried on into the night.

# MOVIE MAGIC

## SIDNEY DRITZ

At first, Marta thought she might be psychic. That would have been okay, and she could maybe even have made a few bucks off of it. "Dave got the place cheap because there was a mysterious death in the basement," she'd told the new kid on concessions, not because it was true but because it sounded good. Ally down the street's step-mom read palms for fifteen a pop and she said that around Halloween, it actually started to pay off. She also said that Marta had a *perceptive aura*, and given the yellowing newspaper clipping about the mysterious death in the basement of the theater on October 23rd, 1993, Marta was starting to think Madame Antiopa might have been on to something. *Authorities have no leads, and an unnamed source suspects that the case will soon be turned over to the FBI for reasons related to the identity of the as-yet unnamed victim*, the article in Marta's hands read.

The new kid had eaten the story straight up, and Marta liked to think it wasn't just because the price of real estate out in the hills was such that there had to be a gimmicky reason why a bleeding heart like Dave could have afforded to buy, never mind run, a passion project like an independent movie theater in the age of conglomerates and the internet. Marta was a good storyteller, and always had been; she was the one who consistently terrified the little cousins when everyone gathered for the big family slumber party thing at her grandparents' place each Christmas.

By all rights, if it were in any other location, the theater would have been an underground, cult-classic location. The flashing, moving, multicolored lights of the sign hadn't been updated since the 1940s, except to move it from its original theater to Dave's place, and to replace the increasingly hard-to-find bulb. The creaky theater seats imported from the same old theater as the sign didn't always snap back to folded-up after they were sat in unless you gave them a good whack, but at least the shabby velvet upholstery hadn't worn away. The posters for classic films on the walls gave the slightly dishonest impression that the theater had been standing there far longer than its actual '80s strip mall origins, and the sweet smell of fresh popcorn lured plenty of people who might otherwise have passed on movie snacks over to the concessions stand.

All of these ingredients together gave the theater the kind of mystique that was *absolutely* what Dave had pictured when he bought a bombed-out theater from a faltering chain of cineplexes, then bought a series of lots being auctioned by sold-off and demolished classic theaters in the Bay Area. He had painstakingly hauled their accoutrements inland to create what was almost a monument to the profusion of independent theaters in the Berkeley of his youth. Even the dry grasses and the occasional flowers poking their way up through the cracks in the sidewalk outside the building, and the boarded-up windows where the sketchy massage parlor next door used to be, added a certain something to the ambiance.

The fact that the place was great, however, couldn't quite make up for the fact that it was stuck just off a highway outside of a small town closer to the central valley than it was to the coast, at least an hour and a half away from any cool or even semi-cool city. There were a handful of diehards who made it out to the theater for the indie horror festival it hosted every year, but the day-in-day-out clientele were mostly young families looking for somewhere air-conditioned to take their bored kids to out of the house when the weather crept close to and then above one hundred degrees in the summer, and their bored teens throughout the rest of the year, trying to outdo each other sneaking into double- and triple-features.

OCTOBER 19TH, 2013

"*Vanilla Sky!*"

"*October Sky.*"

"*October Road.*"

"Pretty sure that one doesn't count."

Chauncey already had the new kid playing one of his little games, which was truly excellent; Marta had four more hours in this shift, and there was nothing she'd like better than to listen to Chauncey brain-tease the new meat with movie trivia until he felt he'd fully established himself as an authority figure.

"We already established that TV shows count," New Meat said, and good, she had a spine; plenty of the high school kids allowed themselves to be awed by Chauncey, who had a film degree and opinions about auteur theory. "You were the one who used *Twilight Zone* half an hour ago out of nowhere and almost stumped me, it is definitely your turn."

"*The Twilight Zone* was groundbreaking in its own time, and is a piece of video-graphic history."

"Yeah, well, *October Road* is notable as one of Laura Prepon's first attempts at a career outside of *That '70s Show*, years before the explosively popular *Orange Is the New Black,* which will change the way people think about the validity of TV produced by streaming sites forever."

"All right, *Road Rules*, then." And okay, that was about to get ugly. When Chauncey dropped the gloves and broke out the reality TV, he was definitely in it to win it.

"Hey, Chance," Marta said, improvising wildly. "You know about the time they wanted to film a reality show here, right?"

New Meat spun toward Marta like she'd forgotten Marta was there, and Chauncey raised an eyebrow like he knew what she was up to, but he played along anyway, asking, "They wanted to what, now?"

"You know, it was when *The Simple Life* was coming out, everyone wanted to laugh about rich people being useless, and I think one of those heiress-starlet types was supposed to be in it, blah-blah-blah spoiled princess forced to do customer service on camera. It was supposed to be, like, cathartic. For the viewer." Marta was warming to this story now. That actually would have been an excellent specimen of the early 2000s reality genre; Marta would have watched it. "But they only got through three days of filming before they had to shut down production. Too many weird accidents. The starlet ran out crying and wouldn't go back. Forfeited her whole advance."

Marta let that hang there for a moment, in the air between the three of them, in the quiet behind the concession stand during the first matinee of the day. One of the tricks to selling a story was knowing where to leave some space. Amateurs just kept filling it in with details until someone interrupted them, and there was nothing believable about *that*. Reality was mysterious, and real stories had weird holes in them, and gaps in the storyteller's memories. Real stories went exactly as long as they went and then they stopped; it was lies that grew or shrank to fit the space you put them in.

"Bullshit," New Meat said into the silence. "And I don't think I believe you about the murder in the theater, either. My mom would definitely have told me about that. Nothing ever happens in this town."

Now, Marta thought, was not the time to double down on the reality TV story. If it were real, she wouldn't care about convincing the kid, because she'd only be mentioning it to pass the time; she wouldn't actually give a shit. Instead, Marta told her, "You can look up the newspaper article in the archives at the library, if a digital native like you even does that." The article Marta had found had been creepy as shit, but that didn't mean she was about to let a good chance for credibility like that slip by.

"Your instincts are pretty good," Chauncey told New Meat, all smug-smiled and annoying. "Marta is actually full of shit a lot of the time. I think I actually saw something about this reality show, though. My brother worked at this theater when he was in high school, and when I started, he sent me this—here, wait, let me find it."

Chauncey dug out his phone from his back pocket, shot a quick look around the theater to make sure Diane-the-manager was still downstairs inventorying, then pulled up a grainy YouTube video from a celebrity gossip news show.

*"MTV's new POP-secret project got blown out of the water yesterday,"* the plastic-

cheerful tones of the anchor said over B-roll footage of the outside of the theater, *"When the show's star stormed off the set. Sources close to the director say that the heiress refused to even go back to the shooting location to retrieve her belongings, and that she claimed to have been followed throughout the shooting process by, quote, 'A chill wind and a darkness, but not, like, an actual darkness, the lights were fine. But I could feel it.' There is no word on whether the series will be resurrected with a new cast."*

When the video finished, Marta found herself glancing down at the description, which described the clip as the first sign of the would-be star of the show's emotional breakdown three years later. It also listed the date of the original broadcast of the clip. October 23rd, 2003.

## OCTOBER 23RD, 2013

Once was a coincidence, twice was a *weird* coincidence, but it would take three times to make a pattern. This was what Marta was thinking as she scrubbed out the popcorn popper at the end of the night a few days later.

"Allison Janney."

Marta was pretty sure New Meat had actually instigated this round with Chauncey, which meant that Marta was absolutely done trying to save her. Besides, Marta had her own important things to think about; she did her best to tune them out.

"Jane Fonda."

It was possible that she was psychic, yes, but wouldn't she know if she was sensing something that already existed? The pet psychic on public access on Sunday mornings didn't think he was making up the parakeet's neuroses, he knew exactly what he was listening for.

"Felicity Huffman."

"Haley Joel Osment."

Unless, of course, the pet psychic was a fake, which he probably was, or he wouldn't be on public access to begin with. He'd be fleecing people like he ran a mega-church.

"Judi Dench."

"No cheating, you know his last name starts with 'O.'"

Unless he was just a psychic with a calling, that would be kind of cool. Marta wondered what having a calling would be like.

"Oprah Winfrey."

"Isn't an actor."

"Oh yeah? Tell that to the Oscar-nominated 1985 film adaptation of *The Color Purple*."

The thing was that she could have been drawn to say the things she did by the psychic, like, currents in the air, or something like that. She'd thought she was making it up, but she hadn't been aware that being influenced was a possibility, which could have made her vulnerable.

"Wanda Sykes."

She'd said things she didn't know were real and then they had turned out to be so, but that didn't mean she had the power to make anything true.

"Sarah Jessica Parker."

That would be ridiculous.

"Do you think 'J' middle names are a celebrity thing?"

Ridiculous.

"Don't think I don't know you're stalling."

Right?

"Patricia Arquette."

There were plenty of things that just weren't true, and there was nothing Marta could say to change that.

"Alyssa Milano."

Well. There was no sense in having a theory if she wasn't going to test it.

"Mike Myers."

That wasn't exactly an opening, but Marta could make it work. She turned around and told Chauncey and New Meat, "Mike Myers is buried in the basement, you know."

There. That was wild enough, that would do it. Marta was almost sure. New Meat laughed uncertainly. Chauncey was even less cooperative. "Mike Meyers isn't dead," he said with all the certainty of a man with an IMDb Pro account.

*Exactly, Chance. That's exactly right.* "That's what you think," Marta told them out loud.

Chauncey groaned. "This had better not be—"

But it was, it was going to be exactly what he feared, Marta stretched a smile across her face, ignored him, and asked New Meat, "Have you ever heard any celebrity body double theories? The Paul McCartney one is ridiculous, but that doesn't mean this one is."


This probably wasn't what Diane-the-manager meant when she said she wanted Chauncey to have a spare key in case of emergency, but it was a serious situation and something needed to be done, so Marta felt no guilt about taking advantage of Chauncey's utter inability to say *no* in the face of peer pressure. Two hours after closing at the end of the last screening of the night, Marta and New Meat stood under a streetlight watching Chauncey fumble the front door to the theater, keeping a furtive eye out for patrol cars, which could definitely have seen this little scene and decided it looked suspicious.

"One of the clues has to do with the album cover of *Abbey Road*," Marta explained to New Meat, who had not, it turned out, heard the Paul McCartney body-double conspiracy theory before. "There's supposed to be this code, because Paul's the only one not wearing shoes, and he's smoking a cigarette, and everybody knows only corpses smoke with their shoes off."

"But what does this have to do with Mike Meyers?"

"Literally nothing. Because Paul McCartney is a conspiracy theory for old stoners, and Mike Myers was supposed to be a guiding light for a generation, before he fell off the map," Marta said, and she meant the first half of the sentence completely sincerely, which she figured would help to sell the second half.

"We *are* talking about the same guy, right?" New Meat asked, furrowing her eyebrows. "Austin Powers, *The Spy Who Shagged Me*, 'Yeah, baby, yeah?'"

"One and the same." Marta had a spiel half-prepared in the back of her mind about resistance in the form of absurdism, and James Bond as an imperialist avatar, but she wasn't sure it would come out convincing enough and she was pretty sure her timelines wouldn't quite line up, so it was a relief when Chauncey finally managed to get the key to click through the lock, and he hustled them inside.

The theater was a little eerie in the darkness, but Marta was fairly sure that was only because if she was caught there she could be charged with trespassing. Chauncey looked a little spooked, but New Meat was cool as a kitten, like she did this every day, so at least one of them wasn't tense enough to blow their cover. Marta pushed herself into the lead of the little group and started making her way down to the storage rooms in the basement. Every stair felt like it made ten times as much noise as it would ever dare to when the theater was open, but it also felt like she barely had time to take a breath between standing at the landing at the top of the stairs and making her way to the bottom, where the maze of the storage room began.

Now, where would someone hide a body down there? Not the closet with the special events lights; those got moved in and out at least a few times a year. Not anywhere that was used to store actual stock, because people were always down doing inventory around it.

"Marta?"

"Not so loud, New Meat. You don't want to wake the spiders, do you?" Marta didn't think it was her imagination that a little rustling sound started to come from the corners of the room after she said it.

But that was the hypothesis, wasn't it? It wasn't about puzzling out where the sensible place to hide a body would be; it was about declaring where the body would be found and going on to find it there. Finding it there wasn't dependent on whether it was sensible, interesting, or even a possible place for a body to be; it was about declaring the place where the body was, and then going there to see if it had, in the time since she said it, come into being as if it had always been there.

"Marta, please, can we make this quick?"

"Sure, Chauncey. Just because I like you."

So not in the stock, not in the events lights closet, but what about the dusty space behind the freezer? It was creepy there. Diane-the-manager always told new kids to make sure they were up on their tetanus shots if they wanted to poke around in that area. Marta strode over to the space like she was sure what she was doing, barely pausing to listen for Chauncey and New Meat trotting to catch up to her.

The space behind the freezer felt bigger than she remembered it. She couldn't see down it, but something about the air moving through the space felt emptier, hollower

407

than it had the handful of times she'd ducked back here for a quiet moment mid-shift.

"Chance?" she asked, shuffling into the space gingerly, feeling along the floor for anything hidden or buried there. "You said you brought a flashlight, right?"

Light, then, Chauncey's cold hand passing a plastic flashlight forward into her shaking fingers, and a beam of brightness bouncing back and forth between the metal back of the freezer and the dusty cinderblock of the basement wall, and under all of that, there was a tarp wrapped around a shape that might have been a body. Marta reached forward, pulled back the tarp, and there it was.

It was desiccated, of course, hollowed out and grayed with time and grime, but there was something in the expression that felt like the old *Wayne's World* grin. The arms were folded like a cartoon body in a coffin. And as Marta stood there, trying to make sense of the strange-familiar face, the floor began to shake.


"Marta? Marta!" Chauncey and New Meat were being loud again—no movie titles this time, but not much better than that, either. "Marta, please, we have to get out of here!"

Marta didn't register deciding to smile, or making any effort to do so, but she felt the muscles in her face stretch just the same. Mike Myers lay on the shaking floor in front of her, in the dim light of the closet, and there wasn't really any question about what to do next. She shaped her smile-stiff lips into the words "I'm the only person here," and it worked; the voices behind her faded. But Mike Myers started to fade, too, and that wasn't right. "I'm the only person here who can speak."

And quiet. Perfect.

# THE WRATH OF OKEANOS

## CLAY WATERS

Two short stories lay atop the desk of the creative writing professor. One was cleanly typed and covered with the white frosting of a title page. The other consisted of three or four stiff, wrinkled sheets of blocky handwriting on clean butcher's paper. The neat manuscript belonged to the neat girl on Professor Keene's left; the grimy hobo foolscap was tagged to the deep-eyed big blonde boy across the table, wafting of sand and surf, whom the professor now addressed.

"First off, Joseph, let me tell you what I like about 'The Wrath of Okeanos.' You obviously feel this ocean mythos deep in your DNA. But one needs some irony, some possibility of an outside perspective." Professor Keene's tone was the type you employ with a rattlesnake when you have a rock tucked behind your back. "What I don't like as much, besides the handwriting," he added tolerantly, "is the relative brevity and lack of character development. You clearly grasp the need to show and not tell, but we don't know enough about the inner life of your protagonist."

"Protagonist?" Joseph's voice was drowsy, like someone deeply ensconced in a bed, or a bathtub.

"Your hero, um, Okeanos. You need to fill us in on him, because while these characters—archetypes, almost—could be interesting. We need an entry point, a way to join the conversation. How did they get this way?"

"They were always that way."

Keene looked over his glasses at Joseph. Actually, the professor wasn't totally sure about the "Joseph"—the first symbol of the boy's signature on the class card resembled a fishhook more than it did the 10th letter of the Roman alphabet. "And as for the victory of Okeanos over the resulka in his rescue of the oceanid—"

"The *rusalka*."

"Sorry, *rusalka*, I'm not up on my Russian ocean mythology—it did not feel sufficiently hard-won to me." He cleared his throat and read. "'*The long-armed Okeanos glided easily through the choppy waves and captured the betraying rusalka, with claws that could open a raw sea bass for supper.*' And the ending is too easy. The *rusalka* simply says, 'I go willingly,' and she dies a merciful death. The End. It's what we in the biz call an anticlimax." The professor knew he should cool it with the subtle ridicule, but *my God* the boy had actually written the words "tenth son to a god." Aquaman was a Shakespearean hero by comparison.

Still, the story would earn Joseph an A. Keene stamped A's on every story that crossed his desk because that was how it was done in the Year of our Lord 1969 at this wave-of-the-future, study-what-you-feel-college. And because Joseph or Hoseph had a blank face and a big frame and a certain dead-seaweed look in his eyes that Keene could imagine scoped to the business end of a rifle if he ever woke up. A good thing the college was under-budgeted for a clocktower.

"But that's what happened to Okeanos ages ago. When the land was empty and the sea was full."

*Oh boy.* Keene had endured this same talk at the boy's last student conference. It had given him ample food for thought. It had even enabled him to work out a plot of his own.

"Joseph, this is Sarah Maloney. She's in the other section."

Sarah extended a lotioned hand. "Charmed." She brushed the bangs out of her eyes, tossing back her head in a lioness sweep.

"So, Sarah, let's talk about 'The Night He Died.' Your story is corrosive and dramatic. An abused girl thirsting for vengeance against her brutal military father. But perhaps crafting an appeal to straight melodrama would have been preferable to this unconvincing attempt at day-to-day realism." The grin became sly. "And what's with the slumming? Do you think you have the chops to convincingly capture a middle-class family? Don't forget that reactionary cliché, write what you know."

An attuned observer would have discerned a second conversation flowing below the actual one. Joseph, blinking steadily at something beyond the wall, was not that observer.

"The story, to be blunt, is a little boring," Keene said into the languid afternoon. "And after all her brooding, daughter pushing father down the stairs is anti-climactic. Why not buy a gun from a pawn shop? Better yet… concoct some mysterious third character who can be persuaded to do your dirty work for you. I'm giving this a provisional A, but it needs more work."

After the session Sarah fiddled with her makeup mirror until Joseph had lumbered across the room and retrieved his sea-green canvas bag, so that they ended up walking out together.

"Mr. Keene's quite a character, isn't he? He knows his stuff, though," she said.

"I like my story the way it is."

The bright, well-trimmed April afternoon was a crinkly blanket of blankness, green with potentiality: anything could happen because nothing *had* happened. It had to be said that Pacific Park College was far from the worst place to tuck oneself away from

410

the world's confusion (and, oh yes, the military draft) and learn ancient Greek, or integral calculus, or all about the local mangrove trees. As for Sarah—she'd spent her three semesters waiting. She would know it when she saw it. Now, she was blinking.

"So where do you get your ideas, Joseph? I've never heard anything like your tales about the ocean."

"I dream about the ocean every night."

"I bet you're a good surfer."

"I would rather be in the water than ride above it."

"I'm going to the Student Union to get a coffee and look over crazy Keene's notes. Want to come?"

"Sorry, I don't drink coffee. It gives me cramps."

For a moment Sarah Maloney just stood there, arm hooked on her hip, like a quizzical vase. "Wow. This is a first. Well, since you can't bear having coffee with me, would you deign to sit with me by the fountain instead?"

Holding hands, she led him under the campus archway, across the Bermuda grass tortured to within an inch of the soil, and sat below the oversized, marble, sun-stripped *Laocoon*, writhing motionless in a clear white silence of distilled agony, a tension the surrounding non-statuary was too narcotized and tranquilized to notice.

"I liked the story you wrote last month. Dr. Keene showed it to me. I hope you don't mind. My favorite character was Okeanos. The hero who saved the mermaid?"

"The oceanid."

"Yes, that's right. And then the slaughter of the evil *rusalka*." She didn't smile when she said it. "You have amazing deep-set eyes, you know? As if you can see right through me."

"Maybe I do."

She made a laugh, then lowered her eyes. "Joseph, I have a confession. My story isn't all fiction. My father really does work in the defense industry. In fact, he's kind of in the thick of it all." Her voice dropped as she leaned in. "The guys that make the Agent Orange that makes all the little Vietnamese babies look like goblins? That's what his company does."

"What is your father or his company to me?" he said, politely, barely curious, staring out at the water.

Sarah's hand moved to her hair, then to the top button of her blouse, then with a sudden hop of inspiration came to rest on the mossy clump of Joseph's knuckle. "You've heard about the depleted uranium from the weapons that poison the fish? Thousands of fish every day, floating up on the beach in San Diego. And my father, seventeen floors up in an office in San Diego overlooking the ocean, seeing it all. Not caring."

Joseph blinked, which made her realize he *never* blinked. "Fish?"

It was a long way down the California coast, and before they got to the end, she had stepped him through the whole shameful story of her father, a fat munching spider in

411

the military-industrial web. Eventually a grunting kind of understanding was reached: one shot, straight and true, in exchange for a lifetime of bliss in a brass bed.

Both now barefoot, they reached a chain-link fence pounded into the sand, surrounding a rocky promontory topped by a small three-story castle that resembled a Gingerbread Gothic. It glinted in the last of the light from the quickly sinking sun. "That's the place." She gestured. "That's where we live. You don't even have to go inside. He'll come out at ten o'clock sharp. That's his way. The moon is full, so you won't miss his silhouette. But you'll have to get him the first time. He's pudgy but he's still strong. And you'll have to climb this fence because you can't swim around."

"I can't?"

"Because it's private beach and the rocks on the shoreline will cut you up."

"I can handle it," he said, without arrogance. Before she could rebut, he half-dove, half-slithered into the Pacific, his 16E feet like flippers, quickly emerging on the other side of the fence. "See?"

"Wonderful, but please come back," she said, apprehending the lights in the mansion. "Daddy's home."

Joseph swam back around and plodded toward her, less graceful on land.

"Where did you learn to swim, Joseph?"

"I don't know. I must have been young."

"You don't know much, do you?" She smiled, and he went quiet.

Returning to campus, they rested in the invisible shadow of *Laocoon*, his suffering in eclipse for the night. "I do feel I know you, Joseph." She unbuttoned his shorts and reached inside. "And I know you can do this."


Ten o'clock sharp found Bradford Maloney pacing his rocky little stretch of the California coast, packing his Irish Army pipe with the first scoop of the tobacco that had arrived

by post that morning.

"Who goes there?"

"Mr. Bradford Maloney?" A surprisingly high, airy voice in the dark rendered the stout Irish name almost mellifluous.

Joseph stabbed him one, two, three times, deep splurging cuts that spilled the older man's thick, scarred heart out in gouts, the blood coagulating on the loose sand. He emptied out too quickly to register there were not one but two shadowed figures on the beach with him.

"Joseph!" a familiar voice exclaimed. On land he wasn't quick enough to dodge the bullet honing in with (ironically) military precision toward his brain.


"Open and shut," Sarah said three nights later, dressing for bed in the bedroom of the house she would own outright, once her father's will passed probate. "Officer Carlton virtually said so. He's a lovely little pig. Troubled boy high on goofballs stabbed my father, who fired his pistol in self-defense. Both dead at the scene. You know, I do believe Father was alive when I shot Joseph. I heard him groaning."

Professor Keene wandered into the bedroom, wearing a robe monogrammed B.M. He sat down on his side of the big brass bed. "I shouldn't be here so soon."

"The door is downstairs."

His easy grin curdled. "Did I forget my place again?"

"This isn't mistress-servant, professor. More like Russians and Americans."

"Just like old times, then. So how did the boy do?"

"He didn't go for the Agent Orange thing. I don't think he even knew what it was. So I went on a hunch and made up something about uranium in the ocean and he perked right up. But he was wavering at the end so I kept his spirits up."

"How—no, don't tell me." Professor Keene wandered over to the dresser. "What's this?" He jabbed at a piece of paper taped to the mirror.

Sarah shrugged. "It's a poem he wrote for me before he left."

"A love poem?"

"Actually, no. More like... goddess worship. You know, I don't think he even wanted me." There was wonder in her voice as she adjusted herself in the mirror.

He looked it over. "Very nice. Freshman Gothic with echoes of schizophrenia."

"Don't start."

"It has an internal consistency that demands attention. Preferably psychological. I see he summoned the spirit of the ocean for you. It's a recurring pattern in Hoseph's work."

"Knee-jerk cynicism is so dull."

"Sarah, folks stared at him when he walked into class. Do you know how hard that is here, short of blowing up the cafeteria or wearing a Nixon button?"

"Wouldn't It Be Nice" came on the radio. First love. Years ago, he'd stuffed a dark spot in his life with reams of awful poems (and a few good ones) on the subject. Keene turned the radio up; he found it affecting in spite of itself.

Sarah smirked. "Look at Mr. High-Brow."

"I like noise." His eyes narrowed. "Are you *certain* he floated away with the tide?"

"I *live* here, Professor. I think I can read a tide table."

*It was a night for strange shapes and silent shambling, the beach still as a sand-globe under the fog. A night much like one six thousand years ago, when the ocean rejected one of its own. Pale gooseflesh puckered and altered into something of land and something of water, cursed and corrupted by both. Five-pronged footprints ended at a thick, useless door.*

With the radio up, the noise of the front door crackling into splinters failed to register with the two heavers upstairs. Only the squishy clomping, closer and closer on the oaken stairs, stirred Sarah, who sat upright in bed and switched the radio off. "Hear that?"

Keene shook his head, then froze. "Now I do."

A final squish; then an abrupt quiet shadow at the doorway, the rankness of small curled dead things billowing into the bedroom. "*Rusalk*a." A serpent's sibilance

413

over serrated shark teeth. *"Rusalka,"* it repeated, remaining perversely in the doorway as if awaiting invitation. The hands were longer now, melted into little scythes at the ends.

Sarah had survived her hateful pit of a high school by playing the angles. Kissing ass so her peers would not hate her quite so fiercely for her military-industrial pig father, intimidating and leading on teachers to massage C's into B's or A's (the A's were where the massaging came into play). But there were no more angles. Even the room's little window was painted shut. Cornered, she took the quick and straight way out. Perhaps that was admirable in her, if nothing else was.

"What did he say?" Poor old Keene hadn't gotten the news yet, though they had both read the story.

"I don't know," she lied, the academic's dooming ignorance allowing her one last bitter grin before the end.

Shaking off his clutches, she rose from the bed and turned toward the creature at the door. *"I go willingly!"* she shouted, opening her nightdress as she rushed forward, the better to plunge herself cleanly, quickly, fatally, onto the scythe-like finger-blades of Okeanos.

# RETRIBUTION

## STEPHANIE R. BROWN

The sound of the ice cream truck's off-tune music filled the air of the tree-lined, picturesque neighborhood. You could hear the sounds of children running down the street yelling, "Wait, wait," as the truck made its way down the block. What also filled the air was the smell of putrid, rotting flesh. With the exception of one person, no one knew that this quiet, residential street in San Jose, California was also the scene of unspeakable crimes that resulted in numerous corpses.

Even though it was a Thursday in early October, summer's warm glow had lingered as Chuck McGowan walked home from the bus stop. He was coming home from his job at the downtown hardware store on East San Carlos Street. Chuck had to take the bus because he couldn't afford to get his car fixed. It needed a new radiator and the money required was nowhere to be found. Chuck was a man of medium height, medium build with short medium brown hair. In short, he was an average looking guy. As Chuck walked home, he passed a telephone pole that had a poster of a beautiful Russian Blue cat. The poster read, "Missing—Her name is Sasha—We miss her terribly—If you see her—Call 555-9876."

When Chuck got to the front door of his home, he grabbed his mail from the mail-box, unlocked the front door and went inside. He threw his keys and mail on the dining room table and went into the kitchen to get a beer from the refrigerator. He popped the top on the beer and took a long gulp from the can. "I really needed that," he said to himself as he walked to a small room that was near the back of the house. Chuck took another sip from the beer can, looked around the room, belched, and said, "Hello, Sasha." There was a small cage sitting in the corner of the room that contained the missing Russian Blue cat, the one that her worried human companions were frantically looking for.

Chuck grabbed a chair that was sitting behind the door, placed it in front of the cage and sat down. He leaned in closely and said, "Did you miss me? Sorry that I haven't been able to feed you for the last couple of days. I just don't have any Kitty Chow in the house." Sasha got as close to the back of the cage as she could, looking at him with her eyes widely opened and her ears flattened against her head. Chuck picked up a thin, pointed wooden stick that was normally used as a barbecue skewer and jabbed it into Sasha's side. The cat yowled loudly and tried to get away from the stick.

As Chuck withdrew the skewer, blood could be seen on the pointed end. He smiled at the cat, finished his beer and sarcastically said, "Oh, did I hurt you? And I so wanted us to be friends. After all, you and I are going to have such a good time tonight. Well, at least I will, you, not so much. So, you see, buying food for you would be a waste of money since you won't be here that long. Speaking of food, I'm hungry. I'm going to fix myself something to eat. I'll be back later and we can pick up where we left off. Don't go anywhere." The hungry man laughed as he stood up, walked out of the room as the injured, shaking cat stared at him in silence.

Chuck strolled into the kitchen feeling rather pleased with himself. This was not the first time he'd had a helpless animal trapped in his house. His twisted mind would think up new ways to lure an unsuspecting neighbor's pet into his home for hours of fun. He would always clean up all the hair and blood before anyone came by, not that they ever did. There had been so much blood that it had seeped under the wooden floorboards of the house. This was why the house smelled so bad, but Chuck didn't notice it because he had gotten used to the stink.

The scent of spoiled blood could be found throughout the neighborhood. That odor hung in the air like a thick fog bank that just wouldn't go away. So did the rancid smell of the rotting animal corpses that were buried in his backyard. Chuck had gotten so lazy that he didn't bother to bury his victims down deep enough to keep them from being dug up by squirrels.

He also had a freezer in the basement that contained the mangled and disfigured bodies of other small dogs and cats that had the misfortune of crossing his path. He had been so busy that he didn't have time to take care of the overflow from his handiwork and bury them.

Chuck's neighbors never suspected that there was anything wrong with their neighbor other than that his house had taken on a look of severe disrepair. He kept to himself and didn't socialize with any of his neighbors, except to say "hello" if they were outside at the same time. One of the neighbor's children mentioned to his parents that he had seen Chuck with his missing Chihuahua, Speedy, on the day of its disappearance, but no one believed him. Some of the children that lived on the block were afraid to walk by his house and had made a game of avoiding it. The loser of the game would have to stand in front of the house and yell, "Come and get me, Boogey Man." Sometimes, the game's loser would be too scared to stand in front of the house and would simply go home crying.

While in the kitchen, Chuck opened his refrigerator in search of something to eat.

When he didn't find anything there, he looked in the above freezer compartment and found two frozen bean and beef burritos. He wasn't in the mood for Mexican food, but since that was the only food in the house, he took the burritos out of the freezer, sighed, and placed the food into the microwave oven. After setting the microwave to the recommended cooking time, Chuck took two beers out of the fridge and brought them to the coffee table in the living room. He turned on the television and changed the channel to watch his favorite crime show, *Murder on the Side*.

No sooner had he sat down on the couch than the microwave oven began beeping that it had finished cooking. He waited for the next commercial break before returning to the kitchen to get his food. Chuck got back to the couch with the burritos just as his show started again. He devoured the tasty, wrapped concoctions like he hadn't eaten in days. That was probably because he skipped lunch since he didn't have the money for it. To wash down the burritos, he guzzled the beers as if they were water. Chuck grew sleepy and quickly nodded off in front of the television set.

When Chuck awoke, he was still a little groggy from the beers but noticed that the ten o'clock news was still on. He also noticed the sound of dogs howling outside. Those dogs sounded more like wolves and their howling seemed to go on forever. Just then, Chuck heard a male voice coming from a darkened corner of the living room say, "It's about time! Obviously, you're someone who can't hold his liquor. Maybe you should switch to non-alcoholic beer."

Startled at having a stranger in his house, Chuck jumped up off the couch and almost fell down.

"Who the hell are you and what the hell are you doing in my house?" He then turned on the lamp that sat on the end table to get a better look at the intruder. What he saw was a tall, slender, middle-aged man with bags under his eyes. He wore a navy-blue baseball cap that covered his salt and pepper hair.

The uninvited guest replied, "My bad, let me introduce myself. My name is Burt Lobos. Until recently, I lived in the house that was on the corner of the next block. You may have seen me walking my Jack Russell terrier, Buster, up and down the streets. Buster and I were inseparable until you took him away from me."

Chuck retorted, "I don't know what you're talking about. You broke into my house and I'm gonna call the cops." When he grabbed the cordless telephone that was also on the end table, he received a severe electrical shock that made him drop the phone. Clutching his right hand in pain, Chuck said, "Ow, what the hell just happened?"

Burt smiled at Chuck. "*I'm* what the hell just happened. There's no need to call the cops. I *am* a cop. Well, I used to be, until I retired three years ago." As he talked, Chuck noticed that the dogs outside had stopped howling.

Burt went on to explain, "You see, my wife passed away four years ago. I should have retired back then, but I couldn't stand being alone in that house. We don't have any children. I thought that if I could keep working, that I would work through my grief. Boy, was I wrong. Grief can make you careless. One day, while out on a call, I surprised a perp during a liquor store robbery in Sunnyvale. I was even more surprised when his partner shot me in the stomach. During my ambulance ride to Stanford

Medical Center, I vaguely remember hearing one of the paramedics shout to the driver, 'Are you crazy? Don't get on 101. Take 280 North, it's faster.' It was just my luck that I got shot during rush hour. I was lucky that I survived. Because of the severity of my injuries and my age, it took me almost a year to recover. I knew at that point, that I had to retire if I wanted to keep breathing. I decided that thirty-five years on the force were enough for me, so I put in my papers. After a couple of weeks of rattling around the house by myself, I went to the animal shelter and got Buster. We hit if off right away. We went everywhere together. We went to the store, to the park, even to the barbershop. Everyone at the barbershop said that I should have gotten a Bassett hound because we would have looked alike on account of the hangdog expression on my face. We were inseparable. If we weren't inside watching TV, we were outside doing yard work together. He was my best friend. Hell, he was my only friend. Right up until the day that he disappeared from the front yard.

"I'd gone inside to get a soda and when I came back out, he was gone. I walked through the neighborhood looking for him but only found his collar and tags. That's how I knew that someone had taken him. I put up flyers with his picture on it, but it did no good. I never saw him again."

Chuck impatiently sighed. "What does this have to do with me? Why are you here?"

"This has everything to do with you. You little turd," Burt said angrily. The volume of his voice got lower as he talked through his teeth. "I couldn't eat or sleep wondering where Buster was and if he was okay. I couldn't take the pain anymore. Losing Buster was the last straw. I had lost everything that meant anything to me. I lost my wife, a career that I loved, and then my best friend, Buster. One day, I decided to eat my gun. Since you watch all those crime shows, you know what that means, don't you? I put the barrel of my revolver into my mouth and pulled the trigger. My body wasn't found until a few days later when the cleaning lady showed up."

At that point, Burt removed his baseball cap and turned around to show Chuck the back of his head. There was a large gaping hole where his skull should have been. All that was left were remnants of gray and white tissue matter that was infused with wriggling black maggots. Chuck was revolted by what he saw and recoiled in fear. When he saw a worm slither out of Burt's left ear, he almost threw up his dinner. He muttered, "This is *not* happening."

Burt replied, "Oh, but it *is* happening. Funny thing. You would think that after you die, you stop learning things, but that's not true. I was reunited with Buster and found out exactly what had happened to him. *You're* what happened to him. You had snatched him out of my yard, took him to your house, and performed the most heinous acts of torture until thankfully, he died."

"That's a lie! I'm innocent!" Chuck exclaimed. He was shaking so much that he could barely stand.

"You dare to stand there and say that Buster is lying? I suppose that all those other animals were lying too," Burt roared. He stepped in front of the television set and

Chuck was still able to see the newscaster reporting a story about pet adoption. Upon seeing this, Chuck gasped and said, "Oh, God!"

Burt glared at Chuck in such a way that it looked like his eyes were about to pop out of his head. "God? You have the nerve to speak his name after what you've done? I'd like you to meet a couple of friends of mine."

Suddenly, Chuck heard the sound of growling and turned around to see what it was. His eyes grew wide with terror because he saw an unusually large, dark brown bull mastiff standing in the corner looking at him with yellow, glowing eyes and drool dripping from his jowls. This dog was so large that you would have thought that it had been on steroids. It was missing one ear and part of its jaw. That didn't stop him from growling at Chuck and showing his extremely sharp fangs.

"Meet Brutus," Burt said. "He was such a happy family dog until he was kidnapped and forced to fight to the death for money and the amusement of some sub-humans that were far too stupid to ever hold down a regular job."

Chuck started to sweat and was shaking so badly that he had to sit down on the not-so-comfortable chair that was near the couch in the living room. Burt continued his introductions. "Say 'hello' to Bella."

Bella seemed to come out of nowhere and stood directly in front of Chuck. The unusually large black Great Dane stood over him and blinked her one eye. She too appeared to be on steroids and was much larger than other dogs in her breed. She stared at the cowering man in the chair with her green, glowing eye. Its glow was as bright as a lump of phosphorus on a black asphalt highway at night. She opened her mouth to display the unusually sharp teeth that she had. Bella had twice the number of teeth that any regular dog had in their mouth. Seeing this caused Chuck to lean as far back in his chair as he could.

"Bella was unlucky enough to know someone just as twisted as you. This is why she has only one eye and half a tail. After being attacked with a kitchen carving knife, she was hit by a car running away from her abuser—someone who also just happened to be her psychotic owner. That freak never paid for his crimes because he was hit by a car too and died that evening while he was chasing Bella. Luckily, you're alive and well and will answer for all of your crimes tonight. Everything that you did to each of those poor animals will happen to you as well. The ones that are buried in your backyard and stored in your freezer will be avenged tonight. You will learn the true meaning of suffering this evening, *Mister* McGowan," Burt snarled.

Chuck's heart was beating so fast that he thought that it would literally explode at any moment. He jumped out of his chair and stuttered, "You, you got it all wr-wrong. It, it, it wasn't my fault—"

The ex-cop's eyes turned fireball red, and he bellowed, "Silence! I've brought the hounds of hell with me. Since you are so fond of using the word 'hell,' that's exactly where we are going to send you. Buster will be coming by later to pay you a visit. For now, let my friends and I get this party started."

Chuck fell back down into his chair.

Brutus and Bella circled Chuck's chair as they growled and bared their teeth at him.

Suddenly, both dogs grabbed each of Chuck's ankles, sinking their fangs deep into his flesh. Chuck screamed as the dogs dragged the helpless man around the room. They continued dragging him through the house, leaving a trail of blood as they went until they returned to the living room where the dogs began a tug-of-war with their prey.

Each dog held a forearm in the grip of their powerful, vise-like jaws, causing puncture wounds so deep that Chuck watched his own blood spurt out. They tugged back and forth until he heard the dull sound of his right arm popping out of its socket. He cried out in agony. "Stop, please stop."

Oddly enough, the dogs did stop. Bella released her grip, too. They stopped just long enough for Burt to open the door that led to the basement. Chuck glanced at Bella and noticed that a few of her teeth had fallen out onto the floor. He couldn't believe it when he saw new teeth replace the fallen ones within a few seconds. That's when Brutus slowly dragged Chuck by the arm down the hard concrete steps.

Once in the basement, the massive animal shook his prey around like a rag doll. Brutus would fling Chuck against the wall hard, wait for him to hit the floor, then pick him up and fling him again. After a while, the dog grew tired of playing and let go of his toy in front of the freezer. As Chuck lay on the basement floor whimpering, Burt picked up a nearby 2x4 piece of wood and hit his host in the face with it, breaking his nose and knocking out a couple of teeth.

"Oh, did I hurt you?" Burt said gleefully. While the 'center of attention' lay on the floor bleeding and crying, Burt tied an electrical cord around Chuck's neck and proceeded to drag him back up the stairs. Chuck gasped for air and tried to loosen the cord, but to no avail; he passed out from the lack of oxygen.

When Chuck woke up, he was on the living room floor, lying in blood and other bodily waste matter. In his dazed condition, he could hear the dogs howling outside again. The house was in total disarray and there was blood everywhere.

As Burt stood over him, Chuck heard him say, "Glad to see that you're back with us. Are you ready for some more fun?"

Chuck started to cry out from the pain again and coughed up a little blood. "Please, I need a doctor. I think my ribs are broken." He was able to raise his bloody left hand and realized that his right collarbone was broken too. A piece of the broken bone protruded through his skin and that made him cry out in pain even louder.

"Sorry, can't help you there," Burt said. "You know doctors don't make house calls anymore. Besides, you haven't seen Buster yet. He's been waiting to see you."

Chuck started to sob uncontrollably with his mouth open wide. Out of the darkened corner of the room, a Jack Russell terrier appeared.

Burt announced, "*Heeeere's Buster!*"

The once-handsome features of man's best friend were gone. Like Bella and Brutus, he looked like he was on steroids and was larger than other dogs of his breed. He glared at Chuck for what seemed like an eternity. His eyes glowed bright white with a tinge of red, like two white-hot pieces of coal. Large amounts of flesh and hair were missing from his body, as was his left ear and right front leg. He couldn't bare his teeth at his attacker because he didn't have them anymore. Buster slowly hobbled over to where Chuck lay on the floor, lifted his left rear leg and urinated into his open mouth. Still sobbing, Chuck spit the urine out and again cried out in agony.

"This is just the beginning, my boy," Burt said with a smile on his face. "My friends and I will be back tomorrow night and all the nights to follow. Each night will be even more intense than the night before. We'll just pick up where we left off. You will pay for what you did to every single animal on this property. Don't even think about moving because we will follow you no matter where you go. You'll be begging us to kill you, but we won't. We might think about it after the last pet has been avenged. But we have a long way to go, don't we? You will atone for your sins. Some people call what will happen to you as karma. Some will call it retribution. I call it *justice*."

Just then, there was a knock at the front door. A voice outside the door could be heard saying, "Police! Open up!"

Despite his many wounds and excruciating pain, Chuck was able to get up off of the floor and open the front door.

One officer said, "Your neighbors reported a disturbance. They heard screaming and loud crashes like someone was being tossed around the room."

"Please help me," Chuck said to the police as he ushered them into his home.

"What seems to be the problem, sir?" the first officer asked. As Chuck pointed to the inside of the house, the second officer said, "I don't see anything."

The house appeared as it did earlier in the evening before Chuck's company had arrived. There was no broken furniture, no bloodstains or bodily fluids anywhere, and no unwanted guests. In fact, Chuck's features no longer looked like he had been dragged behind a pickup truck. His broken bones had miraculously mended and there were no puncture wounds on his body. "Don't you see the mess in here?" he asked the officers.

Looking puzzled, the second officer said, "It's not that bad in here. If you have some free time this weekend, I'm sure that you'll be able to tidy up the place."

Chuck blinked frantically, and couldn't believe that his home was back to the way it was before the police had arrived. He patted himself down and noticed that he was back in one piece and didn't hurt anymore. Just then, he put his hands over his ears and said, "Can't you make those blasted dogs stop howling? They've been doing that all damn night." The first officer said, "I don't hear anything. Do you, Bill?" The second officer replied, "Nope, not a thing."

Chuck looked at the officers and told them, "Wait here, there's something that I want to give you." As he left the room, one officer looked at the other one, raised his hand to his temple and made a circular motion with his index finger. The other officer smiled and nodded his head. That same officer noticed something shiny and white on the floor.

He walked over, looked at it and said, "What's this? It looks like the tooth of some kind of animal. Man, that is one big tooth."

When Chuck returned to the living room, he was carrying the small cage that the Russian Blue cat was sitting in. "Her name is Sasha. I'm sure that her owners will be very glad to see her." He gave the caged cat to one of the officers and began saying over and over again, "Must atone before they come back. Must atone before they come back."

One officer asked, "What's that smell?" Chuck stopped his mantra and told them, "I'll show you. Follow me."

He led the officers down to the freezer in the basement. Afterward, he took them on a tour of the backyard. Within a short time, the house and backyard were filled with police officers and animal control workers. Chuck was handcuffed and put into the back seat of one of the police cars still saying, "Must atone before they come back. Must atone before they come back."

The entire neighborhood was totally shocked as to what was uncovered on Chuck McGowan's property. The children knew something bad was happening, but luckily they didn't know the horrific details. The stench from the house had gotten so pungent that the house had to be condemned and torn down. It took months of dumping lime and other eradicating materials onto the property to get rid of the foul odors.

The next evening after the house had been demolished, everyone in the San Jose neighborhood stayed indoors. Winter was poised to breathe its last gasp as spring was set to start in a few days. The air was cool and crisp and every star could be seen in the clear night sky. One man could be seen strolling down the street with his dog walking slowly behind him.

The slender fellow had to stop and let the dog catch up to him because his companion only had three legs. After the man adjusted his baseball cap, he turned to the dog and said, "Nights like these were made for good friends and good times. Let's see what kind of mischief we can get into tonight. Okay, Buster?" The dog appeared to wink one of its bright white glowing eyes at his two-legged friend and they walked off into the night together.

As the two figures slowly disappeared into the evening's darkness, the sound of howling dogs grew louder in the distance.

# KISSING OFF AMBER

## KEN GOLDMAN

"Hey fiddle-dee-dee
   An actor's life for me…"

— WALT DISNEY'S "PINNOCHIO" (1940)

*Blessed with the brooding good looks of a matinee idol and a modicum of talent, rising star Zane St. George allowed no nubile young thing to stand in the way of his destiny. Love never entered into the equation. There were those women who would claim St. George had no idea what the word meant.*

*"I'm so sorry it has to be this way. It's been great, really great [add name here], but you see…"*

*He could do this with Amber O'Hara too. Hell yes, he could do this. Like any method actor worth his union card he made himself believe it.*

*He was an actor, dammit.*

*All he had to do was stick to the script…*

Zane pulled the covers from him while Amber lay at his side. She was a light sleeper and she yawned herself awake. The digital read 4:48.

"Sorry," he said, already half out of bed and sweating despite the room's coolness. "I didn't mean to—"

"Got to pee again?" she asked, her words muffled by the pillow. "What are you? Eighty?"

"No. Got to talk. I mean, now that you're up." He switched the light on. Amber turned to him, beautiful even without her makeup. Her hair looked like spilled butterscotch, not a bad catch for a kid who was hacking cabs in L.A. less than a year earlier. He was going to hate this.

*[Fuck it. Got to stay focused, like McCaffee says.]*

"Christ, Zane, last night was wonderful. But it's almost morning and yesterday I could hardly walk. Put that thing back in your 'jammies."

"No. I mean I really want to talk." His words sounded serious enough to bring the girl's smile to a full stop. "It's been a great few months. I wanted you to know that. There's no other way to say this, Amber. There's the new pilot, you know, and I have a real shot this time. Maybe you and I ought to slow it down while the networks are looking it over. To keep me focused, I mean. I didn't want to hurt you, but—"

That much was true. Zane had already completed the pilot for "The World According to Sam," some Harry Potter rip-off about a 20-something kid who discovers, with full laugh-track accompaniment, that he's a wizard. St. George personally thought the script was a piece of shit, an obvious Frodo-Meets-Seinfeld stew, but if the new comedic fantasy series deal came through he had performed his last dancing Dr. Pepper commercial. He didn't need to hear his agent lecturing about the necessity of keeping his female fans' panties moist, or how he could never allow any young cooze pot to derail him from the fast track. But Max McCaffee, always laboring for his ten per cent, had preached anyway about the importance of remaining unencumbered and focused on the prize. St. George didn't expect Amber to understand any of this, but the model's understanding was never a requirement.

"Wait. Hold on here—" Amber interrupted, allowing Zane's words to sink in. She sat up. "Let me get this straight. I'm here in your bed with your cum drying on my thighs and you're telling me goodbye? What is this, a joke?"

"Look, I'm sorry, okay? It's just that—"

She turned from him. "No, *I'm* sorry. Because I'm not going to let it happen, Zane. Not tonight. I'm going back to sleep." She fell into her pillow, pulling the covers to her chin.

Zane wasn't certain he had understood the girl correctly. "Amber, did you hear what I—?" Nothing. "Look, you can't just pretend you didn't hear me."

Apparently she could. Except for a cute snort the girl was already gone, sleeping as if she had flat lined. Maybe she was just playing dumb, dismissing what he had told her as if his words had resulted from some bad fish. But a vindictive former lover was no laughing matter for a guy with so much to lose. Zane did not intend his first shot at stardom to be his last.

He remained awake until the alarm sounded. At 6:30 Billy Joel was saying goodbye to Hollywood.

Amber had already commandeered the small kitchen and fixed Zane a cheese omelet with bacon just the way he liked it, even smiled when she placed a cup of steaming coffee before him. She said nothing of the night before. He kept quiet too, conscientiously burying himself behind the new Enquirer, acting absorbed in an article about Britney Spears' fading career. Possibly Amber believed she had dreamed their conversation of the previous night, deciding to keep any negative energy from disturbing her concentration. She was modeling for some weenie bop magazine later in the morning and maybe needed to keep her spirits up for the shoot. Denial worked a whole lot better than Valium.

"Sleep well?" he finally asked as if their late-night conversation never happened.

Amber giggled like he had made a joke. "Weren't you there?"

He smiled unconvincingly and focused on his eggs. He wasn't that skilled an actor to pull off good spirits this morning. After ten silent minutes she kissed his forehead. "Give that peacock network hell today." She headed for the door carrying her overnight bag. "Call me tonight." She blew him another kiss.

Zane smiled and waited for her to fire up her Mustang, certain he wouldn't be making that call. Instead he called McCaffee. He didn't apologize for waking him.

"Max, I think I may need your help..."


At the Green Garden Max McCaffee listened over his second plate of fried eggs, rubbed a thick hand over his bald pate, and gave his client the expected lecture about the disadvantages of thinking with his penis. "So this Amber is going to be a problem?"

"I'm pretty sure she won't go quietly into the night and I don't have the stomach for a round of damage control after the fact. Christ, Max. You know what to do. You're the wizard of Cooz, so just fucking do it!"

McCaffee had been through this before with his young and horny male clients who quickly discovered that in the parallel universe of Hollywood, women were a different breed. He didn't need some vindictive cunt running to the Tattler three episodes into "The World According to Sam" with some story about how St. George couldn't get it up for anyone without a dick. He pulled out a small black velvet box and handed it to Zane. "Your love life is going to break me, kid." The disappointment showed on Zane's face. McCaffee's connections were shady but they were also legion in this town. The man could make things happen, and that included arranging for selected persons to go away. St. George expected a lot more from him than a string of pearls that looked like decayed teeth.

"Jesus, Max, you think Amber's so dumb she can be bought off with a goddamn piece of costume jewelry the fucking oyster was glad to get rid of? She's a model, not a nitwit!" He shoved the junk stones back into their container. "You're going to have to do a whole lot better."

"Not on my salary. Trust me, these pearls are special in ways you can't imagine. You'll see. Hang these babies round her neck and that fashion plate will think you're one class act, kiss you tenderly, and wish you luck with your career. By next week you'll be home free while she's screwing some new guy whose ass is squeezed into Calvin Klein briefs on a Ventura billboard."

McCaffee knew how to put things into perspective. A second inspection of the pearls suggested that maybe, if Zane kept the lights low enough, the necklace ploy might work. Of course, it was even money Amber would tell him to take a flying leap at a donut and flush the stones down the toilet.

Max seemed certain enough to reassure him. There was no pitch man in Burbank like McCaffee, and Zane hoped some of the man's talent had rubbed off on him. The agent scarfed down the last of his eggs with a smile. "I'll handle your bitch kitty myself if you're not satisfied with the results. I have a lot invested in you, kid, just for the record. Now, let's get your ass over to NBC and make you famous…"

**[— From the pilot script of "The World According to Sam" (pg. 23)]**

*… and cautiously, Sam enters the cave of Old Grindolph the wise man, whose face is hidden in smoke and darkness. The elder sits in the far corner cross-legged smoking his holy pipe. He has been expecting this young prodigy but reacts with barely a notice, knowing much more than he will be telling. Sam approaches slowly, standing before the aged master without a word, uneasy and fidgeting in the dancing candle light.*

**OLD GRINDOLPH :** "So, we seek a wizard and a wizard is what ye claim to be, lad? Most curious, a wizard th't calls himself Sam, no less. Come…"

**SAM** *(steps forward)* : "I seek Grindolph, the elder whose wisdom might reveal the truth of who I am. He is whom I seek. You are him… that is, you're he. I mean… *You're the guy!*"

*Shrouded in thickening curls of smoke the old man demonstrates the first evidence of curiosity regarding his strange visitor.*

**OLD GRINDOLPH :** "The nearest mountain tram does not travel to this height. There exists no means by which one so inexperienced might complete this treacherous journey alone, yet here ye be. Tell me, young Sam, is it wizardry helps ye climb this remote mountaintop?"

**SAM :** "Only the wizardry required to follow a map. I hitched a ride on a local donkey leased from some old woman on her way from market. Let me tell you, that trip was murder on the poor ass. And it wasn't much fun for the donkey either"

*[Sam, coughing, swaps at the air to clear the smoke screen surrounding the old man]*

**SAM :** "You ought to break the habit, man. That stuff will kill you."

*The elder looks at him with no change in his expression or in his smoking.*

**OLD GRINDOLPH :** "I should think your concern would lie with your own wellbeing, young Sam, for my destiny is not as yours. If ye be a seeker of truth, then a true wizard must first learn to separate what 'seems' from what 'is'."

*Something suddenly diverts Sam's attention. Old Grindolph's beautiful young granddaughter, Trista, appears as if from nowhere. She notices Sam staring with interest and shyly averts her eyes.*

*Sam, clearly forgetting the purpose of his mission, mutters to himself "I'll show you*

426

*'what is' old man."* He keeps right on staring at the young girl. Finally he turns to Old Grindolph.

**SAM** *(whispers)* : *"Psst! Old guy!* You got a breath mint?"


McCaffee earned his paycheck later that morning. "The World According to Sam" was typical sitcom tripe but the NBC brass loved the tape, even were interested in a call-back within the week because those money grubbers over at "Big Bang Theory" finally finished their last season. The four studio suits seemed especially taken with Zane's performance in the lead, the sole woman among them suggesting the actor had a smart-ass quality with a dark edge, "like the bastard son of Michael J. Fox and Leona Helmsly." One guy seated at the far end of the long table even gave the young hopeful the eye. St. George figured, if that's what it takes to land the series he might even let Mr. Big believe he had a chance at packing some fudge. He smiled right back at him.

Smiling handshakes were exchanged all around, the equivalent of a verbal contract in

Studio City.

Later he and Max shared a liquid lunch on Glenoaks Boulevard and clinked their martini glasses with high hopes. McCaffee reminded him the day's success made the necessity of Amber's graceful exit even more urgent. St. George tapped the necklace inside his sportscoat to assure him the deed was as good as done.

Zane made the call he swore he wouldn't make, performing the best of his acting repertoire in his conversation. The t.v. pilot looked like it was a 'go,' he told Amber; she told him his success required a celebration, suggesting a candle lit dinner at her place. He offered to pick up a bottle of cabernet; she offered him the best oral sex in Santa Monica.

Zane revealed nothing of his intentions. Hell, he wasn't ending it with her completely, not really. He saw no reason they couldn't get together now and then, that's how he would explain it to Amber, although it seemed prudent to tell that to her after the blow job.

He had never been to her place, but it was as he imagined it, a tasteful garden apartment along the trendier section of Wilshire with windows everywhere so sunlight washed each room during any time of day. The lush couch was framed with swivel glass accent tables and the living room low lit with Fuente floor lamps. One wall remained completely blank lacking any pictures, plants, or cumbersome book shelves. Definitely L.A. minimalist chic. There were mirrors everywhere, of course. Models rarely strayed far from their own reflection.

They ate a fantastically cooked duck l'orange. They drank some very good wine. And they fucked right there on her luxuriously upholstered couch. Twice.

Amber was slipping into her jeans when Zane approached behind her and handed her the black velvet box, thankful for the dim lighting. "I wanted you to have this," he

427

said. He considered kissing her, but she could have easily misinterpreted that. He felt vaguely idiotic just standing there.

Amber grinned, clearly surprised but pleased.

"What's the occasion?"

*Well, babe, the occasion is I'm going to be tipping my hat for a while, even though ten minutes ago you were taking it from me in the ass...*

"I saw it and thought you should have it." Simple. Clean.

Amber looked inside and her expression changed that instant. For one horrible moment Zane feared she might turn to him and deliver a haymaker right across his chops. Instead her lip quivered as if she were about to burst into tears.

"Zane, you shouldn't have done this. These must have cost a fortune. Where did you find something so beauti—?" And then she *did* cry.

St. George never could deal properly with a sobbing woman, but at least for now her tears were happy ones. Her reaction touched something inside him, something unfamiliar and mildly disquieting. He didn't have the heart to go through with the rest of his planned speech, not feeling like this.

"Aren't you going to try them on?" he asked instead, dispensing with his carefully planned kiss-off. He had to hand it to Max. Somehow those pearls now looked like a million bucks, nothing like the uncomely boogers he had seen inside the Green Garden. A neat trick, but entirely up to snuff for Maxwell McCaffee. Before a mirror he helped slide the jewelry around Amber's delicate neck, and with a face glistening with tears she looked at his reflection behind her.

"They're beautiful," she said.

"And so are you."

She turned to him.

Amber was a goddamned knock-out even wearing simple jeans and a bra and with her makeup smeared. The pearls added something, some indefinable quality Zane hadn't seen before. He had no idea what that quality was, but his heart felt like a runaway train. Screw Max McCaffee and his red flags. He was going to kiss her, and he was going to do it right now, kiss her hard and kiss her long, because this girl was something special. This girl was...

*... She was gagging??*

*She was trying to scream!* "What the—?"

Amber, choking for air, gasped while the necklace tightened like a coiled snake around her throat, twisting itself with elongated canine incisors until her tendons darkened like thick veins. The string of teeth drew blood, chewing into the soft flesh of her neck.

*"I can't breathe! I can't—!"*

He tried to unhook the necklace but the catch had welded shut. Tugging at it made it worse.

*"Uuuurg—gghhh!"*

"Shit! Shit!"

Amber's face went pale, her eyes flickering wildly like something inside had shorted out. A thick stream of spittle drooled from her mouth.

*[Trust me, these pearls are special in ways you can't imagine.]*

*Max! Damn him! The prick must have known all along.*

Amber fell limp in Zane's arms.

*"I'll kill the bastard! I'll cut his fucking throat! I'll cut his—"*

"CUT!"

Amber shoved Zane from her with a sudden fury, putting as much distance between them as she could. A heavy-set woman appeared from nowhere and rushed to hand the girl a glass of water. Amber gulped a good deal of it down, then spun back towards St. George, spitting her words at him so that only he could hear:

"What kind of gorilla are you? You practically broke my neck in that scene, asshole!"

The empty wall Zane had noticed earlier no longer was there. Instead, he saw an entire crew of people, a technical staff of dozens, milling about behind the array of behemoth television cameras with the NBC logo. The floor was littered with the familiar studio cable rigging from assorted sound boards and mixers.

"That was great, Amber, just great," a male voice called from behind one of the cameras, but Zane could not make out a face. "I really believed that struggling. Sam, you were a little wooden. I need more anger during that scramble to remove the necklace, okay? We'll go one more time."

Zane watched the girl storm off while he squinted at what appeared before him. He could determine some shapes but nothing distinct or familiar.

"Who are you people? What's going on here?"

No one answered, but activity continued all around Amber. The heavy-set woman approached him with a swab of powder. He swatted her away.

"Spray those goddamned mirrors, Eddie!" another voice called out. "We're getting too much glare from Camera Three!"

*"Listen, I don't know what the fuck is happening!"*

A large figure stepped from behind one of the cameras, thick beads of sweat dotting his bald head.

"Max! What are you doing here? Jesus, Max, will somebody please tell me what—?"

McCaffee put an arm around Zane. "Relax, kid, okay? You're making an ugly scene. Calm down before you blow it." He handed Zane a folder. Tugging some pages from it, St. George read:

*Blessed with the brooding good looks of a matinee idol and a modicum of talent, rising star Zane St. George allowed no nubile young thing to stand in the way of his destiny. Love never entered into the equation.*

He flipped through the pages to a brief scene in bed with Amber. Again to another scene over breakfast with his agent. Later the scene with the necklace.

"Max, this is a script?"

Max pulled him aside as if sharing a secret. "Of course it's a script. A manufactured television prime time soaper churned out by a half dozen paid monkeys, like a thousand other horse shit television scripts! What else would it be? Christ, Sam, get it together and stick to the dialogue that's written, will you? This is the third time this week you've pulled this shit. They're already talking about replacing you with Zac Efron."

"Why is everyone calling me Sam? Sam is the character I'm playing for the pilot! I'm Zane! Zane St. George! You've known me for a year!"

Max turned toward the fourth wall to address the camera crew. "Listen, guys. Can we take a few minutes here. Sam's a little confused. Just five minutes, okay?" He returned his attention to his client, speaking low and managing to keep a lid on his anger. "Listen to me and try to take this in, kid. Zane St. George is the character you're playing in 'Amber's World.' Got that straight, Sam? Amber O'Hara's show, her series, her ball game. Not yours. She calls the shots here. Now cut this shit out and let's get back to work."

"But you were with me, Max! You were there just this morning. You gave me that necklace. We had drinks! Don't you remember? Jesus, has everyone here gone fucking crazy?"

A voice called from behind the cameras. "Time is money, McCaffee! Tempus Fugit! Is your boy ready to go, or what?"

"One minute, Aaron, okay? Just one minute."

"I'm counting, McCaffee. Zac Efron is a phone call away. What's it going to be, kid?

Ten... Nine..."

"Sam, please... just get back to the script, okay?"

"*I'm not Sam! Max, I swear to God I don't know what the hell is going on!*"

"Six... Five..."

Amber returned to her mark and she wasn't smiling. "Joey Lawrence, asshole. One phone call. Just wait and see. You'll be forgotten by next week!"

"Stick to the script, Sam. I'm begging you, kid..."

"*Max, I'm telling you, I don't—*"

"...Two... One..."


"ACTION!"

Sam approached the old man slowly, standing before him without a word, uneasy and fidgeting in the dancing candle light. Knowing much more than he would be telling, Old Grindolph blew smoke curls from his pipe even as he spoke.

"So, we seek a wizard and a wizard is what ye claim to be, lad? Most curious, a wizard th't calls himself Sam, no less. Come..."

The old man delivered the lines expertly with a crispness that would have made anyone believe the guy really was a wizard himself. That was the cruel irony of Zane St. George's career. Following years of unemployment checks here he was in the role of a lifetime as the wise elder, Grindolph, and he was too much of an old fart to reap the real rewards of his craft. Christ, was there anything as pathetic as a forgotten elderly actor?

The new kid delivered his lines.

"I seek Grindolph, the wise one whose wisdom might reveal the truth of who I am."

Here the aged Grindolph's attention was supposed to focus on this handsome upstart playing Sam, the character who apparently had wizardly powers of his own. But instead St. George couldn't take his eyes from the fresh and adorable actress in the role of his beautiful young granddaughter. She was dressed in flowing silk and her breasts peeked right through the sheer material like ripened pomegranates. He wondered if she liked the pearl necklace he had left inside her dressing room with the unsigned note: "I saw it and I thought you should have it."

The stones were a little seedier than St. George would have preferred, but it was all he could afford. In the script the girl's name was Trista, and she was the loveliest creature he had ever seen. Zane knew how unseemly it was to gawk at her like this, that somehow he would have to turn off this ridiculous and foolish adulation. Christ, in "The World According to Sam" he was supposed to be the girl's grandfather!

He could do it. He could forget this nonsense and be the actor he knew he was. Just not today, not right now, not while all these heated emotions stirred. A short while ago he had felt certain those long-lost feelings had died, and that made them mean so much more to him now.

No fool like an old fool, wasn't that how the saying went? Well, then, he would be a fool, the biggest fool that ever was, thinking he could be fifty years younger.

Because from the moment Zane St. George first saw that magnificent young girl, the venerable performer could think of nothing else but the budding television actress Amber O'Hara.

431

# GERTRUDE ON OLYMPIAD DRIVE*

## YVONNE

Traveling Shoes. Such a pretty house. Me? Faint?
A Bank in the Sky! A doctor? Come in the Room.
Such an empty home. Trust the Lord. Plain and alone.
Goodwill pennies. Dead babies? Does sweet Clara haunt?
Didn't It Rain? Storm Is Passing Over. Hallelu!
I Opened My Mouth. Trust! Rise up. Trust! Help the lost!
Whose angel, now? I Got Shoes. Packing Up. The cost
In God's hands. Stars He give us! Rhinestones I can do.
What? Stand in rags? Trust! A City Called Heaven.
Awful Day! Down South in a Cadillac! Amen!
Klan took me for possessed. Black devil in
A woman's dress! Trust! Standing on the Highway?
Awful things! Plain. Alone. Trust! Peace in the Valley.
How Far? Home in that Rock. Awful things they say!

*Gertrude Ward, the business brains behind the Clara Ward Singers "brand," moved from Philadelphia to Los Angeles where she lost the house and church Clara had bought for her soon after her daughter's death in 1973.

# HORROR USA

The 51-book HORROR USA series highlights the unique monsters, legends, and stories found in each of the United States.

# HORROR USA

## CALIFORNIA
AN ANTHOLOGY OF HORROR FROM THE GOLDEN STATE

# HORROR USA

## TEXAS
AN ANTHOLOGY OF HORROR FROM THE LONE STAR STATE

# HORROR USA

## WASHINGTON
AN ANTHOLOGY OF HORROR FROM THE EVERGREEN STATE

# WHAT MONSTERS DO FOR LOVE

Love can turn men into monsters... and monsters into men. Come and meet these monsters, and the things they do for love in our new bestselling Horror Anthology Trilogy!

# WHAT MONSTERS DO FOR LOVE

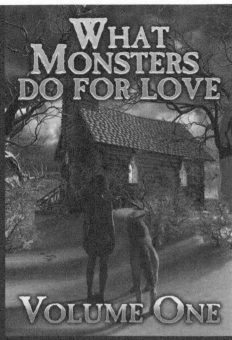

## VOLUME ONE

# WHAT MONSTERS DO FOR LOVE

## VOLUME TWO

# WHAT MONSTERS DO FOR LOVE

## VOLUME THREE

Amazon's
#1 Best-selling
Horror Anthology
Series

THE
MONSTERS
WE FORGOT

THE
MONSTERS
WE FORGOT
TRILOGY

VOLUME 1

THE
MONSTERS
WE FORGOT

VOLUME 2

THE
MONSTERS
WE FORGOT

VOLUME 3

The HARDBLOOD grimdark trilogy by G. R. Dauvois opens the epic *"IMMEMORIAL"* science fantasy saga spanning centuries and worlds.

FAIN HUNTER
HARDBLOOD Book I
G. R. DAUVOIS

BLOODWRATH
HARDBLOOD Book II
G. R. DAUVOIS

RAVENSAGE
HARDBLOOD Book III
G. R. DAUVOIS

WONDROUS
BLOOD

R. C. BOWMAN
G. R. DAUVOIS

Do you want to learn how to make a windigo? Or how to exorcise a
heartbroken ghost before its killer comes after you? Have you heard the real
reason that old boarding school was abandoned? How about the secret TV
channel that only appears on Christmas Eve? Are you ready for the terrible
secret behind the Mandela Effect? Or the dark truth of Morgellons Disease?
    Tragic spirits with unimaginable secrets…. Hidden worlds filled with
monsters beyond comprehension… Family bonds that overpower death…
Obsessions so powerful they reshape reality… WONDROUS BLOOD
presents unforgettable tales of familial fright, parental panic, spousal terror,
sibling savagery, and other horrors you'll only find with family.

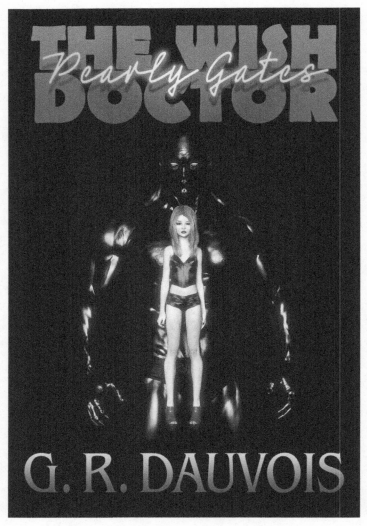

THE WISH
*Pearly Gates*
DOCTOR

G. R. DAUVOIS

Left without any conscience or desires of his own, Harry has been prowling
the world in search of prayers only he can answer, prayers left impotent by
the speaker's fear, whether whispered in church, or shouted out in public—
prayers to save a life, or end it—prayers which Providence has given him the
strength to grant, transforming him into a true-life genie, a purpose he has
reveled in for years… But then he meets Janie, a child prostitute whose
vengeful wish leads him to kill every man he could find who touched her.
Will Harry allow Janie to "heal" him, and thereby risk being destroyed by his
resurrected conscience? Or will he kill her to save them both from the
weakling he used to be?

IN THE UNLIKELIEST OF PLACES, A HAZMAT CLEANER FINDS A
HIDDEN WORLD. IT'S ETHEREAL, DREAMLIKE, EXQUISITELY
BEAUTIFUL... AND FULL OF MONSTERS WHO WANT OUT.
Originally posted to Reddit's Nosleep community where it met with
immense success, this edition of R.C. Bowman's popular horror series is
revised, edited, and best of all, features 10,000 words of new content!

THANK YOU FOR YOUR SUPPORT!

PLEASE CHECK OUT OUR AMAZON PAGE FOR
MORE GREAT TITLES

VISIT US AT SOTEIRAPRESS.COM TO JOIN OUR MAILING LIST AND TO
VIEW OUR LATEST RELEASES.

Made in the USA
Coppell, TX
26 May 2020